I0660555

SHADOWS AND HOUNDS

SISTER SEEKERS BOOK 10

BY
A.S. ETASKI

Published by Corpus Nexus Press
ISBN: 978-1-949552-26-3

etaski.com
etaski.com/sister-seekers
miurag.etaski.com
www.patreon.com/etaski
www.goodreads.com/etaski
www.bookbub.com/authors/a-s-etaski
www.facebook.com/asetaski
mastodon.online/@etaski

Copyright © 2024 A.S. Etaski

Cover Design by Eris Adderly
Book layout by DocKangey

This book is a work of fiction and intended for adults. Sexual activities represented in this work are between adults and are fantasies only. Nothing in this book should be interpreted as the author advocating any non-consensual activity. Violence may be disturbing to some readers.
All rights reserved. This book or any portion thereof may not be reproduced or used in any manner whatsoever without the express written permission of the author except for the use of brief quotations in a book review.

Dedicated to 2014, when the first draft hit its stride, and to the 10 years and every reader, collaborator, friend, and patron since.

This writer discovered how your questions, once left open-ended in the story, needed their past and their future before Book 10 could be our present.

CHAPTER 1

THE REDOUBT, KERUT RIVER MOUNDS

The Guild is ready, Captain Isboern.
~*As are we, Oltere Baradum.*~
Have at, then. As ye will.

Tension broke, and the collective sensation from hours of waiting in worry passed at last.

I exhaled, high on my hill as Willven Isboern kicked his borrowed mount into an easy lope toward the Manalari camp. My willing mindlink with the Human psion at this distance existed by keeping sight of him.

Meanwhile, Krithannia, Talov, and their Guild leads spoke to each other through their Dragon pearls, trading observations and coordinating with the Captain through me and Mourn's newest, malformed pearl attached to my ear. Neither the Guild's chatter nor the flashes of imagery, sensation, or pure thought were constant, so I could keep my mind anchored and aware of my kneeling body while balancing two disparate methods of communication.

The day had just started. Night insects had quieted, and the dew glistened in new light as if dancing to the rising chants of the birds. A distant waterfall added a shush to the steady, warm wind. All this vanished around us when the Manalari people cheered their leader's arrival.

Jael gripped my arm tightly as if she might pull me away and out of view, distrusting the swelling roar rolling toward us. I resisted, detecting subtle clusters of gladness warring with concern as Isboern and his Templars sorted out where to begin among these last soldiers and refugees the Temple City had to offer.

The bustle continued, but no one attacked at once. Several had started weeping, unleashed emotions rising to wails and calls to the sky which I could hear from here.

I pulled my hood up farther over my brow and whispered, "This will be a long day."

"You knew this at the planning," said Gavin, his focus on the living auras swirling around the camp and Templars.

"Of course," I grumbled. "That was before Mourn dragged Mathias out of camp and let him babble about Amelda before stowing him in a cell in the dark of night."

My Deathwalker lifted his bare hands, noting the predictable change of pale white skin steadily greying until it darkened to black underneath direct daylight. We still didn't know why he changed like that. "Hm. Mathias will wait for us. He may be in that magical sleep."

I hoped so. The man was clever and slippery, and I'd only received a taste of all he might know.

As he intended.

I wished for an opportunity before now to find him, but we'd been waiting for Mourn to wake up from *his* sleep, though not for that reason alone. After escaping a massive battle, too many had been injured, exhausted, and in desperate need of cleansing in one form or another.

The skin hunter hadn't been important until the Defender of Manalar had reached his limit staying inside the redoubt. Isboern needed to reassure those camping outside that their Godblood was alive and capable of leading them with his Templars.

I wondered where they would be without the psionic Captain. Who else would be willing to take the fight to the Ma'ab after a complete rout of the city? I doubted anyone of higher rank than Isboern had made it out, except Inquisitor Kegyek, who — according to Krithannia — had accepted the opportunity to hide in Augran under Guild "protection."

"We'll keep watch on him," she said with a smile. *"He's an older man without connections, and he is aware of this. The Inquisitor handed the golden shield over to Captain Isboern in an impromptu ceremony after the Godblood saved his life. I'm impressed he released all control and involvement in the situation."*

"Aye," Talov added with a shrug, *"but don' worry, Kegyek will be back when the dust settles. For all we know, the Godblood might have a use for him that don't involve torturing souls on behalf ov a paranoid sin gobbler like Keros."*

The fact that Mathias had enjoyed a similar role yet hadn't taken the opportunity was of concern to anyone planning to return to Mount Sonai while the Ma'ab camped on its western slope.

Jael swallowed a noise between grunt and a groan but caught my attention anyway. I glanced at her, glimpsing the strain on her face and moisture seeping from the corner of one eye, a physical response with which we were familiar.

How often had she been in daylight over the last few days? Not often, and only when Mourn had to helped relieve the stress on her body from her new mage's aura. When he'd fallen asleep, she'd felt sick. I also recalled how, after discovering Osgrid and Rithal at the waterfall, she'd hurried to the redoubt once we'd run out of night.

"Will you make it?" I asked in Davrin, eyes on the camp.

My Sister shifted as if glancing toward the East before pulling her hood even farther over her face. *"Do you … ?"*

I waited. *"Do I what?"*

"Do you have your … sun mask?"

In fact, I did. I hadn't used it in quite some time.

"Men took yours?" I asked, reaching for my broader pouch.

"Among other things."

True. Mourn had loaned two blades to match her size for the fight in Manalar. She still wore them on her belt.

Jael accepted my mask, donning it at once and breathing out with relief. Her peripheral vision was cut off, but her ears would stand in for most things around us. I waited before speaking.

"You haven't been practicing day-walking."

She growled. *"I didn't have much time to get to the Human ant mound!*

Night was faster."

Her choice of words made me smile, and bearing the weight of my Queen's compulsion, I imagined too well the urgency which must have gripped her many times over, to the point of shedding hard-earned training from Elder Rausery to endure the Sun. Night *was* safer for us, and this might have been why she lived to be captured at Manalar.

I nodded but kept eyes forward. Yellow and green grasses waved around the camp. *"So be it. We'll practice."*

She grunted, though I couldn't note her expression once the Humans took decisive action.

The Manalari set up a large, open shade pointed my way. Krithannia and Talov murmured to Guildsmen to make sure the shelter would be closely watched and ready to welcome their Captain after he'd completed the appraisal of his fighting men.

The majority of Manalari seemed protective of the Godblood. Spies may be among them, but no assassins proved capable of evading this many eyes watching for threats.

Spotted a man leaving the camp, Mourn said.

Stay close to Isboern, Krithannia answered. **Guildsmen are shadowing him.**

An image popped behind my eyes, one of a sandy-blond commoner wearing no armor and walking against the flow.

~This one?~ Isboern thought.

Yes.

~If I may, he is no threat. I know it looks strange, but he is leaving to pray.~

To pray?

~Our minds met a moment ago. His name is Ceri Retulo. He is a speaker in a middle district. I have listened to him before, and he can persuade many here to go to Augran.~

If that is so, Mourn asked, **why is he here?**

~Waiting for a sign. He's received it.~

Ah. Noted.

~Do keep watch. I may nudge others should I find them.~

Keep us informed when you do.

8

I concentrated, allowing the various exchanges to pass through me, understanding but engaging them no more than if I'd been leaning against a wall, observing a conversation in a sealed room.

The Godblood's visit with his people was going well, though we had much to watch at once. The Guild found a few leads, people they would watch. The Captain completed his assessment of his surviving soldiers and the condition of their equipment and weapons. Afterward, he and the Templars retired to the large shade where they could meet with single men or groups and listen to their concerns.

During this time, I did lose track of my body. My spiders finally raised their chime loud enough that I became aware of Jael shaking my shoulder — hard enough to fall over.

Deshi caught me by the shoulders.

"*Janshi?*" he whispered.

"Drink!" hissed my Sister right over him, putting the mouthpiece of a waterskin to my lips. "Eat! Your belly does not stop growl!"

I also had to piss, I realized, but blinked dry eyes and drank deeply first. As cool liquid spread through me, my body gradually came back to me. The day had grown much hotter, the Sun to its zenith. I sweated beneath my hood despite kneeling in shade.

Sirana? Mourn asked a split-instant before Isboern shared his thought.

~You need rest. Thank you for your help. I think the greatest unknown has passed, and the danger with it.~

Aw, no, Captain, Talov protested. *We're not leaving. Guild is still on overwatch.*

~So be it, but let us coordinate in other ways. The mindlink nearly dropped. Sirana has lasted as long as the battle itself but has reached her limit.~

As had Jael, who had grown impatient — or worried — with my glassy gaze and tried to push a bite of rations between my lips. I accepted and started chewing as a deliberate way to settle into my body. At the same time, I struggled to respond to the exchange focused on me.

In that moment, I couldn't manage both, so Isboern let me go.

Oh, Goddess.

Meet Krithannia, Mourn said through the pearl. *She'll let you back inside.*

~Confirmed … ~

I *had* been comfortable when I started that morning, knowing I'd need to stay in the same spot for hours. Now, I most certainly *wasn't*.

"Ow," I grimaced, unfolding my limbs slowly to stretch and deal with a swarm of cramps in order of urgency.

"We done?" Jael asked.

"They are not," Gavin answered, gazing out across the field and lacking the veneer of daytime-wear obvious in Jael, Deshi, and I. "But you are?"

"Yeah," I breathed, pulling up my hood to cover my eyes as my head began to pound. "That's … all I can do."

"I thought you'd tire sooner."

My lips twisted. "Is that a compliment?"

"More an estimate which proved too conservative."

"*Heh*. Good to know."

"Agreed."

I was smiling by the time I reached my feet. The trampled grass around me offered a hint of Jael's movements while I'd been entranced. "I am to find Krithannia and go inside."

"I shall join you," the Deathwalker replied, surprising Jael and me.

"You no watch out here?" she asked him.

"I have seen all I wish."

"Not interested if Isboern makes it inside alive?" I added dryly, watching him shrug.

"My purpose out here was to guard you."

I paused, for certain recalling his volunteering in the meeting. "Ah. Our agreement?"

"Still stands," he confirmed, unblinking, his face the shade of charcoal within his hood. "Meanwhile, the Godblood's understanding on guarding the pool is with my Lady, not me."

I smirked, skeptical. "Your purpose was to break the Bishops' hold on the pool but *not* influence who would take their place?"

"Rather, I do not hold the hand of one on his own quest. That is not my place."

I wondered about the limits on his "place." "But you have ideas to aid the Guild in choosing who moves in."

"Perhaps."

"Can we leave Sun now?" Jael interrupted, copper eyes hidden in the sun-mask, her eyebrows drawing down to vanish behind it. "I am hungry!"

My stomach clamored in agreement, making Deshi smile. Although the Yungian showed interest in pursuing knowledge about his underdeveloped death magic, he did not recognize the second life aura in my belly.

Not yet, anyway.

"What of the Nightmare?" he asked, motioning to Gavin's dark horse. She had regained enough flesh to suggest she'd been foraging further sources of meat and insects since my watch started, crunching continuously on something.

My scholar contemplated her for a few moments.

"I will test her limits of climbing," he said.

"What?" Jael barked as Deshi shook his head in disbelief.

"Climb ... down a ladder?" I asked, my eyebrows reaching skyward.

"Correct. This seems a good time to refine some control."

If Deshi and Jael were any hint, I looked forward to the expressions on the Naulor faces when we reached the hatch.

Not to mention those of Deshi's three battle brothers.

All had either watched or experienced Gavin cutting the barbed Malok weapons out of men still capable of screaming. Even had that not happened, the men of Yong-wen would still hesitate to make fun of *Sho'shien.*

And yet ... the goal!

Would they laugh at Death? Would Jael and I be able to *keep* from bursting out?

This will be fun.

11

My cheeks grew sore from grinning at the range of dawning comprehension. Gavin's proposal ended with Krithannia eyeing the circumference of the hatch and comparing it to the breadth of the rejuvenated, undead mare.

"Are you serious?" she asked as Tami stood with her mouth open.

"When was his last jest?" I remarked. "I don't recall."

The Guild Mistress smirked. "Point taken. Very well, I … think she will fit. It'll be close."

"A good thing if she tilts," Gavin replied.

"You *could* wait until we reopen the redoubt passage."

"I'd prefer not. I would have to wait and lead her."

"I see … Let me warn those on watch duty to stay clear."

"Indeed. Nightmare could fall."

Jael chortled, leaned in, and whispered, *"Give warning lest they be squished shorter still."*

I smirked at the image but nudged her, glad she'd spoken in Davrin. *"Indeed."*

Gavin's intention to push his unliving creation up to some strange boundaries drew an audience below, a handful of Dwarves eager for the spectacle. All the better for the mage to test his focus, from the look of things. I was right about the Yungians making every effort under the Sun to resist emotions shifting away from wonder as Gavin stood beside the hole in the ground, instructing Nightmare to back up toward it.

I held my breath as she took her first blind step, hoof clopping onto the first, flat metal bar. She did so without so much as a whicker. *Good thing these ladders are made for wide feet and hold weights heavier than Mourn.*

"Shit, they're really tryna squeeze her down!" said someone below.

The answering murmurs vanished when Gavin stepped next to Nightmare, where he was finally visible to them. The Deathwalker continued whispering, directing her next steps until her front hooves dragged along the ground and her rump dropped suddenly, bumping into the rim of the hatch.

"Shh! Shh! Get back, get back …"

Not one neigh or burr. Her eyes showed no white at all. A creepy sensation, even in broad daylight.

Tamuril had stepped behind a nearby tree as if she didn't want to watch, despite it going better than expected. The mare was soon standing vertically on the ladder with forelegs straight out along the dirt, her body below ground up to her chest.

Now what? Not as though she has hands to grip the ladder.

Instead, Nightmare hooked her left front hoof through the gap between each flat rung. Achieving success there, her new muscle proved sufficient to hold her balance long enough to hook the right hoof next. Her chest sank down from view, only her long neck and head poking up from the hole, her attention solely on her master.

I noticed her eyes glowing blue and wondered, briefly, if Gavin might be seeing through them.

Then, the Deathwalker kneeled down and spoke into the hatch. "Best move. She can only leap off at this point."

"Gah!"

"Look out, okay?"

"Move … !"

Nightmare's head swooped out of view. An incredible clatter of hooves against metal and stone, followed by a heavy thump and the nauseating crack of bones. Not one cry that wasn't a Dwarf gasping or groaning in sympathy.

Then, though out of my sight, Nightmare heaved her body onto her feet.

"Very good," Gavin said with satisfaction. "That worked better than expected."

"She broke her leg, Deathwalker," called the same Dwarf.

"Only one leg."

"Bone shards are stickin' out!"

"Those I can mend. Make room, I am coming down."

Five or six Dwarves shuffled quickly as the death mage entered the hatch. Peng-lok nudged Deshi and whispered something, and the younger man's face flushed as he shrugged. Meanwhile, Jael and I covered our mouths with our hands, snickering each time we glanced at each other.

Finally, Krithannia sighed, waving her hand to us. "Those going inside, do so now. Lessen the noise, if you please."

I didn't argue; I was still hungry, more tired by the second, and my head throbbed horribly. Nonetheless, I mused how the spectators had been noisier than the climbing horse.

Did not expect something like this today, but maybe I should from death mages. Including the Ma'ab and Sarilis when conflicts arrived.

Once the hatch closed to cut off the day, Jael took off the sun-mask with a moan of relief. I motioned for her to keep it, and she gladly added it to her meager tools on her belt. Deshi remained with us but his three brothers, Torch, Nianzu, and Peng-lok, stayed outside with Tamuril and Krithannia, who intended to see Captain Isboern through his day.

Mourn, as well.

I wasn't sure where Talov was despite his engagement through the pearls. I knew only that three Guildsmen of Reprisal — Wolf, Tak, and Hawk — remained outside near a third hidden entrance as backup for the others.

With another moment of breathing the cool air out of intense light, I grew less concerned about what happened up top and focused on food and rest down below.

We stayed with Gavin in his stained and austere surgery room, tucking his awkwardly lame-legged horse inside. Jael and I ate the food that Deshi brought to us and then settled apart on semi-clean cots. I wished we could lie closer, but I needed to drop into Reverie with Soul Drinker firmly attached and peace-knotted to my belt while keeping distance from my allies, who may or may not sleep at the same time.

Willven was right; I needed the rest so didn't fight it.

I slept, *expecting* to hear the rush of sand in the wind as the queen of the black dagger called to me. I opened my eyes to catch a glimpse of night-blue dunes dissolving, snatched away in a violent blast of scarlet haze.

In place of blue shadows in the Elsewhere, the red dunes of my lucid dreams burned with vibrant heat. The sky appeared like blood as I stood at sunset in the calm center of a sandstorm, braced upon a shifting crest. Soon, my boots sank up to my ankles. Filled with foreboding, I gazed down and ahead of me.

In the trough below, beside a tiny oasis the size of a standing mirror, was the traveling merchant.

Toushek.

The ancient Davrin, who was not a Davrin but had appeared many times in my dreams, seemed aware of me as he lifted his scarlet eyes. He wore a lightly shimmering robe which covered him from neck to wrists to ankles, finely crafted with multiple colors of threads and decorative beads and pearls. Their designs were intricate and abstract, the shades infinite and ever changing.

"There you are, champion," he said in a melodious voice. It should have been too soft to hear him above the circling wind. "Our last meeting was rushed, for which I apologize. I would like to talk frankly with our time alone."

CHAPTER 2

My hand snapped for the red rune dagger.

Not there.

The relic was gone from my belt, vanishing from my dream along with the blue sands. *Shit.*

Toushek chuckled, beckoning to me with a dark, graceful hand. I sought to ground my thoughts, to shield them against the alluring gesture and compelling sound. Whether or not this proved enough with an entity like this, I narrowed my focus to him alone.

The merchant lifted his chin to see me hesitate. "Hm."

Sweeping connections coalesced in the fore of my mind, moments too vibrant to be mere memories. Prior hints and glimpses of this ruler strengthened in my mind's eye.

The traveling merchant had stood first in a Desert stall, coaxing me closer, while Ta'suil warned me away.

"I'd forgotten Toushek," the bua said.

I had never met him *as* myself until now. I'd always been another cait in uniform, serving someone else. Whether I'd stood safe in a market or dying of thirst in an arid wilderness, Toushek was always male, a Davrin Elf working alone, with no matrons or caits in sight. He made offers to passersby or spoke in ways which seemed important but impenetrable, cryptic and incomplete.

Toushek smiled slightly, sounding wry. "So close, was I? Good to know. I wasn't sure of your importance at the time. But then … your aura reacted curiously to the scorpion statue among my wares. Even before you met him in person."

The Scorpion. My thoughts rushed to the moment I'd met Cris-ri-phon at Brom's Inn. *The Deathless.*

I'd witnessed the Zauyrian's memories once while sharing our sleep. Other times I *was* him, walking those dreams whether they had happened in life or not. After I'd escaped Troshin's Bend, I'd continued to see the gold-eyed bua in a remote Desert prison, of the Sorcerer-General promising to free him later.

Only to search and find him gone.

Toushek was at that prison, too.

"How long have you been watching him?" I asked.

The dreamwalker tilted his head with playful curiosity. "Watching *who*, exactly?"

I choose with care. "The Deathless. Yours was the presence in the Sun Temple, was it not? You broke Cris-ri-phon's will when he might have left without a fight."

A hint of fangs.

"I was. He did not deserve such a hopeful way out." Toushek spoke with satisfaction and perfect ease before his nostril lifted in a touch of bitterness. "I told his former grey guardian why. A regrettable mistake on her part."

Houda.

The memory of his icy voice swirled around me, as if he'd summoned those words himself. *Your Cris is gone, Houda. Your time is dead as you are. For all our sakes, do not reveal what does not belong to you.*

My eyes alighted upon a spray of disturbed sand as the hot wind picked up. "She spoke of his Queen's daughters. A hybrid Davrin-Zauyrian?"

"Indeed," the merchant confirmed. "Hers. No longer his."

No longer?

"Still alive?"

"You could ask your 'hybrid' bodyguard about that. You may be glad you did."

My unease climbed as the red dune collapsed in tiny shifts underneath my feet. I recognized the doubt he intended to sow between me and my closest allies.

Much like Soul Drinker in the warp rot forest.

Of course, Mourn knew who this was; he'd confessed that much. But, *as* my bodyguard, he'd also refused to offer me another name which might draw "something worse" in Reverie, something I did not understand.

My protector had seen this mysterious ruler after the battle, too, during his deep Sleep. A bronzed-skinned Elf with auburn hair and red wings, talking with Nyx's agents at the sacred pool.

The Dragon Son had not stayed to engage them but sped past to dive through the waters, coming out in the Red Desert, confirming that Cris-ri-phon existed on the other side in Miurag's Dreams.

And not him alone …

Toushek looked up sharply, eyes narrowing, and I leaned back, swallowing my thoughts in a void as long as I could, until another connection tugged at my Reverie in welcome distraction.

"Who was Captain Xala?" I asked.

I'd lived her memory twice: once while I was dreaming in Tami's hovel — the only time I'd seen the Valsharess I recognized — and a second time when Xala had been exiled and lay dying in the Red Desert. Cris-ri-phon and his older brother had found her by curious luck.

If those events had happened, they must have been millennia apart.

Toushek turned toward me, full of patience I wasn't sure was real. "If you want answers about your Queen, about the Red Desert, I am certain we could make a deal and share a rewarding conversation."

I drew another breath as my stomach sank. "I am not here to make deals, Lord."

The merchant quirked one white brow. "Oh?"

"No. I have only sought answers where they may be found." I half-smiled. "Or are given freely."

The merchant's amusement took on a sinister undertone. "A callow opening. Nothing is free, child, though I understand the temptation to pretend the cost of an ill-defined bond is somehow *less* than an explicit trade." His eyes traced the tops of the dunes. "Such payments are doled out over a long period of time, until you forget to account for their true worth."

I sighed, withdrawing from that direction but not confident about any others. "Very well. I do not want to bargain with you at this time, Toushek. I can barely pay my debts as it is, tangible or otherwise. I know an explicit trade with *you* will tangle the 'ill-defined' bonds I've got, perhaps nulling them before I find the answers I seek."

His eyes glittered as an abrupt smile graced his lips, his expression taking me aback by its open delight. "Thank you for your honesty. Another time."

I folded my arms and waited. The ruler in disguise only turned, peering into the tiny oasis near the hem of his robe. The water was too clear and clean to make sense for its size and placement.

"It seems to me," my keeper began with a slow, deliberate tone, "that your Queen tries to communicate from deep within the Pit. Many intriguing pieces carried by sparse messengers, and all have been mere fragments." He lifted his gaze to meet mine. "The clearest of them come from an oddly fragile champion whose mind nears her breaking point."

My jaw flexed as my calm wavered, my boots sinking deeper in the sand. I tugged out the first after trying several times then worked to free the second. My breath passed through as Isboern had taught me, and I managed to stand atop the sand.

In. And out.

In. And out.

"A fair start," he remarked.

"Have all 'messengers' been 'champions?' " I asked, sensing the wince from the Queen's geas even in my sleep.

"No. You are the first who has made herself known. Perhaps the first to have escaped." He paused as I continued to stare. "May I ask a question regarding this? I am curious about something ... important."

I stood wary. If I asked for an answer to an equally important question in exchange, that was a bargain. "You may ask. I may not answer."

He bowed his head gracefully, his white hair slipping over his shoulders. "Acceptable. First, come closer, out the wind. It is cooler down here and voices carry."

Shit.

"You want me to stand at your mirror-pool?" I asked forthright.

Toushek tilted his head back and laughed, his red eyes briefly taking on an ivory sheen. "Ah. As a matter of fact, I do."

"Would you push me through it?"

"No. I have no interest in disrupting your Dragonchild's plans for Manalar by abducting you, but I am curious about the one … or two Baenar with whom he has chosen to merge auras. You are a first, as I've never seen this touch cloying about him before."

"Yes," I said, shifting my stance on the sinking hill. "He told me."

Toushek smiled; he looked proud. "Good for him. Beautifully effective when you put your minds to it, whether against the Malok or in snatching that one shining Human soul out of reach of his enemies. I imagine the Dragon son has realized he *cannot* try for the pool without you, lest he disturb her true guardian." Another chuckle when I didn't respond. "No doubt a surprise to him, if not to me. But then, he never listened to *me* about such matters."

I stepped partway down the dune while he spoke. The ruler was right, the air was cooler. Pleasantly so. As for what he'd spoken so freely and casually, I set it aside, trying not to inspect it too closely. Easier to assume it must have a speck of truth which might get me to swallow the whole. Truth from his perspective, at best.

"Your question, Lord?" I prompted, stopping midway.

"You cannot see in the mirror," he said, one fang resting on his full lower lip.

"I do not know that I will wake up whole if I do."

"Ah. I frighten you." He breathed in through his nose. "If you understood the weapon you carry, I think talking with me would scare you much less by comparison."

Perhaps. Perhaps not.

Another cool breeze swirled through the trough, carrying an oddly familiar scent from far away. I sniffed the air, trying to recall when I'd caught it before.

My visitor smiled. "Curious? That is home."

"Home?"

"Yes. Mine. Nearby, but unobtrusive to mortal dreams."

I sighed, taking another step down the slope. "Lord. Your question."

"You must look in the mirror before you leave."

"You confirm I *will* leave at all?"

"You shall awaken out of Reverie as any Davrin does." He bowed at the waist, his grace more elegant than any Palace bua back home. "I have no cause to harm you."

"You are forcing a trade."

"Not at all. Answering my question is voluntary, and the mirror has little to do with that question." Toushek waited for me to approach. "Your courage as a messenger and champion is what offers you any reward for accepting risk and opportunity together."

That ploy was not enough to draw me in, given the source, but my bigger concern was when would I awake from Reverie. Would *he* decide that, even if it placed me into a state akin to Dragon Sleep? If I wished or waited long enough, could I choose to wake up whether I peered into that mirror or not?

What the fuck am I doing out here?

Toushek laughed, waiting with patient poise.

Breathe.

Finally, I approached. The chill in the air intensified the lower I went, until the unforgettable scent of morning frost entered my nose, bringing memories of me and my Sisters training in the Western Mountains. It also reminded me of the flecks of white drifting around out from a dark cloud, shortly before Morixxyleth had flown off using a pair of newly grown wings.

Snow.

The sky shifted from an eternal sunset into dusk and night; I watched the red sand fade into black and blue. The oasis, though clear and shining, failed to reflect a single star above.

"*Hey*," I protested, alarmed.

"Don't run," he commanded.

A clear warning.

At the edge of the mirror and right before my eyes, the sand fused into rock, a stone floor spreading like the contents of a spilled goblet beneath my feet. The horizon vanished, as did the sky, as if someone had pulled down the Moons. All pathways disappeared into darkness, shadows surrounding us, as if a mountain had swallowed the trough in the dunes.

The only source of dim light radiated from the rough, clear crystal encasing a disquieting and too-familiar black throne.

Goddess ...

"You are the wielder of Soul Drinker," said the Elven ruler. "Have you checked on the gatekeeper lately?"

"I've ... been occupied," I croaked, my heartbeat throbbing in my ears.

He sneered. "I assure you that demon does not intend to wait until you *aren't* occupied."

Toushek stood in between me and that black throne, and his appearance changed to a form like I'd seen at the first battle of Manalar: a head taller than me, his natural Elven beauty enhanced seven-fold while his skin lightened from Davrin-black to red-bronze and his long, white hair shifted to a shade like burned copper.

No longer covered neck-to-foot in modest travel clothes, the ruler stood naked from the waist up, his chest and arms bare, hands lightly adorned by elegant rings on his fingers. His legs and feet were still covered by the brown leather sarong. Large, earth-red wings rose and expanded freely from his back. Finally, ivory horns jutted through his hair in fine points, taking the shape of a crown.

"Sirana."

My name struck like a blow, the first time he'd spoken it since this dream began.

"You risk *everything* dear to you should you ignore this too long."

I tried to look at his face, his empty eyes subtly glowing the same shade as his horns. "What do I ignore, Lord? And who *are* you? If we're speaking names, you don't look like a 'Toushek.'"

One corner of his mouth lifted. "Thank you. Here, in Ice Heart, you may call me Indrath. But do have caution using it anywhere else."

Ice Heart? Where was that?

"Indrath," I repeated with a nod. "What am I ignoring?"

"Look closer at the crystal you created," he urged, stepping out of my way. "I was not lying to you. Your solution, while unique, is temporary."

Two steps closer to that throne, I stopped, unwilling to peer deeper into the motionless shadow within. Nonetheless, I spotted the hairline cracks at the base.

Damn it all.

"This is the 'mirror' you wanted me to look at before I woke up?"

"Nothing more," he agreed, standing at my shoulder and studying the crystal mass like a fine sculpture.

I frowned. "Are you hinting at a better solution?"

"Mine *is* better," he crooned, "but would require a deal."

"*Pfft.* No. I don't want to end up like Cris-ri-phon."

Or Innathi.

"Very well. I remind you of my voluntary question which you agreed to hear."

Sigh.

"Yes?"

"Who is your child's father?"

I froze, my heart surging, my mind unable to think. I seized on a memory in the Guild's quarters in Augran, as Mourn held his hand to my belly, sensing the new aura and heartbeat of my baby.

"Mm, no," the Ice Lord countered. "To'vah-krav are not fertile, I'm afraid. Although … this could explain the curious gold thread I see in this precious new aura, depending on the nature of your Bargain with him."

Gold thread?

"Indeed. Your child is touched by To'vah magic, the same as your 'sister' is."

What? Had ...

Had he done that on purpose?

"If the father cannot be the Dragonchild," Indrath continued, "who is he, Sirana? Will you answer?"

I tried to speak: *No, I will not.*

My voice was stuck.

"There is another possibility," he continued as if in light conversation, choosing not to notice my distress. "Your Queen bears such a mark. Tell me, does she have any sons? And did you bed one of them?"

Three or four questions I never agreed to answer.

I wanted to leave.

Let me go.

"Not yet, Sirana. You haven't answered."

I bent over, hands clutching at my chest, my throat; my mouth was open but silent. Which ruler was causing this inability to speak my mind? The Ice Lord, my Queen, or both at once? The pain had been much worse before, but mostly, I feared I would never escape.

Because I couldn't *speak!*

I must leave. Let me wake.

"You haven't refused to answer. I would like to know."

Argh!

I dropped to the floor, curling over my knees with arms crossing my middle. *Stop looking at us ...*

"Your actions are too curious for me to do that. Just speak the father's name or say 'no.' The feeling will stop."

I could do neither. I was stuck. I was certain that he *knew* it.

I couldn't stay here until the crystal cracked. I refused to be alone when it happened. I didn't *have* to be.

Not again.

I had to tell them.

~M-Mor ... ~

"Yes?"

Consciously, I drew the strain from my face, relaxing my shoulders as I breathed. *~Morixxyleth.~*

Indrath didn't respond. He looked around and above us.

"M-Morixxyleth!" I growled out from the floor. *"Morixxyleth!"*

"Good pronunciation. Draconic is diffic —"

"Gavin!"

Indrath stopped.

"Gavin! Help me!"

Cold air drifted in as if from outside, and Indrath sighed as he turned around.

"Welcome to Ice Heart, Deathwalker," he said cordially. "Careful where you place your feet, it's a steep drop. Tell me, where is your battle brother?"

"Crossing the shadows, I believe."

My heart thundered in my chest to hear my ally's voice somewhere high in the dark chamber. Gavin's familiar gait took steps one at a time.

It worked?

"Apparently," Indrath said, slightly annoyed.

How? Had they been hovering over me or asleep and dreaming? Had Jael told them something was wrong, or could they see for themselves?

"Aha," the Ice Lord sighed, turning to me. "That would mean —"

I shrieked when dark, clawed hands reached from the shadows, grabbing and dragging me into them.

I came aware some distance from the winged Elf. My bodyguard clutched me tightly, loosening his grip only to push me behind him. His long tail wrapped around my waist as an assurance I wouldn't be snatched right back.

"Exquisite timing," Indrath mused.

I gathered my bearings, realizing Mourn had reappeared behind Gavin on a dizzyingly high staircase, one far too narrow for its height. We stood high above the throne room upon a weaving pathway which lacked any banisters or railings at all.

Nothing but void underneath.

"Do you claim right of contract, Lord?" the half-blood asked, snarling his question.

Indrath huffed a dry laugh. "No, Shadow's son. She told me she is not interested at this time."

Mourn caught the phrasing, I was sure, but did not react. "Then we will take our leave. But first, I ask that you take yours and let the throne be where it is. Give a granddaughter more time."

Indrath's quiet laugh held that worrisome threat from before. "Oh, not to worry. I quite like how it is. Creative. Insightful. Perceptive, even. Work to be proud of. I look forward to the next phase."

My limbs shook to hear this. What did he mean to say?

The Ice Lord offered nothing else, summoning a door much like the one he'd used at the Temple of Manalar. Snowflakes drifted in and landed on the floor, refusing to melt.

"If the gatekeeper becomes too much for you, granddaughter," Indrath said, his ivory gaze tracing the floating stairway up to me, "you may always call. I *will* help you rather than see you consumed." Next, he addressed Gavin. "Herald of the Grey Maiden. Please pay my respects to your Lady. Tell her I am open to new arrangements."

Lastly, the Ice Lord grinned menacingly at Mourn, showing full fangs. "As for you, trespasser, be careful. Lest we meet in Ice Heart *without* a pregnant mother between us."

With this, the winged Elf stepped through a door which ceased to exist an instant later. Gavin, Mourn, and I stood upon stairs leading to nowhere, gazing down at the subtle glow of crystal containing the gatekeeper.

Gradually, convinced we were alone, Gavin pointed beyond the throne. "Is that the way?"

"The way?" I echoed.

"To the Elsewhere. Where you spoke to the ensnared eidolons."

"Uh, I think? … Um, yes, it is."

"Interesting. I can hear them from here."

He could? I certainly could *not*.

The Deathwalker turned toward us, his pupils subtly glowing. "Sirana killed a Hellhound inside the Temple, did she not?"

"She did," Mourn answered, and I groaned as we followed his chain of thought.

I'd thrown the red rune dagger in that tight hall of the Temple, burying the blade in the chest of that pale giant of a man. Soul Drinker had cut through his protective wards, claiming his Vis and Vitas at once. The Hellhound had collapsed without throwing his spiked chain at an easy cluster of opponents.

After the battle, Innathi teased me about the new Ma'ab presence in her realm. *Him and Kurn.*

"You'd have to get past the Davrin Queen," I murmured, unable to hide the tremors as exhaustion crept in.

"We may discuss it," Mourn said, gathering me close. "As we shall all options."

"Indeed." Gavin gazed past the crystal sculpture, perhaps still listening to the dead but disinclined to press the measure.

My bodyguard turned me toward the nearest shadow. "Let us leave and rise awake."

His body blocked the way down so I didn't have to look at the throne … or the larger crack which appeared in the crystal just after Indrath left.

Damn the Void.

And damn the Hells that offered to cage it for a price.

Chapter 3

I awoke in the circumstance I expected, with Jael hovering above me. She vibrated with nerves, drawing my attention despite the Dragonchild being so much closer.

"*Sirana?*" Her throat was tight. "*Can you hear me?*"

I met her eyes. "*Yes …*"

"It worked," my bodyguard murmured above me in Trade. "She is safe."

Jael sagged in relief, and my eyes slid upward. Gavin was kneeling by my head, his dry palm upon my sticky brow. He lifted it as soon as I spoke, his irises rising out of blackness. The Deathwalker got to his feet without a word, putting space between us. Glancing around me, I confirmed laying in his quarters within the Dwarven redoubt, in the same stained cot in the corner where I'd settled down.

Mourn loomed over me, his hand closed tight and entirely around mine, both of us gripping Soul Drinker by its black, red-marked handle. Threads of the loosened peace-knot peeked out from between his fingers.

"Who was it?" Krithannia asked.

I blinked in surprise, craning to see who *else* was in the room. I spotted the Guild Mistress and Tamuril, with Pilla doing her best to smooth her feathers. The greybeard Talov held Mourn's shadow drake, Graul.

And Willven Isboern.

The Godblood had returned inside to come here? How long had this been going on?

Mourn's tail swiped briefly across the stone floor as he exhaled, taking his time to choose an answer. First, he helped me to sit up, letting Jael stay beside me as I rested against the wall.

"The same power who interfered with the Deathless at the sacred pool," he said.

"What?"

"The red-winged lord I saw in my Sleep."

Krithannia paled. "Wh- ... What did he want?"

Mourn glanced at me. "At the least, he wanted to show he can reach Sirana through Soul Drinker whenever he chooses."

My mouth opened, and Tami gasped in alarm. Talov rumbled something in Dwarvish which sounded like a harsh curse.

"Payback?" asked the greybeard.

"I'm certain."

"Fer the 'trespass?'"

"He mentioned that." Mourn paused. "But something else has occurred in my Dreams. I am certain he is following a trail, and I may have interfered again."

Talov's smirk appeared even through his beard. In his arms, Graul scoffed, leaning his head and neck down to signal the Dwarf should set him on the floor. Jael moved closer to hold me, sniffing briefly at my neck and putting her arm around me, while Graul waddled over to Mourn's lap.

"How can he access the relic directly and at will?" Krithannia asked, both stern and worried. "I thought only the wielder could commune in that state."

The Dragonchild lifted his small companion and shook his head. "Apparently not. But we've known for some time he had something to do with the creation of the Deathless, and we all witnessed at the Temple that he controls him. Something we suspected, but this revealed a much longer history with the black dagger than we knew."

"Clearly," she agreed, quite unhappy about the revelation.

"He's sure grinding his heel in it, ain't he?" Talov grumbled. "Think he'll try tah make yer Bargain harder tah keep?"

"Probably," Mourn confessed.

I glanced at the Human Captain and his patient expression, wondering how much he understood. I had been in the center, yet *I* barely followed their cryptic talk.

Mourn's tail suggested he might be worried. I certainly was, having learned I could be "captured" and in need of rescue even when my body nestled in my bodyguard's lap.

The Dragonchild had warned me since Yong-wen about my "lucid" dreams with my buas, that others might be drawn to us. I hadn't understood how or who might have concerned him.

Now, I did. I knew the name of one ancient who wanted to know my baby's sire *and* had tormented Cris-ri-phon for ages — probably through Soul Drinker, if the determined Brom Troshin had worked with the Ma'ab for decades to retrieve the relic of his assassinated queen.

"I understand it's unwise to speak his name," Captain Isboern began. "But I must ask. Do you mean the presence I sensed before the deathless sorcerer turned from the door and cast the strike that opened the rift, allowing the Grey mists and creatures through?"

"We do," Mourn said. "And later, that same presence was speaking with the Grey guardians. I do not know what they discussed."

"That is … concerning."

"You still have the boon from my Lady," Gavin said, his eyes drifting with subtle longing toward his worktable. "She has granted your lifetime to fulfill the oath you made while kneeling in *Pisc'sagrad* waters."

However long or short that lifetime proves to be.

"Thank you." The Captain considered that. "Do I understand we may have opponents beyond the Ma'ab in reclaiming *Pisc'sagrad*?"

"Safe tah assume," Talov said. "The Bishops sure did."

"And if this … um, nameless one —"

"The merchant," I offered. "He's most often appeared as a traveling trader."

"You've seen him *before*?" Krithannia asked, hiding her alarm well in front of Isboern.

"I didn't *know* it was him before. Now I do. He *is* a merchant. He offers what you need but only through deals."

Captain Isboern leaned away as if a realization struck him. "The 'Merchant' is a devil?" He read my Sister's face and put up his hands. "Not the frail 'proof' the *Dios Guerrimos* accepted to interrogate innocents on devilry, but a *true* devil?"

"Devil?" Jael repeated with impatience, her face twisting in frustration. "Called me this a lot. Still don't grab what."

"What the Manalari call devils and demons," Isboern explained, "they do without discretion. I understand they are *not* the same among those worldly enough to see their patterns." He dipped his chin to Mourn. "Each of them corrupts what is generous and loving within us, but the devils do so by negotiation, coaxing exchanges with hidden costs which bind tightly until one's soul is trapped. The creatures *I* would call 'demons' do not have any such desire for trade or structured deals. They consume what they wish and cannot truly be bargained with. They overwhelm and wear down until the soul loses the will to resist."

My eyebrow raised in thought. The psion had skewered the difference I'd experienced, facing both the gatekeeper and the Ice Lord.

"Interestin' that ya heard it like that, Captain," Talov said, smiling wryly. "Aye, tha's the Clans' take on these tempters showin' up in our oldest tales an' sneakin' about our world."

The Godblood smiled mildly. "The world's stories do seem to have a kernel of truth to be found, though much of it may lie beyond life's known borders."

Gavin nodded in thoughtful confirmation, hearing something he'd once told me spoken plainly by another. This made it easier to see how the Abyss and the Hells held conflicting methods but the same goal: to feed an unrelenting hunger for power and dominance over …

Over what? Magic? Life? Vis?

Not unlike the Priestesses of the Sanctuary using the Davrin of Sivaraus, wearing us down to sate their desires and attain their goals of influence. If they and my Valshraress served the Abyss, which I knew to be true, then I understood why the Ice Lord had dropped those remarks to tease or tempt me, fully convincing me that he *knew* something useful about Her.

Like bearing the 'mark' of a Dragon. Or asking me if I bedded one of Her sons ... I shook my head, squeezing my eyes closed as a confused, hollow denial swept through me. *Madness.*

Above me, Talov spoke with a soothing rumble. "Aye. Best we can tell, the 'Merchant' *is* a race ov Elf, but aligned with the Infernal Hells. We don't know how old he is, just that he's been making himself a pain in our Dragon Son's backside fer the last century."

"It's fair to say," Mourn interjected, "I might have thrown the first insult, Talov."

"*Pah!* Seems tah me ya shook 'im last time, so he's tryna shake ya back."

"This does Sirana little good, my friend, if I've pulled her in between us."

"Not how I see it, kid. She was pulled in by Brom an' that dagger. Ya pulled her out before that deal broker could make it worse."

Mourn appeared like he might counter that, but I straightened up, drawing his attention.

"You pulled me out," I agreed firmly. "In the warp rot forest, you *saved* me and my baby. I ... don't know what might have happened to me if you and Gavin hadn't carried me to the river to rest. Either I'd have starved, or the dagger would have gotten me. It took *days* to avoid those outcomes."

Jael's mouth dropped open while the Dragonblood's shoulders lowered. My bodyguard gave up the argument to the greybeard's satisfaction.

"Heh, an' that was *before* yer agreement. Bet the 'Merchant' is annoyed you caught up tah a Dark Elf before he spotted an easy target gettin' in over her head."

"She *not* easy," Jael growled impulsively.

Talov lifted his palms in peace, grinning. "Aye. Yer right. She's tough."

But I am in over my head.

The Dwarf's smile proved infectious, touching Graul, Krithannia, Tamuril, and Isboern before gradually coming to me and Mourn. I squeezed my Sister's shoulder and drew another deep breath or two. She chewed her inner cheek to hold a contrary nature in check, as it tended to bubble over when she was uneasy.

"How went the events in camp after I left?" I asked, looking at Isboern to answer.

The man with blue eyes like mine blinked in surprise, blond eyebrows lifting. "Oh. Well! Nothing too troublesome. Those who cannot help shall leave in the next few days, and I received all the insights I need to bring to the Guild's table."

"And ..." I hesitated. "Mathias Briar?"

"Still in his cell," Talov answered.

"Awake?"

"Oh, aye!" The Dwarf laughed, making me wonder how the Clans were handling him or what he might be saying. "Less worry, *lasschen*. He can wait."

"Until when?"

"At least until you've eaten." Mourn climbed to his feet, cradling Graul with one arm and moving my boots closer to me with the other.

"We're discussing strategy later tonight," Krithannia said as I took one boot and put it on. "After we collect everyone's ideas. I'd like you and Jael to be there before we speak with the skin hunter."

Huh bua ...

"There's enough time to eat and refresh yourself," Isboern agreed. "So, please, take the opportunity."

I stood up, stamping my feet to settle them in my boots before retying the peace-knot around Soul Drinker. "Very well."

"Come to my quarters," Mourn said. "We'll eat there."

"Alright." I checked my spider pouch, alarmed to find it empty. "Um, wait ..."

~Where are you, babies? Come out where I can see you.~

Two chimes, and large, black spiders crawled out together from a shadowed corner. I went to collect them while Pilla clacked her beak, releasing a brief, irritable cry when Tamuril stepped slightly behind Isboern. Meanwhile, Graul turned his head and hissed at the feathered hunter.

"Always forget the spiders until we sense crawling," Jael smirked.

Quite true, but notable to me was how many others had surrounded me while I'd been unaware and in distress, and yet my tiny guardians never attacked.

~*Are you that discerning?*~ I thought, a question they couldn't answer. If not, then perhaps these allies simply felt that safe.

CHAPTER 4

MOURN SHARED A LARGE MEAL WITH JAEL AND ME, GRAUL NIBBLING SOME before crawling into a soft nest of bedding in the corner. Just the four of us for now, and my tender head and ears thanked me for the lack of excess stimulation while I ate.

I'd been outside in the summer heat for half the day, helping to maintain a complex, psionic-magic mindlink for the Guild. I'd gone inside only to plummet into a threatening and thoroughly unrestful Reverie, which was then followed by an intense discussion about an insulted devil usurping a demon's relic.

I hadn't begun to recover.

"I am not certain I am up for the strategy meeting," I admitted once we'd cleaned the bowls set upon the serving tray. "Am I crucial?"

The half-blood considered. "You are where my involvement lies, and I am crucial to the outcome."

Something about how he said it made Jael snort softly, but she waved her hand, telling him to ignore her.

Mourn gave her a look but continued. "After four hundred years, the Bishops I helped to create are gone. I *want* to see Willven Isboern and the men he has trained rebalance the magic of Mount Sonai. I will help make it happen because the Ma'ab would be as bad or worse than the Bishops in restricting her flow."

"*Her* flow," Jael repeated, shaking her head slightly.

"Yes," Mourn answered, sounding slightly annoyed. "She bears a recognized Name among the To'vah."

"A pool of water is female."

"*Yes*. And you benefitted from that while fighting with me in the Temple."

My Sister blinked. "I did?"

"You did." Mourn's tail flicked. "Or the Words I fed you would have you holding your tongue for a week."

It wouldn't last. I bit my lip rather than say that. *We're not in the Cloister.*

Jael's nose wrinkled. "So, what is her name?"

He sighed. "It's not wise to speak it without need."

"*Pfft*. All boast, you."

The half-blood's tail thumped, and Graul's eyes cracked open as the drake lifted his head to prop it on the edge of his nest, peering with annoyance at the argument.

"*Sihe*," Mourn hissed. "Do you want to learn To'vah magic, or not?"

"Want to?" Jael threw up her hands. "I must! Or am crazy from pain!"

"Then stop doubting what I say. You sound foolish."

"Oh! I am not to ask and think? Just wait and obey?"

This time Mourn huffed in disbelief, his spines attempting once to lift beneath his harness. "You haven't discipline for either, Baenar, but need both to learn. Have I *not* proven I can teach you?"

Jael growled without words, matching his glare out of pure spite. Whatever rolled through her thoughts, she kept them to herself before jerking her eyes over to the tub of fresh water, soap, and clean towels.

"Fine. No more doubt." She got up and stepped away, tugging her shirt from her leather pants. "I will wash."

Mourn's irritation filled his large frame before he released it with a quick whip of his tail and a deep breath.

Meanwhile, Indrath's remarks sounded unwelcome in my mind.

"I have no interest in disrupting your Dragonchild's plans for Manalar by

abducting you, but I am curious about the one ... or two Baenar with whom he has chosen to merge auras. ... I imagine he has realized he cannot try for the pool without you, lest he disturb her true guardian."

"A question about the Merchant," I said once my bodyguard had calmed.

"Yes?"

"He called us granddaughters. Was he Baenar once?"

"No," Mourn answered immediately. "Nor was he Naulor. Of that, Krithannia and I are certain."

I would take his word for it. "So, why 'granddaughters?' You used it to placate him?"

He shrugged, glancing over at Jael, who was halfway undressed. "More or less. He is a monarch like your Valsharess, but one who would claim all of those bearing Elven blood on Miurag if he could."

I blinked. "Naulor and Davrin both?"

"Absolutely. Along with half-bloods like me."

Another memory jolted me.

"Hers. No longer his."

"Half-bloods." I repeated. "Like the Davrin-Zauyrians? Would the Merchant claim Cris-ri-phon's children?"

Mourn's tail paused. "He would. If he could reach them."

"You could ask your 'hybrid' bodyguard about that," Toushek chuckled. "You may be glad you did."

"All twelve?" I asked. "They're alive?"

Too direct. He leaned back from the question. "We're losing time. Sirana, will you wash with your Sister so the Dwarves can change the supplies before I leave? I will attend this meeting if you are too tired and lock Soul Drinker in Talov's box to assure your safety. You may stay here with Graul. We can revisit once we better determine your place."

Jael dunked a fresh cloth in clean water. "*Pfeh.* Her 'place.'"

"Place in the mission," Mourn added with a rumble that suggested his patience was on its last thread.

I followed his eyes and smirked despite myself. My Sister was showing us her bare ass, feet planted comfortably apart so I could glimpse her netherlips. She neither looked nor responded to his correction, lifting an arm to start scrubbing, daring him to look or say something.

He looked but said nothing.

"Yeah, I will," I sighed, pushing myself up. "I'll scrub down before you leave."

He turned away. "Thank you, Sirana."

Grinning down, I asked, "Want to help?"

The lingering annoyance wiped clean off his face.

"Or join me?" I added, softer.

He frowned, gold eyes flicking toward my Sister then his snoozing drake in the corner.

I shrugged with an easy smile. "You kept your Bargain, mercenary. I would keep mine."

His expression shifted as he understood.

"I also don't ..." I paused, the smile fading despite myself. "I don't like how his presence lingers. I could use the release, Mourn. And if you could, I welcome you. It might clear my head."

His posture softened. His tail slid closer to him in a sidewinding curve; he fisted the ground to push himself up.

"I will help you wash," he said. "Then, we will see."

I smiled. "That'll be enough."

By the time I'd secured my weapons belt with Mourn's harness on the wall and pulled off my boots and stockings, Jael had finished scrubbing. She hadn't wasted any time, as brisk and efficient as we'd been in the Cloister or training in the wilderness. Her mouth was tight as she left the tub and towels to us, lying down nude on Mourn's bed pallet to let her skin dry in the air, one leg bent.

Subtle.

Rausery would have cuffed her on the head for her attitude, but I'd only done that if I wanted to start wrestling with her. I also didn't yearn to dive in and mediate whatever instructor-learner agreement they sorted out between them each time Jael poked the buzzer's nest.

I had my Bargain or bond with each of them, but neither of those involved telling them how to act around each other. Instead, I preferred to reward Mourn's patience with the abrasive Sister I'd begged him and many others to help me find.

I wasn't too proud to do it where she could see it, either The effect might last longer, anyway.

My spider guardians were out and inspecting the corners of the room while Mourn assisted in removing my armor and clothes. The help wasn't strictly necessary, but the touching was nice, as were calmer gazes as he assured himself up close that my body and unborn were unharmed.

"Let us do you, first," he rumbled, submerging a clean cloth in the tub and squeezing it out with one hand.

I grinned, opening my arms with palms up. "Be mindful of my tits. They're still sore."

Smiling slightly, he began wiping me down, never missing a spot with deliberate, overlapping strokes and an occasional circular massage. Over my face and neck, he caught sweat and grime under my jaw and behind my ears, then went to my shoulders and arms before tracing around and over my breasts with a lighter touch before moving on to my stomach.

My back faced the bed pallet and the nest, so he'd be aware of Jael and Graul, but while they remained quiet, I couldn't tell if his thoughts were on them at any particular point. He concentrated on me, the tip of his tail moving slowly along with his hand movements. I wasn't concerned about scrapes from his claws as he massaged my hips and thighs while wiping them down.

~Oh … Nice.~

A smile touched his mouth, a hint of sensual interest prodding the front of his loose trousers. We'd each hung up our cloaks upon our arrival, so the Yungian-style bottoms were the Dragonchild's singular garment with the magical bracers. A curious similarity with Indrath and his rings, assuming the Ice Lord might also have an aversion to shoes.

Frowning, I closed my eyes to dislodge the thought and let it drift away. When I opened them, my bodyguard's nose had wrinkled somewhat as his tongue flicked out to taste the air near my hip before draw it in through his teeth.

~Uh-oh.~

"Stink of devil?" I asked with a strained smile.

"No more than I'd expect," he answered without concern.

A moment later he spoke through the pearl. *Do not worry, Kiabil. Infernal presence lingers, as you said, but it will fade.*

~And you can smell it?~

A slight nod. *The same as I can smell Abyssal presence, like the Sathoet in the crypt. This is not unusual, nor is it worrisome right now.*

A good point, and welcome reassurance.

Finishing my bare legs and feet, Mourn didn't shy from passing the rinsed cloth between my legs then moving to scrub my back, both of which were my favorite spots so far. I offered a moan of gratitude as he finished up then swiftly rubbed a dry towel all over me.

"Thank you," I said, reaching for the last clean cloth. "Have time for a rubdown yourself?"

The Dragonblood paused to consider our audience as he turned to look at his bed. Jael lay on her back, one arm propped beneath her head so she could watch. Her free hand had been playing idly with her mound fur but stopped when she met his gaze. She lifted it and signed with a wry slant, *I see you.*

"Hrm," Mourn grunted, his Elven ears shifting backward in a way I hadn't seen in a while.

~She did watch at the waterfall,~ I thought through the pearl, taking the initiative to begin wiping down his chest.

He sighed inside my mind. *I know you are correct, but I ... don't recall much as clearly as I'd like.*

~I believe you. How much do you remember?~

My shoulders burning, and that you were willing.

~That can't be all.~ I smirked, learning quickly that it took two different strokes in two directions to clean the transition where his patchy, purple-black scales turned to rough, dark skin. ~You teased her when she called to us, offering my turn to climax. You presented me, remember, holding my thighs open before her? And she sucked on me with you jammed inside my cunt.~

He lifted his arms so I could scrub his flanks, his erection obvious through his pants. *So I did.*

The half-blood might have been questioning why he'd done that as I rinsed and wrung the cloth, starting on his left arm.

You and Jael were in the fertility ritual that healed Tami's curse, he recalled thoughtfully.

~And you said it woke you, yes.~ I rinsed and wrung again, going for his right arm. ~Sorry about that ... ~

No, it was worth it. I can tell the difference in Tamuril's eyes. Especially when she looks at Isboern.

Warmth bloomed in my chest. ~Agreed. Worth it.~

You feel to stand on better ground with her.

~I am. I mean, we are. It's gotten ... better.~

He let his pleasure pass through our mindlink. *How so?*

~I think ... I think it's that she believes I won't hurt her. I could say how I had no reason to, but she didn't believe me. Now she does.~

I am glad.

I finished that arm, doing what little I could to dab in between the metal whorls of the bracers, and got started on his back, noticing how hard and thick the scales were from shoulders to kidneys compared to those in the front. He didn't seem to have much sensitivity, either; I could scrub and claw all I wanted, and he might only feel tapping.

Once I reached his tail, however, that was another story.

~Does that tickle?~ I asked, incredulous that he couldn't keep still.

Well, it's ... Ah! Quite awake.

~Any pain?~

None. Just ... intense. I am always aware of the whole of it.

The prehensible limb kept winding around my forearms as I tried to be thorough. Jael and Graul each chortled at one point through the process.

Finally, I got to his waistline, tugging at the black bottoms before dunking the cloth. ~The rest? Or not?~

Mourn considered, briefly withdrawing from the link to focus elsewhere. *Still gathering. We have time.*

He still had an erection.

I grinned, laying the damp cloth on my shoulder, and took hold of

41

the waist of his pants. Drawing them down, I paused to give him time to draw his tail out of the hole sewn at the back before I freed the stiff cock at the front. My hands stopped at mid-thigh so I could lean in and catch the bobbing head between my lips, giving it lavish tongue ending in a loud suck.

Mourn stiffened. "*Ffff* — ! Sirana!"

"Aha!" Jael commented. "She make the Shadow curse?"

Graul snickered but merely turned around in his nest with a yawn to return to sleep.

"Sorry, big distraction," I said, pulling the material down to his knees. "Step out so you don't trip. I'll wipe your legs."

"No miss the third one," my Sister remarked, her hand digging deeper between her netherlips as Mourn shed his pants.

"I'll come to that, promise."

Retrieving the damp cloth from my shoulder, I smiled up to share in the jest but stopped. He didn't look amused as his eyes slid to the side.

~*I say something wrong?*~ I asked, kneeling to finishing what I'd started.

With a deep breath, he let me finish scrubbing his legs and straighten up before meeting my eyes. *I am interested. But the … scenario is not my favorite. Standing on display while two females inspect and remark on my form.*

~*Ah. Of course.*~ I grimaced, my skin chilling. ~*Just Red Sister talk, honestly. We jest about each other like this, many wearing a cock to remark upon. I wasn't thinking of a slave but a Cloister companion.*~

I believe you. It didn't feel like that time. But …

~*Not arousing,*~ I agreed, noting the dip of his pole.

"What is wrong?" Jael asked, rolling to get up on her elbow. "You stop. All silent talk."

At least she noticed.

"He is not vain," I said.

"Vain?"

"Yeah. Shared talk about his body doesn't give pleasure." I caught his eye. "Is that so?"

A pause, and he dipped his chin. "It is."

The reason or cause didn't matter.

"Hmph." Jael rubbed her chin. "Still likes … *doing* to his body?"

My earlier grin slipped into place. "Last I checked."

She huffed, showing a wider grin. "Last I *saw*."

Before the Dragonchild could think too long about that, I touched his arm and asked bluntly, "What do you want most, my mouth or my slit?" I saw a glint in his eye. "And do you want to stand or nudge Jael off the pallet?"

"*Hai*," she protested, only slightly annoyed because she'd move if I insisted.

Metallic gold eyes looked me over, down to my toes then up, lingering on my lips.

"I want your mouth," he stated, clear and deep. "And I want to brace against the wall with you before me. Like on the rooftops."

My face flushed. ~*Hoo bua …* ~

"Rooftops?" Jael asked.

I held my focus on him. "You liked that."

"I did."

"Come here."

Tugging his hand, I brought him to the nearest wall perpendicular to the door. Facing away from it and toward him, I kneeled in a central spot, where Mourn could see anyone entering from one direction while my Sister shifted for a better view of our action from the other. In the far corner, Graul easily ignored us, burrowing into his nest.

With my ass resting on my heels, I took familiar hold of his shaft, lifting my eyes to meet an intense gaze as he leaned in to brace himself. His hips shifted forward, bringing a full and revived erection closer to my lips. I extended my tongue first, slowly, then took a lewd swipe over his triangular glans and around the prominent ridge.

He stiffened and hissed in pleasure as I tasted slick, salty drops of precum on my tongue. "Mm, yum."

I opened wider, leaning forward to slide him along my tongue and deeper between my lips. He tasted cleaner now than he'd smelled upon first waking up, though a fair bit of musk remained from his exertions outside during the day. As before, I could only fit him halfway, but I made the most of it, using both hands to stimulate the thick base and around his scrotum while my whole mouth caressed and swallowed him like a ravenous serpent eating its meal whole.

"*Mmrrr*, Sirana ..." he said rumbled.

His tail swiped the air with excitement twice before sliding in to wrap teasingly around my right thigh. I responded by spreading my knees and raising my ass so he could coil around it three times. The tip curled against my bare sex, writhing in between my netherlips.

"Mmmm!" I moaned with my mouth full.

His eyes had slid shut, but the noise prompted them to open and watch my face as he thrust his cock in, quite gently compared to most Red Sisters. I let him go deep, relaxing my throat and stopping my breath, suppressing any sensation which might lead me to gag. I held his gaze.

His black member pulsed once as vertical pupils expanded. I held my breath as he took further thrusts, enjoying each slow stroke before withdrawing to give me air. He held still so I could breathe through my nose, sucking and lapping the head and shaft while the tip of his tail flicked and teased my nub. The more it writhed around, the wetter I made those small, fine scales.

So much for washing down before he left.

I licked, stroked with my tongue, collecting a small spring of constant, dribbling lubricant from him. I used part of it to glide in endless patterns and swallowed the rest of it.

~Yes ... ~

"Yes," he echoed in answer. "*Oh* ..."

While not the vigorous fuck of the waterfall, every motion was deliberate, and I believed Mourn was close to climax.

~Spurt in my mouth, please?~ I asked.

He tensed, the cock in my mouth twitching as he flexed, his tail curling stiffly between my buttocks, as if using the cleft for leverage as the rest constricted around my thigh. The sudden pressure playing on my netherhole tightened my jaw, causing my eyes to widen.

The half-blood's gaze hadn't left mine until that moment. He exhaled, breath rattling, his focus dragged away behind tight eyelids as he grunted.

The first gush of cream hit the top of my throat.

~*Oh, yes! Come!*~

I swallowed, making him growl louder though avoiding the full roar. His cock pumped several times, filling my mouth with thick semen, though the only tingling sensation came from how wide my jaw stretched as he pressed in. He smelled and tasted earthy, like a spicy root I hadn't yet dug up on the Surface.

Kneeling in place, slick hands wrapped around his pole, I relished the heat and fragrance, allowing it to cleanse the cloying sensation which had been lingering ever since the encounter in my dream.

He sighed through the pearl. *Kiabil ... *

We parted, an odd little pulse running through my nerves as my mouth came off him, separate from my rapid heartbeat. Behind the half-blood, Graul growled, shifting uncomfortably. Beside him, my Sister was gone.

Jael had left the pallet.

"Wh ..."

Turning my head left I spotted her crouching against our wall to get a better view, copper eyes blazing with interest.

"She not peak yet," she said, lifting eyes to my bodyguard. "Have time to go stiff again?"

"*Mrrm*," Mourn rumbled, sounding wary as he straightened up from the wall and glanced toward the door. "We've not much time."

She huffed. "You gonna take and go?"

"Actually," I interjected, coaxing his tail to unwrap from around my thigh, the wet tip leaving my slit. "I'm still sore from last night. I'll pass on the fucking this time."

"Apologies." The Dragonblood winced, giving me a hand and helping me to my feet. "You offered your sex, though you are too sore?"

"I spoke before I realized it," I admitted wryly. "You picked the ready one, so no reason to contradict myself."

"Heat speak," Jael snickered, agreeing. "Or ... dirt talk?"

"Yes, that."

"I see." His posture seemed too straight as Jael moved closer; he stepped once to give us room.

"How about you lick her before you leave?" she suggested. "You have strong tongue."

"No, not that, either!" I blurted, forcing a laugh to recall how swollen and needy my cunt became each time he slathered it with spit. Sore or not, I'd probably ask for another pummeling.

My Sister tossed an odd look at my tone.

I planted a hand on her shoulder. "It's alright, Jael. There's not enough time before the meeting."

"*Pfft*, what? You serve him best I see besides Jaunda, because he pull you out of devil *he* made angry. Then he leave like a *matron* leave her *bua* to find your finish alone?"

"Jael —"

"She has you to serve her next," Graul remarked from his nest.

I grimaced, and Mourn's tail grew agitated when Jael snapped her gaze at the drake. "Who ask you, lizard?"

"Who asked you, *cait*?" he snapped, his throat pouch swelling, showing purple. "Their Bargain, not yours. Get your nose out before someone bites it off."

"You — !"

Mourn stepped in front of her when she made a sudden move toward the small drake. He scowled down at her, though her eyes dropped to his flaccid cock before glaring up at him.

"Leave him alone, *Vloszia Dalna*," he said in the same tone he'd taken with me in our early interactions. "If my bond-friend gains one injury from your harassment, I will make you pay."

"*Pah!* You never take full swing, 'teacher.'"

"Punishment has *many* options, apprentice."

"You let him say all like a rotted child?"

"You should speak? He is your *elder*, Baenar. Four times your age."

I'd frozen in terror, slick moisture grown cold on my sex as the confrontation snuffed my lingering arousal. At last, my voice broke out of its cage.

"*Stop! Jael! Come here, away from him. No picking a fight!*"

She couldn't pretend confusion when I spoke in Davrin; she obeyed readily enough, lifting hands as she stepped away from Mourn and closer to me. With the breathing room, the large half-blood turned, making eye contact in silent exchange with the drake.

★What's biting your nub?★ I signed to her when he looked away.

★You!★ she replied, teeth gritted. ★And him! Obvious!★

Then she folded her arms, refusing to sign once he turned around.

Damn it all.

"They are gathering for the meeting," Mourn said, his voice rough from his attempt to stay calm. "I am sorry, I must go. We can talk later, and I will excuse your absence to Krithannia."

Great.

For the best, however, given the simmering energy filling his quarters.

"Thank you," I answered. "And I'm sorry."

Mourn pulled his pants on, donning his harness and cloak without looking at me while I ignored the look Jael gave at apologizing for her behavior. At least I had an idea what the problem was.

One of them, anyway.

Then Mourn lifted my weapons belt from the wall.

"Uh, wait," I began in protest.

"I need to know you are secure," he said, "and that the Ice Lord cannot reach you while I am away. I promise I will lock this in Talov's box during the meeting. No one but us will know it is there."

My jaw clenched as my shoulders stiffened. Oh, Goddess, I didn't want him to take it. *Fuck!*

"Fine," I managed, unable to hide my resistance in a tight throat. "Leave. Do what's necessary."

"We will talk later."

"Yeah."

Mourn paused at the door with a parting shot for Jael. "If you dismiss Sirana's good sense and cause Graul distress, I will sense it, and you *will* be sorry you couldn't control yourself."

"Just go!" she barked.

He didn't quite slam the door, but the soft boom took time to fade.

CHAPTER 5

I TOOK A DEEP BREATH, STANDING FOR AN INSTANT IN THE *dorji-ka* OF YONG-wen, one among a group of young Humans also learning to breathe. I couldn't imagine seeing Jael do the same or hold any value in it.

"What?" she said in our tongue, no further relaxed with Mourn gone than when he'd stood in the room. "Disappointed?"

"Confused," I murmured.

"About what?"

I turned. "We talked about this. You *fought beside him*, beside both of us, not long ago. You jumped through shadows clinging to his back and used your new magic to battle invaders from two realms!"

"I didn't do it for the Humans!" she said. "I'd have *left* if I could! But you wouldn't, and neither would he! Now we're going back?!"

"We talked about this, too," I countered with another deep breath. "While he was Sleeping. We had days to come to an understanding. You told the Naulor more than once you would follow me, and you *know* why I c-can't ... I'm not ..."

Free.

Her face fell as she read my discomfort, her life-long resentment of the Palace and Priestesses clear on her face. "Isboern freed me. Why can't he do the same for you? Especially as you've been merging minds with him every chance you get."

"I need a tutor. Or I will die in pain and madness, the same as you." I paused, thinking over the question. An interesting idea, though our circumstances were different.

Maybe if I were going to miscarry anyway ... ?

The Godblood might heal me as he had Jael.

"Assume that he can," I said, overriding those fatalistic thoughts. "What then? I need Gavin to come with me to the Ley Tower, but he won't leave here. Not yet. And I can't go West if this means the Ma'ab will follow me home. Better to help them achieve this goal, since Gavin's Lady left guardians to wait and see how it turns out. And don't forget, this is a grand opportunity for *you* to learn about your magic, and in shorter time than *any* battlemage studies at home."

This swayed her only because we'd discussed this before. I knew these weren't her true concerns. Something else bothered her; it lay deep yet wasn't our Queen's geas.

Her harsh sign returned to mind.

★What's biting your nub?★

★You! And him! Obvious!★

Our quieter conversation from last night followed, while Gavin had summoned Nightmare out of the ground.

"You did so well at the Temple city, Sister. You paid back the cost and never gave in. Mourn can teach you to fight better, please remember that."

"Mm. Better choice, yes. Only ... do not want ..." She made a deliberate motion, like pulling against something attached to her wrists. "Chains. From him."

"Nor does he have any he'd force on you."

"Does he not?"

"No," I said. "I am certain."

She didn't believe me.

I hoped this wasn't like Tamuril *couldn't* believe that I regretted our first meeting until I proved it in a ritual which set her free.

We can't undo what I chose for you, Jael.

"You seemed to enjoy the fun at the waterfall," I murmured.

"Pfft!" She rolled her eyes. "Like we had a choice? He was mad with

lust, Sirana, and *I* caused it, he said so! We could not fight him, *you* had to calm him like a Priestess tugging her Sathoet."

My chest stung. *Ouch.*

Not the same, no.

Mourn isn't anything like Kerse.

Except in how they'd turned against their matrons, refusing to serve as a slave a moment longer.

Huh, bua ...

"He and I have a Bargain," I said, my voice cool. "Carefully negotiated. It took weeks! And I can only abide by it. You may not have understood, but Krithannia and Talov ..." I waved toward the nest. "Even Graul. They warned us!"

The shadow drake lifted his ears hearing his name, eyes opening wider as he shed any pretense of sleeping.

"Warned us?" Jael repeated.

"They warned us when we first got here," I continued, "well before we knew a ritual could help Tamuril. His closest friends *said* that the To'vah in him doesn't always recognize his allies when he first wakes from deep sleep. They've seen this before. You didn't create that, Jael, though you may have been a trigger."

"Maybe," she replied, her face tight. "But that's the thing. You say you 'can only abide' by some binding agreement which involves you *serving* him whenever he wishes! While you may get release as an afterthought. You've never looked so ... so toadish before a big cock before!"

My lips tightened, and I breathed in through my nose, bearing in mind that she hadn't experienced the half-blood when he wasn't being watched. Mourn was plenty generous, but for me to explain what wasn't owed would not help, only give her excuses to twist later.

Crossing my arms, I tilted my head. "You mentioned I sucked him as I do Jaunda. How exactly is that 'toadish' when I simply *want* to do it with both of them?"

"Well, she's a Red Sister, for one," she sniped, knowing at once that argument was weak.

"And he's a Guild leader in a network larger than Rausery and D'Shea combined. Which cock do you think would win a fight?"

Jael made a face. She knew the answer.

"You've seen me do lower and retain my will," I said. "*You've* done lower and kept on fighting. *Every* Sister does!"

A hot, harsh breath escaped her teeth. "Fine! And after you complete your 'bargain' and you go West? What then? What about me?"

I opened my mouth. Not a goddess-damned sound came out. She leaped on my hesitation.

"I'm still feeling this ... this fucker-filch Dragon magic in my skin!" Jael flapped her hands up and down her torso. "And I don't know if it will ever end! Or if it'll ever *belong* to me! I don't know if I can walk away from him and 'retain' anything, or if he has so many enemies that can attack us in our sleep that I'm *dependent* on him to survive up here!"

That was it.

"When maybe, fucking maybe, it's true what the Valsharess saw," she cried with fury, "and I was supposed to die at Manalar! And that pale dark-hair is right. I *have* no place in the Cavern anymore! I can never return home when you have *no choice* but to go back without me!"

And leave her here, dependent on Mourn.

I caught my breath, the insulted sting from before snapped into dust, the sharp edges of resentment softening, spreading into a yearning pain on her behalf. I grasped at last that this was the only path she saw if she lived, because of what we'd done to save her.

She might lose me anyway and be leashed to someone she never chose.

Jael had been trying to say this since Mourn fell to Sleep, in several ways and several times, but she hadn't had the words in the right language, and I hadn't the time or energy to understand its urgency. I understood better why she wanted to fight it, or him, or *anything*. Sometimes the mind was clearer afterward, even with mistakes made.

Would that make any sense to Mourn? Could he understand? I hoped so, or else how could he teach her?

I wetted my lips and swallowed before I found words. "I don't have the answers now. I wish I did. I search for options."

Her face burned from her outburst as her breath slowed. She crossed her arms and shifted her weight to the other hip. "Options?"

My neck was stiff as I just watched her. "I'm not giving up or following along blindly. Give me time. Help me … to give us *both* time. You and me. It's too soon to decide."

Frustration, fear, and a touch of regret mauled her face as she asked, "Too soon to decide what? What do you mean? What do you *know* about what's going on up here? You seem so different, Sirana."

"I *am* different," I said, touching my gut. "I *feel* different. And I've had to decide every step of the way!"

Jael glanced down at my belly; from the way her brows furrowed, she could see the baby's aura. I caught a small nod. She at least got that.

"And because of *this*," I continued before she could speak, "I've needed to try things I've never tried before, ever since we first stepped out of that cave. I *don't* know what's going on up here, or why we were sent. I don't, Jael. The web keeps expanding, there are so many threads, and I *can't* protect myself on every front. I can't protect *you*. I need to try something different to protect … all of us."

Her jaw firmed up. "Like what?"

"Like …" I huffed. "Like recognizing when a Surfacer — or a group of them — shows you they are something you've never seen before, and I tried taking it as truth until they prove otherwise. It doesn't help to twist it ahead of trouble and make it fit something in Sivaraus. That only *causes* trouble, making it harder to keep going."

Jael rolled her eyes, but a smirk appeared before she finished. "*Hmph.* Yet it's a good way to get cornered down below."

"I know. But it isn't always the way up here." I paused. "The world is much bigger, its patterns beyond complex, not simply repeating Sivaraus over and over. I've seen proof even though I haven't witnessed it the way Mourn has, from one mountain range to the Great Lake and beyond over centuries. Can you imagine what he's learned that makes keeping his word essential?"

My Sister held herself tightly; her eyes had lowered and slid off toward one wall. "So, what is your Bargain I'm supposed to keep my nose out of?"

"Mostly what you've seen. Help me find and rescue you. Protect and feed me and my baby." My tone lightened as I smirked. "And in return, I'll give him pleasures in all the ways Red Sisters are skilled, which he's never had with a Davrin before."

Jael jolted slightly, blinking in surprise. "But isn't he *half* Davrin? And came from a second city that's *full* of them?"

"For certain. But he left Vuthra'tern before he was old enough to feel those urges. He hasn't seen any dark-skinned Elves up here, just heard legends of the Red Desert." I paused, hesitating. "He … said our exchange has value to him beyond having a pleasure servant."

"Oh, he did?" Jael sounded wary.

"Yes. It's awakening his mother's blood, I think. Her magic, when he's been favoring his sire's for so many decades."

Tension returned in her shoulders. "He's getting stronger?"

His Hoard would certainly change in some way he'd deemed desirable.

"Probably," I admitted, to which she jerked her chin in a nod.

"See, I believe that."

My turn to sound wary. "Oh?"

"Yeah. I think I can feel it." She pointed a finger between us. "When we fucked by the waterfall. Even if he didn't mount *me*, when you sucked on me and he got up in you … Um. I could feel something. Like when we fought the Malok. You and me and … another."

"Another."

"Th-that's another thing I worry about!" she pressed. "Are we both getting bound … tighter, and he knows but isn't telling us? Or worse! He *doesn't* know! And won't until it's too late."

Damned Indrath's taunt echoed in my head.

"I am curious about the one … or two Baenar with whom he has chosen to merge auras."

How could the bastard Infernal tell so easily?

I was reminded of an earlier thought to untangle his riddle and turned toward the shadow drake lounging in his nest. He was listening, his chin propped on the edge. He'd understood every word so far but did well not to stir the muck.

"Graul?"

He opened one eye, the other drooping with sleep. "Hm?"

"Can you read mage auras other than Mourn's when he is Sleeping?"

Air rattled as Graul inhaled. "Yesss."

"Can you see my baby's mage aura?"

"Of course."

Of course. So casual.

And worrisome.

Jael blinked when he spoke our native tongue but accepted it quickly. She cocked her eyebrow at each of us, dropping her arms to rest hands on her hips as she waited for where this was going.

"In that case, one last question," I said. "And I must have your true answer."

"*Mmmrrr.* First my question, Baenar. Why?"

"Because if you tell me true, you will help protect Mourn, because then I cannot be tricked where I'm vulnerable regarding him."

Graul appeared to understand, and my frank honesty mollified him. "Hm. Ask."

"My baby's aura has a gold thread in it," I stated, making it clear that was *not* my question.

Graul opened his other eye, perking up, his white chin bristles brushing audibly against fabric. He was surprised I knew that, which meant Indrath *wasn't* lying.

My baby is Dragon-touched. My stomach trembled. *Alright. So be it.*

"Was that gold thread apparent to you *before* or *after* Morixxyleth made his Bargain with me?"

The improved pronunciation of his To'vah-krav's name further coaxed the drake to avoid a mischievous or snarky remark. His throat pouch expanded slightly, vibrating in a quiet hum as he exhaled through his nostrils, stiff tail weaving at the tip.

"Before," he said. "*Maekrix* was not aware of the thread until *after*."

Yet Graul had said nothing to his "leader." *Why?*

My stomach chilled down and warmed up simultaneously, leaving me a bit sick. My heart had picked up enough that Jael could hear it, despite calming my mind.

After a long pause, all I could say was, "Thank you."

The little beast smirked. "You are welcome, *Kiabil*."

"What's going on?" my Sister asked. "What gold thread?"

"Can *you* see it?" I asked, curious as I pointed at my womb.

"Wha—?" She tried, squinting at my middle, but shrugged. "Maybe? Not ... consistently. Like I said in the shower, it 'winks' at me. Comes and goes."

Interesting.

"Then what is going on," I said, "is that you aren't the only one I know who is touched by To'vah magic. Somehow, my baby is, too, and Mourn didn't make it so."

"*What?!*" she hissed. "H ... How else?!"

"I don't know." I swallowed. "A choice someone made when I could not, to save my life."

She didn't miss the parallel; she knew the circumstances in which I'd caught.

"Auslan?" she cried, at a complete loss what to do with her hands. "Th-the Consort healer somehow?"

"And the Valsharess knows."

Vague surprise I *could* answer that.

"She knows about Dragon magic in Sivaraus," I finished.

"And She let you go?!"

I could only shrug, shaking my head. To think I'd told Mourn about the golden-eyed bua in my dreams, and he'd encouraged me to practice lucidity during them until I could find the Dragonchild growing wings by a red riverbank. Perhaps the half-blood had suspected even before we made our Bargain.

Ta'suil. Where did you come from? How are you still alive?

And what in the Abyss did Shyntre know that he dared not tell me? The Queen's familiarity with him, and his terror of Her, had been obvious at the trial on Kerse's death.

The moment She placed Her hands on him.

"I do not know what's happening," I repeated like a measured breath in the *dorji-ka*. "But I search for options, Jael, I promise you. It's too soon to say what will happen, or whether we *must* be trapped by compulsion or magic. But, of all these possible threats I've met on the Surface, Mourn and Gavin are the least of them." I met her eyes, seeing them glisten. "And we must help them at Manalar."

She granted me a nod or two as her throat locked up, her hands closing into fists, as if what I'd just learned made it all overwhelming for her. Eventually, she ran out of air trying not to moan or sob aloud and had to gasp for breath.

"Jael?"

"I need air."

"Alright," I reached out. "Let us get dressed —"

"No ... !" She recoiled. "I n-need to be alone."

"Alone?"

"I must go outside for sunrise."

I was dumbfounded as she headed for the door, grabbing her cloak, shirt, and pants, but leaving her belt, boots, and bracers.

"Jael —" I cut myself off, rushing to catch her arm. "No, please, what are you thinking?"

"Let me go!" She pulled free, pushing at the door. "Let me breathe!"

"But if you are seen, if you need help — !"

"You're not my bodyguard!" she barked, voice carrying down the hallway. "I can handle a few marks alone! I'm a trained Sister like you!"

"Jael!"

I had one moment to tackle her before she slipped beyond my reach; I missed it as she swiped her cloak across my face. Her bare feet sprinted down the short hall before hooking around to the stairs, leaping to skip the first three in one jump.

"Don't chase," Graul growled.

I hesitated when I *should have* gone after her. "You jest?"

"Cait is stifled. Guildsmen will watch her from a distance. Let her run until she is tired."

The Guildsmen.

I stilled a threatening tremble. "Aren't they all in the meeting?"

"Of course not. It is for leaders."

But which men would watch her, if not Wolf or Torch or Deshi? Would they know my Sister well enough not to harm her if they saw her naked? Or if she did something impulsive or insulting?

Could they defend themselves, non-lethally, if necessary?

"Sit," Graul suggested, nose pointing toward the pallet. "You are tired. Can't help her later if your body falls down."

Oh, Goddess …

The little drake was right. Small, but still an elder.

The thought made me smile as I closed the door and slid down it to sit on the floor, huffing a few sobs of sheer exhaustion and worry. Once the wave passed, I moved over to Mourn's pallet to lie down. Graul churred with approval.

I fell into dreamless rest, listening to the rolling vibrations of his throat as he purred me to sleep.

Chapter 6

When next my eyes opened, my body knew I was underground. My first drifting thought wondered if I was home in the Deepearth.

No.

No smooth curves in the architecture indicative of magical rock shaping. No subtle engravings to remind the lower Houses of those above, even in the absence of art or tapestry. Just clean, square, Dwarven-built room with a softly snoring drake within. A pocket of air built to withstand time for centuries past abandonment.

Rather like the Ley Tower.

Did Talov know which Tundar Clan had built the fortress out West? Did he know why they weren't there anymore?

He knows about the dark-skinned Elves of the Red Desert. Even Rithal had heard about it. Surely …

I lifted my head and looked around. Neither Mourn nor Jael had returned. Was the meeting still going? Had something happened to delay anyone checking on me?

My gaze fixed on the supply change in the corner as my nose focused on scents. The tub and washing supplies were gone, and a smaller tray of food sat on the wooden table covered by a thin piece of leather.

Shit.

Alright. I'm awake.

I left the pallet to collect my clothes, armor, and cloak, and checked the insides of my boots to reassure myself all was in the same condition I'd left it: good but gathering a persistent, outdoor scent.

My spiders crawled into my periphery, and I glanced up, making a face at how they hadn't warned me that someone might have entered the room as I slept. Or perhaps they'd tried, and I hadn't heard them; the lucky one had simply chosen not to creep close to me.

All was here and satisfactory, except for my belt, which carried all my weapons and pouches. Mourn had taken those along with the dark relic, presumably to lock it in the same magic-masking chest I'd used in Talov's office to protect my Sister and give us peace after that scare when we first arrived.

Jael. Where did you run?

I dressed first, collected my spiders, and tucked them at my nape since I had no pouch for them. Tearing off pieces of bread, I enjoyed familiar Dwarven seasonings in scooping up the thick vegetable mash but didn't linger. By the time I checked the corner nest, Graul had stopped snoring. Red, reptilian eyes watched me with curiosity.

Swallowing the last bite, I asked, "Is the meeting done?"

"No," he answered with a wide yawn, pink tongue curling, one paw flexing clawed toes.

I smirked. "Do you know if Jael is alright? Or in trouble?"

The shadow drake considered but grumped, "No. Neither."

"Very well."

"I'm going to look for her," I explained, picked up her boots and stockings left behind.

"Expected."

At least the drake wasn't playing games or remarking on my intent to leave. Graul wasn't leaving that nest, though.

The room had been unlocked ever since the Dragonchild left, letting Jael escape. Maybe I would have caught her if the door had been secured.

I hesitated. "Should I lock the door? Can Mourn get inside, or you let him in?"

Graul wrinkled his muzzle in annoyance. "Just go."

Sounds like Jael.

I let myself out without further delay. Closing the door behind me, I headed for the stairs leading to the next level of the redoubt, a pair of boots hooked under one arm. The stone wall at the top contained a sliding, camouflaged door, now closed. I wondered how — or whether — Jael had gotten outside if it had been secured in any way.

Halfway up, I received my answer as a male Tundar with sandy-red beard stood and peeked out of his alcove, motioning me forward as he triggered the mechanism to open the door to half-width. He didn't speak but merely stepped out of my way, closing the wall-door after I was through.

Huh.

This area had been secured while Mourn had lain unconscious, but enough ears had heard about it that the Guild no longer bothered to keep the door hidden in plain sight. The doorkeeper must have been instructed not to ask me any questions, though. Our interaction had been nothing like the hatch watchers.

I reconsidered whether Jael *was* outside or had stayed within the redoubt somewhere. I picked up quiet murmurs and droning voices down various hallways, making my way to Gavin's private quarters first, to check if they were either private or empty. The lack of serious bustle seemed to indicate the middle of the night or predawn.

Standing before the heavy door — one of the few I recognized by its unique grain — I raised my hand to rap knuckles on the wood but stopped when a familiar sensation warned me off.

The Deathwalker had left a strong ward outside.

He must be in the meeting.

Should I ask the hatch watchers to go outside and look for my Sister? Who would know where she'd escaped to? Had she eluded all notice, or had she made a commotion?

My next stop was Welden Gherudum's infirmary, where a few days ago the blond Dwarf had managed a roomful of cots bearing the critically injured among the Guildsmen of Reprisal. I knew Brian Wolf and Peng-lok were on their feet after the healer had the time to make his potions, but I was surprised to find his infirmary mostly empty.

The scents from that first, chaotic day lingered, but only a few men and Dwarves slept here as if it were a convenient place to get some rest rather than being unable to stand. One of them was Welden, his cot placed farther into his work area.

He looks exhausted.

From here I could see dark rings beneath his eyes, a trait apparent on the mortal Gavin when he hadn't claimed enough sleep traveling with the Ma'ab. Sighing inside, I left and did not disturb the Dwarf's restful silence.

Where to now?

I didn't imagine the baths or kitchens would be of interest or much tolerance for my Sister in the state I'd last seen her. She might have gone quiet if she were unable to leave and could be hiding somewhere, but unless they locked her up, I didn't think the redoubt could hold her for however long I'd been in Reverie. She might be angry with me and the entire Surface but was still stubborn and slippery when she wanted to be.

Just go outside and look before you stumble on Mathias instead.

Turning a corner toward the closest hatch from the infirmary, I spotted the two Dwarves with a lantern at their card table long before they saw me approaching. Sand-beard was one of them, thankfully; apparently, they were the regular night watch.

A chill passed up my spine, and I stopped, eyes scouring the shadows for any sign of Radiants. Nothing I could make out with the conscious strain to use Dark Sight with a light source nearby.

Hm.

"Oi!" said Sand-beard, not a bellow but sudden enough to make me jump. "Watch my cards!"

"I dint touch 'em!"

"Why is that one flipped, then, eh?"

"I dunno! Ya blew on 'em fer luck?"

"Pah!"

The Dwarves started over, sorting the cards and redistributing them at random. They weren't aware of me yet; a pity I had no other task necessary than to get their attention.

I stepped closer, speaking once the first Dwarf's eyes came up. "Hello."

"*Yakrinshagus!*" he barked, scraping his seat along the floor.

I winced at the stab in my ear, finally thinking to lift my hands as the men did. "Did not mean to scare you."

Sand-beard was on his feet with his darker bearded brother, catching their breaths. "Oh, aye, it's you ... *whew*. Need outside?"

I waited a beat to check if he'd add anything. "Is it allowed?"

"Oh, yeah. The Manalari went tah bed happy seein' their Wall Captain. Just be alert, ya?"

"Always," I said. "Have any of my sisters come by?"

The Dwarf blinked. "Sisters?"

I reached up and touched my ear, tapping the sharp point. "Either pale or dark."

"Ah!" He grinned, glancing at the boots under my arm. "Aye, yeah! The sunny-haired one went outside a couple hours ago."

Tamuril? I paused, but he offered nothing of Jael. "Well, then. I would like to follow her."

"Can do! C'mon. You know the place and the way tah get in."

"That I do."

I followed him to the top of the dark ladder so he could let me out after confirming the night-dark area was clear. Like the Dwarf who'd let me through at the top of the stairs, Sand-beard sealed the way behind me and asked no questions.

Possibly an effect of Mourn's Awakening.

Now I wondered, among the Clans, Guild, or Manalari, whenever someone saw me, how many also thought of an aggressive, black beast seizing the two black "witches" to drag them to a pool of water and make raucous noise.

Hoo bua.

Nothing to be done about it now.

Without tracks or words to follow, and *still* without confirmation that Jael roamed out here, I took a deep breath to enjoy the cooler, fresh air, still humid from the summer day and the rivers all about. Dew would be thick by sunrise.

I chose to check the waterfall first since Jael had been there twice already. If Osgrid and Rithal happened to be there, maybe I could ask them ... or maybe they were both in the meeting with many others.

Sigh.

Near enough to the falls to hear it, I finally spotted the faint edge of a footprint in a tiny patch of soft soil. Not a bare foot, as Jael had been bootless, but it finally struck me that Tamuril *wasn't* in that meeting either.

Maybe she has few thoughts to share?

I picked up my pace, admiring the difficulty of following the Druid's wandering stride as she headed for the falls. At last, I returned for the third time to the pool atop the redoubt, searching for signs of the blonde Naulor.

She wasn't trying to hide but sitting upon a boulder half-surrounded by rippling water, one leg tucked in, and the other knee drawn up so hands and chin could prop themselves on it. She gazed at the moving surface and lines of bubbles, her face relaxed and ...

Calmest I've ever seen her.

I glanced up in case Pilla might be glaring in the trees, about to shriek her warning. No falcon. No sounds above the rushing water, but I thought I caught movement.

Hm.

Moments later, I decided leaves had been caught in a high gust and backlit by the moon overhead.

It's nothing. Now, how to approach Tamuril without scaring her as I had Sand-beard?

I freed Shyntre's pendant from underneath my armor, clasping it with my fist. Watching her, I attempted to "toss" a thought her way, as I had been doing all morning with Isboern, hoping she would catch it and know it was me.

~Tamuril? Can you hear me? ... It's Sirana.~

She lifted her gaze and fixed them in my direction. Goddess, either

I'd learned well from the Godblood, or she had long practice with such precision.

Sirana? Are you across the pool from me?

Had to be the latter.

Will you show yourself this time?

I suppressed a flinch, though she had begun to smile.

~Of course. Didn't want to shout or cause ... screaming.~

Come on out, then. No shouting.

Once she spotted movement, her steady, emerald gaze helped maintain our link. *I thought you'd be in the meeting?*

~I was too tired.~

Hmm.

~And you? Why aren't you there?~

The Druid shook her head. *I am not a warrior.*

I stepped with care around the bank, closing the distance. ~You do not intend to go to Manalar?~

I will go, she affirmed, surprising me. *I must know if Krithannia and Willven will live and what happens to Nalarilin. I must know if we succeed, and she will be cleansed.*

~Nalarilin,~ I repeated, stepping with several strides between me and her boulder. ~The sacred pool.~

Correct. She shrugged. *But I don't like listening to those plans. Willven can share what I need to know when it is time.*

Interesting. The Druid was coming with us. I hadn't yet gotten that far.

~I see.~ I paused, having no lead-in but to say it. ~Um, have you seen Jael out here?~

The blonde Elf tilted her head, finally noticing the boots I carried. *I have not. Have you lost her?*

Damn it.

~Yes,~ I growled. ~She is stubborn and forgot these.~

The Druid's lips smiled so widely that her eyes crinkled at the corners. The soft laughter left me dumbstruck as I witnessed the difference in her eyes.

The ritual *had* been worth it.

I could help search for her, she offered.

Would that slow me down, make it easier for Jael to evade me if she wished? Probably, but the Druid had her own magic and a bird who had called my Sister out of hiding once.

Maybe we can do it again.

Though that would infuriate Jael further.

TAMURIL SOUGHT DAPPLED PATCHES OF MOONLIGHT MORE OFTEN THAN I DID, adding the benefit of covering ground faster. Her quiet steps would slip by most Humans, her long stride steady. Gradually, she moved ahead of me, pausing to listen or scent the air as I caught up.

We combed the multiple rises and slopes beyond the waterfall, searching for any unusual sign. Our mindlink had dropped without my intention, however, and I wasn't sure if I'd failed to hold it or if the Druid had somehow closed it herself. Either way, the vanishing trace of her thoughts had been painless and without awareness.

Within the resulting gap, unasked questions began to crowd the fore of my mind. The major one was where Pilla had gone, for the falcon hadn't revealed herself in sight or sound. Tamuril walking around in the dark without her watchful guardian seemed …

Strange.

Pilla was a day-creature, though. She couldn't see well in the moonlight and may risk injury flying among the trees. The feathered hunter had to eat and rest but had never done the latter in front of me.

Do falcons sleep at all? How? For clusters of minutes or for hours at a time?

Tamuril had reached an apex south of the waterfall, exiting our cover to center herself in a tree-bald patch covered by knee-high grass. I hesitated to follow her out in the open, if only because my spiders had been tickling my neck for the last hour, shifting too frequently for me to think there was *nothing* out here besides an occasional Guildsman on stakeout.

At the same time, we'd spotted no trace of Jael or anything recent since Rithal and Osgrid camping near the falling stream.

I must have chosen the wrong direction.

Assuming she was outside and not in the cell next to Mathias.

Please, don't.

A glimmer of pale blue lit up to my left and caught my eye. Expecting a luminescent bug hovering in the air or clinging to the bark, I met a set of ice-blue eyes just before the toothy, shining smile vanished into a void.

My heart slammed into my throat. *Sucking web!*

Darted out from behind my tree, I rolled once and crouched in the grass. Gripping Jael's boots in one hand, I reached for a weapon at my waist and froze.

No belt.

Mourn had taken it.

Fuck.

"Sirana?" Tamuril asked, turning around.

Shh!

I scuttled backward, eyes fixed to the treeline in front of me. Staying low, I closed the distance with the Naulor. A small gasp escaped as she crouched down.

"What's wrong?" she whispered.

I started hand-signing to her then clenched my fist and growled, "See anything?"

Behind me, she paused to look. "Like what?"

Like what ... Goddess, what was it? *That smile ...*

The memory of where I'd seen that glowing maw before struck. "At the Temple. Those guardian shadows that came through the rift? They blocked Humans from entering the main door."

"Uh ... ?" she stammered. "Wh-what do you mean?"

I grimaced. The Druid hadn't been there. *She's never seen one.*

My knees touched the ground as I exhaled, listening to the thudding in my ears, every muscle ready to sprint. My spiders shifted and moved about my neck as if confused where the threat lurked. Small relief that they ignored the Druid, but where and what?

What in Braqth's twisted guts did Gavin call them?

Calm. *Calm ...*

Breathing through my nose, the word returned in the Deathwalker's voice.

"*Shaegoth*," I whispered.

Tamuril shook her head. "What?"

"Shaegoth. Gavin knows what they are. They are loyal to the Grey Maiden."

I think.

May I not be wrong and the creature was something else entirely.

How had a Shaegoth come this far from Manalar? Would it harm us somehow if it got too close? Should we run back inside and find Gavin?

He's in that meeting ... Damnit.

Tamuril spoke after my indecisive pause. "Perhaps we should stay here a while? Remain in the open."

Her suggestion was the opposite of my usual instincts, but that gaunt, grinning shape had proven I could hardly tell the difference between it and the natural shadows unless the "face" glowed. At least the Sister Moons' light was strong, steady, and overhead with only a few backlit clouds spread out among the stars. As a result, our own shadows lay tight and small.

"Hm," I grunted. "Alright. How long?"

Tamuril settled down as soon as I accepted, sitting comfortably on one hip while I kept my legs folded beneath me, my ass resting on my heels. We scanned the treeline twice.

"Dawn?" she suggested, a curious curl touching the corner of her mouth. "Or until your bodyguard comes looking?"

I made a face, lifting Jael's boots. "And my sister?"

The hint of amusement vanished. "Ah. True. Um." A shake of her head followed by a shrug. "We can go for help?"

The best course apparent to me, but I didn't leap on it yet. "Do you have a throwing weapon?"

"No, just my woods knife."

"More than I have."

"Not even in your boot?" she asked, astonished.

Although she hadn't remarked on my missing belt and the relic attached, my face heated up. "It's in my pack. In Mourn's room."

"Do you have anything at all?"

"Yes. My spiders."

She closed her mouth, quickly glancing around, and I added, "They won't attack you again. I promise."

The Druid managed a nod. "Thank you. I was going to ask ... why are there only two? Did you not have three?"

My mouth twisted. "A fight. A Ma'ab sorceress crushed one after it bit her."

Tamuril's eyes widened. "Did the mage survive?"

I shook my head in the negative. "The venom killed her. Gavin spoke to her afterward."

"Uh, stop." she lifted her hand. "That's enough."

"Alright." I licked my lips, looking for the Shaegoth. "I was going to ask where Pilla was."

Tamuril hummed in quiet amusement. "She's sleeping. She will return at dawn."

"Ah." I smiled. "So, falcons sleep at night?"

"When she can." The Druid lifted her chin. "You made that somewhat difficult when we first ... clashed."

I didn't doubt it. "Can I borrow your 'woods knife?' "

She frowned. "In case you need to throw it?"

"Exactly."

"I am skilled in throwing, and I know its balance."

"Ah, impressive." I grinned. "Except I won't miss."

She rolled her eyes less overtly than Jael. Still a surprise she did at all.

"Not a boast," I said, tugging off my right glove which covered Callitro's ring. "Magic ring. Crafted by a mage back home. It grants a true aim when I *must not* miss."

Tamuril blinked at it, swallowing as she seemed to spot something which convinced her. "Is that ... how you killed the Hellhound in one throw?"

Ah, she'd heard about that, too.

"Yes," I admitted, stroking the new gold ring with the pad of my thumb. "Although the cursed blade also cut through the magic protection woven into the markings on his skin. A normal blade would not have."

She shuddered. "And the relic is locked away?"

"Along with the rest of my belt."

"How could *that* happen?" The Druid's tone somehow matched the concern and a touch of new humor. "Was it the same moment your sister forgot her boots?"

Warmth lingered in my cheeks. "Near enough."

She offered me the working knife in its brown leather sheath, barely larger than one might use to cut meat and vegetables. I accepted anyway.

"I am not certain you can stab a shadow," she said.

"I doubt it," I agreed. "But if something else unwelcome steps out, I won't miss."

"Very well."

We sat alone in the small, topside meadow overlooking the Kerut River Mounds, scenting the breeze as it changed direction. No blue glimmers or moving shadows warped the bending grass waving in silver moonlight. Not much time passed before sitting here felt strange.

Should we leave? Head underground ...

Tamuril seemed less concerned about the creature I'd seen as she gazed out over the lush, rolling hills below. In the far distance, I spotted what must be the Big Ker River bending through the vast and fertile lands.

"I wanted to mention," the Druid began, seizing my attention though she looked elsewhere. "After you'd gone inside to rest, Willven uncovered and arrested some Witch Hunters who had come in from the fort by the river."

"Arrested?" I repeated, controlling the sting of fear to imagine Jael knowing about this. "What does that mean? Where are they?"

"In the Dwarven cell, underground." She blew a breath through her lips. "Probably near the other one you knew about."

"Mathias Briar?"

She nodded.

Mathias and Witch Hunters in the same place. Wonderful.

I wondered how much the skin hunter might taunt the brethren of his first Witch Hunter victim. He might describe what happened to Jacob in the shed behind Brom's Inn. He might say something about me or even Gavin's ritual and where the man's black shard of a soul ultimately ended up.

"And Jael isn't down there with them," I stated, in case the Druid knew otherwise.

Her blonde brows arched with concern. "Of course not."

Of course not.

"Very well."

Now I couldn't sit still.

"Let's return to the hatch," I said, putting on my glove and unfolding stiff legs. "Quickly, through the trees, and watch for sign of Jael on the way."

She blinked twice before regaining her feet as light as a deer. "If you wish."

Odd way to say it.

What else would we do, sit and trade tales until dawn?

I could grant that our Sun *had* caused the Malok to flee and return to the rift, but I saw no benefit in waiting with the hope it would dissuade any shadow from the Greylands, especially if it had roamed this far from the Temple pool.

If Gavin doesn't know about Shaegoth here, he should.

After a final look around and spotting no blue glimmers, I said, "Now."

Sprinting off ahead of the Druid, I made noise with intent so she could follow me through the forested hills. Staying in moonlight when I could, I chose the quicker drops and steeper paths toward the redoubt to maintain momentum. Ducking under a low branch to cross the slanted slope, I cursed when the soil gave way under my heel.

My balance tipped too far to catch myself, and I slipped without the time to shout. My hands flew above my head, scratching for earth or grabbing at branches or brush to stop my fall. Tumbling through the shadow, I expected my next obstacle would hit hard.

Stop!

My hand snagged something slim, rooted deep to the side of the hill. I gripped it tightly as I could, digging my heels in to stop my momentum and find footholds before I broke my bones against awaiting stones. Next, I brought my hands together, grasping whatever fortunate anchor I'd caught, my eyes opening to look above me.

A lipless, ear-to-ear grin spread within a void, misty blue light spilling through sharp teeth. The small hairs of my neck stood on end, and I nearly pissed my leathers. My spiders froze in place.

Oh, no …

This close, the Shaegoth's eyes glowed with icy blue intensity, pupils shaped like crosses expanding and contracting, mimicking the rhythm of my racing pulse. Thick, black tendrils sloped off of a ridged, skinless head which seemed to blend the features of a cat and a drake; the lower ends drifted in a weightless mockery of hair.

A long, gangly body loomed, so dark it blurred around the edges under dappled moonlight. Tiny points of blue on its chest and arms glimmered in a pattern I didn't know how to interpret. I couldn't smell anything, heard no breath or heartbeat, but sure as the Void, could *see* it. A solid form lay beneath my desperate grip, yet no warmth seeped through my glove, and it didn't give like flesh.

What in the Nexus was I touching?

The shadow creature opened its mouth as if to speak, or to laugh, but remained mute. All I could see were thin, pointed, teeth black as the rest of its face, the maw lit like a glowstone thrown into a deep, circular pit.

Sweat had popped out on my forehead, but I had yet to make any sound. Thoughtless, I reached for my dagger, belatedly recognizing Tamuril's woods knife in my hand. The Shaegoth noticed, silently chattered its jaw, and responded by drawing a blade as well.

Shit. Bad idea.

I raised my hand, braced to turn a stab at my arm or face, and the creature stretched out its free arm, crossing blades with me. Metal scraped together in a quiet, tooth-grating sound.

Somewhere higher on the hill, the Druid's voice sounded.

"Sirana?" she called, drawing nearer. "Where are you?"

Should I call her help? Or tell her to run?

"Tam ..." I whispered, indecisive, my spiders barely moving in response.

With weapons braced, the Shaegoth's gaze intense yet unreadable, my eyes flicked down when it scraped our blades together.

Bright metal.

A silver blade. Familiar, tarnished, but I was certain of where I'd seen it before.

The Witch Hunter's dagger from Troshin Bend.

The one Jacob had used to kill Gavin and which I'd later pulled from the Deathwalker's body.

The Shaegoth disengaged first, drawing away. I detected amusement in its poise as it replaced the dagger in its sheath. Like at the Temple, the tangible shadow wore a belt and red sash around a skeletally thin waist. From there, long fingers plucked up a pale, featureless mask I hadn't noticed before, which it then attached to its face before pulling me up to solid ground at last.

I let go of its hand and crouched there, stunned, and hypnotized as the appearance of the white mask changed, taking on precise features and shades of real color. Dark eyes and hair. Pale skin and a delicate bone structure somewhat familiar to me.

Female.

A Ma'ab woman.

The features resembled Commander Vo'traj before she died in the crypt. A sister, if she had one.

The Shaegoth blurred as Tamuril approached, its body losing all sense of solidity and becoming incorporeal.

It moved, and I flinched. Blinked.

Gone.

Just gone.

I turned around, stepping farther from the edge where I'd slipped, and tripping slightly over Jael's boots in the process. Picking them up,

I saw and smelled nothing unusual. My heart throbbed in my ears, the lingering chill in the air receding in a rush of blood as my spiders crawled farther out onto my shoulders, chiming in bewilderment.

~*I'm glad you didn't try,*~ I thought, reflecting on the many things from which enchanted arachnids couldn't defend me, Surface truths which Elder D'Shea could *not* have anticipated when she'd made them.

A Shaegoth with Gavin's dagger. Wearing a mask which looks like a Ma'ab sorceress.

What did that mean? Why did it have that dagger? Had it been stolen? *Or given?*

A moment later, Tamuril reached my side. "Sirana! What's wrong? Are you alright?"

"Back inside," I huffed, realizing I'd never caught my breath. My muscles burned from the strain and tension of the confrontation.

The Druid glanced toward the edge, where the scarring in the turf where I'd slipped was obvious. "Sirana, did you fall?"

"Almost." Still gasping, I returned her woods knife to her. "Here. The meeting is over. There must be news. Let's go inside."

"Alright, but … What about Jael?"

My lips tightened. "The Guild must watch her a little longer. Come on."

I loped off, taking safer if slower paths on the way to the hatch, gripping Jael's boots with the stockings stuffed inside. I gritted my teeth, developing a stitch in my side along the way as my stomach awakened with an angry growl. I shook my head. I would *not* delay seeking Gavin out first.

I had a bone to pick with my Deathwalker.

What in the Abyss have you done?

CHAPTER 7

THE DWARVES WELCOMED US INSIDE WITH THE SAME DEMEANOR AS WHEN I'D gone out: asking no questions, neither sluggish nor in a hurry. They were playing their card game. Nothing seemed out of place.

"Ah, ye found 'er," Sand-beard said, confusing Tamuril.

"I did," I said, deciding I didn't have time to explain. "Can you tell me if *Oltere* Baradum is available? Or how I find out?"

The Clan Dwarf brightened significantly at my request. "Ah, I don' know. But tah find out, take the third left, count five doors on the right, and ask the guards there. They can tell ye."

"Thank you ... ah, how are you called?"

He blinked, clearing his throat. "Admer. Clan Baradum. This is my cousin, Perek."

Admer Sand-beard.

I grinned. "Admer, Perek. You've opened that hatch for us so many times, I thought I should match a name to the beard."

He beamed. "Well, yer the ones mostly going in and out at night. Quiet otherwise. Most wait fer day, even if they ain't sleepin'."

"Do you know *our* names?" Tamuril asked curiously.

"Oh ..." Admer hesitated, glancing at Perek. "Yeah. We do. Think th' whole Clan does."

My smile warped into a dry smirk, folding my arms. "Oh? Prove it."

He responded to that first by lifting bushy eyebrows and swelling his chest, then answered, "Yer Sirrana. The younger sister with red eyes is Zhshahl."

A trill of his tongue struck the middle of my name, and he seemed to choose three different sounds to slur the start of Jael's name. I tried not to laugh as he looked to the blonde Naulor.

"Yer Tamuril," he said, having little trouble with *her* name, "and yer dark-haired sister is Krithana."

"Krithannia," the Druid correctly gently, stressing the end.

"Ah! Krithannya. Pretty."

"Thank you, and yes," she admitted, her cheeks pink. "Those are all correct."

Admer grinned. "A pleasure, Elves."

The last word hung in the air, making me think he and Perek were on the edge of asking about others of our kind.

"I must find Talov," I said, bowing in Yungian style this time to distract them. "Thank you for the direction."

"Ah! Yer welcome."

"And if you let Jael inside, please direct her the same way."

"Ye got it. Be seein' ya."

I motioned Tamuril away with me, lengthening my stride to start counting halls, doors, and turns, only then wondering if they'd noticed the boots I carried and decided not to stare, or if they hadn't thought it important with what I'd said.

Well … hopefully someone has seen her.

My stomach cramped irritably. Despite my thoughts about delays, I kept my nose open in case we passed by food storage. I could imagine crunching angrily on raw purple roots as I cornered Gavin with my questions about the Shaegoth.

Alas, by the time we reached the guards where Admer said they would be, I hadn't smelled anything edible nearby.

"Is *Oltere* Baradum still in his meeting?" I asked them. "I have urgent need to see him."

These two Dwarves had dark brown beards with silver beads woven in. One blinked with pale blue eyes, glanced at his partner, and said, "Nah, they broke up a bit ago. Most goin' fer some sleep 'fore morning, includin' *Oltere*."

Most.

"What about the Deathwalker?" I asked directly, starting to wonder where in the Pit Mourn had gone with my weapons belt.

The Dwarf knew exactly who that was. "He went that way."

Toward his quarters. *Of course.*

"And my sister?" Tamuril asked.

"With *Oltere* an' th' Dragon."

He's not a Dragon.

I bit my tongue as the guard pointed toward Talov's office, where Jael and I had spent some time in private. Gavin's quarters lay in the same direction but required turning left much farther down. Had they all gone to Talov's office, I wondered, or had they split between there and Gavin's surgery room?

Pick one.

Abruptly, I remembered the goddess-damned *Dragon pearl*.

"Thank you," I said distractedly, turning around and picking up my stride to go to Gavin's room, grabbing the smoky-black teardrop stuck to my earlobe. ~*Mourn? Are you there?*~

His voice returned at once. *Sirana. Are you downstairs with Graul?*

~*No, I'm headed to Gavin's room.*~

He paused. *Why?*

~*I want to ask him about the Shaegoth I met outside.*~

Another, longer pause.

He sighed. *Be right up.*

I frowned. ~*Did I catch you on the stairs?*~

Not quite. The guard tells me you left some time ago.

~*I went looking for Jael.*~

Outside.

~*Yes.*~

I will meet you at the Deathwalker's room.

He sounded tired.

I accepted and let the link go, focusing on Tamuril, who waited with a mix of patient befuddlement and curiosity.

"Krithannia is with Talov in his office," I said quietly, "if you want to go there. I'm going to see Gavin. Mourn's coming as well. Talking strategy."

The Druid looked disappointed but accepting. "Very well. I shall return outside. I want to be available for Pilla when she wakes."

Sounds like a good idea.

We went our separate ways, seeking out our next best place to be within the redoubt. Once alone, however, my hunger struck, and I grew thirstier by the moment. I doubted Gavin would have much in his room. Maybe I shouldn't have run off like I had a matron's gem caught between my teeth. *Damn it.*

I seized my ear and shifted close to the wall. *~Mourn, how do I get food? Or water?~*

He was quiet at first.

Then, *I'll make a request.*

~Heh. Thank you.~

He still preferred I didn't encroach on the kitchens.

Given the opportunity to reach Gavin first, I hurried down the hall, tapping on his door once I confirmed the magical ward was gone. After a few moments, I knocked louder. "Gavin? Open up."

"Something amiss?" he asked through the wood, ready to comment on my choice of approach.

"Yes. Quite amiss. Did you ... *do* something? Within the last hour?"

Now *he* paused.

I tapped my foot loud enough for him to hear until the Deathwalker opened the door wide enough for me to slip through. After he'd closed it but before he cast any magic, I added, "Mourn's coming with food and water."

"Hm."

Gavin turned from the doorway, folded one pale hand over the other, and stood facing me while I appraised him. The thick, grey robes given to him by his dead mother and that small insect girl beside the sacred pool had been mended. Holes torn by the black shards once jutting through his skin were gone, the frayed fabric rewoven into a tight pattern, and many of the various blackish-red stains were gone. *Must be magic.*

His face gaunt and pale as ever, his fingernails pitch black, he somehow seemed older than the monk I'd met at the Ley tower despite his skin lacking marks of injury or age. Rather difficult to decide if the death mage had recently expended as much effort as all the others around him who had gone to bed.

I lifted a finger. "First question."

"Yes?"

"Do you know where Jael is?"

His confusion showed. "No, I do not. Have you lost her?"

With a sigh, I lifted her boots. "Yes."

He arched one hairless brow, tilted his head. "Hm."

His only remark on that.

"What about Mathias?" I continued. "Have you seen him since we caught him?"

"I have not. I preferred to wait for you."

I blinked. "Um. Both of us at once?"

"That seems advantageous."

"Alright." I chewed my bottom lip, aware I was delaying the deepest question until I was ready. "Do you know there are Witch Hunters held here?"

Gavin dipped his head slowly enough it looked like a bow. "Talov and Captain Isboern brought that up promptly in the meeting."

I exhaled. "The meeting, yes. Um. Are you missing the silver dagger from Troshin Bend?"

His early confusion receded as his focus on me strengthened. "Interesting question."

"Yes, or no?"

"No, the dagger of Warrant Bictrius is not missing."

Bictrius.

My shooting the man to spare Gavin flashed through my head, as did

Jacob wresting the silver blade from his fallen superior to finish the job.

"But you don't *have* the Warrant's dagger in your possession," I stated, voice flat, eyes as steady as his.

"Oh, dear."

I detected neither amusement nor concern, his expression changing little. His comprehension, however, was total.

"You encountered a Shaegoth before it left the redoubt," he said. "Near enough for you to recognize that dagger."

"Correct." I folded my arms. "Gone? In truth?"

"They have left, yes."

"*They?* How many?"

"As many daggers made of silver as we possessed."

My mouth opened on the next question, but it wouldn't come out as my mind returned to how tired Mourn had sounded before, and that he'd loaned out five silver daggers in the Temple courtyard to use against the Malok that came out of that rift. After the battle, the Dragonblood collapsed into deep Sleep only to wake up five days later.

Did he ever collect them? When did he have the time?

Jael might have one on her belt in the room with Graul.

With apt timing, Mourn knocked on the door. He'd brought food and water and took care of the privacy ward before setting the tray on a scrubbed, stained table. Then he collected two chairs and set them nearer to Gavin, claiming one of them. He motioned for me to sit in the other. Watching the care he took in positioning his tail, I was struck by how often I saw him standing rather than sitting.

He must be tired.

"Tell me about the Shaegoth outside," the Dragonblood asked without preamble.

"Indeed," Gavin agreed, sitting down near the tray and preparing his grimoire. "Describe what happened in detail."

"First," I insisted, taking the open seat, and pointing at Mourn, "why are you visibly tired? Do you need to Sleep again?"

My bodyguard rubbed his eyes, claws splayed out with caution, sighing deeply. "No. But I will explain after, and the Deathwalker can corroborate."

Gavin dipped his stylus in his uncorked ink bottle. "Agreed."

I was mollified enough to detail my night searching for Jael after waking up, starting with the chill and unseen burst of energy scattering Admer and Perek's card game.

"That could have been a Shaegoth," the death mage agreed, "and might have been during the summoning."

"The *summoning?!*" I growled.

Mourn handed me a heavy piece of bread to gnaw on. "Yes. We summoned the Shaegoth here from Manalar."

I poured a cup of water to go with the bread. "Why?"

"We'll get there. But at least one followed you out *after* receiving a silver dagger."

Gavin lifted his icy black eyes from the page when he felt us staring; he shrugged. "I gave them no such instruction if that is what you want to know. As I understand, Shaegoth are quite capable of forming memories and solving complex problems to reach their targets."

"Targets," I repeated, one cheek stuffed full as I sipped water, which at least prevented me from blurting about the white mask becoming the face of a Ma'ab woman.

"Not me?" I asked instead.

"No, not you. Though I'd not be surprised if it might have been curious about you, or about the living in general, before carrying on with its duty to our Lady."

"So, what did you *do?*"

"Part of a larger strategy," Mourn answered. "A few tactical assassinations to see if we can get the Ma'ab camp to break before we arrive."

That explained the pale woman's face.

"The Shaegoth will kill all the female officers while we sit here?" I asked.

Both males shook their heads.

"Each will kill *one* target." Gavin spoke with precision, lifting a long, solitary finger. "Chosen by the provider of the silver dagger who pays the additional cost."

"What *cost*?" My gut froze over as I glared at Mourn. "And what did *you* just warn me about making deals?"

"The Guild paid the cost, and Gavin was the mediator." Mourn rubbed his eyes. "The details aren't to be shared."

"But the silver daggers were *yours*," I said, willing him to deny it.

"Four of them were," he confirmed. "I gave them away."

His statement seemed simple enough, but the silence backfilling that moment seemed loaded with a weight I did not understand.

"Indeed, your daggers were of exceptional quality," Gavin said, almost admiring. "I am still not certain they could have been coaxed through the circle had the first four not shone so brightly."

Mourn acknowledged this without apparent pride. "As it needed to be."

"You certainly proved your determination to help oust the Ma'ab after the Bishops lost the pool."

The Dragonchild smirked. "Isboern would not be thrilled with this decision despite the benefit to his people."

"*Would* not be?" I broke in with a frown. "Was the Captain not at the meeting?"

Metallic gold eyes shifted to me. "He was. Through most of it. We waited until only Guild and the Herald remained to discuss the Shaegoth."

"So, the Templari do not *know* what you did?"

"Not yet. They will later. And you were not meant to know, either."

"What?"

"I am glad that you rested instead."

"*Pfft!*"

"You *did* rest, correct?"

I scowled and bit off some bread, speaking with my mouth full. "Graul muftov told yew."

His eyes brightened; his tail flicked. "He did, but only up to a point."

"Tha's how I losht Jael."

"Ah. Well, she is safe."

I hurried to chew and make room for my tongue to work. "You know where she is?"

"Last I heard, Deshi coaxed her back inside to spar with some Guildsmen."

I stared, tempted to disbelieve yet I could see it. *Yungians read some spirits well, don't they?* "When was this?"

"When Isboern left, shortly before the discussion and summoning. *And,*" Mourn leaned forward in his chair, "it is best if you do not tell anyone else about the latter, not even your Sister. It will come out eventually."

Tension seeped out of my shoulders as he made his condition. "Is she still sparring?"

"Yes. She is safe. I checked before I came here."

And how long before I could see for myself?

Gavin kept writing as he spoke. "Indeed, this might seem sinister, but I agree it may be the only way in which the *Templari d'Manalari* can hold to their service and ideals and yet bear a *reasonable* chance to reclaim their city."

The half-blood grunted. "Or they will soon."

The Deathwalker's eyes flickered, the icy blue winking out before he shook his head. "No. Their chance starts now."

Mourn straightened. "How?"

"The threads the Shaegoth follow do not bear the same sense of time as ours."

I hurried to swallow my last bite of bread. "Wait, your Ma'ab targets are dead *already?!*"

The Herald spoke with the confidence of a messenger and a witness: "They are. All five of them."

The half-blood flicked his tail. "We shall need to speed up on a few plans."

"Agreed, but first," Gavin focused on me. "Describe what happened with the Shaegoth outside, please."

They had given me plenty of insights, so I described as much of what happened outside as I could. Neither of them interrupted me until I'd finished.

"And to your knowledge," Gavin said, "Tamuril did not witness this."

"She didn't act like she had, and she doesn't seem like a good liar."

Mourn smirked but said nothing.

"Very well." Gavin dipped his stylus. "Is it fair to say you fell from a sense of being hunted?"

"Well ... I suppose."

"Not surprising. Shaegoth spread intense dread wherever they linger, possessing an exotic aura unfamiliar to native souls."

"That they do," my bodyguard said.

I could accept that, adding to it how easily they frightened the most devout citizens of Manalar, preventing them from entering their highest sanctuary.

"The Shaegoth might have been playing," Mourn commented.

"Perhaps," Gavin agreed.

"Playing," I repeated.

"Regardless, its intent was not hostile."

That, I believed. How could one escape a grinning blur like that? What could hurt it when it dissolved and vanished in a blink? If it had been hostile, I would be dead.

"What do you suggest for the next time one 'plays'?"

Gavin's stylus paused, his eyes staring in thought. Then he shook his head. "Hope there is not a next time?"

I scoffed. "You jest. Tell me. Should I keep a pretty silver dagger to offer?

"That is unlikely to work."

"So, what would work?"

Gavin and Mourn exchanged looks, and the Dragonchild nodded slightly before speaking. "If you see it again, keep calm and know it is not hostile. Call Gavin or me."

"Even *you* say so? There is nothing to be done with a Shaegoth?"

"Not once it claims the cost of your life, no." The half-blood's tail curled and twisted near the floor. "Not unlike the limits I would face in protecting you should you make a contract with the Ice Lord."

Hoo bua. What have I gotten into?

Gavin tapped his stylus in thought. "I should clarify something for you, Sirana, as I did for those in the meeting."

He had my attention.

"These creatures are loyal to my Lady. They may be creations of hers, for she is the only Greylord known to retain them. Furthermore, Shaegoth are not obligated to accept every offering or any target. The Grave Mother must approve or have no protest. I believe they may reject a given task on their own if the offering is not to their liking."

"This was the only reason we used them," Mourn said. "Were they *not* unique, the risk of retaliation through another Greylord would be far too dangerous."

"The Ascended would never broker a deal with a Greylord regardless," the Herald muttered, completing his jot with a jab.

"And as I said before," my mercenary countered, "there is *always* an indirect way to make a contract which is desired enough. We had only to imagine if the Shaegoth were *not* singular to your Lady, like the Malok."

"Hm. I suppose. The Ma'ab would have to understand what hit them, however, and the souls taken tonight shall not return to Ennikar. Their subordinates in the field will not be able to summon them to ask any questions, either."

Mourn chuckled. "Those were important notes. The Ma'ab army has lost their top leadership and their usual means to communicate up north in one night. How *they* respond determines what *we* do next."

Goddess. Even after completing his task and throwing Jacob's shard into the pool, Gavin had proven so valuable to the Guild. The defenders of Manalar may not have understood the formidable battlefield they would have faced before these two changed it in a few hours.

"What about Mathias?" I asked.

Mourn tilted his horns toward Gavin. "Talov, Krithannia, and I concur with Gavin. We wanted to wait until you could speak your thoughts."

"And Soul Drinker? My belt?"

"Secure."

"Are you certain?"

"Locked in the box you trusted in Talov's office, and never in the meeting room with us."

So be it.

With a tremble of rising nerves, I rubbed my palms together. "What about the Hellhound I killed? Inside the blade?"

Gavin looked up from his book with interest and Mourn breathed out slowly.

"Any information which might be obtained from that source has value," he said with blatant neutrality, "but bears risk as well." Shining irises fixed on me. "And you know what those risks are."

"Yeah," I whispered.

Risky as a web fuck above the Pit.

"So, what shall we do next?" Mourn asked.

"I'd like to see Jael," I said. "And then talk with Mathias. Both without Soul Drinker present. But I'd like my belt back first."

"Alright." Mourn stood up. "Are you coming, Deathwalker?"

Gavin considered but shook his head. "Retrieve me when you have decided what to do about the skin hunter, and if you require aid speaking with the Hellhound in the Elsewhere. I shall be here."

"We shall, Herald. Until then."

CHAPTER 8

I TURNED OUT OF GAVIN'S ROOM WITH MOURN BEHIND ME, REASONABLY ASsuming we headed to Talov's office to retrieve my belt and secure the red rune dagger.

Before we'd fully exited the Deathwalker's quieter area, my bodyguard caught my arm, opened a door, and pulled me in after him.

Whoa!

The space was relatively small and pitch black. I smelled recently emptied storage; nothing which had sat here had been present long.

After setting a ward, Mourn pressed me gently to the wall. His scent had strengthened, his skin growing warmer in a familiar way. His tail looped twice around my calf with a flex.

Now? I signed after dropping Jael's boots.

My vision adjusted to Dark Sight until I made out detail on his face. He managed half a smile, wry and not the least bit arrogant. He leveled a few clawed fingers near my neck, offering my other guardians a spot to climb on before giving them a lift onto the stone above my head.

"Some events will come quickly," he said, voice a quiet rumble. "This could be a last chance, and your Sister was right. I left without reciprocating."

He reached down, sliding one hand between my thighs, touching his thumb to the crotch of my leathers and holding it there. Unmoving. I squinted with mild suspicion, letting the suggestion rest there.

"What is your *other* motivation?" I asked, smiling wider than he dared. "I wager you haven't made a decision since we met that didn't have five other motives attached."

"Exaggeration," he grumbled, smirking.

"Oh? Only four, is it?"

A fang poked out where I could see it, and his tail squeezed with a playfulness I recognized. "Very well. I would like this moment to exchange pleasure, as we've agreed, *Kiabil* —"

"And?"

"And ... doing so will help me rebalance."

"I knew it." I smirked but then added, "Rebalance what?"

He hadn't blinked. "My Hoard and me. As I described in Yon-wen. Your pleasure provides us with ... something tangible. And we've just given up something tangible."

The silver daggers.

"Oh." Carefully, I ran one palm along his forearm, applying steady pressure and encouraging him to press harder between my legs. "And you'll reciprocate this time?"

"Before anything else."

He turned his hand, holding my sex in his palm, patiently churning the heel over and around my mound.

"Ohhh ... yes."

With my back against the wall, Mourn kneeled before me, tugging the knots at my hips and loosening my leathers. Knowing not if he might ever do this in front of Jael, I cooperated to get his tongue on my naked sex without delay because he was right. We could be interrupted at any moment.

"Oh!"

His eyes glimmered in the dark, tail snapping and lively at my cry. Leaving my leathers bunched around my knees, he took my hips in both hands, tilting them forward to burrow a firm, twisting lavender rope in between my netherlips, reaching all the way to my netherhole.

"Goddessss!" I hissed as he wasted no time tucking the tip into my squeezing ring and holding it there. His saliva had thickened further, heat and tingling pleasure spreading between my legs, my back hole and sensitive nub especially.

I gasped from the sudden ache of my cunt swelling, near dripping. At *this* point of readiness, any Red Sister would have bent me over and rammed it in without resistance. Instead, the Dragonblood's tongue continued to slather me with spit and firm, slithering strokes; every moment passing increased the intensity of both.

"Mourn ... !"

His jaws opened wider and a greater length of tongue eased out. The broadest section pressed hard against my clitoris. My hips jerked in his grip, and I yipped at the burst of pleasure flooding my gut. He held the pressure until every little shift and twitch between us helped me to climb. The tip of his tongue lay hidden between my cheeks, dragging itself in lazy circles around the sensitive ring.

"I'm guh ... gonna ... *ah!*"

He could tell.

My netherhole clutched his tongue's tip as my sex fluttered and flexed along the muscular base. I climaxed while upright, suppressing my moans, gripping his shoulders with both hands as I trembled, forgetting to breathe. He braced me up until I'd finished, removing his tongue from between my legs only once I'd squeaked in surprise at the sensitivity.

Mourn supported me as he shifted position. Parting my thighs wider, he ducked both thick arms between them, seized my bare ass, and lifted my boots off the stone floor.

"Wha — !"

My back thumped against a higher spot on the wall, and Mourn's forearms pushed to splay my thighs as wide as they would go to each side. The motion encouraged me to cross my ankles and force my leathers to work their way below my knees.

The Dragon Son's cock was out, stone-hard, and dripping. My gooey, glistening cunt sat on full display right in front of the thick, triangular head.

I looked up. My bodyguard's eyes had fixed on my folds, his pupils widening with interest, hands squeezing my buttocks. His tongue hung partway out, as if to wave in the lingering scents of my orgasm beneath his nose. Speech took immense effort.

"Too thore?"

A grin pricked at my lips. *Not at the moment.*

The soreness was gone, and my holes had relaxed and slickened up enough that he could probably rut either one. It wouldn't take much to overdo it, though, especially if he wedged in that bulge so soon after the last time.

"No knot," I whispered.

He nodded once.

"Fuck my slit."

He leaned in. He didn't need my help to aim. My hole swallowed him, and he grunted, finally pulling his tongue in. "Yesss …"

Adjusting his hold to secure the perfect angle to cycle his thrusts, my bodyguard pumped my wet hole briskly but stopped before he hit bottom, withdrawing to slide it in again. *Perfect.*

~*Yes, indeed.*~

Warm and smooth, short, and steady. Not frantic, not throwing himself into me with abandon to get lodged in later, but eager, focused, unrelenting. His tail did nothing to distract either of us from his rutting prick squeezing in, stretching me out. At this pace, he would spurt me soggy. And soon. Lucky for me, my clasping channel was thrilled, the pleasure running a hair ahead of him to reach my peak a second time.

"Oh! Goddess!"

I held him tighter, gripping straps over his shoulders, and bit down on a muscle at his neck to muffle the rest of my squeals. Mourn huffed in surprise, growled as he held me close in return, his tail slapping between my buttocks as if in repayment for the bite … or to make me squeeze his pulsing rod harder as he released his cream deep in my sex.

Yes!

Our descent was slow and shared, heartbeats overlapping, our breath slowing together. He softened inside me until he fell out, the mixed drip of our juices landing with a splat.

"Thank you," he whispered, eyes drooping. "I feel ... better."

"Sure ..." I wanted a quick nap as my blood sang in my ears, making me dizzy. "I ... enjoyed."

He grinned.

Tricky to unfold my body at the same time he meant to set me down, but I managed not to trip over my pants. Mourn handed me a cloth from his harness to wipe down before pulling them up. I thought I shouldn't be *too* sore walking around the redoubt.

"Ready?" he asked, wiping and covering himself before taking the cloths.

I managed a sluggish nod, reaching up to collect my waiting spiders.

"Let's get your belt and meet Jael in the sparring room."

TALOV AND KRITHANNIA DIDN'T KEEP US LONG, ALLOWING ME TO OPEN THE locked chest and reclaim Soul Drinker while Mourn updated them about the Shaegoth outside.

"Hm!" said the greybeard. "That death mage is growin' his influence as fast as you did once ya hit yer stride."

Mourn answered with a smirk while Krithannia offered a pleasant counter.

"If we were to ask the Deathwalker," she said, "I would expect his journey has not *felt* all that swift."

"No doubt, with th' dyin' part an' all," granted the Dwarf. "Still, wagering th' next branch ov his path'll snap inta focus at Manalar."

"No gambling for me," said the Guild Mistress. "This could not be clearer."

"Fortunate for us."

"Wait," I interjected. "You aren't worried if the Deathwalker might work with an opponent next?"

"Oh, he might at some point," Talov agreed. "In fact, I expect him to.

This day, however, all our goals align. Even his Lady seems tah approve ov the alliance somewhat past neutral."

I tilted my head. "Seems to?"

"Eh," he shrugged, "ya kinda had tah be there."

I shouldn't have missed the meeting. *Sigh*. I glanced at the Naulor next; she was watching me. "What?"

"You aren't concerned about his dealings, either?" she asked curiously.

I blinked. "Um ... no. I know he wants the Ley Tower. I need to return to the Ley Tower. He doesn't yearn for flesh or servitude or wealth, so it doesn't matter what happens in between."

"Yer *that* sure," Talov said with a smile.

"I am," I replied. "He's shown me who he is."

"Aye? How 'bout us?"

I narrowed my gaze with a smirk. "You're cunning. Managing a web of connections through many cities, balancing your pulls and snares over centuries. Who *you* are cannot be as clear as a death monk with one focus."

The Dwarf chuckled. "Fair. Could say th' same about you, *lasschen*."

I laughed. "May as well, greybeard. I *am* from Sivaraus."

"Aye. Ya get Gavin's value like we do." His eyes twinkled without a roll or a flick. "Will yah make a deal with us after speakin' tah Mathias?"

He could tell he'd surprised me. "Don't I have one?"

Talov shook his head. "With the kid, sure, an' he's got our support. But not with the Guild directly 'bout this next undertaking."

"You want something," I said.

The greybeard glanced at Soul Drinker. "Happy tah wait longer, till ya got some answers ya want. Just wanted tah say."

Neither Mourn nor Krithannia were focused on me when he said that. I supposed the eldest closest to death was the least offensive one to suggest I take the risk. I'd have to try regardless, eventually. If only I could be certain about my timing.

"Noted. May I see Jael now?"

"Of course," Mourn replied, turning to open the door and lead the way.

His allies dropped their gazes to grin at the boots I carried. Shrugging, I lifted them higher before seeing myself out.

THE SPARRING ROOM RESEMBLED FAR LESS THE *dorji-ka* IN YONG-WEN AND MUCH more the Cloister, lacking any padding for wrestling while faintly smelling of blood.

Uh-oh.

Gratefully, I recognized the faces or voices of the Yungian brothers and the men of Reprisal, who kept close watch on any approach. Deshi approached us first while Brian Wolf and Peng-lok stood at the doorway, each favoring their wounded side.

"*Janshi!*" the Yungian bua greeted me first with a bow before doing the same for Mourn. "*Wen-yung.* Ah …" He hesitated, pointing at the door. "*Jiji* needs rest."

His word for Jael yanked a smile out of me despite my worry. *No doubt. But how to convince her?*

Pungent scents wrinkled my nose as I got closer, and my face pinched with concern when I saw the young death mage up close. Deshi had fresh strike marks on his face from a fight, although nothing as serious as Jael probably had.

I circled my hand around my face as we kept moving, asking him, "You get those before or after reaching this room?"

The Yungian blinked. "Ah … before. She caught me."

I thought so and arched a brow at Mourn. ~*Deshi 'coaxed' her inside, hm?*~

His eyes managed to shimmer in amusement, though his mouth remained flat. *Coaxed, lured, tempted, ran.*

~*You said she was safe.*~

And Reprisal knows the risks. His tail swayed with his walk. *What will you do, Red Sister?*

As his thought touched my mind, I noticed the wave of movement as Reprisal spotted me and formed a pathway through the cluster at the door. They passed the message forward, much like what happened when Rausery or D'Shea entered a room. Before, I'd always been standing on their side.

Should I mimic my Elders, play into that? It might work for the Humans if Jael went along with it, but she might not. Any earnest attempt to command or push Jael out before she was ready wouldn't work.

What will I do?

Exhaling, I stepped through the men, sensing their interest and curiosity as my eyes sought the center of the room, where she and her newest opponent stood.

Oh, Jael.

She wasn't down yet but was close. I didn't know where her cloak was, but at least she wore her shirt and leathers. Her feet were scraped, bruised, and punctured as I'd fretted, and her knuckles and elbows were bleeding. I'd only seen her in worse shape twice before.

The rest of the injuries among the men in the room seemed spread around. Each one had stepped forward at some point and had taken a strike or two. None had stripped down farther than she had, and her present opponent grappled her with clear intent to remain standing rather than throw the two of them on the floor.

The air lacked animosity despite the scent of blood.

I recognized my guide Tak, sharp-eyed Hawk, and burly, bilingual Kil; each smiled when they saw me, careful not to show their teeth. I wagered the Guildsmen had kept Jael here on purpose and maintained her focus on them for hours, and she hadn't managed to kill any of them by accident or intent.

Goddess, how?

"RRRAUGH!"

Jael tried stomping on the bare foot of her opponent and missed, her sweat and panting greater than any in the room. The man engaged with my Sister had multiple opportunities to win if he pulled the same tricks she was — seizing the waist in a flip, hauling around by the pants, hair or ear pulling, tripping as they swung around. However, he behaved more like a boulder: determined not to be lifted off the ground, not much else.

Surely, she can tell they hold their violence in check.

Twenty against one, all but Deshi seasoned and larger in size than the training buas I'd faced off with. That probably made this palatable.

The Guildsman fighting in the center spotted Mourn and me first and yielded the contest a moment later, bowing and backing up as Jael tried to take one last swing.

"*Web-fucking pucker jab!*" she barked in Davrin before switching to Trade. "Tired so soon … *kiddu?*"

Several Guildsmen laughed like this wasn't a first time, and I imagined her bluster to disengage with each one.

"New opponent," said the last man, presenting his palm up toward me while Mourn kept to the rear, standing behind two men to avoid confusion.

Hoo bua.

Jael's shock from seeing me didn't last, and I hadn't decided how to handle this with everyone watching. The moment my Sister's eyes began to narrow on me, however, I lifted her boots where she could see them. "Ready to leave?"

She squinted. "Leave where?"

I grinned. "Somewhere there could be shit on the floor. You need these." She didn't answer at first, so I made a show of counting each man with at least one visible bruise. "Overtaking my count of *buas*? Impressive."

"*Pfft.*" She blew through her lips, looking about ready to fall over. "*You* be Jee-jee. *I* be Jan-shee."

Deshi shook his head. "But she earned *Janshi, Jiji.*"

"'*Jiji*' too small!" she retorted. "*Jiji* tiny name for warrior spirit!"

"We agree, yes," Torch said, looking at his brothers. "Perhaps … *Janhuren?*"

I caught Kil's smile in my periphery when he showed his teeth. "*Janhuren.* 'Rise with fire.'"

"Ha!" Tak laughed, clapping his hands once. "Perfect. I like it!"

"Why?" my Sister demanded. "What it mean?"

Kil pointed at me. "*Janshi.* Sky warrior." Then moved his finger to her. "*Janhuren.* Sky fire."

"A lightning strike," repeated my jovial guide from Augran. "The spear the sky warrior sends ahead."

My chest warmed with gratitude as Jael's expression softened, even though none of the men here thought we were sky spirits from above the Great Lake.

Still, I liked it. If she hated *Jiji* and wanted a Yungian spirit-name not reliant on me, then she had earned one by wearing herself to a nub in the fastest and hardest way possible.

As usual.

I offered a bow but did not take my eyes off her. "*Janhuren.* Let us clean up. I need you by my shoulder soon. Today."

"Why?" she asked, unaware she hadn't straightened up much. The angry surge had dissipated, and she looked absolutely mauled.

"Come and see, Red Sister," I said, this time sounding like Elder Rausery. It worked.

With a deep breath, as if realizing she needed air, Jael limped barefoot toward me. I guided her out of the humid room first, turning to sweep my eyes over the men of Reprisal. Mouthing, *Thank you*, I received several immediate affirming gestures while many masculine faces split into grins.

"We understand," Wolf murmured as I slipped past.

I had a sense of that truth but not the time to dig into it as Mourn took up the rear, following us down to the end of a long hallway before speaking.

"There's a washroom ahead," he said. "Turn right, then left. Empty for now, but better hurry. The Guildsmen will use it after us."

Jael grumbled acknowledgment, her body language clear she headed that way. This wasn't the same washroom we'd been in with the Manalari women and later healed Tamuril's scars. This was smaller and remote. The water flow wasn't as strong near the end of the pipes but sufficient for Jael to strip down and get clean amid the pained hissing and sucking air as the heat struck her stinging skin.

"Fuuuck," she groaned at one point, head down as she turned the

gems for cooler water.

"Potion, pellet, or nothing?" I asked from outside the stall.

"Depends," she said in Davrin. *"What do you need?"*

Her voice was hoarse.

I glanced up; Mourn confirmed with hand-sign we were alone. *"I want to talk to Mathias Briar in his cell. I need information, but a torturer is difficult to intimidate."*

She paused for a while, letting the water run down her back. Meanwhile, Mourn cleaned and mended her shirt and pants with his magic.

"What do you want from him?" she asked.

I thought about it. *"Anything he might know about Brom Troshin and his daughter, Amelda."*

"And why's that important?"

It didn't take long to find my argument.

"The Ma'ab army lost most of their leadership tonight to assassins," I said. *"Amelda is there according to Mathias, and she is a noble who might have risen in prominence. She's the type to seize the opportunity, and she knows about me and Soul Drinker from when her sire tried to enslave me because she helped him. He's out of the fight, but I'd like to remove her as well."*

Jael lifted her head and turned one copper-red eye to me, her tone dry. *"So, another conniving noble is pushing somewhere that we can't let her stay."*

I smiled. *"Yes."*

"Hm. Wouldn't be the first time." My Sister let the water flow over her, palms braced on the wall. *"Potion, if you have it. Pellet if not, and you can spare it."*

Mourn closed in to hand me a vial, signing that it would take care of her visible wounds.

'Visible.' Rather precise.

I made sure to pass the vial to Jael and watched her swallow its fluid before speaking to Mourn. "If I may ask, what did Wolf mean when we left? About understanding?"

Mourn lifted his chin, exhaling through his nose. "He arranged a non-lethal place for her to purge. He recognizes the fester."

"The what?"

"The anger that has no target. Reprisal understands this. They know a desire for revenge cannot focus beyond appearances, at best. That the *real* target is in the dark of the mind where it cannot yet be reached. Thus, they fight her but have no anger of their own to worsen her wounds."

"Do you talk about me?" Jael said with a muted snarl.

"I do," he replied, unapologetic as he leaned against the stall, tail curving in front of him. "Consider whether you might appreciate the men willing to fight you tonight, as they all fight their own ghosts from time to time, to let out the same poison. None will bear you a grudge for the bruises, whether it helps you straighten out your head or not."

She made a face, wincing as her scrapes stopped bleeding. "They too gentle. Afraid to hit harder."

The half-blood slowly drew in his breath.

"These fighters are not Red Sisters, Jael," he said in his accented Davrin, as if to make certain she understood. *"They fight that kind of fear and torment perpetuated among their own race, such as the sun priests and their enforcers. Their enemies would debase you as you would expect, as your Lead did Tamuril. These males I have chosen would* not. *Will* never. *No matter how you strike them, they'll never force a violating victory."*

Jael scowled through the speech, verbal jabs and all, but made no remarks. Turning over her right hand and forearm, she watched the wounds slowly close. She'd be hungry soon, same as me.

Finally, she looked up — not at Mourn but at me. *"What do you need from me with this Mathias Briar?"*

"The appearance of strength," I said, "and success. He knows I was looking for another of my race, my Sister."

She frowned. *"You told him about me?"*

"No. I was following Gaelan at the time. We interrogated a Witch Hunter who might have seen a 'black sorceress.' My questions were about her." I frowned as well. *"Though I admit ... I am not certain if I gave away that I searched for more than one Sister. I tried not to, but I ... might have."*

I tried to remember but only shook my head.

Mourn spoke. *"Interrogation goes both ways, Sirana, and you were unsafe every moment once leaving the Ley Tower with the Ma'ab. The threat only grew worse in Troshin Bend meeting Brom."*

"Hmph." I smiled with caution. *"True. Except when I was with Osgrid in her hut. She was safe."*

Jael studied my expression and grunted, shrugging. *"Doesn't matter. You succeeded. I'm here as proof if it helps."* She smirked. *"But I won't say much."*

"That would be best," my bodyguard agreed.

"Pfeh."

Jael's tongue was a worm's width way from sticking out at her teacher when he added, *"Leave the skin hunter guessing your thoughts. Watch your expression. The less you give him, the more Sirana has to maneuver."*

"Yeah, yeah. Very well."

My Sister turned off the water before scratching carefully around the new skin and flaking scabs brought by the healing potion. It appeared like a rash — a lighter, purplish hue rather than black. I handed her a towel to dry off, noting Mourn had surreptitiously left clean clothing and boots on the nearest bench.

"Can I get something to eat, first?" she asked.

I grinned, gazing with hope at my bodyguard, who nodded. *"The kitchen is on the way to the lower cell."*

"Convenient," I said.

"Practical. They cannot come to the mess hall."

"They?" Jael repeated as she started to dress. *"More than one prisoner?"*

Oh, right.

"Witch Hunters," I admitted, using their common name. *"Isboern found them hiding in camp yesterday. After we came inside."*

My Sister schooled her expression as she reached at last for her boots, ready to tuck her mended feet inside. *"Hm. Interesting. I see your meaning. There could be shit on the floor."*

Mourn chuckled. *"Not bad but keep trying. They will gleefully jump on your every nerve. Bear in mind on which side of the bars you stand."*

Jael's most unnerving grin broke free. *"This time."*

"Hm." He narrowed his serpentine eyes. *"Correct. This time."*

CHAPTER 9

JAEL'S HAIR HAD DRIED AND FLUFFED UP BY THE TIME WE REACHED MOURN'S deep room to collect her belt and the rest of her armor.

"Where is your cloak?" I asked.

She sighed. "Forgot. In room."

"Hm."

Graul had woken up when we'd entered and offered an obvious if sleepy grin. As we prepared for our next meeting, he asked abruptly, "Weapons good idea in prison?"

"Not usually," Mourn answered his small friend. "But, for this prisoner, Sirana must have Soul Drinker on her where he can see it."

The shadow drake rattled his throat, ending with a strange whistle as he pushed himself up to the edge of the nest. "I come with?"

The Dragonchild considered this suggestion rather than decline it at once. *Interesting.*

"What he do to help?" Jael asked, avoiding insult while dipping into a hint of doubt.

"He does the tasks where no one is looking," Mourn answered. "Especially if something needs to go missing. Metal bars mean nothing to him, especially in dark places with many shadows."

I raised my eyebrows, about to speak when Graul churred, the half-blood lifting him out of the nest.

"Graul will disappear before Mathias or the Manalari see him," my bodyguard explained. "They won't know he is there unless they try to seize a weapon."

"Um. Alright."

They've done this before.

The chances seemed equal to me that either Jael or Graul could cause disruption in the prison. Given my next addition to our entourage, this might not be bad if I expected it while Mathias did not.

"I want Gavin to come as well," I said. "The Witch Hunters will react badly no matter what, and Mathias knew him from the start."

"When?" Jael asked with a nose wrinkle.

"When Sarilis sent Gavin to recruit him. The three of us met while the death mage led Mathias to the Ley Tower." I smirked. "The skin hunter tried to warn me away, saying not a place for 'young girls.'"

Mourn was amused. "Hm. Did the skin hunter also witness the Deathwalker's transformation at Troshin Bend?"

"He did. In the same shed where he tortured Thetri Jacob." I paused. "Mathias knows the specifics of how Gavin made the soul shard he threw in the pool."

"Sounds like someone who has learned where to position himself."

I made a face. "I agree. Unfortunately. And …"

"And?"

I included Jael in my confession. "I should mention we have fucked, Mathias and me."

My Sister blinked but suppressed the blatant disgust as I added, "An exchange only. Strange circumstances. I'd not do it again, knowing what I do now."

Mourn was much better at hiding whatever he thought about this. "That is good to know going in. Thank you for looking forward. Gavin is aware?"

I tried neither to grin nor grimace. "He is."

The first suck got him killed.

"Very good. We shall collect him, some food, then head to the lower cells."

THE TUNDAR DWARVES CONVINCED ME WITHOUT BOAST THAT THEIR "SOLITARY" spaces might be as difficult to enter and exit unseen as the Queen's dungeon.

We passed through two heavy doors, each guarded and with a "trap space" in between. They could not be broken by one of their berserkers with an ax in three tries. As two guides led the way, gem wards reduced their armor's noise while enhancing our footfalls and any whisper bouncing on the walls.

Next came a short but confusing set of stairs. We passed four false passages hiding dead ends along the way, each meant for anyone unguided to lose their direction and be drawn into the range of additional gem wards meant to induce drowsiness and confusion.

Or so we'd been warned.

Graul had vanished from Mourn's shoulder before the first door, however, before the guards could have seen him. Based on the calm of his "*Maekrix*," I imagined the little drake following along, jumping from shadow to shadow without sounding an alarm.

A prison strong enough to keep most Human mages but probably not several Davrin back home, or like one walking beside me.

Hope it's enough.

Fortunately, the Dwarves had given this part of the redoubt as much consideration to its design as the rest. The cells lined only one side of a broad hall, plenty of space to avoid an attack from a desperate prisoner. The ceiling was higher than I expected, too. Neither Mourn nor Gavin had to duck their heads once we passed through the final, guarded gate. One guide remained at a locked door while the other led us into the prison hall.

The walls forming cells presented an odd mix of material. Rows of vertical and horizontal metal bars welded together could form three sides to a cage or only the front of a solid stone enclosure. Farther down, another heavy, slotted door sealed off a small room, such as those underneath the Temple of the Sun.

As if the Tundar want options on whether prisoners can see each other or not.

I wondered which form they had chosen for Mathias, but spotted the largest, middle cage first: four Witch Hunters held together with nothing to divide them. They could sleep bundled together for warmth if they wished although sat apart right now.

"Oi!" the guard barked, making Jael and me jump. "Wake up an' be quiet!"

I didn't see how the bearded one would enforce that command, but then he slapped an emerald embedded into the wall behind him. Suddenly, all movement and voices from inside the cage ceased, and the scene grew clear why we wanted it that way.

The Manalari men had gained their feet, their hairy, ungroomed faces twisting to form acerbic words. Large hands made threats I could not read but understood, nonetheless. Fortunately, we didn't have to listen to any word or screech, whether we knew their tongue or not. A subtle, wavering drone filled the cage along with occasional thumps as if coming from underwater.

"Better," Jael commented with a satisfied curl to her lip.

The Dwarf grinned. "Best part ov my watch!"

"Can they hear us?" I asked.

"Nay. Emerald works both ways, all er nothin'. Need bloodstone tah listen in."

"Ah. Have any bloodstone?"

"Not yet." The Dwarf looked around. "This redoubt ain't that old an' these are our first prisoners."

"We will work with what we have," Gavin murmured, moving forward to study the Witch Hunters.

One by one, they noticed him. With caustic glances at Jael and me and practically no notice of Mourn — strange — the "god warriors" gradually lost their bluster. The gazing Deathwalker neither moved, spoke, nor conveyed expression, yet their offended anger turned to dread.

"Huh," the Dwarf said as he watched. "Yer good as the emerald, Deathwalker. See anything interesting?"

"For three, no, though one bears a chronic fester of some sort dimming his life. It is old. Part of his aura now."

"Hah." The guard tugged his beard. "Crotch rot?"

Jael snorted before Gavin could answer.

"Perhaps," he said. "Your iron bars bear a magical resistance which obscures common markers, so I'm not sure."

"Alright. We'll keep an eye 'im. Which one?"

"This one."

Gavin pointed at a Witch Hunter bearing a red-blond beard like the Templar Erik. The man's eyes flew open, and he stepped away, urgently convincing the others to turn their backs on us and form a circle facing each other. Presenting identical postures, the Manalari stood straight with feet slightly apart and hands folded, their chins lowered near their chests, and lips moving.

"Bah. Praying fer our skin tah peel off, probably," the Dwarf said without rancor, taking a few steps past their cage. "Come on."

We followed, and I asked, "Is the redbeard a Warrant? Or Thetri?"

Our guard was unsure. "Um —"

"He's a Sanctor," said a familiar voice two cells away. "Under the Thetri, the way Jacob was *under* the Warrant."

Mathias.

The skin hunter chortled as we drew closer. I watched an unadorned pair of brown hands pass through two squares in the front bars. The man rested his forearms there, bringing his face close to peer out.

"Nice of you to visit, Sirana," he added with a white grin, eyes shifting. "And Gavin! You've, um, grown. Heh. Sarilis should watch his back."

I resisted the impulse to smile while the Deathwalker stared in that dead way he did.

"I'll rejoin my kin," muttered the Dwarven guard, excusing himself.

When we didn't speak, Mathias pointed his finger at Jael. "You got her out alive? Not easy when the Bishops want something, so good job.

But ... *she* isn't the one you were looking for, is she? What about the other one in the warp rot? Did you find her?"

The interrogator had wasted no time trying to provoke a response, to the point the Dwarf glanced our way, curious. Mathias managed to garner a scowl from Jael while a strange numbness steeled through me. Memories of Troshin Bend started creeping in.

There, and just after.

"No," I answered. "I did not."

Mathias tilted his head, glanced after the guard then lingered on his fellow prisoners. Scratching a dark, thickening beard, he said, "What about that assassin in the trees? The beast with gold eyes Jacob talked about. Where is he?"

Jael and I frowned with genuine confusion, looking up and over our shoulders to make sure he was there. The same moment, Mourn folded his arms, straightening up behind us.

The movement caught the prisoner's gaze, who jumped in surprise then exhaled with a laugh. "Ah, *there* you are! Nice trick. *Heh.* ... Wow, that explains a lot."

Indeed, it did. No wonder I couldn't parse a Dragonchild from a Sathoet as far as half-blood stories went.

The skin hunter looked us over, shaking his head in disbelief. "I can't wait to hear the stories coming out of Manalar later."

"Hear stories?" Gavin asked. "Do you not want to witness it?"

Our old travel mate repositioned his stance for comfort. "That seems particularly dangerous right now. I'm on nobody's side but mine, and everyone knows I'm here."

"Nobody's side," Mourn repeated. "Are you sure?"

"Why wouldn't I be, demon?"

The To'vah-krav didn't react to the misname. *Quite deliberately.*

I asked, "What about Amelda? You mentioned her last night. That she's already there."

Mathias shrugged, his smile tightening. "Oh, yeah. Kill her for me, Red Sister, if you would. I would be far from the warp rot *and* the Ma'ab if not for her. She hasn't given up on *you*, I promise you that, so your new friends might as well put a target on her back. If you don't, you'll be sorry."

His warm brown eyes hardened into that *other* gaze of his, the one he'd shown me on the Midway grasslands. Despite his charm and ease with talking, this Human wasn't soft with anyone. He hunted to consume someone of his choice, and in between, he traded secrets without apparent favoritism.

So far, however, this seemed too easy.

Do not be fooled.

"Did Brom have a hook in you?" I asked next.

"Brom?" Mathias might've pretended to be confused.

"Or was that Amelda's strength?" I continued, trying to prick his pride. "You and the Ma'ab dragged Rithal with you when you came after me and Gavin, but you didn't want to be there."

The skin hunter didn't answer at first, staring at us without a hint if I'd had any effect. Then he sighed. "Alright, so ... First, may I ask what in the Hells you did to Brom that killed him but also *didn't* kill him in the way it *should* have?"

The numbing chill remained in my fingers. "What do you mean?"

Mathias pointed at Soul Drinker. "You stabbed the sorcerer with that cursed blade, right?"

"Right."

The man grinned. "Good work. I take it you distracted him with your cunt once he dragged you out of my shed. Obviously, he got sloppy. And either you *really* wanted that thing, or he was a fool and left it in your reach."

My heartbeat escaped my control, but I took a slow breath. "What happened with Brom after I escaped? I didn't stay to watch him die."

"Heh, the right move to make." Mathias glanced at Gavin, Jael, Mourn, and then me. "The innkeeper I'd known for over a decade *vanished*. In his place was this deranged lunatic tearing through the grounds, vomiting up all these strange voices and languages as he commanded everyone living *and* dead to come to him. I tried to run. I just didn't get out fast enough. Neither did Rithal, but he was lucky enough to get knocked unconscious in the scuffle."

Mathias hissed in a breath before continuing. "That town was turned inside out. Kurn and Castis were acting like Brom was an Ascended god or something, while Amelda was panicking and did *something* stupid, said something to him. The next thing I know, he *compelled* me to stay with her and protect her." He growled. "Going after you two then meeting her father at Manalar was *her* idea. She wanted to drag you and the black dagger back."

"So, the Deathless," Gavin interrupted, "left for Manalar then?"

Hard eyes flicked his way. "Yeah. He knew you would purge the warp rot. And he pulled what had happened to Jacob in the shed out of me. The lich put it together."

"The Deathless is not a lich."

"No? *Pfft!* Stab his body and kill it, but he gets up knowing more than before? Isn't that what *you* did?"

"On the surface," said the Deathwalker. "Liches attain their immortality by side-stepping death, permanently anchoring their soul to one plane of existence."

Mathias rolled his eyes at the lesson. Gavin was undeterred.

"The Deathless and I *have* died and transitioned. We each returned by other means, for another purpose."

The skin hunter made a face and rubbed his eyes. "If you say, monk. The point is, Brom was close enough to what *I* know the Ascended *are*, and what Sarilis would *love* to become."

"As you wish." Gavin's long fingers tapped lightly at his side. "That is an interesting suggestion for my old mentor."

Mathias grinned with blatant satisfaction. "I thought you might like to know. Good thing you didn't hang around much longer. I'm sure he would have strapped you down to suck up some extra life as you did Jacob."

"Reasonable guess. And after you ran off with Amelda in the warp rot forest?"

Gavin hadn't blinked at the comparison. The interrogator recognized the useless tactic and sighed. "It's been a damnable ride ever since, let me say, from there to Manalar to here. Once Amelda was at the war camp, I was stuck in the city reporting to 'Brom.' I couldn't get away until you two finally dealt with the bastard." Mathias looked straight at Mourn as he said that. "I managed to get through the Dwarves' gate before it closed."

"So we see," Mourn rumbled. "Why didn't you run *much* farther when you had the chance?"

"Heh. Maybe I wanted to *thank you* for freeing me."

"Unlikely, given your patterns."

"Ah. Have you been watching me, demon?"

"The Guild has. They know who you are, Mathias Briar, and where you come from. I've been working with them."

"You would." The man looked my mercenary up and down, quirking an eyebrow. "Fine. I stayed in the camp because no one knew what was going on. I wanted to know what happened with Sirana and the dagger, if the Defender of the Wall made it, and how many Templars. Maybe where one could find the scorched, half-Ma'ab monk whom the Bishops should have killed *years* ago." Mathias chuckled with satisfaction, his bare hands drooping outside the bars. "The information would have been worth something to a lot of people."

I glanced up at Mourn's face. ~*Truth, you think?*~

Mostly. I expect he holds something back at all times.

~*He's talking a lot.*~

He wants something.

~*To be released.*~

*He hasn't asked yet. What do you *want*?*

Good question. Gavin had done well coaxing out what had happened in Troshin Bend after we'd left; I was glad I hadn't needed to do it. With most loops closed and nothing starkly tempting, the only part which had something to offer was Mathias's open invitation to assassinate Amelda to prevent trouble.

"How much time did you spend with any Ma'ab officers when you were with Amelda?" I asked.

The prisoner showed me his palms. "Oh, no. Can't help you there.

Men bigger than Kurn started following her everywhere she went, and about every-fucking-thing there looked at me like a tasty brown treat. I got the fuck out of there *days* before the shamblers reached the wall, and was stuck *inside* the city, remember?"

"Inside the city," I repeated. "We saw you in the Temple courtyard. Helping to rile up the crowd."

Mathias was unapologetic. "That was a fantastic display, don't you think? I couldn't dream of better timing to turn the crowd against Keros and in favor of their shiny, new *Capitan* than what happened with the Inquisitor."

"That was your purpose?"

He raised one finger. "That was Brom's. And whoever was informing *him*."

The Merchant ...

"Did Brom ever meet with you inside the Temple?" I asked. "When he was pretending to be that blond Bishop, uh — ?"

"Cognate Horus," Gavin added.

Mathias bore a similar expression to mine. "Ah ... No. I wasn't 'clean' enough to go inside that place, and I wouldn't anyway. He sent magic missives."

Mourn broke in. "So, you never laid eyes on Brom once you got inside the city?"

The skin hunter shook his head. "Nope. I'm kind of glad for that."

His actions could have come as easily from the direction of the Ice Lord as the Deathless, said the Dragonblood through the pearl. *Since the two were setting up stakes during that time.*

~*Where my thoughts headed, yes. But does it matter to Mathias under a geas?*~

Only if that geas is still there, despite what he says about us freeing him.

Unsettling.

~*Are we going to find out?*~

Not yet. We will keep him here for a time.

Which meant the details of what Mathias had been doing after the courtyard were moot under a geas, either then or now. But if he never was? Or was released earlier than he claimed? I didn't have all day to chase him with random questions to uncover something by chance.

What do I want? Why am I here if he can't say anything else about Amelda?

"What *do* you want for your help, Mathias?" I asked.

"*Am* I helping?" He offered an innocent squint and a tilt of his head. "Hm. Well! To be released, obviously. But I'm fairly sure that's not going to happen for a while."

He flicked his eyes at Mourn before refocusing on me. The shift of his smile made me suspicious. *Moreso.*

"So," he continued, "how can I be of service? I'm generally a cooperative captive, rare as this is."

Unlike his favorite Witch Hunter. Jacob had cursed and struggled until the moment he became a black, crystalline fragment in Gavin's hand.

In my periphery, the Sanctor had come alone to the front of his cage, peering balefully down the hall. His mouth opened, and though his voice was muffled by the emerald, my practiced eyes read the skin hunter's name on his lips.

Mathias.

~Mourn — ~

I saw it. One moment.

The half-blood stepped away to slap the emerald the same way the guard had. Meanwhile, the two Dwarves stood at the far end, aware but waiting. Dread became clear on the Sanctor's face at having Mourn so close, but he called down the hall.

"*Mathias, esti el? Truxer o udrim podri?*"

The skin hunter groaned like he'd been caught, smirking with mischief, his eye on the brink of a wink as he answered. "*Esti el. Nontres paenco.*"

Gavin straightened. "You know each other?"

"Eh, not really. We've just been talking for a few hours."

~What did they say?~ I demanded of Mourn.

The Sanctor said, 'Mathias, is this him? Have they brought the warp rot?' And Mathias replied, 'This is he. Do not panic.'

~He? Do they mean Gavin or you?~

Mourn's tail suggested irritation as he touched the emerald, silencing the Sanctor, too slow to answer before the Deathwalker beat him to it.

"Who is 'he?' " Gavin asked Mathias directly.

The interrogator pointed blithely at Mourn. "The 'black devil' that poor Roilos spotted in the warp rot forest. Along with a smaller, *female* one."

His tone was loaded with satisfaction. My bodyguard finally started to frown as my stomach began froze over.

~Female?~

"All the Witch Hunters present at Troshin Bend died there," Gavin stated. "I counted them, met each Vis."

" 'Present' is the key word, Deathwalker." Mathias grinned. "Proper protocol sent one Sanctor and his 'partner' ahead to report to the Warrant at the Kerut Bridge Fort. They never stopped at Troshin Bend. Even I didn't know that."

Until he'd been locked up in the same space with them.

The prisoner focused on Jael and me. "What chance, huh? Did this Elf-demon help to find your third 'sister'? It sounded to me like the good Sanctor spotted them together. She was on his shoulder, or something."

"What noise you say?" Jael growled.

I gripped her forearm, keeping my eyes on Mathias and resisted turning on Mourn. "Jacob said he 'saw' my sister, too. You were there, skin hunter. Even *I* saw her later in the warp rot forest, before we destroyed the core. The forest *mimicked* her, trying to confuse me. We can't be sure of anything these fearful men *thought* they saw in that forest."

Mathias shrugged. "Of course. Makes good sense." A pause. "Sssso, you are saying the big one *did not* offer to help you find her?"

No, Mourn hadn't.

I dared not look at my bodyguard, recalling how determined he had been to dissuade me from "wasting" the time and resources to search hills covered by slanted trees. He could have been right, and no sinister motive existed.

He was trying to save my baby. I needed food … Untainted water … a safe place to rest.

That had been our reasoning. It may have been too late for Gaelan by then, no matter what.

~Mathias plants doubt,~ I said through the pearl. *~Trying to divide us.~*

Wise to be aware. Mourn sounded cautious. **We can leave, Sirana. Come later with better questions and preparation.**

Could we? What if things "happened fast," like he said, and I never knew what this was all about?

"What did the Sanctor describe, exactly?" Gavin asked, folding his hands like the Witch Hunters. "Of the third Davrin."

"Mostly complaining that Bictrius and Jacob didn't believe him at first." Mathias grinned. "Because this was the first sighting of any sort of 'devilry' on the trip. They hadn't gone far enough north yet to see the rot. Just a glimpse of a 'black beast carrying a white-haired witch.' Maybe a partial print in the ground but no track they could follow. They wasted a lot of time from the sound of it but, *whew!* By the time they *did* get up north, they barely got out again. Yeah, they believed the Sanctor then and sent him ahead before returning to town to conscript Brom's help."

I held still, grappling with the possibilities. A Witch Hunter had split off from the rest. He was alive and in the Guild's possession.

Maybe he'd seen Gaelan.

Sanctor Roilos stood holding the bars of his cage, staring to suggest he'd overcome his initial terror of me. We were all loathsome creatures, of course, but …

~Mourn? Could that story be true?~

Let us talk somewhere else. We didn't come prepared, and I think the Ice Lord could still be involved somehow.

"Let us go, Gavin," Mourn said. "Sisters."

"What? Why?" Jael asked, tossing her hand at Mathias. "What of *other* sister?"

I couldn't *feel* anything from Mourn. His shields were up; his mind blank.

Oh, Goddess. Gaelan.

"Done already, are we?" Mathias commented, pulling in a hand to prop his head in his palm. "You seem wary, merc. Did you *not* want her to know that? Oops. But I grasp you. Sirana can be dangerously focused when she catches the scent, can't she? To the point she gets hurt. Makes your job harder, doesn't it?"

Somehow *that* sounded like something Indrath would say.

"Let us leave," my bodyguard repeated.

The plea to obey was subtle, but truth also struck like a stone to my head.

Ohhh, Goddess. He knew something ... all this time.

I followed the guide of his fingers beneath my arm. Mathias said something else to our backs, something suggesting he'd "stick around," but my eyes had locked on the Sanctor Witch Hunter.

The man with the berry-gold hair had blue eyes not as dark as mine. He hadn't meant to meet my gaze directly — I could tell by the flinch and desperate attempt to pull away.

But I *had* him.

His knuckles turned white; hands clenched tight on the bars.

"Sirana!" overlapped several voices as I lunged to grab Roilos by his round ears through the bars.

~Show me!~ I commanded. *~Show me exactly what you saw that Bictrius did not believe! Nothing else!~*

The Sanctor blinked then screamed in nerve-rending agony as colors flooded my mind. The details launched out in front of me, waiting to be caught, slowing enough for me to grasp what I saw through his eyes.

What I witnessed through *all* his senses.

The trees remained healthy. Although the day neared dusk, we were a day or two off from the spoiled forest according to reports. The shrubs were good and full, not the sort which caused a rash, and perfect for privacy.

I need to relieve myself. Badly.

Branches cracked and snapped, and I covered myself modestly, crouching down, waiting to see what cursed thing revealed itself in this wilderness.

A black witch ...

As real as she could be. Form-fitting leather pants, true boots striking the ground. A black shirt torn, bracers upon her arms and gloves covering her hands as if she expected to join a fight. Her hair was pure white, her skin purest black. She acted possessed, sweating, struggling with the forest passage as much as she did the demon which must be within her.

Or the witch was *the demon. Swept up in ecstasy.*

She is heading for our camp.

No ... ! I must stop her — !

Another blackness appeared without snapping one twig.

I froze in place.

A long-tailed, four-legged beast from the Hells ran up behind her, cutting her off from coming closer to me. The male tried to speak but mostly growled. She wasn't afraid. She stared, face glistening with sweat, her eyes like rotted fruit tinged with vomit green.

"Dalhar — !" she cried, falling upon her knees before the beast. "Ussta dalharil ..."

The demon sat obediently on his haunches, lifting partly scaled forelimbs which somehow worked as hands. He grabbed her by the shoulders, held her upright. I waited for him to take a bite and tear out her throat.

"Tesso'ilta," she wept, head lolling, hands pawing him weakly. "Ussta cait ... ussta dalharil ..."

The white-fanged beast threw her across his tall withers and somehow made her stay in place.

Magic.

The monster ran west with the witch, away from camp.

I released the breath I held. "I must tell the Warrant."

SOMETHING WAS WRONG.

Get out ... ! Stop! STOP! Or I'll —

My consciousness hurled itself out of the man's mind quicker than he could see me flee. My head throbbed as I fell, as something stronger *pulled* me, scraping my heels along the stone.

In front of me, a snarl through clenched in his jaws.

"I have her, Graul. Let go."

The shadow drake released the hand of the Witch Hunter reaching through the bars, bite marks bleeding as he vanished before my eyes. Mourn held my wrists, keeping them up and away from my belt as he hustled me toward the exit. I felt sick. Jael's quick gait and Gavin's slower, heavier one sounded behind us.

"That wasn't wise," my bodyguard said. "The man reached for your belt. For the dagger."

"Y-you tracked her!" I retorted. "You f-found Gaelan … !"

"He did?!" Jael barked.

"*Shh!*" His grip on me tightened. "To Gavin's room. Please say *nothing* until then."

"What happened?" asked the Dwarven guard with concern as we approached. "She awright?"

"She will be," said my bodyguard. "Private matter. They jabbed a dagger deep."

"Ah, fuck. Sorry tah hear."

Did they? I thought. *Or did you?*

The Dwarves turned around to lead us out without asking further questions.

CHAPTER 10

"My child ... My daughter ... !"

Gaelan's pleas filled my head, repeating and endless the whole way to the Deathwalker's chambers.

"I have a child ... my cait ... my daughter ... Don't hurt me ... I am sick!"

Although vaguely aware when Mourn picked me up to move faster, I could not oust from my mind the terror on her face. The Witch Hunter may have been afraid, may have only seen a threat, but I *recognized* her.

That had not been the forest trying to trick someone.

That was her.

I read her hand signs begging for help, for mercy. I saw the same sorrow from the night before she left on her mission alone. Fear that she'd never see Natia again, even from a distance, tangled with the green madness in her eyes.

Warp rot.

"What happened to her?!" I demanded as soon as Gavin closed the door, trying to roll out of the half-blood's arms. "What have you done? *What haven't you told me?!*"

Mourn caught me before I could tumble onto the stone and set me onto the nearest cot before stepping back, tail twitching warily as I tried to sit up, struggling to catch my breath. My heart raced with fear as the

Human's had been, my limbs too weak to hold me up. I fought nausea like a writhing eel, and the numbness wouldn't recede.

I could not feel solid ground beneath me.

Jael bared her teeth, her lip curled in a snarl, using everything she had to hold herself in check. Graul was there, too, teeth freshly blooded from the Sanctor's hand. The little beast dared her to close in on his *Maekrix*.

"Talk!" she barked from a safe distance. "Is she alive?"

"It's not that simple," Mourn rumbled.

"It is! Yes or no!"

"I don't know!" He matched her volume then quieted. "She was alive when I last saw her, but it has been weeks."

"Where is she?"

"I cannot tell you."

"You fuck! You will!"

"Not like this, I will not!"

I wept on the cot as they argued, my mind swirling, unable to grasp words from a maelstrom to use for myself. My mouth garbled something as the Sanctor's memory of my sister repeated without cease.

Without. *Cease.*

I could *not* move past it.

"I see an injury in her aura," Gavin said, by far the calmest voice in the room.

"What?" Mourn paused to look.

"It is serious. May we shelve this argument until she is stable?"

I could hear them but couldn't *see* them, could see only Gaelan. My limbs started to shake. My body seemed to float.

"Shit," my bodyguard muttered. Then, "*No! Don't touch her!*"

"Fuck you!" Jael barked.

"You will be trapped as she is! Stand back!"

"I suggest Isboern is best suited to help," the Deathwalker said.

"I will get him. Just keep Jael away from her and Soul Drinker or this becomes *much* worse."

Mourn rushed out, closing the door with another bang that echoed for hours as their voices struggled to fade.

An instant later, Gaelan's pain exploded into jagged shards of color.

WHAT HAPPENED?

Why was I falling?

Don't need to breathe … ?

Liquid swooshed past my ears, rushing through my chest. It might have been my blood or a lake or something else. All was dark, and if I had fallen, I was also *drifting*. When I reached out, nothing lay close enough to touch.

Nothing to seize, to fight the descent.

Void.

I can't scream in the void.

But did I want to?

Held still. Hushed quiet.

Shush!

Floating.

Dreaming … ?

~Always.~

~Always Dreaming, self-child. Come to us.~

~We are One.~

Suddenly, someone opened the cage. Light flooded in.

Pain!

Hands dove into the water, grabbed me everywhere, pulled me up. And out into …

Sunlight?

So cold!

The fluid spilled out of my mouth, my chest. Air rushed in, searing. Heavy. I couldn't stand.

Now I screamed.

~Help!~

Where was I?

Everything is dark!

Worse. The hard, slippery floor underneath had somehow attached to my raw skin. I ... felt ... *Everything.*

Alone! Everything!

~Punishment ... ~

A shard of yellow crystal punctured the black sky.

~Sirana! Take my hand!~

An anchor in an endless sea.

~Sirana, please!~

We knew them?

They knew us?

They still ... live?

~Stay! We are One!~

I seized the shard, the pain of descent lifted in healing radiance.

~Good! Hold on! Let me draw you up, don't struggle. You're safe, I promise ... ~

Mortal sweat touched my senses. I inhaled deeper as a soft hum swirled around me. Gently pushing us apart.

~No ... ~

~Yes. We heal separately. I am Willven. You are Sirana. Each of us must be strong. The fear will pass. You will live. Let it come, allow your life to return to you.~

~But — ~

~Do not give up your body. Your child still needs you, and your greatest gift is sovereignty. Never forget that.~

My baby.

Goddess ...

~What do I do?~

~Let the wound close. Wait alone. Recognize the fear but know you will be alright. That is all.~

That was all?

Tentatively, I smiled.

And waited alone for what seemed like many days.

Until Gavin's quarters surrounded me, until the cot supported my weight, until I smelled dirt, sweat, and a hint of old blood. I opened my eyes and saw Isboern poised above me.

I could breathe. Deeply.

Oh! It felt good.

"Welcome back," the Godblood said with a smile.

"Sirana?" my younger Sister peeped.

I lifted my eyes to her. She looked so scared; my heart clenched in my chest. *"Hai, Jael. I'm alright."*

She swallowed. *"What happened?"*

My mouth tightened as I tried to remember the sequence of events. It happened so fast.

Gavin spoke. "I believe she injured her aura when she forced the mindlink with the Witch Hunter. The psionics seemed caught in the pain of memory, tearing at the wound."

"In a loop, yes," Isboern agreed, straightening up to give me space, enough for me to confirm Soul Drinker lay under my hip. "I have witnessed psions drop into a coma rather quickly in similar circumstances. I am glad you did not wait to get me."

"As am I," Mourn rumbled from farther away. "I could do nothing otherwise."

"Coma?" Jael asked, shaking her head.

"Like a trance," Gavin answered. "But without intention, often because of injury. The connection between body and mind is severed."

Jael reacted with an angry whimper, and I shuddered, rolling to get on my elbow. My body rested on the cot and moved at my will.

~Sovereignty … ~

My thought drew the Godblood's focus, and he offered me a sad smile. "I am sorry, Sirana, but I advise against wrenching a memory from an unwilling mind. This action caused your injury."

My brow creased. "It what?"

He breathed out. "I do not doubt you have witnessed mages with the ability to force their will upon another and not seem to suffer much ill effect. But … psions bear a great cost in doing so. The same as an untrained mage making a mistake which causes them to lose control of a spell, an untrained psion can do the same. And if the Thought is objectively faster than the Word ..."

Isboern didn't have to finish. Once the memory I'd seized from the Sanctor had left my grip, the speed with which I'd spiraled out of control could not be described.

"But our psions below ..." Jael began, pointing at the floor as Mourn touched her shoulder.

"Are either a collective from which an individual cannot escape," he said, "or they are among the cruelest of individuals outside of the Abyss."

My Sister paused while we turned that over in our heads. Clear enough that Mourn spoke of the Ornilleth and the Tragar without naming them, and the latter race was the reason I was like this.

Isboern listened and, while not asking details, nodded in agreement. "Cruelty comes quickly if we yield to our base impulses in fear, as does madness when we cannot separate our wills from each other. Why so few of us live long or contented lives."

"Us?" Gavin prodded.

"My ..." The blond man hesitated.

Only when he turned his head to look at Tamuril did I realize the Druid had been standing silently at the foot of my cot the entire time. She'd seen it all, and the depth of her concern was clear.

"My people," Isboern said. "My clan. Where I come from."

The Naulor smiled with what I guessed to be modest encouragement.

"We are not all psions," Isboern continued, "but enough of us are, so we must be strict with our boundaries and respect the boundaries of others. Otherwise, we will descend into ... a collective, or perpetuate a cruel existence which inevitably becomes a target for the ire and retribution of the legends. This is assuming the mages don't descend upon us first."

"Ire of the legends?" my death mage asked, his curiosity unbound. "Which ones?"

Isboern shrugged as most of us glanced at Mourn. "I have never seen one until now. The Dragons, or the greater beings watching over this world. My elders have always said some do not tolerate psions running amok. Either we control our power or be purged."

Yet somehow, not a concern for psions in the Deepearth.

"And you believe this," Mourn said without obvious skepticism.

Isboern nodded. "Some may choose not to let an unseen threat of retribution motivate their self-control but, regardless, each of us *must* understand the consequences. Our birth number is low enough there are no schools beyond our clan to help, and even though outsiders often do not know what they see, our potential for destroying the lives of others is greater than any mage I've heard of."

When Mourn failed to disagree, my body chilled. The Godblood noticed and offered a warm but cautious smile. "Do I understand you've not attacked a resisting mind like that before?"

"Well," I hesitated, "maybe I have?"

"Self-defense excepted. You did not initiate an attack, while others you've linked to have been willing or unaware?"

Despite my headache easing, memories remained too fuzzy to know if he was right. "Probably. Except for the first one."

Kain.

We'd fallen into a loop together. Neither of us could get out.

Self-defense.

I shook the thought away, scratching my neck, then noticed another absence. "My spiders?"

"Ah, I am sorry," Mourn said, pulling out a familiar, cinched pouch. "I had to take them with me."

He stepped forward, placing the pouch next to me while Isboern and Tamuril moved away. Something within shifted, my guardians chiming for me. Once I granted a response, they resumed patience. At the same time, I caught the mercenary's scent when he'd stepped close, grounding me to recall what had started all this.

"Gaelan," I whispered.

The Dragonchild exhaled.

I sat up with a growing glare. "Where did you take her? Is she dead? Just tell me!"

"Sirana." Mourn closed his eyes, his chest swelling once. "She may or may not be alive. I cannot know because I protect others."

"Others?"

"The *only* others besides the Ice Lord who *might* have helped her," he explained. "But they are in hiding. I cannot compromise their safety in your present state."

My present 'state?'

"I may be able to obtain information for you after our Bargain is finished but little more."

Intolerable.

The moment this coveted half-blood suggested *aloud* that our Bargain would be over soon, and that he might leave to seek news of Gaelan ...

And ... not return West with me ...

The burning intensified.

No. I can't have both ...

I couldn't leave today to continue my search for Gaelan. I couldn't abandon Gavin to face Sarilis alone.

It's too late. The Ley Tower ... the crossroads must be cleansed.

And I could *not* allow Mourn to *leave* and find out what had happened to Gaelan. I could not know if she lived.

I must return before the Ornilleth attack Sivaraus. I ... must ... !

I groaned as the knives pierced my head. Hands clutching my hair, I curled up on the cot.

"Oh, dear," Gavin said.

"What's happening?" Tamuril yelped.

"*Geas*," Jael growled, darting fearlessly close as if to guard me against that which she couldn't see.

"What?"

"Like a curse," Gavin said dispassionately. "She suffers a mental dissonance from it regularly, causing acute pain, but I have not determined the triggers as they seem to change."

"H-how can it be changing?" the Druid asked, aghast.

"Compulsive suggestions can be adaptive, though I've never heard of one as strong as this."

"Compulsion?" Isboern asked my Sister. "Like the spell that was on you?"

"Yes!" she cried, at once desperate and excited. "Free her, like you did me!"

The Godblood hesitated. "The stress on your body nearly killed you, Jael."

"But did not! I live!"

"It *would* have," he replied sternly, "had I not countered that punishing magic to heal your body as the curse ran its course! If I should try the same here, Sirana *may* survive, but her baby will not."

Oh, no …

Auslan's face flashed behind my eyes, the dream of the two of us meeting eyes upon the damp red sand of a Desert river bank.

"You found help …" he said. "Are you coming now?"

"Not yet. I'm safe, but stuck."

"Stuck where?"

"Long tale."

"Then I shall hold on. We shall hold on to hear it."

We.

"Your child is touched by To'vah magic," the Ice Lord said, "the same as your 'sister' is."

I might only be having these traveling dreams because of this golden thread in my womb.

"B-babe — !" I choked, arms crossing protectively over my middle.

"She is *not* willing," Isboern said as Jael tried to argue with him. "I *cannot*. But I can try to understand the obstacle in her way."

"Pulling secret will kill, too!" she retorted.

She was wrong but couldn't know it. D'Shea and I had temporarily lifted her two-century geas long enough for her to tell me. Without magic, I'd found a way in.

My hand struck forward, grabbing Isboern's clothing to pull myself up despite pain which had not lessened. The number of allies who stood in the room doubled, and I could hardly focus on one. I rolled until two Godbloods stood above me, trying to fix my eyes on his gaze.

~Yes. Yes! Hurry!~

I had no idea what I would say, what I might confess, or how it would help. I just wanted someone to hear what I couldn't speak, the same as my Elder after all those years after Shyntre was born. The same as when Jilrina kept me prisoner under her control.

And maybe ... I could find a way to be free.

At a time of my choosing.

The blond man had bared his hands but took my wrist to pull off my glove. Our skin touched as our grip firmed up.

Eyes met.

I was as willing and open as I could be for the Defender of the Wall.

WITH ENOUGH PATIENCE AND CALM IN THE CENTER OF A STORM, THE YOUNG psion found a way in. Evading ancient pain, he slipped behind the haggard wards warning every mage and Ornilleth away.

Only then did I know the Valsharess had assured my death if a mind flayer had caught me.

Willven was not an Ornilleth. He was a modest, short-lived Human man, not part of a collective such as my Queen recognized. He was an individual, a singular will like me, who could quiet his magic such that he did not need to use it. The strange youth also quieted his mind such that the Queen's geas could not sense him passing by.

The Godblood found me inside a Desert tent where I sat shackled, threatening winds howling outside all around us but not in here. He looked about, studying the ornate rug laid atop the red sand, at the stakes holding down the royal purple fabric which made up the walls, at the golden poles which bore up the ceiling.

~Not what I expected,~ he thought, his eyes warm as a sunny, spring day. *~Can you hear me, Sirana?~*

I shifted, pulling the chains along the carpet.

~Talk to me,~ he said. *~Can you hear me?~*

~Yes.~

I flinched, expecting that response to hurt. Several moments passed before I accepted that it hadn't, though the shock must have lingered on my face.

Willven sighed with relief and sat down with me. *~I'm glad. Please, share with me. What begins this terrible pain? How can we help you avoid or relieve it?~*

I doubted my eyes welled up with real tears, but it certainly felt like it. *~I have been trying for many months … to find my Sisters in spite of this geas.~*

Willven nodded. *~You have been fighting it. Finding ways around it?~*

~I don't know … Maybe fooling it by fooling myself for a time, so the magic changes. But … it only wants me to do three things.~

~Do you want me to know what those three things are?~

~I do. But only if you will help me somehow.~

~That is why I'm here. I will start by listening.~

Slowly, I drew in a breath. *~First … Kill the death mage at the Ley Tower. To the West, in the mountains.~*

Willven tilted his head. Recognition glimmered in his eyes. *~Sarilis? The old man at the Dwarven fortress. Your queen wants a Human dead before old age claims him?~*

~Yes, exactly.~

~Is Sarilis meant to cause some disruption?~

~Probably? I don't know what.~

~Very well. What is the second task?~

~And second … To listen for mention of half-bloods of my kind, to seek them out if possible and bring them home.~

Blond eyebrows lifted. *~The Dragon Son?~*

I flinched. *~Him, yes. And the Sathoet captured by the Ma'ab, Vesram.~* I swallowed. *~A mention of the half-blood demon allowed me to leave the Ley Tower without killing the death mage. I made a deal with Gavin to return later, after I'd had a chance to search for Gaelan and Jael.~*

~I see.~ Willven rubbed his chin. *~You did not find Gaelan to the north, but you did find Morixxyleth and convinced him to help you free Jael.~*

My lower lip trembled. *~Yes … ~*

~A needle threaded. Well done.~

~I don't think so.~

~Why is that?~

~I need to bring him to my queen. She wants him. And I cannot leave with *him to search for Gaelan, knowing she might be alive, nor can I allow him to leave me to find her. I need ... him and Gavin to help me with Sarilis. If I fail, I may die. The same way Jael would have when you did not claim the shield in the crypt.~*

~Oh.~ He caressed his bare fingers along the carpet, his eyes looking at a corner as he considered. *~What is the third task the geas wants you to do?~*

My breath quickened. *~Return home before winter.~*

Willven frowned. *~But if the geas kills you first?~*

~Then it kills me, and Her Vision will change to something else.~ I trembled in my chains. *~See? Even returning to the Ley Tower and succeeding in killing Sarilis ... I cannot leave after that to find Gaelan, assuming I convinced Morixxyleth to take me there. There is no time.~*

~I ... believe I understand. It is a small cage in which you crouch, and minor distractions see you pricked by the spikes pointed inward.~

The tears slipped out onto my cheek. *~Yeah. Like that.~*

~Does the Dragon Son know your Queen wants him to return with you?~

I choked. *~Don't tell him!~*

Willven blinked his blue eyes. *~Oh ... oh, no. Your Bargain was based on deception?~*

~No! He knows *I could not say some things. He still accepted!~*

~I see. Perhaps because he also had things he could not say?~

My thoughts halted in place as I stared at the man. Only slowly could I work them out. *~The half-blood ... will find this to be 'balanced.' Yes.~*

Willven offered a sympathetic smile. *~Until the man in the prison blurted it out. Now you must work out a new balance with him.~*

~I do not know how we can do this. Not unless he simply agrees to return with me underground before winter and I give up on Gaelan completely.~

Thinking it hurt, though not in the way the Queen would have it.

~Hm.~ The blond man was silent for a time, eyes drifting around the tent before returning to me. *~It may look impossible today but keep hope close. We may yet find a way tomorrow.~*

I muted a quick denial, and Willven paused, staring at the ground in front of him. *~One question. Your answer must be true without omission.~*

I shuddered. *~Ask.~*

He met my eyes. *~Do you care for the Dragon Son's well-being?~*

I straightened up from my slouch. *~What?~*

~Forgive me for prying, but you appear to be good companions. I see mutual respect. Is that not so?~

Companions.

~He calls me Kiabil,~ I admitted. *~We are … companions.~*

Willven softened as if he understood. *~And do you care for him in return?~*

~I don't … I mean, I do? I don't want to give him to my Valsharess.~

Willven smiled, slightly wry. *~Why is that?~*

~She would enslave him again.~

~Again?~

~Yes! As another did! He will hate me if that happens! He might try to k … !~ I shook my head, squeezed my eyes shut. I didn't want to gaze down so far into the dark. *~And my baby, my Sisters … my buas … oh, Goddess, I don't know how to keep any of them safe or free! Sooner or later, they will all be taken from me! And I must watch it happen, like my Elders before me in the Sisterhood! I have no choice!~*

The truth Willven asked for struck him like a spear in the chest, and tears of his own began to formed from the shock. He was silent for some time as I wept in helpless rage at my fate, working gradually to bring his breath under control.

~And if … ~ he began with caution. *~If I could find a way to free you, as I did Jael … what would you do?~*

I huffed. *~Find out what happened to Gaelan. Get Gavin his Ley Tower. Let Morixxyleth make his Bargains up here however he wishes. Try to convince Jael to stay with him so she can learn and be free. M-Maybe bring the Sathoet home if he wanted to go with me.~*

Willven waited for a natural pause. *~You would still return home before winter.~*

He stated this without judgment.

~If I don't, I will have broken a promise to my baby's sire.~ I exhaled shakily. *~And while I don't understand what the Valsharess thinks I can do against the army*

of a psion collective ... my city might be gone by winter. Consumed by the Ornilleth. And if I don't return, I won't have tried *to warn anyone to get out while they can.~* I met his eyes. *~Like you tried when you knew the Ma'ab were coming.~*

The Godblood swallowed deeply, tears escaping his eyes. *~I understand. Better than I ever could have before.~*

We sat in silence within the tent, listening to the sandstorm outside, until finally Willven got to his feet.

~I shall leave the same way I came. And although I don't know yet if you can be freed without harm to your child, I will seek a way to help you. You have my oath, Red Sister.~

CHAPTER 11

THE HEADACHE HAD STOPPED WHEN I OPENED MY EYES, BUT I BLINKED SEVERAL times before making out Jael sitting at the foot of my cot. Her hands gripped the edge, such tension in her posture she might have broken the frame.

A moment later, I recognized someone holding me, bracing us snugly in a semi-sitting position. Not Isboern; *he* kneeled in front of me, now rising to his feet. The hands were bare and pale.

And delicate.

"Can we break her curse, Willven?" Tamuril asked. "Help her as she did me?"

Her tone was ridiculously hopeful.

"I do not know yet," the Godblood replied. "But I shall meditate on this. Musanlo may offer guidance."

"Ask, if there is anything I can do."

His face softened considerably. "Of course, Tamuril."

"The seizure seems to have passed," Gavin observed.

"Thankfully," Isboern agreed, glancing in a rare distraction toward the door. "I ... am sorry, but —"

"See to your men and your people, Captain," Mourn said, maintaining the most distance from my cot. He cradled his drake in his arms, holding my spider pouch in one hand. "You have my personal gratitude for responding to our urgency."

"Of course," the blond man repeated, staring at the Dragonblood and lacking a more courteous acknowledgment.

My bodyguard noted the hesitation. "I would like us to speak later, perhaps offer a modest payment when you're next available."

I stiffened in the Druid's arms. *Shit.*

Isboern bowed his head. "Accepted, legend. I have duties to take care of, but I will send word through the *Oltere* when I can."

What had I done? How had D'Shea handled this after she'd spoken freely to me, for the first time in centuries? I had no idea.

"Rest, please, Sirana," Tamuril said, firming up her long arms to keep me in place.

I could probably escape if I wished. I chose not to.

"Before you go, Godblood," Gavin said, "may we assume not to discuss the previous topic until you've had time to commune?"

"For certain, yes," Isboern agreed, his tone dismayed. "I am sorry, but further questions will likely cause pain. And she should not reenter the prison cells."

"Indeed. Anything else we should know?"

The Godblood considered, careful not to catch my eyes as I waited for what he would say. "Just hold to your current plans and promises. What you have discussed between you. Do not try to change it yet."

"Easily done."

I released my breath through my nose, seeing Isboern off with a silent nod. Testing a few thoughts which might make decent words, I stopped to realize Tamuril had stayed in the Deathwalker's room.

This could complicate the conversation.

"Jael?" I began. "Are you angry?"

She frowned. "No."

"Why sit away like that?"

Blowing through her lips, she waved at Mourn. "*Capitan* needed someone to lift and hold you. *She* alone could be near soul dagger and help shield body while mind gone."

I straightened up, and Tamuril let me go without resistance as I swung my legs to the floor and checked the weapon at my side. The relic was peace-knotted without a whisper of its magic.

The Druid scooted away until she and Jael sat with me in a row on the cot. Her cheeks had pinkened for some reason. "Um, that is true. I ... do not like the aura of that relic, and I know how to protect psions from disruption while in a trance."

Her cheeks flushed darker. then I remembered Isboern's grandfather, Camden.

"I see," I managed.

"Fortunate she was nearby when the Godblood was summoned," Gavin commented, "and determined to come with him."

That was who was missing.

"Where is Pilla?" I asked.

"Outside," Tamuril murmured. "She truly does not like the underground. Neither do I, but this was important. I ... remember how the curse struck you outside the Ley Tower."

"Mmm, let us not talk about that," Mourn cut in.

She blinked in surprise. "I-I'm sorry? Uh ... What will you do next?"

"Eat, probably." My bodyguard sounded terse as his eyes settled on a wall. "Work in some training. Rest. Wait for news."

That sounded suspiciously like my schedule.

"Would you like to go outside?" the Druid asked.

"Day still?" Jael asked, propping her jaw on her elbow.

"About midday."

"Ugh! Rather work in dark."

"You could use some practice," I said. "And you have my sun mask."

She glared. "*Rrrm.* Fine."

Tamuril blinked in surprise. "We will go outside?"

"Yes," I answered, regaining my feet with care. "I would like to move around in freer space."

"May I come with you?" Gavin asked, shocking all three of us.

"May I ask why?"

"I have some foraging to do. I will leave Nightmare here and help you keep watch."

I glanced into the farthest corner, having forgotten that the eerie, still creature was there.

Guard duty ... ?

Mourn responded. "I welcome your insight, Deathwalker, in case anything unusual remains after last night."

A perfectly reasonable suggestion, considering the creatures *they* had summoned.

Why, then, did it feel like an excuse?

"I will meet you outside," Mourn said, offering my spider pouch for the second time since I'd lost my mind; I accepted gently. "I must be sure Graul is well and settled in our room."

"Of course," I said, unable to speak much else into the leaden silence between us.

Jael donned her new mask and stubbornly exited the hatch into full daylight ahead of me. I sped up on the ladder in case she burst into a sprint to lose us.

"Jael?"

She growled. "To the trees! Too bright!"

"Alright but don't go far!'

Tamuril followed me out while Gavin brought up the rear. The Deathwalker declined to rush his long gait as we trotted toward a thicker patch of trees away from the hatch. The Naulor left her hood down while Gavin and I covered our heads, and a moment later I recalled that Jael had left her cloak behind. She had nothing to protect her ears and face from the Sun.

That explained her hurry.

A familiar cry sounded overhead, and the Druid looked up with a sudden smile, offering her arm as a landing spot for her companion.

"Pilla, baby!" she cooed as the deft flyer landed, gripping the simple leather bracer. "So good to see you."

The falcon chirped in response, accepting the gentle stroke of long fingers on her spotted feathers. She also blinked at Gavin and me quite a lot.

"She appears to have fed well," the death mage said.

I didn't know how he could tell underneath that plumage, but maybe he studied the bird's life aura. Then I caught Jael moving away in the corner of my eye. "*Hai. Don't move.*"

She turned around with a sigh. "We wait on Godblood, yes? No talk about Gaelan. No talk change. Just *sit* and barter for safe space as cocks choose and act all around us."

Jael waited for exactly three ticks for me to deny it, watching my mouth open, but no words came out as I tried to think. She scoffed and spun around, sprinting off with a high sign of her hand: *I will return later!*

My face warmed with added embarrassment as I avoided looking at Tamuril or Gavin. Goddess *damn* this geas!

Damn the Valsharess, too.

My mouth pressed tight when the Druid tentatively touched my shoulder.

"I am sorry," she said. "I ... think you are wise, Sirana. You do what you can and do not give up."

"Indeed, you are slow to run from challenges," Gavin observed, looking pointedly after my Sister.

"Agreed." Tamuril tried to smile. "This will get better. Give it time."

I did not have the time she assumed, but I couldn't say so.

"You mentioned foraging, Gavin?" I asked. "Would you like help?"

"Hm, yes, actually."

"What are you looking for?"

"Any one of five fungi, three molds, and anything dead you might discover. Insects, birds, small fur-bearing bodies. I don't expect large creatures so near a camp like this but would be interested."

"Aha," I affirmed, recalling that the mortal Gavin had searched for such things on our trip across the Midway, too.

Beside me, Tamuril grimaced. "No plants?"

The Deathwalker looked from me to her, his skin a strange, dark grey inside his hood. "Anything acutely poisonous I shall look at."

The Druid pressed lips together. "I shall seek some."

The three of us stayed within shouting distance of each other through the afternoon, moving with caution from hill to hill to gather what we could while avoiding one small group of Manalari women and a few pairs of Tundar Dwarves doing the same.

I foraged alone with my thoughts and my spiders, Pilla occasionally flying overhead to check on me. After a while, I gave up on keeping it easy for Mourn to join us. He was in no rush to resume his post, but at least I had an idea why.

"I protect others. The only ones besides the Ice Lord who might have helped her …"

His confession both clarified my recollection of events *and* confused me further.

Mourn had begun tracking me outside the Ley Tower then followed us across the Midway, even interfering with Kurn's attack on me in that canyon.

In Troshin Bend, after the Witch Hunters had killed Gavin then had come after me, the half-blood had been there to shoot the Manalari who had cornered me. He'd also scared off Kurn a second time when the Ma'ab had followed right behind.

And then he disappeared.

The Dragonblood had told me on the boat from Port Fortnight to Yong-wen that he hadn't witnessed anything after that night. Nothing about Brom recalling that he was Cris-ri-phon, nor of Gavin rising to become the Deathwalker. Nothing with me and Osgrid, or with Mathias and Jacob in the shed … Certainly nothing about Soul Drinker and the Deathless.

Or Kurn in the kitchen.

"I regret that I questioned your actions. I did not know about the rape when I said that."

But Mourn had seen them all defeated eventually. First Kurn and

Castis in the warp rot forest, and later the Deathless at the Temple of the Sun. He'd even warned me in advance about the Sathoet in the crypt, so I did not come upon Vesram unprepared.

I'd grown so comfortable with him.

But if the Witch Hunter Sanctor had seen Mourn and Gaelan on the way north, then the mercenary had broken off from following my group somewhere on the Midway itself. Something must have urged him to do so.

Furthermore, if the half-blood had returned to Troshin Bend to observe Gavin and me for one day, he likely followed the Witch Hunters the night they arrived but then left for another three days after they were all dead or captured.

"I thought," Mourn said, *"that without Sarilis's apprentice, you would either sneak out alone or leave with the Hill Dwarf in a few days."*

But I'd stayed in Cris-ri-phon's town, had met Osgrid, and saw Gavin rise as a Deathwalker.

I did not know what the Dragonblood had been doing in those missing days but wagered it had to do with Gaelan. Perhaps he'd offered her a haven to rest and recover, as he had me, and only called upon these "others" when she did not get well. If this was the case, the mercenary might have been coming for her, me, and Jael, eventually.

I'd made it easier for him with Jael.

And if this goes poorly, my little Sister may hate me for all of it.

Later in the afternoon, I met up with my death mage carrying a small collection of mushrooms, molding bark, a few poisonous plants, dried insects, and a few small bones and tufts of hair. I hadn't been lucky enough to find a dead body larger than a beetle before something else had eaten most of it.

"Sign of a healthy forest," Gavin said, showing no disappointment in my offering as he gathered it all to spread out on a flat rock. "Excessive morbidity and bodies left uneaten by scavengers is always a bad sign."

Tamuril glanced at him oddly but smoothed her expression when he lifted his gaze.

"And what have you to sort, Druid?"

"Uhm. H-here."

Listening to the two of them, I learned some unexpected but interesting things about Surface plants before spotting the half-blood walking up the hill, making himself obvious. Tamuril's voice turned into a muffled murmur as my heart pounded in my ears.

Mourn had been gone for hours, and Graul wasn't with him. Had he met up with Isboern to talk? Had they made a Bargain?

What does he know that I can't explain?

Tamuril stopped speaking when she noticed the new arrival, and Gavin got off the ground to wait with his hands folded, his grey hood pulled low though we stood in the shade.

Mourn bowed his head and greeted us first. "Forgive the delay. I presume no trouble occurred?"

"No," Gavin answered. "All seems well. No signs of disturbance."

"Good. Where is Jael?"

I took a deep breath. "Went exploring again."

Mourn cocked an eye-ridge.

"What do you suggest?" I asked irritably. "Chase her farther from here, until I run out of food and water, only to have her bark louder to leave her alone?"

"No," he answered seriously. "Thank you for staying with Gavin and Tamuril rather than making it difficult to find you."

I shrugged, my stomach gurgling as I crossed my arms over my middle. Mourn was prepared, detaching a full bag of travel mix from his harness to hand to me.

At least he wasn't in a punitive mood.

I accepted and tugged open the pouch, reaching for the first cluster of nut meats and dried fruit stuck together. As I started chewing, Mourn looked at Tamuril. "Hungry? I have another."

"No, thank you," she said politely. "I found plenty."

"Very well." Golden eyes leveled on me. "We shall track your Sister. I need to speak privately with both of you."

My mouth twisted. "I'm not sure which direction she went, and I have been wandering over multiple hillsides the last few hours."

"Um," Tamuril lifted her finger toward the clear sky. "I asked Pilla to keep an eye on her in case she ran into trouble. She is two hills over, near a stream."

The Druid pointed East.

"Thank you," Mourn said, sounding to mean it. "Will you be well here with Gavin?"

"Oh? Oh, uh." She glanced at the death mage. "Yes, I will be fine. I shall stay out when the Deathwalker wants to go inside."

"Not yet," the pale man replied, indicating his half-sorted collection.

"Very well." Mourn handed me a waterskin and the second travel mix, waiting until I'd crossed the strap of the former over my body before tossing his jaw. "Come, let us catch her."

Wetting my throat, I added the food pouches to my belt. "Sure."

PILLA'S EYES HAD BEEN ACCURATE AS, FORTUNATELY, JAEL HADN'T CHOSEN TO hide in the last half hour. She waded barefoot in the cold, trickling water, moving slowly upstream as she turned small rocks over with her toes. She sensed us coming about as quickly as I had sensed Mourn and looked up the slope.

Although I couldn't make out the details of her face this far away, she was wearing my sun mask, and her body conveyed resigned wariness as she left the stream and sought out her boots. Claiming those, she sat down on the most comfortable boulder to wait for us. The sight tugged at the corners of my mouth. At least she wouldn't run off barefoot.

Mourn and I closed with my Sister on the rocky bank, his broad feet pressing the stones gently without knocking any loose. He motioned in Jael's general vicinity. "Please sit comfortably, Sirana. Preferably low to softer ground."

Not a good sign.

I chose a patch of long, coarse grass nudging up against Jael's rock, peeking behind me for anything I might hit my head on if I collapsed.

My stomach had tightened down on its recent snack, but at least I wasn't nauseated yet.

Jael glared through the sun mask. "What now?"

Mourn bowed his head. "I will tell you."

We watched as he sat down on the turf with us, lower than either of us, though he didn't have to tilt his chin to meet our eyes.

"Sirana," he began.

Unconsciously, I clutched the grass, just remembering to breathe.

"Can our Bargain be satisfied?"

My first words sounded to be struggling through a mire. "I don't … understand."

"I've protected you, fed you, and helped find and rescue your Sister, Jael, at Manalar. You are both alive and safe. I have received satisfactory payment in every circumstance I requested, and one extraordinary one. There seems to be nothing lacking. I want the Bargain between us fulfilled."

The first sharp sting lanced through my chest rather than my head. My throat closed as if trying to keep it there, writhing like an injured thing behind my lungs.

He is done with me.

Because he knew the Valsharess was pulling my threads to manipulate him. Perhaps he thought continued sex with me would taint his Hoard. He was right about the stolen moment in the closet.

That was the last time.

"Please, breathe, Sirana," he said. "Speak '*athot*' if you agree our deal is done. Speak '*tuserit*' if you disagree."

Another test.

"A-are you not going to Manalar?" I croaked. "Are you leaving for somewhere else?"

His eyes met mine unblinking. "I will finish what I started with the Bishops."

That slowed some of the rising pain, the panic.

"If I am free of this obligation to put your well-being first, *all* of us have more choices."

Meaning that he could choose *not* to aid me if I were captured or choose *not* to teach Jael about her magic.

Swallowing proved difficult. I couldn't speak either Word. I wanted to say *tuserit*, yet if I were called to explain how he was lacking, what would I say? That he hadn't surrendered to my queen yet?

But if I agree the Bargain is done …

"What about Jael's magic?" I asked. "W-will you help her?"

"We will see. That was never part of our Bargain nor is it your obligation. That is a separate journey she will face and decide for herself with or without you."

Jael exchanged a contentious look with him as she said short of a snarl, "Sirana 'free' you, then she and I stay here while you go? Stay 'out of trouble.'"

"That is also a separate path and discussion," he replied, the end of his tail flicking a pebble, "and one I need not have lingering on the branch of an old Bargain to become convoluted with time."

Because there would be tangible consequences for him and his Hoard.

Which is exactly what my queen's geas pushed me to do.

"I can't," I whispered, filled with fear as the first illness passed through me in a wave.

"Then speak '*tuserit*.'" He waited. His metallic gaze seemed to shimmer, his stare daring me to do it.

I couldn't do that, either. With a groan, I collapsed onto my back before curling up on my side, Soul Drinker digging into my hip and my spiders poking at the inside of their pouch.

Jael stood up, alarmed. "Isboern said no change in plan or promise! Or you hurt her!"

"I change *nothing* about my plans," he growled. "I am asking Sirana if we have fulfilled our promise well before the Godblood gave that advice. She must give me an answer."

I must.

He *had* fulfilled his promise. *We* had. Goddess, did we ever! Fuck this vanishing leverage I might grasp, it wasn't real, and this wasn't *me* or anything I truly wanted.

I had only been afraid of the pain, but pain would always comes, one way or another. It hadn't killed me yet.

"*A-athot*," I wheezed through the flickering vision of the inside of a Desert tent.

Mourn snapped his attention to me. "What?"

"*Athot!*" I said, louder, tears pricking my eyes as the pain swelled for several, terrible moments.

And then broke.

The Dragonblood sucked in a deep, deep breath and let it out, his tail sliding around freely on the ground.

"Thank you, Sirana," he said. "Thank you."

The gentle way he spoke caressed my ears from afar. A sound between a laugh and a sob escaped my lips. *Release*.

"A pity," I said.

"What is?"

"I-I enjoyed … giving you your payments. Seems too few for what you've given me."

His tail curved up behind him, sliding over grass and soil, as a tiny smile touched his mouth. "You gave enough, *Kiabil*. I promise."

Kiabil.

"Still?"

He read the confusion on my face. "The Word is not linked to the Bargain. But if it insults you — ?"

"No," I said, trying to rise. "No insult at all."

At least saying that wasn't a struggle.

"I am glad." He paused. "Is the pain gone?"

My body felt oddly lax. I managed a nod. "No change in plans?"

"Correct. Though I am interested in what Captain Isboern may have to say."

"Haven't you … talked?"

"We have not."

"Where you been?" Jael asked, aware of the lateness of the day.

Mourn displayed modest fang. "Forgive me, *Janhuren*, but you do not need to know."

"Ehh, *fuckemraffinmum*," she muttered, propping her chin on her hand with a familiar scowl as I finally pushed myself up. "What next?"

"We hold, giving the Captain time he asked for. But ... if you will consider, Sirana, the Deathwalker asked me to suggest a time when you might show him the Elsewhere behind the black throne."

My eyebrows lifted as high as they would go.

"And perhaps and negotiate with the Desert Queen on his behalf so he may speak with the newly dead."

My mouth opened. "Innathi?"

"He said he would be willing to mindlink with you, and I can teach Jael to protect your auras from outside interference, the way Tamuril did earlier."

My Sister perked up at this potential new skill, though I swallowed. "I see. And if the Ice Lord shows up?"

"I will be there."

"But you have no Bargain," Jael said, making a face.

Mourn turned a stony gaze on her. "I. Will. Be. There."

Like a star breaking over my head, I finally understood.

More choices.

Once free of our Bargain, the choices *included* protecting and teaching. *When in need. As it makes sense.*

Mourn could call me *Kiabil* without failing either Jael or his Hoard if should he not anticipate everything which could happen. If something critical changed, he would not be obstructed or hesitate to adapt, and *I* didn't need a two-faced geas to keep him close.

He would choose to stay.

For now, at least.

"What say you?" asked the Dragonchild. "You did well when we first landed in Yong-wen, communing with the dagger to prove you should keep it. As the wielder, you can show the Herald the way."

As the wielder.

Although my stomach clenched, I managed to smile. "I can. Suppose it's that or keep picking through forest decay."

Mourn chuckled. "Sounds fun. Gavin should be waiting outside for us." He stood up on his feet, towering over us and offering me a hand. "Let us find him."

I accepted the hand up, succeeding in placing my questions about Gaelan aside to give Isboern the time he requested.

Musanlo may offer guidance, he said.

I smirked, entertaining whether the Godblood meant it literally the way my Deathwalker would. The two mages were already a strange alliance, soon returning to the sacred pool with allies stranger still.

Let's do it.

I held a Hellhound captive in the red rune dagger, and the Herald of Nyx would like to speak with him.

CHAPTER 12

GAVIN WAITED WHERE WE'D LEFT HIM WITH TAMURIL A SHORT DISTANCE AWAY, and I finally spotted Pilla perched several branches above the Druid's head. After a brief discussion, we chose to remain outside the redoubt for the trance with Soul Drinker.

I prepared as I had at Augran, taking food and drink, and relieving myself. All of us did, except Gavin.

The afternoon was warm with a light breeze going into the evening according to Mourn and Tamuril. Regretfully, I agreed to give my spider pouch over to the former to keep them safe, aware of the irony whenever this dagger was involved.

"They haven't warned me about much with you around," I said, cradling the unassuming bag in my palm. "And they are calm with you."

Mourn smiled modestly. "We understand each other. Your small protectors have been loyal back-ups if I was caught away from you."

That had only happened once in the crypt beneath the Temple. I had one less guardian after commanding them to stop a Ma'ab officer from escaping. The sting of that spider's loss returned, but the trade had been a Sathoet freed from his servitude.

Not a death for nothing.

Had Vesram truly run West as we'd told him to, or had he been caught before escaping the area? I couldn't know, and the best case was that I caught neither a glimpse nor word of him until I returned to the Ley Tower.

Tamuril had found a depression on a northern slope which kept all of us out of easy view from wanderers in most directions. She and her falcon stood on higher ground to give early warning of an approach as Mourn repeated his trick from the warp rot forest. The Druid watched with wary fascination as the Dragonchild used his sliders to draw a circle in the soil around Gavin and me, rumbling quietly in Draconic.

"I can feel it," the Naulor whispered, taking a step away from the ward. "It's strong."

"The border will not harm you or anyone else," he assured, having kept himself and Jael inside the circle. "This will only stop all from entering, and, in a Word, prevent anyone from leaving."

"The method works well," Gavin remarked, having chosen his place to sit and sort his belongings on the ground. "As we've seen before."

Oh, we have.

My mouth thinned as I chose a place facing the death mage, removing the red rune dagger from my belt with its sheath. The memory of hundreds of emaciated, bloodthirsty Humans flickered at the fore of my thoughts.

Climbing on top of each other, clawing for us. Mourn and Gavin slicing them into pieces, body parts piling up on that border while Soul Drinker raged in my thoughts ...

Tamuril exhaled with relief. "I can hear you inside the circle."

"Correct," said the half-blood. "The purpose is not to cut us off from our surroundings. If Krithannia or the Captain should come to find us, or if something requires our urgent attention, we will be able to respond."

My fingers curled around the weapon, holding it tight, recalling that moment when the demon had possessed part of my body, trying to force me to pitch the relic at the Dragonblood's back. To let it drink him in.

I would have if not for the Queen's geas stopping me.

The blonde Elf asked, "And ... you wish me to remain nearby?"

I straightened and craned my neck with a smile. "Please, stay. My

Sister will be learning new magic inspired by how you helped me with Willven."

Tamuril smiled tentatively. "Oh?"

"Yes. But this means she and Mourn could be distracted if the mind-link becomes … intense. We need your eyes and ears, too."

"Ah?" Green eyes flickered down to the relic and up. "Ah. Very well, yes, of course."

Gavin set three small pouches atop a rock within his reach. I detected a whiff of some of the items we had been collecting for him. His grimoire and thurible, the chirurgeon's kit, and various tools were all secure inside a satchel resting at his hip.

Meanwhile, Jael stood me with her arms crossed, her silent nerves pouring over me.

"A favor?" I asked.

Her eyes stopped sweeping the hillside and landed on me. *"Hm?"*

"Take a full breath?"

Her lips twisted, but her chest expanded as she breathed in through her nose, shoulders straightening as she held it, along with my eyes, before letting it out through pursed lips. I grinned.

"Better," Gavin observed.

"Agreed," Mourn added with unusual mischief. "More to work with."

"Pfeh," she replied. "So, what first?"

The Dragonchild's tail weaved and flexed along the border he'd created. "One rule."

"One?"

"Yes. You and I do not touch either Gavin or Sirana until they are deep in communion with the dagger. We do not want to slip in with him."

Jael grimaced. "Done."

"Ideally, neither of you touch me at all," Gavin said, his face tightening in a familiar way. "Unless necessary, which I do not see, frankly. I have my own protections to my aura."

"I have noticed." Mourn dipped his chin with respect. "We will only touch you if we must move your body unaware. In such a case, something unusual has happened. Acceptable?"

The Deathwalker grunted. "Acceptable. Otherwise, focus your considerable strength on Sirana and her unborn. Not me."

"That is the plan."

"Good." Gavin rolled up his sleeves, exposing his pale forearms, which darkened to a modest grey as we sat in the late day shade with evening on the way.

"Why you do that?" Jael asked. "Your skin." She titled her hand like a rocking boat. "White. Black. Then like ash. And white again."

I bit my lip at the abrupt tangent, tugging off my gloves with Soul Drinker in my lap. Unfortunately, I hadn't a *short* answer I could give her, and she hadn't asked me the question, anyway.

Gavin fixed his gaze on her in a way she'd have taken as a challenge from anyone underground. As brusque as they both were — and she knew it — she merely stood her ground.

"This is an ancient quality of Deathwalkers," he said, securing his sleeves so they would not unroll. "This change made us easy to recognize in our service, especially in the Desert. Between night and day, for better or worse." His eyes shifted to me. "Although I've wondered if this change is not a 'blessing' of my Lady but a side effect of becoming a soul walking two lands." He looked at the blue sky. "One land with a bright and powerful sun above and the other has no celestial bodies at all."

I frowned. "Is there no light in the Greylands?"

"There is," he answered. "Like a grey dawn. Eternal, unchanging. Though if there is a source to it, I know no soul that has seen it. Nightfall never comes. Nor does morning or midday."

I caught myself imagining that as I waited for him to blink. A waste of time.

"Ah. Well …" I scooted closer until my knees grazed his then lifted Soul Drinker's sheath gripped in my left hand. "I'm curious what you think of the Elsewhere. It feels like night and has stars overhead."

"Or the appearance of them. Interesting."

Gavin placed his cool, dry palm against the back of my hand, long, grey fingers folding around as if he, too, would hold the dagger's sheath. Eerie eyes watched every motion as my right hand took hold of the dagger's handle. My heart sped up as he mirrored me, wrapping his left hand around my right and applying pressure as if to withdraw the blade.

The dagger's aura pulsed. I couldn't see it but *felt* it. A hollow, unintelligible whisper escaped to caress my ears, as if my mere intention to draw had opened some unseen, ethereal door just a crack. A dangerous place to hesitate.

~Look at me.~

Gavin looked up.

~Can you hear me?~

He nodded.

~Pull on two.~

An affirmation.

~One. Two — ~

I pulled the dagger free. The black metal withdrew easier and quieter than before. Compelling power swept in and seized my focus just as quickly but muffled by the hushed voices of many.

⋆The throne room?⋆ the Herald asked, his mind's speech drifting like several winding threads weaving between word and thought. The echo of many I'd heard before.

Wow.

Fear receded for a moment, and I smiled. *~Yes. To the black throne.~*

THE MERCHANT HAD 'WELCOMED' MY ALLIES THERE. HE'D CALLED IT ICE HEART.

… Or maybe Black Heart?

The Infernal Elf had spoken both names to me at different times in regard to Soul Drinker. I wasn't sure if they meant the same thing but, like many things recently, I hadn't the chance to ask. To be standing on the same exposed, vertigo-inducing stairs from last time, I *still* waited to ask, holding my tongue until we'd reached the cracked but thankfully solid floor.

In the center of the platform, my crystal remained intact, encasing the throne and trapping the Void shadow inside. Cracks like spiders' legs remained but didn't seem to have grown. Gavin gave it a wide berth as he took the steps. I followed him.

The place seemed much colder than before.

"Did you catch the name when the merchant 'welcomed' you, Herald?" I asked obliquely.

My scholar glanced over his shoulder. "I did. I am afraid I do not recognize it from my studies."

"Think Mourn does?"

"Possible, given he appears to be in some competition with the figure in question."

I smiled wryly, looking around, listening. All seemed black and hollow.

"Come," my ally coaxed with a motion of his hand, moving past the throne.

I stayed close. "Do you hear them? The souls ..."

"I do. I also feel them."

"Your skin?"

"My bones."

No wonder I didn't have to lead him. "Does it make sense that ... um."

Gavin slowed, turning his neck so his round, shriveled ear aimed toward me. "Hm?"

"That if a soul is taken by the magic of the dagger, only the Vitas is consumed by the gatekeeper. The Vis passes by, whole ... and beyond."

"It does make sense, yes. I am most curious to hear if any plane or entity has a claim on them. Particularly the Elves."

"What?"

Gavin paused, reaching out for my hand. His sleeve was rolled down in its usual position and had been from the start. "I can only know this by speaking with them, wielder."

And he *needed* to know.

I sighed, glancing at the hidden space behind the throne, then took his hand in a firm grip. *~Fine. It's a bit of a drop. Hold on tight.~*

We stepped through; our vision went dark. If we'd been awake in our bodies, he might have crushed the bones in my hand with his grip.

"Oof!"

We hit a titanic slope of a blue dune and began rolling, picking up speed. I lost my hold on the Deathwalker and heard a feminine laugh.

~No, wait! Slow down!~

A mind-shield appeared to catch us both, stopping our fall. As the sand dissolved underneath us as if to flush us downstream, we had time enough to rise and scramble to one side, reclaiming our balance.

"This way," Gavin said, pointing laterally across the dune.

Lacking any landmark beyond the looming slope, I had to trust his sense of direction until mine collected itself. Even glancing down, I was overtaken by a shudder. Reaching the bottom could take a whole night of careful creeping!

We trekked with speed along the endless curve of sand, barely seeing the horizon. I was convinced all the sand in this Blue Desert had formed into *one* dune! Occasionally, I glanced up toward the crest, doubting I saw the actual peak from where I stood. I imagined it like the mountains out West, where a steep climb could have several false peaks while looking straight up.

Sand turned to rushing glitter beneath my boots.

"Whoa!" I cried, my Deathwalker grabbing my arm to hold me steady and to catch himself and wait until the sand ceased sliding.

"Strange," he muttered.

I raised eyebrows in silent comment. He let go, and we continued walking.

Within ten paces, the same thing happened.

"Fuck!" I hissed, wondering if I could twist an ankle in a trance and wake up with a limp.

Gavin grunted, adjusting his grip until we were less awkwardly holding hands, much as he *wasn't* enjoying it. The sand remained stable enough to walk on while we remained in contact, though the death mage needed to test *one last time*, proving the gigantic slope began to flow like water when we walked separately for too long.

"So be it," he muttered.

His long stride kept him in the lead, though I matched his speed by not letting my boots sink as far into the sand with each step.

"What do you sense?" I asked. "You're walking as if you follow a beacon."

"Very good," he said. "I see signs of eidolons concentrated ahead. Quite far, but bright and holding."

"Eidolons?"

He hummed in thought. "A transitioned Vis. One which holds a form based on the strength of its memory."

"Ah. So, would the Queen be an eidolon?"

"She is that. The most powerful eidolon here, from what you've described, as she communicates so clearly with you after so long."

"She is ... when she wants to, apparently."

I huffed behind Gavin for some time, and yet the dune did not shrink. Neither did our goal grow perceptibly closer.

"I wonder," he murmured, taking eyes from his goal to look behind us. "If they are reluctant."

"What?" I panted, catching myself when I turned too fast.

"If we pursue directly, they may stretch the circle larger ..." He rubbed his chin in thought.

I arched my brow. "Thoughts? Suggestions?"

The Deathwalker considered this. Our feet sank while standing still. He glanced down then at our hands gripping tightly. Neither of us wore gloves; there should have been sweat.

"Perhaps I should wait to be introduced by the wielder," he said. "You lead the way."

I blinked, stepping up on top of the sand for a third time. "Hm.

Alright. But I can't see any 'eidolons.' "

"That does not matter. How did you find the ancient queen previously?"

"No particular way. I either fell where she waited to meet me, or I followed landmarks to a canyon with a waterfall."

"Very well. I shall walk behind you."

Whatever insight he'd gained, this change soon proved it. The curve of the dune grew closer, and I soon felt the tug of both my "life tether" *and* that of a familiar presence. Gavin didn't question my direction, and I resisted the urge to ask him if his beacon remained, if we walked toward it.

I listened to the wind instead, to the subtle moans of the lost and, after a time, began to think aloud. *~I'm here. I have brought someone who wants to meet you.~*

A breath in the wind.

* ... *we knowww* ... *

They knew we were here. All the former victims and wielders. Were they agitated? Eager? Hungry?

~Innathi? Your Majesty, I seek your audience. Where are you? Answer me.~

A section of sand collapsed like an avalanche of snow Rausery had once described. Fortunately, it happened far enough ahead to avoid being caught in it. I heard the crack before countless weights of dust and sand rushed down the slope, draining off hard, jagged rock to reveal the mouth of a banded, sheer-walled canyon.

"Interesting," Gavin said.

"Come on," I said, eager to get my boots on solid ground, or the closest I could expect in the Elsewhere.

The Deathwalker said nothing as we approached the new escape from the dune, wholly focused on taking in every detail as we entered the canyon. The tall, pale man gazed all around, walking beneath the stars of a clear night sky, sharing nothing of his thoughts. He showed not the slightest bit of unease or bewilderment.

We were still holding hands, but something felt different.

Finally, he spoke. "Excellent. How do we find the waterfall?"

"I am not certain if that's where we are going," I admitted. "Last time, I 'knew' she would be waiting there to talk and listened for the water. I have no such guidance here. All has gone quiet."

"Ah." Gavin kept his icy gaze high. "Yet the air has a current I can see."

"Follow it?"

"Yes. The current signals an energy flux. If not caused by an active will, then a phenomenon which may draw them."

I wagered if we found either eidolon or "phenomenon," the stoic scholar would uncover some private delight in the search. Lucky for me, his fearless curiosity was contagious. I remained two steps ahead of him, ostensibly leading the way but following the subtle guidance at the canyon's occasional splits, turning whichever way his eyes went. The silent Queen provided no help.

Eventually, we walked deeper into the mists which I had avoided last time.

"I can't see much," I admitted.

"I can," Gavin murmured, tugging his hand free.

"Hai!" I tensed up to imagine what might happen *now*.

"The canyon is a memory," he said, flexing his hand in front of him. "These mists are *truer* than the sands and stars."

"Hm." I had wondered, and the ground lay still beneath our feet. "Do you recognize the name 'Koorul?' "

The Deathwalker shook his head. "I do not."

"The canyon, or one much like it, also within the Red Desert. It is … or was … a real place, according to several ancient memories."

"Koorul," he repeated in contemplation. "A place the Queen has been?"

"Correct. And the Deathless, before he was that. That's where they met as mortals."

"I see. Stop a moment."

Planting my feet at once, I watched as the Deathwalker lifted one hand as high above his head as he could reach. Twining some of the mist about his fingers, he tugged that bit of vapor down to his mouth, drawing it in with a deliberate inhale. His pupils vanished from sight as he seemed to taste it on a grey-blue tongue.

"Hm."

I checked around us, wary of something unseen stalking us within the mists. "What?"

"You have killed two while wielding the dagger?"

My mouth tightened. "Yes. Unless you count Brom, then three."

"True. Have you ever tried calling them to you from the mists?"

A quiet flush of fear spread down my back. "No. Why would I call Brom? A-and Innathi said …"

Gavin's pale pupils returned. "She said what?"

I shrugged. "That … the 'newest' can be among the most desperate to get out. And with my unborn here …"

The Deathwalker glanced at my hands covering my middle. "Hm. A valid concern. Although, for its worth, your unborn is *not* 'here' with us. An attack or a challenge would be against *your* will, not one yet to transition in birth. The child is not here, yet."

I blinked in surprise. "What? But she could tell I was pregnant. She could *see* it as you can. She calls it my 'tether.'"

"Yet the aura is part of you and cannot be seized separately," Gavin said. "Plus, she may not be sensing the child the same way I am. I wonder if that anchor could be so visible here due to the Dragon touch, rather than the mere fact that you are pregnant."

I started. "You know, too?!"

He looked at me. "Only since watching you and Jael together, after you chose her affinity. Your bodyguard may have answered a question or two." He spread his fingers out into the mist. "But of imminent concern, I suggest you may be able to draw the newer dead to you, if you took them with Soul Drinker. I see no reason you require the queen."

Innathi would be grotesquely annoyed to hear him say *that*, but what an intriguing thought! To imagine *me* selecting the voices I wished to hear from exactly when I wished?

Probably not so simple.

Meanwhile, the mist coalesced around us the longer we stood. The night sky had faded from view, and I wasn't certain if the canyon was merely obscured or if it had fallen away somehow, dissolving in silence.

"The mist is getting thicker," I remarked. "Like when I saw you in that dream on the lakeshore. Are *you* doing this?"

"I am unsure. This *could* be an effect of my presence, yes."

"Any eidolons?"

The gaunt man scanned around us. "Plenty, but weakly formed. I would rather you try calling the Hellhound. Or Kurn if you wish."

Ugh. I sighed, reaching first for the pearl on my earlobe as my recent habit.

The hard bump was gone.

Frowning, I checked under my shirt, aware that I wore no red uniform to meet a queen this time.

And no saphgar pendant, either.

"What are you looking for?" Gavin asked.

"My necklace," I said. "The blue stone."

"Manifestations for objects of power are as much risk as aid in the mists, and often not necessary. I start with knowing I brought all I needed with me."

I arched an eyebrow. "Like your black skeleton?"

The faintest smile touched one corner of his mouth. "Difficult to misplace that in any form. My thought is of the thurible."

"Ah. Quite a find. Seems made for you."

"For a Deathwalker, yes." Gavin never stopped looking around. "That *is* an interesting idea."

"Huh? What is?"

"To *know* the blue stone may be part of your bones as you walk here, like the thurible is part of mine. Providing the focus to accomplish what we have while aware of our bodies."

An instant after imagining that, my chest started burning as if Shyntre's pendant glowed intensely. I rubbed the spot it would have been, but no blue light met my gaze. It felt the same and might as well be real.

Son of a Drider ...

"Good suggestion," I commented. "Although, I don't know the Hellhound's name. I may need to call *all* the Ma'ab I've killed."

"So be it."

"Sons of the Ma'ab Empire!" I said into the grey, alarmed how much the hazy wall sucked in and muted my call. *Damn.*

Try something else.

~Sons of the Ma'ab Empire, come closer! Follow my voice.~

"Not bad," Gavin said. "Do that again."

My eyes opened and flicked to him. "Hm?"

"The mist moved in response to your thoughts. Know that your will must be stronger than the Vis you call upon to speak. Draw them out."

"Right." I breathed in. *~Sons of the Ma'ab! Come to me!~*

Before me, the greyed layers beyond mist shifted, rolling over themselves before condensing. A grey shadow started to take form. Encouraged, I focused on the shape.

~Ma'ab sons. Come here. Speak with me.~

A swirl of black tattoos appeared on the bulky body, briefly holding their shape before smearing in the unseen current, falling away like so much ash.

I gasped. *~Yes! You! Come closer!~*

He paused in a slow, shambling gait, turned his head as if tilting an ear to my voice. Then he brandished large, curled fingers and rushed toward me, his silent rage sweeping through my bones.

"*Fuck*," I whispered.

Immense pressure returned on my hand as Gavin snatched it up.

"*Ursurr'religus!*" the death mage snarled, baring his black teeth as he struck at the misty space between us and the hurling form.

Pure ice coursed through my blood; my chest seized, and my breath stopped as something inside compressed before I could release it. Then a barrier appeared, cutting a line between the Ma'ab Vis and us before rising to disappear into the grey. Moments later, phantom hands pressed against it, leading to board shoulders and a size true to the Ma'ab. The bald head and face were obscured as vapor dripped like sweat and tears.

"Ask his name first," Gavin murmured, gripping my hand with a sense of urgency. "Make him remember."

I didn't question as I stared at the pale and partial, vacant face. *~Tell me your name. Remember. What is your name? Speak it!~*

The Ma'ab ghost craned his neck side-to-side. A few threads of black tattoos ran across his chest and arms, creeping onto that thick neck until they reached the top of his smooth scalp.

"Eynkis," he whispered, as dark, piercing Northern eyes finally came into focus.

~Eynkis. What are you?~

"I am dead."

I bit my lip, thinking to reframe my question when Gavin grunted, gradually releasing my hand. The barrier stayed up, and the eidolon before us gradually regained a familiar, Human appearance.

"Unusual for his state to be so clear as he recalls what his body looked like," my ally murmured. "But this one served the Ascended and expected to return to them upon death. He may have been better prepared for this."

I smirked dryly. Only an Empire of liches would know how to prepare a populace for a time when they lacked a body.

~How did you serve in life, Eynkis?~

"I served …" Black eyes drifted up then down. "As a hound released before the mistresses."

~A Hellhound.~

His head bobbed. "One of five. Attackers. Protectors. Breeders."

As I watched, the dark, intricate designs traced across his torso, hips, buttocks, legs, and feet, suggesting a covering from head to foot but in fact leaving him quite nude. His penis had smaller, rune-shaped tattoos, as did his scrotum. Layers of scars and warped markings appeared on his left forearm, earned when frequently wrapping a spiked chain around that limb.

"Why does he not have his weapon?" I whispered. "Or armor?"

Or clothing?

"Manifestations take deliberate will and are a draw on his form," Gavin answered. "He could bring about that weapon at any time, but the resources to maintain it are not infinite."

"In the Greylands," I added.

"For any eidolon in an unclaimed space."

"You have your answer, then? No plane or entity claims him?"

"His gods from the North certainly cannot. I am not certain about anyone else."

"Why am I here?" Eynkis asked, his voice deep and raspy. "Are you to be my new mistress?"

I couldn't tell if he wanted that or not, but the Sathoet Vesram begging me for that same assurance flashed behind my eyes. Hesitating, I glanced at Gavin.

He shrugged. "Be cautious making promises to the dead."

That seemed to go without saying.

I exhaled in slight irritation, drawing breath to answer.

"He is *not,* unless you wish to challenge me for him, *Khalithan!*"

Eynkis jumped as the powerful voice filled the space around us, twisting his head as two figures approached. He growled like a wolf, showing white, filed teeth as he hunched over, ready to fight.

Meanwhile, Innathi forced her way through the mist as if it were a mass of excessive beaded curtains, closing with our barrier but standing on the same side with the Hellhound. She wore the most complex, red and purple warrior gown I'd ever seen, and her eyes had changed from the familiar Davrin eyes with scarlet irises to a solid, ivory blue.

"I have been searching for you," the Queen Elf said to Eynkis, placing her right boot forward and pointing down at it. "Kneel."

"*You* are not ascended," the Hellhound rumbled, his tattoos warping on his pale skin. "*You* are not a goddess! I refuse."

"Only so many times, my promised stud," she sneered, dragging forward another large male behind her by a chain. "You've seen it. You've *watched* it. I shall wait. But first, Sirana! Why have you brought *this one* here? Answer me immediately."

That, I failed to do. I wasn't looking when she made her command, though her gaze burned into me.

My attention was set on Kurn, naked, collared, and on the opposite end of the chain held by the Desert Queen. He was on all fours, appearing stunned, disoriented, and a jutting erection bounced beneath his belly. The glans seemed painfully swollen, the hole leaking fluid over a thick, gold ring attached through a piercing.

He didn't have that when we … ?

"Sirana!"

The Ma'ab exile shuddered when Innathi shouted, the dangling ring in his foreskin losing a drip of clear semen to the grey stone. Kurn looked up. Dark eyes, once glazed over, brightened for one failed instant.

"Sirana …" he whispered. "Release … me …"

CHAPTER 13

"MAJESTY," I ACKNOWLEDGED BEFORE THE LAG BECAME TOO GREAT. "FORGIVE my ... surprise to meet you in such a way."

"How so?" she hissed, the tilt of her head suggesting she kept an eye on the Hellhound as well. "Did you hope to *avoid* me while bringing in *this* behind my back? What is he, exactly?"

"My ally, Gavin Adason." I motioned to him, watching Innathi's face harden, blank eyes thinning to slits. "The Deathwalker who had never seen a Davrin before."

"Also, the one who somehow 'summoned' Houda," she said, proving she recalled the details of our last conversation.

"Not with intent," Gavin said, his lack of inflection bringing a curl to her lip. "I opened the door. The presence of the Zauyrian sorcerer was what drew her."

"And as usual," Innathi responded, coiling the chain twice around her violet-gloved hand before pulling Kurn closer on his hands and knees. "The liaison of Human death has no awareness how to address royalty thousands of years beyond his birth."

"How do you wish to be addressed?" Gavin asked, maintaining his aplomb.

The Desert Queen stepped slow and deliberate, sitting upon the pale

Northerner like a bench. I watched Kurn's awareness wink out. He braced his knees wider and straightened his spine to hold her weight, his cock fully extended and hanging low like his old stallion. He wasn't pleading anymore, just waiting.

Innathi smiled in pleasure, crossing her legs, the royal purple loincloth draping between curvaceous legs clad in garnet red leather. "How, you ask? I have said. Like royalty. Thousands of years beyond your birth. You *strange* man."

I half-expected Gavin to remark on how thousands of years meant nothing to his Grey Lady, who was above Innathi in his every concern. Gavin's slow glance at Eynkis, however, as if to check that the Hellhound was present and paying attention, hinted at why he remained silent about his Greylord.

"Your Highness," he said instead, folding his hands before him, chin slightly down. "I have been interested in meeting you since Sirana first described a 'Desert Queen' within the Deathless dagger. We called for you first, but the dunes swallowed our voice. We merely persisted in your realm."

"Better." Innathi straightened her shoulder so we could admire her surcoat over the fine, flexible armor: a blend of a vine of golden leaves entwining with the firebird of the Desert. "Although, I still think you meant to circumvent me."

"We did not try to avoid you, Majesty," I seconded. "I *did* call you, but the landscape changed too much to know —"

"That is *his* doing, *khali*," she said, pointing at Gavin. "Can you not tell? This Walker has undone *everything* I built, bringing back the mists of old."

"Without intent, Your Highness," he said, otherwise unmoving. "Much of my aura has changed since my transition. I still learn it."

Innathi gazed up from beneath drawn eyebrows. "Be wary, Gavin Adason, lest you tilt the natural powers here to such an extent that you shall become the new master. Should that happen, you will never leave."

When he didn't react, she twisted her torso, splaying her free hand over the intricate warrior dress. "*I* am the one protecting you from that fate, for the sake of my champion and our people's forgotten history."

Gavin bowed his head once. "I have noted your focus for the manifestation, yes. It is impressive."

"You must know how I bear the power." She patted Kurn between his shoulder blades, jangling his chain, making him flinch. "Yet you would simply walk *past* me to summon the tattooed man aside for some private purpose? In *my* realm?" Abruptly, the Queen pinned eyes on me. "What of your promise to learn about your own people from me *before* finding my sister, wherever she has gone?"

"Soon, Majesty," I answered warily, "but I am not heading home yet."

The Queen was displeased. "Why is this?"

"The lands south of the Great Lake face yet another fight over Nalari and the sacred pool there."

Innathi breathed in deeply, releasing it with a sigh. She reached to caress Kurn's haunches, teasing his crack as she smoothed her glove over his tailbone. "Yet another. I presume these two have something to do with it?"

Eynkis growled.

"Them plus thousands, Majesty."

"War."

"Yes. Gavin and I are part of a plot to resolve it in our favor. If we do not, bringing your 'realm' home shall reveal our people's location to our enemies, and to your former husband, whom I seek to evade."

The ancient Queen's blank eyes glowed bluer in the haze as she looked to Eynkis, then warm yellow as she gazed at me. "You do not lie."

"Harder to do with him around," I motioned to my tall companion with a smirk.

"*Hmph!*" She smiled slightly, lips pursed together. "What do you seek from me?"

Gavin answered. "I wish to ask Eynkis, the Ma'ab Hellhound, some questions."

"*Hellhound*," she repeated in a dry murmur.

"Black witch," Eynkis said in response, spoken in observation — and

161

belief — rather than contempt. "I will answer the *maknuut*."

"You will *not* unless I say," Innathi commanded.

"Ask," he bit out. "Now."

"*Be silent.*"

Though the Hellhound's dark eyes shone intensely as he tried to challenge her, the Queen's eyes flashed the scarlet red I knew. The mist recoiled from her as Eynkis did.

"You shall not talk here."

Her caressing fingers slid out of sight and between Kurn's buttocks, giving him little warning.

"I shall have my Palace, first."

The Queen's bench stiffened, his cock bounced as his mouth fell slack. I expected protest and received surprise when Kurn moaned.

"Release me," Eynkis demanded.

"Not yet," I answered truthfully.

"Then we must run."

Gavin and I bore the same thought on our faces: *Run where?*

"I know my new pet violated a Queen's emissary in life, *khalithan*," Innathi said, her voice overtaking our exchange as a deep, growing rumble built around her. "He confessed to me, mistaking the invitation, and he shall receive no leniency for that insult. It is his punishment."

The Queen withdrew her fingers, and the dagger I'd used once upon a powder-strewn kitchen floor appeared in her palm. She grinned with delight. "Indeed, he *well* remembers the vengeance you served him. Everytime I wish it."

With the dagger tip pointed at the sky and the large, round pommel positioned in place, she pressed it in without hesitation.

"A-Argh … !"

Kurn bucked, his voice hoarse from recent misuse, and a squeal slipped from Innathi as she gripped the dagger like a piton in his crack. Her aura shone purple, red, and gold, pushing against the haze.

"Now!" she commanded.

An instant later, the unflagging erection spurted a fiery liquid onto the grey stone, turning at once to heatless steam exposing more underneath in an ever-widening circle.

Gavin and Eynkis backed away from the show, and I moved with them, my barrier dissolving as the glittering, mist-eating ejaculate spread like the contents of a spilled vase.

"Yes!" cried the Queen with a hint of ecstasy as her stallion writhed beneath her. "Give me what I want! See it! See it within me! Let us make it!"

"What's happening?!" I blurted as the stone shifted from grey to pale orange.

"She is consuming his Vis," Gavin answered, "to reshape the land-scape."

"Witch is hungry," Eynkis snarled, circling behind to keep Gavin between him and Innathi. "The fool is weak before her."

We maintained distance, but we couldn't run. Eventually, the fog broke apart to reveal the night sky full of stars, but instead of calming blue dunes, a courtyard of smooth-cut, warm-colored stone formed with a platform in the center.

What — ?

The steps thrust up one at a time, lifting Innathi and Kurn high above us. It kept growing until she must be able to see the Desert horizon beyond the walls of reddish stone. Behind us, a heavy boom. We spun around to see the drawbridge had closed, capturing wind and sand which began to churn in the courtyard. The stone vibrated beneath our feet.

"Trapped," Eynkis hissed, hunched over, flexing his hands as if aching to hold a weapon. He looked between us. "*Maknuut.* Witch. You called me from the mist. Why?"

"To parley," Gavin replied.

"With her?" the Ma'ab growled, pitching his hand at the rising plat-form.

"No. With you."

The large, naked Ma'ab kept his attention on our surroundings, his tattoos crisply visible. "Can you guide me out? I would escape her gullet and return to my gods who await me. If you can do this, I will give you what you want."

Gavin considered while strengthening vortices buffeted us, pushing us away from the pyramid. Eynkis wasn't lying, but what about us? We must free him from the relic, first.

Is that possible?

Our exchange halted as a distant, hollow cacophony shredded the air above us, hurtling closer with chilling threat. The death mage spun to look, his eyes turning black.

"Slaugh swarm," he murmured. "Like what spilled out of the Temple."

"Correct, Deathwalker!" Innathi called from above. "Best climb the pyramid, *khalithan*, where I may keep you safe."

If only at her pleasure.

"Let's talk, Eynkis," I said through gritted teeth. "Stay close. She won't harm me, and I have questions for her as well."

With eerily similar scowls, the Deathwalker and the Hellhound followed me to the first step of Innathi's monument. The sheer size required us to jump and pull ourselves up as if climbing over a wall. One after another, we hauled ourselves up as the pyramid continued to grow underneath.

Behind us, the swarm spilled over the Palace walls and into the courtyard, shapeless shreds of open, screaming mouths and empty holes for eyes. The twisting, writhing cloud began circling the monument like a dark, desperate flock of birds seeking to pluck every insect out of a field.

Fortunately for us, the slaugh could not touch Innathi's summoned sandstone. Although we could not escape the disquieting, constant howls surrounding us, a barrier held them at bay.

"Yes, closer!" came her cry above us.

None of us wished to but had little choice; always better to keep the hungry predator in sight. By the time we reached the top — with me first, then Gavin, and Eynkis crouching behind him — I should have been gasping for breath. I wasn't, and when I stood up straight from my final hop, my clothing had changed from my travel-worn, black leathers to a Red Sister uniform and flowing cloak worthy of standing as honor guard in a Queen's throne room.

"Ah, my champion," Innathi said with a brilliant smile, lounging upon a comfortable chaise of royal purple and gold, wearing a silky, white gown meant for pure leisure. "What do you think?"

The Queen lay with dark legs spread open and gently bent, the slits up the sides of her gown granting easy access to her sex. Somehow, she had converted Kurn's neck chain to wrist manacles which held him secure, belly-down and bent over the foot of the chaise. His knees braced on the stone, and his face in between her thighs.

My eyes fixed on the dagger handle lodged in his ass.

The blade had transformed to coarse, black horsehair, granting him the appearance of a stallion's tail. Despite having climaxed on command, his gold-pierced cock remained turgid beneath his dark-furred stomach, reddish balls hanging lower than before.

My old enemy served her, paying no attention to me, his tongue lapping her slit as if in desperate thirst.

"Is this a satisfying fate for one like him?" she asked.

I didn't have an answer. Intense, unfocused surges of emotion vied for my attention as the howling slaugh whirled around us.

Innathi might know *everything* that had happened in the kitchen of Brom's inn before I'd stabbed then stolen Soul Drinker from her former husband. And if she chose to sentence Kurn to *this* … ? My answer threatened to pitch me from rage to disgust to arousal, all of it dangerously distracting.

"Interesting," Gavin said, saving me an answer as her scarlet eyes narrowed, focused on him.

"What is, Walker?"

"Even here, you create the flux of life magic," he said, remembering to tack on, "Your Highness."

Innathi seemed mildly impressed. "Life magic *led* my rule. I know it well, the flow between me and my Sorcerer-General for *centuries*. Even in death, we do not forget our greatest powers of creation."

"Creation with a cost," Gavin replied. "You cannot create Vitas to reshape your world from nothing."

With a happy laugh, the Queen grabbed Kurn's sweaty, black hair, lifting his nursing mouth up from her mound. "I grant you he is not much, but he is certainly not *nothing*."

She mashed nursing lips against her loins, making the Ma'ab groan as he sucked her folds. She hummed, wiggling her hips. Behind Gavin, Eynkis huffed with contempt.

"Indeed," my ally replied, unfazed by the performance. "I see a semi-generative loop, the least wasteful conversion but unsustainable. Your Desert may remain only until a slaugh is left in those chains with nothing left to give."

"I am *aware*, Deathwalker." The annoyed Queen tightened her core to prop herself on her elbows, eyes sliding past Gavin. "That is why I need the stronger man behind you. He will last to serve us much longer."

Eynkis scowled and opened his mouth; I cut him off. "*We* need him more, Majesty. That is why we came here to speak with you."

"Oh?" Innathi tightened her thighs, trapping her servant's head and forcing him unmoving. "Convince me, *khalithan*."

"War," I repeated, steadfast and imitating Gavin's indifference to Kurn's torment. "I shall send men your way soon. This is inevitable and enough to make up for his loss. How effectively I do so while avoiding death myself *and* losing possession of the relic depends on my preparation."

She hummed. "What kind of preparation?"

"Eynkis has intelligence I need about the force holding Narali." I mimicked Jaunda's stance with hands on my hips. "And he has agreed to provide it, if you will give him to me."

Innathi grinned, further squeezing Kurn's head until her thighs trembled; his cock and its ring bobbed between his thighs. "*Eynkis* will trade his soul for his brothers' to stand in his place?"

"The living," he growled, "the dead. We all have the same purpose."

She tilted her head, relaxing her legs. "No loyalty in this big, pale army, then?"

"The way of the warrior is death," he hissed from behind us. "They know this as I do."

"And the only regret is that you were first. *Hmph*." The Desert Queen eyed me. "I am curious, *khali. How* would you take him?"

"With your permission, Majesty," I said, lifting a surreptitious eyebrow at Gavin while she laughed.

"Well! You know it is not in *my* best interest for you to lose the relic, wielder."

"I know, my Queen."

"Send me no less than five warriors, and permission is granted. I 'give' him to you, to do with as you must. But ..."

Innathi turned onto her side, swinging one leg over Kurn's head and shifting down until his nose bumped her crack. He didn't hesitate to flick his tongue on her netherhole. I'd missed quite a progression since I'd last glimpsed them hiding in a cave behind the waterfall.

"What to do?" she asked, an intense, scarlet gaze fading toward blue as the swarm shrieked louder. "What *will* you do? Just ... take him?" Purplish-red lips twitched. "Or will you interrogate him here and sort it upon a mere promise?"

"I have an idea," Gavin said.

"I'm listening." I glanced at Eynkis, who showed surprise when the Deathwalker rolled up his sleeve.

"If the Hellhound will manifest something with a sharp edge," Gavin explained, extending his pale arm, palm up, "he must cut me with it, then do his best not to let go."

Black eyes skimmed Gavin's unmarked skin with suspicion. "No scars, *maknuut.*"

"There were many as I learned, before I stepped beyond my death."

The Hellhound must have known what that meant for he swallowed, betraying some impression. "A ... sharp edge. Like that?"

Gavin didn't blink. "I care not. It must be yours."

While the Ma'ab considered, Innathi had propped her chin on her palm, smirking. Her irises gradually returned to a glimmering red, and the cries of the slaugh quieted.

"Come, Eynkis," she said. "You have watched me. Manifest something sharper than your wit. That should not be difficult."

His lip curled as he raised his chin.

"Eynkis." I stepped to block sight of her, effective only because the massive Human was standing one step down on the pyramid. "If you wish to return ... ?"

I drifted off, cutting my eyes to the Deathwalker before him.

He grunted, lifting his right arm, and concentrating upon the scars mixed with his tattoos. With visible pain, the first spike tore up through his skin, followed by a second, and a third, until a black metal chain appeared to wrap around his forearm like a constrictor. Several of the spikes crossed the palm, sticking upward but also inward. The whole of it was grotesque but unsurprising.

"Workable," Gavin said.

In response, Eynkis lifted his hand in an uncertain offering to the unannounced Herald of Nyx. The Deathwalker clasped his hand, puncturing his own skin on the sharp points by his own will.

"Mother Divine!" the Hellhound blurted as black blood first stained and then *stuck* to his hand.

"*Horcutrig ferrus,*" the Deathwalker replied, his eyes shutting out all color in a blink. "*Ruiskyn eidolishurra.*"

An instant later, his aura flared a searing, pale blue, prompting Innathi to spring up from the chaise onto her feet. She clutched her arms as if she was chilled, forgetting Kurn as the slaugh swarm grew louder.

"What are you doing?!" she demanded.

"Stand back, Your Majesty!" I called, holding out my palm. "It's dangerous!"

Gavin's blood flowed yet resisted dripping from his hand to touch the pyramid. Meanwhile, the Hellhound's tattoos — or rather, his outline — faded before my eyes.

"*Sssirrrannna ...*" My ally's voice spilled out as the whispers of many, helping to mute the distress of the swarm surrounding us. "*Wake usss. Waaake nnnow.*"

~Yes.~

I took his free hand before any other ghost of the Elsewhere could act upon our escape.

~Wake up.~

I THREW MYSELF BACKWARD AND ENCOUNTERED IMMEDIATE RESISTANCE; SOME-
one was holding me. Two sets of hands held firmly on my wrists, one
from in front and one from behind.

"*Hold on,*" Jael whispered. "*Hold on, let's get it in …*"

Mourn drew his large, strong hands closer to my elbows while my
Sister aided me to secure the red rune dagger. With her so dangerously
close to that edge, my world shrunk down to the point of that blade, to
make certain I wouldn't miss the narrow slot.

Finally, we shoved it the rest of the way. Glowing runes disappeared
inside the casing.

"Fuck," I gasped, my heart pounding, my body shaking.

Behind me, Mourn rumbled, "Deathwalker?"

Gavin had collapsed onto his side within the Dragonchild's circle
of protection, away from his possessions. His eyes were open and fully
black but unaware. A strange, soft wail escaped thin lips. It didn't sound
like him. He shook in a brief seizure before turning onto his stomach,
attempting to rise.

"What happened?" the half-blood asked me urgently. "Briefly. Did
we lose him?"

I licked dry lips. "N-no, ah … H-he's got a Hellhound in his bones."

Admirably short and to the point, I thought. From their expressions,
it didn't help much.

"The one you killed?" Mourn asked.

"Yes. Eynkis."

"You … pulled him out."

"*I* didn't."

"But you … transferred him?"

"Well, yes …"

"Why?"

I grimaced. "Not brief."

Gavin pushed his body up, long, black hair covering his face, the eerie, distant wailing leaking through black teeth. His body shook and shivered as he intentionally scraped the side of his hand on a rock, drawing blood before reaching for the three pouches placed nearby before our trance.

The Herald spilled the contents with far less attention, roughly mixing before cupping into his palm the bits of fresh and dried plants, small bones, and insects which Tamuril and I had helped collect. Crushing them in his palm, sweeping black blood with his thumb to taint it darker, he brought the mixture to his nose, inhaling scents and eating part of it.

Jael and Tamuril made faces of baffled disgust. I didn't know if I'd blinked as Gavin seemed to grow calmer. Soon the strange wailing faded into the night air, though his eyes hadn't returned to normal when at last he lifted his pale, haunting face toward us.

"Ask your questions," he whispered, the voice splitting into several.

The Druid shuddered violently, and the Dragonchild stood up from his wary crouch, tongue flicking out toward our ally. "Who are you?"

"I am the Herald of Nyx. Gavin, son of Ada."

"And ... Eynkis?"

Gavin's eyes flickered. "He is here. Growing accustomed to his chosen fate."

"And he will talk?"

"He will. For a time."

"Let us gather the Guild, first."

"Very well. Do not wait too long."

"We shall do it now." The Dragonblood released our circle with a Word, motioning to us. "Come."

"I will stay out here," Tamuril said, her arms holding herself as she backed up.

"As you wish, Druid. Thank you for your help."

"Mm-hm."

Gavin's presence seemed tenuous compared to whatever happened within him, although he was aware enough to gather his things without prompting. All the same, before long, we guided the death mage inside with the challenges of someone who was on his feet but somehow asleep.

All the while, Mourn kept glancing at me.

"What?" I asked, trying to control my annoyance rising from abrupt head and hunger pains.

He exhaled. "I did not know a soul could ever *leave* that dagger."

The half-blood explained nothing else as practical matters swiftly took over, but the unspoken astonishment and concern hovered over me.

I wondered what might have been different had I given it to Osgrid to bury when she'd asked.

Cursed blade, indeed.

Chapter 14

Jael and I joined this second meeting of the Guild leaders with Isboern and his Templars, but we didn't have much to contribute after convincing the Humans, with the help of Mourn and Gavin, to take us at our word about recent events.

We stood on Mourn's right at the large, round table inside the largest room of the redoubt. The only one sitting at the round table was Gavin, and this only because he and the Templars had agreed on something.

"Best to secure me as you would a Hellhound," the Deathwalker invited. "Eynkis will gain no autonomy through me, but I do not know how agitated he may become with your questions. More importantly, he *expects* to be restrained."

"Awright," Talov said, motioning to one of his younger kin to get the manacles. "Makes sense."

"As much as any of this can," muttered the Templar Robi, rubbing a dark beard which had been shorn close recently.

"Will he be able to see us?" Isboern asked.

"Likely," Gavin answered. "Once I draw him forward to commune with you."

Deshi exchanged looks with his older brother Torch, each man signing a Yungian ward against dangerous spirits.

The red-blond Templar Erik asked, "Should we blindfold the death mage?"

"Who is 'Eynkis' going to tell?" Brian Wolf countered, folding his arms in mild confusion.

"In exchange for his cooperation," Gavin said, observing placidly as a young Dwarf secured his wrists to the arms of the chair, "I have agreed to return Eynkis to his gods."

"Oh? And who *are* his gods?"

"To him, they are the Ascended of Ennikar."

Wolf frowned, and the Templars straightened and tensed as the Dwarf moved away.

Tetente Erik asked, "Do you mean to do this, Deathwalker? Set him loose should he talk?"

Gavin stared at the Templar. "I do not choose the path of the dead. I am to guide them to pathways open for them. I do not force them to take one or another."

"Of course," Isboern exhaled, dipping his chin to his men, "and we will *not* ask our ally to use the same tactics as the death mages of the Far North. We must be on guard for similar interferences in our path to Musanlo."

Every Templar in the room shifted with discomfort, and their Captain turned to our Deathwalker. "*Will* you wear a blindfold, Herald, at my request?"

Gavin's ice blue pupils had reappeared before we had entered the redoubt. He glanced at Mourn and me. "I will," he agreed. "Eynkis need not see through my eyes to understand your questions."

My lips stretched into a smile as the same younger Dwarf reached for a band of cloth produced at a moment's notice by someone in Reprisal. Of course, Wolf and his men would have blindfolds among their gear, and covering Gavin's eyes *might* make the entire event less unsettling for most here.

When the "communing" began, an odd, rasping echo escaped from the scholar's throat any time he spoke.

"*Manalari ... ?*" the pale man whispered, the creepy undertone growing louder. "*Asal ... asal'tikasal.*"

The Templars stiffened, exchanging glances; Imran tried to suppress a shudder.

"Won't speak in Trade?" Wolf muttered, glancing at Talov and Krithannia.

"Prolly better he speaks native," the *Oltere* replied. "We got this."

"The Deathwalker speaks Ma'ab as well," the Templar Erik countered. "How do we know this *is* the Hellhound?"

"We're trustin' Sirana's word," Talov said, receiving a formal nod from Captain Isboern, who stood patiently. "An' it'll get clear soon enough, assuming we ask our questions. Like he's invitin'."

"We'll start," Wolf said. "I doubt a former monk from a monastery is going to know the answers to what I want to know."

"*Asal'tik,*" the blindfolded Deathwalker whispered.

The Guild had worked out a system for when to speak, probably from the first meeting I'd missed. Mourn and the rest would place a smooth, black stone on the table before talking. If two or more placed the stone at once, they spoke in order of rank. Among the Templars, only Isboern asked the questions, though I knew he listened to his men through a mindlink.

All this made for an astonishingly smooth interrogation as Eynkis truly seemed to have come to the fore. Even the manner in which our restrained ally held his head seemed different, not much like Gavin.

Although the questions came in Trade, the answers returned in the Ma'ab language — fortunate for those who had made effort to learn the former, including Krithannia, Talov, Mourn, and most of Reprisal. This was a relief to me that they wouldn't need a psionic link to decode the Dead tongue instead.

Unfortunately, this left Jael and me somewhat in the dark about the details. We could tell Eynkis was moderately cooperative, speaking through Gavin's mouth without inflection, favoring neither eagerness nor reluctance. If he lied or attempted to evade a question, this wasn't apparent to me.

Meanwhile, most of the Guildsmen and Templars seemed convinced that this *was* a captured enemy. Even Erik settled into the exchange, his blue eyes growing intense and hungry for each response. Still, I detected a hint of wary skepticism from several non-Yungian men, both Guild and Manalari; they didn't *want* to believe the capture of such valuable information could be so easy.

In contrast, Deshi and his three older brothers were not only willing to entertain it but responded like Mourn: taking in the information without needing to decide on the truth or accuracy at once. I could have felt the same as any of these males if I hadn't *been* in the Elsewhere to witness all that happened.

"Are you betraying your gods, Eynkis?" Isboern asked, waiting until after the Guild nailed down the numbers they wanted. "In your desire to return to them?"

Gavin's neck craned around; his nose pointed toward the Godblood. His eerie voice sounded content as he answered in his native tongue.

"That is not mine to judge," Krithannia translated quietly, for this seemed important enough to do so. "I have been lost to them. I do not know how long. To return upon death, as I've sworn to do, I come to whatever punishment is mine to bear. Regardless, I bring honor to their ascension, and I am the victor over our enemies. I await the final embrace promised me."

That sounded oddly familiar.

Most in the room took time to ponder that, and upon whatever else they'd gleaned thus far. Suddenly, Tak placed his token on the round table, awaiting nods of acknowledgement from Talov and Wolf.

"Name one weakness in a Hellhound's tattoos," he said.

"*Hadya laeed suudlan*," Gavin-Eynkis replied, deadpan.

"That is not a question," Krithannia translated.

The Guildsman smirked. "Fine. *Where* do we find *the greatest* weakness in the magical protection of a Hellhound's skin?"

A snarl appeared on Gavin's lips. After a brief but apparent resistance, Eynkis answered, "*Eabu alrahanu shaqri*."

"Across the winged center of the spirit," Mourn confirmed.

"Where is that?" asked Wolf.

"Eynkis described it precisely," the half-blood said, volunteering me to use as his example. "Turn around, please, Sirana."

I did so, feeling Mourn sweep my cloak to one side and touch my spine, a few vertebrae down from the center of my shoulder blades.

"Will be closer to your eye level, of course," he remarked, a comment on our relative height that made several men chuckle, "but this is the point he means."

"Is it the same place on every Hellhound?" Talov asked.

The gaunt Deathwalker answered: *Nearly all.*

Close enough.

"We know all the markings are different," Tak murmured. "Wouldn't mind knowing why."

"Maybe later," Wolf said, placing down his token next and leaning toward Gavin. "Are there traps in damaging the tattoos of a Hellhound?"

Gavin's body held perfectly still. Then, to everyone's shock, he grinned broadly, showing pure black teeth.

"*Tathyr*," he answered.

"Many," Krithannia translated.

"Where are they?"

The Naulor shook her head upon hearing Eynkis answer. "Different on each man and not shared, even among each other. He could only tell you what his had been."

"Then do so," the Hand of Reprisal pushed, scowling. "Where were your traps on your body, Eynkis, and what would they have done if the black relic hadn't killed you?"

This was a complex answer, as Gavin couldn't point to sigils or runes on his body. None of us enjoyed hearing the translation.

"My body might burst with an infectious pus and spores, or a caustic liquid might cover and scorch my flesh until I drip scarring blobs on anyone in contact with me. Another might tear my entire body apart in a fiery eruption, engulfing those around me."

The placement of his "trap" tattoos varied widely, but all sat within reach to trigger himself, to extract a heavy, final cost from his adversaries as well as destroy his markings before an enemy mage could study them.

Fortunately for me and everyone else, the mage artist for Eynkis hadn't predicted a magical dagger piercing through his chest bone in one strike.

"Are these same traps on *all* Hellhounds?" I asked on impulse, lacking a token to place down.

Gavin pointed his nose in my direction, staring with his void-like eyes. He answered in Ma'ab.

"No," Krithannia translated, hinting at a mild relief. "Only those chosen for the Temple raid. An honor."

Quite a few Ma'ab had hurled their spiked chains around inside the sanctum. Suddenly, I wondered about Jael's glee when *something* had exploded, surprising even Mourn.

The Dragonblood smirked, following my thought. *Yes, I think Jael and I found one such trap by accident, but we weren't close. Better to know what is possible.*

"By your own count," Isboern stated, "a greater number of Hell-hounds roam around the city than we saw inside the Temple. Are any 'packs' of Hellhounds likely to retreat north with the living host?"

"*Qata*," Gavin answered with a small sneer. "*Jat'al tiwaban baqai.*"

"Not ever," Krithannia murmured. "Brothers came south to stay."

The Captain looked around the room. "So, we do not know which Hellhounds are 'trapped,' but they must all be dealt with."

Gavin's body chuckled briefly. "*Qata* …"

The Deathwalker shuddered, jolting once hard enough to cause the legs of his chair to scrape the stone. He took no deep breath but tilted his head as if trying to stretch or relax. As I watched, the tense lines from Eynkis had vanished.

"Gavin?" I asked. "Can you hear me?"

He filled his chest with air, speaking next without the ethereal whispers.

"I hear you," he said. "Sirana."

"What happened?"

"His memories became ever more vivid under interrogation," my ally answered. "The spirit succumbed to temptation to try and seize this body." Gavin flexed his fingers, wrists restrained to the arms of the chair.

"I have put him to sleep."

"So, interrogation is over," Talov stated.

"It is."

"Let's get the restraints off, then. An' I'd say we got enough."

"Agreed," Isboern said. "Beyond expectations. Thank you for your extraordinary contribution, Herald."

"Quite," Krithannia pondered. "Especially as we must assume the Ma'ab sorceresses can perform interrogations like this as well."

"Unfortunately," Mourn agreed. "Our death mage is a high-value target for them the same as theirs are for us."

Nods from many of Reprisal and Clans. "Aye ..."

Gavin grunted. With free hands, he removed the blindfold from his eyes. A subtle tension spread through the room as some of the men waited to see if we'd been taken by a baited response, though Deshi seemed to have the most confidence in what he saw.

Meanwhile, I smiled to recognize my ally when he stood up, from his distant, sullen face to the slightly hunched shoulders, down to his long-fingered hands with their black nails.

Talov noted my expression with a softening of his own. "Welcome back, Deathwalker. I presume ya heard most ov what came out ov yer mouth?"

"I heard *all* of it," Gavin corrected.

"Ah, good. Let's go over it again, take notes. Everyone, break for a quarter if ya need it. Afterward, let's talk strategy."

"Yes, *Oltere*," said the Clans, Guild, and several Templars.

Yet another full night inside the redoubt.

Jael's eyebrow lifted high in silent remark on the complexity and zest with which the men and Dwarves argued their favored tactics and contingencies.

Are you following all this? she signed, one-handed and behind the shield of her spare.

★Yes,★ I signed near my belly. ★But I doubt I can repeat it without the map.★

Not even close.

The only two *not* pushing to be heard were Talov and Isboern, both of whom asked questions at precise moments, having the effect of either scrapping an idea or pressing Torch, Reprisal, or the Templars to find ways to strengthen it. Meanwhile, Mourn, Krithannia, and Gavin spoke when asked a direct question pertaining to their areas of expertise.

Gradually, my younger Sister and I accepted that novice enforcers like us — granted power by the will and protection of an absent Queen — did not make us war-makers or negotiators on the level of these Surfacers.

These men displayed their expansive knowledge of language, culture, and landscapes well beyond anything Sivaraus could boast, not to mention the centuries of practice and far-reaching travel, especially among Talov's Clan.

Tamuril was wise to stay outside with her bird if she wouldn't understand any of this anyway.

I doubted Gavin understood it all either, but he didn't have to because they weren't building their plan with the unique races or magic users as their lynch pins. We would be the "enhancers, disrupters, and communicators" on the fringe.

Wise strategy.

"So," said the Templar Imran, proving a thoughtful speaker, "the 'Eternal Hellhound' boasted by our prisoner … ?"

"Kreshel Divigna," Mourn clarified. "Perhaps not the same body or man, but for certain the same name and role for at least a century."

Several of Reprisal exhaled in a sudden rise in tension, some grumbling under their breath. Every man present hadn't been born when Divigna started leading the "packs."

"Thus, he is the strongest rallying point for the Ma'ab, correct?" Imran continued. "Like our *Capitan Dyos Saung*."

The To'vah-krav nodded. "A good parallel, Sun Blade, but less from the number of men under his direct command and more the *speed* with which his packs can move to break down defenses for their mistresses leading the true numbers."

"Understood. Can we recognize *him* among many bald, tattooed men?" The Templar looked about the room. "Has anyone seen his present face? Or better, did anyone lay eyes upon him at Manalar those days ago?"

I had. *And so did Mathias.*

A sudden, sick wave overtook my middle, wrapping around my shoulders like a damp blanket. My mind's eye saw him standing across the stream. I shifted my weight, drawing Mourn's notice.

"*You* have," he stated, as if recalling Mathias's boasts the night he was caught.

So many eyes fixed on me.

"Can you show us, Sirana?" Wolf asked.

"We would avoid mistakes or misdirection," Imran added.

I breathed in through my nose. "Of course. Now, if you like."

"Thank you," said the Godblood, gently mindlinking with me as he'd done many times.

An instant later, we stood for a flash in the knee-deep stream leaving Mount Sonai's southern face. A chill steeled through the Godblood to witness how close Divigna had stood during our retreat.

"Brightest God ..." he whispered.

"*Capitan?*" Sohl asked, expressing concern for the others.

"Divigna could have killed us before we ever reached the Dwarven gate," Isboern said bluntly, making eye contact and sharing my memory, one after another, with his men. "On the cusp of our escape. He stood with his pack while you carried me through the water. He chose *not* to attack. It was deliberate."

"Why, *Capitan?*" Erik asked, visibly rattled.

"I do not know. He was ... he made eye contact with Sirana. He was not looking at me."

Wolf straightened up. "Let me see, Captain. Please."

Isboern did as asked, and the Hand of Reprisal blinked several times, focusing on me while Jael touched her shoulder to mine in solidarity.

"I am sorry, Sirana, but," Wolf asked, "is there a ... connection between you?"

Shit.

Nausea took me by surprise as Mourn moved partly in front of me. The Godblood spoke before Krithannia could.

"There is," said Willven. "Forgive me, I hadn't realized until now. She has confessed to me but is forbidden to speak in detail. I must ask that you trust that she had been searching for multiple prisoners beneath the Temple. She recovered one —"

"Two," Deshi said, fidgeting as he looked at Wolf. "A skirmish with the Ma'ab in the crypt. I *also* did not make the link."

The Hand scrunched his face. "What link? I'm *still* not making it."

"The white-maned demon," Peng-lok answered, Torch and Nianzu confirming in sign. "A servant to the Ma'ab witch no longer. *Sho'shien* stopped her. *Janshi* freed him with her mind magic. And *Wen-yung* convinced the demon to take his freedom and escape."

"Hm," Gavin grunted. "Correct. In simple terms, we released a valuable slave of the Ma'ab before we found Sirana's sister. He was a demon with Elf blood."

My lips tightened. *Or a Davrin with demon blood ...*

"And now that we speak of this, I am certain Kreshel Divigna would have orders to capture any Elf discovered alive. Given the opportunity to target Sirana and the Godblood, I don't know which he would try for first."

Several Templars' faces paled along with mine; I kept one hand gripped on Mourn's harness as I fought vertigo.

"But he did *not* come for her," Sohl said, "or for our *Capitan*, though they met eyes?"

~*I don't know why ...* ~ I said through the pearl, shaking. ~*Something about it ... I don't understand ...* ~

Something of which to be wary, Mourn answered, adding aloud, "The threads of that encounter are complex and rooted in past centuries, yet to be untangled. All we can do is urge you to be mindful that Divigna's behavior *cannot* be predicted as you might another man your own age.

We do not believe he bears Human concerns any longer."

"Sagely said, legend." Isboern looked around to his men. "Take him at his word, please. See the First Hellhound *not* as a parallel to me, but as a parallel to the elders revealed to us." He motioned toward Krithannia, Mourn, me, and Jael. "You *must not* presume Divigna's concerns are grounded in *our* lifetimes. This may get us killed."

"*Ci, Capitan*," said the Templars with many nods and salutes.

Soon enough, all men and Dwarves in the room had the true face of Divigna in their minds, and the meeting moved on to speak of other things. Gradually, the fear and sickness faded, though my head still hurt.

Goddess, I want to be free *of this … !*

I must appear as fragile and uncertain to them as Tamuril had to me before I knew about the scars that truly troubled her.

OVER THE NEXT FEW DAYS, SUPPLIES ARRIVED FROM AUGRAN TO PREPARE WHAT remained of the Manalari army to head south. During this time, the Godblood and his four trusted lieutenants learned about the Shaegoth — or at least of their actions — from Gavin, and about the reports sent to Talov and Krithannia from Guild spies in the field.

"The hierarchy falls into disarray," the Naulor interjected before the Templars could debate Guild tactics, "but slowly. Looted resources in the city are plentiful enough for their living army, and the officers seeking to fill the void of their superiors have yet to contact Ennikar, as far as we know."

"What of any prisoners?" Isboern asked. "Our people. Those who did not escape but yet live."

Cool-faced, the Guild Mistress bowed her head to acknowledge him. "Most civilians were killed, and their bodies may be ensnared by the Ma'ab death mages, either now or later. An estimated fifteen hundred living, breathing Manalari have been rounded up into the Northeastern quadrant of the city. We expect the Ma'ab may begin moving them North before long. Probably before we arrive."

Several Templari shook their heads in denial as Isboern asked, "Is there anything we can do?"

"Maybe," Talov said from his wide chair, aged hands folded over his chest and decorated beard as he settled, breathing deeply. "Depends on the Kurgan taking our deal."

"The Kurgan?"

"Aye. The Steppesmen loathe the Ma'ab. Lots more fights between them th' last three hunnerd years than here in Paxia."

Two of the four Manalari natives did not appear to know this, Isboern looked between them before asking Talov, "What deal have you offered, if I may ask?"

"Nothin' on yer behalf, Captain, promise." Talov grinned. "These are dealings for the Taiding Clans. Takin' opportunity tah make nice with neighbors while we can."

Krithannia agreed. "The living army will escort living prisoners. We have seen this in the past. Thus, the Clans have offered generous rewards of horses, tools, weapons, spices, and anything useful to the Steppes in exchange for *living* Manalari prisoners recovered and brought to the outskirts of Augran or Taiding."

The Godblood blinked then stared at the greybeard. "You are offering to … craft for the Kurgan? In exchange for *any* Manalari soul they wrest from Ma'ab hands?"

"Precisely, Captain." Talov shrugged. "Kurgan don' carry or collect a lot ov gems an' coins. They're fast, often said tah sleep in their saddles. Don't give a shit 'bout silk 'r luxuries. Giv'em somethin' they can use in exchange fer whatcha want, an' ya might tempt 'em onto yer side for a time."

"What about an additional bounty for Ma'ab heads?" Erik asked. "Or Manalari recovered for burial?"

The Dwarf shook his head. "Nope. Bad territory fer th' Clans tah trade in, *Tetente*. Besides, the Kurgan will take heads anyway, an' we don' offer rewards fer Human body parts, no matter th' city. We *will* offer rewards fer a living, breathing person, though, no matter the age."

"I am sorry," Krithannia added to the room at large. "This is the best we can do from here."

Willven's eyes shone with tears as he bowed deeply at his waist. "No, please … I am grateful. Reclaiming Manalar and *Pisc'sagrad* must be our priority, but I shall not forget your compassion and generosity for prisoners of war."

"Related, Captain," Talov said, pointing one thick finger toward the ceiling, his facial hair displaying a grin. "We were wonderin' if ya wanted tah renegotiate the maintenance ov the bridges around the Kerut River Mounds? On behalf ov th' city of Manalar, as its highest-ranking commander."

Several expressions passed over Templari faces, some of them hard to read, but I could see none were fooled by the cunning timing in the *Oltere* bringing this up.

"Renegotiate?" Isboern asked. "With you?"

"Nah, not me." Talov waved his hand. "Clan Baradum has no claim on those mounds."

The Godblood proved not the least bit slow in following his lead. "Ah. Rithal Hobgaer? You want me to renegotiate with him."

"As th' last survivor ov Clan Kerut, aye, I would."

"For the land of his kind and the Dwarven bridges, I presume."

Talov gave a pert nod. "At minimum."

"I see. Compensation for past wrongs done?"

The *Tetente* beside Isboern grimaced. "*Capitan*, be careful. That massacre happened *centuries* before we were born. We had nothing to do with it."

"True, but what do you suggest for our own lifetime?" Isboern asked his man. "That we continue to use the *Dyos Guerrimos* garrisoned there to extract wealth from the river traders at the expense of those same bridges built by Rithal and his deceased kin?"

"We've lost everything, *Capitan*. If he wants the land, give it to him, but what more do we owe?"

"I disagree, we have *not* lost everything, and we owe something beyond the land seized. If we do not acknowledge the families and knowledge lost, then I say we have *everything* to do with what happened back then, for we join each complacent lifetimes since and pass it on to our children."

Erik puffed through his lips, shifting in his seat. "What are your thoughts, *Capitan*?"

Isboern turned to him. "Have you been listening to the *Oltere, mei Tetente*? They have opened their forges, stables, and entire marketplace to the Steppesmen who ride countless horses, and who *may* be motivated to recover some of our people."

"But … that has not happened yet."

"I trust his word that it will. Clan *Oltere* is known for keen judgment in looking ahead to the days of their grandchildren. They advocate for their kin not yet born, unmotivated by greed he shall not live to hoard."

Isboern waited, looking between his closest officers, while Talov, Krithannia, and Mourn each confirmed their approval of his description. Eventually, Imran and Sohl indicated their agreement, and Erik sighed and sat back, making a salute.

"*Confio entoa, Capitan*," he acquiesced.

I glanced at Mourn, who translated for me through the pearl: *I trust your far-reach judgment, Captain.*

Good to hear.

We took a quick break and, soon after reconvening, Rithal entered the room with Osgrid. The eve witch held his arm firmly, her poise presenting every kind of support.

The red-beard's blue eyes hinted at the emotions roiling under the surface, and I recalled Gavin's memory of him in the shed. When the Clan-less Tundar had been mourning his family over Jacob's bloodied body, granting the Deathwalker's ritual greater strength by his grief for the dead.

Everyone stood up from the negotiating table, so Jael and I followed suit. The first Dwarf I'd met on the Surface looked at Gavin and me. Rithal managed a wry smile and a shake of his head, as if amazed at how we'd all gotten here. At a loss, I returned the smile.

"Come in, Master Hobgaer," Isboern said, offering him a chair at the table. "Let us talk about the Kerut River Mounds and the bridges there."

Rithal took a seat next to Talov, his eyes blazing as his dark-haired companion balanced him on his other side with a cool enough air to keep his first words civil.

"Don' have much tah talk about, Godblood," he said honestly. "I only wanna hear one thing."

The psion smiled. "Manalar releases all claims to the bridges and to all lands between the Ker River fork. We shall help revert control to the Kerut Clan and his allies of choice. If you are willing to speak further, I offer to escort you there, to inform the *Dyos Guerrimos* that they have been relieved of their duties. The Templari shall assist in removing all Manalari at the garrison." The blond man paused. "With only one condition."

Rithal's eyelid twitched, his lower lip quivering an instant before he stopped it. Taking a deep breath, he sat up straighter in his chair. "What condition, Captain?"

"Allow, without obstacle or sabotage, a launch of my men onto riverboats provided by the Guild of Augran, so that we may sail south to fight for our home."

The Dwarf pursed his lips tightly, a great many conflicting thoughts and ideas for response sweeping his mind. Osgrid took his hand and squeezed, lifting her chin, and waiting beside him.

Finally, my old travel companion exhaled; I could hear his heart before he spoke. "Yer lucky yer more tolerable than *any* Ma'ab I've worked with, Captain."

Isboern chuckled. "That is not luck, Master Hobgaer."

"Hmph. Rithal."

The Captain bowed his head. "Rithal. I am Willven, and for what little it is worth, I am sorry for what happened two hundred years ago."

"Ye weren't alive, kid," the Dwarf muttered. "Ya ain't even from around here. I don' blame you."

"Thank you for that grace," Isboern said. "But I am alive *today*, and I am here in my position. If we are successful in routing the Ma'ab from the Temple City and I retain favor with my chosen people, I give my word to offer you every diplomatic effort to make amends to the Kerut Clan beyond closing the garrison and acknowledging your claim."

The red-beard dug his chin into his chest, either thinking it over or overwhelmed. "We'll see. As it stands, I would rather have Templars downriver o' me than the Ascended, so …"

He shrugged, looking to Osgrid, who smiled and straightened up, eyes bright as the moons.

"We're on yer side, Capt'n," she said. "Let us talk 'bout that garrison bein' empty, then fillin' up those riverboats goin' south."

Chapter 15

Negotiations and planning surrounded us for four days, their reach and consequences stretching farther than my eye could see. Mourn and Krithannia disappeared during most of that time, and I learned they would take Gavin with them during the last two days.

"Rithal has requested the Deathwalker," Mourn said, a fang showing in his smirk, "to make the removal of Witch Hunters at the Ker River garrison further infuriating for them."

Interestingly, Captain Isboern had agreed, though no word if the red-beard might have requested me and Mourn had said no. I didn't ask; I knew why. Jael would insist on coming as well and likely thrill in antagonizing Witch Hunters as they had her.

Mourn and I wanted to save such risks for Manalar itself.

Before Rithal and the rest left the redoubt, however, I found an opportunity to talk with Gavin alone about Innathi. And Kurn.

"Now that you've seen the Elsewhere and the spirits there," I began, sitting with elbows propped on my knees in his surgery room, "what are your observations?"

My ally scratched in his grimoire. "Many. Though, not without speculation."

"I'd like to hear some."

"Anything in particular?"

"Not yet."

Gavin fell utterly still, as he often did while giving an idea his full attention.

"With the mists," he began slowly, "and the swarms. With the unfixed distances …" He turned to me. "The Elsewhere felt like an eddy of the Greylands themselves, somehow isolated by a small and strict means of entrance. I admit I do not know if my presence had a greater impact on this perception than it might with any other visitor."

"Hm," I grunted, discomfited by the thought of bringing anyone else with me.

"Lacking the relic's history or knowing its maker," he continued, "I must guess that the means of passage into this space, this trap, must have been part of the forging of the weapon itself. The gatekeeper, I am not so sure. The runes could have been added later, I suppose, binding that demon there."

"Ah, correct, yes. It … the demon told me. More or less."

"Hm. Interesting. I would say that throne room blocking the Elsewhere feels … wholly separate. Yet, they *are* connected. It is most strange."

I swallowed. "Did you see any other spirits besides the Ma'ab and Innathi? Anyone who could have been a past wielder? In the mist, or … among the swarm?"

He considered. "Nothing I'd recognize as such. Have you?"

I shook my head. "Only when Innathi drew my attention to them. And they were vague. The land and sky were always empty whenever I stood alone."

"This makes sense to me, given how long one powerful soul has existed there."

I tapped my fingers together, preparing to speak it. "And … *was* she eating Kurn? As you and Eynkis suggested?"

"Quite slowly."

I swallowed. "So she can hold onto her memories?"

My ally hesitated, brow furrowing with doubt. "Not … exactly, I

189

don't think."

"What *do* you think?"

"That she is not the queen in fact, not with the lessons of a full life guiding her, though she may bear memories of it."

"Is she a slaugh as well?"

"No. Not yet. Though that risk remains, and she knows it." Gavin dipped his stylus and began writing as he spoke. "What I believe I met were the points of her memories that remained the strongest past a violent death. Cannibalizing the essence of others to anchor herself will have caused alterations we cannot gauge without having known her in life."

He paused. "This could have enhanced parts of her base personality. After so long in that dagger, I believe what has survived is a twisted shade of her original soul, concerned most with its continued existence. And possibly revenge."

Revenge. I rubbed my palms together. *Definitely revenge.*

"So, I have two devourers to contend with?" I asked. "The gatekeeper who may break out of my crystal — when, I do not know. And a ... a vengeful shade who was once the sister of my Valshivess and a queen of the Red Desert."

"The demon seems capable of causing you great harm," Gavin replied, "but I do not believe Innathi can do more than haunt you, as long as you do not welcome a true possession. With your talents, training, and further practice, I do not believe you are as vulnerable as she would have you believe."

"And she needs me."

"It seems so."

"Thus tormenting Kurn before us, claiming it to be for his actions against me when she would have done it anyway."

Gavin nodded. "Such as I saw. I am familiar with the method of show."

I exhaled, thinking things over. "This explains why she had no strong response to the possibility that one of her daughters could be alive."

"Did she not?"

"No. She wanted me to focus on her sister. In exchange for history. I don't know what she means to do if I bring her to Sivaraus."

"Like most memories, she can do little but torment you," Gavin said, "in whatever way works. Many unknowns remain before we know whether you will have the option to bring the relic underground."

True. Especially if the gatekeeper broke free.

"Do you …" I paused. "Have thoughts about the merchant? And what he said to you about welcoming contact with your mistress?"

Gavin shook head. "I have received no insights on this."

"Alright." My mouth twisted. "Maybe he was hinting that he wants you to ask her about it."

"Perhaps." He leaned forward. His stylus scratched parchment "Regardless, it is not time to ask."

I released the breath I held, recognizing soon after that he was finished talking.

"Right." I stood up. "I'll get something to eat. And … thanks."

"Mm-hm," he grunted as I let myself out.

DURING PREPARATIONS, MY ALLIES NEVER LEFT THE REDOUBT WITHOUT TALOV telling me about how long they should be gone. The strangest one was knowing that Gavin had gone with them.

"We wanna assure the Guild's and Isboern's aligned goals can come to fruition," the greybeard said, "an' the Deathwalker is the best early warning we have for other death mages in the area. Deshi's learnin' a lot by stickin' close, too. Really helps the kid and us!"

Half of me regretted missing out on that; the other half just wanted to train with my Sister, maybe suck between each other's legs in private, and try not to think about Gaelan and my geas holding everything down like an anchor on a ship.

"I *shall* return," the Dragonblood said each time he was about to leave, meeting my eyes. "If you need me, try the pearl first. If I don't answer, I am out of range. In this case, find Graul."

An interesting implication for how far that bond may work.

"Tell me what Graul likes best for treats," I said, crossing my arms, "so I am better prepared to tempt him when I need him."

Mourn's unbidden grin held decades of nostalgia. "He's fond of eggs when they're fresh and fish wet from the stream."

I made a face. "Messy. And hard to get."

"Mm-hm. If none of that is available, the dried meat or fruit you've seen would be enough. But not the hard biscuits. It's too much for his teeth."

The first time, especially, the Dragonblood might have wanted to appraise whether my belief in his Word to return was enough to keep the geas from killing me while he was gone. I couldn't ask but had assumed he and Willven must have spoken about what the Godblood had learned.

He must know about the Valsharess and the Ley Tower. About the timing.

I couldn't tell for certain, though; the half-blood excelled at covering his emotions when focused.

In the meantime, Jael and I had agreed to stay away from Mathias and avoid communing with Innathi. Instead, we'd eat well, improve our endurance and strength, but also, rest and help around the redoubt.

For a greater part of the time than I expected, we kept Tamuril company outside, sometimes jogging and climbing with her through the Kerut Hills. Whenever we sat together to eat or rest, Graul often appeared out of the shadow of a tree to watch us from a thatch of cushioning grass.

"Little spy," Jael muttered, louder than necessary, smirking as he vibrated his throat pouch from afar.

I smiled, tossing a handful of harvested seeds into my mouth. "Always better 'f we see him."

"Yeh. He fake age well. Hops like a tree biter as he likes."

I wondered about that. "Or conserves until hopping is necessary."

"Not unknown to me," Tamuril said, "that an elder creature might conceal his true limits when outside the safety of his den."

Wise thought.

I had witnessed Graul at his safest and most comfortable in the underground library in Yong-wen. He had been sore and aching then, but also playful and curious. I could assume this demeanor was still true for Mourn's companion from the Deepearth.

"You are doing better in the sunlight, Jael," the Druid added with a brave smile.

My Sister grunted, turning over a couple rocks for no apparent reason. "Is necessary."

The breeze was strong today, but I enjoyed the fresh air as green leaves threw shadows from above to dance over Jael's face. She was peering around with a cautious squint, the tension around her eyes suggested a stronger headache while mine was mild.

I caught Tamuril watching me and lifted my eyebrows. "Thoughts?"

Her pulse quickened, but she inhaled through her nose and let it out through pursed lips. "Um. Well, yes. I … I asked Krithannia about … our Druids, once exiled."

I blinked in surprise. "You did?"

The blonde Elf blushed as she swallowed, managing a soft laugh. "Ah, she appeared as surprised as you that I asked. I have not … sought as many answers as she has."

Jael glanced my way, chewing the bark off a thin stick to prepare the inner fibers to clean her teeth. Something for her to do to keep her thoughts while I gathered my wits.

"What did she tell you about them?" I asked the blonde.

"Well, I … would like to trade. Questions, I mean."

I showed my interest. "Of course."

"Alright." Tamuril smoothed a lock of hair. "First, the Deathless sorcerer told you true. Naulor Druids once protected *Nalarilin* atop the mountain known as Mount Sonai. Krithannia estimated this was … around thirty-three centuries ago. But we did not hold it long because we were too few in number, though we were influential. Our name persists to this day."

"Huh?" Jael grunted in confusion.

"Nalari," I murmured, plucking a strand of grass, "Nalamar. Manari. Manalar."

Tamuril blinked in astonishment. "Yes! Exactly. The names passed over the last three millennia. How did you know?"

"The Infernal Elf crooned it inside my head," I muttered, digging my fingertip into the soil like a determined worm. "Taunting me."

"Oh!" The Pale Elf glanced at the dark relic but breathed deeply. "So, he knows."

"That and more, I'm sure." I smirked. "But nothing will be given in kindness."

Tamuril shifted uncomfortably. "I would not expect so."

"Why? Have you met him?"

Tears of fright appeared in emerald eyes. "Probably. I ... ran. Rather than stay to be certain."

Always a choice.

At least this helped me anchor Innathi's reign beyond a vague mist of the past. Thirty-three centuries ago, Cris-ri-phon was traveling outside the Red Desert, aiding the Naulor Elves to win the sacred pool. Eventually, they would be forced out, and the sorcerer would bring them with him to the Dark Elf Queendom, where the shapeshifting Wilder would later appear among Innathi's Davrin people ...

Some of them with blue eyes who could also change their shape.

The Wilder.

"Does Krithannia know," I asked, "what happened to the Naulor exiles after they lost control of the sacred pool?"

Tamuril exhaled. "She was not specific, only that she imagined they may have found somewhere to hide from us all these years." She fiddled with her fingernail. "Not unlike ... those Davrin hiding from your queen? Where Mourn comes from?"

She told you about that?

"Your queen is fester crotch, too?" Jael asked, gnawing on the twig.

The Druid sputtered. "What?!"

I broke out laughing, losing enough strength to flop onto my back.

"Do you ... do you not respect your queen?" Tamuril asked above Jael snickering.

"We *fear* queen," she said. "Different from respect."

"Quite true," I said, staring up through the tree branches, noting Pilla was far enough away not to poop on our heads. "We respect elder sisters, like you do Krithannia."

"Ah."

"Not the first sister," Jael growled. "Fake respect! To avoid pain."

I pointed at her. "Also true."

As I sat up, Tamuril stared between us, her face losing any shade of pink. She licked her lips. "But you *do* respect some sisters?"

We nodded together.

"Yet *not* your queen?"

Neither Jael nor I answered at once. The power of the Valsharess was immense, for certain, dogging our heels every moment we'd been up here. Knowing the *minimum* age of our Valsharess, and the lasting enemies She had made up here …

"Intimidating," I granted. "Compelling. Frightening."

"Full of power," Jael agreed. "Punish. Not respect."

True. If I could have made unfettered choices since stepping out from that cave underneath the sky, I doubted I'd be concerned at all about returning before winter.

"What about you?" I asked, staring into Tamuril's eyes. "Do you respect your queen?"

The Naulor shut me out even as we held gazes without blinking. A willing mindlink would have been impossible. She looked away without answering. She wasn't ready.

"Why did you ask me about mimicking an animal?" the Druid asked instead. "Or about your eye color compared to Naulor?"

I blinked but started to smile. "You're still thinking about it."

"About what?" Jael asked.

"If the Nalari Druids hid in the Desert Queendom after losing the sacred pool. If they ran where the Naulor Queen couldn't reach them."

Hearts sped up to consider what Innathi had told me.

"And this could be why I have blue eyes," I said. "Some shared children, long ago. Krithannia may not know where they went, but the ancient queen in Soul Drinker did. She told me Elves with brown skin once lived in her Red Desert. That they hid as animals."

195

Tamuril whispered, "Oh, God ..." before covering her mouth with her hands.

Jael's mouth hung open for several moments until she inhaled sharply, pounding a fist onto the dirt. "Gaelan!"

I jumped. "What?"

"Mourn said! Others who *might* help her, but not Ice Lord! Brown Elves have Gaelan, I bet."

Now *I* was stunned. *Possible ...*

"Mourn knows," she insisted, looking at Tamuril. "Maybe Krithannia, too! They keep location from two queens, will not tell us because *we* fear the touch on us!"

Goddess ... She could be right.

What else could it be?

Had Mourn been lying in Yong-wen when he said he hadn't visited the Red Desert? Had he taken Gaelan there? *Impossible.* How could he move her so far and return in mere days to meet me and Gavin in the warp rot forest?

No, they must be somewhere else ...

Unless he'd used a Dwarven Gate, which meant Talov was in on all this as well.

Goddess damn it.

How many had known where Gaelan was while standing so close to me, and I couldn't realize it?

Above us, Pilla chirped rather than screeched, and Tamuril's head whipped downhill.

"Oh!" she gasped, bracing to stand as I jumped to my feet.

~*No, no, please sit,*~ said a gentle but tired mind. ~*I did not mean to disturb.*~

Willven walked up the hill toward us, alone for the first time I'd ever seen. He wore his heavy armor, holding his helm under one arm and carrying the golden shield over one shoulder. The man's face was smeared with dirt and dried sweat, his body betraying utter exhaustion with every step.

~*May I join you?*~ he asked as if he couldn't muster the strength to move his mouth.

"Uh?" I blinked.

~Only for a short time. I must rest ... ~

"Of course, Willven!" Tamuril settled down against her tree, preparing herself to sit in comfort. "Please, join us."

Jael's bemused face demanded an explanation as I reclaimed my spot. Her hand signed to ask where his retinue was, but I could only shrug.

"Is there danger?" I asked. "Or concern?"

Sleepless, blue eyes flickered in my direction. ~No ... not yet ... ~

The Godblood set the shining shield beside his Druid. We watched him awkwardly get down on the ground with armor and boots on, placing his helm next to the Druid's tree. Then Willven flopped atop his shield with a grunt, face-up, apparently intent on using the relic as a rough bed pallet.

Metal scraped against stone as he shifted, and Tamuril scooted closer, so he was within reach. Carefully, he settled his head into her lap, breathing out slowly, his eyes closing.

~Thank you ... ~

"Of course," Tamuril whispered, combing his sweat-damp hair from his brow with her fingers. The glimmer in her eyes surprised me, especially as she smiled so tenderly. "Rest now."

The Captain relaxed in visible stages, gradual and clear as frost melting in the sun. I wasn't sure of the moment his consciousness slipped away, but I recognized Pilla and Tamuril shifting into guard duty.

"Is he ... alright?" I whispered, checking if any of his men were on their way up the hill.

"Hm?" The Naulor blinked. "Oh, yes. Sometimes a shield needs shielding in return, that's all."

Jael's mouth twisted in sarcasm, her hand moving: ★Simple! How could we miss it!★

"Too many people?" I hazarded a guess. "For too long?"

Tamuril shrugged, her fingers lightly caressing his round ears. "I am not sure he has received a full rest since his first day in the camp. He knows methods to revive himself in brief trances, but this cannot continue forever."

"He feels safe with you," Jael observed bluntly, making the Druid blush. "Unlike non-mountain Humans."

"Mm. Yes, I suppose he does."

"You do this often?" She grinned. "Or more?"

"Wha — ?" Tamuril's blush darkened to hint at anger. "What do you mean?"

"I mean no clothes."

From the way the Druid's mouth turned into a straight line, not only was she offended, but the answer was negative.

Perhaps with regret.

"We have never!" she confirmed, voice low and hissing. "How dare you! That is not yours to ask, do *not* ask again."

My Sister's face screwed up in baffled annoyance at the pushback, looking to me for guidance.

★The two have private rules as companions,★ I motioned. ★I cannot explain them, only give space.★

★But we have seen her naked.★

★And you saw her desire to hide her skin. Naked is neither comfort nor status to her. Why remind her?★

"What are you saying?" Tamuril demanded, her face heated.

"Sirana confirm your rules," Jael grumbled, propping her chin on her elbow. "Sorry. Won't ask again."

The Druid blinked at the ready yield, noted my confident nod, and, fortunately, chose to take it as stated. "Well. Thank you. Willven m-m … means much to me. I have watched him grow from an infant into the man he is, and I could not be prouder."

A good reminder.

For all Willven Isboern's clear talents, influence, and capabilities to organize men to battle with the Ma'ab, this Human was not far beyond his boyhood. He had lived a mere quarter-century, much of that isolated in the West away from large cities. From that view, a young man resting his head in the lap of a gentle Druid who had lived many times his years made a strange bit *more* sense than the Templar Defender slinging sun spells from atop a wall.

We let the man rest, although I began to wonder if we were truly alone. What if the Templars frantically searched for their Captain after an hour had gone by? Who had convinced them he was safe somewhere out of their sight?

~Are you outside the redoubt, by any chance?~ I asked through my pearl.

Mourn chuckled through our connection. *I am.*

~Can you see us?~

Yes.

~Is Graul around?~

He is. Enjoying a relaxing massage.

I smiled. ~May I ask you a question?~

About?

~Something you said. About who besides the Ice Lord might help Gaelan.~

Somewhere behind me, he exhaled. *I cannot tell you where she is.*

~I know. But we were talking with Tamuril about Pisc'sagrad and the Druid exiles, comparing with the Desert shapeshifters Innathi told me about. Jael guessed it must be the Wilder you sought for help with Gaelan. My question: Is she correct?~

He paused.

~A yes or no will do.~

Another, longer pause.

~It makes sense to me,~ I continued. ~That you would have some agreement in place to protect them from both queens, given they are of two bloods. Yes? They are much like you.~

We disagree there. The Wilder are fertile, full-blood Elves with many children. Not infertile hybrids.

I smirked. ~So ... Jael was right?~

He sighed. *Correct.*

I relished that confirmation, knowing something at last! Mourn might have expected me to keep prodding him, but I set the feeling down somewhere safe where I could find it again.

Returning my attention to the two sun-haired Surfacers, I watched how gently Tamuril's fingers touched the psion — upon his brow, his temples, his cheeks, ears, and chin. Her eyes half-closed, her subtle breath weaving a pattern inside a soft hum.

~*Is the psion alright?*~ I asked Mourn. ~*Do you know?*~

He will be. Tamuril knows what to do.

~*Oh? Can you see her aura? Is she using magic on him?*~

I can see it. She does not use overt magic, but her aura mends and strengthens his. She is intimately familiar with its song, as one of her nature would become holding an infant.

Song?

I watched, listened, imagining her holding a pale-skinned baby with round ears, bearing the smile she did now. The rhythm of the mending seemed to flow with the breeze while the gradual tilt of the shadows led even Jael and me to lie down in the grass for a while.

I didn't sleep but soon drifted, choosing not to disrupt a moment of peace deliberately sought.

THE TEMPLE OF THE SUN APPEARED IN THE FORM OF HIGH STONE WALLS WITH many balconies, but this did not last. Nor did the Temple topple. The walls merely faded away, the skylight expanding into vast blue space.

The metal gates once obstructing the platform dissolved into glittering particles, lifted by the first gust to be spread over the forested valley below. Every sharp edge caught the strong light of the Sun, dotting the peak of a stony mountain rising high, a wave of black-barked trees encroaching upon the once-clear slope.

Around the pool itself, raw, pockmarked stone returned, the smooth, polished stone once carved, dressed, and cleaned so meticulously around the spring buckling beneath pressure and time.

I stepped closer to it and to the blond man beside it. He wore plain clothes, down on one knee, his lips moving in silent prayer. The pool's water, clear as a jewel, was lit from somewhere unseen and deep below the rippling surface. Threads of color arrived and interspersed throughout the currents like a bloom of tiny fish flitting with abandon.

"Thank you for answering my call," Willven whispered, his eyes closed. "You are the first."

Am I?

"Let us give the others time."

Others.

That Tamuril stepped from the trees next should not have surprised me. She gazed in wonder, turning in place, and eventually peered into the colorful waters as I had. Upon recognizing her mountain man, she smiled.

"Have you heard?" she asked. "Anything?"

Willven's nod became a bow. "I have. Let us wait for the others."

Tamuril was patient and only mildly surprised when she recognized my presence. She said nothing on it.

Gavin was next to arrive, walking up the rockiest side of the grand slope with the least amount of grass or brush. Curious but cautious, his unearthly eyes moved gradually across the clearing until they settled on me. He grunted, chin dipping as if this explained all, and drew closer to stand with us at the pool. With him, our positions loosely touched each quadrant.

"Still others?" Gavin asked.

"Two more," Willven replied, "if they will come. We shall know soon."

As it happened, they arrived together.

The golden-eyed Dragonchild arrived in silence from down the vanishing slope, boosting my Sister up and over the edge. As she stood up from her crouch, Jael froze, peering around, and soon became flustered, disoriented by whatever she saw.

She spun around too quickly but Mourn had gained level ground behind her and caught her by her shoulders. They continued the turn full circle until she faced us.

My Sister recognized *me*, at least. "Sirana, wh … where am I?"

The plain-dressed psion stood up, his blue eyes opening. "You are in my mind, Jael. I wanted to share something privately, but as directly as I can to soothe all doubts."

"Why?" she asked, glancing up warily at the half-blood, whose large hands covered her shoulders.

"You know I tell no lies," Willven answered. "This way nothing will be lost in translation. You need not hear it interpreted through another's mouth."

She looked around, clearly worried. "Hear what?"

Willven smiled modestly. "Something hopeful. A revelation to me as I've prayed for a way to help break Sirana's curse."

Tamuril gasped softly. "You have been given the answer."

"In a sense. I have been shown that which must be done should we win *Pisc'sagrad*. We must perform a bonding and rebalancing of the pool's magics."

Mourn nodded once in clear agreement but said nothing.

Willven looked at Gavin. "I know that I will need *your* presence to do it."

"Indeed," the Deathwalker peered around the rustic mountain clearing. "I've been shown something similar."

"Please share what you have seen, Herald."

"A raw flux of natural energies, like a river made up of lightning storms flooding the continent." He motioned toward the colors flicking through the water. "Starting here."

"Yes," Willven said. "The difference is our presence, whether the flux is the rain which nurtures a field of grain or the landslide which tears out the roots of ancient trees."

As the two described it, I believed I could see it happening down the slope in front of us, two versions of the valley below laid atop each other: one golden and thriving, the other all churned soil of muted brown.

They didn't mean this materially, did they?

"How does this help Sirana?" Jael asked.

"Well …" Willven opened his palms to us. "For a short time, I will have near limitless strength for healing. And … I have seen Elvish threads within the pool. Naulor magic, like Tami's."

A hopeful smile confirmed her agreement.

"With enough will and magic," he continued, "I believe this ritual is our best chance to unravel the curse while protecting Sirana's child from harm."

"I will help you!" Tamuril cried at once.

"We must *win* the pool, first!" Jael griped.

"That is the goal, regardless," Gavin commented. "And I agree. May as well make full use of any surplus when we know its source."

Not to mention the added motivation for me and Jael in going along on this challenge.

Mourn hadn't spoken yet. I knew the reason *I* seemed unable to speak in this connection — an abundance of caution from the Godblood against discussing undermining the Valsharess — but the Dragonblood's silence in this context seemed odd.

"Well, another question?" Jael prodded.

"Yes?" Willven invited generously.

"Why does the pool look like this in *your* mind? Where is the Temple?"

"This is how *Pisc'sagrad* appeared before the Temple was built," he answered. "This much, I *do* understand in what I've been shown in my prayers. Although the place of worship built around it will likely stand through this challenge, raw magic will *feel* like this. We must be prepared." Willven laid his eyes patiently on each one of us. "Anything to say?"

Placid Gavin shook his head while Tamuril clasped her hands before her chest, shaking her head in firm and contented belief.

"We can *do* something," Jael said, testing out the purpose of this mindlink. "We can find enough magic to free her from the geas."

"Yes," Willven replied. "I believe we can."

Next, my Sister turned to Mourn, lifting her chin high. "And if we succeed? What then, *To'vah-krav*?"

The Dragon's son smiled with chagrin. "Then we may discuss your third Sister to your satisfaction. We may negotiate what can be done in the time we have left."

My eyes teared up to hear him speak. I *knew* he meant it. This meeting held no room to worry over lies or half-truths.

~*Thank you,*~ I thought.

Willven made the Templar's salute to Musanlo over his heart, murmuring a prayer for courage and direction before opening his eyes.

"Now, let us wake."

The armored Captain climbed to his feet, lifting his helm and shield. The way he moved recalled that deep tiredness in which he'd arrived on our hill.

"The riverboats leave before sunrise on the morrow," he announced. "This is my last night in the redoubt. We have room to accommodate you if you wish to sail with us, but part of the Guild is going by land and know our rallying points. How and when the rest of you reach them is up to you."

"We will meet you there, Captain," Mourn answered, having emerged from cover with a dozing Graul in his arms. "We shall aim to arrive before you and provide reconnaissance."

"Anything you can do is appreciated, legend. I know you have wanted this many times longer than I've been alive."

"True, but we both live now." His tail completed one long wave from side to side. "And the time has come."

"It has," Isboern murmured, watching the sun set in the direction of the garrison. "And I am ready, come what may."

He turned eyes to Jael and me, offering a relaxed salute, which I answered even if Jael did not, before turning to face Tamuril.

"Promise me you'll stay with your sister," he said. "Trust her judgment as events shift."

The Druid flushed. "I p-promise, *duriladan*. I shall."

Willven smiled wider, gazed into her eyes, then bowed his head, hand over his heart. "*Edaintril.*"

Soon enough, or too soon for some, the Godblood strode down the hill toward the shrunken camp. We watched him go, and I wondered what plans Mourn and Krithannia had made for our intended route.

Jael couldn't resist poking Tamuril. "Ee-*dayn*-tril, hah? A promise name, ya?"

"It means 'lady with beauty,' " the Druid snapped. "A compliment."

"Uh-huh. And 'doo-*ree*-la-dan?' You said first."

"Cherished man," Mourn translated. "Nothing surprising from what you've witnessed thus far, apprentice."

Jael looked annoyed by the interference while Tamuril cooled her cheeks with her palms, looking to me for reassurance. I granted it with a smile as the large half-blood continued.

"And I guarantee you shall be too tired in the coming days to concern yourself with the Druid's friendships."

"*Hmph!* Will see."

Graul snickered in Mourn's arms. "More challenge. Fun to watch."

Jael peered at the old drake. "But you not going, lizard."

"But I *am*, novice."

"Why?"

"To teach you."

"*What?!*"

"He is," Mourn confirmed. "I hope you're ready to learn some new tricks from an old trickster."

The banter had caught and tickled my ear. A good sign, but my stomach cramped too hard to think of any good quips myself.

"Would you like to eat inside with us?" I asked the Druid. "A last big and hot meal?"

Tamuril blinked, glancing up at Pilla, who leapt off her branch to take her mistress's arm. Beyond the rustle of feathers, the falcon was blessedly quiet.

"We would like the company," she replied, gazing in the direction Willven had gone. In her eyes lay an expected touch of worry and sadness, not as acute as it once was.

"Let's bother the Dwarves," I invited, leading the way.

CHAPTER 16

WE LEFT THE REDOUBT AN HOUR AFTER SUNSET. MOST OF THE NIGHT LAY AHEAD of us. No one spoke as Jael and I grew accustomed to our mounts, concentrating on the navigation of the steep ravines between hills and over brush lines.

Each of us had a passenger as well. Jael leaned forward atop the Dragonchild's long back with Graul tucked beneath my Sister's chest and fenced in by her arms. She stabilized the old drake as they clung to Mourn's harness together. Quiet Words of magic from the half-blood and his familiar seemed to ease the worst of Graul's aches.

Meanwhile, Gavin sat behind me as I used his knucklebone talisman to guide Nightmare. We didn't take long to reclaim our rhythm from when we'd run out of Troshin Bend and toward the warp rot forest. The Deathwalker held onto my waist even lighter than before yet seemed not to strain; his body's strength and endurance no longer followed the same rules as mine.

Ours wasn't the only reconnaissance team which Talov and the Guild had sent ahead of the main force soon to be sailing down the Big Ker River. We expected the surviving members of Reprisal in their own time alongside other allies from Augran whom I wouldn't necessarily recognize, except to say they'd be the wrong size and coloring for full-blooded Ma'ab.

"*Try tah get there first,*" the greybeard said to us in a final, private meeting with Krithannia. "*Even ahead ov our best.*"

"*We will,*" Mourn assured.

I believed we would. The redoubt lay a six-day merchant's journey from the outer fields of Manalar, and none of us needed to sleep as long as Humans. Given that Gavin's mare stopped when I did and Mourn had stamina to keep up with the only horse which never panicked around him, we could run for stretches twice as long as any cavalry.

The other stealth teams would arrive without mounts yet also ahead of the boats, thanks to a combination of five cache stops to exchange horses followed by endurance potions to finish the last stretch on their own two feet.

"*Ma'ab scouts could spot some of 'em comin' from the north and east,*" Talov said with a smirk. "*But not every team, unless we're sloppy.*"

Meanwhile, Captain Isboern and his warriors planned to arrive from the west along the riverbank. Krithannia and Tamuril would be with him, along with the Yungian brothers as their protectors, and another contingent of the Guild's less stealthy members.

"*Please bear in mind,*" Krithannia said. "*Men and women capable of casting magic or using imbued items shall be in one place, concentrated compared to any recent time of which we know. Be wary of spells going wild while the sacred pool settles. Suppress your auras as often as you can before the eyes of the enemy, and do not underestimate our opposition.*"

Not a hard shift of mind for Jael or me, given the Ornilleth battle where we first met; still extraordinary, given what Gavin had told me about the prevalence of mages among Humans in "ordinary" times. The fight for *Pisc'sagrad* may well be decided not by battle alone but by whomever wielded the strongest magic or adapted quickly to the unexpected.

"*What about psions?*" I asked before the meeting ended. "*Do the Ma'ab have any among them you know about?*"

Talov, Krithannia, and Mourn all paused with unique expressions preceding that answer: relief, worry, or wryness.

"*They don't,*" the Dwarf answered, adding a shrug. "*Er, none sane enough tah rise in their ranks, anyway.*"

"*The Godblood has a keen advantage there,*" Krithannia agreed, her face stern with arms crossed. "*But again, do not underestimate them.*"

Mourn rumbled, "*Especially if victory seems close.*"

The pressure to attain that moment was certainly there, given the frequency I overheard Jael and Graul squawking at each other once we reached level ground.

"*Mahhn,*" the shadow drake crooned.

"Mahn?" my Sister repeated.

"*Mahhhn!* Longer, and up at the end."

"Up? How long?"

Graul followed up by snapping, "*Mahhn kagh gethrisja!*"

Jael received a rumbling echo from their mount several times, back and forth. The two males said nothing else until she exhaled, another shiver seizing her. Finally, after allowing the half-blood's rolling gait to grant her some calm, she spoke.

"*Mahhn ... kagh geth-risja.*"

"Good!" Graul piped.

"Did it ... work ... ?" she asked.

"Almost. Again. Without pause!"

"Hm," Gavin grunted after she tried thrice, as if spotting something I hadn't.

"What do you see?" I asked over my shoulder.

"Masked auras," he answered. "Obscured without suppression, lacking a need for consistent concentration."

He is correct, Mourn said through my pearl as his open mouth huffed with deep breaths. *Though any aura becomes readable while using strong magic.*

The added protection this provided a novice would help all of us during a risky approach. When Jael glanced my way, I grinned, encouraging her.

She didn't return it.

My bladder and belly kept us on regular breaks, which Graul seemed to need more than me though he tried to hide it. Perhaps he used some magic Words to stave off the pain, though he did not seem to be mending.

~*Could you heal your companion?*~ I asked Mourn curiously, biting into my ration. ~*With a Word?*~

The cautious regret in a golden gaze told me the answer.

Healing by Word or by touch is a rare talent, he answered, pacing around in a circle on four legs to cool down. *And not one of mine. I can try to enhance a potion, at best.*

~*A potion?*~

~*Yes. Imbued with magic guaranteed effective because of vast, collective knowledge from thousands of years studying and experimenting with the components. The Word empowers and accelerates the aid provided by natural properties of Miurag.** He paused. *Graul and I agreed to save the potions for dire circumstances.*

~*Aha. Just checking.*~

His wry smile looked less familiar on that longer muzzle. *Many a time, I have wished I could simply mend where he hurts. Touch healers seem much rarer than death mages. A life mage with talent in fertility isn't necessarily a healer, and those few I've known were vulnerable to abduction or exploitation.*

It was the same as in Sivaraus, and Osgrid said I carried one.

"*The father is a healer, ain't he? He passed his gift.*"

I swallowed another absent bite, prodding my stomach to confirm the hard ball of my womb as I drank from my waterskin. Mourn didn't notice; he was looking at his aged companion. The drake had found a thick patch of grass to plop into and wait for our break to end.

The Dragonchild added to our exchange, spoken like a weight upon his mind. *Graul will not accept either potion or Word as often anymore. There seems to be a … limit where the return of his aches is worse than the state which had been taken away. He has told me … enduring what exists is easier than manipulating the scale.*

A sober pause, then: *He knows he is dying.*

My brow beetled as I tried not to stare at the softly wheezing bundle of wings and black scales in the green grass. ~*Yet we're bringing him with us.*~

Golden eyes shone in the dark, fixed on me. *For Jael's sake and this *opportunity, yes. He will hide and wait outside Manalar. We will not carry him into battle.* *

I shook my head, thinking over how flustered Jael had been with the beast's constant demands. *~Why not make another pearl and teach her yourself while we're traveling?~*

His smirk looked odd on his shifted face. **Those are not so quick to form, and I have Slept since I made yours.* *

~So?~

**You noted I am somewhat larger since Waking, correct?* *

~Well ... yes.~

**There are ... other changes. I am still learning them. Planting the seed to irritate my jaw glands hasn't been at the fore of my mind.* *

~Hm. Reasonable.~ I pushed the last, large bite into my mouth. *~What does Graul think of her? Or of your suggestion to teach her on the way?~*

Mourn paused in walking the grounds, noting where Jael came out after fussing around in the brush. He showed me a small smile. **Graul's idea.* *

I blinked twice, forgetting to chew. *~Huh?~*

Jael's mount showed fangs in an open smile. **Not the first time he's attached like a burr to a mage with no direction. In truth, he is helping me to learn your Sister's aura slower, as the intermediary rather than my aura overbearing hers like at the start.* *

I returned his smile, at least until he added his next thought.

**I also think she is learning from him how to manage the pain this can cause naturally, with less overt thought, than she would from me.* *

~Uh ... She hurts still?~

Mourn dipped his head. **She has grown better at hiding it from you since the ritual with Tamuril. The pain has not disappeared.* *

Damn.

Jael tromped over the thick grass, staring between us as we looked her way. "What?"

I shook my head, pushing the partial mouthful into my cheek so I could say, "Finished eating?"

"Not hungry." She shrugged, belying any irritation. "Ready with you."

In my periphery, Gavin stood up from against his tree, his grimoire tucked away in a smaller satchel at his side.

"As am I," he said.

I finished up the meager meal and washed it down with another swallow of water as Graul lifted his head from the grass. "Let's go. I see the first dawn light."

THROUGH THE HEADACHE OF THE DAY, I PAID ATTENTION TO JAEL AS SHE WORE her sun mask, held Mourn's harness, and practiced speaking To'vah with Graul tucked under her chin. Even seeking her pain, I couldn't reliably tell it from frustration, especially when Nightmare couldn't gallop close enough to listen or see her full expression.

"Any read on her aura?" I asked Gavin instead, giving him a long time to study the other riders.

"Volatile," he said at last.

I waited before prodding, "Concerns?"

"Well, she is not masking it."

Sigh.

"Is it pain?" I asked outright.

"Perhaps. But I do not know the intended effects of her words."

I had a guess by the start of our next two breaks that day, based on how little stiffness she showed compared to me.

"Endurance spell?" I asked her with a good-natured groan and immense stretch.

She wrinkled her nose. "Leech spell."

"Leech?"

"Not *my* enduring," she said, flexing her arm and waving vaguely where Mourn was crouched like a large cat, drinking from a running stream. "His. Shifting balance, is all."

"Well," I shrugged. "That's good. Sharing strength is what we were doing in the last battle, right?"

"He not guiding this time," she grumbled, hands on her hips and her face in a scowl. "It ... hard. Coming through the lizard."

That explained the "volatile" aura, then.

Quickly, I searched for that "lizard," spotting Graul belly-down on the loosest mound of dirt he could find. I began to worry about him making it through the next three nights. Surely, Mourn wouldn't let worse happen.

"How you control dead horse so well?" Jael asked abruptly, sounding annoyed.

I blinked. "How? You know about Gavin's talisman."

"So easy? You just *think*, and she *do*?"

My lips tightened. "Mm, no. It was hard at first. I've practiced. We rode her for a long time before Augran."

"Hmph."

My Sister spotted Mourn returning and chose to end our conversation there, moving away to refill her waterskin and start chomping some food by the stream. Graul lifted his head to watch her go but soon fluttered his throat pouch and slipped into a quick nap before we were to leave.

~*How is it going?*~ I asked Mourn.

The quadruped glanced after Jael, his barrel chest expanding in a deep breath. *She is conscious of something which she refuses to let go. This slows her learning, distracting her focus and thoughts away from her efforts.*

~*Refuses to let go of what?*~

I have not sorted that out yet.

~*Hm. Where do you want her magic to be when we reach the outskirts?*~

Mourn considered that. *As far as she can get. She can mask her aura. That is good. She knows how to draw mage strength from me without depending on my initiating it. Also good.*

~*You're giving her mage tools?*~

Of course. He met my gaze. *I cannot fight beside her without drawing on her raw potential first and using her like a familiar or a focus.*

I blinked. ~*What? Using her?*~

*She was aware of this when we fought in the Temple, do not worry. This *might be part of what troubles her, though. Wielding these tools without my help made her realize the extent to which I pushed her to keep you both alive. She 'knew' much in that moment but could not retain it because the knowledge was mine, not hers.* *

Now I had a better understanding. Free of his Bargain, the To'vah-krav had neither obligation nor temptation to compel a raw resource in its most effective direction. What she retained depended on her, which was better for both. She must know that.

Yet, something is holding her back.

Could I gain that insight? Would she tell me?

By her expression and evasion of eye contact late that morning, the answer was, *Not yet.*

Later, however, we found a cave — or rather, Mourn led us to one — where we would take our Reverie during the hottest part of the day. Gavin and Mourn would be awake to watch over us, and the Deathwalker agreed to lean against the rock hiding Soul Drinker so I could snuggle close to my Sister. Nightmare could forage for dead things while Graul, Jael, and I claimed much-needed rest.

After a period of quiet, peaceful blackness, my Sister and I found ourselves upon the bank of red sand beside the Desert river. We lay on the side where Morixxyleth had grown wings after Jael had touched him but ran away when he'd begun thrashing.

"Where … ?" she whispered.

"You're safe," I said. "This is our dream."

Jael studied our appearances. We wore our Red Sister uniforms from Sivaraus, cloaks spread out as we rested on our sides, facing each other. I didn't sit up immediately but watched her, fascinated by a faint, purple glow around her. It traced the lines of her body like a fine brush, teasing my eyes like an iridescent candleflame, here and gone.

Is that what an aura looks like?

I smiled, reaching to brush white hair from her temple and tuck it behind her ear. "Heard you're learning some new tricks."

She bolted up, back stiff, copper eyes staring across the river into the Desert as the stars glinted off the water's surface. "What are you doing?"

"I wanted to talk somewhere private." With effort, I stayed on my side, tucking my arm beneath my head. "I can let you go. If you don't … want to be here."

Jael tossed a dry glance my way before she scanned the landscape. "I was … here before. Wasn't I?"

"Yes. Or at least your memory of it. You found the To'vah Morix-xyleth while he was Sleeping, I think."

"Hmph." She dug the fingers of her left hand into the sand. "You're getting better at this. Like Isboern."

A smile touched my mouth. "He helps make sense of some things when I'm not awake."

"*Pfeh*. Wish my teacher did that instead of letting the lizard bark orders."

"You've barely begun. At least you got a taste of how far you could go."

"Almost wish I hadn't," she grumbled.

"I dunno," I countered, propping up on my elbow. "I stumbled around with psionics for several turns, in pain and terrified of a void-end with no pathway or teacher. D'Shea couldn't help, though she tried. She was better than having no one."

My Sister took a deep breath, letting it out. "Alright. I hear *that*. But … it's just more words. Echoing like a bird. He needs me to learn another language, a *harder* one, when I can barely speak Trade! I'm not *good* at languages, Sirana. You and Rausery both knew that while we were in the cave!"

"Ah. Well —"

She turned at the waist to meet my eyes. "Your thoughts move *much* faster now that you have a teacher. I've noticed, believe me. And … and unlike you, I don't know *why* I'm like this! The Black Dragon spoke to me in the crypt, now suddenly his son is here to instruct me through his shadow drake. I shouldn't question it?"

I sat up at last to be level with her gaze. "You haven't asked Mourn about that yet?"

"No, and neither have you!" she barked, flipping her hand. "And

214

you're the one he would trust to answer if you asked, you said."

I shook my head. "You were annoyed about my bargain spilling onto you. Now we can start over. Sort it out with him clean."

"Easy to *say*." She pulled her legs up to hug her knees. "We're *only* on a four-day endurance trek to seize that goddess-damned pool from an army of pale giants so we can free you from the queen's noose! And I've got *so much* to learn before we get there, or I'll make it worse for all of you." She paused. "And I *hate* every tick of it. I don't *want* to be a mage. I'm not a scroll cait, I never have been. I'm a fighter!"

I bit my lip. How could I not believe her when she spoke *exactly* what held her back?

Hating the experience, the tutoring itself.

I wasn't sure how well she could read and write in the Davrin language, and she'd proven to have little ear for Surface tongues. I might not have either, except for the "thoughts" moving faster than the words, as she suggested.

"I see." I laid down on the bank. "And ... you're right." Sensing her modest surprise and confusion, I added, "What do you think about doing when you practice the Words?"

"Using the blades he loaned to me, of course," she grumbled, propping her chin in a palm. "He hasn't even mentioned Blade Song though we've done it."

"*He's* done it," I said. "You drew knowledge from him as he drew power from you. Or so he said. You're beginning."

Jael muttered unintelligibly then cleared her throat. "Impractical swinging a sword while we're riding all day, anyway. I'm not blind or stupid."

"I know." I gave it some thought. "Want some sword practice before we get there?"

She hesitated to speak the affirmative sparkle in her eye, her mouth stuck in a frown. "Or just some fucking answers about his sire."

Her quiet exasperation made me grin. "I'll make the suggestion. Nudge with the one *and* the other."

She arched her eyebrow as if weighing a potential tug of her threads and sighed. "No, no need. I'll focus. I know this is important."

I shrugged. "It is, but I don't think he has *taught* anyone before. Why not change a method if the pupil loathes it?"

Her lips tightened. "Maybe it's the best way, but I can't learn it."

"Drider shit." I held up my pointer finger. "The first day, you can mask your aura better than I can suppress mine."

"Huh?"

"You do. And you can *knowingly* influence another aura with intention. I can't, Jael. I do it by accident, and I can't sense *anything* until after it's happened." I bumped her shoulder with mine. "You're learning, Sister. Graul squawks directions at you, doesn't he? He hasn't blown the air from his pouch and given up."

My Sister was willing to accept this but made a face. "I wish …"

I leaned in, brows held high. "You wish?"

She sighed, shaking her head. "Nothing." Her mouth twisted in dry amusement. "So, you were enjoying those 'payments,' you said, before he said he'd had enough?"

Of course she'd turn our conversation to sex. I arched my eyebrow and smirked. "Did I look like it?"

A shrug. "Maybe. I saw the two ruts, and he *took* those payments."

My lips softened with memory. "Oh, we didn't start like that."

She perked up. "How *did* you start?"

"With far less confidence."

"On his side?"

A knowing grin.

"Nope. On both sides."

"*Pfft!* I don't swallow that!" she laughed. "You're a Red Sister. You know how to fuck."

Her eyes scoured my leathers, finishing with an expectant arch.

"No, I don't," I said. "Red Sister in a strange land, Jael. Even fucking has different rules up here."

"Hmph. Didn't look like it." She shrugged. "Not from *him*, anyway. He's got enough Davrin blood to …"

"To what?" I prompted, wondering. "To feel familiar?"

She hunched her shoulders, twisting awkwardly. "Close, I guess. You know. Kind of like a Sathoet."

Silence.

I imagined Rausery's rescue of our youngest recruit from the four Sathoet attacking her, whether Jael implied that or not. I had witnessed the likeness in the half-bloods' forms, their snarls in the dark. Mourn had frightened me for a moment in Dandan's bridal bed, looming above me the way Kerse had.

But when he'd seen it, he stopped. Lifted me up. He had held me safe until the shadow in the room passed.

He understands. Remembers his helplessness despite all strengths.

Meanwhile, Jael had only experienced the towering Dragon's Son seizing us, escaping out of the redoubt to the waterfall, randy to the edge of his control. In hindsight, he should have terrified me but hadn't. Even then, he'd kept his Word.

Yet I couldn't convince her of anything beyond what I'd said. She had to see for herself.

"So," I said, reaching to touch her glove. "Maybe a different method than bludgeoning you with Words?"

Jael glanced down at my fingertips resting on her hand, waiting as if to let shared heat seep through leather.

"Or," I added, "some reason why his Sire might have spoken to you?"

Copper eyes held to our gloves, she swallowed. "Yeah. Either would help."

"Alright."

We stopped talking but stayed close until, gradually, we faded apart in our Reverie.

Anything you wish to share? MOURN ASKED AS WE PREPARED TO LEAVE THE cave. He knew I'd been in a mindlink in Reverie.

~Yes, but ... not yet. Let me think. Continue as you planned.~

The Dragonblood didn't argue, knowing the distance awaiting us. Only halfway to Manalar.

The late-day sunlight remained bright and strong, stretching our shadows ever longer as the Sun approached the horizon. We stayed far from roads and villages, crossing a broad stretch of open grassland. The summer heat lingered without breeze above the tall, swaying bristles, the song and buzzing of insects laid over us like a thick blanket. Fortunately, we were either moving too fast to be bitten, or the strange nature of our mounts kept them away.

Jael's verbal lessons lasted shorter than the previous two days; all three seemed tired of the drills as progress slowed. When we stopped for another stretch break, the evening was young.

Mourn curled protectively around Graul to keep the insects off the little one then asked me, *What did you learn of your Sister's state of mind? She tries, but not for her own sake.*

So, he could tell.

My mouth full of rations, I could still answer. ~She isn't a scholar. I've never seen her write, I am not certain how well she reads, and she claims she has no ear for languages like you. Even Graul speaks six languages. The present method grinds this into her face every moment. She feels the lack keenly.~

Mourn considered, looking down at his dozing shadow drake. *She is not doing poorly for the circumstances, Sirana, and I have told her that. We both have. Is the skill comparison alone which brings her confidence so low? Could it be anything else?*

~First, let me ask, could there be other methods to teach a mage? Something aligned to her talents?~

He sounded surprised. *There are other methods, yes. Many which I intend to present. This is rudimentary at best, only because we must divide our attention in a short time. It is not ideal, the difference between supplying a travel pack in a city versus a hermit's cabin. I have told her this, too.*

~I'm glad to hear it. It'll help.~

Given enough time.

To our right, Gavin's patience, or obliviousness, was extraordinary as he practiced writing in the earliest moonlight. His skill had grown in adapting his vision like the Guild mages. As always, Nightmare made not a sound standing beside him. Jael had gone hunting for small game, saying I needed "fresh meat" and ignoring the capable set of claws and teeth resting nearby. Mourn had let her go to talk to me.

What else? he asked, the thought tinged with the slightest impatience.

I thought over what she'd said at the last: '*Kind of like a Sathoet ...* '

~*What thoughts can you share about the Bargain your Sire mentioned to Jael?*~ I asked directly. ~'*Huge gold eyes' appeared to her once the geas had broken in the crypt. She said they were like yours, and a male voice said she was the first 'unfortunate' daughter who must leave the nest.*~

His familiar wariness seemed habitual for anything concerning his Draconic parent. Graul stirred in his nap.

~*I'm not asking for all,*~ I added. ~*Just ... something. At least I recall the catalyst that made me psionic, for good or ill. She experienced no such moment. She was never a mage, and never wanted to be.*~

*Hm. Well ... *

I waited.

Captain Isboern recalled the Dragon's speech clearer than Jael did, Mourn admitted. *The To'vah spoke to him directly, and he and I have spoken at some length recently.*

A telling glance.

I smiled in dry response but, as always, must stay silent on the matter.

My Sire's remarks seemed unusually clear to me, Mourn said with discomfort, *Jael did not spontaneously change into a mage. She always had the potential, but it has been magically suppressed until now.*

I straightened. ~*What?*~

Isboern was the catalyst. The release of her mage's aura was a To'vah Bargain fulfilled, I am certain. Something which took centuries to come to fruition. But she is so young, I can only imagine the original Bargain was made with someone in her bloodline who met him while he was Awake.

My mouth hung open; I was breathing through it until I had to puff away a gnat which tried to land on my bottom lip. ~*So, she already had a To'vah magic affinity?*~

Bestial Mourn shook his head on a stout neck. *No. That was you and me.*

~Oh ... Strange luck.~

Agreed.

~Could you ask him for advice about tutoring her? The Black Dragon?~

Mourn's serpentine pupils thinned as he drew his chin back. *Sirana. Believe me when I say it is unwise to invoke my Sire to show you a shorter path in anything you desire. I have found it always best to find your own way.*

I couldn't ignore the chill which prickled along my spine. ~So, 'no.' Are his Bargains like the Ice Lord's, then?~

In a brief turnabout, the Dragon's Son looked annoyed at the comparison before giving that some thought. He shrugged with a sigh of acceptance. *Alike in that the outcome is true but never what you'd predict, yes. I grant you that. But in all other ways, no. The two are not alike in their motivation to make deals with the young races in the first place.*

Interesting bit of defense of his Sire. I couldn't help but smile. ~What else did Isboern say about that encounter with a legend?~

Blatant worry escaped Mourn's careful expression before he leashed it. *That the To'vah of the Deepearth is Awake and your Queen has been searching for him.*

This time, I swallowed, seeing at once that couldn't be good. My stomach clenched.

Shyntre and Auslan. What could be happening with them?

~So, we teach Jael ourselves,~ I repeated. ~Don't ask your Sire for help.~

Correct. We will be well and shall assist Willven Isboern to anchor and rebalance the sacred pool of Manalar.

~Got it.~ This was the key to my freedom as well, yet, I added, ~I would offer something to bear in mind.~

What is that?

~Suppressed potential or not, she is not a mage at her core.~

She is, Mourn returned. *And she must become a mage or lose herself. There is no choice here.*

~There is one choice,~ I retorted, smiling tightly without baring teeth.

He waited, staring. Then with a sigh, *Tell me.*

Jael's footsteps sounded. She was returning to camp.

~You know many languages, To'vah-krav,~ I said, ~and you also know that some are wordless.~

Of course.

~The Sisterhood has a wordless one, and she excelled in it. Maybe consider using some of what I've taught you so she can hear and understand her teacher.~

Resistance.

No, he stated. *I do not teach by brutalizing those weaker than me.*

Despite that sting of truth about our Cloister, I met his eyes moments longer. ~I showed you another side in Yong-wen. More than once.~

His eyes played through their memories but did not light with understanding.

~She wants to use your blades,~ I continued, ~but is new enough to need the mats, right? Maybe imagine her in a dorji-ka.~

His resistance eased, and I sensed his amusement.

A dorji-ka. Out here?

I shrugged. ~Where else can her elder meet her where she is? The Guildsmen gave her that at the redoubt after arguing with you and me. The 'potential' is just that. She's already a fighter.~

His thoughts churned, and Graul opened his eyes, lifting his bristly chin to peer at his companion with a pleasant smirk. The drake's throat pouch vibrated in a low purr as Mourn met his eyes.

I left them to their private exchange, standing up to meet my Sister as, coming through the grass, Jael held up her burrow's catch with pride, high enough for me to see.

CHAPTER 17

Mourn and Graul gave Jael a break from the verbal lessons when we mounted up.

"Must make speed," said the drake as Mourn drew long, deep breaths, preparing for the next sprint. "See Manalar far-fields by next eve or sooner."

Gavin, Jael, and I had no strong sense how difficult that goal might be to hit, but Mourn had been setting the pace, anyway, and had run this trek before. Or so he'd said.

My Sister dove whole-heartedly into this last stretch with her reptilian companions, focused only on speed, leaning and rolling with Mourn's curving and jumps to keep Graul in place. I didn't know what the old drake said to her once, but that was the only time Jael grinned on this trip.

We suffered through the high point of the day, keeping our stops brief. Toward the end of our trek, the air cooled some but remained moist and sticky. I also caught the frequent scent of manure. Breathing deeper, I half-expected hints of metal and leather, blood and rotting meat.

Not yet.

Perhaps the winds blew to spare us this first sign of Manalar's loss from ten days ago. Would the Ma'ab expect us to return so soon, or would the Shaegoth assassinations keep them distracted?

That is what we are here to discover, Mourn said through the pearl, long strides and talons skimming the ground. *We have two days to look around before the boats are planned to arrive. The more information we can send as Krithannia gets closer, the better.*

We would hole up in another hidden cache Mourn had built, not unlike where we'd rested once out of the warp rot forest. According to him, none of the other Guildmembers knew it existed, much less which hill it lay beneath.

I have made it my practice never to use the Guild's caches in case they need them. His smile was feral in this form. *I am not alone in the practice, but I have a longer memory.*

We entered the narrow "finger" of the Raguruos Mountains, where the foothills and dark wood forest crept some distance to the west instead of following the bulk of their peaks in a steady march south. I'd seen the Guild maps how this massive land barrier reached from Augran, past Manalar, and continued far to the South Sea.

The warmer lands that Sha-rish, the dark-skinned Guildsman, calls home.

I had no cause to ever stand on that distant shore, though I imagined it, surrounded by the Desert's descendants. Alas, an army from the Far North squatted directly in my way, not to mention a time-sensitive geas yet unbroken.

Much yet to be seen.

Late sunlight faded into deep shadow as we arrived in a tight, rocky hollow not far from where the forested hills gave way to the agricultural fields leading toward the City of the Sun.

I guided Nightmare slowly through this difficult terrain, her hooves scuffing the moss off rounded stones and crushing rotted tree trunks. A challenge to keep me, Gavin, and our supplies from spilling off while keeping an eye on the Dragonchild while he climbed stones and sprang over brambles as he wished.

Any ordinary horse would have refused to tap-toe along the second ledge especially. I held my breath as Gavin assisted, silently commanding a precise, if unnatural, gait for his mount to cross that last line of brambles, easing around them without having to drag us *through* them.

I couldn't imagine any Guildsman building a private cache here but *could* see a hoarding half-blood drawn to a hideout near Manalar. This place would be too troublesome to dismantle with axes and remain familiar for half-centuries at a time.

Here, I also detected the faintest scents of smoke, shit, and rotting meat drifting between the branches. A Human wouldn't be able to smell it yet, but those from the Deepearth took a sniff of the air as we stopped beside a boulder.

How close are we to the army? Jael signed, frowning with concern after dismounting Mourn.

The Dragonchild stepped beside a rock ledge large enough for Graul to slide off then he met my eyes. *Our first sight will be three ridges over at a distance. A brisk jog for another hour if we wanted to let the perimeter see us.*

I signed that for Jael, noting my death mage's pale stare as he waited for his explanation as well.

"We may speak," Graul said with confidence. "Too far to be spied or heard. We will set cloaking wards soon, use no fire. Wise that you mute your presence by habit, Deathwalker."

Gavin grunted while Mourn transformed into his birth form. With bones and joints popping and grinding, he groaned in pain. I winced in sympathy, given the impression he wouldn't shift back to his runner's form unless necessary. After four days and watching him straighten up, I'd forgotten his height.

He does seem larger since he awoke.

There were other changes, too, he'd said, but these weren't obvious to me.

As Mourn prepared to roll the boulder to reveal the entrance of his cache, I gauged that he'd have to duck down to get inside. The cave also wasn't deep.

"Where will we keep Nightmare?" I asked Gavin, who shrugged.

"She will do well lying down along the rock," he said. "She can warn me as I look outside through her eyes."

Alright, then.

We settled inside and, after a quick bite, I quelled the worry about my food supply and how we'd supplement going forward. Fresh kills and foraging along the way worked well enough given our speed, but we sat on the border of a land invaded and a city looted. Mourn and Jael would need as much to live as I would, Graul much less, and Gavin almost nothing at all.

Two days before the boats arrive. Watch, don't get caught, and meet up.

And if we were lucky, we'd reach an untainted resupply before the fight started in earnest …

"A small stream lies nearby," Mourn said, removing his cloak and harness with care, "if you wish to wash with me."

"What about Word?" Jael asked. " 'Clean and mend?' "

"Be my guest."

She exhaled with annoyance. "Me? No. Tired, and spell didn't work before."

The Dragonblood shrugged, naked but for his trousers and metal bracers. "We will try again when I return. You can help make sure our gear is in good condition. I would prefer to wash my hair in actual water, however."

I blinked in stark surprise. "Wash your hair?"

"As you have done many times."

"But you've never … uh …" I hesitated.

He smiled. "I am now. Consider it a last luxury for a while."

Scowling between us — at his amusement and my fluster — Jael grumbled and got to her feet. "Right. Water. Wash."

Wordlessly, I followed with soap and a cloth, staring at the queue looped at the base of his neck. Usually tightly plaited and intricately wound so hardly a strand could fall out, this was the most unkempt I'd ever seen it.

Have I ever seen him take it down? At the waterfall, perhaps?

I didn't think so. Before he Slept, my bodyguard had always done his hair grooming when I wasn't looking. Whether he'd fought, fucked, run, or swam, the plaited rope of black hair had been sleek and tidy so soon afterward, it must be by magic.

Why was Mourn doing this the long way? Was it truly a luxury?

Jael and I took advantage of the chance to wash but were understandably distracted, studying the half-blood male doing something either of us would have only seen in a Matron's manor or at the Palace Court: a bua unraveling his braids to show us just how long his hair was.

Once free of the loops and bands, the end of Mourn's queue splashed into the running stream from his kneeling position, floating like a lure for some fish before he began unwinding it.

I stared. *Where was he hiding all that … ?*

Neither thick nor wavy like other buas, the sheer length would have allowed Mourn to create infinite designs if he wished. All I saw and had ever seen was a glossy rope, plaited simply. My thumb and pointer finger could meet around it, yet the ends might brush his ankles when he stood up.

Why did he never cut it? Or had he, and it still grows like this?

Mourn's claws combed through small snares as he slowly worked his way toward his scalp, unraveling his queue. He caught my ear with his exotic accent speaking Davrin. *"Will you help tug out knots near the top, Sirana?"*

Knots.

When I didn't reply, he smirked, throwing me a knowing glance. I exhaled, making my mouth move. *"Sure. I mean, yes."*

He leaned down to give me some slack as I took hold. Straight, black hair flowed in the stream near where Jael had finished scrubbing her face and scalp. When she saw me crouching to help smooth out the rough spots before dunking his head, she snorted softly.

What are you doing? she signed.

I shrugged. *Letting him use my soap?*

"Pfft." She shook her head, wrinkling her nose.

I knew exactly how this looked to her, and I wasn't sure why I was so eager to help. Buas either tended their own hair or had others to help with the ornate designs. They didn't ask matrons or caits to do it for them; they might sit to have their hair combed by a servant if they felt secure enough.

For Jael in particular, growing up without servants at all, I also imagined each took care of their own hair in House Aurenthin.

Who would let others so close for such a long time under most circumstances, anyway?

Yet here I was, feeling secure and rather enjoying the process, as Mourn showed me without speaking how he washed his hair in sections, using a light touch and barely any scrubbing. As each length was smoothed, lathered, and rinsed clean, the strands felt strong and rich between my fingers. Quite alive.

And Goddess help me, heat crept into my face as I watched the droplets falling from his ivory horns and the tips of his ears, not to mention the small streams running down his naked shoulders.

Hoo bua …

"Thank you, Sirana."

He took that clean, black rope from me, methodically wringing it out from the top down.

"Would you like to plait it before I band it up?" he asked, turning an eye on me. *"Or shall I?"*

This isn't fair.

"If you trust I'll do it well," I said, lifting both hands, wiggling my bare fingers.

He smiled, a fang poking over his lip. *"Of course you will. I have watched you braid your hair many times."*

Jael cleared her throat. *"And you never helped?"*

He met her pointed gaze. *"She never asked."*

I lifted my eyebrows. *"Would you have braided my hair if I had asked?"*

"Of course."

Damn.

"Why?" Jael asked, shaking droplets from her own hair like a bird caught in the rain. *"To play 'Palace?'"*

Now Mourn huffed a breath. *"Not at all."*

But he didn't explain it to her, and I wasn't sure that I could make sense if I tried. I was halfway down the length, twisting idly, when she said, *"I can take over. Get it done, give you a break."*

"*I'd rather you not, Jael,*" the half-blood rumbled.

"*Hmph.*"

Their tones made me tense. Jael hadn't yielded and Mourn spoke in a way that only made her try harder. I braided faster, but once my Sister rose from her knees and left the stream's edge, I knew it didn't matter.

"*You're not his servant, you know,*" she said, crouching at my right shoulder and reaching for the tight weave above my hands. "*You don't have to —*"

"No, wait —" I blurted.

"*— do this for him.*"

She grabbed and tugged on his queue, jerking his head in trying to lift the rest from my reluctant hands. Mourn bolted to his feet and whirled, knocking her over with a well-placed strike of his forearm.

"*Ow — oof! What in shit fuck … ?*"

Mourn positioned himself between Jael and me as she sprang to her feet, his half-finished queue competed with the swing of his tail. His broad back covered my view, but the dangerous, white spines laid flat.

"*I told you not to touch my hair, Red Sister,*" he growled.

"*No, you didn't!*" she protested. "*You said you'd rather I not!*"

"*Then you understood. You simply didn't care.*"

"*Care about what? I didn't hurt anything. I was just saying Sirana doesn't have to style your hair for you!*"

"*And yet she chose to, lacking all threat and magic. You are not in the Deepearth anymore. Can you not watch and learn?*"

"*Not when you're displaying your ass and teasing her even after ending your pit-damned Bargain!*"

He inhaled deeply, but I couldn't see either of their faces when he spoke. "*Apologize, Jael.*"

She sputtered. "*For what?!*"

"*For yanking my queue without permission or understanding the insult, and for dismissing Sirana's choice.*"

"*Oh, fuck my spinnerets, if I shouldn't have stepped in to question Sirana, then don't speak for her now! She isn't as sensitive as you are!*"

Shit.

Mourn backed up a step, nudging me to move with him.

"And stop crowding her!" Jael added with intense aggravation. *"You're not her bodyguard, remember? You wanted 'freedom,' right?"*

Why were all the words I wanted to say stuck in my throat? *Stop it! Let it go. We can't go into Manalar like this —*

If I'd had the chance to wet my throat to speak my mind, all breath hitched to a stop when Mourn summoned glimmering weapons from his bracers.

"Catch," he said, tossing her first one sword, and then a shorter one, giving her the chance to grasp them both.

"What the f — ?" she started.

I peeked out and glimpsed her admiring the edge of the first sword in her grip. Then Mourn summoned his sliders, and I jumped.

Fuck!

"Would you rather apologize, apprentice?" he asked. *"Or take an impromptu lesson in persuasion?"*

"You're fucking jesting," she snarled in disbelief. *"You wanna call all the Ma'ab here and give away our position over a hair tug and wreck the element of surprise? May your hubris choke you first!"*

"So be it," he said.

With a slider positioned for defense, Mourn pushed me out to one side. His half-plaited hair followed the white spines before sliding to the right of his tail. I made sure our eyes met.

~*Don't, please!*~ I pleaded.

His eyes glinted with something warm but feral. *Trust me.*

"Apologize, Jael," he said aloud. *"I insist."*

She scoffed. *"Make me, half-breed."*

"To first blood, then."

Fuck.

I hurled my body away and to the side when Jael did the incomprehensible thing: she lunged first. Mourn *could* have ended it right there. He had the opening, had drawn her in, and she leaned too far forward. I saw him turn his blade and come from above, aiming for the back of her neck. My protest stuck in my throat as denial froze me in place.

His wrist turned smoothly, striking her with the flat of his blade. Jael grunted at the contact, pivoted out of easy reach, and touched the skin of her nape.

"*No blood,*" she sneered.

"*Pity,*" he replied. "*I suppose you must try again.*"

"*Pah! Should have knocked me out when you had the chance.*"

The tip of his tail flicked playfully. "*Then I wouldn't get my apology.*"

Jael lashed out, her blade caught and sliding away at the hybrid's direction. His return swipe forced her to yield ground as he blocked her sight of me. Instead of irritating her, it helped her focus on the one beast in front of her.

"*Will you make them sing?*" she asked, her teeth bared as she tossed her chin toward his weapons, holding hers ready for a competent defense.

"*You want me to?*" he asked, showing a particular twist and twirl with his left slider, sending a faint hum into the air. He also unlocked them both and began moving freely.

Jael growled, backing up, "*You'll take a limb off!*"

"*You could apologize.*"

She pressed her lips tightly closed, signing, *Pucker sucker.*

Mourn's tail snapped to one side in a way I couldn't read; an instant later, he pushed her farther on her heels with his superior reach. She scuttled deeper into the trees and brambles, where it took true form and skill for the hybrid to be able to thread his ever-shifting weapons between them. Jael grinned as she rolled and danced as she pleased with stationary blades.

Mourn's response was to cut her off from slipping around three different tree trunks, one after another, protecting his flank and startling her more than once. I noted when she realized the difficulty of predicting his reach and movement at any given time. Growling audibly, she kept darting in close, blade swiping at empty air.

I crouched beside a stouter tree. *Good luck, Sister.*

Memories of the Cloister and the *dorji-ka* blended before me. Then, as the hum of the Dragonblood's blades rose louder, however, I began to wonder whether Jael was right about the risk of attracting the Ma'ab.

Mourn drawing this out suggested otherwise — unless he *was* choking on hubris somehow.

A familiar thrum sounded behind me on my left side, and I jerked my head to look. Graul had slipped into my view, resting atop the boulder closest to me. His hazy red eyes stared at the movement deeper in the trees, his purplish throat pouch partly expanded, vibrating gently.

The drake seemed to concentrate on his *Maekrix* while I tried not to be distracted by humming and clashing blades or my Sister's cursing when Mourn slapped her a second time with the flat of his blade, this time on the thigh.

"That will leave a bruise," Graul churred, irritating me at once.

"What good is leaving her limping?" I growled.

"Wait."

"What if they get louder than this? Or he starts casting?"

Graul's throat vibrated. "Why I came with you. No one will hear. Or feel."

No one would feel … ?

Even I could sense the magic accumulating like an invisible fog flowing along the ground, and my saphgar had begun to warm underneath my armor.

Not just martial sparring anymore.

Foliage rustled and bark tore as Mourn bounded off two trees from an abrupt charge, springing high enough to land behind Jael. Before she could spin around, he'd slapped her backside with the flat of his slider, which *infuriated* her.

"*Fyaegr!*" she hissed, pitching the smaller of her blades with full intent to injure.

Mourn swatted it out of the way, and looked as surprised as I was when the impact of metal on metal sent out a burst of light and sound like a small thunderstone. I flinched, flickering lights obscuring my vision. A moment later, Jael scrambled away then flat-out ran, gaining distance with one blade. Mourn kept on her as blind as we were, with no intent to give her a rest.

I murmured, "Did she do that?"

Graul purred. "What you think we been doing these four days?"

I saw spots for a while but eventually made out green leaves and shadows of the trees. Shifting closer to Graul's boulder, I watched behind some cover as Jael was cornered next to a dense cluster of trees. She spun around but Mourn twirled his sliders on either side of her, speaking a Word below my hearing.

She shuddered and dropped her second blade to cover her ears with her hands.

Shit.

Nothing but the whizz and hum of the metal in motion and the shifting vegetation beneath their feet as Jael jumped sideways over his blades skimming low toward her ankles, required to retreat and leave her last blade behind. She tried to circle about and reclaim one of them, but the Dragon's son made her work for that, punctuating a near-miss by cutting down a young tree in one strike.

At her peak frustration, she grabbed a fistful of dirt, threw it in Mourn's direction, yelling, *"HETHA!"*

That small handful blossomed into a brown cloud obscuring everything in my view.

"Suaco," Mourn responded, satisfaction reverberating in his voice.

A wind came up, immediate and strong, to brush the cloud of dust aside. Jael brandished the small blade in her hand and came close to tagging Mourn's side before he dodged.

His tail slapped her wrist with an audible smack, and I winced when she dropped the blade again. It looked like it hurt; her hand wasn't working properly.

"See?" he said. *"You have learned more than you think."*

"Wasn't this about an apology?" she snarled, flexing her hand, using her boot heel to drag the blade handle closer.

"Or first blood, yes."

Driven hard and fast by Mourn's long arm and longer weapon, Jael ducked low from the first slider then jump over the second before reclaiming her weapon.

Graul's breathing had changed, and I glanced to the side, worried for a moment. The drake had extended his wings up, the clawed tips trembling, though he did not intend to fly. A response to the shiver passing through him.

"What is it?" I asked.

"She draws on him," said the drake, sounding pleased. "Else he'd have caught her in exhaustion by now."

The little one sounded like a proud instructor.

Mourn may not have "caught her," but she remained weaponless. He changed his tactics then, keeping her on intense defense until she was nearer to wearing out. Jael could tell; she snarled another Word and pitched a rock at his brow with an intensity and strength I didn't know she possessed.

Mourn dodged it, barely, and the stone took a chunk of bark off the tree behind him.

"Come on!" she taunted. *"Closer for first blood!"*

The Dragonblood grinned, cutting down another two young trees in his pursuit, shouldering them to block her path. The noise of each fall had me checking to see if Gavin was coming while Jael stumbled more often but slipped through the makeshift fence.

Mourn provoked her to use her last weapon, her boot dagger, but she missed with that as well. With nothing left but her hands, she had the good sense not to try bleeding his nose with her fist.

Finally, Mourn swept in close in a successful feint, spinning around and tripping her with his tail.

"Ungh!" she grunted, landing on the ground.

Graul stretched out his neck, and I leaned forward as the Dragonchild planted his sliders vertically in the ground. He pounced immediately, grabbing Jael's leather armor, one hand at her neck and the other at the small of her back.

He hauled her up.

"Hai!" she barked as her feet left the ground.

The half-blood slammed her chest-first against a sturdy tree, one small enough to encircle with her arms. First, he wedged his knee between her thighs, supporting her crotch as he lifted to keep her off the ground entirely. Only then did he release her armor to force her arms forward, crossing her wrists on the far side of the trunk before gripping them with one hand.

He paused, tongue flicking out, his mouth opening.

Shit!

I sucked my breath when Mourn champed Jael's nape with his teeth and she emitted a startled shriek, failing to get free. My ears strained to listen as Mourn removed his teeth and growled.

"First blood, Red Sister."

My heart throbbed in my chest. I believed him from the way his tongue flicked out and across one fang, tasting something, but my eyes could spot no red upon her neck from here. I'd have to look closer.

Meanwhile, Jael's muscles trembled visibly with fatigue, her chest stretching urgently for air. Strands of her short hair had fallen into her face, sticking to the sweat. She groaned roughly, and I didn't miss the shifting of her hips as she essentially sat on his thigh with her legs dangling.

"Apologize," he demanded, loud enough for us to hear. *"You have listened well enough to hold a line briefly, but you must listen in all ways if your blades would sing for you. Anger against life itself will not save you from it; believe that I know and understand."* He took a breath. *"Blade Song is not for pupils who attempt to cut brick walls with their swords."*

Once, Jael might have considered this a weak finish for the victor, even considered getting fucked in her current position a better outcome than apologizing. I knew well how fighting like this aroused us in the Cloister; she would get pleasure out of yielding.

Yet today ... I witnessed her think twice.

"Can I learn it?" she asked. *"The Blade Song. No lies."*

"You can learn it," he answered. *"It is your heritage, Aurenthin."*

She released a shuddering breath, licking her lips. *"Sorry."*

He tilted his head. *"For what?"*

"For pulling your hair. Without asking. Won't do it again."

"Hm. Apology accepted."

He released her then, and Jael staggered on quivering legs, staring around her as if recalling where we were. She sought me, next, and I lifted my hand to make it easier. Mourn grunted and motioned for her to go while he summoned to him the blades he'd tossed to her to fight, making them vanish into his bracers before pulling his sliders out of the soil and doing the same with them.

With Jael in front, the two retraced their path of destruction toward me and Graul. At some sign I missed, the shadow drake released the air in his pouch, and the subtle vibration, which *had* been continuous, stopped.

Suddenly, I could hear all the evening crickets and frogs. Gavin still hadn't come to see what the noise was about.

Huh.

As Jael drew closer to me, I recognized the shine in her eyes; thus, I wasn't surprised when she leaned down to grab me by one shoulder and kissed me. I smiled against her lips; she was sweaty and gritty, the wash in the stream undone.

"No further," Mourn said as a simple command, sounding unaffected. If he'd ever held an erection in those loose pants of his, he'd kept it well hidden.

Simple or not, my Sister jerked in surprise. *"What?"*

"No distractions of that nature," he said. *"You can't afford to expend the energy."*

I couldn't help the sardonic face. My bodyguard had cut out encounters of "that nature" close to the actual fighting the last time we'd gone to Manalar. Although, I couldn't recall one touch meant sensuously once the missions began.

"But you can't —"

"Yes, I can," he cut in. *"Keep listening, apprentice."*

Jael showed irritation but with less insult than she would have earlier. A good sign, maybe.

I exhaled and kissed her softer than she'd done me, touching her cheek with my fingers. *"I agree. You* are *my Sister, but this isn't the Sisterhood. We shouldn't forget that, and we have much to learn about the Surface."*

Jael's face was stuck in a grumpy pout as she leaned back to look at the half-blood. *"Hmph."*

I expected her to start the friction all over but, for the second time that evening, my Sister surprised me.

"*If you are our Lead, but this isn't our Sisterhood, what do I call you?*"

I blinked. A fair question. I'd asked the same thing and had received "Mourn" only after several tries.

The half-blood smiled wryly. "You may use Graul's name, *Maekrix*, if it suits you. I could use *Dalkrix*, if you wish."

Graul snickered but churred in approval. I showed my confusion, waiting for a translation. After a patient gesture from the To'vah-krav and his companion, I received it from Jael.

"*Maekrix*," she repeated. "*Leader.*"

"*Mm-hm.*" Mourn motioned her to continue. "*And?*"

"*Dalkrix*," Jael pronounced it with care, "*means 'learner.' *"

"*Correct. Although Graul and I don't use them, Maekrix and Dalkrix are formal companion Words. Speak either using your aura, as you've learned, and I will be able to sense where you are.*"

She crossed her arms. "*If I'm not already under your tail.*"

Mourn chuckled, and I smiled proudly.

Jael noticed and tossed her chin my way. "*And her?*"

"*She is Sirana, of course. The name she's given you.*" His smile remained. "*Or, if you need another name with the young races, remember Janshi.*"

Nothing Draconic, obviously. I didn't mind; I wasn't the learner in this particular struggle, much as I had been in others. I held the feeling of relief that a stubborn obstacle had finally been shifted.

"*Let us return to the Deathwalker,*" Mourn said. "*No need to mention the fight. He'll not have heard it.*"

I thought so.

Graul appeared smug as his *Maekrix* lifted him up

"*What about your hair?*" Jael asked, clearing her throat to add, "*Maekrix.*"

He paused, sharing a considering look with the drake. "*I would prefer Sirana help me to plait it at the cave.*"

She exhaled, waving her hand at the disheveled length. "*It's covered in dust again.*"

"*I shall take care of that.*" His eyes shifted to me. "*May I have your help,*

Sirana? I enjoyed how you were caring for it."

My face heated up unexpectedly. *"Uhm, yes. Certainly. If you can get it clean, I'll use my comb this time."*

He smiled, showing fangs. *"Thank you, Kiabil."*

The warmth rushed from my face into my chest. *Oh! I **do** have a Draconic name.*

Managing a wavering smile, I motioned toward our camp. On the way, I was reminded to check Jael's neck for puncture wounds that might be at risk of festering and need one of Shyntre's few remaining pellets.

"Just a scratch," she grumbled.

I found it; a mark from one canine, more than a scratch. But it had scabbed over quick and clean.

Hmm.

"I'm fine, I'm fine," she said, waving me off. *"Come on, we're falling behind."*

Watching her move ahead while I brought up the rear, I recognized a lightness to her step which I hadn't seen since our training on the Surface — when we'd been doing anything else but the language lessons. Her familiar spring had returned.

Maybe we'd figured it out, finally, the four of us. Just in time for a harder fight, too.

I hope this works.

I hoped to be free at the end of it.

CHAPTER 18

OUTERLANDS OF MANALAR, PAXIA

I SPIED THE MA'AB ENCAMPMENT BEFORE MOONRISE. A LONG AND DISTANT string of flickering fires and steady blue spots glowed at the base of Mount Sonai. Subtly teeming shadows clung like moss to the damaged wall of Manalar, the abrupt end to the broad swath of northern fields trampled by horse, Human, and cart.

Graul remained safe at the cache. Although he'd hidden it well, by the time he'd rested long enough then tried to move, I could see the pain from the multi-day journey.

Mourn had made sure his drake was tucked warm in a soft nest he'd built from weaves of grass, lined with down feathers taken from a recent kill, and covered with a small blanket. With food, water, and resources nearby, the two had exchanged quiet words in Draconic. Jael had shaken her head when I glanced at her. She hadn't understood what they'd said.

"*Dalkrix*," the little drake had said with a mischievous grin. "Follow *Maekrix* and try to pick your trouble, not have it pick you."

Jael had rolled her eyes though her smirk held a hint of acceptance, even fondness.

On our way to this first vantage point, our focus had shifted to Gavin, who walked the ground with us, Nightmare following steadily behind him. The Deathwalker had made no remarks since we'd stopped — on our behavior or otherwise — but had worked one task after another on either mundane camp chores or preparations for tonight.

One of those, like it or not, was joining me and Jael in a surface-level mindlink so Mourn could speak to all of us through my pearl, thus assuring both our silence and overcoming language barriers.

Always stop with cover above you, if possible, Mourn choosing relatively easy shelter beneath a large tree and crouching down, peering ahead. *Reports all mention the skin kites. They are ubiquitous and will look like bats in the light of the Moons.*

Gavin agreed. *Most any animal could be a sentry. Look for signs of death or decay if they get closer.*

And I will teach you to recognize such things sooner than that, Mourn said, eyes landing on Jael and me. *This is within both your abilities.*

My pale ally agreed. *Some will be blatantly obvious. Some may be like Nightmare when she is well-fed.*

We had to take them at their word.

Although too early to see signs of Guildsmen from the redoubt, Mourn silently pointed out those of men who had never left the area when the Dwarven gate had been collapsed. Through the days of recovery to the arrival of the Shaegoth and our days of speedy travel, the sheer distance and speed in which reports had come to Talov from this unseen group boggled my mind.

They must be relieved, thought the half-blood. *Exhaustion is high and the risk of discovery is great.*

Our first mission tonight was to leave signals for the loner spies to withdrawal to a safe distance, to confirm that their relief had arrived. At the same time, we'd be doing some counting so that, later, we could give Krithannia and Isboern forewarning as they sailed in on the Big Ker.

I will trace the perimeter and leave the signs, Mourn said. *At the same time, I will carry two bloodstones to send what I see and hear through the pearl. Sirana, keep Gavin mindlinked so he may experience them firsthand. Jael, keep guard over them.*

We hand-signed an affirmative, even Gavin as he learned our simpler signs. With the Guild's spell, his Dark Sight almost equaled ours in the night. Once Mourn slipped away, however, we couldn't track him.

Test, please, said the Dragonblood.

The Deathwalker and I had taken maintainable positions by the time Mourn quickened the bloodstones which would speak to each other and to us. Refined in two ways from those I'd shared with D'Shea in Sivaraus, the scrying spell did not have to run its course before we accessed the sound and sight they absorbed, and the two senses would be synchronized. Thank goddess.

What can you see and hear, Deathwalker?

Within my mind's eye, I beheld a view as if I was passing through a forest, not sitting in a grass patch. The brush around rustled from other animals but not Mourn.

I see a young sapling ahead which splits into a near-perfect fork. A banded forager just growled and ran from you.

Excellent, the half-blood responded. *Well done, Sirana.*

I shivered as their exchange passed through me, somehow more intimate than when Isboern had anchored us at the redoubt. I certainly felt present compared to communing with D'Shea and Gaelan.

… Gaelan.

Mourn fell silent, and the view sped up as he approached the massive camp in the distance. Several times, our vision winked out before reappearing at a new vantage point. We'd been warned he would be shadow jumping. The leaps made sense to cut down distance, so I anticipated them even as my stomach lurched, threatening queasiness in a jolt or two.

The number of large-boned skeletons standing on their own unnerved me at first, though I wasn't sure why. The cleanliness and better maintenance compared to living soldiers? Their bones had been scraped clean, pale in the rising moonlight, and lightly armored around vulnerable joints, though they all lacked helms. Their hands grasped sword, spear, or scythe in a manner suggesting they remembered how to use it. None of them bore shields.

Confirming two hundred fighting skeletons, north side, Mourn reported. *Unused from the first assault, kept in reserve. The Manalari reported this many had also been present when the wall broke, tiring the defenders before the living* invaders breached next. Blunt weapons only; don't bother with arrows or blade.*

I know, Gavin responded to my smirk.

Once past the pristine skeletons, Mourn counted far fewer living men compared to the corpses recently brought to their feet. Their armor was damaged and flesh slowly decaying. Although my nose breathed in the familiar smells of a night in the trees, I recognized, somewhere beneath the mindlink, that the Dragonchild scented air much fouler gliding across his tongue like a vaporous slime.

These fallen warriors were kept in clusters like docile livestock and away from the tents and the horses. The size differences alone confirmed both Ma'ab and Manalari dead among them, no longer opposing each other but meant to fight on the same side of the battlefield. The Templars had been warned about this, but we still expected a strong reaction from the survivors upon first sight.

The Ma'ab no doubt counted on it.

Upon leaving those informal corrals behind, Mourn's centuries of experience as an assassin and spy became apparent as he gauged the perimeter of the living center of camp. A slew of animal skulls set upon banner poles or large sticks had been lodged into the ground, their vacant sockets pointed haphazardly in all directions and varying heights. Some skulls were pale and plain; others decorated with muted yellow and reddish-purple strips of cloth; many bore visible carvings granting the impressions of magic runes.

Our infiltrator passed too close to some to be prudent.

Not all are intended to sound an alarm, Mourn answered my concern. *And those that will aren't the ones you think.*

Gavin intensified his concentration on those skulls and their markings. *Those scratches are gibberish.*

And they lack any taste of magic, the half-blood agreed. *The plain ones or the ones with simple strips of cloth may have runes hidden from sight, for they will let their maker know if something of interest appears in range.*

Assuming the 'maker' lives to focus upon it, the death mage added.

Indeed.

I smirked. "Something of interest" certainly had, and yet the Dragon's son skimmed past them like one invisible, unseen to those Ma'ab he passed among the tents, carts, and crates. I had a first-hand observation of how he had followed Gavin and me for months, where we'd sensed the mercenary only when he'd let us know he was there. Each time had had something to do with his marks, Kurn and Castis.

Choosing his pathways and his timing to leap between shadows, Mourn located and counted the number of horses and wagons, weapons and supply tents, mess halls, and officer tents where the magical supplies would be stored. I could tell Gavin was making notes.

All numbers far down from their first arrival, Mourn said. *Plenty of evidence that a host left several days ago with slaves and spoils. Their camp has shrunk to less than half the original size.*

All information we'd heard at the redoubt, but good to confirm.

Our infiltrator approached those larger officers' tents, the material stiff and drab grey. The banners at the door flaps echoed the colors of the strips upon the watch skulls, the designs elaborate. Enormous, tattooed men appeared in almost every glance, forcing Mourn to hide or to alter his direction several times.

Eventually, we made out the pattern. Pairs of Hellhounds stood guard at each bannered tent, whether a light showed inside or not. One tent light from inside revealed the silhouettes of three additional Hellhounds inside, completing the typical "pack" we should expect, each bearing the distinctive spike chain wrapped around one arm. These men watched over smaller forms who might be talking with another, have their head bowed over a desk, or reclining on a cot. We counted seven tents with these elite guards, with another eight similar sized ones interspersed without them.

Interesting, Mourn thought.

Plenty, Gavin agreed. *Anything specific?*

You can't smell it, but there are at least two women per tent, sometimes more. The pungency of some bring a slave to mind.

Or the maknuut.

Possible. In addition, five of the dark tents lacking Hellhounds are also empty, and I detect old blood.

I sensed a base satisfaction from Gavin. *The Shaegoth.*

Agreed. No Hellhounds in the five kill sites. I want to examine them.

By all means. I will speak if I see something of note.

Like the spider at the center of a web, I maintained our mindlink, witnessing all they saw and discussed around me but making no sound myself.

Each tent had been stripped of anything valuable — scrolls, codices, components, chests, clothing, weapons — leaving behind a stained cot with soiled bedding. The tents themselves remained, their purpose undecided while none took shelter there.

What might they have done with the bodies? Mourn asked.

Gavin considered. *It depends. Sent them north with the returning host, perhaps. Collected them into a single place for better preservation and ritual. They would not have burned or buried them, not allowed carrion feeders access. Not unless they meant to somehow hide the deaths of their betters from Ennikar, which seems foolish and pointless.*

Mourn hummed in thought before leaping through several shadows, spying on areas whose vantage points turned my sense of direction around before long. I didn't know what he searched for, but my ears practically perked up when he deeply scented the air.

I found her, he thought quietly.

Her?

Found who? Gavin asked.

Amelda Troshin.

My thoughts darkened, recalling the conversation she'd been having with her sire about enslaving me to the Northern Empire.

Mathias had told us she would be here.

Gavin must have sensed something as he tilted his head. *Hm. Shall there be another mysterious assassination tonight?*

Tempting, my former bodyguard admitted, *but that is not the mission, and I don't know whose lives we'd be risking. If harrying becomes part of the plan, or if she bears value as a prisoner.*

Very well.

~Can you lay eyes on her?~ I broke in, making them pause.

Probably, Mourn answered. *May I ask why?*

My lips stretched. *~I want to see what she is wearing.~*

He doubted that.

Reasonable, Gavin seconded. **We might know what rank or house she claims, if any.**

Mourn acquiesced but chose his next Words and path to approach Brom's daughter with care, taking pains to avoid a gleaming wolf's skull set at an inconvenient place: where the footprints were fewest. He was still and silent for long enough, my mind began to drift ...

Until all went black.

I jerked my focus to where he'd ended up, crouched behind a short stack of crates *inside* one of the dark officer tents.

Even here, five animals' skulls had been posted on sticks or rested on raised surfaces. They appeared to be from the smaller hunters that sought the nut finders and burrowers, but I couldn't tell which were active, beyond one which glowed subtly, lifting an oppressive void enough to see the bodies in their full color.

Mourn didn't move, counting twelve women and two Hellhounds. The men stood, alert, and only two women rested in cots; the rest bundled upon the ground, some lucky enough to claim a spot upon a large travel rug spread to create half a floor within the confined space.

One small woman hissed something to another close by.

'Too hot here,' Gavin translated.

I smirked as the complainer stuck a pale, ritually scarred foot out of her bedroll as if to manage her body heat better.

Maknuut, my grey ally said with certainty. **Five mages from the slum caste.** He paused. **I wonder, do the officers attempt to protect their servants and power sources from another attack? Interesting ... **

This seemed a personal interest to him, and I had no answer beyond what we saw. I overlooked them in favor of one familiar to me.

There, Mourn said, inhaling slowly. **On the rug in between the two ranking cots.**

Interesting position to find her in.

Amelda's black hair had been neatly plaited and bound closer to her skull, mimicking the hair of the women in the cots, which vaguely resembled helms in shape. The drab bedroll appeared borrowed but in good shape. I couldn't recall detail during the chaos of the last battle as these sorceresses in grey armor had ridden on the backs of their tattooed bodyguards. Regardless, I knew that I had *not* seen their hair flowing in the wind.

Amelda shifted inside her bedroll, turning over so that Mourn could see her face. Eye closed, her brow was furrowed, her mouth downturned. A small complaint slipped through her lips, either her body or her dreams discomforted. She sniffed, groaned …

And sat up, dark eyes wide, her pulse showing briefly in her throat.

"*Fahdi*," she squeaked before gulping down the rest.

Amelda peered around the dark tent, aided by the soft, blue glow of a propped skull. Mourn didn't drift one claw's point as her eyes paused on his corner of the tent before moving to the women in cots and on the floor. The *maknuut* who'd been complaining about the heat was awake and aware Amelda had seen her.

After deliberating, the young noble reached for her boots, striking the bottom of each to dislodge any creatures which may have crawled in before emerging from her bedroll to don them. She dressed fully but for the cloak she unfurled from beside her, giving a shake before draping it over her arm.

Cris-ri-phon's daughter stepped off the rug and onto the dirt toward the Hellhounds, both of whom watched her in silence.

"*Shika*," said the *maknuut*, also sitting up as Amelda traipsed by. "*Oyin tihab?*"

Mistress, where do you go? Gavin translated.

The half-blood Ma'ab did not answer, until two men twice her height blocked the exit with their bulk. She looked up, and I could imagine the indignant scowl.

"*Daani akruj*," she demanded.

Let me out.

They did not, though neither spoke as the slum woman awoke a second who could have been her sister. The two began donning their boots.

Amelda noticed and scoffed at their intent to join her. "*I have much stronger magic than them*," she said, suppressing a snarl. "*I do not need them.*"

"*They stay with you*," one Hellhound responded, his expression barely changing and his voice a low vibration which did not disturb the sleeping officers. He and his brother-in-arms shifted their weight as if to open the way only on that condition.

Amelda looked beyond them to the outside. "*Very well*," she grumbled. "*They best not be slow.*"

The men opened the flap for the three women, the night sky peeked into the tent as they passed through. Mourn backed out undetected but had lost sight of them by then; he began tracking their footprints and scent through camp.

~*Did she sense you?*~ I asked, finally. ~*Is that why she woke?*~

I did nothing intentional, but I believe so.

~*Really.*~

A mental shrug. *She may be sensitive to unusual auras from living with her sire, whom she lost to this war days ago.*

Goddess, he was right.

~*Do you think she saw him fall?*~

If she didn't, plenty of other witnesses who did.

Which meant her hatred of Gavin and me would be white-hot, and she might know about a second Davrin at the Temple. Mathias's warning in the prison niggled me.

"*Kill her for me, Red Sister. ... She hasn't given up on you, I promise. If you don't, you'll be sorry.*"

I already was.

~*Perhaps we should kill her,*~ I suggested. ~*While we have the chance.*~

Not yet.

Mourn's response was firm and final. His desire to know what she sought in the middle of the night tremored through the uncommon threads connecting us.

~*Sigh. Alright.*~

The two *maknuut* slowed, hesitating at a subtle line in the ground. The soil and grass had been churned by creatures much heavier than them.

"*Come!*" Amelda barked.

"*Mistress,*" said the one in the lead. "*We enter here, we asking for it.*"

"*Then stay here. I shall not be long.*"

The slum of Ennikar scratched her scarred scalp through lank, tangled hair. "*Mm. You be 'til morning, if not having care in those rows.*"

The young noble smirked. *"A pity.* *Won't the new commander be so disappointed you let that happen?"*

The *maknuut* watched Amelda pitch herself forward onto the uneven ground, cursing under her breath before tugging her sister's sleeve and hustling to catch up. As soon as low, male voices floated through the air, they practically attached to her elbow. Amelda wrinkled her nose and hissed insults several times, but it made no difference; they stayed close.

They've entered the infantry camp, Mourn said. *Skimming the border. Moving fast, no eye contact with those awake.*

~Huh. Are they at risk from their own men?~

Their scent and body language say yes.

At risk of what? Gavin asked. *Dying?*

*No ... *

When Mourn hesitated how to say it, I grinned and filled in for him. ~Mating, whether they want to or not.~

The Deathwalker made a face. *Oh.*

A few soldiers had begun to follow the three females at a distance but Mourn did something with his aura as he passed by which gave them serious pause, granting Amelda time to slip from view.

~You're helping her?~

I would see where she intends to go, not wait out a gang rut.

The wiser option, of course.

Amelda led us to another pocket of Hellhounds amid the fighters. Ten giants stood around a field table with an orange lantern in the center, with strange shapes placed upon a ragged piece of parchment. When she raised her arm and spoke to prompt their attention, I was startled to see one familiar head above the rest.

His eyes lifted, his face showing no surprise — no emotion at all but for simple recognition.

Memory struck from the first time I'd met those eyes.

~*Kreshel Divigna ...* ~

Amelda had gone to meet the Eternal Hellhound in the middle of the night.

CHAPTER 19

I dare not get closer, MOURN SAID, *unless we would attempt to assassinate him in the middle of his men and his camp.*

Seemed foolish *not* to take the opportunity despite the risk.

And yet ...

Amelda approached without fear, the cowering *maknuut* in tow. Unlike the trek in, none of these Ma'ab men appeared to be contemplating her cunt.

When all looked to Kreshel for guidance, he said something brief and low which we couldn't hear then moved away from the table to approach the noble. The others broke down the parchment and objects before Mourn could study them, a process seemed expected regardless if this interruption was brief or not. They dispersed to take on some other tasks.

Plenty of shadows surrounded Divigna as his men moved away. Someone who used them to transport himself small distances would have had options ...

Why do you hesitate? Gavin asked, leaning forward. *What do you see?*

I will try to show you. Sirana, please open up more.

I didn't know what this meant at first, then became aware of his stronger tug on our psionic link, similar to when we'd been on the boat.

He was drawing me closer, voluntarily; all I needed to do was allow it.

Then, suddenly, my sight changed. Threads of colors began to outline certain figures, Divigna, Amelda, and the *maknuut* included. Dim at first, then growing vibrant, intense, until I could see mage auras as clearly as the Dragonchild in peak focus. I stared with awe, without knowing how to interpret the patterns and designs of a living world.

Gavin, however, knew.

By the Grey Lady, what … ? he murmured, uncharacteristically revealing shock as he studied the Eternal Hellhound.

I gave him what time we had, holding my focus until the threads of colors began to unravel from the sheer volume of other details which flowed in. Mourn followed as Divigna stepped away from the main path with Amelda and her entourage, the half-blood's attention on evading detection while using the best angles to observe and listen.

The Deathwalker volunteered nothing about what he'd seen, and I didn't break the delicate balance as the four Ma'ab stopped underneath a supply shade. Amelda ordered the two slum women to keep watch at the front corners while she stood with the large man in the darker shade near the rear. She craned her neck up, her tongue on the cusp of a crucial conversation.

Hold, wait, and listen.

"*Any hint of the skin hunter from among your eyes, Wargan?*" Amelda launched without introduction or hesitation.

Slowly, Kreshel shook his head. Said nothing. He never blinked.

"*What of the sacred pool? Have the Grey guardians left yet?*"

The Hellhound tilted his head as if questioning whether to answer. If she didn't know this from one of the officers sharing the tent already, I was surprised.

Amelda hissed with impatience. "*Your true superiors are dead and somehow silent. I am the only one who has met this Deathwalker and his black Elf ally! Speak to me as you would one of them.*"

"*Out of their presence,*" he stated, his deep tone level.

"*Yes, and the lieutenants recognized me in your presence. The only way to move forward. They speak over me and each other despite the threats of inaction.*"

They crave control yet do not listen and know nothing! Your men are paralyzed, Wargan, and I can help. I insist we go over your report again without *their interference.*"

She paused. When Divigna offered no outward reaction to an argument I wasn't sure should persuade anyone, let alone him, she pressed harder. "*I can grant you a better chance of bringing success to your hunts, and I must find the soul blade. That is my legacy as the Daughter of the Deathless One. We must turn over all stones left to us. Speak freely with me.*"

After several beats, the Hellhound Wargan nodded, a slow bow of his hairless, decorated head. He'd accepted.

"*So,*" she prompted. "*The Grey guardians.*"

"*Still present,*" he answered.

"*And they answer to the Grave Mother and, by images uncovered in the Temple, we know why. She was worshipped here first and has blocked the Ascended from claiming the true power of Manalar out of spite.*"

The Hellhound shrugged massive, marked shoulders. "*The guardians do not speak. The only appearance to me is that something has been left unfulfilled.*"

Amelda seemed miffed at his refusal to speculate but took his direction. "*Unfulfilled. Regarding the Deathwalker or the Shield Defender?*"

"*Unknown. Most likely the Walker, given what you know of him. Possibly both.*"

"*Why do you think this, Wargan? You weren't granted the chance to say before.*"

He grunted. "*My last eyes witnessed that the Defender summoned the Grey guardians.*"

"*What?! But the Deathwalker is the servant of the Grey!*"

"*The Walker destroyed the Bishops' control, opening the rift which summoned the Malok. The Defender knelt to pray in its waters.*"

Amelda paused, in denial before forcing acceptance. "*So, both may as yet return, despite the days' silence since the killings.*"

"*Agreed. The army's assault won our gods the city, but a magical pact from more than one faction keeps the central jewel protected.*"

"*More than one,*" she repeated, tapping her chin. "*Including the Elves who have appeared. The pale and dark ones at once, but so few.*"

"*The opposition brought forth their divine feminine with masculine guardians,*" Divigna stated like this was absolute. "*An exact counterbalance recognizing the strength of Our Vermillion Lady.*"

The sorcerer's daughter sneered to hear such an opinion of us, enough for me to chuckle about if he hadn't also confirmed our visibility and value as targets.

"*What are your thoughts on these feminine powers of our enemy?*" she asked slowly, curious but contemptuous.

"*I have none,*" he said. "*They do not matter in my objectives.*"

I believed him, and Amelda refined her question.

"*Would you capture them alive or kill them?*"

A question which spoke much about the productiveness of recent meetings if they hadn't sorted out this much.

Kreshel Divigna closed a fist, the first unconscious motion he'd made. "*Commander Vo'traj passed on a standing order from the Third to capture Elves alive and bring them to her. This is still in effect.*"

Brom's daughter seemed to think about how close she'd been to that achievement and what it had cost her. Her mouth turned down, tightening as a flare-up of strong emotion gave her pause.

"*Vo'traj,*" she repeated, an acid reminder.

"*Not found,*" answered Divigna as if she'd asked the question. "*Not her or the Hellhounds with her.*"

"*Hmph. Perhaps they encountered the same 'masculine guardianship' that my father did.*"

"*Possible.*"

"*What of her slave, the demon Elf?*"

"*Nothing confirmed, though one report suggests he may be inside the city.*"

What?

Amelda appeared discomforted. "*Has he been released?*"

"*If Commander Vo'traj is dead, then Vesram is released.*"

She cursed, staring at his chest tattoos. "*Who else knows his complete name?*"

Divigna shook his head once. "*No one both in camp and alive.*"

"*Then nothing will keep him in check if he lingers nearby.*" She blinked at a sudden thought. *"Could he have been the assassin? With the restraints gone?"*

The lead Hellhound shrugged, granting no real indication of likeli-hood or whether he cared. *"Him. The Deathwalker. The Guild. The black guardian. Too little is known."*

"How could a half-demon have prevented their Vis from speaking, though," Amelda countered herself. *"Unless he learned far beyond what they knew ..."*

She paused, lifting her eyes as Divigna waited without comment. *"You have known of him a long time, haven't you, Wargan? How long?"*

"Since before you were born, mistress."

An obvious rote response for a man who should have withered long ago. The honorific softened the dismissal as Amelda hesitated to push him for a number.

"Does Vesram fear you?" she asked instead. *"Or any here you know about?"*

Divigna stared as her confusion shifted to wariness. She shifted half a step before he spoke. *"If he has no mistress and will not leave, best we kill him."*

"No!" she protested without thinking. *"No, there must be a way to draw him in!"*

"Not without his name, mistress."

"What about the black witch? I mean," she corrected herself, *"the Dark Elf? Would she attract him if we captured her? I heard ..."*

Amelda stopped at some chill in the air.

"Heard what?" Divigna asked.

"I-I heard we once had the mother, and that was how we caught him. He would not leave his matron."

A long pause. I wasn't sure if Mourn could sense my nausea, but my concentration wavered.

Divigna's voice grew quieter. *"Who told you that?"*

My stomach lurched as the Ma'ab noble verbally squared her shoul-ders. *"You know who my father is ... W-was."*

"The gods kept the deathless one from knowing the demonblood existed."

Spoken with such brittle, crystalline certainty that Amelda hesitated. *"Well, uh ..."*

"They hid the demon son as they sought the soul dagger for him. Again, when

he returned to conceive you. So, who told you?"

She broke loose from freezing up. *"I have said! M-my father!"*

"When?"

"As the siege began," she said. *"H-he visited me. One last time. He must have seen Vesram in the Commander Vo'traj retinue."*

Divigna did not look convinced, and I doubted whether Cris-ri-phon could have dug up a century-old story so quickly from a war camp in the mental state he'd been in. He'd only begun to be suspicious about that at Brom's Inn while he'd been waiting, setting the trap for me.

Amelda had been dodgy around the question then, too.

~She's lying,~ I told Mourn. *~She must have a contact who told her about Vesram before I arrived at Troshin Bend.~*

He rumbled a mental acknowledgment.

"But you mention the soul dagger," Amelda continued to Divigna, a clear distraction or a return to topic. *"Do you know who has it?"*

I stiffened as Divigna dipped his chin once in an affirmative.

The small, dark-eyed noble showed her surprise. *"You do? Tell me."*

"The 'black witch' with the Deathwalker has it."

"How do you know this?" she demanded, not hiding her irritation.

"I saw her with it. And one of my men was killed by it."

The pale woman's face could not become any whiter; she turned green, instead. *"Y-you … saw her? When?"*

"During the evacuation."

"How did she escape if you laid eyes on them both, Wargan?!" she snarled. *"Did you let her go?"*

Something *I* wanted to know, too, but the Hellhound stared distantly, the same as he had from the riverbank. Amelda's body language suggested she did not wish to let this go but had no way of forcing him to answer when he chose not to. A strange dynamic, given he could intimidate her enough to compel her to lie to his face but also choose whether to discuss a topic or not, and she could do nothing about his choice.

~If nobody remains to control Vesram after the Shaegoth assassination,~ I thought to the others, *~could this be the case for Kreshel Divigna? He cooperates with these lower officers and nobles as it suits his objectives.~*

Agreed, Mourn answered. *He has stated part of those objectives stem directly from the Third.*

~The Third what?~

The Third Ascended, Gavin interjected. *Called the Divine Physician, to whom Kreshel Divigna almost certainly answers.*

Oh? asked the Dragonblood, like he tested the death mage. *Why so certain?*

Because of what you showed me of his aura, Gavin replied, betraying a thread of disgust. *The Physician made him, I am certain of this, and she used Elven essence to do it. This is why he lives to breed a century later. He is a violation of the natural cycle of Miurag, life magic harnessed into an unnatural form by a death ritual.*

A whimper arose inside me. ~You mean, the Priestess?~

Standing before us, or what is left of her, Mourn said, apparently satisfied with the Deathwalker's deduction although I sensed him hiding his own emotions. *It makes sense for Divigna to bring any Elven captives to the Physician. Now we know what she might do with them.*

Part of my geas thrashed like a fish in a net, twisting so tightly within its throngs that it snapped in the depths of my mind. I gasped in thought-less pain, wordless fear dissolving and leaking like pus. Our connection wavered as I wanted to collapse and curl up in a ball.

"Why won't you speak?" Amelda demanded, checking around them, her agitation growing. "What happened? How did Sirana escape yet again with Soul Drinker?"

Still, no answer.

Then, "Perhaps you should return to your tent before dawn, mistress."

"I shall report your confessed failure to the Third if you don't find her," she threatened.

His mouth twitched, barely a response but large enough to make her growl.

"Very well, Wargan, know this. She is also pregnant but not with a demon child like Vesram. She carried another Elf, pure."

Her words punched me in the gut. I couldn't focus on them but still heard her snide play to rock the heavy man's composure by spilling my secrets.

"*Say that she returns at all, and you see her. Capture her as you are required. Would you allow your brothers to take their turns on her? Hm? Would you try her fit? I can only imagine the damage that would cause. Care to explain how you lost for the Physician only the second mother-child bond discovered in a century?*" She paused only to twist the dagger, as if she knew I was watching. "*Though you could sate yourself on one of the other Elves, if you bring her to me, first. I can check for you. If her womb is empty, perhaps you can impress the Physician with a catch of four.*"

Ah, Goddess, I was going to be sick.

The last vision I saw was Divigna's icy posture cracking as he reached to pluck Amelda off the ground, tucking her under one arm. The *maknuut* women broke their cover and ran after him, sticking to his elbow across from their noble's kicking feet.

The warrior, in no hurry himself, took long strides across the disturbed ground to lead them out of the infantry section of camp. Mourn didn't have to help to keep the women unmolested this time.

My focus unraveled when a psionic headache roared in to throw me out of my trance. I pushed the other two away, got them out of my mind before my body rolled belly toward the ground. Braced on my elbows, I retched nothing but bile into the grass.

"Sirana!" Jael exclaimed, kneeling beside me, opening her waterskin once I coughed, the heaving slowed. "You are here? Speak!"

"Here," I confirmed, a cold sweat beneath my clothes and a warm spot on my chest from the pendant.

She helped me up, and I accepted a drink. By then, Gavin was aware and composed, if he'd been disquieted by the abrupt finish at all. He reached for his pack and tools.

"We stay?" Jael asked, baffled as she picked up the bloodstones we'd dropped.

"For now," Gavin said. "It's safe enough."

She looked out and around for any sign of Mourn.

"He is in the camp," I rasped, sipping water, my middle jumping in startled protest. "I couldn't ... hold it anymore."

"Discussions became rather personal, didn't they?" Gavin muttered, opening his book to begin writing.

"Personal?" Jael demanded. "How?"

"We found Amelda," I said, placing a hand to my skull. "The Ma'ab daughter from the inn where we met the Deathless. As Mathias Briar warned us, she wants revenge against us. She would send the lead Hellhound," I quieted on that word, "um, she would send Divigna to capture you and me alive."

"Hmph," she rolled her eyes. "Surprising you, how?"

One corner of my mouth lifted. "I suppose you had to be there."

"*Been* there," she reminded me, grousing.

"You were lucky the Inquisitor hadn't the time to determine what they had," Gavin remarked, scratching his pages, "and made only a blunder which Sirana and Mourn could mend."

" 'Only?' " she repeated.

"Indeed. Another of you wasn't so fortunate."

My Sister scowled in silence, and I almost heaved. The inside of my head pounded, persistent and numb around the edges, such that I couldn't tell if this was the aftermath of the geas, the mindlink, the pearl, or the bloodstones.

Or all of it.

"How you say?" Jael probed, growing impatient with us both. "Another. Where? When?"

Despite my weakened state, I tested myself. My shaken geas.

"The Sathoet captured a century ago is freed," I said carefully. "His Priestess ... was not. Sh-she is ... um, dead?"

Though uncomfortable to say, I *had* said it, and Gavin expanded for me.

"Her body likely is, given the time passed," said the scholar without looking up. "Her Vis is present but in a condition which has no natural path. Not to its birth nor its death."

Jael shook her head, rubbing her face and grumbling in Davrin before ending with, "What say you? Do not ... grasp."

"I do not fully understand it, either." He lifted dark, Ma'ab eyes to her once he'd finished his cryptic note. "But in the Eternal Hellhound, I witnessed a crushed yet potent aura, jagged in its forced flow, yet flush with true life. I saw Human and Elven at once, yet the Ma'ab body bearing this aura is no half-blood."

Jael's mouth opened, eyes blinking widely.

"The Sathoet's matron … *exists* in some form," he finished, peering down at his notes before adding something else. "And I *must* know how this was done."

I swallowed. "And how to undo it?"

"Kill him," Jael said, opening her palm to the plain solution.

Gavin's dry expression tugged a surprise laugh out of me before he grunted and explained. "Unique patterns of Existence often require unique conditions both in which to exist *and* to unravel. I suspect this may be the source of his persistent presence over the decades. It's simply not so easy to kill the Eternal Hellhound, and for good reason. We do not know the unique conditions which created him."

My Sister seemed to understand, grudgingly accepting. "Same that it not easy to make you stay down, Herald. Unique pattern."

"Hm. Less common, at least." Gavin ducked his head down, dark hair falling into his face to hang above the grimoire, as if to pull the curtain and end the interaction.

Jael rolled her eyes but took the hint; she wasn't curious enough to persist in his "existence" anyway. She turned to me. "You said the Sathoet is free. You sent the beast west, I thought?"

I shrugged. "Vesram may not have obeyed me. He ran down the passage which led to the canyon. I went up to the Temple looking for you."

Her arms crossed, Jael used that as a salve for her irritation and discomfort. "You know his true name?"

I shook my head. "No."

Thank Goddess, because he'd tried to give it to me.

"No one knows," she said, echoing Amelda's concern.

"Correct. And he may have stayed around here after the battle."

"To pay cost?" she asked, shrugging at my baffled expression. "For one century in chains. For ... ah ... forging? Yes, forging his matron into a smelly man while he watches."

"Insightful," Gavin muttered, making a note.

Jael glanced his way, arms tightening. "That why *I* would stay. If Ma'ab army stays."

I had to agree. Vesram would have less reason to assume we would return, especially when we'd told him to meet us at the Ley Tower. If he was here, it would be for another reason.

Sirana?

I turned around, searching for the source of that cautious touch. ~Mourn?~

Are you alright?

I winced. ~Better, I think? Headache. Hungry.~

Softly, he chuckled, and Jael started looking for him.

We have time to eat but should move soon.

~Did something slide sideways after I lost the link?~

No. We had already pushed the spell beyond its typical capabilities, yet neither of you fell unconscious. Well done.

A shadow moved in my left periphery, and Jael took position between us, one hand on her sword hilt. Mourn stepped out, and my Sister exhaled.

"You," she grunted.

"Glad I did not surprise you," he replied, approaching our small cluster.

"What happened after the spell ended?" Gavin asked bluntly. "You apparently did not stay long."

Mourn shrugged, nonchalant. "Divigna carried Amelda to her tent and left her there. The low-caste women made it and were relieved of responsibility."

"The officers did not wake?" I asked.

The Dragonchild shook his head. "Quiet and cooperative was in Amelda's best interest once they got close enough. She gave up the struggle and none made enough noise. She returned to her bedroll."

"Officers heavy sleep," Jael commented, disapproving.

Mourn's tail weaved as he considered other matters. "Important to note that Amelda expected Mathias to return. Either she never knew he escaped to the redoubt or ..."

"She knows but anticipates his return if his will is not truly free," Gavin finished. "One seems as likely as the other."

"We will include that in our report. He may try to escape his cell if he can't bargain his way out. Let us travel west and south and check for signs of allies nearby. By dawn, we shall study Manalar itself beyond the Ma'ab camp."

"But first, food," I reminded him.

His gaze drifted to my belly, a darker thought passing through him before he smiled with fang poking out. "Of course. We have time to eat, and I saw edible roots nearby. Good for long rides and marches."

"Where?" Jael asked, suddenly interested.

"I will show you, and how you can roast them for us with a Word."

Jael's mood brightened beyond either of us, not having heard the particulars of Amelda's last threat. Mourn demonstrated but let her do the digging and washing, and then the magic; he stayed near me the entire time.

Bargain or no, he said after giving my headache time to ease, *I will not accept the fate Amelda spoke of for you or Jael. If I cannot watch you every moment or prevent all harm which may come, please believe I will not abandon you, your Sister, or your unborn to that corruption.*

I watched my Sister delight in her new-found smokeless cooking method, shaking her fingers from the heat as she worked to peel one before handing it to me. I smiled, accepted, and bit into the stodgy vegetable as I replied.

~Thank you. Truly. But ... ~

But?

*The Ma'ab have threatened me this way since the day Kurn grabbed me and pulled me onto his horse outside the Ley Tower. And I believe Mathias that, given enough time, the Ascended could track Soul Drinker if they somehow found it for Cris-ri-phon. So, if I go in there to Manalar ... I ... I want ... ~

Mourn waited patiently for my answer.

~If it cannot be over and done forever, I want it to be decisive.~

A mental nod. *What would 'decisive' look like to you?*

~Amelda dead,~ I answered. ~Kreshel Divigna ... undone, however he was made. Jael ... Tamuril, Krithannia, each of us alive and free. Vesram leaving Manalar for good to head west for the Ley Tower. The Ma'ab defeated and the grey guardians giving way for Isboern to cleanse the pool, so that he can ... can ... ~

So that Will might free my will and grant me *all* my choices upon the Surface.

Heard, understood, and acknowledged, the Dragonchild said, standing patiently next to me. *I am here to do all I can to help make this happen.*

~Of course you are.~ I smiled. ~You've been waiting four hundred years.~

Not just waiting. Planning.

~Impressive planning.~

His brief amusement faded. *Not exactly. I remembered, spied and planned from Augran, and yet I never knew these final hours would look like this, Sirana. Your presence alone hammers in the lesson. Our best laid plans shall be rendered moot the moment conflict truly starts. Beyond that ... ?*

I swallowed my root, accepting another. ~Do what it takes to win. All futures means nothing if we lose.~

You understand.

~When it's my fight, yes. I didn't see the first battle as my fight, I suppose. I only wanted one thing, threaded through the throngs at your lead.~

Mhm. But now?

~Like it or not — and I don't — this is personal for me, as it has been for you these decades. I know what I want it to look like at the end.~ I mentally shrugged. ~Fortunately, it looks like what you want.~

Mourn grinned, accepting a cooked root from Jael and confusing her with how many teeth he seemed to need to show her.

And that, Kiabil, is why we do not need a binding contract to fight together in the same mess. I only ask that, despite all impulses you've learned below, despite the secrets I keep for your sake and others, believe what I have said. I will not leave you or Jael or the Naulor Elves in Ma'ab hands. Not under any circumstances.

My hunger had eased after consuming my third root, and I made sure Jael at least took a second.

~I believe you, To'vah-krav. Thank you.~

CHAPTER 20

THE NEXT DAY, WE TRAVELED ACROSS THE EMPTY FARM FIELDS NORTHWEST OF the city's mountain slope with great vigilance and care.

The skulls on sticks had disappeared, but Ma'ab skin kites fluttered above our heads in a periodic pattern and packs of Hellhounds would appear at random. The tattooed bands were startlingly quiet on foot; often we watched from sparse distances as their bald heads and marked, naked shoulders slipped through the grasses and underripe grains like fish in a river.

Fortunately, Nightmare could drop to her knees at a speed that would cripple a living horse while Gavin hid her aura and his own. Mourn did the rest so long as Jael and I cooperated.

Through the daylight hours, Mourn led us closer to any structure made of stone, be they rocks stacked upon each other at a crossroad, a border fence, a cart bridge, or a burned-out cottage. His tongue usually told him within moments whether to search deeper for Guild sign.

Reprisal is here, he said after our sixth checkpoint. *Wolf directing three teams of four. Barely a few hours old.*

My brows lifted. ~Wow. And after his losing so much blood to that Greylands barb.~

Mourn's mouth set between a smirk and a grimace, his thoughts closing off to leave a brief gap in our mindlink. He looked around, pointed ears open and on alert. After a few moments, he returned.

Bear is on watch. The rest are holed up sleeping.

Wait, who has the pearls? Jael blurted into the tenuous connection.

I recited this easily. ~Wolf, who is the Hand. Bear, Hawk, and Crow, who are each a Focus, heading a trio of Flames.~

Flames?

~Mageborn Guildsmen.~

She chewed her lip. *Uh-huh.*

~And one more with Krithannia on the boat: Torch with his three Yungian brothers.~

She rubbed the knuckles on her right hand with her left palm. *I think I remember Bear. He can take punches. ... A lot of them.*

Chuckling, the Dragon son used his hands to make a notable change to the arrangement of scratched rocks tucked inside a broken hearth, adding an additional five markings with his claws.

What is your message? my Sister asked curiously.

That 'Shadow team' is here as well, numbering five.

I resisted counting with my pointer finger. He must be counting Nightmare. ~Heh. Not the 'Dragon team'?~

The corner of his eye crinkled before he rose from his crouch. *The Yungians claimed that name, and I'll not confuse their signals at this stage.*

~I see.~ I paused, frowning. ~But if Bear heard you just now, why would Reprisal come back here to check this message?~

A shrug. *They wouldn't unless they must retreat. This is for those yet to arrive whom we've not met but are Guild-vetted.*

~Oh.~

"Kites," Gavin said, black eyes peering up at what I would consider an empty, blue sky yet we didn't question him. We found cover yet again, masking our life signs until they flew out of range.

"Two or three per mark," Jael grumbled in Davrin.

She was right. The Ma'ab must have swarms of these things to cover so much land with such frequency at all times of day and night.

"Whose eyes do you suppose are watching?" I asked Gavin.

The Deathwalker shook his head. "No way to know. It could be the lowest *maknuut* slaves, a series of rank and file, or a bored officer in her tent."

"So much death magic," my Sister commented.

"Such is valued by their gods."

"It remains to be seen," Mourn said, "how close the boats may get before the Black Army sees them and mobilizes. Before then, let us approach the southwest wall near the quarry. See if the refugee tunnel is further damaged, rebuilt, or merely guarded."

I signed my readiness to continue. After Mourn had damaged the mansion's foundation to fill the cellar and block the escape route, no chance the victorious Ma'ab could not have found the rest of the passage through which a thousand Manalar citizens had escaped their grasp.

Especially given the position from which Divigna watched us.

Standing on the *opposite* bank from his own army.

He followed us.

The Eternal Hellhound and his pack had to have come down by that same quarry, scaling the mountain well ahead of the moment we'd been surrounded at the mansion's courtyard, long before the jump-port spell Mourn had cast to get the rest of us off that crest.

With no stories among the refugee of attacks or captures on the way down, this one Hellhound pack must have moved on speed and discretion alone. They neither killed nor abducted, going against orders.

Why?

Grasping the horror of what Kreshel Divigna was, believing Vesram could have been nearby, I didn't know the answer.

I feared how we might find out.

By the earliest evening, Mourn's keen senses and Guild experience located two of the three hideouts for Reprisal without giving them away, despite swarms of kites continuing to scout for Ma'ab enemies.

Bear huddled with our friendly guide, Tak, multilingual Kil, and another I didn't know and, later, we found Wolf with Hawk's team. They were glad to see us, and how oddly *reassuring* to meet these known, determined faces and exchange our collective knowledge directly. The Guildsmen seemed to feel the same before their Hand confirmed it.

"Thanks for sticking with us in this," he said, his familiar, light blue eyes scanning each of us as if seeing us anew. "I think this would be a fool's run otherwise."

Mourn smirked. "Likewise, thank you, Hand of Reprisal. You know better than most. When plans fall apart, fight to win."

Brian Wolf smiled in a disconcerting manner. "Always. The sun shines brighter after a long night passes. We only need to last long enough. It'll come."

"Indeed."

We left shortly after, looking for Crow's team as we scouted out the quarry. We spotted them wide awake and staked out watching the steepest, most naturally reinforced part of the city wall above the quarry. So intent were they that we got close enough that I could read some of their hand sign.

What holds your focus, Crow? Mourn asked through his pearl from a distance, letting me listen.

Gah! Prick ... Right, Shadow. Living up to your moniker.

I try. Recently found others whose natures allow them to be better.

Yeah, we heard the talk. The tense, dark-haired Guildsman signed reassurance to his teammates and breathed in. *Something took out the top five commanders in camp, and the Ma'ab couldn't find them. Couldn't do shit about it.*

Is that what has your attention?

Not exactly.

Tell us anything you want Isboern and Krithannia to know.

Crow peered at the south wall lined in moonlight. *So, uh, you've seen the half-filled camp out north where they first came in from the mountains.*

We have.

Well, they didn't all abandon their tents and head north. A fat portion of them *have taken up houses in the wealthy districts with Manalari captives.**

Expected.

Yeah, but it also means any way the Manalari can hope to enter, there are Ma'ab on both sides ready to pinch. Meanwhile, they're fattening themselves up while they can, and I can't help but wonder if these are their elites or something.

Hm, I do not think so. We confirmed both the officers and lead Hellhounds are in the camp yesterday. Laid eyes.

Yeah? Weird. So … the luxury-sniffers are the lower ranks, and the doyen don't care? They'll stay in a smelly camp with less food, worse bedding, weather, everything?

Mourn looked at Gavin and summarized the question for him. The Deathwalker gave it some thought.

"I hazard to guess the 'doyen' do not eat or sleep as much as the lower ranks," he said, "and the powerful death mages have muted sexual urges. Exceptions are the Hellhounds. These men are enhanced by mages but not mages themselves. They must need substantial sustenance and have clear reputations for taking spoils of war yet do not claim the best of the city. They remain in the camp or roam around watching empty fields."

Mourn repeated that through the pearl.

Well … fuck, Crow muttered. **So, their better forces have discipline, the ones deliberately working on less to stay sharp, while the hedons with all the appetite are their blast fodder?**

A reasonable conclusion based on observations.

Guess that neuters our plans, the Guildsman grumbled. **Wouldn't do enough damage to the right assholes.**

Correct. And the Guild plan is to wait and watch, not interfere in their doings or harry them. Not quite yet. The watchtower is no longer occupied by friendly eyes, and you would spoil the Captain's approach.

*Yeah, yeah … *

Altogether that night, with Reprisal's help, we pieced together a fuller picture of the City on the Mount. Starting with the vastly shrunken camp clinging to the northeastern side, the breach in the wall had been expanded to a gaping gateway. This led into the poorer side of Manalar, lowest in elevation and farthest from the Temple, where most structures had been damaged in the battle and used for rough storage or short-term shelter.

From there, we confirmed the Ma'ab had taken over the wall on both sides of the massive break. Big men of the Far North walked or stood guard along the slanted stone pathway high above the street, rotating watch at each of the regular city gates which, by all appearances, seemed functional.

Within those walls, the highest and most wealthy sectors were packed with people forgoing the illustrious architecture of the Grey-touched Temple for the comfortable surroundings once belonging to the Manalari nobles. That occupation grew less dense as they approached the middle of the city, remaining quite sparse until one reached the opposite wall and the string of cisterns underground.

We spent the rest of the night climbing through the canyon to confirm instead of circling to approach the main camp. The Ma'ab jealously guarded this precious source of clean water, blocking the exit we'd known about with stones piled high.

Was not expecting that, Mourn thought. *They used that northeast passage to pitch the final battle in the river, correct?*

Correct, Gavin confirmed.

They sealed up the only way in from this direction. I wonder why.

The answer appeared once we got a look at the scraggly grounds and dirt roads on the slope between the city wall and the Raguruos Mountains. We stared for a while before I asked the question.

~Why so many ... um ... ~

Shamblers, Gavin supplied. *Animated but unguided.*

But not collected like those standing in camp, Mourn pointed out. *Is this not a waste of their magic?*

I think it an aftereffect of the pool surge and does not drain their concentration.

~If that's so, why so many bodies walking around on this side?~ I asked. ~There aren't any on the quarry or farming sides.~

Gavin shrugged. *Path of least resistance from the streets, I suppose. They could be summoned without keeping them in camp, and a death mage may choose to look through their eyes at any time if they've done any preparation at all.*

His tone suggested that a death mage worth their rations should be prepared for such things, yet I wondered. These bodies seemed so aimless.

Could you summon them, Deathwalker? Mourn asked.

Now?

No, not now. But later?

*If other death mages are between me and them, I am likely to get into a contest of wills and capture a handful at a time at best. Unless ... *

I waited for his continued thought when Jael nudged me and pointed across my nose.

Dead beasts, she signed.

I turned my head. She was right; among the shamblers were a small herd of wandering, dead horses that had stood up after the battle. Belatedly, I realized these were what had caught Gavin's attention in the first place.

Just in time to watch him roll up his sleeve to expose his long, pale forearm.

~Uh-oh.~

Deathwalker, what are you doing?

If we have nowhere to go the rest of the night, he said, offering his flesh to the sharp teeth of his remade mount, *then I may be able to plant a seed of advantage when the seizing of these bodies begins.*

Won't they sense your blood? Jael asked.

Not until I use it.

Nightmare opened her misshapen muzzle, biting deeply into Gavin's arm, chewing to coat her sizeable tongue and drench her lips in thick, black ichor. Jael grimaced and looked away while Mourn weighed the wisdom of this.

Gavin's icy pupils glowed in the moonlight. *If you would, Sirana, use the talisman to guide her into the fields. Instruct her to bite every shambler and horse corpse she can reach before dawn.*

I understood him perfectly but blinked. ~Me?~

Yes. Do not rush. Be subtle.

So the blood will be inert, Mourn clarified. *You are just spreading it around.*

*Yes. And Sirana's method of command creates far less of a magical ripple than *my direct guidance.* *

  **Hmm. Very well.* *

Thus I spent the final hour before dawn puppeteering Nightmare from a distance, willing her to open her jaws and use those carnivorous teeth on flesh animated like hers. Once I had to creep closer to extend my range in our last remaining moments and Mourn helped to camouflage me. In my hurry, however, Gavin's mare twisted her neck too much and seized the narrow neck of a weak man, stopping short of decapitation.

  ~Oops.~

  **It is alright. No one noticed,* * Mourn said. *Keep going, not much longer. Good work.* *

Jael heard all this, keeping her peace as well as her watch. When he praised me, however, I detected a shift of interest and warm pleasure — a sensation like when we'd been on another mountainside with Rausery.

  Encouraging.

I wasn't sure how much of Gavin's blood was required for what he intended to do, but I crawled to the blind and casually drew Nightmare out of easy line of sight of the wall before guiding her to her master. At once, the death mage seemed especially interested in how much stagnant blood his mare had smeared on her mouth from the other bodies. Gavin began collecting as much of the mixture as he could from her muzzle onto a wrap cloth.

  **Excellent,* * he said, cleaning her thoroughly before pausing in contemplation.

I half-expected he might bring the dark stained cloth to his own lips or touch it with his fingers. He just stared at it.

  **I would meditate on this, if possible,* * he said, finally.

Mourn set about finding us a better, defensible place to hole up in enemy territory. We would wait until later in the morning to cross the canyon and gather any last intelligence from Reprisal. Isboern and Krithannia were expected on the Big Ker that next day, and we planned to speed toward them on four legs to bring our collective report.

Once we'd all squeezed into a tight blind with wards of protection set, Gavin became senseless within moments, black-nailed thumbs pressing firmly into the corpse blood from his mare's lips.

Jael and I exchanged curious glances but took Mourn's signal and settled for some Reverie while we could. An outbreak of violence approached though I could not know exactly when.

Plan while we can but fight to win.

And may the Templars and their kin be able to look past the Ma'ab captives to see their own goal, or they'd lose the chance to reclaim and balance their sacred pool. *We'd* lose that chance, and much more. At minimum, I would wait longer to be free, with no choice but to let Gaelan go.

Wherever she is.

THE NEXT MORNING, BY THE TIME WE RECROSSED THAT CANYON TO REVISIT Reprisal in their new hiding places, we ran out of both food and the opportunity to hunt or gather. I'd eaten the last of it long before we left the quarry behind us, unable to press Mourn's and Jael's gentle refusals to share.

You eat it, they signed though their stomachs had to be empty as mine.

Once we reached some forested land both level and far enough from the watchtower, Gavin and I mounted up and Mourn shifted his body once again to carry my Sister. Awkwardly ignoring the pops and cracks and a brief groan of pain at first, Jael took hold of his harness, swung her leg over, then gasped in surprise, wrenching her hands away and tucking at her chest.

"*What the fuck … ?*" she hissed.

"S'rry," he replied, teeth gritted.

"*Your scales burned through my gloves!*"

His tail whipped in agitation. "*Need a few moments.*"

I pressed my lips together, reaching through the pearl. ~*One of the recent changes?*~

Not really. He craned his thick neck, meeting my gaze with one eye, his thoughts brusque. *Just worsened. Makes it harder to shift.*

~What has worsened?~

I will be fine. We must go.

Reluctantly, I let it go.

We began at a lope, crossing ground underneath the trees and far from the road or the river. Gradually, we stretched out to a swift but sustainable pace. We wouldn't slow until midmorning when we saw three sail boats large enough to carry the last of Manalar's army. They were anchored near the reaching bank of a long bend, resisting the current as they waited for the insights we'd brought with us.

Krithannia! Mourn called the moment he was in range.

Oh! You are here.

Intensely relieved.

The two Naulor and their Yungian guards stood amid tall grasses with Captain Isboern and the Templari. Behind them, activity picked up aboard the boats, and Paxian men lined up at the rail as word of our approach spread in ways unseen. The Pale Elves and their Guildsmen sprinted to meet us, though the heavily armored men hesitated to follow at first.

In a glimmer of light, Isboern disappeared and reappeared ahead of everyone else, barely giving us distance to stop before running into him.

"Were you seen?" asked the Captain, blue eyes vibrant, his wind-reddened face tense. "Or followed?"

"Neither," Gavin answered, "to the best of our knowledge."

"Perhaps better to assume you were."

"Why?"

As the Templari started jogging to catch up to their leader, Krithannia and Tamuril drew close enough to read their concern; it echoed the Godblood in front of us.

"What happened?" I asked.

"We received a message from the redoubt," Krithannia panted. "At dawn. Mathias is gone from his cell. We've checked every man. He's not among us."

Icy skyfire struck my gut. *No.*

"They don't know where or how," she continued. "Or exactly when. None of the other prisoners escaped, and no one was hurt."

Mourn growled low as his lip curled, and he said what I was thinking. *The Ice Lord.*

The Guild Mistress grimaced. *I pray not. We have no sign or contact, just the message of the skin hunter's disappearance.*

With no conflict or traceable method. The man would have had to pass through five checkpoints, Krithannia, and he is no sorcerer. It must be so after his intrusion into Sirana's Reverie.

A gentle mind-tug coaxed me to look at Isboern, and then he was there with us. ~*We sent Tamuril and Pilla ahead to scout our path. How strong is the link between Mathias Briar and the Ma'ab? Strong enough to be a concern?*~

Jael and I glanced at each other as Gavin beat us to it, answering bluntly as always.

We witnessed Amelda Troshin ask Kreshel Divigna if his scouts had spotted Mathias Briar yet. They are expecting him. He may have arrived in the two days since.

Isboern's shoulders slumped as his Templars gradually closed the distance behind him. ~*So. Quite strong, and of immense concern.*~

Unfortunately.

The psion looked between us. ~*Are we fighting this Infernal as well? If he has helped them to recover this prisoner of war.*~

Unknown, Mourn answered, his tail hovering stiffly above the ground. *It depends entirely on his motives and the particulars of his agreements.*

~*On which we can only speculate. Very well, we shan't waste the time. Last question. Do you know if the Infernal competes for the pool?*~

He does not want it. The Dragonchild surprised all except Krithannia with the certainty of that statement. *Of this, we can be certain but do not ask me how.*

~*Alright. Then I think it is best we move now. The boats are unloaded, and it won't take long for the last men to disembark. The merchants will sail upriver to Rithal's Bridge, and we will make haste down the valley. I think if we have any element of surprise at all, it won't last the day. We have a few places to retreat to if necessary, but none between here and there to lie in waiting.~*

Mourn's black tail weaved slowly. *You want to march directly and attack.*

~We want to arrive as loudly and brightly as possible to draw out the bored and anxious among them. Our aim is to reduce as many of their remaining resources as possible outside the walls *before* we must fight within them.~ The blond man smiled grimly. ~Unless you have a better plan, legend?~

Not with Mathias missing, Mourn admitted, meeting Krithannia's eyes and sharing her nod. *Prepare to march with your men, Godblood. We will catch you up on what we know, and the Guild will escort you to Manalar.*

Chapter 21

Gavin and I rode Nightmare beside Captain Isboern and his four top officers. We had swapped places on his horse, him sitting in front and me behind, able to peek over his shoulder if I stretched up. Our group muddled in the middle of loose formations while most of the Templari led the march on foot.

The last handful of battle mages in shining armor rode with a small cavalry comprised of thirty destrier mounts with barding which the Clans had been able to gather and bring aboard the boats. I watched them separate from the host and drift north to do their own scouting, though not too far from the Captain, as we all expected trouble sooner rather than later.

Mourn and Jael had vanished from my view but remained in range of the pearl on my earlobe and the one hidden on Krithannia. For the second or third time — *The fourth?* — I sat as the center anchor, bridging communications at some distance between the Manalari, the Guild leads, and the "elder races."

Krithannia and Isboern had asked me, of course, but in a way that made plain they didn't have an alternative for this keen advantage if I could not continue in the role that I'd fallen into during the first battle.

~Why do you think I've been practicing ever since?~ I'd thought, glad for

the two days' psionic rest after Mourn had spied on Amelda and Divigna, but also for Isboern's stable and reassuring mindlink.

~*I am grateful, Sirana,*~ he'd replied. ~*We know we are greatly outnumbered. Passing orders and accurate information faster than the Ma'ab can move is the only way we might overcome this and spare us the unnecessary loss.*~

I exhaled. Necessary or not, loss there would be.

We traveled on the north side of the Big Ker, passing over and around constant rolling hills and through tall, mucky grasses buzzing with insects and rustling with hungry birds in pursuit. Soon enough, the river turned away from us, disappearing to eventually join the stream passing out of Mount Sonai's southern cliff face. Meanwhile, we continued in broad sunlight toward the Mount's long, western slope.

All of us who had hoods wore them over our heads despite the summer heat, regardless of which city they hailed from. Certainly, I needed the extra shade for my eyes, while Gavin's face retained an ever-shifting gradient of grey, never as pale as he was at night but sometimes approaching my skin tone.

While I could not be certain who might be Guild amongst the marchers, a couple groups among the five hundred Manalari chattered enough to hear their language, their laughter brash or strained to cover their nerves. Most were quiet, waiting through what must have been an interminable stretch of time to see if today was the day something would change, breaking the exile they'd faced that first night after retreating through the Dwarven gate.

Would it be enough?

Do you mean to present yourself at the front? Mourn asked Isboern, somewhere unseen. *If you intend to be 'bright and loud' in your approach.*

~*That depends on the Ma'ab,*~ the Captain said. ~*I am easily recognized with the Sun Shield, but I can protect myself and those around me. The invaders must prove themselves capable of attacking beyond the front line if they wish me to forgo any exchange with their leadership.*~

About that, Gavin interjected, *their leadership is in shambles, so we are not sure exactly how they will respond to our arrival, or who it shall be, though they expect it.*

Isboern offered the death mage a rueful smile. ~*Yes, Krithannia informed me that their chain of command had been ... shortened significantly.*~

The smirking glances exchanged between Erik, Imran, and Sohl told me Isboern let them listen in.

~*With the heads cut off on both sides, we are left with many unknowns to rise in their place. Quite ruthless, Deathwalker.*~

Gavin's back stiffened. *Are you saying I broke some rule of engagement?*

~*I am not. This is a war, and you've proven yourself determined to spite both sides in their hubris. I would admire your clarity of purpose even if our goals did not align.*~

The Herald of Nyx grunted acceptance. *If you admire clarity of purpose, I remind you that the Hellhound leader is the one least shaken by the disruption in camp.*

~*I believe you, and I have not forgotten him or his threat.*~

A threat Isboern only knew by a fraction, for while we had told the Godblood that Divigna served the Third Ascended and would consider any Elf or strong mage a valuable capture for the lich, we *hadn't* told anyone but Krithannia exactly *why* the Eternal Hellhound had been alive so long.

I do not see it as relevant or helpful for the Manalari to know, given our speculation, Mourn had said. *Most in the Guild cannot use this knowledge in this battle.*

The Guild Mistress had agreed, though remained troubled. *Need-to-know basis, then.*

Later that day and with Kreshel Divigna brought up, I caught Captain Isboern glance in Tamuril's direction. Despite her present distance from him and the pre-determined escape plan with Krithannia should violence break out, I caught a flitting regret from the psion that his Druid was present at all.

I glimpsed Deshi in my periphery, drawing closer to Nightmare. The Yungian moved in between lines and clusters of men with paler skin than him, walking a few paces beside them until he could step toward us alone.

I frowned, and my focus drew attention from those closest to me in the mindlink.

~Where are your brothers, Deshi?~ Isboern asked with mild concern, earning a warm face from the young man as he blinked up at the Godblood.

With their charges, Captain, I swear, he answered, adjusting to the mental speech quickly. *The pale elder spirits have their defenders.*

Then what are you doing here? Gavin asked like he suspected the answer.

Impressively, Deshi met the Deathwalker's eyes. *I am meant to help guard you, Sho'shien. To learn about the Grey Maiden.*

A tricky time to be concerned about tutorship, and I do not need your protection.

Anyone can use another watching their back, Sho'shien. If not you, then I can aid Janshi while she rides with you.

Hm. That might be the better idea. Guard her, yes.

I blinked. *~Hey. Who has the soul blade, Deathwalker?~*

Which requires your target to be within arm's reach.

~Same as Deshi's dagger.~

*Which reminds me, Sho'shien — * began the Guildsman, withdrawing his prized weapon.

Blessing it a second time will change nothing, Gavin groused.

Are you certain? Deshi asked. *Has your power not grown since you lay in the sacred waters? Revived by suckling from the mother guardian with obsidian eye?*

The Deathwalker scowled at the ground while Isboern looked between them with interest.

~If you are certain it changes nothing, Herald,~ he suggested, *~then it cannot hurt. Perform the rite anyway. For morale before another big battle.~*

With a sigh, Gavin extended his arm toward Deshi, his skin turning black in direct sunlight. The Guildsman placed his dagger and sheath into his palm, giving ground but keeping pace with Nightmare. Those around us witnessed what was a familiar sight for me: Gavin rolling up a sleeve to draw his own blood with the dagger's tip. The wound wasn't large, nor the contrast as sharp as I'd seen; the black blood on black skin added only a wet gloss.

The Herald reanointed Deshi's dagger, pressing both sides of the metal to his stained flesh, murmuring in that shiver-inducing language of the Greylands. Nightmare's haunches seemed to grow colder beneath my ass, as did the air around me. If not for the hint of decay and throat-coating dust, it might have been a pleasant change in humidity.

"A drop of your blood," Gavin rasped, the eerie echo suggesting his eyes were solid black.

With Deshi's dagger held deliberately out of reach, the Yungian had to draw a second dagger to comply, nicking himself on the back of his hand. Once the Guildsman could squeeze a bright red spot between his fingers, Gavin reached down to seize his wrist, keeping us on the move as he scraped the drop up, using the clean, dull edge closest to the hilt.

"Good," he said, completing the ritual on horseback, re-sheathing the weapon, and returning it to the young death mage like he'd borrowed it to trim excess length from a rope.

At first nothing seemed to change, as Gavin had said. But as Deshi cradled the dagger, whispering something earnest in his native tongue, I thought, for an instant, his dark, familiar eyes glimmered blue.

Uh ...

Had that happened the first time? Had I just missed it?

"Thank you, *Sho'shien*," Deshi said aloud with a broad smile, bowing the best he could while in motion. "I shall mark as many as I can for the Grey Maiden."

"Indeed," Gavin said blandly. "Though don't forget to watch Janshi's back."

"I will! And yours! *Huafo*!"

I resisted rolling my eyes but shook my head slightly when Isboern met my gaze.

The Captain offered a warm smile. *~Don't underestimate one so devoted, Sirana. I've witnessed his developing magic at the garrison, and I've heard about how he confronted the walking dead to defend the evacuees on the riverbank. Rest assured, he is quick, brave, and he can use his magic in a fight. Quite different methods from the Herald, but another death mage who wishes to defend life. That is a good thing.~*

~Hm. As you say then.~

Though lacking specifics, Isboern may yet be right. Deshi had neither needed nor cared if his brothers witnessed Death granting his weapon a second blessing. This was for him, what he most desired.

I didn't know how to feel about a bua I barely knew, and so much younger, putting himself in between me and a Hellhound. Hard enough to trust Mourn with that task; at least the Dragonchild matched or exceeded the Northmen's size.

"Janshi," said Deshi with reverence, dipping his chin when we next met eyes.

I sighed inwardly but returned the bow. "Deshi. Ready to fight like a storm bringer above the Great Lake?"

"*Hai, Janshi,*" he breathed, his eyes lighting up as he withdrew his blade partway, admiring the clean edge. "Remember, always, to take the next breath."

I smiled despite myself. I might not grasp the meaning from his home, but a simple goal like that didn't need questioning.

MY STOMACH FULL, SITTING IN A SADDLE IN A LATE-DAY GLARE, I'D COVERED my eyes with my hood.

I must have dozed in the saddle.

By dusk.

The words startled me. For an instant I thought we rode upon the Midway, crossing the flat grasslands. I searched desperately for the hailstorm.

No, wait —

The Ma'ab are on the move, Krithannia said. *The two armies shall meet by dusk.*

Oh, crystalline piss.

So much for 'bright and loud,' Gavin commented. *I'd think they waited until the Sun Shield would be rendered moot.*

~Probably,~ Isboern agreed, not as dismayed as I might have expected.

~*A smart tactic.*~

So, we fight through the night, Wolf broke in, his rising intensity singing through the Dragon pearl. *Strike and flee tactics?*

~*For the Guildsmen, yes,*~ the Captain agreed, lifting an arm and sending a second thread of thought to capture the attention of the Templari ahead of us. *The Manalari will stand our ground.*

I could picture Wolf's grin. *Goal is to last until morning so you can blast their sick bones back to the glaciers?*

~*The sunrise shall come as early as he can. We shall create our own light until then.*~ Isboern stood up in his stirrups, peering around at the landscape. ~*No easy retreat. We have little time to choose where to burrow in and thin their lines into a perimeter you can harry.*~

Dread spilled into my gut. Was he jesting? Stay in the open? Fight in the dark and center of a full-bore attack? All *night?!*

Madness!

A mental tug, and then the psion's eyes met mine. ~*Time to join Tamuril and Krithannia. They will help you keep me in sight but out of view of the Ma'ab. As long as we can all link, we can force them to retreat with far less than they brought.*~

Agreed, Mourn weighed in. *We can do this, but we must be in strategic positions. Above all, communications **cannot** go quiet, or we will be split up and taken down piece by piece.*

~*And Jael?*~ I had to ask.

I'm here, she said, her mind's voice antsy but excited. *Tell us where to hit, Sister, and we'll hit hard. Give us the bird's view.*

Take Nightmare, Gavin said, shifting backward to force me to give him room, signaling we were about to dismount.

I threw my leg over to drop to the ground. ~*But — *~

Ride with Deshi, he insisted, grounding his own feet before turning to gesture at the Yungian. *It is better if I am closer to the ground. I need not see the dead to draw them. And remember, Nightmare can tear flesh off bone or kick to shatter it. Use her as your first weapon before the soul dagger or spiders.*

Huh? Spiders? Wolf asked.

Unpleasant surprise, Jael replied with a mental snigger.

Shit. This was happening.

Captain Isboern motioned for us to get moving, offering me his hands with fingers interlaced to step into. I accepted, daring not to hesitate in front of so many eyes. The Godblood boosted me up near the undead mare's withers before assisting Deshi to climb up behind me.

~*Get into safe position before they see you,*~ Isboern said. ~*Then talk to us and keep us talking. For as long as you can.*~

Communications could *not* go quiet.

Or they'll get picked off.

Piece by piece.

Shit. *Shit.*

"Take in breath, Janshi," Deshi whispered from outside the tightening net inside my head.

Breathe.

I exhaled, positioning my knucklebone talisman in my palm beneath my glove to turn Nightmare toward the distant river. Directing her into a trot then easing into a rocking lope, I guided us through the fighting men moving out of our way. My tension rose as we shed the familiar protection while still quite far from another.

If I were Mathias or Indrath watching, I would strike now.

The thought made my back itch as chatter through Mourn's pearls slowed unexpectedly. My heart together with Nightmare's hooves thudded in my ears.

~*Can you hear me, Sirana?*~ Isboern asked.

~*Ah, fu ... ! Um, yes.*~

~*Good. The Dragon son can close off excessive voices crossing the pearls if needed. He wanted to test this in case one of us must make sure you receive a message.*~

~*Got it.*~ I paused. ~*And if I must make sure one of you receive a message through the din?*~

Project my name, Mourn said abruptly, making me jump a second time.

~*Ahm?*~

Like you did when the Ice Lord threatened you.

~Ah. Understood.~

~And the same,~ said the Godblood.

~The same?~

~'Willven.' You and Tami are the only two likely to use it. I grant you permission to use it get my attention.~

I breathed out. *~Alright. Willven.~*

~You are clear ahead. Stay safe.~

Gavin's mare carried us over the ground as our shadows stretched and warped at the end of a long day. Pilla flew lower above us, circling, showing us which direction to go. I glanced tensely at the horizon but spotted no smudges which could be the Black Army.

Tamuril's falcon called my attention with a screech somewhat less powerful than her full capability, swooping into a sharp decline, her legs stretching out to land. Only as she clutched her Druid's leather-bound arm did the camouflage break to where I could make out the outlines of both Naulor sisters and the three Yungian brothers. Their coloring had little to do with it, especially with Krithannia in her city clothes, not dressed for wilderness.

That masking must be pure magic.

"This way," Krithannia said aloud, motioning for Deshi and me to remain seated on Gavin's mare. "We have a place to watch but have care what you say about our location through the pearls. Just in case."

I followed her, hiding my skepticism. When Isboern had mentioned having no place to retreat, he'd meant no defensible rises or passageways were large enough to be worth defending among the rolling landscape. Advantages existed only for small groups like ours, as copses of trees dotted the crowns and gullies among the many hills, allowing for hundreds of places to hide, scout, and ambush.

We'd start with the first two but must be prepared for the third.

The Sun touched the horizon behind us, and a deepening purple crept into the sky ahead as Krithannia and Tamuril led us up a hill on the southwest edge of the anticipated battlefield. At first, I grimaced at a height simply not tall enough to see the whole of the Manalar force, much less adding the Ma'ab to the churning chaos.

We kept climbing and another crest appeared before my eyes, then another when I believed we'd reached the top.

"Um," I began aloud, cognizant of Krithannia's warning. "Where?"

"This is the tallest hill in the area," she said, as she huffed to keep up with the Druid's long strides. "The Manalari know it is here. They call it *Miraderio*. The Lookout. The Ma'ab aren't likely to know it is 'missing' during this conflict."

Tamuril smiled as if she were finally pleased about something within this whole mess. "My sister holds great knowledge from our elders, enough to cloak the Lookout in a masterful mirage."

My mouth sagged as we attained our fourth crest and paused at last, gazing out at the land below. *Now* we were high enough to gauge sweeping movement across the fields, presuming the Manalari would indeed hold their ground.

"Isboern chose this spot," I guessed, my spoken voice sounding strange in my ears that moment.

"He would have preferred to get closer and attack at dawn," said Krithannia while Tamuril gazed out for the third time, the same worry in her leaf-green eyes. "But as the Ma'ab come to him at the end of day, *Miraderio* was our best place to halt and wait."

They had had plenty of time to strategize on the boat, so I could believe this was one of many contingencies or opening gambits discussed.

Meanwhile, conservative chatter murmured through the pearls, and my understanding allowed Isboern to hear it, too. The psion made a noticeable effort to mute the brief exchanges shared with his officers, to a point I could listen or choose to ignore, like standing in the same room but near different walls.

I paid attention once I had dismounted and released my spiders to settle beneath my hair, crouching behind brush. Ready as I would ever be. Between the Guild and the Templars, I understood and shared plans to illuminate as much of the fighting grounds as possible.

The Ma'ab will use thunderstones, and half their infantry doesn't need to see, Mourn said to the Guildsmen. *The best counters are the strongest light spells we can cast, as high in the night sky as we can set them. Expect fires to catch* and spread, but it will be less disorienting for those fighting if light above remains in play.*

And the skin kites won't be as useful, said Wolf as the first stars winked into the sky. *Might as well shoot them down or net them as we can.*

~Be cautious,~ Isboern said. ~Be sure it's not a falcon.~

Check.

I began to wonder if they would keep talking to fill the time — better than standing in agitated silence — when Gavin's distracted thought filtered into the discussion.

*The dead ... *

What?

Tension vibrated through our bonds.

Where?

To the East in the direction of Manalar, the light faded from dusky shadows, and a disturbing rumble preceded the approach of uneven lines.

There.

He must have pointed.

I see them! Wolf said. *Meat shields first, armed skeletons behind them.*

Disrespect! Erik cried out, reacting on behalf of several. *Our brave fallen are not 'meat shields'!*

The Guildsmen barked an incredulous laugh. *Some are both, holy warrior, and others are just enemies you'll have to kill again! We told you this would happen.*

~Can you usurp control from their mistresses, Herald?~ Isboern asked, a calm thought stepping in between both men.

I believe so. We shall find out soon.

~Whomever you claim, send them to our rear as a buffer for my light casters.~

Understood.

Among the mass of armored men repositioning and before any light spells had been cast, my sight had shifted in the dim. I recognized Gavin from his posture and gait alone as he stepped out front.

~Not too far out, Deathwalker,~ I said.

He paused, looking around for me by habit.

~You make an easy target.~

Hm. Noted.

Four packs of Hellhounds spotted! Bear bellowed, out of breath as he proved my point. *They skim the edges, two on north and south, moving fast. Aim is for the rear as the fronts meet.*

Was Divigna among them? My stomach clenched. At least they didn't seem to know where Gavin and Willven stood in the crowd.

~Cavalry!~ Isboern ordered with force. ~Flush them out. Drive them toward the center. Illumia! Prepare to blind them.~

Guildsmen, Mourn rumbled. *Let us put a few obstacles in their way. Watch your eyes.*

At the same time, Gavin's aura flared noticeably to Krithannia, breaking through the ambient rise of magical activity below.

Hata Ri! the Naulor ordered. *Help mask him as he calls the dead! Now!*

Twenty men broke ranks, sprinting to the front line to surround Gavin in a loose arch. They were armed and armored as battle warriors but not at all dressed consistently, and the way they had sped past the Godblood without a glance confirmed he was not their superior.

Voices arose from all ends of the fighting stage, boots and hooves cut through the grass and ground, and corpses moaned while bones and metal clattered. All of it filled the evening sky as the black mass from the occupied city closed fast in the distance.

Other than the early sighting of Hellhounds, I couldn't see any bodies who were sure to be alive. The death mages who controlled the lurching lines hung farther back, and we had yet to see whether the soldiers lounging in the wealthy districts had been roused for this march.

Meanwhile, skin kites fluttered into view, too high and too small for those on the ground to strike with arrow or spell, and Pilla had left on a gust while I wasn't paying attention. I only realized this when the falcon appeared amongst them, disrupting the view of their mistresses, her beak and talons tearing the kites apart mid-air with furiously determined precision.

"Wow," I muttered. "A pity we don't have ten of her."

Tamuril heard me and turned her head, her brow wrinkling in dismay.

"Not good enough?"

"Didn't say that." I smirked. "It will take time to clear the sky, but I have no doubt that she will."

The Druid smiled despite obvious apprehension, rolling her shoulder to bring down her long bow. I'd seen how many others from the boats carried the weapon with quivers of arrows, but Tamuril somehow made it less obvious as she walked in her full leathers and gear.

"How far can you hit?" I asked curiously.

"Quite far," she said, dipping her chin as if too modest to say.

"She can hit those closest to us on the battlefield," Krithannia said, "although we must *not* do this lightly lest we give away our position."

The Druid nodded as if she had heard this before. "Only if Willven is unconscious. Otherwise, save the shot for us."

That sounded like something the Guild Mistress had made her repeat, and the dark-haired sister appeared satisfied.

I chewed my lip as a thought passed underneath the other voices. "You will be focused on Willven."

"Yes," she replied.

"And if you must shoot, you cannot miss."

She pressed pink lips together. "Correct."

I hesitated before suggesting something I'd never said to another Red Sister. "Remember my ring? The true aim?"

"Huh?"

I lifted my gloved hand, wiggling my fingers. "When the wearer *cannot* miss."

"Oh!" She remembered. "Um. Yes."

I tugged at the fingers my glove. "Will you wear it? I would share the command word."

Her heart became audible for an instant, coinciding with the strong pink flush of her face. She didn't speak as Krithannia watched with lifted eyebrows. The Yungians had spread out to keep watch, so at least they weren't staring, too.

"What?" I exposed my hand and started working the ring off with a twist. "I can only defend myself at this point. I can't help anyone on the battlefield."

"You *are* helping, Sirana," Krithannia murmured, like me, trying to split her attention between Tamuril's answer and the opening of Gavin's challenge for the walking dead.

I held out my hand to the Druid as men shared details and orders in my ears, Callitro's ring sitting in my palm. "One shot where you cannot miss your target. And you can do it again the next day."

"At dawn?" she guessed.

"I don't ... know," I admitted, glancing to check on the twenty men obscuring the Deathwalker's aura as best they could. "We crafted it in the Deepearth. It takes time, less than a 'day' up here, but I have not counted, and its magic depends not on the Sun."

With a sigh, Tamuril had slipped off her tanned glove and opened her hand for the ring. "For Willven."

"Agreed." I placed it in her palm. "Don't put it on yet. I need you to recite the command."

She closed her fist, her focus deepening.

"*Ilbauseke*," I said.

She flinched, and Krithannia appeared further interested.

I sighed. "Yes, the 'Dark tongue,' what else would it be?"

Tamuril swallowed but repeated the word for me.

I shook my head. "Not quite right."

"*Ilbauseke*," Krithannia said, her pronunciation perfect as she touched the Druid's shoulder gently. "It means 'grant true aim.' There is nothing harsh in it."

She added something in Naulor I couldn't understand before repeating Callitro's command word. Something translated well for Tamuril when tried again.

"Just like that," I said, relieved once she spoke it correctly three times.

"I ... I have it," she said. "May I ... ?"

"Put it on," I urged, the crisscrossing voices in my head testing my focus, but I wanted to witness as she slipped it onto her finger.

"Good," Krithannia murmured soothingly.

Moments later, as the Druid pulled her glove on over the ring, my eyes darted over the hills searching for Gavin, or at least the signs of his work among the Ma'ab. I could see it, I thought, as the frontline began to warp, some shamblers slowing, some moving ahead, others breaking formation and spilling off to the sides.

It's working, Wolf said. *He's siphoning some off.*

Just the ones Nightmare bit, Mourn said, followed by a chuckle. *Hm. What happens if one of yours bites one of theirs, Deathwalker?*

I couldn't begin to understand Gavin's response, the vibrating hiss of multiple voices I'd once heard in our dreams plainly not of this world.

What was that?! the Guild Hand cried.

~Calm, calm,~ Isboern said. ~That was the Herald of the Grey Maiden. He says he will find out.~

*Weird damned way to say it … *

The light spells once talked about hadn't been summoned though the Sun lie well behind the horizon, the night sky growing intense with stars. Pilla was forced to return to her mistress to await the change as several score skin kites overtook the air above the main Manalari force, who had nothing to do but listen to the approach of the corpses and skeletons in the dark.

~Hold,~ Isboern reminded them. ~Wait for the living, the light will come. Let us give the Herald time to disrupt and position the dead. Keep an eye for if the Hellhounds emerge.~

They are running into problems escaping the trees but cannot see why, Mourn answered with a mental smirk. *Though we cannot keep them corralled indefinitely.*

~For as long as you can, legend. This helps.~

On the chosen battlefield, Gavin was surrounded by non-uniformed Guildsmen standing in his defense. They were doing what they could to obscure his aura with theirs, though I was not sure if he was aware of this.

The Godblood once again muted the overlapping whispers of the Grey so that unnerving sound wasn't so prevalent in the cross communications. We both watched as the shamblers split off in groups of five or ten, thinning the wave in front of the cleaner and better armed skeletons. As we did, the knowledge spread throughout the men, strengthening their resolve when the plan bore results.

Roughly half of Gavin's bonded corpses sought to leave the front line, placing themselves on the flanks of our living force as another obstacle for Hellhounds reportedly coming from these directions. Meanwhile, the other half turned on the "unbitten" closest to them, reaching out with hooked fingers, jaws opening wide.

Odd to recognize Ma'ab and Paxian together in their sizes and features yet expect no patterns of attack based on them. Some of each belonged to Gavin, the rest to the Dark Army.

Distant moaning and rumblings accompanied their inelegant twitching, bodies jerking as at least two death mages wrangled for control of the first wave. I wished I could see the sorceress's face as Gavin siphoned the strength off her talismans and spells through his unearthly blood. Gratifying to imagine if he contested Amelda's magic, though I couldn't see the pampered noble in the thick of this fight.

Once the corpses under the Herald's guidance started biting, the advance practically stopped in its tracks.

Oh my shit, yeah! cried Crow. *Look at that!*

Most of the corpses had fallen under the weight or attack of another. Some crawled away on all fours with another scratching and clinging to them while avoiding the Manalari. Others regained their feet and joined the steady flow to our flanks. Some spasmed on the ground, lay broken or unresponsive, heightening our chance of tripping up the skeletons behind them.

The Hellhounds reported hadn't yet appeared, and Gavin had disrupted the battle-claimed bodies in swift order, revealing the lines of bones solidly under Ma'ab control.

~Templari valentre,~ said the Godblood. ~Line up. We have our first true targets without defense. Let us make it count. Everyone, protect your eyes. The blast will be powerful. Dragon Son, how close are the Hellhounds?~

You have time for this spell. Do not delay.

~Understood.~

Although not explicitly thought, I recognized the coalescence of the Templar "sun spell" used to clear the streets at our final retreat in the first battle. This time, as the focus and silent anticipation escalated beyond my first experience, even *more* battlemages stood together. None were occupied by helping refugees or watching the rear as their fellow warriors ran for the gate.

Every Templar was here. About fifty of them.

Hata Ri, Krithannia commanded. *Drop prone. Cover your heads.*

The unspoken order to take Gavin down with them was an amusing thought right before it happened. I didn't have time to enjoy it as the mind's voice of the Godblood sang through the web of mindlinks, the "words" unknown yet the thought as clear as the starlit sky.

~Liesti, Templari! Guerrimos, protexintes!~

Two instants later, I obeyed, dropping my gaze, squeezing eyes shut, pulling my hood down to cover my entire face. The chant of the Sun Warriors collected into one, audible to my physical ears even at this distance. Confused, chaotic shouting arose somewhere new upon the field just as the spell reached that critical pivot point, where their will became manifest.

Light flashed into intense silence, a burst of release leaving the crack and subsequent destruction of a massive number of bones to catch up, only to reach my ears much later. I wish I'd been able to see it but, like everyone, we could only appraise the aftermath.

Great Musanlo ... Wolf murmured, an oath to which many responded with great heart.

Hiya-Yo, hua shien, Torch concurred.

Beside me, Tamuril squealed happily, covering her mouth with her hand, and Krithannia chuckled in a way which held both a simple amusement for her sister and a darker satisfaction of the results.

I stared mutely alongside many others, witness to the empty space where the skeletons had once been, grey dust filling the air above. A few stragglers stumbled around toward the rear, but the armed bone warriors we'd spied in the camp, waiting endlessly to be used, were gone. The tall grass had been cut short by the blast, revealing a field littered with warped weapons and broken shields. Wisps of choking smoke arose to suggest small fires smothered by the settling dust and ash.

"Walked right into the battering ram," the Guild Mistress said, the grim grin plain in her voice.

Beyond the skeletons, we caught sight of the real force from the camp, those of living flesh and blood like their opponents.

The Ma'ab lines were standing still.

"*Dyos sange!*" a soldier bellowed at full force. "*Dyos sange!*"

"*Dyos sange!*" another took it up. And another.

The chant rose above the Templari, hurled with thundering glee at the pale faces of the Northmen, a slap of insult and a challenge in one. The heightened sense of power and bold desire to fight filled me, looping within and through me, as Isboern allowed as many of his men as he could reach to *feel* that elation.

"*Dyos sange! Dyos sange!*"

The lingering fear, which had clamped down on some when the Sun had set, was now severed as their Godblood shouted in Trade, projecting his voice beyond Human capacity.

"*We shall fight beneath the light burning in our hearts!*"

Guild, Krithannia barked, dropping her eyes into the crook of her elbow, *Protect your eyes.*

Fuck.

Although I did the same, I sensed the delight of the Sun warriors as the illumination spells went off from the hands of ready mages. Isboern showed us how the natural starlight disappeared behind a cloud of intense, dancing lights cast in short sequences, shedding white light upon the battlefield.

Gavin was getting to his feet, no longer restrained but surrounded by the *Hata Ri* — whoever they were. Behind him, the Manalari roared as one and charged forward, their Godblood with them, running at the confused Ma'ab foot soldiers, most of whom clutched their heads or rubbed their eyes from the blast, many others having been thrown from their horses.

They're asking what's happening, my Deathwalker remarked in understated translation of their shouts.

Isboern's amusement tagged his focus for the ride. ~Good. They shall *learn the answer.~*

Then Wolf broke in. *Hellhounds charging the flanks with chains!*

~Is Divigna present?~

Negative, Mourn said. *No sorceresses on their backs, either. Keep the charge. Blasts incoming on the sides.*

~Acknowledged. Look ahead, my Manalari.~

Gavin's pilfered corpses provided no true shielding from the Black Army's packs, but at least they made a running target harder to hit with those flying, spiked weapons. A couple close calls for our side, as several shamblers were ripped down in place of someone still living.

Suddenly, four separate bursts of force dropped into the center of each pack. No light exploded with these spells, but dirt and shorn grasses sprayed up around the tattooed Ma'ab, either knocking them down or causing them to stumble. Wicked chains retracted to wrap around its owner's scarred arm as each warrior climbed to his feet.

Hata Ri! Again!

The Hellhound packs were struck by the same spell, less effective as the Ma'ab had learned quickly, spreading out. Still, the blasts kept them from the delectable targets of the Herald and the Manalari light-bringers concentrating on their spells.

Hold further attacks until they move, Mourn said, though I did not know who he spoke to if not the *Hata Ri.*

I couldn't see *him*, or Jael. I didn't spot any Guildsmen near the hesitating Hellhounds, yet the air thickened with imminent intent.

Meanwhile, the gap closed at last between the Manalari and the invaders, the Godblood summoning a blinding ray of light to flash into their faces at the last moment. Clashes of metal and launching of arrows erupted amid bellowing shouts, the air filling with screams and grunts of lethal contests spilled over the ground. The first lines of Ma'ab soldiers might as well have been fighting in absolute darkness.

~Sever the heads lest we be forced to fight them again!~ Isboern ordered.

Kill the women the moment you see them, Mourn added, a necessary reminder which tugged at the reluctance of many men.

Many, but not all.

Archers took their shots at the handful of Northern sorceresses behind the first lines, guarded by Hellhounds.

Fucking Hells, the bulls are taking the hits for the dolls! a Guildsman griped. *The arrows bounced off those bastards!*

I smirked. He was surprised?

Remember the anchor tattoo between their shoulder blades, Wolf said. *Best chance of getting through their skin.*

Yeah, well, they don't turn around very much. Also recall some of them will spray who-knows-fuck all over us before he dies.

Can't worry about that, Crow. We know what we signed up for.

Indeed, there was a lot we couldn't take time to worry about.

Battle lust and rage underscored every thought passing through me while pain and mute fear receded into the figurative corner. Isboern wasn't even winded, and his tight connection with so many of his warriors formed the anvil against which they smashed their hammer, breaking a much weaker resolve as untested officers tried to pass orders to those alive while wrangling the newly dead onto their feet — often without limbs or heads.

The sorceresses from camp gave ground to the Godblood. The four Hellhound packs, however, stood firm, surrounding a separate and critical group of mages. They didn't taunt or make any noise, only shuffled forward, searching for their opening to get at Gavin and the illuminators.

Chains at the ready, and only one at a time, they took out the Death-walker's stolen corpses with an unnerving display of unhanded spinning and constricting of their spiked chains, cutting off heads and limbs and leaving a pile of meat before the weapon was summoned to return.

They're protecting each other's backs and aren't getting impatient, Wolf murmured. *We can't get close enough and be sure to hit that spot, and they're too far apart for concussive spells. One spell each if we're lucky, and we know two force blasts doesn't stop them.*

Very well, Mourn said. *Let us choose one pack to distract, one to attack.*

Hold, Krithannia interjected. *We haven't seen Divigna on the field yet but must assume he's watching like we are. We were waiting for him before you showed yourself.*

My former bodyguard grunted. *If they get close enough and even one triggers a trap upon himself, they will threaten the Herald and will disrupt the light above the entire field. We cannot wait them out.*

I know, the Guild Mistress acknowledged, chewing her lip in hurried thought.

Seeing as the shamblers are fallen, Gavin said, his mind's voice attaining that eerie multiplicity, *allow me.*

In a visual and direct response to the Hellhounds' approach, the Death-walker summoned a familiar bramble of black, barbed vapor which encircled him and roughly fifty Humans, entwining, becoming thicker by the moment.

"Kazin!" one bellowed, flinging his chain forward in a straight shot from over ten horse lengths away, as if trying to shatter Gavin's spell like a stone throne at a mirror.

Shield! Krithannia commanded.

The flying chain darted like an eel through the writhing black barrier but struck something unseen and fell to the ground. At the same moment, the Hellhound nearest to the one Gavin had provoked jerked hard, head thrown back as if attacked from behind.

Got'im! Wolf crowed, his elation spreading through the rushing layers of thoughts and actions coursing through the field.

"Akhi!" shouted the weaponless Hellhound, turning to see the Guildsman suddenly appear, his sword buried in his brother's back.

Four chains rattled at once, three whipping around like serpents toward Wolf while the fourth and nearest one slapped at his flank. The next moment seemed thoughtless as Guildsmen acted, their illusions dropping startlingly close to the pack as they took full advantage of the distractions.

Men roared with aggression, in disbelief, grunting and screaming as defenses failed, striking out in retribution. With the constant din of the battle on the east side, it took time for me to grasp what had happened.

First pack down, two of ours wounded! Bear called out.

Watch out! Hawk cried. *They're charging to center!*

Two from each of the three packs, six in total, had returned their spiked chains to their arms and sprinted toward our mage group from three directions.

They're touching tattoos!

One's blistering up!

Trap!

Fuckin' stop them!

A fierce rush passed through my arms and chest the moment I saw Jael and Mourn appear on the field. Leaping through shadows, they barked a few Words in front of two dashing Ma'ab before moving to the next, gone before the Hellhounds landed on their backs ten paces away.

Stay back! Mourn ordered. *Cover your nose and mouth!*

"Oh, no," Krithannia whispered, recognizing as I did that none of the self-slaughter Hellhounds had gone up in fire. The bodies were soon to be all pus and rot or melting in a caustic sweat becoming a choking vapor.

"Sister!" Tamuril cried softly, grasping her hand as we looked out above the brush.

The elder Naulor took a deep breath, closing her storm-grey eyes and tucking her Dragon pearl in a pouch, removing herself from the network. Standing up tall, she lifted her arms and hands and began chanting, soft but intense.

"Tol theul rhun, rashia duin cala ..."

The wind came abruptly and in as much favor as we could hope, sustained from the east and heading due west. Moving the air that way was the surest way to spare many on the battlefield from exposure to disease or poisonous air.

Even the Ma'ab.

Good work, Krithannia, Mourn said through the pearls.

~She can't hear you,~ I responded awkwardly. ~But ... she'll be back.~

Very well. We will take out the rest of the packs now that they've broken.

That, he accomplished alongside Jael and the Guild's mages.

Although two Hellhounds thrashed several Guildsmen in their charge into Gavin's ethereal vines, they might have regretted their directness as the tendrils visibly sapped their strength. Vengeful men from Augran came up behind them, taking advantage of that one spot, their protective designs falling vulnerable.

Two other Ma'ab failed to close with the Deathwalker as Jael relished shoving them away multiple times with her new favorite To'vah Word, until Mourn cut the play short and appeared behind their targets.

My Sister slashed across the spine of one before ramming her sword into him, forcing a final, hoarse cry from his throat. In the same moment, Mourn clawed the triggering tattoo on the other, giving Jael another target once she'd wrenched out her blade. I couldn't make out articulated thoughts from her; she was full in her moment and eager for more.

I breathed out in relief. Eynkis had told us true. Destroying that specific tattoo on a Hellhound made it easier to kill them as several protection wards stopped working all at once.

This skirmish wasn't without cost, as from the chatter I understood a third of Reprisal had been raked by those chains, and one of them had a broken arm. But they had time to drink potions while the wind blew steadily, making it possible for those in the fight to avoid the worst of the danger.

With that part of the field under control, I shifted my focus to where Isboern worked tirelessly as the steadfast Defender in the thickest part of the battle. Rarely swinging his sword and using the Sun Shield as a psionic and magical focus, the Godblood directed components of his forces with a silent strength the Ma'ab could neither see nor understand.

Wounded Manalari strengthened before their eyes, rediscovered their resolve in the face of loss, resisted distraction in moments of confusion, and displayed no fear. Gradually, the uprooted men of the South chipped away at this first barrier on the route to return home.

Isboern had been right. The Ma'ab *must* withdraw behind Manalar's walls soon or simply lose everything they'd brought outside of it.

The retreat itself would be costly enough.

Torch, Mourn said. *Tell Krithannia we need her focus. The air is safe enough down here.*

No response.

Torch?

Ice filled my middle as I forced my attention on recounting the overview upon the Lookout. The only Yungian whose dark eyes I met were Deshi's, and he read something in my face.

"*Janshi?*"

★Sirana?★

"Where is Torch?" I asked, my mouth dry, a distressing thirst and hunger swept over me, seizing too much of my attention.

The youth pointed to the right. "Standing guard. Peng-lok and Nianzu in the other dire —"

A twig snapped.

Shit.

Pilla wailed, launching from Tamuril's shoulder as the Druid sprang up, nocking an arrow on her bow.

"Krithannia!" she cried. "Wake up!"

~Morixxyleth!~ I screamed into the ether. *~We're in trouble!~*

CHAPTER 22

COMMUNICATION CEASED BETWEEN THE GUILD'S PEARLS AND THE PSIONIC GOD-blood. Isboern himself had withdrawn at sensing my cry, shielding his closest officers from the primal fear which gripped my guts in its fist.

The Captain was gone.

Mourn hadn't responded yet.

And I couldn't fucking worry about any of that right now!

Deshi and I drew our daggers as Tamuril drew on her long bow. Each of us stood and faced danger just as Kreshel Divigna emerged from cover, Torch's body lifted above his head like a sack of beans. The Eternal Hellhound tossed the lax Guildsman straight at us before we could react.

~NO!~

I lashed out with a pure, searing thought, trying to "punch the sand" like I had in my dream, hoping I could shove him off his feet the way Jael had with his subordinates.

The Yungian struck solid air, landing on the ground without a sound, crumpled and unresponsive as Krithannia shook herself out of her spell.

"*Groa!*" Deshi cried. "*Wo'huida?!*"

Torch didn't move. Divigna smiled slightly, ignoring him, dark eyes boring into me.

Tugging, *daring* me to look deeper.

I can't.

A second Hellhound burst out of the brush beside of his leader, black-marked hands open as if to seize one of us around our throat.

With a nerve-jangling yell, he rushed us.

"*Ilbauseke!*" Tamuril shouted, releasing her arrow.

"*Hgkk!*"

Blood thundered in my ears as the Druid struck the Ma'ab in his open mouth, bringing him up short as the collision snapped his head back. The Hellhound's hands quivered and jerked as if tempted to pull the shaft from his throat—

When something snapped within the ground snapped, cracking into open air in a vividly familiar way.

"Get back!" I shouted at Krithannia, gesturing as I scuttled out of the way of the disturbed soil.

Shaking off her daze, the Guild Mistress obeyed, crouching beside me and Deshi as Tamuril summoned her spiked vines right at the Hellhound's feet. They entwined and constricted around the hapless attacker, as I expected.

Divigna, however, neither interfered nor tried to rush through the hostile growth. Instead, the Ma'ab Wargan watched as Tamuril's vines formed a barrier between us, with our attacker who'd swallowed the arrow in the center. The Hellhound wasn't dead yet, but blood spilled from his mouth and down his throat, his breath rattling and gurgling in the grip of the woody binds. He flexed, his arm snapping one of the vines.

"Y-you s-stay … *right there!*" the blonde snarled, pointing her finger.

Suddenly, the arrow's visible fletching splintered into four pieces as the shaft broke apart within the Ma'ab's mouth, anchoring like thatched hooks in the flesh around his lips. He squealed and thrashed before he began to choke, wide-eyed, as a fountain of red gushed from his deepest wound.

Goddess, what … .?

The vines from underneath his feet began burrowing into his skin, thorns puncturing him in greater numbers than had ever pierced me. I saw evidence that the broken arrow had somehow lengthened *through* his torso. The vicious fragments would soon burrow *out*, as if trying to reach the twisting vines and join them in the middle.

Tamuril stared, recognizing this as her rage slid from her face like melting wax, transforming into mute horror.

"Tami!" Krithannia gasped, a belated attempt to touch her wrist.

The Druid jerked her hand from the touch as if it burned, her scream so shrill, I flinched.

Fuck!

"Morix is coming!" I blurted for Krithannia, scrambling between the Druid and the Hellhounds to brandish Soul Drinker.

Deshi joined me, holding a couple of pellets ready to throw in one hand, his own death-blessed blade in the other.

"*Lung-di!*" he shouted into the trees around us. "*Peng-lok! Nianzu!*"

Divigna stood impassively from the other side of the thorny barrier, his spiked chain wrapped dormant on his right arm. The tiny smile had vanished, but his sharp eyes glanced around briefly before returning to us.

Had he not gotten to them? Had any others?

How many of Divigna's packs lay in wait all around us?

Buy time.

"I saw you across the water!" I said, my voice hoarse and on the edge of a quaver.

A slight nod, acknowledging that.

"Why didn't you attack then?!"

The terse line of his mouth showed no sign of parting to speak, but one broad, bare hand reached for Tamuril's thorny wall, taking firm hold before subtly touching a marking lower on his body. With a rip and an orange flare, one vertical section of the barrier went up in smoke, charcoal and ashes falling to the ground. He stepped through, past the twitching corpse of his man without a glance, extending his hand.

"Your guardian will be here soon," he said. "Give me the swallower of souls. I will negotiate on your behalf."

Absolutely fucking not.

"Negotiate with who?" I asked, gritting my teeth, failing to pretend

I'd consider. "Who would it help?"

"The relic first."

"I am not a fool."

"I imagine not. To remain uncaptured on the surface world."

Shiiiit. Don't let it be Vesram's mother looking out through his eyes.

Behind me, Tamuril moaned in broken dread as Krithannia pulled them behind Nightmare. The bonded beast stood rock still, awaiting any command from me. Gavin had said to use her first, but Divigna could go through her as easily as he'd gone through the Druid's barrier.

"Once the Dragonblood arrives," he intoned, "we shall be too late. *Nothing* is satisfied."

The pressure of his gaze had no respite. Not even in a blink.

"Where are my brothers, Hound?!" Deshi demanded as burgeoning rage threatened his focus.

"Dead," Divigna replied. "Necks snapped." He was close enough to kick Torch with the toe of his boot. "Like this one."

The youth's voice cracked, his exclamation unintelligible.

"Deshi, *wait* — !"

Too late.

With a yell, the young death mage threw his dagger away, whipping it straight at the Eternal Hellhound's chest. I held my breath, waiting for it to bounce off, trying to choose my next words to recapture his focus.

Divigna flinched, glancing down at his chest with a quiet grunt. Then he peered down where the weapon had fallen before reaching to pick it up. Every thought shriveled on my tongue when I saw that Deshi's blade had been blooded.

Bright, *red* blood, matching a slashing wound on his chest as long as my palm was wide.

Before I could move, the Eternal Hellhound changed his mind about what he was going to do next.

"Dodge!!" Krithannia shrieked in a rare terror.

Flinging myself to one side, I rolled to put Nightmare between us. Behind me, a crunch. Deshi started screaming.

"Who made this?"

I glanced over my shoulder.

Divigna held the youth off the ground with one arm, his giant's fist crushing the Yungian's right hand as he bared his teeth. "Was it Adason?"

Deshi couldn't stop wailing long enough to answer, gripping the Hellhound's fist with his left in a hopeless effort to free himself.

"S-stop! *Stop!*" Tamuril screamed, gasping for breath through her sobs. "L-let him *go!*"

I expected Divigna to use Deshi's own dagger to kill him for the insult of that bleeding cut. With both his hands filled and his attention occupied, however, Pilla darted in from close by and swiped her talons across his face before flying off. The falcon left not a single mark, but she gave me two instants to prepare my arm.

I *couldn't* miss, and yet …

Some extra sense warned him, and I did.

Divigna dodged, evading Soul Drinker and glancing where the relic landed, free of its sheath. Nausea overtook me as I cursed the stupidest mistake I'd ever made in my life.

If *he* picked it up, of all possible souls …

And the demon on the throne broke free—

What have I done?!

"SIRANA!" Jael bellowed. "We here!!"

We couldn't see them yet, but the warning prompted another decision in the Eternal Hellhound. He threw Deshi over his shoulder, the young man alive and shouting in pain, and fled with the Herald-blessed dagger in hand.

"Takhur!" he shouted over his shoulder.

Two Hellhounds appeared to cover Divigna's retreat, each holding a gagged and struggling Yungian brother in an obviously painful grip.

Peng-lok and Nianzu.

Alive.

"Stop, drake!" the left Ma'ab barked as Mourn and Jael appeared from the shadows. He palmed Nianzu's head, ready to twist it in a full circle. "Mother Elf is unhurt."

"For now." The right Hound grinned, tapping a tattoo. "You leap?

We *all* die."

Mourn's and Jael's eyes both narrowed, an impossibly low rumble filling the air around them. My Sister's face was sweaty, streaked with dirt and blood the same as her blade.

"No leap," she said, "they die, yes?"

"No leap, find breathing at bottom of lookout."

The doubt was palpable.

Then Isboern broke through the blurry tension in my head.

~*Retreat!*~

My spine jolted straight as I clutched my head. *"Augh!"*

Kiabil?!

~*The Ma'ab commanders have ordered the retreat!*~ the Godblood announced, elated. ~*Survivors are leaving the field! We're in pursuit!*~

Mourn heard that. *Thankfully*.

"Retreat," he said aloud to the Hellhounds. "Captives alive and unhurt at the bottom of lookout."

"Or we give chase," Jael growled, making a jabbing motion with the point of her blade. "Pierce fleeing star-holes."

By the arch of their brows, I got the impression that the Hellhounds didn't hear such threats often.

"As bidden," one said.

"Lucky for you," said the other with a victorious smirk.

At once, the men dragged our Yungians onto their shoulders and sprinted after their leader as if the two brothers weighed nothing.

Shit.

Had we failed them as I had Deshi?

"Shit, shit, *shit!*" I hissed, scrambling to retrieve Soul Drinker before Mourn had to ask me about it. He made note but didn't comment, waiting to launch after our captives.

"Deshi's blade hurt Kreshel Divigna!" Krithannia blurted before Mourn might leave.

He craned his neck toward her. "What?"

"It drew blood!" she gasped. "That's why he took him!"

"Divigna captured Deshi," Mourn repeated.

303

"H-He's not going to trade him for a head start," I added, unsteady on my feet as light-headedness increased. "I missed."

A pause as Mourn and Jael focused on the gruesome centerpiece of the Druid's barrier.

"Tamuril didn't miss," I finished, noting how she clutched her fingers.

"T-take it back!" she cried, pulling off her glove to twist off my ring. "I-I don't want it! It's evil!"

I stared twice. "Evil?"

She flung her naked hand at the dripping corpse. "It darkened my magic! The one who made it must have added that twist! I never … ! I would never — !"

Insult twinged on Callitro's behalf. "If you were to meet him, you'd find a *bua* capable of as much guile as yourself."

Haunted, green eyes blinked as doubt and shame touching her face. Nonetheless, she held out the golden ring. "Please. I-I don't want it anymore."

Plain enough.

Within an inward sigh, I stepped to retrieve Callitro's gift. Few of my measured gestures had landed well with the Druid, and perhaps that would always be the case no matter what else I tried.

Such is the results of a Red Sister attack like Jaunda's.

"Torch's pearl?" Mourn asked as I redonned my glove.

Krithannia's eyes widened, and she rushed to kneel beside his body, searching as quickly and thoroughly as she could. "*Jitauthan* … it's not here! Divigna must have it."

The half-blood's lip curled in obvious anger and frustration. "Communications compromised."

As I redonned my ring and glove, Mourn shared one last announcement.

Hands and Foci, there's an echo in the canyon.

A profound quiet took hold as Morixxyleth withdrew his power from the Dragon pearls. I couldn't see Isboern; beyond the message the Godblood must have pushed by his own strength, I'd lost the mindlink with him and the Manalari.

And the Guild had lost the links with each other because Kreshel Divigna had sneaked up on us at the Lookout.

Who told him? Did he see through the illusion?

"Run with us," Mourn said. "We must stay together."

With no Yungians alive atop *Miraderio*, I mounted Nightmare and offered one of the Naulor a ride. After green eyes slid to one side, Krithannia accepted and climbed up behind me. Tamuril kept up admirably well on her own two feet as we followed the Dragonblood and his rider down the slope.

The Hellhounds were easy to track, but we kept to one side, wary of ambush spots, holding our breaths to see if Peng-lok and Nianzu would be alive at the bottom as agreed.

I didn't expect they would be.

~*How did Divigna find us?*~ I asked, tears threatening to bring heavy despair.

Mourn sighed through our private link. *I made a mistake.*

My face flexed through several emotions, most notably confusion and disbelief. *He* made a mistake?

I showed myself on the battlefield first. We were both watching, I knew it. He outlasted me.

~*But ... that doesn't explain how he knew about the Lookout.*~

He may have before and noticed it 'gone.' A known risk.

Maybe.

~*Or another mage might have sensed Krithannia when she changed the winds and discovered the camouflage that way. She seemed anxious to be casting at all.*~

Mourn considered, his prowl toward the bottom unwavering. Jael glanced between us, aware we were "talking" but said nothing, her face placid and unusually patient. Maybe she was tired after all the bloodshed.

Perhaps, he granted. *The Ley Lines are affecting the mages in unusual ways.* His thoughts paused. *Do you remember if Divigna said anything notable?*

At first, I shied from the sweep of chaos that returned only too easily. With heart pounding, I picked one place to start while tugging odd snags on my cloak through the sparse forest.

~*Divigna wasn't there to capture or kill us. He asked for Soul Drinker. Said he would 'negotiate' on my behalf.*~

Negotiate with who?

~*He wouldn't answer except to say when you arrived, we were too late and 'nothing' was satisfied.*~

Hm. And then?

~*Deshi reacted badly to the Ma'ab kicking Torch's body and taunting him about Peng-lok and Nianzu.*~

And the wound from his dagger was a surprise.

~*Yes. Divigna almost looked angry.*~

Almost. And then he took Deshi and the blade with him?

~*Not before asking who made it. And making a guess.*~

Oh? What was his guess?

I paused, the moment crystalizing as if the Hellhound stood before me on the side of the slope. ~*Gavin. Except he called him 'Adason.'*~

We seemed to share the same chill down our spines.

Didn't Reprisal give the Deathwalker that name in Augran? Mourn asked. *Son of Ada?*

~*Yes. And Deshi spoke it in the crypt. Sho'shien Adason. I remember because we caught Vesram's attention.*~

Mourn rumbled. *The Sathoet who knew Ada.*

My stomach clenched with a painfully rising appetite. ~*Divigna reported Vesram to be in Manalar somewhere.*~

He grunted. *Then I am certain he is and might assume the two have spoken recently in order for Divigna to learn that name.*

The Eternal Hellhound and a demonblood from the Deepearth. Talking in Manalar.

About Gavin.

~*He has Deshi ...*~

First task is first, Kiabil.

I breathed. He was right. We approached the bottom of the Lookout, Mourn's tongue extending frequently into the air as he sought his Guildsmen or any hint of a trap. Though he led us unerringly close without an attack, the tall Druid spotted them first.

"There," Tamuril whispered, her voice thin on hope.

Krithannia hurried forward, dropping in between the downed men to check them over, the rest of us guarding every direction. She chanted, touching Peng-lok and Nianzu gently, checking them over before a soft shudder overtook her.

"They're alive," she said, eyes shimmering with silver. "Unhurt, I think. Though ... I sense something imbued within them. Probably tracking magic."

Farther away, the mage lights shining upon the battlefield started winking out one at a time. Watching this for a few moments, Mourn bowed his head, tossing his head to Jael, signaling for her to dismount.

"I will carry them somewhere safer. We will cleanse them before regrouping with the others."

CHAPTER 23

THE HELLHOUNDS OF ENNIKAR PROVED TO HAVE SOMETHING IN COMMON WITH the Red Sisters. The "imbued objects" which Krithannia sensed lay low in their gut and, at first, the Guild Mistress expressed uncertainty how to reach them.

On the one hand, they were too low to have been swallowed. She may have expected something bloody and damaging, such as creating a wound in which to stuff the object before closing it up in some rustic method. On the other hand, Divigna's pack hadn't had a lot of time, and neither Guildsman was bleeding from his abdomen.

"They inserted it," I said, pantomiming my finger penetrating the circle formed by my thumb and forefinger.

Jael smirked as she read me. "In stink hole. Could be worse."

The elder Naulor's mouth tightened but she agreed. Tamuril winced in sympathy, covering her mouth and turning away. I granted if Peng-lok and Nianzu had been conscious at the time, the Hellhounds had either intended distress to their minds over their bodies or the Ma'ab had merely had greater concerns.

Rightfully so.

"I can help remove it while they are unaware," I offered, hesitant not because of the job but because I knew better than to assumed too much about netherhole stuff with Surface males.

Or Naulor females, for that matter.

"Me, also!" Jael's grin didn't help. "Easy! One man each."

Mourn was *trying* not to smile, rather to my surprise. "In the interest of time, yes. One each. Slowly. Have care for anything barbed."

Ouch.

A good reminder there was always a crueler way to treat opponents.

"Understood," I conceded, deciding to leave on my gloves. "Can you help clean after?"

"I can."

"Excellent."

Without delay, I rolled Peng-lok over and loosened his belt and trousers while Jael prepared to handle Nianzu. With Pilla on her shoulder, Tamuril stepped somewhere she didn't have to watch.

"Stay where we can see you," Krithannia said.

"Mmm," was her reply, along with a baleful glance from the falcon.

At least they weren't protesting.

It's necessary.

I caught myself staring at the muscled curve of light brown skin and blinked, shaking a confused mix of Bohai's awed smile and unfocused worries for Deshi out of my head. I got to work, hoping this would go smoothly and I wouldn't have to try to remove a barbed sliver from Peng-lok the way Gavin and Isboern had from his leg at the redoubt.

With my finger deep in his ass, carefully searching, I thought of Callitro and the games we'd played in his room in the Wizard's Tower. Interesting how, like the Red Sisters, the Hellhounds wouldn't flinch from pushing a "little something" into this hole. Then again, Amelda had made it clear they "played" in groups as well.

I didn't like the parallels.

This brought my thoughts to Callitro's ring and Tamuril's horror for the corpse she'd made atop the Lookout. *Could* that have been caused by my bua's crafting magic? Or was it hers gone wild from the massive Ley Line surge two weeks ago … ?

If only she'd hit Divigna.

Unhelpful.

Argh. Back to it.

"Something round, hard," Jael said, her pointer finger in between Nianzu's cheeks to the third knuckle, as far as she could go. "Just touch. Can't ... grab."

"The Hellhounds do have longer fingers than us, yes," I murmured.

Earning a fearless grin, Jael pulled out and started again with her first two fingers, quite focused on catching the foreign object. I followed her lead without assuming I would encounter something smooth and firm.

Not until I did.

"There," I said. "Same."

We had to stretch their tight rings quite a lot to reach deep enough to curl our fingers around the small, polished tracking gems and tug them out. Both men would feel it when they woke up. I wondered if Krithannia would explain or one of us? Would I have preferred the Yungians be aware as we did this?

I didn't know.

This is war.

Krithannia held out an open pouch for us to put the gems into, cinching it up, then Mourn cast his cleaning spell to banish the odor and slime from it and our gloves before we righted the Guildsmen's clothing. Meanwhile, the Guild Mistress took a few minutes to cast a spell upon our findings along with a tracking suppression ward.

"That was interesting," she said, staring at the pouch.

Jael chuckled. "Hounds think we *not* search holes?"

"The Manalari might overlook it, I think," the Naulor answered with a shrug. "Some others might hesitate."

"They may have counted on neither Guildsman feeling it," the Dragonblood added, speaking clearer in his quadruped shape the longer he wore it. "Would be worth the try."

Indeed. The Sisterhood would do the same.

In a reminder of those "others," she turned toward the brush and cleared her throat. "We are finished, Tamuril."

"Thank you both," said Mourn to Jael and me. "Please strap them to my harness. We shall find our allies."

Indeed. We had many allies to find.

WITH THE PEARLS AND THE GODBLOOD SILENT, WE NEEDED TO FIND GAVIN AND Isboern with mundane but reliable ways. With Mourn carrying two unconscious men across his back, Krithannia had offered Jael her space on Nightmare.

"Short legs?" my Sister questioned, white eyebrow arched.

The Guild Mistress smiled. "Shor*ter*, yes. Tami and I can also obscure ourselves if necessary."

"Fine."

I admitted it was nice having her beside me. She smelled like her own sweat and a fair bit of strange blood and dirt, her eyes bright despite the turn of events. She sat closer than Krithannia had, sharing warmth, touching my thighs casually as if checking their tone.

I asked quietly in Davrin, *"How was the fighting?"*

"Mmhmm," she hummed, prompted to recall the excitement. *"He set us upon the right spot every time. I only had to practice my Words."*

I smiled. *"Is the pain lessened, then?"*

She paused as if trying to recall it. *"The pain is ... gone for now."*

Gone. *Good.*

"A relief to hear."

If only my headache would fade.

Our search started where we could not miss it: an entire field trampled and churned, bloodied and charred by fire, with many piles of bodies burning and smoking. Based on size alone, the male Ma'ab dead far outnumbered the Manalari and Guild, although I didn't know how many had been killed at the *first* battle and reused here.

Either way, fire had been the quickest way to deal with the dead before reaching the walls of the city. We followed such piles for half an hour, witnessing how long the Ma'ab had been chased and cut down in their retreat. I wondered how many returned to tell those loitering in the city what had happened.

"Here, eat," Jael said later, pressing a ration she'd gotten somewhere into my hand.

Despite the smell of smoke and opened guts, I didn't argue and bit gratefully. She'd ignored the noise from my stomach the first time but not the second when her hand had been on it. Not only had my middle been empty for hours, but the energy surges had worn off, both from the confrontation with Divigna and the sustained mindlink with so many others.

I didn't want to think about the struggle if Gavin hadn't given me Nightmare to ride. I wanted to lie down in the grass and take Reverie, also worried when I might be safe to try. I didn't want to pass out at the worst possible time.

Another two hours passed for us to find the spot on the Big Ker river where Isboern's men and most of the Guild had gone once the Ma'ab's retreat was final and confirmed. The night was about half over, the sky alight with the two half-moons.

So much for fighting until dawn …

Once we were spotted, word spread fast, pearls or no. Isboern and a few Templars borrowed cavalry horses and torches to ride out to meet us.

"*Ahoi!*" called the Godblood, raising his hand in the air for the last few strides of his mount. "Need you healing?"

"Not at once," Krithannia answered. "We need food and water, and rest."

Isboern exhaled, daring to smile as he found us upright, bowing his head to Mourn bearing our Guildsmen. If he had worried he might not see us alive after the battle, he tempered it well in front of his men. "That, you shall have, elders. Come. I must know what happened at the end."

Gavin had insisted on walking far behind the Manalari riders because he made any living mount nervous these days. He met us on our way back, dark ice eyes scouring us, taking in nuances difficult to describe. He didn't have to ask if we needed a healer.

"What happened?" he asked.

"Let us go into the tent," the Captain suggested. "I'm sure they will tell us."

Gavin peered closely at the lax Yungians and frowned. "Where are Deshi and Torch?"

The mild grimace on Mourn's current face looked strange. "Let us go inside. That and more shall be discussed."

The Deathwalker grunted and turned around, leading the way to "the tent," a hastily erected square of poles and flaps no larger than five others currently housing the wounded. I'd been aware that a separate contingent had trailed the main force with carts and supplies, but was impressed they had gotten here so fast, not knowing how the battle might turn.

The space inside was a tight fit with Captain Isboern and Templars Imran and Sohl, Gavin, and the rest of us. The walls were incredibly thin, but magic would prevent our words from carrying and our silhouettes from the single lantern showing too crisp. Isboern unrolled two blankets for Peng-lok and Nianzu, allowing us to lay them down, while he took his own turn to check them over.

"Seems drugged," he said.

"Agreed," Krithannia prompted.

"How long have they been out?"

"About three hours."

"I take it with the pearls going quiet, one has fallen into enemy hands," Isboern continued, fingers pressing gently to Nianzu's temples. "And Torch is dead."

"Correct," Mourn confirmed.

Blue eyes lifted to me, slid to Gavin, and returned. "Deshi?"

Why look to *me* to answer?

"Captured," I managed.

Not what Isboern had been expecting to hear. "Captured? A ... Alive?"

I glanced between them. "Kreshel Divigna found us somehow, and that, uh ... remember the second ritual Gavin performed on Deshi's blade?"

Concerned, the Godblood looked to the Deathwalker.

"Merely reaffirmation of his service and for my Lady to be aware of him," Gavin said. "I did nothing terribly different."

"Even so, the blade *hurt* him," Krithannia stated. "The Eternal Hell-hound, when it shouldn't have."

"Oh?" Gavin's eyes narrowed in contemplation. "Interesting."

"Worse, I'm afraid," the Naulor replied. "Divigna took Deshi, I believe, because he was at once in possession of a dangerous weapon and valuable to interrogate for its information."

"*Mierda*," Imran cursed quietly.

"Agreed," Isboern said in an exhale, the flush from the ride paling with the news. "He has a Dragon pearl and a non-Ma'ab death mage in his possession. I had hoped to see him on the battlefield but did not think he would be easily led."

"He is not," Mourn agreed with a low growl. "With the most power-ful spellcasters assassinated and other mages lost tonight, this Hellhound is your greatest threat and obstacle by far. His primary target may be the Herald."

The Captain exchanged another look with the Deathwalker, who merely frowned deeper at Mourn's proclamation.

"Because I blessed a blade in my Lady's Name?" he asked.

"You made him bleed," I said. "And more."

"More? What else have I done?"

Mourn cut in. "We have reason to suspect that the demonblood captive knew your mother before she fled Ennikar, and that Kreshel Divigna did as well."

"*What.*"

Mourn paused as if to appreciate Gavin's incredulity. "Ada stands in the Temple, where either Vesram or Divigna *could* have seen her, correct? She is in another form, but what if they recognize her all the same, as Sirana did you?"

Gavin's mouth stretched into a thin, tight line. "How does the possi-bility of recognizing my mother make me a 'primary target'?"

"That depends on what Divigna wants. He took Deshi alive and called out Adason, so he wants information about you."

"Is there any chance we could save him?" Isboern asked. "Whether or not our enemy gains such information from him?"

"We do not know where they went," Krithannia said with sad eyes, "though our Guild will try to find Deshi."

"We must focus on approaching the city," Mourn added. "Recognizing that our only death mage may be a higher priority to the ranking Ma'ab."

"Unsurprising," Gavin muttered with a grim smirk. "To them, I am the worst kind of heretic and traitor, after all."

The corners of Isboern's eyes crinkled in a smile. "I know the feeling." A sigh. "But many need rest before we move in daylight. We need guards who need less sleep to give them that chance."

The Dragonchild and Guild Mistress nodded at once.

"We will help with that," said Krithannia.

"I'd like Sirana to stay here," Mourn added, "and if you have any way to soothe her mind, I believe the aftermath of the battle linking still affects her."

His comment startled me out of my daze, and my eyes fluttered. "Huh?"

"I do, yes," Isboern answered with a smile. "Although, I believe another among us could be as effective when I'm not within reach."

He turned to the Druid, who jumped at his focus.

"Oh, I-I've not …" she stammered. "I mean, I have never …"

"Please, try."

Something private passed between them, and the blonde sighed. "Very well."

" 'Very well,' what?" Jael asked, frowning.

"Feel free to take your rest with Sirana and the Guildsman, Jael," Isboern said to her. "And there is some food in that pack with the two waterskins. I do apologize, but I must step out. My men and I have much to do before dawn."

Enough that he couldn't stay to further tutor the neophyte staring into the void. I kept my mouth from twisting with my thought.

"I guard here!" she insisted. "Not rest."

"That sounds excellent, mage blade."

Her face softened to hear that.

"Agreed," Mourn said. "You know how to summon me, *Dalkrix*. Keep them safe."

Jael jerked her chin in a perfunctory nod.

Gavin stood up as Mourn and Krithannia prepared to leave.

"I do not need sleep," said the Deathwalker. "I shall remain on watch as well."

I didn't know how Tamuril could help, but no one would stay to watch her except my Sister. I was too tired, hungry, and thirsty to open my mouth and delay them further.

"Eat, first," the Druid suggested, reading my expression well as I glanced toward the small pile of supplies. "Pilla and I ate on the way here. We are fine."

I accepted, convincing Jael to eat, too. With every swig and bite, my focus between sustenance and sleep finally shifted in favor of the latter.

"When you are ready, um," Tamuril extended her legs, her back lightly resting on one tent pole, "put your head in my lap."

Jael's eyebrows raised with mine, but she pointed with her recollection. "Oh! The trees! You humming over Godblood." She grinned. "Thought just sleep, but was more?"

The Druid blushed but nodded without speaking.

"Does it take ... familiarity?" I asked, doubting if this could work.

Tamuril blinked. "Mm. Yes. And I *am* ... familiar. With you. I can help your aura as I did his." She paused. "As you did me."

Despite the recent stress and upset over Callitro's ring, a close and arousing peace returned as I recalled the ritual bath inside the redoubt.

Vividly.

"Oh," was all I managed.

At least my doubt had vanished by the time I laid my head down on warm, worn doeskin. I could have been disconcerted with how steadily Pilla stared down from her Druid's shoulder, but the bird seemed to accept my nearness and what was necessary.

And Tamuril was right. We *were* familiar.

"Breathe," she said, touching my brow with bare, warm fingers. "And close your eyes."

I obeyed, my body growing heavy with repose, eager to fully relax. I began to drift, my mind slipping under shockingly fast, although the instants dragged on as I ceased hearing the camp around me.

All grew quiet. Dark.

And still.

Then …

Breathing.

Humming.

Not someone's voice. Not a melody.

A different hum … Intangible yet …

Colorful. Flowing and cyclical.

A gentle plucking, like fingers picking strings to make a song, and I noticed … I *knew* somehow that where the colors constricted was where I was most exhausted. The pattern was warped but malleable. The humming grew louder. The pattern, clearer. Colors brighter, until …

All at once, the exhaustion fell away like dried leaves.

~*Ohhhh … wow …* ~

The plucking slowed, and I sensed confusion, but then she continued. I hummed in satisfaction.

Welcoming.

Opening my eyes.

I sat with Tamuril in the shallow water covering the floor of the shower room, warm steam rising to partly obscure our mutual nudity. The Druid looked around, face flushed pink but the familiar weight gone from her eyes.

And not a mark upon her pale breasts.

~*Nice,*~ I said with a lopsided grin, too relaxed to form anything complex.

She was tempted to smile. "Hm. Camden would do this sometimes."

~*Do what?*~

"Draw us in somewhere safe. To pass the time while his body rested. To 'talk.' "

~*Talk* … ~

"Is that what you want?"

…Was it? Had I drawn us here?

Somewhere both of us had once been safe.

~*I don't know,*~ I admitted. ~*Maybe.*~

Tamuril watched me, head tilting expectedly. "What is on your mind?"

I chortled. ~*Too much. Can't answer that.*~

"Ah. Well …" She shrugged. "Then you ask me a question."

Ask her a question.

~*You used that word again,*~ I thought before I could stop.

Not a question.

Tami's eyebrows drew down. "What word?"

~*Evil.*~

Her face fell when I lifted my hand; the plain gold band was there.

~*Do you think Callitro's gift is evil?*~ I asked.

Her bottom lip trembled as she heard the name. She shook her head, her voice squeaking. "No. Truth, I do not. I think, um, Callitro crafted an impressive tool for a shape so simple. I could feel it working."

~*So … that was you? Without the penance scars suppressing your magic.*~

The creeping blush traveled down her bare shoulders, chest, and upper arms. She shook her head vehemently.

~*Or did you lose control of your magic?*~ I thought, offering her a way out. ~*Because of the Ley surge?*~

She opened her mouth as if to agree. I waited for her head to nod. Neither occurred.

She closed her mouth as a tear welled up suddenly and escaped onto her cheek. "Th-that was me. I *did* lose control but not … of my magic." Green eyes pleaded for me to understand. "Of my temper."

I stared, my thought flitting out before I could stop it. ~*You have a temper?*~

"Of course!" she flipped her hand, looking irritated for the first time. "Everyone does!"

Fair point, but why did that not sound quite right?

~*You were scared, for certain. But you were also angry?*~

She bit her lip, fear entering her eyes. "I am not angry."

A lie.

~*You* are *angry,*~ I replied, one corner of my mouth sticking in a smirk. ~*But ... not at that Hellhound you caught, right? We didn't know him from any other brother.*~

Her face tightened as, with ankles crossed, she reached to cradle her bare feet in her hands. The pose squeezed her tits quite nicely.

She didn't answer, but the last word echoed between us.

Brother.

I hesitated. ~*You ... are angry with your brother.*~

"I am not!" she barked.

~*You look angry.*~

"I am *not* angry. I understand the position I put him in! He didn't have many choices given his station."

I sneered. ~*Spider shit.*~

The Druid was on the verge of weeping, and I sighed, neutralizing the venom in my expression. ~*Never mind. I don't know. I better understand the position you were in. I was angry at my sister as well. Until I 'lost control.'*~

She stared in disbelief. "You what?"

I shrugged. ~*More like the threat of punishment was no longer enough to make me obey everything she wanted. She lost control, not me.*~

"And ... where is your sister now?"

~*Dead.*~ I offered a thin smile. ~*In truth, Tamuril, the path to becoming a Red Sister wouldn't have been open to me with her standing on it. On me.*~ My thoughts drifted down that path. ~*I would not be here on the Surface, either.*~

Tamuril frowned, weighing this. "I am ... out there alone on account of my brother. Without his decisions, I would be home."

Like warped mirrors to each other, though I wasn't sure which one twisted beyond the other.

~*And you were scared and angry,*~ I thought, ~*but Callitro's ring isn't evil. It did as you commanded. You didn't miss.*~

The Druid sighed. "Agreed. I am sorry, Sirana. I-I wanted ... a reason I could face in that moment. But I don't believe it."

~*That's good enough for me.*~

"That's all?"

~*Yes. I like Callitro, and if you can see me as not 'evil,' then he is even farther from that measure.*~

"Hm." She raised her eyebrows slightly then tentatively smiled. "Well, may I ... see the maker of that ring of true aim?"

I blinked rapidly. ~*See him?*~

"A memory, perhaps?"

My turn for face and chest to flush hot. ~*Ohhh, well, um* — ~

Tamuril saw *something*, for sure. Her face darkened to red as green eyes sparkled. Her mouth opened to gasp. "Oh!"

~*Oops. Sorry* — ~

"Oh, um. No, he's ... quite handsome."

Laughter slipped out of me. ~*'Handsome'?*~

"Yes. For male beauty."

~*What?*~

"Well, you don't call an *adan* 'pretty,' do you? Or beautiful?"

I thought about it. ~*I call buas beautiful all the time.*~

She huffed, letting a smile slide in to be seen. "Well, I think he's handsome. Callitro, I mean. The ring maker."

~*Ah. Well!*~ I grinned so my cheeks hurt. ~*Thank you. He was a lot of fun.*~

"Fun?"

~*You know fun. You knew Camden.*~

Tamuril's face hadn't let go of the heat yet. "Alright ... yes. Just ..."

~*Just what? Can't imagine 'fun' with an adan back home?*~

Her blush receded, skin paling. Her expression conveyed the answer well before she shook her head in the negative. "No. Um. I cannot. Nothing like Camden."

I stopped grinning. *Shit.*

"I'm sorry," she said. "For ... everything."

My eyebrow quirked. ~*That's a lot to be sorry for.*~

"Well, I'll not cast anger."

~*Pfft! Do you jest? I hope you do. Tomorrow! If it's not the Ley Lines, then your magic is more powerful than I knew. I'll count myself lucky you weren't this angry when you caught* me *in those vines.~*

"Oh, but it *could* be the Ley Lines," she hurried to say. "I don't ... try to ..." Tamuril saw my expression and gave up. "But ... it doesn't matter now."

No, it did not.

I chewed my lip before asking. *~If we need your bow, planning out for a far shot, not facing down Hellhounds a few strides away, then might you wear Callitro's ring again? If needed?~*

She looked worried but, in the honesty of this mindlink, reaffirmed, "If needed. You or Willven. I would."

~Excellent.~

She exhaled, looking away from my delight and at the ceiling. "You have rested, Sirana, and have done well. We should ... wake up. Give your sister a chance to sleep."

~That we should.~

Within a few moments, the humming stopped, and I opened my eyes in the tent, aware of men moving around beyond the thin barrier.

My headache and fatigue were gone.

Jael straightened up, expectant, and I turned my head on the Naulor's thigh.

"*Much better,*" I said in Davrin.

"*Hmph.*" My Sister offered a curious nod rather than dismissal. "Not take long."

"About how long?" I asked, sitting up.

"Hm. Hour? One."

Wow.

Tamuril didn't appear drained, but I asked, "And you?"

"Better, also. It ... is a mutual wellness method."

Her face remained pink from lingering memories of our conversation, her focus on stretching and flexing her legs once I had lifted off them.

"That's good to know." After checking that Peng-lok and Nianzu slept, I turned to my Sister. "You want to lie down next?"

"Oh!" Tami gasped. "I-I am not as ... familiar ..."

"No, no," I corrected. "I meant a natural rest for her. Since we have time."

"Mm," Jael wrinkled her nose. "Not tired."

"Well. Lie down anyway. While you can." I smirked. "We're going to Manalar once the Sun comes up."

White teeth showed in her dark face. "Joy."

I chuckled; a deadpan delivery almost as good as Gavin.

"Fine," she agreed, lying down as she'd been trained in a Cloister of bare floors and thin pallets. "Just close eyes."

"Better than nothing."

And yet, as I half-expected and hoped, Jael slipped into Reverie despite herself. I smiled at Tamuril to realize it, and she gently returned it. The Druid and I sat in a comfortable silence, listening to the rise and fall of activities around us, awaiting the next daybreak.

And the next fight.

With more of our vulnerabilities known.

CHAPTER 24

CAPTAIN ISBOERN RETURNED ALONE TO CHECK ON US. AT THAT MOMENT, THE camp was pulling up stakes with light on the horizon on the cusp. He had waited as long as he could but was concerned to see the Yungians' barely stirring.

"I am sorry," he murmured, touching each man's forehead. He did … *something* which awoke them with a start. "See them on their feet, please. I will return in a moment."

Although Tamuril's mouth sagged open as if this were unexpected, I imagined Rausery or D'Shea doing exactly that in this circumstance, if it were within their capability.

Such was the price of leading an entire fighting force.

"*Janshi?*" Peng-lok whispered, his cat-like eyes finding me.

"*Ji … Janhuren,*" Nianzu echoed, peering up at Jael hovering over him.

The middle brother had almost called her *Jiji*. Having been one of the Guildsmen who had met her in a fistfight, he'd corrected himself quickly.

"Up!" she said, taking Nianzu's shoulders and helping him to sit. I did the same with Peng-lok, and the brothers came vertical with disoriented winces.

"Where are we?" the elder asked with intense concern. "Not Lookout

—"

Nianzu gasped as he remembered. "Hellhounds."

His brother both paled and quietly cursed. "Team L-Lung? Are we ... last?"

"If so," Nianzu murmured, "we failed the spirits."

"No!" Tamuril blurted. "We *all* failed to sense them. Krithannia could not maintain the illusion and guide the winds at the same time. Our enemy saw a new hill appear."

Was that true? Neither the Guild Mistress nor the Dragonchild were here to ask.

"*Wen-yung* brought you here," I said. "We watched over you."

The Yungian brothers displayed mixed feelings about that but pressed their hands together and bowed their heads. The elder gathered the courage to ask, not without dread. "What of ... Groa and Deshi?"

"Groa is dead," I said. "The Eternal Hellhound found him and took his Dragon pearl. He died quick."

The two looked nauseated.

"Deshi," Nianzu repeated.

My mouth tightened. "Captured."

Part of me wondered how many times I would have to explain this; the other part knew the answer: exactly as many as necessary.

"He is a death mage who caught the attention of *Sho'shien*," I said, "so Divigna knew better than to kill him."

"*Hainai* ..."

Tamuril was swift with an empty sack, helping to guide Peng-lok as he vomited into it. Nianzu managed to hold his stomach but only with effort; tears slipped onto his cheeks instead.

"What do we do now?" he asked me.

"Guild looks for him," Jael said, clasping a hand on his shoulder. "You leave to them. *We* go to Manalar wall."

"The Manalar wall ..." The youth breathed deeply but was trembling. "It is not over."

"No," she said. "Not close. Need to stand up."

She was right. Slowly, I got to my feet first, offering Peng-lok a hand while Tamuril took the sack outside.

"Walk with us," I said, having little else to say at this point. "We will get you some water."

The movement of supplies and pounding of footsteps was getting louder when Isboern finally poked his head in. He seemed heartened that the Yungians were on their feet. "This is the last tent to take down. Are you ready?"

"With waterskins, yes," I answered.

"You'll have them. Come with me. The Herald's waiting for you."

The Yungians swallowed but obeyed, and we did not go far before I discovered either the Godblood or the Deathwalker had had the foresight to load up Nightmare with saddlebags stuffed to the maximum.

Including waterskins.

"Let us walk," Gavin said as Isboern peeled off once more with a quick farewell and Tami's dismay. "We should stay toward the front of the host."

The Yungians bowed deeply to him, some mention of Deshi on the tip of their tongues as they straightened, but Gavin didn't notice before he turned away. With nowhere else to go, we followed his lead.

"What about Mourn and Krithannia?" I asked, seeing only Humans around us.

"Gathering information, I believe."

The Deathwalker's robes were smeared with dirt and spattered with dark spots, a swath of yellow grass blades stuck below knee level. No obvious new tears, no black spots where a wound might have closed. "*Hata Ri* seems to have done well protecting you in the thick of battle."

He grunted. The cadence of his long stride and Nightmare plodding behind us reminded me of our days on the Midway.

"Where are they now?"

"Summoned where needed, I presume."

"Do you know any of them?"

"They are nameless to me. I am certain that is the point."

"But you'd recognize their auras if you saw them."

Hood up against the rising Sun, his pale skin turned the shade of ashes, one visible blue iris growing brighter. "Likely but not expected. We'd be foolish to use the exact same tactic the next day."

As if we could with the Dragon pearls all quiet. I reached to touch the one on my earlobe, attempting to reach out.

No answer.

So strange after the past weeks as new companions. I'd known the Dragonchild was invested in the outcome of this conflict from the start, but his absence enhanced my impression of how badly he'd wanted to be free of our Bargain as my bodyguard, to need to come and go as he pleased. To do what he could to influence the battlefield thus far, then on to whatever he would do next.

At least Jael has the means to call him from a distance.

"Your thoughts on how this is going?" I prodded.

"We haven't reached the difficult part yet."

That landed upon my ears as wholly true, yet the mood and alertness of the Manalari rose with the daylight. Jael and I pulled our hoods farther over our faces as I listened around us. Little outright laughter, but the tones within their spurts of conversation sounded uplifting to my ear. The tension remained but with less of the unknown clinging to them. They had seen battle with neither reliance nor interference by the Bishops and held a greater focus and determination compared to the previous dusk.

The Godblood had led them to victory in *full* darkness, before the moons had risen. Musanlo watched over them with the Sun Shield catching His Eye.

They must be excited to see what else he can do.

In the same fearful way, so was I.

WHOEVER REMAINED OF THE MA'AB LEADERSHIP TRIED NEXT TO PARLEY, LONG before fighting men could approach the wall.

The Temple City was visible in the distance, its levelled construction and streets climbing their way up the mountain slope like a careful, serpentine skeleton. A series of cobbled and packed-dirt roads led away from the large, semi-circular settlement, suggesting either the rays of the Sun or the uneven spokes of a wheel.

About halfway between here and there, a Ma'ab entourage stood atop one of the few shallow hills in the fields, comprised of fifty large horses and their equally large riders. In each case where there was a woman, a man sat behind her steering the animal. Other men rode alone; ten of them were bald and covered in tattoos, a spiked chain wrapped around one arm. This was the first time I'd seen Hellhounds atop any mounts.

After some swift and private mindlinks with his Templars, Isboern came to find us, seated on a spirited destrier horse so he would be level with his opponents.

"They want me, the Deathwalker, and the 'black witch' to come forward," he said. "And whichever bodyguards we wish to bring."

Tamuril petted her falcon to soothe them both while Peng-lok and Nianzu worried the edges of their gloves. Jael scowled, folding her arms and exchanging looks with me.

"Is Divigna one of them?"

The Captain appeared wry. "Unfortunately, he is not in view."

Great.

"How many do you want to bring?"

Now he smiled with genuine amusement. "Truthfully? Just the three they requested, and Jael."

The Druid's mouth dropped open; Yungian eyebrows lifted in surprise.

"Four?" Jael growled.

"Against ... ? Ah ..." Tamuril hesitated.

"Fifty," I answered, equally surprised but waiting for what I assumed was a plan.

"Correct. The Sun is at full strength —"

"And in our face," Jael added.

"Somewhat, yes." The Godblood smiled despite that, or because of it. "If you trust me to shield you while up close to the Ma'ab *and* believe we are watched and protected from afar, then yes. Four. I'd like our forest spirit out of sight and behind the Templari, since her presence has not been requested."

Another exchange with my Sister, and I nodded an affirmative.

"You taunt them," my Sister accused, smirk twisting. "Dangle bait in front of Hounds."

The blond man shrugged. "We'll hear what they have to say. If they attack, we engage, and we are not alone. The Guild is ready, they won't get away. This could result in many fewer Ma'ab for my men to fight at the wall and further damage their morale, as I don't expect they will offer what we want."

I turned to Gavin last, who shrugged.

"I am curious enough," he said, preparing to mount up on Nightmare. *Curious, and without apparent fear.*

"I will carry one of you," Isboern said. "The Herald, the other. We use two horses."

"I prefer Sirana as my passenger," Gavin said bluntly, gathering up his reins as if he needed them. "She can control my mare if I leave the saddle."

"Good suggestion." The Captain offered a hand to my Sister. "Jael?"

She screwed up her face, checked that her blades were secure and within reach, and snatched his hand an instant before springing off the ground. The Godblood assisted her lift so she could swing her leg over his mount's haunches on the first try. She settled easily, the Sun Shield squeezed between them.

I followed suit, Gavin's grip reminding me that he was stronger than he looked. After I'd gotten comfortable and the animals started forward, Isboern caught my eye.

~How are you?~ he asked. *~Well enough to link with me through this?~*

I exhaled in relief. *~After whatever Tamuril did, I'm doing fine. And I thought you'd never ask.~*

He chuckled as we rode forward. *~You are doing well and thank you for accepting her help. I think it went as far as your Elven ritual to remove her curse.~*

My mouth stretched, slightly downturned. *~Her magic is stronger* *without the curse, and the Eternal Hellhound knows she can be a threat.~*

He paused, letting me feel his concern, though tempered for the situation given my timing. *~In what way?~*

~She grew angry in a way I've never seen when Divigna threatened us. Shot his flank man with her arrow and turned him into a bloody barrier with her vines. So ... she killed him.~

Isboern kept his eyes forward with the Ma'ab in view. *~Well, I always knew my clan's 'forest spirit' could be an ardent defender when pressed, though I don't believe she's known war before. Certainly not like this. I can accept the unexpected from her, but thank you for warning me about what our enemy has seen of her capabilities.~*

Leaving it there, I turned my attention where it should be: the potential and ever-increasing threat in how truthful the Ma'ab intended to be about this "negotiation."

We'd find out at any moment.

A few heads turned amid the Ma'ab entourage, the smaller females exchanging looks or shaking side-to-side in silent comment. Most of the men didn't look away or show possible confusion, whether sitting on a horse to protect a charge or standing facing us upon the ground. Some had tensed up when the Captain shifted his golden shield into a different position, however, and I wondered how this same group might have looked with higher ranks among the living.

The Godblood did not speak but drew us to stop within "speaking" distance, if we were to project, raising his free hand above his head, fingers pointed narrow and straight at the sky. Gavin made no gestures at all, his blackened face partly covered by his grey hood. Jael narrowed her eyes peering out from behind Isboern's shoulder; I did the same from behind my Deathwalker.

~Goddess damn her,~ I snarled. *~Amelda Troshin.~*

The Captain gave nothing away in his expression, focusing where my attention had landed. *~Recognize anyone else?~*

I did, but only because his Paxian frame was so slender by comparison, his hair a lighter brown.

~Mathias Briar behind her.~

The skin hunter appeared not to have changed clothing since I last saw him in the Dwarven cell, but he wore borrowed leather armor, stained dark enough to seem black during overcast or in the slightest shade. He also had a bow and arrow quiver — something I'd seen him use to hunt his meals — and two short blades at his belt.

~So,~ Isboern thought, ~*the torturer escaped only to be compelled to come here.*~

I agreed that Mathias would be smiling if this had been his idea. Meanwhile, Cris-ri-phon's daughter laughed in theatrical delight, causing the four female officers to go stiff in their shoulders.

"Sirana! Gavin!" she called. "So good to see you again."

Jael questioned in silence, and I signed out the names of Amelda and Mathias. After translating sounds in her head, she nodded brusquely, her expression shifting into a tighter scowl as she studied the sorceress and her leashed mercenary.

A moment later, Isboern shifted his golden shield to catch the Sun's light and pitch it into the women's faces. Amelda yelped with indignance as the Godblood cleared his throat.

"You have requested an audience with *Capitan il' Templari*, noble-woman, not an errand boy." Isboern's voice carried so well, it must have been enhanced by a magical trick. "I have answered. Let us not waste the day. Have the Bone Caste speak with me on military matters first before you address any grievance with my allies."

Fury flooded Amelda's face as Mathias broke into a familiar, unrepentant grin behind her, doing nothing in the face of her indignance. I couldn't help chuckling.

"Enough, *tiflajay*," said a well-dressed woman of rank, lips drawn in a tight smile. "Be silent. More to this all than your revenge."

"My 'revenge' also redresses your failures to the gods, *nilazim*," Amelda hissed. "Or have you forgotten?"

"I have not, but you overstep time and again. I grow weary."

"*Pah!* You cannot kill me. The end will be the same."

Hearing this, Mathias's humor faded as an unknown consideration took over his thoughts. The officer and her three subordinates appeared displeased to have this thrown in their faces.

But Amelda must be right because they did nothing.

Quite like home.

"*Anfazi, tiflajay,*" the officer repeated in an understated threat before lifting her chin, her black-eyed focus on the blond man. Her accent was thick, dragging itself across many borders by the time she finished. "*Capitan il' Templari* Willven Isboern, yes?"

"Yes, commandress."

"I am *Nilazim* Vo'yara, and these are my death hawks. We are indeed of Bone. Surprised you even know. Further to acknowledge."

The armored women glanced at Gavin with expressions promising violence as Isboern smiled, allowing only a bow of his chin.

"Introduce your allies, *Capitan*," said Vo'yara with a wave at Gavin and me.

"Why, *Nilazim*? Has Amelda Troshin not informed you, given your missive?"

She bared her teeth, a restrained, feral smile. "Formality."

"I think we are beyond formalities, *Nilazim*, unless your intention here is to discuss Ma'ab withdrawal from my city and the release of your prisoners."

Vo'yara blinked but recovered well, tilting her head with sly consideration. "Mm. What would you pay? What ransom for a useless pool of water and a great many well-bred prisoners?"

Willven wasn't taken off guard, but the jab landed without a believable offer in response. I sensed him taking a long, slow breath.

"Your lives," he answered.

And stopped there.

Given pause, Vo'yara and her officers laughed loudly, their tones high. Some of the male warriors began to smirk.

"*Capitan Templari* is generous," Gavin said, the Greylands sibilance in his voice as he adjusted the thurible at his belt. "I would offer you and your men their Vis, and enough Vitas to carry you to Ennikar without your bodies."

Whatever had been done so that the negotiators could hear one another apparently included those of us who hadn't spoken yet. The sorcer-esses stopped laughing, looking at Gavin, their flashes of rage and insult reminding me of Priestesses with old grudges frayed and ready to snap.

"*Maknuut* will not speak to us again, *Capitan*," Vo'yara demanded with an imperious sweep of her arm. "Or this meeting ends."

I caught Mathias rolling his eyes, and thus, so did Isboern.

"What is his offense, *Nilazim*?" the psion asked curiously. "You called this meeting, requesting his presence. You wanted his introduction a moment ago."

She scoffed. "The heretic claims the power to overcome our gods but is only a treasonous coward. An ungrateful tongue misusing his gift granted by the gods he denies. Imagine a fool shouting that *he* decides if the sun's rays reach you or not, this is what he says to us."

"A stark difference and false comparison, *Nilazim*," Isboern replied. "One is *kept* from daylight which exists regardless, while the other would deny the next sunrise from ever coming, thus killing our world. You exalt the threat of a challenger of old ways, nothing more."

The Bone officer jerked her head as if avoiding a blow, her injured pride spilling over onto the Manalari Captain. Jael enjoyed a snicker at her expense, patting his shoulder as if impressed.

~*You've done it now, Willven,*~ I thought, darkly amused as Amelda leaned to whisper something urgent to the officer. ~*They're much like Priestesses of the Abyss clinging to their place on the web.*~

~*So be it. I am not here to placate a non-negotiator or her 'gods.'*~

~*Then why are we here?*~

"Give us the heretic," Vo'yara called out as Amelda straightened up on her horse. "Give us the two black witches, *and* the red rune dagger they stole. That is enough ransom for this miserable city of sows."

The Godblood laughed at once. "They are not mine to give, *Nilazim*. Ancient power beyond my ken would revoke such a trade before the next nightfall."

An exasperated curse.

"Then why do we speak to *you*?"

"Because I speak truth you should hear. If Amelda made that suggestion to you, she already knows about the old powers which would prevent such a simple exchange. She will turn against you at the first sign of trouble."

Vo'yara and her women glanced at the noble as if they could believe that. Until now, I hadn't seen Amelda's eyes so wide and furious when she wasn't blaming me or Gavin. With effort, she shrugged them off, lifting her chin toward the Godblood.

"You deal with dark creatures, sun warrior," Amelda said. "Do not pretend you aren't expendable to them."

"Accusations from those acting on bad faith are always confessions. What darkness have you dealt with, noblewoman, which you cannot let go? Perhaps you are not free to do so."

Mathias looked up, gazing at me. We weren't close enough to make any sort of link, but …

He peers toward Lookout.

What was he thinking? Or trying to say?

Did you know the hill was there all along?

"No chatter!" I shouted. "Show me Deshi!"

Two moments, and fifty pairs of eyes refocused on me.

"Who?" Vo'yara sneered. "We have many captives, black witch."

Mathias grimaced or maybe smirked, while Amelda smirked for certain.

Son of a netherhole.

~We must break this off,~ I said. ~Our eyes are on them, not our backs. They haven't any power to negotiate and don't know what Kreshel Divigna is doing. Either we attack and kill them, or we confront them later after they've killed or caught more of us.~

Isboern's horse pranced with the rising tension while Gavin's Nightmare didn't so much as flick a fly off her ear. The Godblood and Deathwalker exchanged looks, and Isboern shared my concern with him.

Agreed, Gavin replied. *I will detain their Vis, if I can.*

As he had not Commander Vo'traj in the crypt.

The Captain addressed the Ma'ab officers. "I know how many of you there are, but you do not know how many of us lie in wait. Try to hold my city if you must. It shall be difficult, the cost greater than you believe."

The *Nilazim* tossed her head. "*Hah!* As for you, wall scrambler? *Aiaya, vo!* We shall hold the pool to your last ally, *Capitan*, until every womb drops her last seed, and all Manalar is part of the Ma'ab Empire by *birthright*."

Isboern lifted his shield and disappeared from his saddle, Jael lunging forward to seize the reins.

"Stay on," Gavin rasped, practically falling sideways off his mare rather than kick me with his long, swinging leg.

Simultaneously, the Godblood reappeared *among* the Ma'ab officers, standing on the ground and surrounded by massive, dark steeds.

~*Buenreisol!*~

Brightest day ...

Shit!

Jael and I threw an arm across our eyes just before daylight exploded to engulf the Ma'ab.

CHAPTER 25

DRAGON PEARLS OR NO, MOURN APPEARED WITH A MASS OF GUILDSMAN, LEAP-ing into the fray the moment the Godblood and his light had retreated with a second shield-leap.

Sound and light hit me like a fist as the pitched battle erupted into chaos. Stunned enemies struggled to match glimmering weapons and sense-robbing spells in close quarters, casting blindly, swinging spikes chains and mauls at any moving target.

"Get behind Sirana!" Isboern shouted, running up to snatch the reins of his rearing horse as Jael lost control of the huge beast.

My Sister slipped off and rolled clear of pounding the hooves, sprint-ing to leap onto Nightmare's back. I shifted forward, making room behind me just in time, and engaged the talisman beneath my glove, looking for Gavin.

~*Eyes open for Divigna!*~ the Captain warned in an open thought.

I would try, but choking dust bloomed from the intense skirmish roiling so close on the field. I couldn't see what was going on, surprised as an errant arrow struck an invisible shield in front of us, making me jump.

"Back up a safer distance!" Isboern commanded, his hand outstretched in our defense, shield pointed toward the enemy. *"Templari! Unete!"*

Chains whipped about, grunts and hoarse cries preceded throttled breaths and death rattles.

"Gavin!" I called, turning the mare. "Come on — !"

An explosion erupted like inside the Temple. Men and women cried out as shredded limbs and offal flew outside the obscuring veil, rolling and staining the grass.

"Puckerfuck!" Jael cursed, gripping my waist, her voice muffled as I moved us a short distance, spinning Nightmare around. One ear mostly numb as blood spattered over the ground, our mount, and our leathers in sticky wet drops.

"Gavin!"

Already facing away from me, the Deathwalker took two long strides closer to the lethal contest. Lifting his thurible in his left hand, his eyes gone black, his quiet murmurs sent chills down my spine despite barely hearing them.

Two figures broke out of the cluster, stumbling before gaining their footing. The larger one dragged the smaller one by an arm, signs of magical shielding in place as they ran toward us.

Mathias and Amelda.

"Surrender!" the skin hunter shouted, waving a stained, pale scrap of cloth above his head. "We surrender, Captain! Please, don't kill us!"

Isboern hesitated and Mourn broke in through my pearl.

*Do **not** allow them near the Deathwalker!*

Nightmare charged in on my command, standing between them as Jael drew one sword, grabbing my opposite shoulder. She was prepared to leap off.

~*Do not kill them!*~ Isboern ordered, his attention split defending us against the chaos. ~*We will take prisoners!*~

"What?!" my Sister blurted, lacking any binding tools. "Sirana, no!"

Mathias had said we'd be sorry if we left Amelda alive, yet the same man kneeled before us, forcing the Ma'ab noble facedown into the dirt. With his palm on her head to prevent any mischief, she squealed in protest.

"We surrender!" Mathias repeated as I drew my hand crossbow, his pitch urgent, body hunkered down, brown eyes desperately seeking mine. "We know about Divigna! And Deshi!"

*Goddess **fuck!***

"Stay with me," I said to Jael, commanding Nightmare to stand in between them and Gavin while aiming my weapon. I asked the skin hunter, "What about the Ice Lord?"

"The what? Who?"

My eyes bore into his. If he was faking, the performance was a good one. I wasn't sure what to do. Shoot a leg? Drop to the ground and squeeze the blood from their heads? Strike their temple with the pommel of a dagger? Keep my distance, send my spiders, and *hope* my last antivenom prevented their deaths?

No, I only have one left.

Most options would require getting too close, and I didn't want to waste my last vial on either of them.

Behind us, Isboern's Templars and the cavalry closed in with their Captain as organized units of men tightened ranks, awaiting their orders.

There's an idea.

"*Templari!*" I shouted as Isboern's most trusted men got closer, the horseback riders passing by. "Take this man and woman prisoner!"

"*Farrimus!*" Robi answered.

Seizing Amelda, he dragged her away from Mathias, who was at once tackled by the much bulkier *Tetente* Erik. The skin hunter grunted, pressed flat with a knee on his back.

Good enough.

Meanwhile, Gavin drifted closer to danger. To people dying.

"Wait, stop!" I called, turning Nightmare closer, aware of the next three times the Godblood outright blocked the spiked chains thrown at the Deathwalker.

~Sirana, away! He can't hear you!~

Shit. And how obvious the Hellhounds *wanted* my Deathwalker, equally as much as they would take the Godblood if they could reach him. However, the spells and tactics of the Guildsman alongside the Dragonchild and the mounted Manalari countered their ability to disengage from close quarter combat.

Instead, the psion defended us from the reach of those thrashing

337

chains while the Guildsmen cut down the Ma'ab one-by-one with a few surprises. Two "bursting" Hellhounds meant to punish everyone were trapped inside an invisible "bell," containing their deadly aerosol. I wasn't sure whether Isboern or Mourn had clamped down on that putrid, bloody cloud, but ...

~*Brilliant move.*~

Unable to assist directly, Jael and I kept watch, flinching, coughing in the constant din and dust despite our best efforts. For now, the Hellhounds and Northern officers were trapped in a tight arena Mourn had drawn with his singing blades, and an opposing response was not yet launched from the city walls.

The Godblood was aware of his vulnerable position on the battlefield, needing Sohl and Imran to take up orders with the other Templars to defend him in turn while he defended us. They could meet this challenge and, behind them, the rest of the Manalari force stirred and moved forward to close the gap.

"They're running!" someone shouted.

"Don't let them get away!"

The "parley" had been useless, the fighting resumed, and yet ...

Where in the Abyss is Kreshel Divigna?

"Expect ambush," I said to Jael. She squeezed my shoulder, head swiveling while I peered closely at Gavin.

The black-eyed Herald held his thurible aloft, grey lips muttering within his hood, gesturing with his free hand. His concentration held fast on numerous things which I could not see. Without a rift to the Nexus open, the "current" of Vis and Vitas which had been plain to see atop Mount Sonai remained hidden from my senses, yet I wondered if Gavin could be overwhelmed by this whorl of violent death and its abrupt transition.

Was the Ma'ab Vis fighting him, a collective a score stronger than Eynkis by himself, or did someone interfere?

Amelda had been bound, gagged, and blindfolded by Robi, who dragged her farther away while Erik kept Mathias face down in the grass. The skin hunter hadn't been gagged yet; men were exchanging words.

Bad sign.

"Don't listen, *Tetente!*" I shouted. "Gag him!"

"Behind us!" the Templar returned. "Attack incoming, he says!"

~Tamuril.~

I flinched as the name darted into my mind and my chest, but the thought was not *mine*. The Godblood spun around, looking up at the sky. His expression led me to do the same.

Skin kites.

They harried Pilla as she darted her way through them rather than fight. Had she been trying to warn Isboern?

Simultaneously, the charge of the Manalari had slowed as confusion spread from the rear.

Then a man screamed.

And another.

A discordance of shrill calls rose as whole pockets of men broke ranks and turned around, lifting weapons toward horses trampling the dirt. I turned Gavin's mare to better see, finally spotting the Eternal Hellhound leading a score of bald, marked Ma'ab. Each enemy would be head and shoulders above the Paxian men even if they *weren't* mounted on gigantic warhorses.

~Behind us!~ I clutched the dark pearl attached to my earlobe, forcing the warning through whether it worked for anyone else or not. *~Divigna and four Hound packs behind us!~*

The chains launched in unison, leaving their masters' arms like flying, thorny serpents released from their restraints. Ten of them whipped into the mass of soldiers, concurrent attacks shaped like the spokes of a cart's wheel. They seized one enemy in view of many, grappling, puncturing, and shredding armor and flesh, a horrific sight seen no matter which way our allies turned.

"*Musanlo nospritec!*" someone shouted.

Once these unlucky ones had been snared, the Ma'ab dragged them in behind the massive horses and kept running. Chain-wrapped bodies worked together to trip lines of other fighting men, disrupting casting attempts in the swirl of painful screaming and shout of confusion.

Crossbow bolts and arrows, though well-aimed, glanced off the Northmen's thick, marked hides, and the Hellhounds countered by casting spells themselves, striking and shoving the Manalari out of their way, only too pleased to catch several on the ground to be crushed under hooves.

Sirana, gain distance! Mourn growled from inside the scarred battle ring. *I'll be there!*

~Yes, go!~ the Captain seconded. ~Tamuril and Krithannia have fled. You do the same! Let us confront him!~

Yet I could sense how Willven strained to keep track of the flying, spiked chains surrounding us, closing in, trying to protect every man while watching some fall anyway.

Heart thundering beneath my pendant, I glanced at Gavin. He had *no* idea what was happening. If I fled, no one would stand between him and Divigna except for the blond psion who, if *he* died, lost us the entire war.

Along with my best chance to be free.

~I can't ... ~

Drawing Soul Drinker to add to my tiny crossbow, grateful *this* horse couldn't panic, I called my spiders should I fail to summon my shield and stop the first chain. Jael squeezed my shoulder, brandishing her borrowed blade, and feeling like she might spring off at any moment.

"Mourn's coming," I warned.

"I know," she growled.

"I'll block, shoot, and stab."

"Aye. I pound Ma'ab beast with Words."

Divigna broke out of the Manalari force in front, his armored stallion ignoring his wounds, his packs leaving a thick trail of dead men behind them.

"Takfa!" the leader shouted.

The packs split in half: ten aiming for Isboern and his Templars, with Divigna plus the other ten coming for us. Bloody chains unwrapped from the grit-encrusted corpses who had tried to slow them down.

We were next to try.

"Thrae ternesj!" Jael shouted, spinning and pointing her sword.

340

Her Word caught the front stallion's legs, flipping them off the ground as he screamed in fury. Divigna moved fast, snatching then pressing something to his steed which broke the spell and freed the horse's movement. His men reacted at once, splitting into two packs of five on either side of him.

"Gavin!" I shouted. *"Wake up!"*

In the same instant, I thought, ~*STOP*.~

Another warrior took the command meant for their leader; as Divigna had slowed, another darted out in front, smashing into the psionic shield I'd summoned with a barbaric yell. The collision caused such a cacophony in my head, I couldn't hold it. The shield splintered as others ran through, the horse I'd struck squealing in pain and confusion, gathering its bearings under the brutal hand of its rider.

"*Fyaegr!*" Jael roared, sounding hoarse as she sacrificed another dagger to pitch at the nearest Hellhound.

I remembered that Word, knew to close my eyes and cover my ears best I could as the cracking flash went off. Multiple horses shrieked and stamped in terror. Further thunderstones erupted around us until I didn't know which way to run. The Hellhounds coughed, growled, and slowed …

But did not stop.

The battlefield collapsed further into roaring chaos, voices seared with rage and bafflement and fear. I wasn't one of them, but the sounds filling my ears threatened to shatter my skull. I didn't know what was happening!

Should we run? Which way?

Where the fuck was Mourn?

With a fearful flick of my eyes, I checked to see how Isboern fared. Circumstance had grown worse for him, and *that* was where I spotted the Dragonblood.

He's trying to keep the Godblood alive.

The Ma'ab engaged, fearing nothing before them as they tried to overrun the Templars. Mourn spun his sliders, snaring and yanking two spike chains midair; he slammed them into the ground, breaking their momentum and trajectory. Two other chains snaked past him to torment the Templars, wrapping around sword arms and weight-bearing legs, grinding against their armor.

I blinked to see the golden shield on the ground near the psion struggling to get up. Mourn braced between him and the three closest Hellhounds, blocking and harrying them with near-equal reach.

What the fuck just happened?

It didn't matter.

I raised Soul Drinker, wondering if Callitro's ring would work for me. Had it been long enough? Maybe not. Dare lose contact with the relic, especially for *this* target, when I could hardly see with such pain filling my ears?

No. Not with his men coming in first, and fast.

"Enough, Kreshel."

My body shuddered with the voice behind me, cool air touching my sweating brow as an ally I *should* recognize rasped louder than seemed natural.

Gavin had turned from where the fight had begun to where opponents raged about five paces behind me. The only good sign for us was the response, as gore-thick chains wound around their forearms, thick-boned steeds surrounding us.

The Deathwalker's face had shifted to pure white despite the sunlight, void-black eyes staring out from beneath his hood. His posture and face were strained as if magic or ritual was barely under his control; his thurible remained in his black, right hand.

"What do you want?" he asked.

Despite Mourn and the Templari still fighting, Divigna heard the Deathwalker. Pulling a dagger from a sheath in his boot, the Hellhound slashed the rope which strapped a body to his horse's haunches.

I cringed in dread, having not noticed the passenger until now but recognizing him at once.

The Eternal Hellhound dragged Deshi off and around with one hand, gripping him with a thumb at his collarbone and the rest clenched at the base of his neck. He lifted the Guildsman with one arm, showing us his battered and mutilated form, stripped naked but caked in blood and filth.

"You can see it, Adason, yes?" Divigna waved his prisoner like a cut of meat to a dog. "Aura imbued with Vitas, but not much longer."

"*Pucker suckers*," Jael muttered through clenched teeth.

"Agreed," Gavin answered, his voice sounding somewhat less like a maelstrom howling through it. "Do you return him to us?"

"Would you 'call' him if I did not?"

The Deathwalker chose not to answer, though I didn't know if he was thinking about it.

"What do you want?" he repeated.

Divigna chose not to answer either, but the small smile which appeared on his lips chilled me to the bone.

Suddenly, bright light streaked past us, striking the Hellhound farthest from his leader. The Ma'ab shouted and tumbled from his rearing horse as another two blasts hit his brothers.

Isboern called out. "Run or fight, Ma'ab! Those are your options!"

The Hellhounds which had been fighting Mourn and the Templars were down. The surviving Manalari were preparing to cast into our circle. Because of me, Jael, and Gavin, they had to be selective about the effects of that light spell.

Mourn was finally coming in to help; Divigna was aware of this.

The smirk lingered.

Behind me, Gavin gasped, his boot crunching on husks of tall grass, catching himself before a stumble. My stomach turned to witness my ally pulling a dagger from his lower back.

"F-fool," he uttered, his voice quieter ... no, *singular*. "What have y-you done?"

Bright metal coated in viscous, black gore rapidly *changing*. Gavin's blood became watery as it turned from black to red only to *burn* in blue and orange until the blood dried up like red sand falling to the earth.

The Deathwalker's eyes wavered, ice blue pupils winking in and out as he dropped the thurible. The dread on his face grew, and I focused on the dagger.

Silver.

The metal had once severed connection to his body at Troshin's Bend. Only its removal had allowed his Vis to return to his body.

What just happened with all the Ma'ab souls he's linked to?

My eyes darted along the path from which the blade must have come. There, in perfect position to have thrown the weapon at the Deathwalker, was Mathias Briar crouching behind one mounted Hellhound.

Bastard.

"Sirana!" Mourn shouted, sprinting to match the speed of Divigna's horse as the lead Ma'ab launched toward us.

My heart clogged my throat. *"Shit!"*

Neither Jael nor I prepared a defense before the Eternal Hellhound pitched Deshi's body at us. The Guildsman hit hard, engulfing us with the stickiness of blood and the stink of shit, dragging us halfway off Nightmare from sheer dead weight.

The Yungian grunted weakly next to my ear.

Alive?!

Divigna rammed his horse into ours the instant before Mourn caught up, throwing us to the side and into his path. The Dragon's son barely had space to pull his long blades away to avoid cutting us into segments.

"Sargt!" my bodyguard barked, equal parts furious and startled.

Deshi had landed on top of me; my spiders clung to my neck as I was clinging to Soul Drinker. Something else weighed down one foot but my senses hadn't caught up to tell what.

"Deathwalker!"

"Stop him!" I wheezed, struggling to get free.

How could such a lithe young man could weigh so much?

"Jael!"

"What! How!" she yelled, working to pull Deshi's body from me.

I rolled over, tugging my foot so hard that I lost a boot underneath Nightmare as she lay unmoving on her side. Scrambling up to my knees, I tried to ignore the shooting pain lancing through my ankle. Instead, horror enveloped me as Divigna traded Deshi for Gavin, ignoring all the Elves on the field except in how we served as obstacles or distractions.

"She said you would *end this*," the pale giant growled, picking my ally up by his neck and choking any words the death mage might say.

A second Hellhound dismounted, going for the silver dagger and thurible which landed on the ground.

"*Stop!*" Mourn shouted, swinging singing blades. "*Mahnrah!*"

The seven remaining Hellhounds froze in place for a moment or two, but Divigna did not; he launched away at full speed toward Manalar, clutching my long-boned ally to his front.

~*Isboern, do something!*~

~*We can't! We'll hit all of you as well!*~

The lead stallion's legs out of reach, Mourn growled, using both arms against the Hellhound going for Gavin's relic. The Ma'ab bellowed in shock and fell back as the magical weapons severed his arms, tattoos and protections unraveling within moments. The hybrid ran him through the chest, a final blow before he could die by explosion.

The other six Hellhounds had broken the mage paralysis and kicked their mounts into top speed, galloping after their leader. One of them extended a hand for Mathias, hauling the torturer up to straddle the mount.

As they fled, the battlefield finally began to quiet.

Or it was shock.

They took him.

Gavin.

And Mathias got away. *Again.*

A mere glance at what they had done to Deshi, and I couldn't help it; my stomach already heaved at the smell. Painfully, I retched over the grass, my forearms braced, though my stomach had nothing left to offer.

Left to wonder who had conducted the interrogation, dreading the images which came unbidden to my mind's eye, I still recognized part of the skin hunter's work.

Either the Hellhounds joined in, or Mathias is capable of sadism surpassing my darkest expectation.

CHAPTER 26

THE WORK WHICH FOLLOWED THE SECOND CONFLICT WAS SMALLER IN SCOPE than what I'd missed the first time. Although half the night wasn't required to address it, the cost of doing so was greater, heavier in the chest of the survivors, granting this same necessity a crippling impact.

Manalari and Guild joined together, taking swigs of water and potions without food; they moved with purpose, without pause, to search and then drag the bodies into a pile to burn them.

The losses on our side were numerous. We may have taken the first fifty Ma'ab which had approached us then a few Hellhounds after that, but Divigna and his twenty men had broken and trampled almost a hundred Manalari from the rear up to the frontline.

Not all the Guildsmen had made it, either. Melee and spells used on tight grounds would never guarantee anyone's wellbeing. Wolf led Reprisal, but his unit had shrunk to eleven. The only one I knew for certain was Kil from his size. Most of *Hata Ri* were here, but the mages numbered fifteen rather than twenty.

Tamuril and Krithannia would find us in time, I'd heard they were well, but I doubted the Yungian brothers' count would climb from two to three. Until then, I stayed by Deshi's body, waving away the Templar Erik when he approached with a limp, his leg wrapped from the scoring of chains.

"The Guildsman is alive," I said, watching Deshi's filthy, naked chest which barely moved. "This one is not ready to be burned."

"I ... I am sorry, Blood Sister," the Templar said, keeping a respectful distance rather than looming above me. "The mercenary escaped me. I ... I do not know how, but you were right. *Dyos sange ... mion Capitan* was in danger, and this drew your Shadow away from your protection. Perhaps as intended."

I ground my teeth. "You are not the first Mathias has fooled, *Tetente*."

"What can I do to make amends?"

Nothing right now.

"We will retrieve my Deathwalker," I stated. "You and your brothers will help with that."

"*Ci, farrimus. Capitan* agrees." He glanced behind him. "What of the Ma'ab sorceress?"

Amelda. My nose wrinkled. "Make her wait. Keep her blind, deaf, and mute. I will see to her."

I doubted I would follow Isboern's lead this time.

Erik placed his hand over his heart and stepped away so that Jael was the only other near me.

Mourn *had* checked on us before the *Tetente*, satisfied we were mostly unhurt, and he suggested that we come with him.

I'd been staring at the ruined tattoo on Deshi's left arm, the skull and winter rose deliberately defaced to be unrecognizable. If I hadn't already admired the beauty and detail in the *dorji-ka* in Yong-wen, if I hadn't understood what was gone, I would have taken those wounds to be oddly crude for Mathias's pride in his skill.

"No," I'd answered. "Just ... let me be. Let me think. Keep Peng-lok and Nianzu away. *Please*."

The irritation crumbled into wavering tears.

The Dragonblood had said nothing and left, finding plenty to do with the Godblood in trying to salvage any morale from the bitter defeat. The survivors witnessing them working together helped more than either of them could say or do for me right then.

Meanwhile, I braved Deshi's face after Jael did us the favor of speaking a "cleaning" Word which helped with the smell, if not the blood and dirt.

How are you alive?

His eyes would never focus on me for they had been pierced, the eyelids cut off either before or after. I dared not count broken bones or missing teeth, although difficult *not* to note the severed digits.

Only one left on each limb.

I did not want to understand the reasons for those left attached, nor why his tongue still leaked blood. Deshi's flesh had also been whipped and beaten much like Jacob had been, with too-familiar injuries of restraint and violation eerily matching Reishel after her "trials" alone with the Prime.

"Sirana," Jael said, soft but firm. "Look, I find."

Find?

She had already brought Gavin's thurible and the shining silver dagger which the Ma'ab had failed to claim. What else had she spotted?

With reluctance, I turned my head.

Deshi's "blessed" dagger.

Pristine. No blood on it.

No sheath, either.

Where had it come from? Had that been the weapon Divigna had used to cut the ropes from his horse's burden?

Perhaps one small gladness that it used on him.

With Soul Drinker secure and the silver dagger in the grass beside me, I reached to accept this third blade, turning it over in my hand as a thought intruded too quickly for comfort.

Any Vis marked by this blade will be in the view of the Grey Maiden's agents.

Nyx would send guides to find them.

Should I ... ?

Could I assist Deshi in his limbo and send him to the Grey Maiden he revered? Or could his body be healed by the Guild, the Godblood, anyone? Would that only make it much worse, imprisoning him in a disfigured existence he no longer wanted?

"*I must ask him a question,*" I murmured to Jael.

"Huh?"

I couldn't hide my discomfort. *"Like Reishel when she lay senseless after the Ornilleth attack, or after the Prime 'tested' her. I asked if she ... wished to come awake into the pain. Or if she wanted to slip away."*

"Oh." My younger Sister's face twisted with concern. *"Oh, I don't like that, Sirana. What if you ... get trapped in his last day?"*

I swallowed. *"If you see something in me like with the Witch Hunter and Gaelan, break my touch to him, but* without *touching me. Get Isboern, like in the redoubt prison."*

She squinted with doubt. *"But ... why? Why suffer it if he will die in time?"*

My vision blurred, surprising me. *"I-I don't know. What if he holds on from his will alone? Or worse, what if he doesn't but is lost? I can ... find out. Maybe set him free."*

My Sister's lips thinned as she considered. Finally, *"Alright. Do it. I'll watch you."*

Grateful for a clear path, I secured my spiders and removed my gloves, flexing my fingers as I considered where to touch him. His abraded brow? His scored chest? His broken stump of a hand?

Before I could decide, a whisper rushed in from my left. I jumped, seeking where I'd set the Temple's relic and silver dagger, waiting until the sound returned.

Voices ...

Drifting from the thurible.

Chills overwhelmed me beneath the bright, hot Sun. I shouldn't be able to *hear* that. I certainly wouldn't pick it up!

Deshi's head shifted, his tacky brow brushing my fingertips. I gasped, nearly yanking my hand away in fright.

Janshi ... ?

Oh ... Oh, Goddess.

So confused.

Where ... ? How did I ... ?

His consciousness lay upon cusp of his last memory, about to fall into it.

349

No!

~*You're safe, Deshi,*~ I soothed, taking hold with a mental shush. ~*Don't think, just listen. Listen to my voice. I am Janshi. I am here with you. Listen to me.*~

He tried but could spare me only a few moments. *I ... can't feel ... ! Why ... ?*

I scrambled for something to say; all I had was the truth.

~*Your body is dying, Deshi. Sho'shien cannot be here, I am sorry ... But listen. I have your blessed dagger beside you.*~

He didn't respond, confused but listening.

~*Do you ... want to transition? The Grave Mother's agents will come to you. They will find you as they did Sho'shien. Or do you want the Guild to try and mend your body which ... may or may not succeed?*~

For an eternal instant, the boy was so frightened. His Vis, so young. Starkly bright.

Why will Sho'shien not come to me now? he asked. *How have I offended him?*

~*You haven't!*~ I rushed to say, fighting the squeeze in my chest. ~*I'm sorry. The Ma'ab ... Divigna captured him when he returned you to us. Our Deathwalker is in trouble ... his body is —*~

Abruptly, Deshi *remembered*.

No! he cried. *My fault!*

Hit, I screamed alongside him, drowning in a whirlpool of utter silence.

"*Urtren'shila ... Rashin tra'gall. Isshrugren, miurssbluen ...*"

A prickling sensation spread up the back of my skull as I attuned my ear to the flutter of sound like a moth's wings ...

Touch without harm, She whispered. *Lift memory to shed life's pain. Be not afraid, world's bloom.*

With Deshi's dagger in hand, I touched two fingers to the top of the thurible as spiritual incense leaked out of the many holes in the metal. Awareness of a blood-soaked field swept away, along with the fading wail of Deshi's mortality.

We kneeled upon an ashen plane where light diffused through a grey veil, its source indeterminate and any suggestion of rain clouds questionable.

It was … quiet.

"Janshi?" Deshi asked, not too loudly.

His eyes were open.

I stared at a gaze clear and perfect, one I'd believed I would never see again. The youth lifted his chin to look around, his form whole and dressed only in Yungian style pants. His hair trimmed the shortest I'd seen, his bare arms and chest were much as I remembered in the *dorji-ka*. The tattoo of the skull and white rose decorated his left arm as I remembered it.

"Janshi." Deshi pointed behind me. "Who is she?"

She … ?

"You know, child. I am here."

The whisper held care and restraint, like a Dwarf trying to handle a butterfly fresh from its cocoon, as if speaking a measure louder posed a danger to him.

To us.

The Yungian quivered and bowed until his forehead touched the grey dust, his chest resting upon his thighs, arms outstretched, hands splayed wide, his palms up.

"*Huin'sho*," he whispered, awe immeasurable. "*Y-you* came to me …"

Not her agents, as Gavin had said.

Her.

I didn't *want* to look, but I must. Twisting my neck and body, I looked without turning full around.

A grey woman's form stood not far away, swaddled in pale, worn cloth, the frayed, loose ends swaying in an unfelt wind. Her figure was contained in roughly our own size, yet I could not dislodge the certainty of kneeling in an enormous presence, her far-reaching gaze reaching leagues beyond my Valsharess.

Her face, hidden behind a white, featureless mask, reminded me of the Shaegoth playing with me on the hillside. The marked differences were the dark cracks which began around sightless eyes, spreading onto her cheeks in such a way that suggested the mask could *move*.

I read neither thought nor expression in that moment. If her gaze landed upon me, I did not feel its weight.

"Come," she said, beckoning Deshi. *"It is time."*

The youth hesitated. "What of *Sho'shien*?"

A black beetle climbed out of the mask's right eye, pausing on the broken cheek. She tilted her head curiously, seemingly unaware of the insect. *"Your life is past. What of him makes no difference."*

"B-but ... he is captured by a warped soul because of *me!* He could be truly destroyed if he is given to the Ascended, and it will be my fault! I know our home *needs* him, please! If you are who I believe you are, tell me you will help him?"

She shook her head once. *"That is not to be."*

"Not to be?"

"Release this world, child. For your service, I grant safe passage to the next."

Pain shocked the Yungian, and he shuffled backward on his knees. "No. I do not believe you."

The beetle resumed crawling with the next tilt of her head, crossing the bridge of her mask's nose, only to stop on the opposite cheek. *"What is there to believe? Existence is."*

"Not by chance! Janshi is here! She bears witness!" His voice cracked. "The sky spirit gave me a *choice*, to s-stay or go!"

"Oh? Has she that power?" The grey woman's mask tilted toward me, acknowledging me at last.

Now I felt the weight of her gaze.

I couldn't *think*. The air — if air existed — seemed too dry to swallow as I wondered how deeply I'd stepped in sucking mud. The edges of my thoughts quivered in doubt as I exhaled.

Tiny motes of light left my mouth, forming a visible cloud of glittering breath which took me by surprise. Deshi's eyes flew wide, fixing on it intently; my breath caught in my throat from the way he stared at me.

What in the web?

My next breath exited through my nose, yet the space around me filled once more with shimmering, golden swirls.

"Aha, she does. By proxy." The masked woman hummed with slight, breathless amusement. *"Very well. Choose."*

Deshi blinked. "Now?"

Instead of tilting her head, she bowed it forward, and the beetle climbed off her face and onto her neck. *"If you would travel under your own will, it must be 'now.' Beyond this small eternity lies the realm of Soraveri, into which we gaze but cannot tread, and the Nexus itself. Do understand, if you turn back now, you would straddle living Existence at best."*

I hoped the youth grasped that better than I did.

"If … if I forfeit safe passage and return," Deshi said, "will you grant a different boon for my service?"

She dipped her chin. *"Speak it."*

"I ask for a body which cannot be killed again. I shall use it to protect and defend your Deathwalker from threats which might undo him."

The Grey Woman lifted her chin the barest bit, the motion seeming to bear the greatest weight thus far. *"You may be granted a sturdier form, one bereft of a natural death. To make you unkillable would be a mockery to this world. You have spoken of purpose, but what is your desire?"*

Another flash of pain overtook Deshi's dark eyes, turning them briefly blue like Gavin's. Anger took its place, and he confessed.

"I will make certain Mathias Briar cannot hurt another like me again," he intoned. "And after I find the skin hunter, I will hunt as many Hellhounds as I can, especially the warped one. He is long overdue for his crossing."

The swaddled woman achieved an uncanny stillness to the extent I wondered if I had fallen into a second trance. Her mask remained unreadable while the black beetle finished its journey down her arm and into her palm. She lifted her hand to peer at it, as if just noticing its presence, before extending it out in offering.

"Eat this," she said to the Human before tilting her head toward me.

"Then breathe in the native breath. Take it in deep, harrowed soul, and do not let it slip away. This is your anchor now."

Deshi crawled to her, moving around me and stretching to reach for the insect without brushing the drifting tatters.

~Deshi — ?~

The crunch between his teeth made me grimace. When his head turned, his pupils had taken on a firmly pale, iridescent blue. He crawled from the Grey Maiden to me, hungry still.

"Breathe for me, Janshi," the youth pleaded.

Chilled with fear, I *could* have fled, I knew. Only one pathway was open to me, however, one where he could not follow.

If I fled, I abandoned him.

"Touch without harm," the Grey Maiden repeated.

I stayed. Frigid fingers framed my face, icy blue eyes making every promise without guile.

"Let me breathe again," he said. "Let me will my body to mend, to become stronger, and I *will not stop* until we reach *Sho'shien*. We will find him!"

"Are you sure about this?" I whispered.

His eyelids fluttered in bliss, snatching the air of my words like a bird catching a grasshopper. His head dropped as if it was too heavy to hold up. A soft whimper slipped out alongside his single thought.

Home.

Lifting his eyes, he leaned forward. ""I have made my choice. Thank you, Janshi, for offering it."

He covered my mouth with his, but not for a kiss. He was waiting. He was cold.

Breathe for me.

I couldn't withhold my next breath if I tried. Exhaling, I pushed the sparkling current into him, where the light caught like a flame on a wick and became visible within his core. His chest brushed against me, expanding so much he might have just broken the surface of water where he'd been drowning. He drew on my air, sucked it in, *ate* it alongside the beetle.

Until the two became one.

Until they became *him*.

And a harrowed soul came screaming back to Miurag in his entirety.

I came aware on a gore-strewn, daylit battlefield, my lips hovering above the mutilated face of a corpse.

"Sirana!" Jael called, likely not the first time. Her arms hooked beneath my pits as she prepared to haul me away. *"What are you doing? Can you hear me?!"*

~I hear you.~

Yet my open mouth wouldn't move, and too little air remained in my lungs to push words. Light-headed and shivering, I gripped Deshi's dagger in my bare hand as Jael dragged me a dozen body-lengths away. The ancient thurible sat upright in the grass near his naked body, getting smaller as the whispers gradually left my ears.

Mourn hurried toward us, responding to the pitch of my Sister's voice and her long, hurried scuttle for distance. "Sirana! Does anything hurt?"

If he meant my *body*, no.

Just cold.

Finally, my chest filled with air, and I moaned with relief.

"What happened, Dalkrix?" he asked in Davrin, drawing me from Jael's hold to cradle and check me over himself.

Goddess, he was *so warm!*

"W-well, um," Jael stammered, *"sh-she wanted to ask Deshi if he wished to stay alive."*

The half-blood paused. *"She mindlinked with a dying man?"*

"Well. Yes."

She didn't try to justify it.

"Shuiblith." His thick neck twisted to search behind him, probably for Isboern.

"W-wait," I forced out. *"I'm here. I'm alright …"*

I was staring, though, and hadn't blinked. My body was coming under conscious control in pieces.

Intense gold eyes met mine. *"Your name?"*

Heh.

"Sirana," I said. *"Sirana d' Vloszia Dalnanin draeval uz'Thalluensareci."*

Mourn smiled, showing his relief, far fess reluctant to take the jest compared to when we'd first met. *"Very well. Do you need anything?"*

"Water."

Jael gave this quickly while Krithannia and Tamuril appeared in my periphery with the Yungian brothers. I almost choked.

"Uh, shit, wait," I muttered in Davrin, *"they shouldn't stumble on him."*

Mourn glanced up. With a nod, he passed me back to Jael and moved to intercept them. We tilted our ears to catch what they said.

"A warning," the Dragonchild began. "Deshi's body is gruesome."

Tamuril hesitated, but Krithannia stood tall. "We understand, *Wen-yung*. His brothers know and have asked to see him anyway. I would grant their request given how we left Groa's body amid the thorns atop Lookout."

Peng-lok and Nianzu confirmed this desire, bowing respectfully to Mourn while abjectly miserable. The Dragonblood's tail swayed, somehow conveying acceptance and patience.

"As you wish."

Mourn led the three forward while Tamuril hung back with Pilla, glancing my way before coming to join us.

"Do you need a hand?" she asked, offering hers.

Jael made a face as if tempted to pout that Tami beating her to it. I chuckled and accepted the Druid's help, testing my footing and balance. Both were good, but my head swam until deeper breathing helped that fade.

"Is it ... truly bad?" the Naulor asked.

"Oh, aye!" Jael replied with disturbing certainty. "Vicious. Ma'ab match our leader's prison underground."

I winced. She had seen that truth, too, yet a potent discomfort rose in me to hear the comparison spoken so glibly.

At least Auslan said he got out in time.

The Prime didn't have him around for sport.

Tamuril swallowed. "I'm … sorry."

I blinked. *For what?*

Nearby, the Yungian brothers cried out in alarm, rattling off words I couldn't understand.

Uh-oh.

"Sirana!" Jael said as I sprinted toward Deshi's body.

"Come on!" I replied.

Tamuril followed more slowly, if only to not to appear idle while all others worked. I wasn't sure how to help her, but I could look at Deshi again with an emotion beyond grief.

I could find out whether that vision had been real.

Mourn's tail twisted in a way I couldn't read, and he turned to me as I approached.

"What is it?" I huffed. "What are they saying?"

He frowned. "Their brother is breathing but has no pulse. Deshi's heart lies still within his chest."

How … ?

Oh.

Once close enough, his moving chest didn't catch my attention but rather, it was his eyes. His cheeks were still caked with blood, but the eye sockets weren't empty anymore. His eyelids were whole, closed, and uncut; he appeared asleep, as if he had been weeping crimson tears, not blinded by knifepoint.

I inspected his left arm next, grieving anew at Mathias's cruel distortion of the winter rose which the Yungian had held sacred. *And yet …* These blade marks shrank as I watched, much like Gavin's wounds when he cut himself. The lash marks faded as quickly, and …

"*Chindi,*" Nianzu whispered, his body shaking and his face becoming pale. Peng-lok took his arm with both hands as if to steady him. Or himself.

"His fingers," Krithannia murmured without pointing hers.

If I hadn't spent time with her like I had, I would have missed her supreme effort to sound like a calm observer. Disbelieving, I witnessed his bones reemerging out of the stumps, growing at a visible pace, layered by the rise of dark red flesh — muscle and sinew — and eventually cloaked in skin.

His missing fingers would reform, as would his toes.

"Sirana," Mourn asked softly, "what happened just now?"

What *had* happened? What had I *done?*

"Did you create another Deathwalker?"

"Wh-what?!" I spun to face him. "I didn't create the *first* one!"

Only then did I realize Mourn was smiling, as if pleased with my reaction.

"Was that a jest?" I demanded.

"It was."

Mourn's smile grew as easy to see as Deshi's new digits. Peng-lok and Nianzu stared at the Dragonblood with odd hope in their frightened eyes. Jael squinted at us all before gauging the unresponsive body healing at an unnatural speed.

If 'healing' is the correct word for this.

"Not Deathwalker," my Sister said. "Aura is different."

"Agreed," Mourn said. "What do you see, *Janhuren?*"

She caught on that he asked on behalf of the Yungian brothers.

"Mixed," she answered, moving her hands like stirring a bowl. "Like Deathwalker, but also like *Janshi* b ... ." Jael stopped, licking her lips. "Yellow light. Like the blue mist and sun together."

The Yungian brothers seemed joyful, as if she had confirmed something they hadn't dared believe. That emotion turned my way and, for whatever reason, I grimaced.

"Sky-blessed!" Peng-lok said. "Our young brother will return to us but awaken as a spirit warrior to serve *Sho'shien.*"

My mouth was dry. "That was ... his choice."

"How so?" Krithannia asked.

"He *said* it," I said in a rush, my shakes turning to nervous exasperation. "Or at least h-he ... *thought* it!"

She frowned. "I think we are missing key details."

"I think we are missing *all* of them," Mourn remarked, bizarrely amused.

"And I don't know where to start," I growled, narrowing my eyes.

"You tell me you will ask if he need help to die," Jael said. "You use Deshi's dagger to mark him for the Grey Maiden if he said yes."

"Right. *Thank* you, Sister."

My face burned to have that difficult decision spilled so bluntly, and I expected Deshi's brothers to be watching me in horror for what I'd done.

They weren't. They bowed.

"You offered him this honor, Janshi," Nianzu said with blatant relief.

I resisted shuffling my feet. "Well, yes? But I didn't kill him."

"Our brother chose." Peng-lok bowed. "And you honored this, too."

"Not me. Not alone."

"Not alone?" Mourn echoed. "Who else was there?"

Damn my babbling.

"He met the Grey Maiden," I said stiffly, "when I touched the thurible. *Deshi* told her he wanted to stay, not leave, and *she* granted his wish, not me. A-at most, I was the ..."

Conduit?

"Middle link," I finished. "That allowed them to talk."

I think.

Yungian eyes widened with surprise and awe. Instead of more bowing, they seemed at a loss. Reverent hands formed a series of slow gestures above their brother's body.

Meanwhile, Tamuril had stepped into my periphery, willing to approach now that Isboern and two Templars had arrived to discover why we loitered in a bunch.

Now I felt sick. *What will I tell him?*

Mourn's bemused comment looped in my head. *"She mindlinked with a dying man?"*

Goddess, not him, too ...

At least Deshi's kin weren't upset for the moment.

"What is your concern, legends?" asked the Captain, though it didn't take long for his gaze to be drawn to Deshi's body. If any of us had answered him at once, I doubted he'd have heard and understood the words.

"Has he not died?" Robi was somewhat reluctant to ask.

"Oh, he *has* died," Krithannia said without hesitation, tapping lips with gloved fingers, her dark brows knitted in concern.

"But we shall not be adding him to the pyre," Isboern added as a confident guess.

"Correct," Mourn confirmed.

The Godblood needed something more. He looked at me.

I swallowed. "I believe the death mage will wake up again. He only needs time, as when Gavin arose with his new purpose."

Isboern's eyes widened. "You've ... completed a ritual?"

~Not intentionally. I don't understand it.~

The blond man's face was sweaty, streaked with grime and blood; his mouth twisted slightly with my pleading thought. He stepped closer as if to better study the man we'd gathered around. Robi and Imran followed him to keep watch around us while Tamuril eased next to my side, hugging herself with her arms. Pilla hunkered down warily on her shoulder.

"*Beindi Musanlo*," the Captain murmured, placing a fist over his heart. "He's breathing."

"But no heart," Jael added, thumping her own chest. "Is still."

Peng-lok and Nianzu had kneeled protectively on either side of their brother's body while we talked. They seemed ... stunned after I'd told them Deshi met the Grey Maiden.

"And his ... injuries?" Isboern asked.

"Are closing," Krithannia confirmed. "Or regenerating. Similar to the Herald."

Several heartbeats became audible then as I listened to the wind and the laboring men in a trampled field.

"Perhaps ... wash his body?" Imran suggested. "Before he, *erm*, wakes? We can find some dress from ... another who no longer needs it."

Isboern gauged our reactions. "I agree. Deshi need not wake up nude and covered in his own blood."

"Hm. A good suggestion," Mourn said.

Peng-lok and Nianzu bowed to them both, eyes glistening.

"A small stream lies this way," the Captain added, pointing north, "behind that stand of trees. We will bring you a set of clothing soon."

"Ah, may I ask," Robi cleared his throat. "Do I see h-his fingers ... healing?"

"Rebuilding," Mourn replied.

"What do you mean?" Isboern paused as he took a second look. "Ah. *Mutilondio?*"

"Correct."

"I ... am sorry."

"Mathias Briar took part in it," I growled. "Much worse than he did to the Witch Hunter."

The Dragon's son motioned a subtle warning as Isboern and his Templars stared.

Oh, yeah, they don't know everything about that ...

"Retaliation for our imprisoning him?" the Captain asked.

"Unlikely," Krithannia said, matter of fact. "I believe only the Death-walker's need to create the Bishops' undoing spared Jacob a similar end. Given the opportunity, Mathias would have taken it."

"Agreed," Mourn said. "This man has a compulsion to torment. Deshi was an opportunity, nothing more, but thanks to Sirana, his body becomes whole. He may help us locate the Herald. He only needs time to rise."

And when he does, he comes for the skin hunter.

I kept the thought to myself.

Deshi would make that clear soon enough.

Chapter 27

Mourn offered to carry Deshi's body to the stream, and Krithannia was willing to bear his "blessed" dagger and Gavin's thurible.

Probably a good idea.

Every brush against Soul Drinker's pommel brought a chill, though it might have been me thinking about the demon inside the crystal. My spiders could sense the stress of my psionic trances yet must be still, lest they interpret the threat as *me*. I didn't need to carry anything more to do with death and required my hands to eat rations anyway.

Baby and I are starving.

Isboern stayed behind to continue guiding the clean-up while his Templars disappeared on other duties, one of them presumably to retrieve clothes that might fit the Yungian. Once again, Tamuril waved farewell to her clan psion from the West and joined me and Jael with Peng-lok and Nianzu. She seemed sad about it.

At least she waited until I'd finished eating and Mourn was passing Deshi over to his brothers when she spoke her mind.

"Is it too soon to ask for your ring?" she murmured near my right ear.

Only Jael heard her, arching her eyebrow with suspicious confusion. She hadn't been with us on the Lookout, but she'd learned about it.

"Um. I suppose not." I started to tug on my glove. "But … why now?"

"I had another shot at Divigna," she whispered, sounding about to weep. I couldn't tell if guilt or dread weighed heavier in her tone, but her falcon cheeped tenderly near her cheek.

I twisted Callitro's ring, pulling it gently from my finger. "If you missed his mouth, would you arrow pierce his hide?"

She whimpered; Pilla chirped encouragingly. "I-I don't know."

"I'm certain the rune dagger will, but I do not want him that close again. And maybe you shouldn't try."

"What?"

I offered the mage's jewelry in an open palm. "I would rather you do as you said. Use it to protect Isboern, the way Mourn had to, no matter where Divigna was at the time."

The Druid took in my words gradually before reaching for Callitro's ring. "But — ?"

"He *can't* die, archer," I said, lowering my voice, "or the Ma'ab and their Ascended gain a foothold south of the Great Lake. How long do you think the Ascended will wait before their Hellhounds travel West toward your forest? Toward your people?" I paused to make certain she imagined that. "Divigna is not your focus. Isboern is. He *cannot* die before the sacred pool is reclaimed."

Her pale skin warmed as she donned my ring, the resolve clear on her face. I was glad for only my Sister's judging gaze witnessing this while everyone else was distracted at the stream.

"*What if you need it?*" Jael whispered in Davrin. "*You know, to not miss when he gets close? Because you know he will.*"

I smirked. "*I'd rather the archer have a sure reach much farther than you or I have any skill to aim. My mind shield will have to get stronger, and your Dragon words almost toppled his horse. Hit harder next time. Slap him onto his ass.*"

I caught Jael's face in an amusing scowl of delight at the possibility before she rubbed it away with her hands, exasperated. "*Urgh. Fine.*"

The distinctive song of the Yungian language touched my ears as Mourn and Krithannia exchanged words with the surviving Guildsmen.

Deshi's body was greyish-pale compared to his warm-tanned brothers, and appeared clean from where I stood, floating spread-eagled in the slow current.

Peng-lok and Nianzu had removed their boots and rolled up their pant legs and sleeves to do the work; they appeared to be performing a ritual of their own. I didn't know if it would have any tangible effect other than having something to do while awaiting the unknown.

How much longer?

What was happening with Gavin and the "twisted soul"? What did Mathias expect do against us next? Could I "wake" my Deathwalker's would-be protector the way Isboern had nudged his brothers after being drugged?

I should wait until we have clothes to offer … My gaze drifted toward the battlefield. Finally, I spotted Robi and Imran returning, the latter carrying a bundle. *Perfect.*

I'd stepped forward, lifting my hand to acknowledge and greet them, when Peng-lok and Nianzu called out behind me.

"Deshi? *Deshi?!*"

"*Nuvrenshu wen-ma?*"

I spun around, gauging whether the two living brothers were helping the third to stand up …

Or if they tried to hold him back.

The haunting screech which left the young man's mouth jolted my ears, darting down my spine like a sky bolt. Everyone froze in place, Templars included, and stared with horror as Deshi pulled free of supporting hands and scrambled dripping out of the water.

Naked and huffing for air, his teeth bared like a feral animal, *something* about the lines of Deshi's flesh quivered — yet he wasn't trembling. The whites of his eyes had turned black like Gavin, and although the irises appeared ice blue, something was different about them.

"*Shundi!*" Peng-lok reached out. "Deshi, *shinu Peng-lok!*"

Deshi's body jolted at the voice behind him, moving three steps forward before his brother could take his shoulder. He sucked in a deep breath, releasing it as that shrill, frightening cry.

Imran backed up, and Robi made a protective gesture across his chest. "*Revenante*," he whispered.

I wasn't certain but also not the only one worried the death mage would attack them. Mourn and Jael broke into motion when I hurried to stand in between them.

"Deshi?" I called.

His head snapped toward me, unnervingly fast.

Was this Deshi?

"It's Janshi!" I called, my palms forward, hands empty as I stood in front of the Templars. "Janshi! You are home, Deshi. You made it. Listen to me. *Sho'shien* needs you. I need your help finding him."

His eyes blinked once, refocusing on me. Yellow-gold rings outlined his irises, separating ice-blue from the black of his sclera. A change similar to Gavin's but …

Not the same.

Something lower distracted him. The Yungian youth stared at my middle with rising intensity until understanding broke over his face, spreading to soften the hard lines.

Damn it.

He could see it, too.

"Life spirit," Deshi said, his voice hoarse and rasping. With another blink, he exhaled softly without that creepy sound. "Janshi … !"

He remembered.

Straightening up from his wild-man hunch, he bowed, his form solid to my eye. The ritual gesture grounded him, and only then did he lift his hands to study them and the rest of his body. All appeared healed, even the tattoo on his left bicep.

Although that looks different, too.

In place of the skull was a woman's mask.

Mourn had detoured to take the clothing from Imran, who mutely released them. The half-blood whispered a cleaning spell at once, making certain no stain or gore remained.

"Do you feel the sun, Deshi?" Krithannia asked, stepping up as he did this.

The young death mage turned such that I couldn't see the image on his skin. "Yes. The light is warm."

And yet his skin remained deathly pale, his lips slightly blue, without a tremor of color shift elsewhere.

"How about the breeze?"

"Yes, *Yunze*." He breathed in deeply. "It is beautiful and strong."

Cloud keeper.

The Guild Mistress smiled hearing her mission's name. "Do you feel chilled?"

"No, *Yunze*, I do not."

"Not your feet? Your back?"

"I am ... well, great spirit."

He also didn't seem aware of his nudity despite the rest of us surrounding him fully clothed.

Krithannia's expression remained gentle and welcoming. "Will you accept a gift? We would offer clothing to draw fewer enemy eyes to you."

His own eyes narrowed, a flicker of anger passing over his face, air rattling in his throat before he blinked. Hurriedly, he bowed, expelling the bitterness before speaking. "I accept. Thank you."

But not all of it, as it turned out. Mourn gave him plenty of time and space to inspect what the Templars had brought.

"Nothing to bind my feet," Deshi said, rejecting the boots and stockings. "I must feel the earth."

The half-blood chuckled. "This, I understand, *zimengsi*."

Deshi glanced down at Wen-yung's long claws and rough feet, his answering smile not-quite-Human. Our revived mage eschewed the padded armor, belt, gloves, and helmet without further explanation, donning only the plain brown tunic and trousers, leaving his head, hands, and feet bare.

"That is enough, I suppose," Krithannia said with dry appraisal.

"I mean no insult, *Yunze*," he murmured with real regret. "I ... listen to my body."

"As you must. That is the greater gift by far. No insult taken."

Precisely what he'd asked for: a sturdier form, and one that apparently needed clothes only for the comfort of those around him. In addition to that freezing shriek and a body losing definition … *What else can he do?*

After a disorienting delay, Deshi finally noticed his brothers. Upon seeing their faces, his own collapsed in sorrow.

"*Dubiqi, cingdumei,*" he said, not a single tear touching his eyes the moment they would have if he were Human.

His next words cracked around the edges, drawing Peng-lok and Nianzu through any lingering fear to approach him, to pull him into a close, body-shaking embrace. Gradually, they sank down onto the ground, holding on through a wave of emotion which needed to pass before we could do anything about Gavin.

I sighed quietly, drawing in my patience as Mourn asked the Templars to retrieve the Godblood "when he was next available."

So be it.

I didn't have a next step, anyway. The Sun was well past its zenith, and I wasn't sure where we would end up by nightfall.

How quickly everything changed.

Mourn and Krithannia seemed to notice and smiled with understanding, motioning for me with Tamuril and Jael to give the Yungian brothers space to sit with each other for a time.

"A good sign Deshi can still grieve with the living," the Guild Mistress murmured once out of earshot.

"Is it?" Tamuril asked, not disagreeing but curious.

Krithannia nodded. "If he could not, we would have a true revenant on our hands causing further grief without care. Jael is correct, this is not a Deathwalker, nor is he merely a vengeful spirit, but something different." She looked at me. "I've not seen it before."

"How many standing dead you *see* before?" Jael asked, dumbfounded.

The Naulor smiled. "I have lived among Humans for over five hundred years, Jael, and witnessed a few wonders among their death mages. Human 'Vis' is potent leaving their bodies, and far more malleable than ours or that of the Dwarves."

"*Hmph.* Maybe good thing they live short."

The Guild Mistress chuckled. "I think a short life is why they remain so bright."

My hands crept to cover my gut while they spoke, unable to ignore an unarticulated thought which lingered since the ritual bath with Tamuril. Deshi had given it a voice, as had Nyx.

"Has she that power? Aha, by proxy. Very well. Choose."

I cleared my throat, drawing their eyes, showing the worry on my face.

"What is it, *Kiabil*," Mourn asked.

My face warmed with the tone of his voice. "Mm. You and the Naulor ... suggested, at different times, that my chosen sire has passed on his gift to my baby. He's a healer by touch."

Krithannia and Tamuril brightened, glancing down with the mention of my unborn. Their looks held a distant yearning and wonder which seemed so odd until I remembered how old they both were.

Compared to me, at least.

"I believe we could see this gift in the bath," said the elder as the Druid blushed. "Osgrid could, too. That is why it worked."

"I could feel it, for certain." Tamuril caressed Pilla's feathers to soothe them both. "Life magic in harmony with all else when my ... brother would insist it must be corrupt somehow."

Krithannia scoffed. "They should peer into the mirror."

The Druid swallowed with discomfort and regret to have brought it up. The Guild Mistress granted her an escape by turning to me. "Is that all, Sirana?"

I shook my head. "No, not close. Deshi isn't merely grey-touched, but life-touched, yes? That's why you haven't seen it before?"

"Well, yes. I suppose."

I hated saying it but wrung it from my tongue anyway. "What is ... I mean, is it 'usual' for a *mata* to feel and ... and to use an unborn's magic?"

Mourn's tail had started moving as I formed my question, but he looked elsewhere, keeping thoughts to himself, and letting the females answer first.

Jael shook her head, folding her arms. "Never heard it, never saw it."

"Mm, indeed, it's not 'usual,'" the Guild Mistress granted, "but not unheard of, especially as the new aura becomes potent in the first year. The mother is usually a mage with a compatible magic, but I've been thinking that your psionic gift may be taking the place of that as you've learned from Isboern, thus easing the pathway, and strengthening the bond between you and the child."

Tamuril was giving Krithannia a strange look, as if she couldn't understand where her sister was getting this opinion.

She noticed and sighed deeply. "Ancient memories speak to me, sister, and have for centuries. Our people *have* lived through hard times, when a pregnancy *empowered* a wife's magic and body. Giving life did not drain and diminish her. Mother and unborn sometimes had to work together to survive." Krithannia appraised me. "That is how I see this. I am unsurprised to learn Davrin can do the same. In fact, I am impressed."

I trembled beneath her gaze. My baby was Dragon-touched like Jael, *and* healer-by-touch? *Like Auslan.* Yet unborn, my baby passed magic to Tamuril and Deshi through me because I had desperately wanted to mend my allies.

Because they will help me survive?

If the Valsharess had Seen even a fragment of this, She must have been satisfied with my methods to live to return before winter, with or without the helper in my womb.

Looking at Deshi, I watched him gather his strength to stand up, offering a hand to his brothers. At the same time, the hard, hot spot in my gut had become so … *real.* I didn't know if I held a cait or bua, but no life would be easy under the direct gaze of the Queen.

Still … Not just an endless hole into which I toss food.

"What word did you use in the bath?" I asked Tamuril.

The Druid looked startled. "Huh? I don't understand …"

Of course, I could do better. "When you apologized for using thorns on my stomach, you said you didn't know."

"W-well, I didn't —"

"I know, and it's forgotten. But what did you say?"

"Say?"

"You used a word. Um." I pointed at my stomach.

The Druid needed two moments to bring that word to her tongue. "*Pinn'ionne?*"

"That was it!" I crowed, a smile tugging at my lips. "What does it mean?"

"Oh! Uh …"

Krithannia's eyes twinkled as she translated. "Smallest treasure."

Treasure.

My hidden treasure.

As I'd named my child's sire in secret.

"Or smallest blessing!" Tamuril added, spinning on her. "Blessing is also a good word."

The dark-haired Naulor shrugged with good humor. "I suppose it depends on the millennium."

"So, which part means 'smallest?' " I asked.

Krithannia pinched her thumb and forefinger together. "*Pinn.*"

"So, *'ionne'* is the treasure? Or blessing?"

"Correct. *Ionne.*"

Ionne.

That would work until I decide on a Davrin name later … Once I "saw" his or her face in a dream, as Krithannia and Innathi said I would.

If that becomes relevant.

"Why do you ask, *Kiabil*?" Mourn prodded gently, trying to read my face if not my thoughts, while Jael appeared equally curious.

"Mm, well," I began. "If the presence is so obvious, as are the results of magic which is not mine …"

Only by proxy.

"I wanted a name," I finished, my heart thudding harder in my chest.

"What?!" Jael asked, alarmed. "A Naulor name?"

"Not unchanging," I replied. "Like a Guild name. Or Yungian. Just *another* name besides … what I don't want everyone saying."

"A code name." Krithannia's grin fixed into place. "I love it. I'd say it is well-earned."

"Agreed," Mourn said with a brighter swing to his tail. "So, Pinn? Or … ?"

"Ionne," I confirmed. "No one will know what it means, but we can use it as needed."

Jael glanced around the circle and shrugged without putting up a fight. "Good sound."

"We should tell Deshi as well," Mourn said. "He recognizes the aura now."

My heartbeat throbbed in my chest as I agreed. *Yeah ...*

"Ionne," Tamuril breathed wistfully, green eyes bright as she placed less accent on the sound as if to make it a name. "I ... wish I might meet Ionne one day."

My lips compressed out of habit, withholding my expression of doubt. A large, warm hand rested in comfort on my back.

"That is why we need Captain Isboern alive," said the Dragon's son, "and standing victorious at the sacred pool."

Tamuril's eyes glanced down, thumbing Callitro's ring beneath her glove. "Of course. I recall his vision and will support it with my last arrow."

The wind carried the sound of approach to us. On one side, Deshi and his brothers were on their feet and leaving the stream; on the other, Imran and Robi were returning with the Godblood.

"Next goal in that vision then," Mourn said. "Find the Herald of Nyx."

Chapter 28

The Templars waited for us beside a small copse of trees. Amelda was blindfolded, gagged, and bound at Sir Erik's feet, who had taken his role seriously while we'd taken time for Deshi.

The afternoon sun lengthened the shadows over the open ground; the mage-controlled burning of bodies ongoing. My words from a few minutes ago echoed in my head, unsettling me despite Mourn and Krithannia's reassurances.

"Amelda knows about Ionne. Brom must have told her after I stabbed him and ran with Soul Drinker. She didn't know before then, but she told Kreshel Divigna. I don't know if either of them told anyone else."

We'd spoken in a huddle which had included the risen Yungian but not his brothers.

"I recall no mention around me, Janshi," Deshi shared, his expression darkening. *"Though I understand ... this cannot be taken as proof."*

"Did Mathias ask about Sirana as well as Gavin?" Mourn asked.

"He did, Wen-yung. But no questions or ... taunts about the new spirit."

Deshi's pale form had begun to shift as he spoke, to become less substantial as a subtle but spine-chilling howl had entered the breeze blowing past us. Ice blue irises had begun to sink into the black sclera, though the yellow ring remained in stark contrast. Mourn had lifted his hand slowly, placing it on the young man's shoulder, drawing his attention at once.

"*Good, Deshi. Thank you. Stay with us, please, but say nothing directly to Amelda, for she will use it for diversion. We will question her.*"

Deshi's eyes had regained their colors, his outline fully defined as he bowed to the Dragon Spirit. "*Yes, Wen-yung.*"

The young man held his tongue but indeed stuck close to me while I'd coaxed Nightmare to her feet to come with us. We rejoined the Templars, Deshi and I approached from the front with Jael and Mourn flanking. Gavin's old mare made enough noise with her hooves to alert our noble prisoner of a new arrival.

The Naulor Elves diverted with Peng-lok and Nianzu, approaching in silence from a different direction to observe from within the trees. Meanwhile, Pilla arrived on her own, selecting a branch extending out above Amelda and Sir Erik.

~May the falcon see fit to void her gut all over the Ma'ab's head. Maybe it'll land in her mouth while she's threatening us.~

I sensed Mourn's mental smirk, but he said nothing as Captain Isboern turned, raising his arm to greet us.

Sky blue eyes landed on the Yungian, unsurprised but concerned as his gaze shifted to me. *~Is this a good idea, Sirana? Amelda was present during his torture.~*

I wondered how he was certain but also saw that as likely. *~We have limited time and no secure space. Would you rather I send him off and he wanders a field of death without aim?~*

~No, I would not. Just … a regrettable circumstance.~

~I agree. Deshi respects Morixxyleth. He will hear his word.~

~Very well.~ Isboern looked quite serious. *~She will try to provoke us once the gag is off. I must warn about what happened when you forced the Witch Hunter to give you answers.~*

My smile twisted. *~I remember. No forcing a mindlink. I have greater concern for Ionne than to try that again.~*

Willven's expression flickered with confusion, but a willing memory from me filled the gap for him. His mouth turned tender with a hint of a smile. ~*I am glad. Alright. Let us work with what we have.*~

The big, redheaded Templar stood at attention behind our prisoner, though the rest of the Templars had spread out to stand guard or touch base with the gathering army. The fires were under control and the smoke, while constant, no longer billowed in large, black plumes.

We didn't have long.

Amelda was surrounded without any of having spoken aloud. I crouched in front of her, crushing twigs on purpose. She tensed up, growling a question through her gag. Looking up to meet Sir Erik's eyes, I gestured like I was pulling a blindfold from my eyes. The Templar understood and reached down, tugging the cloth off the Ma'ab woman's face.

Amelda focused her dark eyes on me quickly. The moment she recognized me, I reached out, pinching her nose between the knuckles of my first two fingers. She jerked away as I squeezed hard, yanking my fingers from her face, baffling her vision before slapping each cheek with my open hand. She yelped in protest, blinking rapidly.

"Pleasant day, sour slit," I said. "Looks like Mathias traded you to the enemy for a chance to run, and Divigna doesn't care. He rode off without you *and* left his ranking officers to die." I lifted my hand and signed to Jael. "It's just you, Amelda."

My Sister drew a dagger and stepped forward, causing our captive to throw herself into Sir Erik's armored legs. Her face twitched as Jael reached forward, snatching her gag with one hand and giving it a jerk before cutting it off with her blade.

Amelda's freed mouth sagged with surprised insult as my Sister tossed it aside and returned to her position. Then the Ma'ab sneered, opened her mouth to respond, then snapped it shut as she thought better of it. Surprisingly wise.

I clucked my tongue. "Are you *certain* you learned from a city led by mothers? Or did your years at the inn with *Fahdi* accustom you to men who do what they want despite your plans?"

Simple rage flooded her face.

"The Third take you!" she hissed. "You *will* pay for what you did to him, whore."

"Yet Brom left you saddled on the back of a man-sucker who could not wait to off-load you," I replied, propping my chin casually in my palm. "Deals were made, clearly, but I can't begin to fathom who is fulfilling theirs, much less getting paid. You're all so sloppy."

Amelda growled then wrinkled one nostril in a smirking. "Just wait. The Eternal Hellhound will pay whatever price he's earned for his actions, but I do not need him or that pucker-fucker to watch you and that Deathwalker suffer on your knees!"

She caught her breath, eyes flicking up to Jael before her gaze landed on Deshi's scowling face and paused. She might have paled further but hid any confusion or fear behind a disgusted wrinkling of her nose. Eyes dropping, she mumbled something.

"What did you say?" I asked.

The Ma'ab noble made note of the Godblood next, who stood impassively to her left. *His* presence seemed a comfort to her.

"Impressive healing on the boy," she said to the Captain with false sweetness. "You must have caught him in time."

Isboern said nothing. No one did. Amelda's attention swept past Mourn, the tallest one observing from two steps behind me, without acknowledging him at all. The rest of us could see him, I was certain.

How the fuck does he do that?

"Hmm, where *is* Gavin?" asked our captive, a thread of delight twining with her voice. "Did you *lose* your repulsive heretic in the heat of battle?"

I offered a dry smile. "Part of the plan to parley, I'm sure. What does Divigna want from him? I wager there isn't anyone left at Manalar the Hellhound is trying to impress. You're running out of capable mages who can also lead."

She scoffed. "To give him to the Ascended, of course."

"Planning to drag him all the way North, is he? That's a long way to hope circumstances don't change."

She had no ready reply as her eyes narrowed, sliding to the side before coming to stop on Soul Drinker at my belt. Then, "You should know, if

I am killed, particularly by that dagger, the Ascended *will* come here to Manalar. They will know what happened, and they will come for you and the Deathwalker." She looked up. "They will come for *all* of you!"

Sir Erik shifted his weight, but the rest of us did well at appearing nonplussed with what would be the worst outcome of this campaign. I wasn't sure whether to believe her. Was that the threat she had held over the other three officers? Why would they think it possible?

"Borrowing Father's connections while he's not using them?"

"So amusing," Amelda crooned. "The words you choose."

Her grin held such brass, my gut *had* to pay attention. Our eyes locked, though I could feel the mental barrier in place; she was accustomed to guarding her thoughts.

"Who told you about the mother and son?" I asked, mimicking Divigna's tone when he'd asked her during their midnight meeting in camp.

Her composure cracked. "I do not know what you speak about."

"*Fahdi*, wasn't it?" I continued, offering a sweet smile. "Supposedly. While you waited outside the walls for the first assault. Although I'm certain Brom was *inside* the Temple during that time, impersonating a Bishop, and most certainly *not* thinking about you."

"Cunt," she snarled, leaning forward from her waist, hands bound behind her. "You will get nothing else. You will have to wait and see! I will *laugh*, you hear me?" She took a deep breath, raising her voice to shouting. "I shall *enjoy* watching the Ascended pull out of your gut that ch —"

A strange, cyan light passed in my periphery, like a flame with a black center. I jolted, blinked, and Deshi was beside me, his arm outstretched. He had touched Amelda on the chest, above her heart, and her words stopped before she could give away Ionne's presence. I stared as his fingers became incorporeal and shifted forward, moving ...

Into her.

The summer heat disappeared. Ma'ab eyes flew wide yet saw nothing. Amelda used what air remained in her chest to scream, the pitch rising fast from surprised pain to unadulterated terror.

"Deshi, stop!" Isboern cried, reaching for him, but Mourn blocked him.

"Do not touch him," he warned the Godblood before twisting his neck to speak to the Yungian. *"Kungchi, tongku-jen! Rangtuo huixi."*

Deshi withdrew his hand, breaking contact but remaining beside me in the grass. *"Kihua, Wen-yung."*

The Yungian hadn't taken his eyes from Amelda yet, and while most of his form appeared as a paler version of his living body, his right hand was ... translucent. I could see the inner structure of his hand, dark, articulated bones backlit against a bluish-green glow.

"What did you do, Deshi?" Isboern asked with concern.

"Protected Janshi." His voice held a shrill undertone, like an echo of Amelda's shriek. "This woman should not speak to an elder spirit in such a way."

Sir Erik seemed none the wiser. "Indeed, such threats only serve to delay and intimidate."

"Thank you," I murmured, more for Deshi, although Isboern's *Tetente* blinked in surprise but acknowledged me.

The Yungian hadn't looked away from our captive, waiting for Amelda to reclaim her senses. Then he smiled, displaying teeth sharper than I remembered, allowing her to study his hand with mounting horror.

"Like what you see?" I guessed.

"Y-you *can't* let him touch me!" she cried, first to me then to the Godblood, scrambling against the Templari blocking her retreat. "Please! Promise! That is torture! No one is meant to bear that alive!"

Isboern glanced at Deshi. "You would know better than me, woman. What would you tell us to be spared another touch?"

The Ma'ab noble quaked, her face truly white, her lips turning blue around the edges. "I ... I can't believe! H-How can you — ?"

Deshi's smile dropped; he reached for her.

"Stop!" she screamed, thrashing such that Sir Erik had to take her shoulders to stay upright.

"Hold," I said, lifting my hand, merely *hoping* Deshi obeyed.

He paused, at least, while Amelda continued her struggles. His eyes had gone black and yellow, and I could see bones beyond his hand as the spectral light spread up his arm.

"Oh! Oh, my gods, no!" she wailed. "No, please, don't. Don't touch me!"

"You laughed when I said the same." The bua's Human voice frayed like a thousand hollow needles had punctured it. "You *laughed*."

Deshi swept his hand through her middle, raking her and yet drawing no blood. Hysterical wails bolted far out onto the field as Amelda lost all senses to whatever she was experiencing. This drew a lot of attention. Mourn had moved into a better position to act while Krithannia drew closer as if to get involved.

"Hai, hai, listen!" I seized Amelda's jaw once she'd somewhat calmed down, forcing her to look at me. "Tell me what was so amusing about my choice of words."

"Wh-wha — ?" Her eyes locked on me with pleading dread.

"Borrowing your father's connection? Why did those officers *believe* they couldn't kill you?"

"I-I c-c-c — !" Amelda convulsed.

She couldn't say.

Fuck.

"Let down your guards," I commanded. "And Deshi won't touch you. My oath."

Her face was drenched from the sudden but continual weeping. "Let down my … ?"

"Share your thoughts without speaking." My smile didn't reach my eyes. "Please."

"Sirana," Isboern said disapprovingly.

"Let her answer." I cocked my eyebrow. "Well? Open your thoughts to me?"

"To *us*."

The Godblood's tone brooked no argument. Amelda glanced up in gratitude, leaking eyes moving from him to me and then, hesitantly, to Deshi.

Then away.

"Yes," she whispered. "I will give what you ask, Captain, but you must protect me. Take me prisoner, but do not kill me, and do *not* let th-that ... that —"

"Harrowed," Deshi said, his inhuman voice making her shudder. "That is what I am thanks to you and the skin hunter."

Amelda swallowed. "Do not touch ... No more. Please, I-I surrender as captive of the Manalari Captain of the Wall. I beg his clemency."

She believed and accepted it.

I wanted to know *what* Deshi had done in those moments of contact to break her so utterly, but my glance at Isboern reminded me we didn't have much time after all that screaming.

Or in general.

"You shall have clemency," Willven said, "if you hold to your word and share with us all we need to know."

Brom's daughter nodded urgently. "Yes! Yes! I am open!"

That was good enough for the Godblood, apparently, for he kneeled on my other side as Mourn quietly coaxed the Yungian out of arm's reach. The Godblood mindlinked with me before turning to Amelda, gently touching her forehead, and drawing us together into an enemy's mind.

I braced myself for what I was about to learn.

"So, devils and demons are real," Mathias reflected on the long ride to join the siege down south.

"Of course they are real!" Amelda barked, at a loss of how an essentially clever man could be starting so far behind.

"Eh, my father always insisted they were mages using smoke and mirrors to scare commoners into making up stories." He shrugged that off. "But Sirana was proof enough, and she said the two are not the same. That she is more familiar with demons — the Abyss — than the Hells, while Gavin denied dealing with either of them. His 'Lady' stands somewhere in the middle."

"Clearly," she said acidly.

"Ah-ah-ah, *not* clear, darling," he crooned with that hint of masculine distaste he'd hidden better in the past. "Does that mean angels are out and about as well? Inspiring men to wholesome restraint and selfless greatness? The Wall Defender of Manalar, perhaps?"

Amelda made a face. "Probably, but even Father isn't sure who guides his hand."

"And the Ascended?"

"They are *the* Death Gods of our world, opposed to that heretic's enslavers, the Greylords. If left unopposed, the Greylords will invade us and usurp our existence, stealing our souls for their own power."

"Right, right. So many factions. I had no idea. What about dear Father? Who is whispering in the sorcerer's ear? *Not* the Death Gods alone, with all that rambling about the Red Desert and sovereigns and traders."

Amelda hid her disappointment the best she could. "He never spoke of this before. I do not know."

Not before that char-skinned demon-worshipper appeared to tempt him far beyond his capacity to resist. Amelda had thought the deathless sorcerer held command over his past centuries, but one night with a Dark Elf and chaos had erupted from within. The Deathless had become as volatile and unpredictable as Kurn but with terrifying power at his fingertips. Amelda could do *nothing* to persuade him to wait in pursuing Sirana!

I must get that soul blade before he does.

"I don't imagine any mage so old," Mathias remarked, "would share *all* his intimate secrets with a recent spawn he's known for five years. But he's sending us to Manalar, expecting us to do his bidding on pure faith."

Bastard.

Her mother's plans certainly hadn't worked out. The Deathless lay beyond their realm of influence now. Amelda was on her own to elevate their status but still had options. She had only to make certain the skin hunter couldn't stab her in the back before she found another protector, a better one who *enjoyed* the company of women.

How blatantly the Paxian *chafed* to flee and leave her alone in this Ma'ab-hostile land. If only Sirana hadn't stabbed Kurn, *too!*

What does she know about all of this? What lies about the Ascended was Gavin feeding her every day? Amelda breathed out the sudden flash of rage to imagine.

"Trying to swallow that dick of defeat she fed you, huh?" Mathias prodded like a graceless elbow in her ribs.

"Be quiet," she groused.

At least she had been able to hear about Kurn sharing Sirana with *Fahdi.* The whore deserved such pure Ma'ab treatment with *her* attitude. A pity Amelda had fallen to the Dark One's trickery moments before and could not watch the Elf get fucked against her will. She would have laughed.

I will find someone she and the heretic can't *outrun, and they will be sorry.*

That night, the sorcerer's daughter had performed a ritual to call for that help after "encouraging" Mathias to oversleep his watch. Its crudest form had been developed by the slum *maknuut* but refined by the nobles, otherwise Amelda would not have dared. However, she possessed enough hair from Sirana's stay in her father's bed to be confident the *right* kind of creature would respond.

The spell had claimed most of the night and *all* the strength she had possessed, but then, as she'd been on the verge of passing out, *he* appeared.

At last.

And he was stunning. Elegant and beautiful, his ears a similar shape to the Dark Elf, though his skin was lighter, brilliant as burnished bronze. He had red wings and ivory horns, his eyes without iris or pupil, glowing with soft white light.

"Pleasant night, child," he said, his voice gliding smoothly past her ears. "I heard you and have answered. I believe I know you. The daughter of the Deathless, yes?"

Amelda fought to remain upright, overwhelmed by his presence. "I am. Amelda Troshin of the Blood Caste of Ennikar."

"Ah."

"Who are you, great one?"

His lips turned up in approval. "I am the one your mother came to, some time ago, to uncover the soul blade for your father."

Amelda gasped. Had her magic been so strong? Or her, so lucky? Somehow, she'd summoned the Ice Lord of Vinter Hjem!

~Fucking son of the uroan!!~

~Sirana, calm! Steady!~ Willven placed the golden shield between me and Amelda's memory, strengthening our separation of identity. *~Do not become entangled in another's memory. Do not interact — ~*

A stark chill cut through me as the Infernal Elf turned his head toward me, starkly out of sync with Amelda as her form kept moving, continued talking as the memory played, but the Ma'ab woman was out of focus in her own mind.

"*Hello, Sirana,*" Indrath said, his fangs clear and sharp in his smile. "*Captain Isboern. I must admit I did not see you two learning from each other so swiftly.*"

Startled at the direct address, Willven moved closer to me, until he had one arm around me and raised the shield guarding us both. I could only see the Ice Lord from bare shoulders up as he shifted his body to face us in full, his red wings rising above his crown of horns.

The Ice Lord studied Willven's manifestation of Mitneh'thran. "*That relic suits you well, Captain, and seems pleased enough to answer in your time of need.*"

~You made a deal with Amelda,~ the blond man replied without acknowledging the compliment.

Indrath's lips lowered to cover his fangs though his smile remained in place. The Infernal Elf splayed his clawed hands with a small, casual shrug. "*I am the Deal Broker. But I cannot allow you to eavesdrop on the details of her bargain with me, for that is not your business.*"

~Is it true that the Ascended will come to Manalar if she is killed?~ Willven pushed. *~Was that part of the deal?~*

"She has been wielding that aspect with all the grace of a toddler with a club," the Ice Lord chuckled with derision. "So I shall answer. In a sense, yes, it is true."

~'In a sense,'~ I snarled. ~Were you the reason Kreshel Divigna offered to 'negotiate on my behalf' if I handed Soul Drinker over to him?~

Indrath's expression was one of pure delight. "I am impressed he could ask you, if only once. A sure sign of the Elven essence subverting part of the Third's control. But ..." A blithe shrug. "You denied him, so that door is closed. He won't ask again."

I growled. ~If you want the blade so badly, why don't you just take it?~

"Whoever said I wanted it at all?" His eyes shimmered with amusement at my expression. "You may as well become accustomed to my presence, Sirana. Human souls are once more fighting over Soul Drinker while I merely wait and see what you will do about the Black Heart. I always keep eyes on events of interest from every vantage point. This will never change."

~What about Mathias?~ I asked. ~Did you help him escape the Dwarven redoubt?~

Ivory eyes flashed. "The easiest aspect of the deal to fulfill, though I believe he might have preferred to stay in your keeping."

~Does he have a deal with you, too?~

Fangs appeared. "Not yet. But he knows, the same as you do, that I can help at any time."

~Grrrr. I can't tell whose plans you try to help or foil! What in the Void are you trying to accomplish?~

The Ice Lord's brilliant gaze took on a crimson tint. "A loaded question I have no inclination to answer, granddaughter. Worth remembering most Humans are short-lived tools which break easily. Although, well done with what you've helped accomplish for the Deathwalker and this new creature, the Harrowed. I am most intrigued. Perhaps I see why Ishuna took the risk to send you here, even if she is unsure how this all ends for you."

~You keep suggesting that past connection. Are you from the same time in the Red Desert? You went to serve the Hells and her, the Abyss?~

Genuine laughter escaped him. "Oh, my dear. No, I'm afraid not. First, I do not **serve**. Second, Ishuna is as much my granddaughter as you are. I have been watching over our families for far longer than you can comprehend, welcoming many generations and helping them come into their own. Whether they know this or not."

I had the sense the Infernal would have pointedly focused on Ionne's aura in my womb if Willven hadn't been blocking his view with the shield.

Next, Indrath addressed the Godblood. "What about you, hm? The Grey Maiden seems to think you are the best choice to realign Io'sulta for the next millennium. Is that what you want?"

~I want a freer and fairer existence for the people of my city,~ the man answered, psionic thoughts unwavering and clear as crystal. ~I have the ability and thus the obligation to help them achieve it in my lifetime if I can.~

The Infernal lifted a nostril. "One like you, resisting the larger view?"

~I listen to those 'easily broken tools' low down and hear what you miss, Lord. That 'total view' of yours is made up entirely of small moments like me. You can't distract me from the gift of this life or persuade me to serve a devil's vision of it instead.~

Indrath's expression pinched before he dismissed it, relaxing into regal grace. "You know your place, then. Not a disagreeable position between us, Captain." Red-tinged eyes slipped to me. "I have one last question for you, Sirana. Then I shall release you both to the Dragonchild before he makes this awkward."

A reminder that I could call Mourn if needed, yet unlike last time, my thoughts remained clear, no tug on a leash or manacles dragging me down while in Indrath's presence.

I narrowed my eyes. ~I have a question as well. Like for like?~

The Infernal's wings relaxed; he hummed pleasantly. "Terms?"

~Sirana, please reconsider,~ Willven murmured.

I shook my head in refusal, eyes fixed on the Ice Lord. ~You ask your question first.~

"Ah, so you may change yours to match it in nature and scope?"

~Yes, and you get to tailor your answer based on the value of mine. If a Dragonchild can do it and come away with what he wants, so can you.~

Indrath chuckled, folding his arms, and drawing in his wings, lifting them higher. "Very well. Agreed."

~And, if possible, we must answer who, what, where, when, and why. It must be succinct, without tangents, and the truth to our experience, even if negative. Not by omission, and not the borrowed words or perceptions of another. It must be answered in full with no presumed continuation of the exchange later. Once this meeting is complete, we owe each other nothing.~

"*Interesting.*" His eyes shifted along with his question, the crimson fading into warm ivory.

"*Do you agree?*" I prompted.

Indrath smiled at Willven before answering. "*I agree, granddaughter.*"

~Don't call me that.~

"*Oh, apologies, I hadn't realized you have a grandsire you preferred in the role.*" The Lord smiled as he guessed the answer. "*Or worse, you do not. You haven't a sire who holds any care for you. Quite an isolated child, never to know the powerful love and protection of a father. Just as your Mothers wanted.*"

~Stop,~ I snapped. *~That is not a question.~*

He smiled serenely.

Waited for three beats.

And asked, "*Who is your child's sire?*"

My hands clenched. His question was what I'd suspected but at least I was not caught off guard this time. He didn't have a stranglehold on my thoughts, and I wouldn't be giving it away for nothing.

~A mage healer owned by the Valsharess,~ I answered.

Indrath's eyes sharpened. "*His name.*"

~He goes by many different names given to him.~

"*Tell me what name he goes by now.*"

~I call him Auslan. Before that, he was Enoquis at the last House that bred him. Others from Priestesses and Matrons which I've never known.~

Indrath frowned. "*I want the name he calls himself. You must speak what you **do** know to the best of your ability.*"

Indeed, I had to, and if not for Willven's powerful shield, the Infernal Elf would have picked up my hesitation, my struggle. I knew one name to be true, and another name which the Merchant *wanted* to be true.

Fortunately, both *were* true from my experience.

~Avel,~ I thought with the utmost care, meeting the devil's gaze

from across the shield. ~*My child's sire introduced himself to me as Avel.*~

"Where? When?"

"*In a dream. Shortly after I reached the Surface.*"

The Ice Lord's eyes were difficult to read. He craned his neck up and took a deep breath through his nose, wings unfurling with the exhale through his lip before drawing in close again.

"*Thank you,*" he said. "*Now, your question for me.*"

I'd expected him to nudge my boundary for a mark, to wear me down as he had before. The abrupt shift of the scales gave me pause. Had I made a huge mistake?

Too late if I did. Match the nature of the question. Like for like.

~*Who is Cris-ri-phon's living Elf daughter?*~ I asked. ~*The one mentioned by the Red Desert Deathwalker, Houda, at the sacred pool before the rift split open to let in the Malok.*~

Indrath grinned. "*Such precision. Clever cait. Hmm.*"

He contemplated the blurred forest and campsite around us, reminding me that we'd met this time in Amelda's head.

"*She is the eldest Human-blood in our family of which I am aware,*" he answered. "*I have been watching her since her Queen-Mother's assassination.*"

~*Her name.*~

"*Shunraeki. Named for Ishuna, her mother's sister.*"

I resisted that distraction from the whole of my deserved answer. ~*Where? When?*~

"*Hidden among the Wilder Elves. I've seen her within the last decade.*"

~*The ... Wilder?*~

The Ice Lord enjoyed my startled shock. "*Oh, yes! And, according to Mathias, you sought a* third *sister before the fiery Jael, and all signs point to her being with the Wilder as well. I could negotiate a family visit for us when this matter of Manalar is settled. When you are next available, of course.*"

Had I been awake, I might have been shaking.

~*Are we finished here, Sirana?*~ Willven asked.

A simple question. No anger, irritation, no impatience — those seeped from Indrath despite his smile — but the tone was firm, requiring a decisive answer.

With effort, I dragged my gaze from the Elf Lord's glimmering, fey eyes to the calming blue of the Human Godblood. *~Yes, Captain. We are finished here.~*

~Then let us return to our allies.~

With greater ease than I might have managed alone, Willven closed the link with the Ice Lord and gently withdrew from our captive's thoughts.

When I woke up beside Willven, Mourn, and Jael, no one was screaming. Not Amelda nor Deshi.

Not even me.

Chapter 29

Undercroft of Manalar, Paxia

The Hellhounds did not drag Gavin through the front gates as a prize for the eyes of the Northmen occupying Manalar, though the Death-walker had anticipated this. Instead, they galloped with neither pause nor word until they reached the eastern slope of Mount Sonai, their thick-limbed horses charging up the field where animated battle casualties had once wandered.

The wall bore many eyes as the Deathwalker listened to unanswered calls and cheers for Kreshel from the sentries, though they did not seem to realize the significance of the enemy prisoner he'd captured. Perhaps they did not know what had happened on the western fields and awaited the return of their leading sorceresses.

The lead Hellhound would let them wait.

Kreshel and his men entered the city's catacombs through the once-blocked cisterns, removing the massive stones themselves as if they had been the ones to place them. The passageways were tall enough to lead the horses single-file by their reins, traveling underneath the wall and into the city's complex undercroft.

Gavin had been bound chest to the saddle before they entered, Kreshel leading his horse with the Deathwalker's tool pack over one shoulder. Although the Deathwalker recalled dropping the silver dagger which

Mathias Briar had pitched at him, Kreshel had produced another one from his harness which he used liberally, any time he wanted to shatter the death mage's concentration.

The method worked exceedingly well.

Mathias was with them, but Amelda was not, nor were any of the Ma'ab women from the parley. They had all been killed in the skirmish and drawn into Gavin's thurible for temporary holding. No man present showed a fragment of concern for this, and Gavin's intuition suggested he may not be carried to the next female in a dwindling chain of command. For all he knew, the Guild had killed so many sorceresses that Kreshel Divigna was his own head of command in the field.

Regardless, the Third's creation seemed to be operating under his own goals.

"She said you would end this."

Gavin waited for an elaboration.

"Horses, here," Kreshel ordered gruffly, opening the wide door to a well-kept stable in what Gavin guessed to be the basement of a wealthy house.

The Hellhounds fixed torches to their sconces, swiftly stowing their mounts while Kreshel dragged Gavin off the horse to the ground by his shoulders with wrists bound together.

"The maggot says nothing of his circumstance," said one Hellhound, glancing side-eyed as he regained his feet. *"Have we missed something, Wargan?"*

"Word for the wise," Mathias said, brushing horse's hair from his coat. "He understands Ma'ab far better than the last one, and staying mute until he tries to poison you is his preferred method." He grinned. "Right, Gavin?"

Several Hellhounds grunted acknowledgment, though the Death-walker did not.

Ghostly whispers had begun in the undercroft now that Kreshel had withheld the silver long enough. Gavin sensed a presence down a passage to his left, one quite strong and angry enough to make the horses uneasy. He tried to listen closer, attuning his ear and heightening his focus.

The sharp jab of a knifepoint hit his side, followed by ragged blindness breaking behind his eyes and white noise filling his head as the silver burned in his blood.

"Argh!"

"You look at me, maknuut," Kreshel said, holding the blooded point beneath his chin. *"You listen to me."*

"I await an explanation," Gavin grumbled in kind. *"Otherwise, any number of ghosts in Manalar might want my attention in the given moment. One is nearby, and it is hostile."*

The Ma'ab looked around, noting the sounds coming from the stable, and seemed to believe him.

"You will quell any souls which are threatening," said the Wargan.

"Not if you continue to prod me with silver without provocation," he replied, touching his brow where it throbbed. *"I can work no magic for some time afterward, and hostile spirits will do as they please, then."*

Kreshel's black eyes narrowed; he held up the silver knife, wiped off the blade as Gavin watched, and sheathed it without a word.

Mathias whistled in low remark. "Cold as snowmelt. The monk I knew was easier to rattle, heh! Here's a question. *Can* you tell lies, Gavin? Or are you one of the dead?"

The Deathwalker turned his head and glared. "What are you doing among Hellhounds?"

"Long story. But," the skin hunter smiled, looking at Kreshel, "it worked."

The Wargan gave a disinterested nod, motioning for his men to check the four tunnels around them.

"What worked?" Gavin asked.

"Surrendering Amelda to the Templars." Mathias's grin widened. "Apparently that's a safe enough place for her to keep their situation happy."

"Still compelled to be her bodyguard?"

The grin flattened into a grimace. "I think that spell broke with Brom's dearth."

Gavin did not correct him. "Another spell?"

Mathias shrugged, turning his neck as if it were stiff. "I said you and

390

Sirana would regret not killing her."

"Enough," Kreshel rumbled.

The Paxian man closed his mouth, winking one eye at Gavin.

I do not know what that is supposed to mean.

"Three passages clear," said one Ma'ab as they reconvened, *"but the maggot is right. The air is bad in the fourth passage."*

"Sun-worshippers have more rogue spirits in one rotting city than all of the Empire," muttered another with contempt.

"They exile their spirit-talkers," said a third with a spit on the floor. *"Leave their ancestors to decay and grow hungry. Blind fools who bring it on themselves. The Divine Prime will cleanse the city in moments and bring all the lost to her."*

Gavin agreed with his first statements, but the last must not happen. *"Where next, Wargan?"*

"Take him to the temple? Or hunt the demonblood?"

Mathias rubbed his hand across his mouth, watching with interest and wariness when Kreshel focused on the Paxian first.

"We do not require your service with this one, and the noble is in other hands. Leave now if you will it."

The skin hunter wasn't about to do so. "Well, see, um, there could be other tricks he can do that I'll help watch out for. And Amelda isn't dead, so I can't 'will it' yet."

"We will not kill her for you. Best hope the enemy does. Find your entertainment elsewhere."

Mathias stifled a sneer. "Pretty sure the rank-and-file aren't going to know what I've done for you all."

Kreshel tilted his head. "Then do not be seen. You are skilled in that. The city is large and riddled with Dwarven hollows."

Tolerance toward the smaller man shifted, the sense of unwelcome palatable as the Hellhounds position aligned with their leader. Mathias wasn't a fool, but Gavin could only guess that such obvious hesitation meant the skin hunter had hoped for private contact with their captive.

Mathias risked a quick crouch to speak. "Good work keeping the 'Sho'shien' legend with that Yungian," he murmured loud enough that

Kreshel could monitor him. "The boy hadn't learned much about you that we didn't know, and centuries of lore got in the way. But at least he'd seen that silver dagger which killed you before." Mathias shrugged. "He said you didn't have it anymore, gave it to the shadows or something. Got rid of it. Pretty smart, *heh*. At least I didn't have to stop to let *you* take over the torture this time, hm?"

Gavin and Kreshel watched him with thinning patience. Behind the largest man, spike chains slid and rattled in warning.

"A lot of eyes watching this fight, eh?" the skin hunter finished jovially, standing up with clear intent to leave. "Pity Brom got taken out, but you know ... voids and roles filled ..." He cleared his throat. "And all that."

"Get *gone*," Kreshel snarled.

"Right." Mathias took a step away. "A reminder this 'maggot' was once a southern monk. Personally, I'd take him to where the scrolls and codices are stored."

"You have said."

The cool air of the undercroft chilled further, and the skin hunter exhaled. "Right."

Finally, the multi-faced mercenary chose a path, disappearing down one of the three cleared tunnels as two Hellhounds grumbled under their breath. Only once the man was out of sight did Gavin lift his hand from his most recent wound, checking his blood by torchlight.

His body's fluid had grown darker, thicker, but wasn't usable for magic and his wounds weren't closing.

Meanwhile, Eynkis and many others who hadn't entered the thurible slept in the Herald's bones, but he did not know how much silver would shatter the peace. Events would become rather sticky if this became the Hellhounds' goal.

"*On your feet,*" Kreshel ordered, speaking his native tongue as he adjusted the dark satchel which contained his grimoire and kits.

Gavin complied, observing in silence as the Eternal Hellhound led them through the underground maze with a destination in mind. The weeks since the city's fall had been enough time to explore the eastern cisterns and their waterways.

Meanwhile, the fourteen Ma'ab who had come through the skirmish visibly grouped into two sets of five with Kreshel making up the fifth of a third pack. They passed two ladders marked with a knot of dirty string; from there, one pack would split off to climb to the surface, their orders given in sign rather than spoken, until Gavin remained with Kreshel and only four other Hellhounds.

Gavin neither expected nor witnessed a moment of laxness in his captors keeping watch on him. Their leader had a supremely effective way of neutralizing him if he was uncooperative, and the Ma'ab had used these tunnels before.

Despite the Deathwalker experiencing two transitions, Mathias was correct about Gavin's mortal habit of waiting and observing in silence until something noteworthy changed. He had outwaited many driven and aggressive souls, living or dead, and he remained while they did not. None had been mixed with an Elven soul until now, but until Gavin's task regarding this ill-fated mortal became clearer, his base duty would always be to observe and study.

To learn.

Whispers arose and faded as he passed crossways and pit stairs leading further down, but his captors seemed not to hear them. The Deathwalker glimpsed faded or misremembered faces huddled in a high corner or drifting through walls. None of them spoke or approached like the one avoided near the cisterns, or like her in the library and him beneath the Temple.

When Kreshel and his pack finally rose to the surface streets, they pushed Gavin up the ladder in between them. The group emerged into the late-day shade, the shadow of Mount Sonai spreading over the eastern side of the slope.

They stood in a quiet, narrow passage separating two walled gardens in the wealthy district, the broad-leafed vines in summer bloom despite everything. Gavin guessed they were hidden from all known eyes, for the closest residences contained no noise from the occupation of soldiers, and no open windows despite the heat of the season.

"*Come,*" he said. "*Look.*"

The four Hellhounds followed his hand motions and took hold of a large tarp partly draped over the body of an animal. A *large* animal, on which Gavin glimpsed thick, grey hide before the Ma'ab pulled the covering off to reveal the recognizable body of a Malok mount which had flown through the Rift.

Gavin stared at the crumpled creature, dead from a crash landing.

"*What is this?*" Kreshel asked in Ma'ab.

"*Roh'ghast,*" Gavin answered in the tongue of the dead.

A glimmer of recognition showed in his dark eyes before it faded. "*Meaning?*"

Interesting.

"*It means 'screaming terrors,' *" the Deathwalker translated.

The four Hellhounds smirked as if they remembered the bone-chilling sound the flyers had made.

"*Did you summon them?*" Kreshel asked.

Gavin shook his head. "*The Deathless One cracked the door open further, giving opportunity for others with no alliance to either of us to step through.*"

"*Why did he do that?*"

"*I do not know. He tried to leave the Temple but was compelled to stay, perhaps by another will. In his frustration, he added to the magic surge and fractured the stable link to the pool.*"

The five Ma'ab did not seem to fully comprehend what he'd said. Gavin did not repeat himself while the Eternal Hellhound contemplated the alien animal.

"*Could you make this fly again?*" he asked.

An intriguing idea.

"*Not quickly,*" Gavin answered honestly.

But, he considered, *if given enough time … ?*

"*Not quickly,*" the Eternal Hellhound repeated in a murmur, staring at the beast.

Another captive might have asked what Kreshel would want with an undead Roh'ghast in the first place, but what other answer made sense than to fly? The Herald didn't care while the answers were theoretical.

"What would you need to make it happen?"

Gavin lifted his chin, breaking his focus on the creature which held his gaze, refocusing on Kreshel with modest surprise.

"Besides time," he added, standing as unblinking as the Deathwalker, though his lieutenants seemed annoyed that the "maggot" dared to meet eyes with their leader.

Gavi hadn't missed that the Eternal Hellhound had ceased addressing him as anything at all, slur or otherwise, since the last time prodding him with the silver blade. He checked that wound.

At last, it mends.

"Have you found other corpses of the same creature?" he asked. *"Where it may be better to replace sinew, bone, and flesh than to repair it."*

The Hellhounds frowned but were startled in turn when Kreshel answered, *"Not yet. We can look. What else?"*

"My blood as my mistress intends it, untouched by silver."

Upper lips curled as the four men bared their teeth, showing understanding that Gavin made no reference to any Ma'ab female, ancestral god or not.

Something about it made Kreshel smirk. *"What else?"*

"Wargan, his power when —"

"I promise nothing. Be silent." Kreshel addressed his man but kept staring at Gavin.

"A cool, dry workspace out of the sun," he answered with a meaningful sniff. *"I am surprised it has not rotted further in the past few weeks."*

"Our sorceresses slow the decay. Anything else?"

Ah, so the Wargan did not keep a "whole" secret.

"I must begin a study to contemplate that further. Is that why you've brought me here?"

"For now."

Kreshel brought down Gavin's satchel from his shoulder, rummaged around, and brought out his writing kit and grimoire. The Deathwalker watched as the Hellhound placed his writing supplies on the stone with decent care. Then, after skimming through some of Gavin's cypher and drawings, Kreshel found the empty pages painstakingly threaded into his book in Yong-wen and tore out a handful to toss them atop the kit.

Gavin clenched his jaw but otherwise masked his reaction.

"Begin the study," the Wargan ordered, placing the grimoire in the bag with the surgical kit. *"It will be cool and shaded here through the night. Show me progress, and perhaps you will receive what you need."*

Kreshel prepared to leave two men to guard the Deathwalker, giving clear orders not to disrupt his work, then stabbed Gavin in his side with the silver blade.

"Argh!"

"No magic while I am gone, scholar. I will return soon."

Three of them left as the other two stood looming over him, chuckling. Slowly, Gavin knelt beside the Roh'ghast, bleeding red from the deepest wound since the skin hunter's pitch from behind.

Worms rot their bellies.

GAVIN'S THOUGHTS WANDERED LITTLE AS HE TRACED THE MUSCULATURE OF THE unfamiliar beast with his fingers, finding the fractured or broken bones from the fall out of the sky and, where possible, resetting them to better suggest their true, functioning form.

Only once he'd gone over the body three times, tilting and turning it where possible, did he begin making careful sketches. Within his concentration, Mathias's voice returned.

"A lot of eyes watching this fight, eh? Pity Brom got taken out, but you know … voids and roles filled … and all that."

What did that mean? And if Brom's compulsion had been broken with his defeat — not his death — then why did Mathias need Amelda to die to leave Manalar?

"We will not kill her for you. Best hope the enemy does."

Unlikely while the Templars had her, unless Sirana decided to even the score from Troshin Bend for the noblewoman's role in Sirana's abuse at the hands of the Ma'ab.

Voids and roles filled.

A lot of eyes watching this fight …

Why did none of that sound like what he'd come to expect from the mercenary? Similar to oddities spoken while in the Dwarven prison, not to mention the little matter of his mysterious escape unseen from the redoubt.

"A lot of eyes watching," he murmured aloud, lifting the heavy head of the Roh'ghast with both hands and turning it to better see the shape of the nostrils and strange horn-like structure which made its nose seem upturned.

Out of his periphery, someone blinked. He would have dropped the beast's head, but his fingers clung to it without drawing the Hellhounds' attention.

Turning his death mage's gaze with care, Gavin spotted a pair of floating grey eyes without pupils. Eyes he'd seen before.

The demonblood Sirana searched for since the Ley Tower.

Once the death mage held that anchor in relation to the rest of the form, he confirmed a solid body crouching in the deep shade of the narrow passage, across the Roh'ghast from him. The Deathwalker's eyes began detecting a life aura, something suppressed while recovering from the silver, but it matched what he recalled of Vesram's form in the crypt.

The Sathoet shushed him, under-breathed and short-ranged, much like when Sirana whispered: enough to detect but not harsh enough to draw the Hellhounds' focus, despite how frequently they glanced in Gavin's direction.

Although the strength of the Deathwalker's aura had not recovered from the silver dagger, he recognized the push of magic when he encountered it.

Ada's son, yes? You hear me?

Fortunate that he'd had enough practice with Sirana in putting his thoughts into words. He focused, sliding them to the fore of his mind. *I hear you. And yes, Ada was my mother.*

Yesss. Ada. Remember her. She said you would come.

Gavin frowned at what sounded like … affection. Lowering the flying creature's head, he picked up his loose pages to test which ones had dried. *When was this?*

Three decades past. Ennikar.

The Far North?

Well before Ada had met his father at the monastery of Gavin's birth in Paxia.

Impossible.

While she was mortal? the Deathwalker asked.

A young woman, yesss. Slave to Vo'traj, like me. Spoke with me. Her maiden showed her things.

Her 'maiden.'

Yours, too.

He sighed inside. *I am aware.*

But was Vesram aware of Ada in her transitioned form? Had the two spoken in the Temple since Gavin had fled to the retreat? Should he open that volatile box if Vesram remained ignorant of her proximity?

No. Gavin had noted that affectionate tone, and he was not in a favored position to deal with a demonblood's emotional surprise.

Instead, he asked, *Did she speak of what I might do if we met, you and I?*

The mind's voice of the Sathoet fell silent for a time, as if considering or trying to recall. *No. Not you and me.*

Then what have I presumably come to do?

Stop the Physician's Hellhound.

And ... how do I do that?

Kor Nigram.

What?

You must take Kor Nigram.

Gavin translated in his mind. *The Black Heart?*

Vesram's eyes widened in surprise. *Yesss! You know it?*

The gatekeeper bound Soul Drinker? How did this have anything to do with Kreshel Divigna?

I do, he said warily.

Will not be easy, the demonic Davrin replied.

Certainly not.

One touched by the Abyss would know.

*But is possible — *

The Sathoet gasped, his thought ceasing abruptly as grey eyes vanished. The messenger spell ended like a ghost crossing over, the lightest footfalls possible teasing Gavin's ears, as if merely suggesting their reality.

Behind him, Kreshel returned, carrying Gavin's satchel, with two men flanking him.

Cursed timing.

The Deathwalker checked his recent wound, aware of how lengthy the blood stain had grown on his left side. The color darkened toward black, the flow slowing toward a seep. He sighed.

Right on time.

Gavin stood up straight with his smudged sketches, ready to explain what he had gleaned about the Grey flyer's anatomy, however much the Physician's creation cared to listen for displaying his next move.

Kreshel did not ask. He reached for the pages, took them without pause, and flipped through them briefly, too quick to comprehend much. Bringing the Deathwalker's satchel off his shoulder, the Hellhound removed the grimoire and tucked the torn pages back into it.

"Clear the western most tunnel," he growled to his men. *"All of you."*

With the slightest hesitation, they obeyed. Kreshel and Gavin stood alone; the silver dagger remained sheathed. The Deathwalker *could* stand and wait for him to speak; he felt no particular urgency. But … this wasn't what Sirana would do were she in his place, and worth noting this soul *did* possess Elven influence.

Could he engage in a similar trade of knowledge, for which the Red Sister from the Deepearth had been so hungry?

Should he?

"Why is Mathias Briar here?" Gavin asked. *"The trickster fled the city once without care for Amelda Troshin. We held him prisoner once he was discovered among the Manalari ranks but he escaped somehow."*

The Ma'ab smirked, black eyes narrowing, his large hands causing no further damage to the grimoire as he placed it in the satchel. *"The tormentor tried to tell you at the end."*

"Indeed. The 'lots of eyes watching' remark?"

"Correct. As if he thought you might know whose those are."

Gavin shrugged slightly. "Still cryptic enough to be useless."

Kreshel grunted. "It matters not to me which leash-holder she has invited in to counter yours, but I expect they will reveal themselves soon."

"Leash-holder. She? You mean Amelda?"

The Hellhound dipped his chin. "Any deal can be found in the Far North if desired enough, and the Daughter of the Deathless is overconfident in her protections to impress our gods. But she is hardly the first. She has her own leash on the tormentor, but not for long if she doesn't keep eyes on him."

Gavin frowned, wondering about Kreshel's own leash also knowing the Eternal Hellhound would be as unwilling to talk about it as the Herald was the specifics of his own service. As an alternative, Vesram had given him some quite recent insight.

"I expected the black-skinned Elf would be a higher priority for capture," the Deathwalker said. "Yet you seized me, claiming another 'she' who told you something."

Kreshel's expressions *had* seemed more Human, or at least *living,* during this exchange. Yet, as Gavin watched, any nuance withdrew, and his ritually scarred hand folded around the handle of the silver blade. The Deathwalker nearly stepped away but refrained, refusing to give in to doubt.

"Was 'she' my mother?" he pushed.

Neither blinked, and Kreshel rumbled, "Which one was your mother?"

A test.

"Once a slave to Commander Vo'traj," he answered, "alongside the demon Elf who recently escaped with her death."

"You know about that. Are you responsible for her disappearance?"

Gavin stretched his lips in what seemed an appropriate place to smile. "Did your tormentor not succeed in pulling that information out of the Yungian you captured? Hm."

Kreshel's stoic chill remained. "Is Vo'traj dead?"

"She is. And the demonblood is free. Not in our possession."

A grunt, as if that confirmed what he suspected. "And the assassination *of our generals? Was that you or another power?"*

"Which other power concerns you?"

"An admission."

"A question. You said you cared not about other leash-holders brought in to counter ours. I can only think your primary objective is not to hold the city, but I am somehow to 'end' something for you."

A tiny muscle twitched near the Hellhound's dark eye. He said nothing.

"Did you once know my mother?" Gavin asked again. *"While she was alive."*

"I did not. But I remember which slave she was." Kreshel smirked. *"A favorite of the demonblood. When she needed to avoid Ma'ab men, she went to the Abyssal creature to hide. He would protect her."*

Gavin did not want to ask but recognized when motive was critical to explain a pattern. *"She had a 'need' to avoid Ma'ab men. Why?"*

The Hellhound stared, standing so still that Gavin believed he would not answer.

Then, *"The bitter bloods of the slum hold greater value than the nobles will acknowledge. When an officer's female slaves are both powerful in death magic and conceive a child, few live past the birth. The nobles are always there during the labors to capture their Vis to hold for the gods."* Kreshel paused. *"Your mother went to great lengths to avoid that fate. She escaped her mistress, and the demonblood helped her, knowing his punishment would be less than hers."*

That both explained and corroborated Vesram's whispers, and indeed, Ada had evaded a truly horrible transition. Dying in childbirth under the abuse of a zealous hypocrite seemed preferable to the Ma'ab nobility.

"What of the drinker of souls?" Gavin asked. *"You asked the dark Elf for the cursed blade. Do you still need it?"*

"No. She refused. That opportunity is closed."

"Oh? Does the Black Heart not have anything to do with you?"

The flinch on Kreshel's face looked so out of place that Gavin wasn't certain he'd seen it until the Eternal Hellhound withdrew the silver dagger from its sheath. His intent to use it could not be clearer.

The Herald backed up, able to see that unnatural, blended life aura alongside the flare of magic from Kreshel's tattoos; simultaneously, a familiar rush arose in his aura. He would *not* allow it to be taken away. Gavin would tear his flesh open with his own teeth if need be—

"*Ssstop!*"

The Hellhound jolted, accompanied by a strange double grunt. Belatedly, Gavin connected he'd witnessed an impact with some unseen body, making Kreshel stumble though he did not drop the silver blade.

Suddenly, all went black, as if the sun had plummeted from the sky. Someone hissed, grasped him, and lifted him from his feet. If Gavin still needed air, the shoulder jammed into his gut would have knocked it out of him.

"*Vesram!*" Kreshel bellowed, his howl erupting solicitous rather than enraged. Regardless, distant chains rattled in its wake, a clear threat as his Hellhounds approached to join a chase unseen.

For the Herald, void darkness encased him as his jostled body finally purged the poison of silver. The river of otherworldly wind and whispers returned, passing through his mind in a welcome caress. The hope and calls of the Vis in his bones echoed, answered, granting their strength for his promise of safe passage.

His connection had returned.

Should he try to escape? Disrupt the Sathoet mid-stride and force him to drop his burden? Could Gavin escape *both* Hellhounds and a demon Elf chasing after him?

Unlikely.

"Wh-where do you ta-ake m-me?" he asked, struggling to take in enough air to convey the question.

His bestial bearer lacked the breath to answer, his pants bursting through his muzzle. At least his unshod feet avoided slapping the stone which might have led their adversaries on.

Vesram ran blind yet without hesitation, turning this way and that through the alleys of Manalar. Though sightless, Gavin estimated he was a significant height above the ground, equal to the Ma'ab from which they fled. His only certain sense of direction of was they were headed downhill and, somehow, the sounds of pursuit grew muffled. Distant ...

Gavin did not understand how a demonblood carrying him could outrun unburdened warriors who had just lost their prisoner. Not unless Kreshel had called it off.

Finally, after an unnaturally long sprint, the air changed and he sniffed. *Offal?* Old blood, for certain.

The Deathwalker had long become inured to the heavy, cloying scents of a body dismembered, to gore and decomposition. He could detect them nonetheless and knew they approached a place of death.

Simultaneously, a familiar sensation arose, gathering around them like freezing fog.

Anchored spirit.

Like the elderly monk below the temple and the historian in the library. It even reminded him of the unknown by the cisterns whom the Hellhounds did not want to meet. However, they were nowhere near that underground maze, and this place smelled like a slaughterhouse.

Abruptly, Vesram slowed, coughing as if to expel sickly-sweet scents from his lungs. He deposited the Deathwalker on the damp, sticky cobblestones. The magical darkness lifted, but Gavin's vision did not improve much.

He could make out they were inside an unlit butchery. Hooks swayed on the end of long chains, empty of all carcasses to process, the stains and fluid trails barely visible in the dying daylight, leading to iron grates on the floors.

"*Masssked,*" the demon-Elf said in Ma'ab, panting, crouching onto the balls of his feet and peering into the dark rafters. The thick, white mane spanned from crown to tailbone, curving with his spine as he caught his breath.

"*What do you mean?*" Gavin asked, having a guess.

"*All to do with death, here, Adason,*" the other answered, pointing a claw at the ground. "*Difficult to track for beast, mage, or Hellhound.*"

"*I thought so.*" He looked around warily. "*Would this not be the first place to look for a hidden death mage, whether one could detect me by any other sense?*"

The Sathoet drew back his lips to show teeth. He said nothing, as if wanting him to guess. Gavin didn't have time for that. "*I also sense a* presence here. Could be dangerous."

Vesram was pleased with his answer. *"Yesss. Officers did not wrangle this ssspirit before being ssslain. Too strong for those remaining. But not for you."*

"So certain."

"I am."

Gavin supposed the former slave *had* been observing the Ma'ab death mages up close and for far longer than him. He rose off the floor, moving slowly in case Vesram took it as a threat. Strangely, the grey-eyed hybrid remained in his crouch, tilting his head up rather than straightening to meet the Deathwalker at eye level.

Gavin asked, *"Have the … officers 'wrangled' any of Manalar's ancient spirits?"*

"Know not. Been hiding sssince the crypt."

"But you know a guardian spirit is here."

"No. Ada tells me."

Gavin held still, gradually moving his eyes away to watch for any soul to manifest in the corners. *"Hm. Have you seen her in the Temple?"*

"Yesss. Guarding the pool." Vesram chuckled. *"She was right."*

"About?"

"Many thingsss. She suggested thisss place to hide."

"Does the spirit not bother you?"

The Sathoet rumbled softly, covering his teeth in an apparent gesture to seem contemplative. *"Hrrrm. Part shadow by now, recognizes blood of the Void. Ssso it waits. Watches. I cannot sssee it. Feel it."*

Part shadow. This made a certain amount of sense. Even partially cognizant shadows lay closer to the Nexus than they did the axes of the Eternal War.

Might he … ?

Is it possible?

But he didn't have his grimoire or surgical kit, worms rot it all!

"You have your mother's ears," Gavin muttered, an impulsive observation as he thought about his larger troubles.

Vesram displayed his teeth. *"Yesss. You have your mother's eyesss and mouth."*

The Deathwalker squinted, at loss how to respond.

"Do you feel morrre ... Ma'ab or Manalari?" the Sathoet asked, curious.

Surprised, Gavin grappled for a response. *"Neither one over than the other. Something ... apart, yet both. I recognize the effort of the womb bearer, though in her absence upon her death, I cannot refute that my father did not slay me as an infant. Much as I loathed him."*

Vesram grunted, granting a bob of his head, solid grey eyes blinking. *"My sssire, absent. The womb-bearer and she who gave care were one. I feel more ... Elf. Through her. She balanced the Abysss in me. Though none believe to sssee me."*

Gavin could admit he hadn't expected this snarling face to express complex thoughts on his upbringing through their shared connection, yet his gut instinct to think of the hybrid as another type of Elfblood, not unlike Mourn, hadn't been unfounded. *"Hm. That is ... common among the living, unfortunately."*

"Truth."

A second later, the stripe of Vesram's mane puffed up, the hairs standing on end along his head and spine as he sniffed the air. At the same moment, Gavin detected the chill on his skin and picked up the sooty, vaporous movement in the upper corner of the butchery.

The Deathwalker stood up, his hands fisting in a brief surge of frustration as he felt the lack of his tools then looked around. The cleanliness of his cutting edge mattered in the reliability of his blood magic, but surely there were sharp edges aplenty in a place intended to dismember carcasses!

"What will you do?" Vesram asked, glancing in the general vicinity of the spirit. Impressive that he was even that accurate.

"I would snare it long enough to speak an exchange," Gavin answered, lifting his palm, letting his sleeve fall as he considered his pale, unblemished flesh. *"But I must draw my blood to do so."*

The Sathoet lashed out, swiping at Gavin with his claws then backing up. He was out of reach before the Deathwalker realized he'd been gashed. He stared at his forearm, as the black blood started flowing.

Vesram crab stepped to a bucket full of ashes nearby and plunged the dark-stained tips of his claws into it — an intriguing response Gavin had not expected — while motioning with his other hand. *"Ssspeak. While you can. I ssstay and guard."*

"Very well."

Gavin took his longest stride, closing with the butchery shadow as blood filled his cupped hand. Before the shade could decide either to threaten or fade away, the Herald flung his blood at the wall and ceiling, speaking his command in the Dead tongue. The spatter became a veil of mist which swept around the spirit, blocking off the dark cracks through which it might evade him. A wail of protest sounded, and it started thrashing like a fish in a net.

"Enough," the Herald growled, his voice taking on the multitudes within him as the mist grew brighter, erasing the last scrap of shadow except the misshapen one in the center. *"My time for options grows short. In the Name of the Grave Mother and the Winter Throne, obey me."*

The spirit quieted.

Aware.

Gavin could not tell how ancient this spirit might be or even which race it might have once lived as, for something about it did not ... *feel* Human. Older than the monk and librarian, for certain. Feeding upon the continual release of Vitas from the slaying of animals had allowed it to remain in Manalar, evading the fate of hungry self-cannibalization which led to dangerous ghost swarms.

Yet, gradually, this had transformed a once-sentient Vis into a some-what clever "living" shadow. Not a Shaegoth, not yet, although his mistress might be interested.

"We shall reach into the shadow realm together," Gavin intoned, *"and sum-mon aid."*

The spirit responded, and Gavin's vision became the inverse of his waking world, the darkest of energies mirroring the light. A blinding crack appeared, much like what had appeared when the Deathless had disrupted the bridge at the sacred pool, but smaller, for that was all the ancient spirit had ever needed.

The mist dispersed at Gavin's will, and the shadow slipped through, taking a fragment of the Herald's Vis with it. The world he knew turned quite literally upside down, a reflection rising like the forest upon the surface of a lake against the backstop of an evening storm. A thread of light connected the two realms, anchored by the Herald's body, its vitality a clear representation of the time which remained to return from his travel.

We stand upon the crossroads, he chanted, weightless and free. *Past, Present, and Future are as one to her. Her reality is all of time. Life and Death. Real and Unreal. We serve the Maiden of Shrouds, the Grave Mother ... I am here. Are you? Answer, and we shall talk.*

Gavin did not doubt his method of earning an answer from the Grey in such crude circumstances, only the precise nature of that which might respond. Regardless, he would repeat the chant until another acknowledged.

Or until he ran out of time.

*We stand upon the crossroads ... *

*Life and Death ... *

*The Maiden of Shroads ... *

*Answer ... *

Chains rattled. Once.

And again.

Closer.

Tension swept through the thread linked to his body; he expected it to fray and fade as the Hellhounds captured the demonblood and tried to wake him from his trance. Perhaps they were about to stab him with silver.

"*Intriguing concern to my favorite introduction,*" said a smooth voice. "*You peer inward first? Have I come too late to partake in an outward joy?*"

Gavin drew his attention from Miurag, his gaze flung out into the infinite shaded valleys.

The figure approached with a sway to their gait, traversing the realm as if material dirt existed to walk upon. The amber pools of their eyes cast a soft light, illuminating a scarred, androgynous body with blue-grey skin, some of it sewn on in patches.

"A Herald of Nyx, hm?" cooed a low, smoldering voice. "You must be newly awakened. I don't believe we have met."

The head was bald with jeweled needles piercing the scalp in through one spot and out the other, creating the hint of a halo. A veil of fine chains tipped with tiny hooks hid the face from those glowing eyes down, a few tiny bells playing a delicate song of pain.

Deliberately chosen straps of black leather covered the groin and chest, woven into the skin and muscle in ways reminiscent of Ada after she'd stepped through the rift. They granted him a bow from the waist which did not seem mocking despite their brazen state of dress.

"The Grey Maiden's agents have offered such delectable offerings for my assistance in the past," they said. "Tell me what you need, Herald, I listen most raptly."

"Hm. What kind of assistance?"

The creature tsked. "You haven't said what you need. I did not answer your call only to stand here guessing."

"First, tell me who and what you are."

The figure straightened up, eyes crinkling at the corners to suggest a broad smile beneath that swaying veil. "You may refer to me as an Artist of the Exquisite Host. Some purportedly 'wise' mortals call us 'chain devils,' pfft! As if we serve those warmongering Lords above the Art itself?"

The name of the collective arrived in his thoughts.

"You are a Chenkyte," Gavin said. "The body-makers always reweaving their essence across worlds."

"Excellent." They leaned one way then other. "I am glad your education has not been lacking, for I so admire your Lady. Now, what is your dire need to call out so?"

Gavin thought over something specific. "You have some fondness for chains?"

The Chenkyte purred. "Oh, I do. A most brutal and oppressive restraint." Metal links rattled where Gavin could see none. "The sound alone threatens the soundness of bone and the choices of the uninitiated. Add a few twists at each link's joining with another, and some souls forget they ever had those choices."

"Twists? You mean barbs? Or spikes?"

"Oh, yes. Would you like a demonstration?"

"Well —"

"Hold yourself."

The scarred figure lifted their eyes briefly, shuddering with delight and not a trace of fear. Links of black metal struck like vipers from the darkness, crisscrossing each other near every facet of Gavin's presence, every hook and barb a near-miss. They hemmed him in within instants, sharp tips teasing at his aura; he couldn't move if he wished to avoid punctures.

"You see?" they said.

Rather than take the demonstration as pure intimidation, Gavin recognized a finer control than the Hellhounds possessed. Much like summoning the Shaegoth at the redoubt, Gavin wagered his Lady's hand may have guided this eventual meeting.

"Very impressive," he murmured. *"A pure artist's hand and mastery of control."*

They cackled. *"Thank you, Herald."*

The Chenkyte withdrew one vicious chain after another, preventing any one hook from tearing to his essence. When Gavin was free to move, he asked, *"If the help I needed involved ... contesting the control of such chains used in a homebound conflict with the Ma'ab, would you be able to assist?"*

"Ohhh, a beautiful tapestry," they breathed. *"I can, yes, and you call at a most fortunate time, for I am alone and receptive right now."*

"Do you ... not wish to be alone?"

The figure shrugged, their posture touched by sadness. *"My last acolyte failed to create a lasting vision of themselves, and it destroyed them. Practicing the Art is endless exploration, but what use is unveiling untrodden pathways if not to become a guide to others? I know you understand this, Deathwalker."*

"Ah ... perhaps but ... you do not suggest I join you as payment?"

"You? Between worlds, no!" The creature laughed heartily, the bells and hooks jingling in their accompaniment. *"Wise as you may be in the ways of enlightened transformation, you are spoken for by the one who urged you to achieve it! No, I require my own offering. I want a fresh mortal soul, one with **potential** that I may nurture in the Art far beyond the limits of the life they once*

knew."

Gavin considered. *"Must they volunteer to be your acolyte?"*

"Not at all. You only must convince me of their prospects. I will do the rest."

A face passed through Gavin's thoughts, and the Chenkyte seemed to sense it. They prowled a step forward, amber eyes aglow, voice dropping so low it sent a tremor through Gavin's anchor thread.

"You have a soul in mind," said the Artist, tiny hooks dangling.

"I do. A skin hunter."

"Oo. Self-proclaimed?"

"Quite."

"Intriguing."

"We may have to catch him first. I believe an Infernal is pulling some puppet strings on him."

The Chenkyte's eyes narrowed, a tiny squeal escaping through the shimmering veil. *"Invite me onto your world, Herald. I would not miss the chance to woo a soul with true prospects to be free of a devil's cage."*

"Assist in disarming our enemies of their chains and other weapons first."

"Of course. Just reveal to me where they are."

Gavin extended his hand, and the Artist grasped it at once, their grip powerful, crushing, and the Herald's aura responded enough to see them both through the border of their realms in a spray of stars and sparks of gold.

When the Herald emerged from his trance and regained his physical senses, his body was no longer inside the butchery. Vesram had hauled him somewhere else. Somewhere dark, the Sathoet as the only life aura close by.

"Where am I?" he asked, touching his nose which was dripping blood. He checked the texture. Properly thick.

The Sathoet shivered in a corner, his mane puffed up like an angered cat. He appeared to be scowling at the Deathwalker and, at first scan, the two seemed alone.

"Could not ssstay," Vesram hissed with resentment. *"You draw eyes. Dangerousss eyesss ..."*

"My gratitude for choosing to move us, then. Where are we?"

"Under Temple."

"What?"

"Crypt. Where you and Sssiranna discovered Vo'traj and me. Where you ssstopped us."

A focused inhale confirmed dry bones and ancient stone surrounding him. Gavin looked up and around the blackness, neither cool blue wisps nor any bright-burning life auras besides the demon-Elf visible to him.

Where was the Chenkyte? Had they not passed through with him? Was their agreement not set?

Then, at the edge of his senses … *movement*.

The Deathwalker recognized the ghost of the ancient monk he had seen before coming down the wide stairs into the crypt. The old man stopped, beckoning him with a transparent hand, his dead man's voice touching Gavin's senses.

"The way to the sanctum is clear," he rasped. *"Your mother asks for you."*

Chapter 30

"We do not know the exact chain of events which would occur with her death," Captain Isboern explained to his men. "Only that it would draw direct attention from the Ascended to our city. More than one elder believes the liches *are* capable of interfering from afar."

Mourn and Krithannia bowed their heads in clear agreement to the Godblood's assessment. I did the same, if only because Jael and Deshi looked to me for a signal. Evening would be upon us within two hours. We stood in the open, in the presence of the Templari and in view of the resting army, an obvious mix of Manalari and Guild.

The only man missing was Sir Erik. He had volunteered to continue his guard of Amelda in the nearby shade of the trees. We were visible to him but out of earshot while Willven conveyed our encounter with the Ice Lord during the mindlink with the Ma'ab noble. Neither Dragonchild nor Guild Mistress showed surprise, only the familiar aggravation when the Fey Lord came up.

At least we know what it takes for someone to escape a Dwarven prison, Krithannia had remarked.

A literal deal with a devil.

"We can't risk bringing the Ma'ab noble with us to the wall," Isboern continued, "yet we can't release her to cause further trouble for us through her connections. Certainly not without a protector. My granting her clemency has as much to do with protecting our chances to reclaim our city as it does any code of conduct in this war."

"We understand, *Capitan*," said Sohl.

"You do right by us, *Capitan*, always," Robi added, a sentiment echoed by several other men.

"Thank you for your trust," Willven replied, dipping his chin. "I am only sorry this is not a straightforward contest of wills between us and the Ma'ab. We navigate a convoluted path from events set in motion long before any of us were born."

"*Nomilu sancji,*" the Templari murmured together, crossing their hearts before placing armored fists upon their chests.

"The day nears its end, *Capitan*," Imran said, "and many are too tired to move on. We lack the ability to fight in the dark a second time."

"Yes," Sohl agreed. "We cannot attack the wall at night."

"Understood," said Isboern, meeting each of their eyes steadily in a semi-circle. "We are more vulnerable here than where we were last night and are farther away from water. I also cannot discount our lack of a powerful death mage as we must consider the Ma'ab camp outside the wall."

"We have suggestions, Captain," Krithannia said, drawing each man's attention, "to address all those concerns."

"We are open to hearing them, elder," the Godblood replied.

"The Guild can offer a great deal of traps and illusions to dissuade an enemy approach at night, and we shall use these far beyond last night. In addition," Krithannia smiled at Tamuril, "while she cannot bring a whole river to your men, my sister has much skill in finding the hidden sources available. She can help you prioritize where to lead those most in need."

Isboern bowed from his waist. "We are grateful for anything you can do. Thank you."

The Druid blushed, and the Guild Mistress looked to Mourn with a nod, who took over.

Here we go.

"As for the Ma'ab camp," he said, "although we lack the valuable

413

insights and strategic advantage of the Herald of the Grey Maiden, we have a new combatant of the same vein, sworn to help us recover him." Mourn dipped his chin to Deshi. "One who can inspire terror in the Ma'ab soldiers if we make our moves well."

Discomforted, the Templari shifted their eyes to the Harrowed, whose expression darkened as if the night was coming early. Deshi pressed lips together as if to remind himself not to speak.

"Does this ... have to do with the Ma'ab woman screaming, legend?" Robi asked.

"It does," the Dragonblood confirmed with a subtle, somewhat inappropriate smile. "The Grey Maiden has granted Deshi a powerful gift for his courage and his pledge to continue service in this war. I recognize his choice to return. He could have left us. He did not."

Several Paxian faces paled to imagine, and the newborn revenant's gaze landed on anything but a living face.

"I do not assume to know the limits of his power," Mourn continued, "but I *do* recognize its nature. The Harrowed has a talent the Ma'ab fear above all."

Willven took a slow, calm breath while Tamuril looked on with a sympathetic hope to understand.

"Please explain it to us, legend," the Captain prompted.

After our interrogation, I wagered that the psion had a strong idea.

Mourn watched all Humans in the huddle. "First confirm you understand that your enemies have pledged their afterlife to their gods of the Far North, the Ascended."

The Templari spoke affirmatives, some making reverent gestures for their own god.

"You also recall how Deshi put down attackers living and undead, helping to cover the retreat to the Dwarven gate."

Further nods, and one Templar said, "He used a dagger blessed by the Herald of Nyx."

"Correct. The Harrowed no longer needs a dagger. His touch is enough, and this can affect the Hellhounds. Their tattoos shield their body from a material attack unless we strike the right spot, but they shall do nothing to stop a direct wound to their soul."

"What?" Imran asked with rising concern. "How do you mean, legend? How does one ... attack a soul?"

Mourn turned to him. "The touch of the Harrowed causes pain to the spirit of the living."

Watching their horrified expressions, I spoke up. "He means the Vis and Vitas."

"The what?" Sohl asked me.

This confirmed what I suspected. *They don't know what makes a death mage what they are.*

Then again, neither had I until I listened to one for several weeks.

"Vis and Vitas are the dual aspects of the soul," I explained, "which *every* death mage can sense if he comes into his power." Using the male word nudged the Templari harder to pay attention. "These are the memory of one's life, the Vis, coupled with the power and will to live, the Vitas. This is the nature and foundation of *all* death magic. Attuning one's aura to these aspects is how their magic works."

The Dragonblood smiled, pleased as my small lesson earned us nods of comprehension and astonished revelation. Gavin's horseback teachings had come in handy.

"She is exactly right," Mourn said. "Deshi's aura interacts with these aspects by touch, disrupting the connections to that which many of the living deem divine: the capacity for memory and that powerful drive to live. This incurs a solitude beyond comprehension for mere moments, an unbearable terror for most. The prisoner Amelda confirmed that her Ascended can do this as well, and her desire to resist answering our questions collapsed in the face of this experience."

Bodies shifted warily.

"The Harrowed of the Grey Maiden," Imran repeated, incredulous, "now has the power of the Ma'ab gods?"

Mourn's tail curved with pleasure. "Yes. One such power."

Deshi's pale face pinched with strain at the thoughts flying through his head. Krithannia, his brothers, and I moved closer to him in support, but only a little tension eased.

415

"I have a plan," the Dragon son continued, "for tonight. I will lead a small, focused team with the Harrowed as the foundation. The fear he can cause *could* spread like wildfire if we play it right. Our aim is to disperse the Ma'ab camp outside the wall and further reduce their leadership in the dark, thus, opening the way for the Manalari army to gain entry by the morning."

The Templars straightened up; they liked this idea.

"If we are lucky," Mourn finished, "it will draw Hellhounds out of the city where we may deal with them, so you do not have to."

"And if Divigna shows himself?" Robi asked.

"He will regret it," Deshi said, his voice taking on that shrill, haunting edge which made multiple men shudder.

Mourn showed many teeth in agreement. "Indeed, all the better. We will ask Divigna directly where the Herald is being kept. Meanwhile, you keep Amelda safe and the Ascended away while we chip away at the invaders squatting in your homes."

The reminder went far in gaining their acceptance of this plan, the anger and dread visible on their faces. Robi had a question, however.

"What if Deshi is cut down or recaptured before such 'wildfire' takes hold?"

"He will not be," Mourn assured.

"Because you will be there?"

"He does not need me, but I shall be there regardless."

Deshi peered up at the tall hybrid, tempted but wary to take that reassurance. The Templars, however, were not convinced.

Noting this, Mourn motioned to Robi. "Unsheathe your sword, *Tetente.*"

"What?"

"Bare your weapon and threaten the Harrowed with it."

Isboern nodded to his lieutenant, who obeyed while the rest of us made room. Deshi's hands fisted as he glanced at Mourn and me.

"Should the Templar threaten Janshi to invoke the gift?" asked the Dragonblood.

The youth shook his head at once. "No, *Wen-yung*. That ... is not

416

necessary."

Mourn bowed his head respectfully, waiting patiently as Deshi moved in front of Robi. With the deep breath, the pale blue disappeared from the eyes of the Harrowed, leaving only the yellow ring floating in darkness.

"Cut me down, Templar," he invited, opening his hands to each side. "Or ... *Try.*"

"God," Robi whispered, looking to Isboern for reassurance.

"Have faith in our allies, *Tetente*," said the Captain with a brief nod. "Give our brothers a demonstration."

Our huddle yielded to make room, and Robi's heartbeat ramped up as he gripped his sword with both hands, taking a stance as if to drive the point into Deshi's middle. I didn't know what inner voice the Templar silenced to thrust forward without hesitation, but Robi obeyed his Captain, and the sword pierced Deshi's body, jutting out the other side.

The Harrowed's form burst into something from a nightmare, causing his brothers and several others to cry out in alarm. His entire skeleton appeared, starkly defined against a swell of bluish-green light which mimicked ghostly flames. Any hint of Human expression was gone. The edge of Robi's sword fell to one side without resistance, passing through without a drop of blood or gore to dim the shine of its edge, as if Deshi's body had become a spirit of its own.

"*Musanlo salbami!*" the Templar cried, a palm pressed above his heart, his right hand nearly dropping his sword as he backed up. "*Capitan! Verdai terrovi!*"

"*Baixin,*" Isboern answered, offering his hands for Robi to take. The man did so gratefully after sheathing his sword. His upset eased and the color returned to his face as the two met eyes.

Meanwhile, Deshi solidified to the point where I could recognize him. Everything except for the sadistic smile of satisfaction teasing his lips.

That reminded me of Mathias.

Finally, Robi could speak. "Th-the legend speaks true. The Grey Maiden's warrior ... invokes terror for one's own soul."

417

"The bua didn't even touch him," Jael whispered to me, scratching her jaw.

"A good thing," I whispered back.

A Templar who had gathered his faculties swifter than the others spoke up. "This lad ... this Guildsman returned from the dead, is ... invulnerable in battle?"

"He may as well be," Mourn answered, a deliberate distinction not everyone caught. "The Harrowed will be our point man to break up the Ma'ab camp. The Guild will back us up. If we are successful, you shall have a clear path by morning, and the contest for the soul of your city can begin."

"Then we must prepare and hope for that success," Isboern said.

Mourn agreed, nodding to Krithannia, their exchange curtailing further questions. Willven caught my eye, however.

~*Stay a moment, you and the Dragon son. Please.*~

~*Ah. Alright?*~

~*I will return.*~

The Captain stepped forward to give his officers their orders before dismissing each one. I tapped Mourn's shoulder as he'd finished signing to the Guild Mistress, and he looked over his shoulder.

"Isboern asked us to hold here," I said. "You and me."

"And me?" Jael asked, crossing her arms as Krithannia and Tamuril coaxed the three Yungian brothers to come with them.

I smiled. "Certainly, Sister. Stay."

She arched her eyebrow, grumbling something about Willven but kept watch with us until the Captain could join us and share his concern.

"I admit I feel only injury," Isboern said bluntly, "at the thought of exploiting Deshi's pain like this."

"That is why I shall lead in this, Captain," Mourn answered.

"I understand all you've shared, legend, but ..." Blue eyes fixed on us. "The boy hasn't had time to grieve, and I *saw* his realization during your demonstration."

"What realization, Captain?"

"That he is no longer Human." Isboern paused with a swallow. "That every man he meets from this day forward will see him as the ghost he is. A night terror and tormentor like those who killed him."

Mourn paused, bowing his head slightly. "That is what he must be today, Godblood. What he has chosen for the rest of this war."

"And if he breaks?" asked Isboern. "Loses control of this death power. If he turns on *my* men because he can't tell the difference in souls in a grip of battle lust?"

"I will be with him," the Dragon son replied sternly, tail flicking behind him. "I will help."

"You can't take responsibility for his actions."

"Neither can you nor *any* man hold him in check once the fighting resumes. The Harrowed will not value any word of restraint."

"How do you know this?"

"Because he barely restrains himself now." Mourn took a breath. "The best path forward, for us *and* for the boy he once was, is to point the Harrowed at the Ma'ab and set him loose."

The shield-bearer grimaced, shaking his head once. "How is *that* a path forward, guardian? To be a fighting dog taught in pain to seek revenge on any flesh set in front of him? All for the benefit of his masters who released the chain. That is much like the Ascended and the Eternal Hellhound, is it not?"

Mourn paused, granted a nod. "I can see the parallel."

"I do not want to use their tactics."

"You do not. This was between Deshi and his Maiden, and I say letting him loose is the only way to avoid further tragedy."

"Then please convince me, ancient one, how that is the case. What path forward do you see that I do not?"

Mourn's tail stopped moving as he drew in a calm breath, glancing at Jael and me. We shrugged, and I signed, ★Your move.★

Something about it made him smile.

"I was in their place once, Captain," Mourn said, turning to Isboern. "Deshi *and* Divigna. Centuries ago. Captured by those powerful enough to hold me, helpless to escape, and young enough to fear being killed while sometimes wishing I had been. Each trial I went through was for the entertainment and enrichment of my 'betters.' "

The blond man's eyes widened in a way that reminded me that he wasn't much older than Deshi despite his experience.

"When at last I found my power, I used my freedom to make my tormentors pay the cost of holding me prisoner. Nothing in the Void could stop me."

The Dragonblood and Godblood held eyes. Willven believed him.

"Deshi will do the same when he meets his tormentors," Mourn continued. "But afterward, *when* we win the pool, after you cleanse it and begin the era of peace you dream of on Mount Sonai, the Harrowed might seek a peace learned from *your* example. As I did from Krithannia's."

Isboern began to look convinced. Even hopeful.

"As I see this, a decisive victory, followed by your vision of a better life for all Manalari. *That* is the best way to give Deshi his chance. The *necessity* to fight demons every day must lessen before peace is possible."

Jael whipped eyes to me, eyebrows raised, as if amazed to grasp an idea she hadn't expected. She may have recognized his enslavement in the Deepearth but not what it took to become the young teacher he'd been.

I smiled warmly. Reluctantly, she returned it.

"Understand, Captain," the Dragonblood finished without noticing our exchange. "Deshi's spirit will not heal while the Ma'ab hold the Herald and Manalar. The Harrowed *is* a revenant returned to the fight, a willing and effective weapon against our foes. Best to view him as such for the sake and safety of your men."

The Godblood exhaled, tense shoulders lowering though the regret remained. "Thank you for sharing that with me, legend. I ... admire that an ancient such as you can be moved to empathy for one of us."

Mourn smiled, his tail curving gently. "I have lived among you a long time, Captain. Bearing witness to life patterns on a shorter scale has helped me to recognize my own."

Isboern returned the smile. "Then you will help to guide him?"

"As I can with what I know."

"And that would be a lot. My gratitude, truly, on behalf of all who depend on us."

"Well said." Mourn glanced where Krithannia waited for us, answering as she signaled. "Watch for Pilla and signs of Tamuril, Captain. We will be out all night but are working on an alternative to keep in contact and pass information."

"Again, my sincerest gratitude. We will keep Amelda safe and await word. We shall be ready before morning to breach the wall."

ALTHOUGH A PARTICULAR NAME INDRATH HAD SAID WAS NIGGLING IN MY THOUghts for hours, I wouldn't ask until after I had eaten my fill and after our small team of four had resupplied with what was available. I also had to wait until Mourn and Krithannia held their private meetings with three Guild teams — including some from Reprisal and *Hata Ri* — and had released them for reconnaissance.

"Just four," Tamuril commented anxiously, arms tightly crossed. She and her falcon stared at the elder sister.

"Four," Krithannia confirmed as she scanned the settling campground. "With others waiting on the fringe if needed. The smaller, the better at the start. Fewer allies to get in the way as chaos builds."

The Druid exhaled. "But … a direct attack? You could be so easily surrounded and overborne."

"Not so easy," Jael countered, hands on her hips.

"Agreed," Mourn said without elaboration, focused on checking over his harness.

I smiled. "Willven taught me some shielding, but sometimes the safest place is behind those with the longest reach."

Deshi waited patiently in his drab clothing, his hands and feet bare. His face was set, morbidly placid, as he watched Peng-lok and Nianzu assisting the Templars.

"We have plenty to do here, Tamuril." Krithannia touched her arm. "And we need your help to keep watch while making sure the men have enough water."

The blonde Naulor was willing to play her role but glanced pointedly at my belly.

"Guard Willven first," I reminded her, rubbing my ring finger with my thumb where she could see. "Ionne and I have our own protectors."

"That they do," the Dragonblood agreed, finishing his inspection.

"To go for her," Jael added with a mean smile, "only gives me anger."

The Harrowed turned tri-colored eyes to our group then, echoing her grin with one of his own as he gave her a bow. "True, *Janhuren*. Me as well."

"Are we ready?" Mourn asked.

The Sun had set about three hours ago. The Little Sister Moon would rise first in another two, the Big Sister another two after that. Dawn was about six hours away, and we were only an hour's fast ride from the camp along the wall.

Enough time to level the Ma'ab camp, one charge at a time.

"Ready," I said, summoning Nightmare closer so that Jael and I could help each other mount up. Mourn and Deshi would run beside us, neither wearing boots.

"Stay safe," Tamuril said rather helplessly.

"I will try for 'unhurt,' " I replied with a confident grin. "Promise."

"I will hold that promise."

I held the smile in place as I turned Nightmare to the east, until we were out of sight of even a falcon's eyes, then gave my face a rest to focus on guiding Gavin's horse toward big trouble.

Fortunately, it did not take long for us to find a rhythm. I knew Mourn's endurance, but he had assured me Deshi would not tire for as long as he could breathe. I could accept that. The only life sound I heard from the Harrowed *was* his breath, which he'd somehow received from me.

"Breathe for me, Janshi," he pleaded.

"Take it in deep," Nyx said, *"and do not let it slip away. That is your anchor now."*

With brow drawn down, his face set in determination, the Harrowed ran beside Gavin's mare as steadily as the Dragonchild. His limbs pumping, his feet often passing *through* obstacles, Deshi leapt over ditches and stayed with the galloping beast, maintaining his speed as if he could go all night. Far beyond Human endurance.

Though awe-inspiring to watch, a name Indrath had spoken returned to my thoughts.

~*Io'sulta.*~

Mourn's eyes flickered toward me in the dim starlight, aware I was speaking to him. *Yes?*

~*The Ice Lord knows about Isboern given his lifetime to win the pool after Gavin broke its constraints.*~

Yes. I told you he stood with the Grey guardians as part of my Dream as I Slept.

~*Right.*~ I guided Nightmare between two brambles which hadn't yet grown together. ~*Io'sulta is another name for the sacred pool? For Pisc'sagrad. An older one?*~

The oldest, he confirmed. *Draconic.*

Together, we dropped off a tiny ledge, quickly regaining traction on the soft ground.

What about it? he asked.

Far too casual.

~*I heard it before. From Cris-ri-phon in the Temple. When he was about to spill that young priest's blood into the pool. I didn't know what he was talking about, but you said not to 'awaken the Sargt.'*~

Something we want to avoid if possible. A To'vah Awakening would have far stronger and lasting effects on this war, on this entire region, than small bands of raiders slipping in through the rift.

A flash of fear rushed through at the thought, but I didn't fully understand why. ~*Why would the Deathless want a blood sacrifice to awaken the Red Dragon?*~

I have reflected on that, and I do not think that is what the sorcerer wanted. My guess is that was the will of the Ice Lord, who would have been ready with a plan of his own. Meanwhile, the rest of us would have lost every opportunity we have now.

My mouth tightened at the next swerve around brambles too dense and high to take on directly. *~I don't think the Infernal tried hard enough if he wanted that.~*

I agree. It might have been a counter to something or someone we couldn't see or a response if the Bishops started working together. I think Indrath backed off when we arrived. The Deathless certainly did.

Not before a lot of taunting. I frowned. *~Indrath has been watching what we do every step of the way since, making things harder if not outright sabotaging us.~*

Mourn didn't respond at first; he focused on his breath, on his and Deshi's paces beside my horse. *The Ice Lord has made some things more difficult, yes, but we aren't his true adversaries, Sirana. If we had been, he would have already destroyed our chances.*

Not comforting.

~Oh? So who are his 'true adversaries?~

Other Outsiders. Other devils, demons, celestials, and sovereigns.

I sneered. *~So with Elves, he would rather claim 'family disputes' instead of enemies?~*

I think that's a wise way to see it, yes. It would explain many of his remarks about your queen and the sire of your unborn, which he seems focused on even over Soul Drinker.

~Ughhh.~ I scowled resentfully. *~So ... Was it a mistake to give him the name of the sire?~*

Too early to say. I'm only glad Willven Isboern was strong enough to help guard your full thoughts on the matter. If what you've given the Ice Lord buys us time from his interference tonight and tomorrow, that may need to be good enough.

~And in the meantime, I have the name of Cris-ri-phon's living daughter if the Deathless shows up.~

Ahmm, yes ... He likely won't. But we will talk about that.

I leaned forward. *~When? And when will we talk about the Wilder?~*

Once the Grey Maiden's guardians leave Miurag and pass the task of reviving Io'sulta to the Godblood.

I exhaled, choosing to take that on its face.

My eye caught the first skull on a post, that first sign leading us to the Ma'ab camp.

Jael growled eagerly behind me. "Almost there."

Deshi's pale skin shifted toward a familiar shade of aqua as he grinned, his canines visibly sharper. "We are, *Janhuren*."

"They will see us coming this first time," Mourn rumbled, large hands flexing. His metal bracers gleamed as if ready to send all his favorite weapons into his palms to address this matter. "We shall see what greater minds and mages remain. We will wear them down."

Shyntre's pendant warmed against my chest as Jael drew one sword and brandished it out to one side. I touched Soul Drinker's hilt, and then my spiders' pouch, ready to release the latter to guard from my neck the moment Nightmare slowed enough.

The two males would dive in first, incapacitating and cutting down every Ma'ab still in the fight. Meanwhile, my Thoughts would shield my Sister as her Words set everything they had left on fire.

And we'd let Chaos spread.

Chapter 31

Vesram had his nose open as they climbed out of the undercroft of the Temple, constantly sniffing the stagnant air.

"Concerns?" asked the Deathwalker, taking the stairs one or sometimes two at a time without pause.

"Not yet," the Sathoet murmured.

"What would your nose detect to give us concern?"

"Othersss …"

"I would expect that."

"*Outsider* othersss."

This made sense. Mourn had paused in this underground passage weeks ago, his Draconic senses detecting the Abyssal blood of the same creature following Gavinn now.

"Have you smelled Infernals in the city? Or others?"

"Yesss."

"Which have you smelled?"

"Hellsss. And Heavenss …"

Concerning. Neither Manalar nor *Pisc'sagrad* needed the attention of those two factions at this time and place. Worse if they grew frustrated nudging their agents and arrived in person to come to blows.

"Both sides would threaten you on sight," the Herald murmured.

Vesram rumbled. "They would dessstroy me."

No wonder the demonblood Elf had seemed so shaken when Gavin came out of his trance, after drawing "dangerous eyes," apparently. The Deathwalker *still* didn't know where the Chenkyte had gotten off to.

Invite me onto your world, Herald ...

Gavin supposed he hadn't specified any particular constraint on that invitation beyond disarming the Hellhounds before hunting Mathias Briar. Tactics and timing were not his strongest suits.

Let us hope the Artist is stronger.

"Would you recognize the scent of To'vah?" the Deathwalker asked suddenly.

"Yesss," Vesram answered quietly. His bare feet made hardly any noise on the stone. "Also Nexusss and Abyssss."

"You have a valuable ability to discern such nuance. Should you sense any of these nearby, Elfblood, tell me which one they are."

The Sathoet paused, perhaps surprised by the clear favoring of his maternal side but answered in kind. "I will, Adassson."

Adason.

Gavin decided he had grown accustomed to that name, which was just as well. They weren't far from the sanctum.

Mentally, he prepared to meet his mother again.

This time, he'd be conscious from the start.

"Welcome back, Herald. And you, too, Vesram."

The Nexus guardians stood present, all four around the sacred pool. Although all signs of a rip in the world's boundary had disappeared in the weeks since the first battle, the waters themselves glowed with a familiar misty blue color. The light cast enough shadows that Gavin expected Shaegoth to be present, though he could not detect them.

Houda was the one who had spoken. Although the former Desert Deathwalker was not the tallest in stature, the dusky-skinned warrior stepped forward from the others: the delicately vibrating wasp girl, the thick-boned, greenish brute, Oskar …

And of course, Ada. Elegantly grotesque in her black gown attached by silver hooks and needles, a smooth orb of pneuma flint filling her right eye socket. Upon closed lips she held a tiny smile.

"Where are you allies?" Houda asked.

"We've been separated," Gavin answered. "We misconstrued which captive might be the priority for Kreshel Divigna."

"And Vesram found you?"

"Abducted me, rather. From my abductor."

His Ma'ab mother showed teeth in her amusement. They were black like his, though some had grown jagged and carnivorous. Her false eye glimmered in a rhythm mimicking laughter, and Gavin turned his head to the side, expecting the Davrin half-blood to be the one garnering that attention.

The Sathoet wasn't there; the Deathwalker had to crane his neck farther to find him. Vesram had slowed down when Gavin hadn't noticed, crouching on the floor quite far from the platform.

Strange.

"Can you not approach *Pisc'sagrad*?" he asked.

"I can," the Sathoet answered, the low tone neutral. "But I draw eyesss if I come clossser."

"He is correct," Oskar rumbled, muscled arms crossed. "Though you will not, Herald."

So, the former slave to the Ma'ab seeks to aid this meeting.

The Deathwalker faced his Lady's emissaries, folding his hands before him. When they only watched him, he spoke. "I was told Ada requested my presence."

Houda and Oskar seemed surprised, though Gavin could not tell if the wasp girl shared that sentiment. His mother's enigmatic smile broadened further.

While Ada had retained her small Ma'ab build, pale skin, and one black eye past her transition, Gavin took the chance to study the style in which her black gown and adornments were attached by metal piercings and hooks through her flesh. He could not help but note a similar masochistic aesthetic to the Artist of the Exquisite Host, with whom the Herald had made his agreement in the shadow realm.

"My son intends to challenge his old master?" she asked with a voice intended to be spoken behind the backs of others.

"I do," Gavin answered. "I shall send the old goat on his next path before winter."

"The task has grown more difficult than my son believes," she responded. "Upon the moment he freed this pool, the crossroads transitioned to a new stage of Existence, and Sarilis with it. He will not give up what he has gained easily." Ada lifted her chin in a smooth gesture to indicate the Sathoet behind the Herald. "My son will need Vesram and what he has learned. The Sathoet must keep his newfound freedom; he and his allies must help him. Vesram has earned it for what he has suffered in the stead of your mother."

"He is worthy of such trust," Gavin said, not quite a question, but Ada nodded regardless.

"That protection he once gave your mother," she said, "he gives to my son for whom he has been waiting."

Behind him, Vesram rumbled with that unsettling hint of affection. The half-blood's actions and words had strongly suggested this, and thinking on it produced a strange sensation in Gavin.

"One of my allies has been searching for him," Gavin said. "I believe she is meant to bring him to the underground city of his birth."

"*No*," Vesram growled. "Will *not* return to Abysssal queen. Will *not* ssserve her again."

At least that was clear.

The Herald turned around to address him. "Then it is doubly important Sirana is freed from her queen's constraints as well. Captain Isboern is her key to unlock those manacles. The man must live to regain the city and take over guardianship of the pool."

The blank, grey eyes narrowed. "Or shhhe may die."

Gavin frowned. "Agents of the Nexus, the To'vah, the Hells, *and* the Abyss have all either suggested or sworn to act to see that she *won't,*

Sathoet. I am inclined to accept their visions and motives for what they are. I am also one who has sworn to act. Although the path is not clear yet, *her* freedom may be linked to yours."

Vesram hissed, his muzzle rippling to expose a carnivore's teeth. "Undersssstood, Adassson."

Ada laughed softly, and the shadows of the dimly lit sanctum quivered. The wasp girl's wings buzzed, antennae shifting independently as large, insectile eyes focused on the damaged front door. Houda and Oskar appeared as if they could understand the mute child's language for they gazed out above Gavin's head, in the direction of sunrise.

"Another assault begins," Houda said, dark irises filling with mist. "You may join them when you wish, Herald."

"What of the Eternal Hellhound," he asked, mostly to his mother. "Kreshel Divigna is an unnaturally wrought soul. Any word for what is to be done about him?"

All four emissaries fell silent, even Ada, her smile all but vanishing. Gavin was taken aback.

After a pause, Houda shook her head once. "No, Herald. Nothing." *Impossible.*

Behind him, Vesram growled, looking away when Gavin turned.

"Nothing of the Black Heart?" he asked any that might answer.

"You should go, Herald," said the Desert warrior. "Take what you know. Do with it what you will in service to our Lady."

At once so clear, yet pockets of mist remained.

"As always, then."

The Deathwalker strode past the Sathoet on his way to the front door of the sanctum, noting the lingering look the half-blood gave his mother. He frowned. "Come, Vesram."

The Sathoet turned away, joining Gavin with a barely restrained expression of demonic wrath on his face.

The Deathwalker had questions, of course, but when two in a row had been blatantly refused, all that remained was the waiting. Sirana might have pursued further questions with the silent former slave. She might have asked for clarification of his earlier statements.

The Herald knew when matters of his concern were not helped by prying.

After leaving the sanctum but before exiting the Temple, Gavin took a detour down a hallway, testing doors in search of a room which led to a north-facing, exterior balcony. From there, he might be able to see what was happening at the wall.

Once he found one, Gavin went in, expecting the Sathoet to follow without further coaxing. Not only did Vesram enter these quarters but moved ahead without asking once he realized they headed for the decorative doors leading outside.

"I check firssst," the half-blood grumbled. "Ssstand out of sssight."

Suddenly, Gavin knew what Sirana had experienced with Mourn guarding her every step. An odd annoyance when one simultaneously accepted the dynamic and then found unconscious choices obstructed.

"Very well."

The Sathoet vanished from view while he watched, a fascinating display of bending the available light which also obscured his life aura. Then one balcony door opened slowly, quietly, and wide enough for the demonblood to slip through. Gavin heard no footsteps.

He waited.

"*Sssafe*," Vesram whispered from outside, invisible when Gavin joined him.

Starlight alone lit the midnight sky for the smaller moon had yet to rise. Small fires from torches, lanterns, or hearths burned in the wealthy districts high on the mountain slope but also farther down on both sides of the shattered wall. Gavin couldn't discern any magical lights yet, not until he noted a larger fire which seemed to be spreading within the Ma'ab camp.

A sustained wail had taken to the air, distant but somehow stirring his mage sense, a preternatural presence rising above the drone of mortals crying out in alarm.

What is that?

His first guess was the Dragonchild, yet the sound was oddly familiar. The glimpse of a bluish green witchfire had been the source of it, he was sure; the sight and sound moved together toward the center of the encampment.

Another assault begins.

And the Guild had chosen to attack the Ma'ab outside the city at night. Interesting.

Would the Chenkyte appear to fulfill their agreement? Possibly yes, if Kreshel led or sent his packs outside the wall, or not if the Herald of Nyx wasn't there to confirm their alliance.

Gavin was too far away to arrive on foot and assist with this phase of the attack. Chances weighed in favor of the Godblood and his army arriving at dawn. Eventually, they would have to breach their own wall, and the timing would be determined by the success or failure of this night attack.

"Vesram," Gavin said.

The Abyssal Davrin shifted. *"Hrrrm?"*

"Can you guide us unseen toward the damaged wall?"

A soft hiss. "Yesss, but ..."

The Deathwalker turned his head. "But?"

"No way under," he said. "Tried. Flush pipes too small."

"What do you mean 'flush pipes'?"

"Manure."

Ah. Of course.

The Guild had discussed how the middens ducts passing through the walls were too many and too small for even Yungian men to crawl through, thus, the necessity of the Ma'ab breaking said wall and their elite forces climbing farther up the mountain to pass beneath the wall into the cisterns there.

That the Temple City chose *not* to use their raw middens to flood directly outside the wall, creating a disease-ridden moat at the expense of their poorest citizens, had to do with the early Dwarven crafting and design over choices the Bishops might have made centuries later. The poor were not as miserable as they *could* be, although enough for having the undesirable but critical task of turning fume-ridden waste into earthly gold for the city's fields and food supply.

"Ssstay here?" Vesram suggested. "Wait for allies?"

Always an option to stay in one place. Gavin being recaptured while traversing the city wouldn't help his allies while viewing movements from higher up had its advantages.

At the same time, he could not ignore the sense he would be forgoing an opportunity of some sort to sit truly idle. Though accustomed to waiting, he usually had his grimoire to write in, which Kreshel may or may not possess, or at least something to read.

"A reminder," Mathias said, "this 'maggot' was once a southern monk. Personally, I'd take him to where the scrolls and codices are stored."

Gavin hummed as the idea set roots, and the Sathoet perked up to listen. "Have you seen the library?"

"*Hrrrmmaybe?*"

"I will describe it, then. You help us avoid enemy and Outsider."

Point the Harrowed at the Ma'ab and set him loose.

The screeching, black skeleton lit up the camp before Jael had cast her first fire spell, drawn to anyone with breath and a heartbeat. Deshi found them the moment he was close enough, whether they were charging to meet him or hiding inside a tent or behind a cart. A few large fighters struck first and would have landed a solid blow if the Grey Maiden's warrior wasn't what he was.

Deshi attacked the Ma'ab without hesitation. With a swipe of his arm as if gripping a dagger or with a series of punches and kicks like in the *dorji-ka,* the Harrowed swept through their bodies, drawing no blood at all. Yet with the force of his aura, each pale Northerner stumbled and fell, screaming on the ground, eyes bulging, clawed hands clutching their chests.

Deshi would leave them in terror to dart after the next one and Mourn was always behind him. With his sliding blades, he cut them down with as few strokes as possible, conserving his energy. Most didn't seem to see him coming in time to resist anyway.

Whether targets were man or woman, alive or undead, it didn't matter. People screamed, guts spilled, limbs and heads bounced onto the ground, their pieces kicked and spread through the camp amid the panic.

The final battle had begun, and only one way to end it.

Kill them all.

We had four hours to sunrise and eight scouted locations to hide in the dark outside the perimeter. I had Gavin's thurible and some food in a sling bag; the former in case we found him and the latter for me to devour on horseback.

The goal was to reach the center of camp and cut swaths outward with unexpected changes in direction. We'd leave abruptly and wait in camouflage while Reprisal and *Hata Ri* attacked from the shadows, casting their own attacks to keep the Ma'ab within the camp or bunch them up for the Harrowed's next charge.

Ideally, we'd keep up with rolling attacks until the place was levelled or until the resting army behind the walls spilled out. We had to stay close, not stop or be stopped while we were inside the perimeter.

No matter what.

VESRAM COULD NOT SHARE HIS INVISIBILITY UNDER ANY BUT THE DIREST OF circumstances, requiring utter stillness and practically full-body contact to become one with the wall.

"Noted," Gavin grunted. "Scout ahead, then. Choose our path. I can wait."

The Sathoet was accustomed to this role, apparently, and was smarter at planning a route and conveying each segment than the Deathwalker had expected. Though Gavin had used stealth his entire mortal life to avoid hostile attention, he could learn from this half-blood.

Avoiding full or noisy houses, guard posts, standing horses, or Ma'ab on the move were all obvious choices, of course. Vesram also kept them to the deepest shadows, which he seemed able to find like a thirsty man listening for a steady stream.

The half-blood selected the slightly fouled pathways littered with the flotsam of death auras never properly released, those "haunted" places which made most Humans unconsciously uncomfortable enough that they tended to avoid it. Even the ordinary, invading Ma'ab were Human enough to recognize it.

While they traveled in the shadows, Gavin kept his senses open for the Chenkyte but detected none of those distinctive ripples in his reality. He found himself wanting to ask Vesram about Ennikar and how often he explored the city of the Ascended, but he refrained based on his mother's recent advice.

My son will need what he knows ... protect his newfound freedom.

Now was not the time to distract; they were in Manalar, not the Empire's capital. Gavin could inquire on their way to confront Sarilis. The journey would be long.

Meanwhile, the wailing on the wind continued, not much louder than it had been at the Temple but consistent and always coming from the direction of the camp at the wall. Likewise, the lights of multiple fires became noticeable against the night sky, growing enough to block out the northward stars once the first moon began her rise.

Too many distractions for Gavin to assist whatever came next, and although they made good time traversing the city at night, he knew they were not halfway.

"One question," the Herald whispered when he and Vesram paused for a moment.

"Hrm?"

"Has Kreshel spoken to the Grey guardians at the pool?"

Sharp, Elven ears lifted in surprise as the Sathoet shook his head. "No. Avoidsss temple."

"Why?"

Vesram shrugged. "The Third learnsss all he learnsss, each time he returnsss to her. Divigna learned not to be curiousss."

Unfortunate but unsurprising.

"Hm," the Deathwalker replied. "Then it must have been you who told him who I was."

Another shake of his head. "He sussspected. Ada esssacaped into Manalari territory. You are half-breed Manalari *maknuut* of the right age."

"Adason," Gavin said firmly. "Divigna spoke it to Deshi. That name is not widespread."

The white-maned creature with oddly bright grey eyes appeared guilty. He admitted, "Hellhounds almossst caught me ten nights ago. I disstracted Divigna, said you'd come back if we wait."

"Hmph."

Vesram put his clawed finger to his muzzle. "No more. Mussst go."

Gavin waved them ahead. "As you will."

They could only move forward. What happened when Sirana saw Vesram or when *anyone* saw the Artist would only be his concern once the gap in their distances was closed.

AFTER THE LOSS OF THEIR FIRST WAVE OF GUARDS, DESHI MET A CLUSTER OF THE walking dead. This must have been disappointing to the controlling mage. Even without a Vis to terrify, the Harrowed's ghostly flames snuffed the spark of Vitas keeping them on their feet, causing them to collapse much the same as he'd done with his Nyx-blessed dagger by the river.

"*Hai*, look!" Jael shouted, pointing. "She goes!"

Without using his eyes, Deshi sprinted after the mage as she launched out of hiding. For an instant, I didn't know whose wail was loudest when he caught up to her.

Behind me, my Sister's focus latched onto pure destruction as she began using one useful phrase, over and over.

"*Docar Svorlim!*" she cried like a battle yell.

With these Words, a ball of deep orange light the size of her fist formed along the edge of her borrowed blades. With each swing, the intense spots flew on that momentum, colliding with tents, carts, and crates to scatter like bugs before igniting them with flames not easy to smother. Horses screamed in panic as the fires grew, voices shouting orders which could not seem to coalesce into effective action to either stop the enemy or extinguish the flames.

Meanwhile, I moved Nightmare fast and close enough behind Mourn to protect our front but not get in his way. I also had to split my focus between guiding our mount and guarding our flanks and could only manifest a psionic barrier when I was aware of a potential threat. My shield didn't last long before I was distracted by an obstacle over which we had to leap or the startling collision of an arrow or stone.

Better than leathers alone.

We'd known this going in, but my companions and I had agreed. Like Jael on her budding journey as a battlemage, I had no luxury of time to worry about matching the skills which had taken Isboern decades of practice with his mind.

My mount took several arrows to the throat and haunches behind Jael's ass, each with a thump to which Nightmare did not react. None of the Ma'ab mounts would go anywhere near the Dragonblood as Mourn consistently bellowed a roar at any cavalry. He also cleared the sky of spying skin kites with fire, his voice booming in between Ma'ab executions as he blasted the diving annoyances with scorching heat.

I kept my ears open for the first clink of chains, knowing we were on borrowed time. That was the moment Blade Song would truly begin.

GAVIN AND VESRAM WAITED A FEW TIMES FOR SOME OF THE WEALTHY HOUSES to empty out.

Mundane soldiers on their way to the wall to confront the disturbance in camp.

The Herald stood stiffly as the half-blood wrapped his arms around from behind. Vesram tucked them around a corner, bending light and shadow to the point neither could see their feet.

Meanwhile, Gavin's thoughts drifted from the library ghost he expected to see to the ancient monk who had come to him in the crypt, then, finally, to the feral spirit in the butchery. Perhaps later he would have the opportunity to offer the first two a new path and release that strange essence feeding on the slaughter of animals.

If they won the pool.

Not 'if,' he thought to himself. *We must.*

The consequences of failing in this would disrupt every path the Deathwalker must walk from now on.

Over the next hour, the distant howling and noise of combat rose and fell while the fires grew ever brighter. Vesram led Gavin into the quieter neighborhood he'd described, to an alley across from the old library long ignored by the Bishops.

The front door was ajar.

Gavin had no way of knowing when this had happened; it could have been this evening or several weeks ago.

"Check firssst," Vesram whispered. "Divigna may wait for you."

Sigh. That was a good supposition. Mathias had told him about it and Gavin's proclivities.

"Very well," he murmured.

Spotting only the smallest of signs that the Abyssal Davrin had crossed the street, Gavin observed the iron gate swinging open just enough for the half-blood to pass in. A few moments later, the open front door did not move, but some dirt was knocked off a stone step.

The street remained quiet. *No clinking of chains, at least.*

When Gavin sensed the Sathoet approach; he lifted his chin slightly as if to meet eyes he could not see.

"Paxian man searches," Vesram whispered.

"What?"

"The torturer."

"Mathias?"

"Yesss."

"Searches the library."

"He looksss for sssomething."

"Well, that won't do. Anyone else?"

"Not unless strong magicsss."

Good enough.

Gavin launched into a long stride, heading for the front door, ideally before the skin hunter came out of it.

A couple monstrous constructions had been summoned to meet us on the fringe of camp.

Golems, Gavin had called them.

Physically sturdy and magically warded beyond a simple risen corpse or walking skeleton, the Harrowed and the Dragonchild required time and coordination to deal with one of them. Much like facing the grotesque giant in the warp rot forest, I aided them by catching the attention of each and leading it in a circle until Mourn broke the wards of protection. Then Deshi would either pass through it or leap upon its back, draining the Vitas until it fell flat on its face.

Living Ma'ab soldiers shot arrows from the wall, aiming often for the Dragonchild, who deflected them with humming blades. A few targeted our mount; they seemed hesitant to kill Jael and me. Those for which I was unprepared sank into Nightmare's shoulder and thighs without a flinch, collecting several on each side.

Nightmare charged, unbothered by the howls and roars, by the fires, or the clash and noise of battle. Jael broke off the shafts if she could reach them, but Gavin's stalwart mare kept running regardless, turning tightly around obstacles under my command. Behind me, my mage Sister retaliated with spells of fire, scattering Ma'ab units daring to form outside the wall.

No Hellhounds had appeared yet, which was odd. Observance in the first battle then spying on the camp at night had shown them guarding the female mages especially. We had slaughtered another twenty women in camp without a Hellhound bodyguard, all of them ill-prepared to meet the Harrowed in close quarters. Deshi's ghostly hands cut into each the same whether he confronted nobility or a slave from the slums.

The more we alternated with Guild mages in attacking the camp, the greater number of traps the Ma'ab set up for us. The first two were poor attempts to ambush us, ineffectual as long as we stayed close to Deshi, who always sensed the living bodies.

After that, they set trigger spells and mundane tripwires. I sent Nightmare into two of them without warning. Three others would have spewed filth and disease but Mourn detected the foul scents and moved us away while Deshi, unaffected in his phasing state, threw flaming wood on top of them.

Once, the Harrowed chased a duo of Ma'ab into their own surprise. The men inhaled, choked, and struggled only until Deshi rammed his fist into their backs, pausing long enough for his ghostly hand to seize their hearts. Each Ma'ab collapsed, comatose.

The shrill, otherworldly call which escaped through Deshi's open jaw never ceased as he stole the will of the withering army to fight. Alongside him, Mourn's blades sang a resonant tune as he sliced through the air and dismembered their bodies. Meanwhile, Jael and I saw their unmounted horses stampeded, all their supplies, shelter, and weapons destroyed.

Eventually, the remnants of the Black Army fled their camp outside the wall for the protection behind it. A blur of morbid aqua-fire screamed in victorious frustration right behind them.

"Stay outside the wall, Harrowed!" Mourn bellowed. "It's almost dawn!"

Deshi dogged their heels right up to that point, catching a few stragglers without leaving the camp's perimeter. Meanwhile, the Dragonblood joined Jael in destroying everything of use outside of Manalar.

Ma'ab soldiers watched the carnage from atop the wall, doing nothing as perhaps they lacked orders. Hellhounds remained out of sight, presumably somewhere up the mount and hidden in the tight streets. The lack of a single jangle of linked metal was truly concerning, though we continued to routed the entire camp while another shadow flew in a circle above us.

Pilla, free of harassment from any skin kite, was also high enough to be out of range of spell or arrow. I imagined Tamuril peering through the eyes of her falcon even from this distance, witnessing the camp collapsing far below, the ring of fire obvious in the fading dark.

With a distinctive, drawn-out cry, the falcon swooped around and darted away. That was our signal to vanish from view and leave the survivors on the wall, wondering where and when their inhuman foes would appear next.

The Ma'ab wouldn't see us again until we stood next to the Godblood of Manalar.

CHAPTER 32

GAVIN ENTERED THE OLD ARCHIVE, DOOR HINGES AND FLOORBOARDS CREAKING. He brandished nothing with his hands. The main floor contained neither life aura nor anchored Vis, so he went up the stairs. He didn't see a start to this confrontation in his mind, only that it must occur, nor did he expect to spy upon the mercenary to learn what he sought. That did not matter.

Vesram lingered behind him, cautious and unseen. The landing and the three rooms on the second floor grew so quiet, Mathias could only be hiding. Perhaps preparing an ambush.

"Skin hunter," Gavin said, focused on the subtle hum of life in the third room at the end of the hall. "It's me."

A pause.

Quiet bootsteps approaching the door then a man peeked out.

"Gavin!" Mathias said with relief and bafflement, shifting enough to display a dagger at his waist. "You made it. Ha. I was wondering if I'd see you here." He listened. "Where is Divigna?"

"Not here."

"No Hellhounds with you?"

"No."

The man licked his lips. "You got away?"

"I did. What are you searching for?"

442

The man worked through his skepticism before he could answer. "Ohhh, you know." He shrugged. "Anything of value to pay my way. Before it all gets burned."

"You can determine that?"

"Not as easy as I'd hoped, I admit." Mathias grinned. "You want to help me with that, monk?"

"Bold presumption, given you are the reason for many of our obstacles and my capture."

"I haven't had a choice, Deathwalker. Not since the shed." He smirked, a self-deprecating shrug. "I'd be glad to trade. What do you want to know?"

Gavin folded his arms. "The Black Heart."

"Uhhh." Mathias shook his head. "Doesn't chime a bell."

"Hmph. The Ice Lord, then."

The man started, blinking. The silence stretched as several uncomfortable sensations passed over his face.

Finally, he hissed, "*Fuck*."

"I know his are the eyes you tried to warn about. Any others?"

Mathias's face relaxed. "Ah. That I might have something for you. Help me pick out three rare books or scrolls, tell me their subject. I can decline if it's not enticing enough."

"For each one you decline, you owe me another name you've heard discussed among the Ma'ab and its context."

"Oof. Learning to negotiate, huh?" The former nobleman straightened, lips spreading into another wide grin. "You're a far cry from the apprentice I met under Sarilis's boot."

Gavin placed his hand on the railing and took a step forward. "Assuming the deal is practical. How and when do you mean to leave the city?"

"Before Isboern tries for the wall." Mathias snorted. "Then, out the way we came in, but I'd climb down the south side like the first retreat. Follow the river."

"You don't have much time to cover the distance."

"Oh?"

443

"The Ma'ab camp is being destroyed as we speak. The confrontation at the wall is likely at dawn."

Mathias appeared as though he were counting the hours of darkness.

"Less than two hours," Gavin supplied.

"Shit."

Mathias glanced behind him at the books, coming to realize what Gavin already knew: that it would take over an hour to reach the cisterns if the mercenary left this moment.

His pulse flashed in his throat, followed by an emphatic, "*Shit!*"

"You may leave the library," said the Herald. "I will not stop you if you take none of its contents."

The skin hunter narrowed his eyes in suspicion. "Don't you want to know some names?"

"They will come to me eventually. The same as my allies. That matters not unless you remain here. We may also stay here and look through scrolls and you may decline what you wish."

"Heh, once a scholar ..." Mathias made a face. "No 'payback' for your capture? Exposing your weakness to your enemies?"

Gavin watched him for a few moments, long enough that the mercenary glanced out the window as if searching for the sunrise.

"As it happens, so it is," he murmured. "I imagine others seeking reprisal long before I might get around to it."

Mathias's face scrunched in doubt, but he decided to laugh it off. "Fine, then. You haven't changed much after getting stabbed in the heart."

He left the room and started for the stairs. Gavin stepped to the side.

"Tell Sirana I said hel — *umf!*" The skin hunter looked to have bumped into a wall before he reached the first step. "What in fu — ?"

Vesram's camouflage vanished, and suddenly Mathias stared up at the Sathoet looming over him, white mane puffed up and his sharp teeth on menacing display.

"Shitting fuck!" he shouted, throwing himself back and reaching for a weapon. "Gavin, move!"

"No need. That is my ally."

Vesram's light grey eyes crinkled at the sides as his snarl leaned toward a smile.

"Ally!" Mathias kept his hand tight on his sword's grip. "What is this?"

"This is a half-Elf. Of Sirana's people."

The mercenary looked him up and down. "What's the other half?"

"You can't extrapolate from what Sirana told you?"

Mathias looked for a way around the Sathoet but stayed where he was. "Um. Abyss? He's a demon?"

"A demon's son, yes."

"Must've been quite a show. Given how nasty they can be to get some cock."

Vesram growled and took a step forward.

Mathias backed up. "Wait, he can understand me?"

"He can," Gavin answered, nonplussed. "He speaks when he chooses to."

"Fuck. Uh, look, demon son," Mathias lifted his hands in the air, his sword in its sheath. "Are you looking for Sirana?"

"No," Vesram said, clearly displeased.

"What are you doing with Gavin, then?"

The half-blood spit with the abruptness of a horse's kick. "Sssearching you for booksss."

"Good idea," Gavin said. "Let him, Mathias. Then you may go."

"Damn it, no, get back —"

"You could run," the Deathwalker suggested. "He's quite a tracker."

Mathias pitched a disgusted, bitter look as Vesram pawed him, sniffing various places on his body from two fingers away, and generally making the interrogator squirm. Without a hint or prompt, the Sathoet removed two small journals which Mathias had slipped beneath his tunic.

"Is that all?" Gavin asked, accepting them from the hybrid.

"Yes! Bastard."

The Deathwalker glanced at the Sathoet, who bowed his head in a nod of agreement. "Very well. The sun will rise soon. Good luck."

On cue, Vesram shifted to make the stairs accessible. Mathias didn't hesitate, launching forward to scuttle down the stairs as fast as he could manage. He may have slowed down to glance outside the library before sprinting into the open, but the pause wasn't enough to have entered the main level room and steal something there. Vesram crouched on the stairs regardless, watching him leave.

"Gone," he said.

"Good." The Herald turned over the journals in his hands, wondering if he could find where they went on the shelf.

Or better yet …

Answering a familiar feeling, Gavin turned around. The pale, hollow-eyed specter from his previous visit stood in the doorway of the room Mathias had been searching. Vesram was silent but his mane hadn't smoothed down yet; he wasn't focused on the ghost, likely couldn't see her, but he sensed her.

"There you are," said the Herald, holding up the purloined texts. "Show me where these should rest."

She bowed her head and motioned for him to follow her.

As Gavin entered the room lit by a single candle, he thought he heard the rattle of chains outside. Wary of the source, he pressed himself to the wall and looked outside.

Night. No boots, no life auras, no undead.

But there was an … unusual shape.

It appeared to be blowing a kiss up at the library window before sauntering off into the shadows.

Gavin grunted. *As it happens, so it is.*

He turned to the spirit of the library, unsure what dawn would bring but willing to wait.

I have something to read until then.

DESHI WAS SHAKING WHEN HE RESUMED HIS HUMAN FORM IN HIDING, GASPING as if he couldn't draw enough air. He ignored it as he crept up one side of the depression in which we hid, either keeping watch for enemy approach or staring at the broken wall of Manalar in the distance.

"What do you need, Harrowed?" Mourn murmured quietly as we huddled, Jael and I dismounting, all of us temporarily masked and muted by his magic.

"Hm?" The Yungian glanced over his shoulder. "Nothing. I will be fine, *Wen-yung*. When do we join the Godblood?"

"Soon. If you shall be fine, what is your new body telling you? I am curious."

Deshi blinked, glancing down at his bare hands and feet clinging to the grass and earth. He huffed harder than the rest of us.

"You need to catch breath," Jael said. "It escapes you."

I smiled at the mental image. "She is right. We've rested long enough yet you are shaking."

He turned, careful to look away. "That will settle, Janshi."

"Are you certain?" Mourn asked.

Only the breeze filled the silence.

"What is your new body telling you?"

I noted Mourn's tone, as if he knew or had been in a similar place before.

"Hollow …" Deshi murmured. "But filling."

"Filling? With what?"

"Dirt." He paused as if knowing this made little sense. He tried again. "Like a hole. Filling with dirt."

"Like an earth grave?"

Deshi flinched. Given how his breath held an underlying hint of panic, that was easy to imagine.

"Suffocating?" I guessed.

The youth hesitated, his eyes on the grass. "Maybe."

Maybe?

"Your breath is shrinking," Mourn interpreted. "The breath Janshi gave you."

Deshi shuddered, stronger and more obvious than shaking from fatigue. "I … cannot …"

"Cannot what?"

"T-take another."

Mourn glance at my expression before asking, "Why not? Do you need this to continue the battle?"

The young man's fingers sank into the earth. Finally, a whisper.

"*Yes ...* "

Uh-oh.

"I am ... sorry," he stammered. "I-I don't ... understand. What has happened ... to me."

Mourn's tail moved in a long curve. "You will, Harrowed. For now, listen to your new form. Believe it." Then he asked me, "Can you give him another breath?"

"I can ... try," I answered, guilt and discomfort rising in my gut.

Deshi shifted around, staying low as he rejoined us. I wasn't sure where the obvious reluctance was coming from — *pride, stubbornness, revulsion?* — until I met his eyes.

The sun-yellow ring around his ice blue pupils brightened as he stared. An intense flash answered my thoughtless exhale, reflecting something far more basic.

Hunger.

The Harrowed seized me, his pale, cold hands darting out to clasp my face and draw us together, mouth-to-mouth. He inhaled, pulling the air greedily from my chest. The ache inside exploded, spreading at once to the rest of my body and, suddenly, *I* was the one suffocating! I panicked, trying to pull away, to get loose! I couldn't make a sound, my eyes open but unfocused.

~*Stop! Let me go!*~

"*Hai!*"

Jael darted in to separate us, and she wasn't the only one. Mourn seized Deshi's hands, peeled them off my face, and hooked his arms under the Yungian's pits to pull him away. My Sister grabbed hold of me before I could collapse. Grateful she was there, it took me three tries to fill my lungs. In the meantime, she used her body to shield me from Deshi, who wailed once in frustration as the Dragonblood locked him into a hold he couldn't break.

"Not good!" Jael barked. "No!"

"I-I am sorry," Deshi said miserably, as he shook. "P-please forgive ..."

The pain in my chest faded with each gasp, until I could grapple for words. "I ... see ... I see it, Deshi. I didn't mean to ..."

To do this do you.

I didn't know.

What had I done? Did he *need* me this much to survive? Were we shackled together? The Harrowed had no natural pathway to death, Nyx had said, but what of when *I* died? This was worse than caving to the pressure to take Vesram's true name!

"We cannot do it this way," Mourn murmured, his voice deceptively calm and pondering.

"*Must* be her?" Jael asked, hands out as if ready to block Deshi. "Could be me? I offer."

"We must find out," the half-blood agreed. "Deshi?"

The youth's head was bowed, eyes down and closed, hanging limp and shaking in the Dragonchild's grip.

"Can you hear me?"

"Mm."

"Will you try to breathe with *Janhuren* instead? Let her touch you if needed?"

"I-I will try, *Wen-yung* ..."

The Harrowed sounded scared, but he didn't resist as Jael approached cautiously. She bent down, put their faces closer together.

And blew in his face.

Deshi gasped, drawing in deep to fill his chest. The tension eased on his face, but he kept his eyes closed.

"Good sign," Mourn said, speaking to both. "Try again."

Jael took in successively deeper draws of air, as if preparing to dive beneath water for as long as she could handle. She kept the hand-width gap between their faces but refrained from touching him. Pursing her lips, she exhaled, a long, steady stream of air pouring over the Harrowed.

With soft moan, Deshi lifted his head and breathed her in; his efforts lost their desperation, the rushing air growing quieter. His tremble gradually vanished.

"Good." Mourn sounded as relieved as I was. "Is the sensation of suffocation lessening?"

"Yes, *Wen-yung*." Deshi responded with a deep draw as Jael gave him another breath.

"Are you sated or need more?"

Tri-colored eyes avoided me as he glanced around, aware of our exposure. His lips tried a few times to form words.

"Want," he said with care. "Not 'need.' "

"Dawn is *here*," Mourn said bluntly. "Are you ready to fight all day or not? Do not lie, Harrowed."

The revenant took too long to consider.

Jael huffed, shaking her head, tossing me an encouraging smirk as she leaned down and blew even closer to his mouth. Deshi couldn't resist; he strained against the Dragonblood's hold for a telling instant.

Mourn rumbled low in his throat.

"No, *Wen-yung*," the youth admitted. "I am ... not ready."

"Knew it," Jael said.

And gave him more of her breath.

Deshi drank it like someone parched and guzzling water. The ball of horror I'd been wrangling broke to watch him, my eyes tearing up from relief.

He doesn't need me.

The Yungian needed *someone*, but here was proof Deshi could survive without me, even with his limits unexplored. Did he require Elves, or specifically Davrin Elves? Was it the breath of a mage? Or one Dragon-touched? Would a mundane Human do?

He could simply needs the living.

We had neither time nor ability to test it now.

Jael fed the restrained youth for a quarter of an hour, until she withdrew on her own, placing a palm on her brow and a hand on my shoulder. "*Oof.* Dizzy."

"That is enough, then," Mourn said, gradually releasing Deshi, allowing him to step away on bare feet. "How do you feel, Harrowed?"

"Better, *Wen-yung*. Much ... much better."

And he was obviously as relieved as we were.

Deshi bowed formally to Jael. "*Janhuren*. Thank you." Then to me. "Janshi. Please believe ... I am sorry."

"I understand," I said. "You are ... newborn."

He looked so sad. "Did I ... harm Ionne?"

"I don't think so." I touched my gut in reassurance. "Can you see for yourself? The Herald can. He described a white aura with purple thread."

With my gentle reminder, Deshi let go of his shame long enough to concentrate. After a pause, a tiny smile flickering at the corners of his mouth. "Ah. I can see, yes, Janshi. Still strong."

"Then no harm done." *Anything else to say?* "Um. I forgive you, Harrowed. Just don't do it again."

"Oh ... !" He bowed, his knees wobbling as if he would fall to his knees. "*Thank you*, Janshi. That will *not* happen again."

"Aye, will not when I here," Jael agreed, sounding like Talov as she grinned, and I laughed, needing the tension breaker.

Mourn was reserved in his smile, choosing not to speak further about it. Each of us were aware of how fortunate we were to get this far before dawn.

"I am ready to fight all day, *Wen-yung*," Deshi stated with believable confidence. He straightened up, looking us in the eyes.

"Good to hear, Harrowed. We need you."

The Dragonchild looked East and then West, ears moving forward to catch the earliest sounds of horses and armor on the breeze.

"The Godblood is here," he said. "Let us join him."

CHAPTER 33

THE WALLS OF MANALAR, PAXIA

THE URGE TO LIFT MY HOOD TO SHADE MY EYES STRUCK HARD AS THE PALE orange and yellow stone of Manalar brightened, sloughing off the bluish hue of night.

~*We're here,*~ I projected as soon as I could see Isboern. ~*The crest, your front left.*~

The Godblood walked near the front on foot and among his warriors on horseback. A few men coughed in the face of the smoking camp, their mounts whickering nervously.

~*I see you,*~ he responded. ~*You are safe to approach.*~

I didn't think any of us could be mistaken for a Ma'ab ambush but better not to startle anyone. Tensions were tight as a drawn bow ready to snap. No Ma'ab jeered or shouted insults from the wall, though officers blared orders into a breeze losing its pre-dawn chill.

Wolf, Tak, and the other members of Reprisal, and the mages of *Hata Ri* came out of hiding. We joined Isboern and the Templari, while their cavalry moved to either flank to keep the nervous horses calm as Mourn got closer. Apparently while he could "trick" the rest of us into forgetting he was there when he wished, the horses could not ignore their own noses.

"Good work," said the Captain, looking mostly at the Guildsman, at Jael and Deshi. "Having the camp dealt with makes the next decision easier."

All of them responded well to the acknowledgement.

"Who will we be 'negotiating' with next, I wonder?" said Robi.

"Who is *left*?" Tak chuckled.

"Not to prick this too finely," Mourn said, "but Kreshel Divigna is left, and he may have the Deathwalker. If they hold strengths in reserve behind the wall, even at the expense of their camp's destruction, we must be ready."

Deshi might have meant a growl or grunt to agree, but it came out like a dreadful moan, making Imran and Robi shiver.

"I will offer surrender," Isboern said, "though I understand they may refuse it."

"As you will, Captain. We are with you."

That we are.

Most of us, anyway.

"The Naulor?" I asked, looking around.

"At the rear," Isboern said, "with Peng-lok and Nianzu and our crafters. Guarding our one prisoner of war."

I wondered what Amelda thought of that, to see Elves as pale as she was, each of them posing a danger far less obvious than the one she expected of me.

I wish we could kill her.

Shaking off the thought as quickly as it came, I lifted my eyes to one of the clearest skies I'd seen on the Surface. *There*. "Pilla watches."

"Good." Isboern nodded. "The skin kite numbers seem to have shrunk."

"Ashes," Jael said with a plain grin.

Plenty of burned spots and black marks passed beneath our tramping boots. Although the Manalari host skirted the edge of the camp on their way to the wall, we had to step over Ma'ab bodies who had failed to escape last night's spirit of vengeance. Some of the horses kicked them regardless.

Fortunately, the Manalari knew how far out to stand out of reach of all but the luckiest arrow. Roughly four hundred natives and another hundred Augranites drew to a halt outside the broken wall, orders passed from the front as they formed loose lines across the road and into the fields on either side. Insects and birds had long gone quiet, and the strong taste of moisture as I breathed suggested a stifling heat to come by afternoon.

I assumed Isboern couldn't issue a command to surrender from here, but he and his closest officers soon proved me wrong. Together, they had a spell to amplify his voice so much we were warned to cover our ears. He also intentionally flashed the golden shield in the morning light, drawing the faraway eyes with a rhythm.

"Listen, Ma'ab occupying Manalar! We give you one chance to leave with your lives, and it must be today. If one among you can speak of surrender, send your messenger outside the wall. I will hear the message and send them back alive."

At last, my head stopped ringing with the sound. Jael and I lowered our hands with care, sharing the same expression: *Ouch.*

How effective would *that* have been with a host of House Guardsvrin standing outside an opposing Matron's House? Not greatly, but all in Sivaraus would know they were there, extrapolating that their own plantation was too lightly guarded.

Ultimately, the Ma'ab answered the Godblood.

The messenger who stepped outside the wall was a Hellhound. My thoughts froze watching him unwind the spiked chain from his arm and hand it to another behind partial cover. By the time the unarmed giant turned toward us and left the protection of the city's barrier, I recognized his build, his gait, and his mannerisms.

Divigna.

"Well played," Isboern murmured, adjusting his shield on his arm.

"Indeed," Mourn agreed.

"Side-fucking stalactite," Jael cursed in Davrin.

"We shouldn't stay bunched up," Wolf said from nearby. "In case he … I dunno, explodes?"

I doubted this Hellhound could do that on demand or he would have already. We couldn't explain, however, so Mourn and Isboern agreed and rearranged the greeting party into a large semicircle, as if we stood waiting to hem the lead Hellhound in, while the force behind us formed up in protective trios with space between them instead of lines.

Divigna's expression didn't change in the face of this movement; he stared ahead with an empty expression, not mildly curious or tense. He knew we couldn't take him down easily or simply wanted us to try.

"What do I do, *Wen-yung*?" Deshi whispered. The trembling had returned, though not from suffocation.

"Stand with us," Mourn replied, indicating the Captain. "Honor the Godblood's word. Wait until it is time to fight."

Templars within our hearing straightened up, a few dipping his chin. These may be mere standing orders for them, but harder for Deshi. The Harrowed gathered the nerve and breath to try, but stilled unexpectedly once concentrating on the enemy approach.

"What *is* he?" Deshi asked, uncertain.

So, he can see it.

"He is not —"

"*Later*," Mourn whispered, distracting the nearest two Templars and causing Isboern's jaw to flex.

The Eternal Hellhound had covered half the distance, not once raising his hands or making a gesture. He wore no belt, no weapons we could see. Like Mourn, he was shirtless but the density of markings on his body made this easy to forget. His only garments were tough leather trousers and boots.

I nudged Jael, signing, ★Can you see his aura?★

She squinted. ★Tattoos are magic. He is not.★

Fair response. But she knew this fact already.

★Anything else?★

A brief jerk of her chin; a negative while keeping an eye on the enemy approach.

The Harrowed could see something strange about Divigna's living aura, as could Mourn and Gavin, but *not* my To'vah-mage Sister.

Good to know.

Divigna kept walking.

"What if he does not stop?" Imran murmured. "Or will not leave?"

"Then I push him," his Captain replied, his shield ready. "And we fight."

A moment later, the armored psion stepped forward ahead of the horses, lifting his empty, gloved hand. "Messenger. I am Captain Isboern. Stop if you can hear me."

The Hellhound was about forty paces away; he stopped in the wide, paved road. The Godblood did not allow silence to fill the space.

"Do your men and women behind the wall surrender?"

Divigna's mouth moved; his low voice was hard to hear, and I didn't think he spoke in Trade.

" 'They are not mine,' " Mourn translated, stepping closer to the Godblood, who turned his ear toward him.

"Do the Ma'ab people behind the wall surrender?" the Captain asked again.

Hard lips moved around another answer: " 'They cannot.' "

"I see. Do you hold prisoner the Deathwalker of the Grey Maiden?"

The Hellhound gave a slow blink before countering. " 'Do you hold Amelda Troshin?' "

Isboern breathed through his nose. "We do. She is alive and whole."

" 'Proof?' "

"Do you have proof of wholeness for our prisoner?"

Finally, Divigna showed some emotion; he smirked. " 'Maybe. Shall we trade?' "

"Bad idea," Mourn added.

~*I know.*~

The Godblood asked aloud without missing a beat, "And then what? We fight?"

" 'Of course. The Black Army outnumbers you. We have the high ground and all the food.' "

"By my count, our mages outnumber yours."

" 'Mage flesh shreds in chains just as easily. Or I crush their hands and pull out their tongues before they can stop me.' "

"So be it," Isboern replied without flinching. "Will you go behind the wall to wait for me, Hellhound, or do you have another intention out here? Another question?"

Divigna paused to consider. His bottomless black eyes rested on the shield shining on the Captain's arm then up again. " 'The spirit canister. Do you have it?' "

"Canister?"

"The thurible," Mourn answered, pausing in translation. "And yes, Captain, we do."

"We do!" Isboern said.

" 'And the dagger blessed by Walker with Death?' "

"Yes. We do."

" 'Fight your way in, Captain. Bring the two relics *and* bring Amelda. Find me at the Temple or the archives. I will wait with my Hellhounds.' "

Isboern narrowed his eyes. "You will hold the chain-wielders back until the rest of your army is defeated?"

Divigna nodded once.

"Why would you do that?"

A cold stare. " 'Message is delivered, Captain.' "

The oldest pack leader turned around, exposing his back in defiance. Every Guildsman tensed up, searching for a weak spot in his tattoos and permission to act. They received none. Isboern reinforced it, signaling to his Templars to stand steady.

Once the Hellhound was out of earshot, Wolf hissed, "Do *not* like that offer."

"Nor do I," growled Sir Erik.

"Yet the morning burns on," said the Godblood. "And, as planned, we will attack the wall next, regardless of what happens afterward."

I was frowning, chewing on his wording. *Something about it —*

"Who has the thurible?" Isboern asked.

Thrown out of my budding thought, I raised my hand to sign it but cleared my throat instead. "I do."

"Krithannia has Deshi's blessed dagger," Mourn added. "And is watching Amelda, too. Given the circumstances, she and I will be in contact as we were in the first battle. If Divigna overhears us, it will only suggest we are following his instructions."

Isboern sounded relieved. "Good. We will need that link. Sirana, will you be my other link if battle separates us?"

He surprised me by asking.

"I'd be foolish to refuse," I replied. "He can't overhear *that* link."

"Thank you. Then, as invited, we shall fight our way in."

Deshi exhaled then, a striking rasp which sent shivers up several men's spines. The Harrowed's body lost definition as a hint of blue-green flame licked around his shoulders. "I am ready, Godblood. Set me loose. I will open the way for your return to the Temple."

Every man around us fell silent, not a single doubt in their eyes. With a solemn bow of his head, Captain Isboern landed intense blue eyes upon Deshi, Mourn, Jael, and me before turning toward the rising Sun.

"So be it," the psion said, repositioning his own relic so its reflection wouldn't blind his men. "Allow my Templari to clear the breach in the wall for you first, Harrowed. Once we've begun, do not stop. We shall be behind you every step up the mount."

INTENTLY FOCUSED ON THE TEXT IN FRONT OF HIM, NOT EVEN GAVIN COULD ignore the burst of golden light which filled the city and flooded every window.

Curiously, while he *was* caught off guard and temporarily blinded, his eyes did not react as quickly as they used to. The white blur impeded him like a veil lifted by Human hands rather than the instantaneous club to his eyes when he'd been alive.

Seems to be fading faster, too.

"Vesram?" he asked, belatedly realizing he'd heard a yelp of pain and standing up from the reading desk.

The Sathoet moaned, "Wasss looking *straight* at it!"

"Unfortunate. Was it a light spell?"

"Enormoussss ..."

"Could you tell the direction?"

An annoyed grunt as Vesram kept rubbing his eyes. "Low gate."

"Ah. The attack has begun."

Gavin rolled up scrolls and closed his selection of books, replacing each where he had gotten them. Without searching for her, he could sense the library spirit watching him, approving of the care he took with her materials.

The Deathwalker hadn't found anything particularly relevant to immediate concerns, neither for him nor his allies, but what texts he *could* read had begun to get interesting.

Perhaps later.

If this building remained standing after the conflict.

"Do we leave?" Vesram asked, reluctant but recognizing the inevitable.

"I'd rather not draw factions in conflict to this archive by staying here. Although this place is not on the main route to the Temple, we're not far enough off of it for my liking."

"Join Sssun worshippers?"

Gavin hesitated, thinking it through. "If mages remain to puppet the casualties to continue fighting, I could help with that. But ... any Hellhound knows how to disrupt my concentration amid the carnage."

His frown deepened as another unpleasant thought struck him. *Where are my tools and grimoire now?*

Magic wasn't impossible without them but certainly less efficient and precise. He would seek them if only he could be certain the Artist would arrive when needed.

Hmm. How far has Mathias gotten, I wonder?

Vesram hissed, hunching lower to the floor as he peeked out the window. Gavin turned his neck to look. "Hm?"

"Hellhoundsss, watching."

"They know we are here," the Deathwalker sighed. "Well, Mathias *did* tell them. How many?"

"Five."

A pack of them, but not *all* of them.

"Could we escape through the undercroft?" he suggested.

"Could meet a second pack down below."

True. Kreshel bore decades of experience; if he wanted the library scouted, he wouldn't have clustered five pairs of eyes all watching one entrance.

"They won't destroy me," Gavin said, fully facing him. "If we are trapped, I can draw their attention while you slip away unseen."

The Sathoet rumbled, his ears flattening like an angry dog.

"Ada said we must protect your newfound freedom," Gavin added. "There isn't much to debate."

"Don't like it ..."

"We exist with much we don't like."

The creature glanced sidelong, cocking a brow ridge. Neither one of them had much that one might call eyebrows, but the meaning was the same.

"If you find my allies —" Gavin continued, regrettably seeking to damage the sturdy grey robes recently given to him, tugging on the sleeve.

"Will not look for them," Vesram interrupted, shaking his head. "Too dangerousss in a fight."

"Fair. The Temple?"

"Abyssal alssso unprotected."

"Hm. How about tracking Mathias for me?"

Pupilless, grey eyes narrowed. "Why? You let him go."

"Indeed, I did. But there may be another from the shadow realm following him."

"Sssshadow realm?"

"Yes. A Chenkyte."

Vesram's mane started to stand up as recognition showed on his face.

"With other options set aside," Gavin reasoned, "I should like you to deliver the message that the Hellhounds have me surrounded and I call in my favor this morning."

The Sathoet scowled but turned it over. "Appearance?"

"Bald with a halo of needles through the scalp. A veil of small chains weighed with tiny hooks covered the face beneath the eyes, which are the color of amber. Bluish skin with many scars. Their stated title is the

Artist of the Exquisite Host."

"*Hrmm*. Understood. You ssstay here while I look?"

"Can you get past the Hellhounds if they are watching for you?"

A muzzle of fangs showed. "Have before."

"Without a distraction?"

"Will wait for one."

Gavin supposed the outcome might be the same if the packs grew impatient and barged in over his outright surrendering. The same if they started chasing the half-blood down the street should they spot him.

Meanwhile, given this pause, a distraction may be well on its way.

"So be it. We shall give it a try."

~*Cover your eyes. Cover your horses' eyes.*~

The message went out as if quietly spoken in one's ear. With my help, enough Manalari and Guildsmen on the field heard it for word to spread. The riders had little time to blindfold their mounts, all others to protect their faces before Captain Isboern blinded every Ma'ab watching from the wall.

The power of his morning Sun erupted in a flash, an instant when the entire world turned white. A few of the enemy might have been prepared but not enough, based on the wave of voices which rolled down the slope toward us.

"*NOMILU SANCJI!*" the Godblood yelled, amplifying his voice above the alarm. "*CHAARRGE!*"

"To the Temple!"

"*Ao Templi dul Sohl!*"

The roar of Manalari and Augranite answered together. Jael whoop behind me, and I grinned.

Deshi lunged for the broken wall with a screech of resurging rage, all Human expression vanishing in an aqua blaze. Mourn followed next, and the Templari charged together behind him while Isboern joined the cavalry, a Manalari rider offering his Captain a hand to climb up behind him.

Were it not for me and the small herd of war horses losing their tolerance for the Dragon's son, the Godblood would have been leading his mage warriors right behind the Harrowed. Instead, Isboern had deemed the best way to get past the front assault and find Gavin was to ride behind them, using all of his psion's focus on communication and shielding.

At least until the Ma'ab gave way.

"Go, go!" Jael murmured as I squeezed Gavin's talisman, moving Nightmare into a deceptively quiet gallop compared to the steeds around her. She hadn't drawn her swords yet but watched every stride for the moment the others gave her enough room.

Poorly aimed arrows dotted the ground and glanced off our collective shields, be they mundane, magic, or psionic. The lack of mages among the Northerners to counter us during this final stand was obvious, tilting the penetration in our favor despite their numbers.

Once Deshi and Mourn arrived to disable and cut down those who volunteered to meet them, the Ma'ab might have thought to clog the way with bodies, yet To'vah Word and Templari spell shoved those limp forms away before they'd fallen, clearing the path for the rest of us.

They could not surrender, Divigna had said, and every fighter that we killed would return to the Ascended, according to Gavin.

~Forward, courage to all! The way is open! Do not stop!~

They have thunderstones. Hurl them back!

The din of bellowing horses and exploding projectiles swamped me until my ears were numb. I could not discern the threads of noise, nor could I follow the battle with my eyes amid the dust and desperate actions. Isboern's and Mourn's voices grounded me, however, and my body endured the impact of sound and the strengthening heat of the day.

Meanwhile, the Hellhounds waited for us farther up the mount, a conflict meant to test what weaknesses we had left and drain our magical strength.

Find me at the Temple or the archives ...

The archives? Was that the library? And why one *or* the other?

Doesn't he know where Gavin is?

I held my thoughts until the horses slowed, their riders turning and regrouping in the streets to cut down or spell bash the sheer number of staggered Ma'ab visited by Deshi, missed by Mourn or the Templars, and struggling to breathe. Thick-boned horses without their riders bolted through us, champing and kicking at some of the Southern mounts while avoiding Nightmare.

Meanwhile, the Guildsmen had been climbing the walls and structures, taking out soldiers and blunt weapons meant to be dropped on us. No enemy had gotten close enough to require me to do anything apart from guiding my mount and giving Jael space to cast. The crumbling streets were lined with the broken forms of the invaders, and some were running.

~*They fall behind a new barrier,*~ Isboern said, freeing the thought shared by so many minds at the fore.

Mourn translated an order he'd overheard. *The gate to midtown. Be wary of area bursts. They do not care if they die with you. Many want to go down in battle.*

With a verbal call from Mourn, the Harrowed's flames turned up the widest main road, an eerie light leading the way.

Onward, then.

This wasn't the clear sweep of a deliberate encroachment but a scattershot rampage which would allow some Ma'ab to hide if they decided not to stand their ground. Soon they could be behind us, behind cover, and for that reason, Krithannia and Tamuril had begun moving their way through the friendly fighters, trying to catch up to us and dragging Amelda every step of the way.

Mourn couldn't wait on them, but Jael and I held back as Isboern organized his cavalry and Templari into a dual force with him in the center. I didn't understand a lot of his orders passing through the mindlink but it didn't matter; his men knew how to respond. Part of their goal involved opening a pathway for the Naulor to reach us, guiding them through secured areas, and switching the horsemen to the front as the Templari moved behind, catching their breath.

"Sirana!" called the dark-haired Naulor, weaving through the debris and bodies. She held the Ma'ab noble on a leash made of tight cord and gave the shorter woman no time to dawdle. Krithannia was also either notably stronger or had some way of discouraging outright rebellion. Amelda's face was pinched with fury and fear, but her feet kept moving, kept in between the Guild Mistress and Druid.

Tamuril's eyes, wide and sharp, took in everything around us, especially above our heads; she kept her bow ready should a distant target present itself. She spoke no words, no greeting, strangely with no blush or horrified awareness of the violence, as if she dared not lose sight of changing signs in a hunt. Pilla probably helped.

~Temple or library?~ I asked the elder sister.

Krithannia met my eyes. *What?*

~Between the two, where do you think Gavin will be?~

Her pink lips twitched in humor. *The library.*

I grinned. ~That's what I thought.~

To the next barrier, then.

The Godblood made it his sole mission to protect our central bubble from threats in every direction while everyone else protected *him*. Ma'ab males charged us with mace, sword, and pole weapons, few getting close enough to swing but keeping every Manalari defender busy and focused on the ground.

Thunderstones and flaming arrows dropped from above until either the Guildsmen took the high-ground attackers out with a stealth attack, the Druid's arrow found their eye, or my Sister's Word set them on fire. Only a few were lucky and persistent enough that, as a last resort, the Templari collectively blasted the floor out from beneath their feet, leaving a hole in the ancient building rather than lose another man on our side.

By the time we reached the gate to midtown, the barrier once set up weeks ago had been shattered, the ground littered by contorted bodies touched by the Grey Maiden's warrior and executed by the Dragon's Son. A few hidden Ma'ab attacked from above, only to meet the same fate as their brothers.

Ahead, I made out a fresh rise of mixed voices. Soldiers exiting the wealthy districts where they'd indulged in Manalar's resources, but also frightened screams, begging and weeping, had joined Deshi's haunting howl. They weren't pleading in Ma'ab.

~*The prisoners,*~ I thought.

The rush of true anger caught me aback, entering through my link with the Godblood and his bonds to many others.

COWARDS!

Their collective fury was something I'd never felt before, overwhelming *pain* in their helplessness to act fast enough, though they would try anyway.

~*We knew the invaders would hide behind the helpless,*~ Willven commanded with iron determination to temper the threatening conflagration. ~*Remember your training! Caution with your targets and change the angles of attack. If the lead Hellhound reveals a lie, it will be when it hurts most.*~

A cool focus darted through the red haze, drawing the powerful response forward over extinguishing it. Without thinking, I kicked Nightmare's side, trying to keep up with them until I tugged enough of my thoughts free to nudge her through the talisman.

"Sirana!"

Just in time for the Godblood and I to make eye contact, I remembered not to leave Krithannia and Tamuril behind.

~*I need to be there,*~ the Captain said, apologetic. ~*Will you be alright peeling off? Find space to wait this out if possible.*~

I got it. We were the only females among the fighters: the Naulor, Amelda, Jael, and me. We would serve mostly as distractions in what happened next.

~*For certain,*~ I answered. ~*Promise me you'll fight to win.*~

~*We will, and we shall win.*~

The force of his will amplified through his men, his eyes were the bluest I'd ever seen.

~*My oath, Sirana.*~

CHAPTER 34

THE TEMPLE CITY OF MANALAR, PAXIA

GAVIN CRACKED OPEN A STUBBORN WINDOW ON THE SMALLER THIRD FLOOR. The angle was less likely to draw the attention of the surveilling pack waiting around the corner alley yet allowed him to listen to the distant cries of conflict.

Not as distant as before.

The Manalari force would enter the wealthy district soon, his library located on the lower end. An oddly compelling wail carried on the wind as if leading the advance, mixed with higher pitches of mundane Manalari not trained for war.

That the loitering Ma'ab pack hadn't been summoned to join the combat surprised and annoyed Gavin. He was even skeptical the Hellhounds were among those fighting, for he heard no chains.

Kreshel waits.

Meanwhile, the Godblood must be alive and well enough to lead such a cohesive assault through the morning, his strength of will lasting beyond the sun-bright flash signaling the start of this fight.

Mourn would be lending a strong arm and vast experience to the battle. Ending his Bargain with Sirana at the redoubt surely meant, when the struggle became most intense, he would guard the psionic Human meant to rebalance the sacred pool over the pregnant Davrin. At the least, the Dragon son would have the choice.

And where is Sirana in all this?

Would she or the Guild Mistress think to look for him here? Should he stay rather than run about and potentially miss them?

Or make things worse.

In the end, one location drew them all. The Temple of the Sun was the one place on the battlefield where he had the opportunity to sway the success and failures of the leaders' tactics.

They always intended to come back.

Where Kreshel knew and must be ready.

We don't have much time.

Not on finding Mathias or the Artist. Not on waiting for that distraction.

Gavin closed the window against the dirt and the noise and headed down the stairs, intending to inform the Sathoet of his change of mind.

If only I'd been precise with the Artist.

"Vesram," he began as he reached the landing.

And paused.

The Sathoet stared out the window from an extremely low angle, his white mane full and somehow reflecting his state of alert. Before Gavin's gaze, the half-blood wrapped the daylight about himself and vanished from view. Gavin shifted his sight and made out the life aura only because he knew where to look.

"Vesram —"

"*Shh. Now.*"

"Now?"

"*Pack turnsss away. I find Mathiasss …*"

Three crawling steps and one open door later, Vesram slipped outside as they had discussed. By his Lady, *what* could have distracted the Hellhounds in that exact moment he'd decided it would not happen?

Uncaring about matching stealth with a century-old former slave, Gavin looked out the window to confirm that the pack had vanished from sight.

Indeed, they have.

467

He turned his head. Two angled streets away, two Dark Elves sat upon an intimately familiar mare with another two Pale Elves as escort.

Oh, dear.

To make matters worse, Vesram underestimated Sirana's apparent sensitivity to a mind she had encountered before, whether she could see him or not. Her head snapped to an empty wall, tracking some unseen motion as a small skid of gravel betrayed the Sathoet's presence.

"Wait!"

Unfathomably, Sirana turned Nightmare as quickly as she could and launched after him down the street. Jael hung on, helpless to stop her as Krithannia and Tamuril — *and Amelda?* — stared after them with mouths gaping open.

Now he heard chains.

Gavin seized the door, opened it only wide enough to step outside, and closed the library door behind him.

SOMETHING ... *something* WITHIN ME SHOUTED TO PURSUE HIM.

I *had* to reach him.

Now!

"Wait!" I called. *"Stop!"*

How in the Pit did he move so fast?

We'd reached the library, avoiding the worst of the fighting and evading potential threats. No Hellhounds had appeared.

But then I'd *sensed* him along every nerve.

Taking advantage of our distraction to leave.

Why was he *here?!*

"Sirana!" Jael shouted, alarmed as we galloped down the paved road. She twisted on our mounts' haunches to glance behind her. "Where are we going?! What about the Naulor?!"

Pain.

~No, no, no ... Damnit!~

I couldn't slow down; *everything* started to hurt if I did. My conscious thoughts seized on the proof that Vesram *hadn't* gone West to wait for us. As the Valsharess's geas roared alive with spine-jolting power, I could no longer skirt the truth or fool myself.

I followed the wisps of intense dread preventing Vesram's mind from going quiet, relying on Jael to watch our surroundings. I could barely see beyond Nightmare's ears to pick up the harried thoughts of a moving target.

"*I don't see anything!*" she cried. "*What are you chasing?*"

Vesram answered that for me.

"*Won't go back!*" he shouted, his voice bouncing off the stone.

Jael's fingers dug into my shoulder when she realized what he was. Once Gavin's mare had helped burn up that initial sprint, the Sathoet paused at the mouth of a curved alleyway. his dark, feral body appeared ahead of us as he abandoned the drain on his magic.

"*Fffuck!*"

"*Misssed your chance, Red Sisssterss!*" he snarled in our native tongue. "*Suck her spinnerets and leave me!*"

He sounded like Kerse on his last cycle. But older.

We couldn't slow down. *I can't.*

I *had* to chase him down that alley.

"*Wait!*" Jael screamed. "*Trap!*"

Of course.

We arrived at the edge of a startling decline, a dry channel rather than a walkway, and the mare was going too fast into a curve that was far too tight. We had no hope of staying upright; not the talisman nor psionic commands could overcome forces in motion as Nightmare's hooves skidded and her body tipped, about to collide with the stone wall.

"*Jump!*" my Sister barked as she threw herself backward off the horse.

I wasn't so lucky. My best option was to cling to her neck and lift my leg out of immediate danger. I had time for nothing else.

Nightmare hit the wall and my thoughts on her dropped, cutting her strings. She had no voice, no air, though meat smacked, and bones cracked before pain exploded in my shoulder. We bounced off together, collapsing in a sliding heap which took several seconds for me to realize I was on top, clinging to her like driftwood in a flood.

Yet all I cared about was the sound of Vesram running away.

~*No! Stop!*~

Sirana!!

I clutched my head. ~*Owww!*~

Mourn tempered his intensity through my pearl. **What happened? Krithannia said you ran off and left them! Where are you?**

I hated this. ~*No, no … Not now —* ~

Are you alright?! Tell me!

~*Stop. Y-yes. I'm alive. Jael is with me. Focus on the Temple. On the Godblood. I-I have to …* ~

Mourn seemed about to say something sharp but our connection fell. Instead Deshi's wailing scored the air not far away as I dragged myself to my feet.

"*Let me help*," Jael panted, taking the arm I *wasn't* clutching to my chest.

My right shoulder had gone numb, but I'd escaped crippling pains in my legs. My spiders had clung to me for their lives, their song one of shrill concern, and Soul Drinker remained in its sheath.

That had to be enough.

"*Come on*," I said, giving Nightmare the command to stand and follow the talisman before leaving her behind.

"Sirana," Jael protested, knowing she was helpless to talk any sense into me.

I knew it made no sense, that it made everything worse.

How could we catch up to him on foot? How could I persuade him to stop, to listen?

What would I even say?

I just had to reach him before—

"*Eeeeeeeaaaaargh!*"

The hideous scream broke over us like a wave the instant we spilled out of the narrow decline. Jael and I spasmed mid-stride, clutching our ears.

"What is that?!" Jael cried.

"Vesram?!" I shouted, catching a whiff of the Sathoet's musk. Once I focused on that direction, I did not understand what I was looking at.

The next moment, my body went cold.

The Ice Lord had the Sathoet gripped by the mane. The demonic half-blood was a head taller than the Infernal Elf and twice as wide at the shoulders, yet Vesram's legs had buckled and he kneeled on the pavement, having no strength to resist.

"Disgusting," Indrath murmured, a faint rumble underneath his voice adding a chilling depth to his tone. "It is about time I dealt with you. In light of the circumstances, I shall make this fast."

No —

"You festering, chainless corruption."

The Lord tossed the former slave away so that Vesram struck a stone wall harder than I had before falling with Nightmare. The Sathoet yelped and crumpled onto his side with a terrified whimper, covering his head as the Infernal lifted his hand threateningly with palm out and claws splayed. A potent, peridot flame appeared and began to swell, and in Vesram's wide, grey eyes flashed the knowledge that he was worse than dead.

"Fucking goddess, *DON'T!!*" I shrieked, pitching myself forward.

"Sirana!" Jael shouted in terrified disbelief as I threw myself onto the Sathoet's sweating, quivering body.

Above me, the Ice Lord emitted an exclamation — of surprise, of horror, I wasn't sure — but he hissed and turned his body, lowering his arm and extinguishing the green flame.

"*Fool!*" the Lord barked. "Do you *realize* what you almost made me *do?!*"

"*Don't touch him!*" I snapped, shaking as my spiders came out onto my shoulders, ready to jump on the devil.

"*Move*, Sirana," the Infernal rumbled, ivory eyes cutting like glass. "This beast has no life in this world while he has no mistress."

"He does! He had been living without one for weeks!"

"He does *not*. And he *cannot*." The Ice Lord squinted. "Unless you volunteer? I'm sure he would give you his name rather than suffer what I intend for him."

Tears stung as anger swelled my chest, and my shoulder suddenly flared with overwhelming pain from my fall. My spider guardians chimed, baffled by my insistence that they do not move as I faced sources of pain they couldn't poison.

All I could manage aloud was, "F-fuck off!"

"If that is your answer, then ..." The devil's eyes turned crimson. "*Move away from the demon.*"

I nearly obeyed as one compelling command clashed with another.

"No!" I shouted, fighting in place, panic unspooling in my chest as the Queen's magic enforced Her Will without the ability to explain.

Indrath's wings snapped the air; his patience was gone. "Make no mistake, Sirana, if you do not take his name, I will rip it out myself and imprison him rather than allow his taint to spread. If you'll have neither, better to simply put him down now."

What could I say to convince an Infernal Elf to let the demonic one go?

"I-if you do that," I stammered, "you kill Avel's child as well!"

The Ice Lord stiffened, his lip curling. "What do you mean?"

~*I ... I can't ...* ~

My throat closed and I couldn't blink, couldn't stop shaking. My true thoughts lay behind an iron veil, yet, with gritted teeth, I covered the tight bump in my abdomen.

"Ah. I see."

The Ice Lord offered more distance, his footstep soundless and hidden beneath his leather sarong. Jael filled the space at once, swords out, her glare turning to a smirk as Indrath crossed arms over a bronze-red chest, dark red wings expanding.

"Calm down, my granddaughters. I'll not intensify your distress over this matter."

I sucked in a badly needed breath as Vesram's arms slipped around my waist, his wrists crossed, and hands fisted where I could see them. His surrender was clear, but only nausea arose in place of my panic as the Sathoet shuddered, pressing his brow to the square of my back rather than meet the gaze of the Ice Lord.

"Your Queen wants this fouled son to return to the Deepearth," he said, gaze narrowed in thought. "Intriguing. Rather surprising, too, given what she did to her own Abyssal daughter."

Daughter?

That was a hook I dared not swallow.

"But then," Indrath continued, reflecting, "only she and her father ever approached any pinnacle with their gift of Sight. Is *this* why you're here? And with such a *specific* bond in your belly. *Heh*. Curious."

Jael stepped up and scoffed, batting his teases away like annoying flies.

"Go away," she said. "You have other 'outsiders' to watch, yes? Not us. You watch us *win*, but not make it harder."

Indrath hummed, eyeing my Sister up and down with the sense that he was reading her aura more than admiring her body, though he may have been doing some of that as well. "So be it, D'Shauranti. It is a pleasure to see other Guardians are finally getting involved. They are overdue."

My Sister bit her lip rather than correct him on her House name, as if she might have received a similar warning from Mourn about giving Indrath too many names to work with. "Go, please, Lord."

"A moment. Allow me to ease your sister's shoulder."

Indrath waved his hand, and I flinched as a startling, yet soothing heat seeped into me, removing the swelling which had already begun to stiffen my muscles. I couldn't hide the new sense of health and ease from him.

Had he healed me without touching me?

The Ice Lord smiled with pleasure before peering at Vesram with a sinister edge, his presence large and compelling even without eye contact. "Queen's Creature, listen well. These Red Sisters are your governesses on the Surface. If you leave their care, you are fair game to me. If you rebel in *any* such way that costs Sirana her unborn child, I *will* find you, and I shall place you in the depths of Ice Heart and make you regret it for a *very* long time."

"I hear," the Sathoet grunted behind me, afflicted by a low, constant pain. "Underssstood."

"Good." Indrath revealed fangs in a broad smile. "I am satisfied for now. Carry on with your battle, my children."

In a stark rush of cold air and snow, the Deal Broker disappeared.

The Deathwalker had nothing of use in his hands as he ran toward three females standing on the street. He lacked a plan for the confrontation but knew only that shedding blood concerned him far less by comparison. His vision flickered as the nuances of life, death, and magic stood out in greater contrast before his eyes.

"*I am here!*" Amelda shouted, wrist bound and a leash around her neck. "*Come get them! Capture them alive!*"

Cris-ri-phon's daughter was healthy but seemed to have an imbued foreign object in her pelvis. The Naulor were unharmed, their auras flaring with alarm and magic as they chose their responses to the five Hellhounds approaching from four directions, revealing themselves in a coordinated display.

Simultaneously, the Herald entered the scene but kept enough distance from his allies to determine what he needed to know. The Ma'ab had spotted him and the leading threads of ice-blue magic on their chains all pointed toward him.

Good.

"Gavin?!" Krithannia blurted, her attention splintered between the Ma'ab noble covering her pleas as commands, Tamuril drawing her bow, and the rattling links of metal and heavy boots.

"Duck," he said.

The Guild Mistress showed whites in her eyes, reacting with admirable speed to take his advice. She didn't disrupt her sister's aim or focus on her target but dragged Amelda to the ground by her leash as Tamuril released her arrow on the Hellhound to her right.

The fighter barely slowed, grimacing in pain, but his skin remained unbroken as the sharp tip glanced off his tattooed chest rather than embedding in it. The Druid froze up, unable to choose another response. Fortunately, flying chains sailed right past her, wrapping around Gavin's limbs and torso, the thick, jagged spikes biting into him with the first constriction.

The pain, as always, was the focus, further intensified once the chains started pulling past each other, grinding, and dragging their wicked points through his flesh. He seized command of his aura through his blood, drawn and flowing.

Gavin fractured the remainder of their collective spell, dispelling it before the chains could return to their masters. Heavy weights slid off him, crashing on the ground in a tangled, impotent circle. Black blood stained his robe from his shoulders down, trailing long, viscous drips along his pale skin.

"*Fantastic display, Herald,*" cooed a familiar voice in the Greylands tongue.

It came from the longest shadow behind him.

"*I have been waiting, Artist,*" he replied in kind.

"*Seize the heretic!*" Amelda barked, fury and frustration spilling out of her mouth before Krithannia stuffed a cloth into it.

Gavin heard the cluck of a mismatched tongue. "*Bland choice. Does she take suggestions for her exhibition?*"

"*The chains,*" he growled.

"*Already mine.*"

Dormant, serpentine threats came alive, much to the alarm of the Hellhounds, the stained spikes keeping a respectful distance from the Deathwalker's body. Three Ma'ab snarled their command words, hands outstretched in a familiar gesture to call their favored weapon. Not a tremor suggested this might happen. The living men instead hissed with discomfort, broad hands clasping at tattoos as if they burned.

At last, the Chenkyte stepped out into the sunlight. Every grotesque scar, needle, and suture rippled in sharp relief against the lusterless, blue-grey flesh and tanned, dark leather.

"*Underwhelming effort,*" they said. "*These fine tools deserve the touch of an expert.*"

The Hellhounds seemed not to understand the words but reacted quickly to the new threat. The pack charged together rather than retreat — a questionable choice — drawing shorter melee weapons and touching their tattoos, their muscles swelling.

The Artist laughed behind the veil of tiny chains and hooks, opening their arms as if to embrace the sight before them. Predictably, the spiked chains whipped around to ensnare their former masters. Less predictably, Ma'ab boots left the ground, their bodies catapulting up into the air.

Amid their shouts of protest, Krithannia and Tamuril dragged Amelda to the nearest doorway in obvious desperation to find cover. Meanwhile, Gavin stood bleeding and bearing witness.

Near the top of a shaded wall, the spiked chains threw themselves and their captives against the stone, burrowing in to strap down and anchor the large bodies in a disordered net. Two lay in the frame of adjacent windows while the other three had been turned in various orientations and pinned around them.

If the pattern was intentional, Gavin didn't grasp its significance.

The Chenkyte lowered their arms and hummed, swaying out of direct light to better inspect their work. *"Hm. What will it take to puncture their skin?"*

"A marring of the correct tattoo located on their back," Gavin answered. *"Though this may trigger a trap spell in some of them. We don't know which ones as we do not recognize all the symbols."*

The orange in foreign eyes deepened. *"Ooo. Clever use of skin. Whose idea was that?"*

"The Ma'ab Ascended."

"I'm impressed. Perhaps I shall get to meet one."

"If you do, the rest of us are in the depths of trouble."

They lifted their gaze to admire their display. *"Is this all of them? Am I finished, Herald?"*

"No. At least a score of them."

"Excellent."

"And their leader is not among these."

"Is this leader notable?"

"He is. You'll see why."

"What intrigue." Amber eyes gleamed as the men started to groan and complain about their position. *"May I save these bodies for later? They clearly have stamina for discomfort."*

The Deathwalker glanced up. *"If you can be sure they will not escape."*

Another chuckle. *"Any who challenge my work shall deal with the chains."*

"Hm. Could be quite a drop."

"Oh, yes! One of my favorite techniques in any grounded world. Heh!" The unseen grin was evident. *"Though, you did interrupt observance of my acolyte, Herald."*

"Mathias? Did you confront him?"

"Not yet. I enjoy a bit of anticipation."

Gavin frowned as the Artist's eyes crinkled at the corners.

The Naulor dared to look out of the doorway in which they'd hidden, and the Guild Mistress called out to him.

"Herald!"

He turned his head. "Yes?"

She paused as if waiting for him to speak, glancing away to clear the street. "Is this an ally?"

"Not really. A mercenary I've hired against the Hellhounds."

"Ahm ... That's good." She may not have been sure about her own statement but at least had stood in that position before.

Then Tamuril was tugging on her sleeve.

"Sirana and Jael," the Druid pressed.

Oh, yes. Of course.

"The Davrin rode off on Nightmare," Krithannia said. "We don't know why."

"I do," said the Deathwalker. "Vesram was here. Sirana must have caught the Sathoet's thoughts and pursued him."

Both Naulor looked distressed.

"We must catch them!" said the Druid.

"A moment." Gavin turned to the Artist, *"Do you understand this trade tongue?"*

The Chenkyte shifted their weight, leaning slightly away with a hand bearing the fingers from more than one body resting on their hip. *"It's gibberish. But my grasp of bodies' languages is on point. They are concerned for others of their kind."*

"They are."

"Shall I seek the other hound packs, then? I do not want my acolyte slipping away while you corral your wayward Elves."

Gavin was slightly amused. If he somehow managed *that*, their stillness wouldn't last.

"A moment," he said with an internal sigh as he switched tongues for Krithannia. *"Will you convey to Mourn that I am sending him help? Offer a description."*

The Naulor lost focus in her storm-grey eyes for a moment, then nodded smartly. "Done. He says we must meet him near the Temple once we've found Sirana and Jael. They are close."

So soon.

Gavin turned to the Chenkyte. *"A Dragonchild knows you are coming toward the Temple."*

"Oh?"

"Dark, black and purple scales. Gold eyes. Long, twin blades."

"Wings?"

"No, no wings."

"Strange but noted."

Gavin pointed in the direction of the watchtower. *"That way. Seek the other three or four packs of chain wielders. Do not underestimate their leader."*

"I cannot wait to see why." With a bow, the Artist backed up toward a darkened doorway across from the Naulor. *"Until we meet again, Herald."*

The sudden lack of presence convinced Gavin it was time to leave. With his longest stride, he approached the Naulor.

"Let us find them," he said simply to which Krithannia and Tamuril responded at once.

Gavin wondered why Amelda was here while also dismissing this as a Guild concern. Her bindings and new gag seemed secure enough to wait on that matter.

First, he would find Sirana. Vesram as well.

He would explain between his allies as it became relevant.

THE QUEEN'S GEAS RELEASED ITS GRIP ON ME FOR THE TIME BEING. AS THE bodily distress receded, however, a mental one took its place.

The guarded cavern imprisoning the mindflayer lay wide open in my head. Tears blurred my eyes, and I couldn't get up. I couldn't speak, couldn't hear my guardians …

I wasn't sure how to close the prison, if it could be.

"Sirana?"

Jael crouched down; I couldn't meet her eyes.

"Move," she said to the Sathoet. "Hands off. Get back."

He did so without resistance, making no sound, yet I could *still* sense the resentment against his matrons.

Long-buried, Abyssal wrath seeking a focus. A way out. Escape.

Danger stayed behind me.

"These Red Sisters are your governesses on the Surface. If you leave their care, you are fair game to me."

Responsible for another one, and not by my Queen alone but the Ice Lord, too. Both had *thrown* him onto me!

I can't …

I couldn't survive their cruelty again.

Just leave me alone!

My expression must have unnerved Jael. Her thoughts leaked out.

⋆I don't know what's wrong! What do I do?!⋆

A quiet gap of time where I wasn't aware of much, then she embraced me protectively, her tone oddly tender as she spoke.

"I'm here," she said. "I'm here, Sirana. He won't touch you. Can you hear us?"

That took a moment.

~ … Us?~

*⋆Sirana. Can *you* hear us?⋆*

His calm voice anchored me, loaned strength which wrapped around me through our connection alongside Jael's embrace.

~ ... Mourn?~

I am sorry I shouted before, he said. *I understand what happened. It wasn't your fault.*

~Wasn't it?~

No. Keep protecting your child however you must. We will free you, Sirana. Stay with us. The Godblood is almost to the Temple.

Willven. I wanted to cry. ~Free me ... ~

We will. I promise. Stand up. Find Krithannia. She has found Gavin.

Gavin.

A burst of concern. ~Gavin! Is he ... ?~

He is doing quite well. Even as a captive, he never stopped working toward our goal. The Dragon Son's amusement and admiration were clear. *Can you stand up?*

~Ah ... Yes.~ I placed a palm on the ground, trying to lean away so I might push myself up.

"Here, I'll help." Jael said at once, releasing me and holding me steady as I fought through sudden dizziness to get upright.

The smells of the Human city flooded in, along with the reassuring chimes of my spiders as they sensed me. Somewhere to my left and behind me, Deshi wailed unceasing, fighting against an entire army, while the shouts of the Godblood and his Templars sent concussive bursts of magical tremors through my feet and teeth.

Only Jael and Mourn had stopped in the middle of a battle to wait for me as I stopped to gather up the broken pieces.

As it should be. The world can't wait for me.

We were lucky it hadn't cost Willven his life or his victory.

With every breath, my weakened body came further under my control until I mustered the courage to looked at Vesram. He crouched on the ground not far away. Intense relief washed through me when he didn't stare.

The Sathoet wasn't pleased with his situation, not one mote, but neither his anger nor desires focused on a Davrin for the moment. Separating him from Kerse was easier because of his grey eyes, and I took those seconds to study his features.

Vesram hadn't grown enough to have the extra set of arms or wings Kerse had gained suddenly upon releasing Ullipmious. His elongated face had the muzzle, the sharp predator's teeth, the sprout of white hair under the jaw plus the stripe of a mane from his brow down his spine to the small of his back. His Elven ears weren't curled or wrinkled like other Sathoet, and the patches of fur on his elbows and back of his knees weren't as long or wild.

Vesram also wasn't sitting with that barely restrained agitation, searching for the next distraction or thing to want. His expression bore a calmness, a patience that I'd never seen in the demon sons of Sivaraus.

Angry and fearful though he may be, he studied his surroundings, sniffing and listening, taking in many of the same details I was. He had taken the time to scavenge for useful things, storing them on a sturdy belt with several hanging pouches. He hadn't added clothing over his loincloth, though, and I wondered how adapted he was to the cold by now.

I asked him quietly in Davrin, *"Why are your eyes grey?"*

His attention snapped to me, and those eyes squinted. *"Born with grey, Mother told me."*

"But ... they were red in the crypt."

"They changed with my new mistresss."

I swallowed. *"Were they yellow at any time?"*

His tufted chin bobbed once. *"In Sssivaraus."*

I suppressed a shudder in how he said the name, somewhat at a loss. Was this true for all Sathoet? Yet another thing the Priestesses kept to themselves? Or was he ... different? Did the Valsharess truly want this specific half-blood, as Indrath supposed? Had She seen something, thus needed to place the geas on me?

Perhaps She had never known Mourn the half-blood existed, and I'd tortured myself for nothing.

"Why are your eyes blue?" he rumbled.

"H-huh?" I shook myself out of my spiral.

481

Jael huffed, smirking as she kept her body between us. *"She was born with them."*

Vesram smiled oddly. *"How? Priestess Consorts?"*

He remembered those, too.

"No," I answered. *"Lineage. Happenstance."*

"Hrrmm. Sssame."

Nightmare hobbled around the corner, breaking that awkward moment. Loud and irregular clopping of her hooves matching the broken bone in her left hind leg.

Jael said out of the corner of her mouth, *"Shouldn't we be looking for the Deathwalker?"*

I grimaced. *"Yes. We should."*

"Maybe he can fix her."

Vesram perked up. *"I know where Adason is."*

"Oh?"

"Library." He pointed in the correct direction.

My Sister and I tightened our lips against a double laugh. Krithannia would have found him there, according to Mourn.

"Let's backtrack," I said, seizing a stronger link with the mare through the talisman in my glove. *"We were going there anyway."*

Vesram's features tightened before he moved ahead to lead the way, walking mostly bipedal but using his knuckles for balance when the incline was sharp enough.

"Were you watching him?" I asked. *"To know where he was."*

The Sathoet glanced over his shoulder. *"I was guarding him. How you imagine he escaped from the Hellhounds?"*

Jael's mouth sagged alongside mine as Vesram kept us moving. We exchanged looks, but my Sister was baffled. She hadn't been in the crypt to witness Gavin's initial disbelief that his mother had known this creature before he was born.

Vesram and Gavin's mother were both slaves to the same commander, I signed, trying to keep it simple.

She squinted her eyes in doubt. *Explains the name. Since when is a Sathoet loyal to the son of a dead female he once served with?*

That was a good question.

A hundred years alone among Humans is a long time, I replied. *Plenty could change.*

Like with Mourn and Krithannia.

Even Tamuril.

He must want something, my Sister insisted.

I smiled. That went without saying. *Everyone does.*

We stepped up our pace to keep up with the half-blood on the steep incline where we'd fallen earlier. Nightmare continued to make a clatter as we favored speed over stealth.

Yet, huffing my way up the street, my stress lessened to think Vesram *had* been intending to go to the Ley Tower, but to follow Gavin. Not me. I couldn't have known that, and Indrath had been about to kill the demon's son regardless. This forced arrangement wasn't all for nothing, but …

He's not interested in me.

The unspoken weight lifted off my beleaguered mind, convincing my silent spider guardians to add yet another thread to the web of nearby bodies which they ignored. The Surface held plenty of threats for us, but I wondered if D'Shea could have ever imagined this many others standing between those threats and her gift to me.

The street leveled out, but the library wasn't yet in view when Vesram stopped in his tracks, crouching lower and putting up his hands.

"Don't shoot him," said a gruff, familiar voice.

Gavin.

"Sirana!" Tamuril called with relief, relaxing her bow, and dropping the arrow tip from its aim on Vesram's chest.

"You found him," Krithannia said as we closed the gap.

I glanced at the Deathwalker, unable to stop my grin from spreading as I replied, "So did you."

Gavin's new robes were badly torn and stained with blood, both dried red and glossy-wet black. Dirt patches and smears suggested a variety of places he'd been since yesterday. All of it made me envision the rough shape he might have once been in since we last saw each other but had since mended. The impulse to ask if he was alright was there, but I also saw the look he'd no doubt give me in my mind's eye.

He's been through worse. Probably.

"Here," I said, hurriedly dropping my pack to pull out the bulky thurible. "Before something else happens."

I'd rarely, if ever, seen pleasant surprise on Gavin's face but witnessed it now.

"My gratitude," he murmured, stepping forward to accept it.

The metal handle turned cold as I released it to him, and Soul Drinker trembled in its sheath. The pale blue of Gavin's irises shone intensely for an instant as the relic responded to his familiar aura. The Deathwalker said nothing of this adjustment as he looked at Vesram.

"You returned with them," he stated.

"Ice Lord found me before Sssirana," the demonblood hissed. "Now, must ssstay with her, or he killsss me."

Vesram had pulled in most signs of his resentment explaining that to Gavin, a self-restraint which was … interesting coming from a half-demon.

My Deathwalker showed his amazement. "You convinced an Infernal *not* to kill the Abyssal?"

My mouth tightened. "I had to, or Ionne and I may not survive. Fortunately, he believed me."

"Hm. Well," the death mage said slowly, "that's not the worst out-come. I intend to stay with you, and my mother said I would need both you and Vesram to confront Sarilis."

I blinked. "She did? When?"

"At the Temple."

"You've been there already?"

"Last night."

I started to smile. "And then the library."

"Of course."

So Divigna had been right about both.

"Speaking of which,' Krithannia said, helping to clip off further delay,"are we ready to meet the Godblood at the Temple? They need us as soon as possible."

Jael cleared her throat, motioning behind her. "Broke the mare chasing Sathoet. Need to fix."

Gavin appraised his old cart horse. "Sirana, do you have a dagger I could borrow? A plain one."

"Sure."

I gave it to him, unsurprised as he used it to draw his Nexus-touched blood and feed his risen horse without her gnawing on him. Tamuril looked to the sky while Amelda emitted a muffled scoff through her gag, wrinkling her nose in distaste.

As if Ma'ab magic is any cleaner?

Gavin attached his thurible to his belt, prompting me to note he did not have his satchel. No surgeon's tools, no writing supplies …

No grimoire.

All of which I'd never seen him without before.

Where was it? Had he lost it?

We had little time and less breath to talk as we took to the streets. Vesram dragged Amelda by her leash; he wouldn't take no for an answer as this small measure gave him obvious satisfaction. Gavin rode Nightmare as Jael and I intended to stay with the Naulor and help guard Amelda's life. Nonetheless, I made the space to mention one last change since Gavin's capture.

"Deshi," I said.

"Hm?" Gavin grunted from atop his mount, and Amelda's eyes grew wide.

"He died from his torture. But he came back somewhat like you did."

My ally's face frowned in confusion. "Came back? As a Deathwalker?"

Nyx's empty eyes flickered behind mine, her whisper seeping through my thoughts.

"Has she that power … ?"

"No," I answered Gavin's question. "Something new. He wanted to help us rescue you."

An insight passed over the Herald's face. "Is he the source of the wail

I've heard on the air since last night?"

Wetting my dry mouth, I swallowed. "Yes. That's him."

Amelda growled something, somehow sounding intensely distressed *and* poisonously insulting. Gavin glanced her way.

"Hm," he grunted, dismissing her.

We sped up to confront the Hellhounds at the Temple once more. *Back to where I killed Eynkis in the fight before.*

CHAPTER 35

ONCE I SPOTTED THE LIGHT REFLECTING OFF A GOLDEN SHIELD, I REACHED OUT hoping he could sense me.

~Willven, I see you.~

A powerful psionic touch responded, linking us from afar.

~Sirana. I am glad you're well. We have control of the district but have caution. Divigna hasn't shown himself yet.~

Neither Mourn nor Deshi would leave Isboern because of this, so Krithannia, Gavin, and the rest of us had to make our collective way through scores of tense and exhausted soldiers guarding and guiding large groups of crying recent captives.

A few streets up lay the main gate to the Temple's courtyard. The all-morning push up the mountain had paused where they had space for Manalari soldiers and captives alike to gather. Behind them, headless bodies and streams of blood spread down through every level, most of them large enough to be Ma'ab. I also didn't see any large male prisoners among the Paxian army and civilians. Many of these noncombatant Manalari screamed and blurted curses upon sighting Gavin and Vesram.

"Capitan Dyos Saung valesitos!" the Manalari officers repeated constantly, placing their bodies between us and them, though a few could not hide their revulsion at the Deathwalker's gaunt and bloodied appearance

487

or the Sathoet's hunched and bestial form.

"Valesitos! Nun medis, nun medis, Dyos Saung valesitos …"

Jael and I grimaced at the flood of voices and choking scents of sweat, blood, and bowels. Gavin seemed to ignore it as he held his thurible aloft, eyes black as he silently gathered the Vis from the battle. Tamuril peered around in sympathetic distress, reaching to squeeze Krithannia's hand. The Guild Mistress returned the grip but kept her focus calm and serious in dragging Amelda along.

The four of us had pulled up our hoods to seem less threatening by comparison and used Nightmare to shield us from some ill-fated choice made by the populace. Thankfully, the Templars Erik, Imran, Robi, and Sohl soon rushed up to us, providing additional escort and visible reassurance to the rumbling crowd. They didn't flinch seeing Vesram; in fact, something else seemed to be on Sohl's mind as he sidled up to me and Gavin.

"I must ask, Herald," he said. "Did you send, um, assistance?"

"I did," Gavin replied as if he'd expected the question, lowering his relic at last. "The Artist. A mercenary familiar with Hellhound weapons."

The Templars weren't reassured but at least their concern for being duped had lessened.

"And, uh?" Robi gestured to Vesram.

"Ma'ab defector," the Herald replied. "We killed his commander in the crypt during the first battle. He has joined us against the Hellhounds."

That sounded so much simpler. No doubt Gavin made this "Artist" sound equally understated.

~What mercenary?~ I asked.

The Godblood heard me. *~The Dragon son and Guild Mistress vouched for their presence when the Artist stepped out of nowhere. Quite … ah, recognizable. They resemble Gavin's guardian mother but is much taller and somewhat masculine.~*

~Somewhat? What does that mean?~

~Ah … I see both man and woman in the form, but not … as one.~

I had to wait and see what that meant. *~Did they mention the price for this assistance?~*

~The Artist has not said much of anything beyond invoking the Herald of Nyx, and I don't recognize the thought patterns on the surface. They are … not from here.~

Of all the things I'd seen recently to give me a shiver. *~Stepped through from the Nexus like the Malok?~*

~No. This is different. Even from that.~

This conflict over a pool of water on a mountain grew stranger by the moment. How had Gavin reached an entity like that as a captive? I glanced at my Deathwalker, but he looked ahead, his thoughts elsewhere.

"Is that Deshi?" he asked.

Oof.

"Yes, he is," I said in measured. response "What do you see?"

The Harrowed stood still but not calm, his blue-green flames not as striking in full daylight but brightly enfolding the odd sight of a dark, Yungian skeleton.

"I am not sure," he replied bluntly.

His tone made me nervous. I imagined my ally might see Elven magic mixed with death magic, like Divigna.

But they aren't the same.

Deshi was one soul. He had chosen this.

Vesram's mother had not.

"The Harrowed *can* take his Yungian form," I added. "The one we recognize. This is when he is battle-ready."

"The Harrowed." Gavin grunted with curiosity despite himself. As the Templars guided us into the open square, he slid off Nightmare's back and walked between me and her with Vesram on her far side.

"I am shielding us," Isboern said, projecting his commander's voice. "Have no fear standing out in the open while we regroup."

I spotted the Artist at once, a hairless, greyish-blue horror with blazing, amber eyes, decorated in hooks, needles, and chains, barely dressed in leather which I doubted could be shed like standard clothing. The creature stood closer to Mourn while keeping farthest from Deshi, an odd detail eclipsed by the disturbing presence of this new mercenary.

I gaped at the nauseating arrangement of torture metals and sutures.

They seemed to hold the humanoid body together equally as much as granting its morbid aesthetic. Isboern's likeness to Ada was believable and yet, in comparison, the small Grey Ma'ab either showed restraint in her self-mutilation or was a novice in such modifications to her transitioned body.

~Mourn?~

The Dragon son's tail moving stiffly, his every sense on alert as he gestured us closer. We had to approach the Artist, which thrilled none of us, yet how many other times we could have gotten squeamish but hadn't?

I breathed out and led the way.

Gavin spoke to the creature in their shared tongue, receiving a graceful bow and jingle of their veil of tiny chains. They gestured with a hand bearing six mismatched fingers.

"I will return," the Deathwalker said to us. "Stay near the Artist. This is the safest place for you with Hellhounds about."

My eyebrows lifted near my hairline, though Gavin didn't notice. He left Nightmare with me and headed directly for the Harrowed, Vesram following behind him.

Krithannia and Tamuril responded in solemn agreement to my questioning glance, the former explaining. "The Artist can seize magical weapons from their bearers from afar."

"Chains?" Jael guessed.

"Yes. We saw them counter five Hellhounds at once after you left in pursuit of the Sathoet."

Gavin had found such a precise and practical choice of aid, I had no trouble imagining him making it.

An eerie chill disturbed my spiders at the nape of my neck. The Artist gazing at me with deep, lantern-like eyes. The eyelids seemed stiff as if rarely used to blink.

~Why do you stare?~ Based on Isboern's thought, I had no expectation they understood me.

The chill grew colder as those eyes crinkled at the corners in the strong suggestion of a smile behind the veil. Their thoughts barely made sense to me, much to my consternation.

The life flower coaxes the greenskeeper to uphold cycles to which they're disconnected, thought the disturbing soul that was the Chenkyte. *The deeper the roots, the better for all. More so when that life is touched by a sleeping god.* They laughed in silence, and didn't *stop* laughing. *Careful lest you wake it.*

I lost my nerve holding that gaze, turning away and closing my mind, seizing Jael's hand to ground me. She blinked but her hand squeezed mine.

Distant, delighted laughter faded.

"*You alright?*" my Sister whispered.

"*Mmhm,*" I grunted.

Now was not the time.

Across the square, the Harrowed had avoided dropping into his Yungian form before the Herald so he would not need life's breath to continue the fight. Deshi was difficult to read except for the bowing, and I couldn't know what insights Gavin had gained in this short time.

Not until he glanced my way, eyes void-black.

My stomach fluttered. His pale, placid face and empty eyes reminded me far too much of Nyx granting Deshi's final wish.

"What now?" I asked mostly to Mourn.

He grunted. "Divigna told us, 'Find me at the Temple or the archives.' He is not at the library, yet we found Gavin. So we go to the Temple and face the Hellhounds."

I tried not to fidget, noticing that Mourn had taken a few lucky blows from the crush of enemies from the high ground. One puncture wound in his thigh, barely on the edge of a patch of scales and the flesh around it singed, plus a handful of shallow slash marks or scrapes from debris on his face, arms, and calves, all of which had scabs already.

"Any new insights on what Divigna wants?" I asked.

My former bodyguard shook his head. "No. Nothing new."

I gazed down the sloping street at the visible survivors, Manalari and Guildsman alike. Plenty looked worse off, exhausted and their clothes stained with blood in areas where Mourn had his sire's scales to protect him: around his shoulders and upper back, trailing down his flanks and lightly covering his thighs, and all along his tail. I wouldn't be able to tell how many blows had struck that Draconic armor but imagining how many others he had shielded indirectly by drawing Ma'ab aggression.

Glad I was able to release our Bargain.

"Ma'ab prisoners?" I asked mostly for confirmation.

"Just Amelda."

Mourn glared in a way which conveyed he would rather this not be the case. Her face collapsed as she bit down hard on her sopping-wet gag, though that ever-prideful shield rallied with the knowledge that he wouldn't invite the consequences of cutting her down.

Divigna had asked for Brom's daughter along with Deshi's dagger and Gavin's thurible, but we didn't know why. Lacking that insight, we hadn't a strong counter, and we knew it. Gavin was with us, however, which at least removed the leverage of a trade.

~*Do you think Divigna wants to kill her to bring the Ascended directly to the Temple?*~ I asked privately.

Assuming that would happen, Mourn replied, *I see it most likely with the occupying army vanquished.*

~*But he allowed us to vanquish them. He stepped away and didn't lift a single chain to help them.*~

The half-blood shrugged slightly. *Ma'ab culture is ruthless, more so the older they get, apparently.*

And Kreshel Divigna was, in an unsettling yet practical sense, older than I was.

Meanwhile, the Godblood would not be distracted. The blond man concentrated visibly on his psionic shielding while his Templars guarded him, all patiently waiting until we gathered and shared information. By the time Gavin, Vesram, and Deshi finally approached the rest of us, the Artist appeared bored, pulling on a hook binding cured leather to the thick skin on their flank. They tugged and stretched it short of tearing.

Then held it there.

"Stop it," Deshi said, his voice touched with anger and carried by that underlying shriek. He kept the most distance from the rest of us, though that didn't make him any less distracting. I could feel the chilled air dancing within his flames.

The Chenkyte lifted their eyes to the Harrowed, the visible part of their nose wrinkling in a silent snarl as their gaze intensified. Calmly defiant, the mercenary tore the hook out with a distinct rip of flesh that made everyone flinch. They sighed in relief, oozing red blood, and laughing softly before speaking.

"*Yigista rrentrugl vencoasshra?*"

My ears perked up. *The Dead Tongue of the Nexus.*

Gavin and Deshi seemed to understand as the former squinted in thought and the Harrowed grudgingly tilted his skull toward the cobbled street.

"What said they?" Krithannia prompted.

The Deathwalker turned his head. "They asked whether or not the mind mage's shield slides beneath our feet." With a brief pause, he added, "The Hellhounds have become familiar with the undercroft these past weeks."

Mourn's white spines lifted halfway up his back; his tail lashed once in a hard whip.

"*Shuiblith,*" he growled, scanning the survivors of the uphill battle. The Manalari soldiers, Guildsman, and captives all crouching and resting in spaces where we didn't know if an underground passage might abruptly open.

Shit, indeed.

The Dragon son said, "I do not hear or smell them or their magic yet. What do you sense, chain dancer?"

Gavin translated, and the Artist seemed to like the description enough to answer. They pointed to the far side of the Templari and their Captain.

"*Ithkari besshrageth tiyroin,*" they crooned with distinct bliss.

Deshi snapped his focus that way as Gavin repeated, " 'Two souls in great agony stand close to the divine-touched one.' "

To Isboern.

Yet we couldn't see them.

Now that the idea had taken hold, I spotted within the protected square several drainage grates and two circular, Dwarven-made metal plates among the cobbles, each of which *could* be covering a hole beneath our feet.

Above us, a falcon screeched. To my left, metal scraped against stone. Mourn hauled Jael and me off our feet and behind him, Vesram crouching in our defense as Tamuril's voice broke into a shriek.

"*Willven — !*"

The heavy plate nearest to the Templars burst skyward with a loud bang, hurling toward us by concussive force. Before the spinning projectile could collide with one of us or the ground, a spiked chain struck like a snake ambushing from its burrow. A second later, another chain launched from the nearest grate a quarter-turn to the right.

"*Look out!*"

"*Duck and roll!*"

Light flashed, the metal plate striking the cobblestone, chipping off fragments as it turned end-over-end down the street, missing armor and bone. Likewise, two sets of chains sounded to hit walls rather than wrap around bodies, clattering against themselves in their drop to the ground without any scream to accompany them.

The shield is gone, Mourn said through the pearls, squeezing my wrist tightly as if he wanted me to do something. **Hellhounds incoming from three directions.**

I wasn't sure everyone heard that but the Guildsmen behind us were moving faster than the Manalari while Deshi's unearthly scream ramped up. Likewise, the Templari drew up into a familiar defensive form.

Isboern began, ~*We must move forward while we can* — ~

A brief clatter of wood, feathers whipping through air, and Tamuril's bow creaked from sudden tension which also flooded her voice.

"*Ilbauseke!*" she shouted.

I blinked, frantic to see where the Druid aimed as she released.

A Hellhound with his shoulders through the Dwarven street hole suddenly sported an arrow from his left eye. Visible shock lingered on his face long enough for his skin to turn sickly grey as putrid black and green spots spread on his skin with alarming speed before his dead weight dragged him beneath the street.

Contagion! Wolf blared through our stout, revived communication.

Draw back, seconded Hawk. *Take everyone down a level to the merchant gate.*

Cloths over noses and mouths, said Bear. *Now!*

The Naulor hustled somewhere behind me, and a wind picked up from the West, blowing downwind from the Godblood. The second Ma'ab who'd thrown his chain through the grate never showed his face, but three packs of his brothers had come out of hiding with their own weapons rattling.

The majority of Hellhound emerged at last, flanking the square and everybody in it.

Mourn summoned the sliders from his bracers and into his grip. *Deshi and I will take the pack to the west!*

~And we shall continue to push south.~

Isboern lifted his shield, choosing his pack of adversaries in front of him, blocking the most direct route to the Temple, to eat their next meal off his relic. Three of them dodged but temporarily lost their guidance on their spiked weapons, while two came to a sudden halt, hands gripping their faces as the light struck them. They dropped their chains entirely.

Deshi took this moment to relaunch his endless sprint, aiming to meet the Ma'ab coming from our right, but the Chenkyte looked on with mild curiosity.

Gavin! Will the Artist engage?

The Herald spoke to the Artist, gesturing toward the limp chains on the ground near Isboern and the Templari. He received a response while Jael and Tamuril dragged me behind a street cart with Vesram, Krithannia, and Amelda. Meanwhile, Mourn peeled off from us, spinning his blades to chase after the Harrowed.

They will once the weapons draw fresh blood, Gavin answered, though Mourn wasn't nearby anymore. *The usurpation of control is secure then.*

Fresh blood?

The Godblood prevented the first two from drawing any.

*For Sargt's sake ... *

My blood counts, To'vah-krav. Allow me.

"Good, Sirana." Krithannia squeezed my shoulder as Gavin set his thurible near her and left. "Let them hear each other."

So long as she didn't expect me to run at the same time.

Jael and Vesram guarded me and the Herald's relic as Tamuril took shots with her bow. Meanwhile, I grappled for any awareness of my body as the pitched battle closed in, and so many voices and splinters of thoughts not mine filled the square.

The Godblood was there somewhere, among them, but he wasn't here to guide me, nor was I his anchor to hold the mind-net down to the earth.

"Ao Templi dul Sohl!" Isboern called, his voice rising above the rest as armored men answered and charged up the street.

~We shall meet you at the Temple!~

To the Temple!!

Meanwhile, my Deathwalker moved faster than I'd ever seen him to reach the abandoned chains. Gavin wasted no time gripping them, puncturing his hands intentionally to stain them, and then tossing them in the general direction of the Artist.

The blooded chains did not brush the stones before they spun upward in a scintillating, vertical dance as if thrilled to be alive.

"Another fine gift, Herald," the Chenkyte said, stretching an arm up to caress the length of twisting, wicked metal, slashing their own palm in the process. "Let our path to your sun be varnished with crimson earned in captivating savagery."

I shuddered, my heart accelerating into a choking rhythm as my hands covered my ears, fingers digging in behind them. The words, the devotion in them, made too much sense!

"Sirana?" Jael asked, clasping my shoulders, consciously avoiding my spiders.

I shook my head. I didn't understand.

How could I understand the traveler from the Between?!

The third and final pack of Hellhounds entered the square from our left, unchallenged but for a few of Tami's arrows which bounced off bare, tattooed chests. They charged straight for Gavin, who stood empty-handed and held his ground.

"Oh! Krithannia," the blonde fretted, voice shaking.

"Duck down. Let him do it."

Do what?

The Druid and I watched in twinned horror as the Ma'ab pack ensnared Gavin as one team, their chains grinding over each other as they wrapped and tangled up around my Deathwalker in a fierce play to bring him down once and for all. His black blood, once drawn, soaked fast into robes, which were further torn to tatters. One magical jerk ripped off his ear where it bounced to the cobblestone.

"*Augh!*" Jael gasped as my stomach heaved.

The Elves around me flinched as if their vision was taken by a bright light, but I saw the magic without obstruction. Gavin stood with his hands balled into fists as the chains gave one last constriction before going limp and sliding off him, crashing in a dark woven circle around him.

His enemies were as stunned as I was.

"*Mutakia!*" one cried in disbelief.

"*Luqad fastul!*" blurted another, hand outstretched, his face in a grimace as he attempted to summon his chain.

★The packs haven't shared reports,★ Krithannia confirmed through the pearl.

★Acknowledged,★ Mourn answered, a subtle thread of strain in his thought.

The Chenkyte swayed into view, strutting forward so light on their feet, willing the abruptly obedient bundle chains into the air. Arms up, thirteen fingers subtly guiding the metal links and barbs, the Artist created a harsh, waving design which reminded me of the ceiling for a butcher's cold storage if it had been made into a script.

"*Sacred number seven,*" they said, counting the chains. "*My favorite.*"

"*Mind the distances from my allies when you puncture their protective markings,*" Gavin growled, bending down to pick up his ear.

"*Yes, yes, or they may explode into festering bits. Surely one of them will oblige. I want to feel their wet flesh sliding on mine.*"

The otherworldly mercenary pitched themselves forward without awaiting a response, diving into the midst of the Hellhound pack and bringing all those stolen chains with them. Screams of pain and terror bound up with cries of delight, all of it echoing off the solid stone buildings.

Suddenly, I grasped how it wasn't *my* ears taking in the language of the Nexus, but Gavin's. I had merely absorbed his understanding, his mental translations through a mindlink which seemed to be growing ... *Stronger*.

"Which way?" Jael said, raising her voice over the noise, unnerved by the writhing debauchery close by.

Which way, Shadow? Krithannia asked.

Another concussive blast answered from his direction. Deshi's wailing cut short. A terrifyingly intimate pain leaked through the link, jolting me to my core.

~Morixxyleth!~

Alive! he answered at once, unable to hide the stress and pain. *We are still up!*

I groaned as a scorching stiffness climbed up my back ...

Wait, no.

His back.

Burning. Like at the redoubt. Under the waterfall.

What about Deshi? Krithannia asked, numb to the pain.

I've got him, he assured her. *I have this. Follow the Godblood. We will meet you there.*

Gavin had returned to lift his thurible with one hand, holding a slippery curl of flesh to the side of his head with the other. His robes were damp and thick with black blood, torn to such an extent that I glimpsed his lean legs and breis, and a few of the black, hardened ribs emerging from his skin.

~Will the ear ... reattach?~ I asked.

Night-ice eyes met mine; the former monk seemed to have less revulsion at this than in the past, yet he spoke aloud. "It will soon, yes. The Artist will play. Let us move on and find Kreshel."

"Yesss!" Vesram seconded, the thrill in his voice suggesting a doubt to hope. "Sssstop the Physsician's Hound."

Gavin glanced at me then at the red rune dagger at my waist. "The Black Heart, yes."

What?

I jerked in surprise, at both his suggestion and the eruption of fury behind me.

*Are you all **mad?!** You **mustn't!***

Amelda struck Krithannia from behind with a loose brick across her head, making her stumble as the Ma'ab seized her, scratching for Deshi's dagger on her belt.

"Hai, roach!" Jael barked, whipping around and catapulting into our prisoner. She dragged Amelda into a full-on Red Sister wrestling hold before anyone else could react. The Ma'ab noble shrieked and yelped through her gag, the pain sharp and intense as my Sister pinned her.

"Krithannia, are you alright?" Tamuril asked, trying to see underneath where the Guild Mistress pressed her hand to her dark hair.

"I ... I will be," she said with a grimace.

I watched Amelda's face as Jael secured her hold. Eventually, the sorceress met my eyes long enough to attach another link, so I tugged her to one side of all other noise in my head.

~*What is mad about using Soul Drinker on Divigna?*~

Black eyes wide, she growled, drool leaking down her throat as she worried her gag with bared teeth. *The dagger is mine, whore! It belong to my father! Don't you dare strike the Physician's Hound with it! You could destroy them both!*

She heaved as Jael pressed her weight down on the square of her back, squeezing air from her lungs and turning her face pink. My Sister reached with a gloved hand to squeeze her throat just enough to cut off the blood to her head.

As Amelda passed out, she bore enough resentment for one last, bitter thought.

Strike him down ... Go on. And may we be blessed as the Desert relic claims you, too!

CHAPTER 36

THE LAST CONFRONTATION WITH CRIS-RI-PHON HAD ENDED JUST OUTSIDE THE Temple courtyard. Signs remained, prompting tense memories for me as my heart pulsed in my ears and my stomach threatened to cramp.

"Were you planning to use this?" he asked, setting the vial down on the table.

I frowned. "Not unless survival forced me —"

The sorcerer picked up the metal plate and smashed it down, shattering the vial. I jumped in shock. "No! What have you done?"

"There is always another way!" he thundered. "I won't have this poison in my town, but especially if you might be the one to drink it!"

My stomach boiled. How dare he?

"Any poison on my belt can cause miscarriage, 'life' mage! You destroyed the safest one for me!"

The ancient sorcerer had come closest to trapping me before I'd achieved anything in my mission. He had certainly done the most harm, stripping me of options which had been between the Sisterhood and me and leaving me with much worse ones.

A hungry demon and a mad queen heavy on my belt.

At least Gavin had returned and stayed with me. At least Mourn and Isboern had chosen to help rather than hurt.

Thank Goddess the Ice Lord didn't find me and my Sisters first!

Whole walls and the corners of Manalari buildings had been scorched or demolished by the combined mage force from the Desert General, the Dragon Son, and the Godblood, during which my Deathwalker had guided the collective effort to tear free the man's warped, unnatural anchors that kept him alive without aging. The spot where the Deathless had lain defeated appeared as though half a mountain had fallen from the sky yet shrank down to smash only a tight circle of the street.

Cris's body was gone now, and I was filled with a moment of awe to consider the willpower and magic it had taken, all the focus beyond what we could see and touch to disrupt his existence enough that he would vanish from our path, passing into a place where Mourn would see him in a Dream.

A living body so hard to kill, he walked elsewhere until he found his way home.

Would Divigna prove to be the same? Had the Physician somehow duplicated whatever had been done to the ancient Zauyrian, a Human returning to claim another life layered over many others?

I walked on toward the Temple, far from alone. Tamuril hovered around Krithannia while Vesram carried Amelda over his shoulder so that our group could close the distance and join the Templari. Gavin had stopped trailing blood along the street though he looked like a battle-slain corpse which had dug his way out of the ground, doggedly followed by the dead horse he rode in on.

~*Careful, all,*~ said Willven with his open, silent voice. ~*Any warning, anything at all. Be prepared to push as hard as we can.*~

Min Capitan.

Ci, Dyos sange.

Hearing Erik's and Sohl's salute surprised me, and the hint of exhaustion and pain was concerning. I peered closer as we approached the warriors of the Wall's Defender.

Although Isboern and his men had managed to overrun the five Ma'ab blocking their way, neither the psion's shield nor the golden relic could protect them all. About half were missing armor as parts of the Templari uniform must have been damaged enough that the fighters had simply stripped it off.

A handful had ragged scoring on their flesh from chains which had gotten past the armor, though the bleeding had been stopped or slowed. Some tried to cover a limp or a favored shoulder, and I sensed a depletion of endurance from which they might not recover in a short respite before confronting the Eternal Hellhound.

The pack had not gone down easily, extracting the cost which most benefited their leader.

Yet ... it could be worse.

If any of that pack had been meant to erupt with arcane harm or disease upon his death, the Manalari defenders must have neutralized that danger before it took them down.

Meanwhile, I waited in constant worry for any sign that Mourn and Deshi would catch up next. *They* had been caught in the hidden sequence of offensive magic that Eynkis had told us about. The Harrowed's wailing had stopped, and the Dragonblood kept a careful guard on what information came from *him* through his pearls.

~Come on, say something ... Where are you? What's wrong?~

The Guildsmen's chatter rolled in the back of my head, but fortunately, Krithannia wasn't reliant on me to hear them and communicate as needed. I could suppress the murmur once I understood the gist.

The Augranites were doing well to keep survivors calm, moving them farther away while the Manalari managed some post-battle cleanup. The war wasn't over for them, and none let down their guard. However, they understood how numbers crushing the streets could not help the Godblood here as they had through the morning. They might only hinder the confrontation with Divigna and his Hellhounds in the streets around the Temple.

Meanwhile, Amelda had come awake from Jael's rough treatment, hanging over Vesram's shoulder and drooling through her gag, her wrists tied together. She squealed and struggled, kicking in protest though not so hard as to risk falling; she stopped when the Sathoet squeezed her calf, threatening his claws, and growling his annoyance.

We slowed as the tarnished, pale stone wall guarding the Temple courtyard came into view. We waited long enough to survey the area and for Isboern to meet eyes with Tamuril as her falcon circled high above.

Next, Godblood broke contact with her and turned to me. ~*Anything from the Dragon Son or the Harrowed?*~

He couldn't hear them, either. Not good.

~*Not yet,*~ I replied, wetting my mouth. ~*He said they were standing after the explosion but then withdrew from the link.*~

~*Understood. We may not be able to wait or leave to find them — *~

Kreshel Divigna appeared head-to-shoulders above the courtyard wall as if to agree; there he folded his forearms and rested on his elbows. I needed a moment to grasp that he must be standing on a ladder or stack of crates to lean with such leisure. A scrape of metal on brick to his left suggested he was not alone behind that wall.

"*Capitan*," he said in a fair Manalari accent, his tone bland but loud enough to hear. Black eyes panned over the rest of us, lingering on Gavin and Vesram. The latter rumbled in his throat.

"Divigna," Isboern responded, his shield in place and his men at attention. "Here we are. We fought our way back to our Temple. What will see you leave it to us?"

The Ma'ab may have smiled, ever-so-slightly. Through the Dragon pearls, he answered. **The will of my gods, or by my death.**

The shock of his mental voice struck the Guildsmen, Krithannia, and me. Isboern and Gavin seemed able to hear him for they reacted to the Ma'ab as well.

You have brought all the pieces to determine the outcome, Divigna continued. **Either the one or the other.** A pause. **Well, almost all.**

A coat of ice swept through me as I listened. Somewhat like Gavin's multitude of voices when he bore the souls of others and used their strength, I sensed more than one thought-voice entwined around itself within Divigna.

Inseparable and strong, as one, but …

Cold and removed.

Deep chill entered the mindlink, such that I feared my muscles would lock up. The Godblood's warmth countered it, touching me with sunlight as he witnessed the same.

~*This is how it shall be?*~ the Captain asked. ~*You will not speak where Ma'ab ears can hear you.*~

Divigna shrugged, ignoring the subtle scrapes and shifts of other men out of sight.

It may be in your interest to guard our negotiations starting out. The lead Hellhound scanned the streets. *Have you lost your point men?*

Mourn and Deshi.

Fear for its truth tried to creep in, but I focused on my earlobe. The pearls still worked. Surely that meant my bodyguard was alive and could *hear* all this?

~*Will you wait to find out?*~ Isboern countered.

Gradually, I recognized the presence of the Templari among expanding mindlinks along with Tamuril's terrified determination. Krithannia and the Guildsmen had been with us a while. I caught Jael's and Gavin's eyes to bring them in though shied away from drawing Vesram's gaze.

Or, for that matter, the Artist as they appeared in my periphery.

"*Ah, I am late. My apologies.*"

The Chenkyte exited the shrinking shadow of the nearest building, dragging the blooded, contorted bodies of five Hellhounds by their own chains. Daylight illuminated the grisly torture few of us wished to study for long. Divigna frowned in confusion rather than anger as he took in the mess of surreal details. The rest of us merely made room near Gavin.

"*How curious,*" they said, looking up at the wall.

"*What is?*" Gavin prompted after a pause. "*His aura?*"

"*Oh ... agreed, quite enticing. But I mean something near him. Or ... someone.*"

I couldn't tell who else understood the Dead tongue by mindlink; Krithannia did not appear as if she did and Isboern kept his attention on the Eternal Hellhound, encouraging his men to do the same despite the flagrant rise in tension.

"*Someone near him? Who?*"

"*My intended.*"

I squinted. *Intended? For what ... ?*

Before I could ask, Deshi emerged from the other direction ahead of

Mourn, and relief swept over Krithannia and me, spreading quickly to Jael, Tamuril, the Guildsmen, and the Templars.

Our late arrivals drew Divigna's attention, as he accepted the presence of Gavin's strange ally and discounted his captured subordinates in the same moment.

Ah, he said as if events had shifted where expected. *The revenant can bleed.*

Deshi's green-blue flames had gone out, and he wore his Yungian form. The pallid face and simply dressed body bore large, ugly bruises from blunt strikes and red gashes from flying debris, none of which seemed to have bled much. Compared to Gavin's streaks of red and black, these dark crimson stains were contained to their wound sites.

Beside him, Mourn suffered fresh wounds but not as if he'd been caught in a set of grinding chains. His agitation was obvious and persistent through his tail, though his face was like stone.

~What happened?~

The Dragonchild would not speak through the pearls, nor could I sense anything psionically. The circumstances demanded I let it be.

I have something to trade, Divigna said, reaching down behind the courtyard wall to grasp something reasonably heavy.

I blinked. No. Not some *thing*.

Mathias.

"Oh," the Artist crooned. "He ordered a proper presentation of my gift?"

The skin hunter was indeed bound and gagged, with greater restriction of his arms and torso than we had tied Amelda for the simple need of dragging her along as we crisscrossed up the mountain streets.

"Purely pragmatic," Gavin grumbled, drawing baffled glances from Krithannia and Tamuril, "for as many captives as the Ma'ab take."

Meanwhile, I stood beside them as that sank in.

My gift. My intended …

I thought the snarl was Mourn's, but it came from Deshi.

~Trade for what?~ Captain Isboern asked, inviting an answer without eagerness or curiosity. ~Or whom?~

The Godblood focused on Divigna, and abruptly I realized these

505

weren't open thoughts or negotiations. Deshi saw Mathias dangled in front of him but couldn't hear us.

"Sirana," Krithannia whispered. "What do you see?"

~*Uhhh ...* ~

Choose from among yourselves, Divigna offered. *Trade to me Amelda with the revenant and his dagger, or the Deathwalker with his thurible. Should either one enter the courtyard through the gate, and you shall have your betrayer along with the peace to choose his fate.*

The Eternal Hellhound lifted Mathias higher with one arm, until we could see the skin hunter's boots were bound as well. The man's eyes flew wide as Divigna hefted him up and above his head, holding tight to the ropes crossing over his back.

"What is he doing?" the Artist asked.

"Oh, my Lady," Gavin murmured with a shake of his head.

~We do not wish revenge on him enough to make that trade,~ Isboern began.

On the contrary, Mourn interjected, jolting me in his brusqueness, *we should ask the Harrowed. He may well wish it.*

Divigna's slight smile returned as Isboern wrenched blue eyes from the Ma'ab on the wall to focus on the Dragonblood. Around him, the Templars shifted uncomfortably.

~We cannot trade Amelda,~ the Captain reminded. ~A bad idea, you said yourself. Besides, why would Deshi submit himself to the Hellhounds yet again only to see Mathias taken prisoner?~

Mourn didn't answer, but his metallic eyes slid to one side as the Harrowed's face darkened further, his outline flickering as if trying to vanish but failing.

Gavin was the one to speak it. *Mathias would not be taken prisoner, Captain. Several who are present see a different fate for him regardless.*

~But — ~

He has made his enemies. His fate is not in your hands. Do not protect him. Isboern's face tensed. ~Be that as it may, what of Amelda?~

Trade myself and Deshi, Gavin suggested, *instead of Deshi and her.*

Agreed, Mourn rumbled.

No, Divigna declined. *By the will of my gods or by my death. The one *or the other.* ✱

What did he mean?

"What are you saying to them, Herald?" asked the Chenkyte, amber eyes narrowing in suspicion, hands tightening around the barbs on their chains. *"I hope you are not negotiating. The skin hunter is* mine *to woo."*

"I have not forgotten, but you knew there might be competition." Gavin tilted his head toward Deshi. *"One of them is his last victim, blessed by my Lady not a day ago."*

"Well! You weren't there for that, I know. Who then is responsible for raising such a creature?"

Gavin focused on keeping these simultaneous threads of conversation separate. If I'd been smart, I'd have been looking somewhere else when my Deathwalker noted my presence.

"Eavesdropping, are we?" they whispered, sending pure ice up my spine, eyes crinkling in amusement. *"How lovely. You understand us both. You can show me what happened —"*

"Drop him!" Deshi shouted up to Divigna, his voice hoarse and young. "What are you waiting for? Give him to us!"

Divigna frowned, looking disappointed at the rest of us. My eyebrows shot skyward as Isboern and Mourn reached out together.

✱*Sirana?*✱

~*Can you* — ?~

✱*Tell him.*✱

~ — *help him understand?*~

Not yet skilled to handle so many voices, I took my eyes from the Artist and focused on the Harrowed.

Turning my back was a mistake.

Blood-scented fingers grazed the pearl attached to my ear, pinching my earlobe with sharp fingernails.

Breaking the skin.

It hurt so many ways for a wound so small.

~*Owww!*~ I groaned.

✱*Hai!!*✱ Jael cried in alarm.

✱*If you are negotiating for the bound man, Mathias Briar,*✱ the Chenkyte hissed malevolently through the mindlinks, *I have a firm claim by way of my agreement with your Herald of Nyx.*

That is so, Gavin confirmed, his tone neutral.

Isboern's mind held no thoughts at first. His mouth hung open at the abrupt appearance of this outside entity within our mental web.

Divigna's composure cracked, a surprised understanding as he gazed at Mathias with a new wariness.

* I shall be most displeased if I receive no compensation for my work,* the grotesque creature continued. *Unless you want me to return these chains to their former masters? I shall rearrange their bodies in ways most unpleasant, gift them with my tolerance for pain, and leave them for you all to deal with.*

Shit.

~Slow down the threats,~ I tried. The Artist released my throbbing earlobe as I leaned away. ~We're not trying to cheat you. I need to explain to Deshi — ~

Alien eyes glimmered. *Oh? I would enjoy listening, life flower.*

I have changed my mind, Divigna broke in. *Give me the Herald and his thurible, and the revenant can have Briar.*

Before we could respond, the Eternal Hellhound made eye contact with Deshi. "Here," he said aloud. "Take him."

And released Mathias, dropping him on our side of the wall.

~Oh, no,~ Isboern moaned as he shouted aloud, "Deshi! Wait!"

The Harrowed was faster than any living man present with or without his cloak of ghostly flames. He launched at his target before any Human could get their feet under them. Mourn, Jael, and I were next to react, the Artist behind me, their chains jangling, their laugh one of delighted pursuit.

Details came into stark relief as we closed in on the skin hunter. Mathias had fallen a distance twice Mourn's height and landed on the cobblestone, bouncing on his hip before he could roll. No awareness of injury had touched his face before Deshi was there, spinning him onto his back and sitting on his chest.

Their eyes met, and Deshi ripped off the gag from pure force. The action and furious, ghoulish face of the risen Guildsman pulled pained denial from Mathias's lips.

"*Argh!! N-no — !*"

Rough, solid hands gripped his face beneath the jaw, digging in with intent to hurt. Deshi breathed in another groan of discomfort from the interrogator, bliss crossing his face, then forced their mouths together.

The Harrowed started feeding, drawing the air from Mathias's lungs the same as he'd begun with me when he first struggled with his hunger.

No such struggle existed here; Deshi released all control.

He'll kill him if we don't get him off! Jael said.

Oh, we can't have that. The Artist tossed out a chain. *Far too soon!*

Mourn summoned a hooked sword to catch the weapon.

Absolutely not! he snarled, winding up the clattering links with an ease which suggested he'd done it a lot lately. Both his sword and the chain disappeared into his bracers. *I will get him off.*

Cheeky Dragonchild! the Artist laughed, unrattled at the theft of their tool. *Best reach him first!*

With powerful arms, the Dragonblood seized Deshi around his chest before his dark skeleton could begin to show through. With a mighty yank, he wrenched the Harrowed off Mathias, leaving the man gagging and heaving as he struggled to relearn how to breathe.

"*Give him to me!*" Deshi shrieked, blood on his bottom lip where he'd bitten Mathias's mouth. "He mustn't get away! *Not again!!*"

"He will not!" I said, grabbing his forearms as he kicked in Mourn's grasp. "Deshi, let us feed you first!"

He squeezed his eyes shut, wouldn't look at me, and I feared dragging him into the net of mental links in this frenzied state.

"Deshi, please! We need you here! Can you hear me?"

He began to wail, but it lacked his ethereal echo.

Just him. His mortal cry of pain.

Of grief.

"I will quiet the pearls," Mourn said through gritted teeth, "if you will withdraw from the Godblood's links."

I stared. "Go in together?"

Draconic pupils expanded as I watched. "Yes."

"Not without me!" Jael barked, seizing my arm.

I didn't have time to argue, actively shedding the weight of excess presence and voices, none of whom knew how to hold on if they wanted to stay.

None except Willven. He let me go with a last thought.

~*I will shield your bodies. Good luck.*~

Canyon is flooding, Mourn told the pearl-holders. *I will report when it's past.*

A strong, cool hand seized my shoulder at the last moment, and the wound on my ear throbbed around Mourn's pearl.

The traveler of shadows whispered in my ear, their ethereal eagerness plain to hear over Deshi's rising wail. *Not without us, either, life flower.*

"No! Stop!" Mathias protested, managing his first breath. "Let me go!"

Too late.

The daylit streets of Manalar disappeared, turning to twilight before I landed us all …

~*Elsewhere.*~

CHAPTER 37

THE SPACE IN WHICH WE BECAME AWARE *was* FAMILIAR, EITHER TO EVERYONE or someone, but didn't exist anywhere on Miurag.

The black throne of Ice Heart appeared, missing the Black Heart encased in crystal. Neither demon nor shards were there.

I might have panicked but also recognized the shed at Brom's Inn where Gavin had arisen and where Mathias — and I — had questioned and tortured Jacob the Witch Hunter.

And beyond that ... ?

The cavern where the Drider had guarded the Ornilleth prisoner.

I shuddered.

Next to me, Jael bared her teeth against the prison cells underneath the Temple which once held her, alongside the sky-lit quarters where the Archbishop and Inquisitor had questioned her through the night before the first battle. Although she whimpered at the memory, my Sister *knew* she had been fortunate, owing Isboern her reprieve from the worst those men could have done in the days before I found her.

She knew because Deshi and Mathias recognized a private space they'd shared. Closed by brick and Dwarven-hewn stone, the room deep in the undercroft maze of Manalar, one's cries of pain and the other's maniacal laughter never reached the surface.

Mourn had witnessed most of these places before and focused on us. Meanwhile, the hint of his aunt's bedchambers in Vuthra'tern seemed present only because I was looking for it. Like when the To'vah-krav quieted his presence so our gazes passed over him.

All these places — the cages, dungeons, and traps — existed together, seamless and surreal, with a flowing quality contrary to their purpose. This shadow vision presented an imperceptibly grand space, enormous despite the locked doors, the walls at our backs, and hard floors beneath us. Somehow it invited freedom of movement, teasing a possible release from the oppressive memories they contained.

How could that be?

Beside me, the Artist chuckled. Chains rattled in absolute darkness into which I couldn't see.

"Beautiful," they said, spoken as though they were native. "I did not waste my trip answering your Herald's summons."

Gavin.

How had the Deathwalker managed to call an outsider like this? A curiosity for later, I knew, accepting the implicit understanding that others like the Artist were *not* common on Miurag.

Meanwhile, our minds came to full consciousness. Mathias was unbound, not gagged, and stood on his feet. He spun around, near panic as he tried to make sense of where he was. Jael slipped between the skin hunter and the Harrowed while Mourn rested both hands on Deshi's shoulders.

I stood apart, aware as I'd never been that *I* was the one maintaining this strange realm. The anchors holding us together were mine and seemed solid, as if I could touch them. If needed, I could move them like stones lining a brook to redirect a stream of water, for as long as the change might last.

"*There* they are." The Chenkyte focused on Mourn with a smile in their voice. "I'd wondered."

The Dragonblood glanced their way, granting a brief nod with an expression I couldn't read well. Even here, he guarded his thoughts, although what the Artist referred to was obvious.

A pair of large, shadowy wings attached to Mourn's back but did not seem as tangible as the rest of him. A significant sight and not surprising when I thought about our dreams lately, but also something he wished not to speak about here.

I could probe the Chenkyte about why they seemed to *expect* to see wings on the Dragonchild but only at Mourn's expense and privacy.

That was not why we were here.

"Where the fuck am I?" Mathias demanded, trying to mask a keen edge of fear. "Another fucking jail?"

Deshi leaned forward, balling his fists, and Mourn's hands tightened to hold him there. "You cower in the dark with me," the Guildsman hissed. "Rabid dog."

"Yeah, um …"

The skin hunter rallied when he focused on me, as shared memories of us partnering on Jacob's misery overtook the other quarters of torture around us.

The naked Witch Hunter was bound face-down over a table, his body laced with old scars from the punishments of Bictrius. Although Jacob's colorful protests had filled the shed with sustained vitriol, his back arched, his buttocks opening as Mathias leaned in, piercing him swiftly and full length. The jouncing which followed seemed painful enough, an acceptable penance for giving away his desire to an unbeliever.

As Deshi shrank away, Mathias gathered his confidence into a sneering grin. "Might've gone easier on you if you'd talked, boy, but no. Guild secrets and all." He indicated to me. "Can't help but wonder if you would have spilled if I'd been ramming *her* ass in front of you, like Jacob did."

That memory flickered then came alive, mute in all its lurid detail until I recalled my motivation and the questions I'd been asking at the time. Enough to know the Witch Hunters had seen Gaelan, and enough to realize later that Jacob had been railing about what Mourn had done to Manalar's leadership three hundred years ago.

"I needed information," I said calmly, mostly for Deshi. "Nothing forced on my end."

Behind me, the Artist hummed with curiosity. Deshi cursed in Yungian as he turned his head away, Jael incredulous and disgusted while Mathias laughed.

"Jacob had information about Gaelan," I said without regret, catching Jael's focus as I arched my brow disdainfully at the skin hunter. "And I know removing fingers is ineffective for hearing the truth."

"Depends on the truth you seek," the Artist interjected with a chuckle. "But do go on."

Mathias ignored that, scoffing. "Embarrassed, Sirana? We weren't interrogating *anyone* when you wrapped your mouth around my dick. Thought Red Sisters couldn't be shamed that way."

I shrugged. "Your idea. I wore the face of a young boy, if you recall, chosen by the sorcerer who caged you. You didn't want me but were feeling your other pressures. I agree with Deshi, you seemed rabid asking, and in hindsight, not so interesting for *me* as to be worth the trouble which followed. Just regretful."

"Ouch," he mocked. "Easy to say I regret filling your loose ass. I could tell how often you were on bottom with your 'sisters' down in your pit. Wish I'd never dipped in. Jacob was no virgin despite his claims, but at least he couldn't babble about anything *else* while it was happening."

He paused, flashing a cruel grin at Deshi as blood-spattered stone tunnels surrounded us. "*You* were fresh, slant-eye. So enjoyable that you couldn't hide it until it became too much to handle."

The Harrowed lunged, unsuccessful in escaping Mourn's grasp. The underlying wail returned, if not the aqua flames. "You made certain you will have no peace, murderer. Not while you live. Not after you die. Not *ever* again!"

Mathias tried not to flinch as his face flushed with anger. He turned a stubborn gaze upon me. "How did he come back? Gavin wasn't there. The Ma'ab took him. Was it Captain Isboern?"

~*No, that was me,*~ I thought.

Everyone heard it. At that moment, my voice was everywhere.

Mathias paused. He tried a charming smile which wavered as he began to doubt. "*You* did? How? Fucking Hells. Was there *another* silver dagger for you to yank out or something?"

"A distasteful oath," the Artist murmured.

I didn't respond aloud but instead shared the memory of the Yungian's blood-soaked weight pressed onto me after Divigna had tossed him from horseback. All of us felt it, even Deshi, whose eyes recognized that he would soon awaken, whole in spirit if not in body, moments before I had curled my hand around his own blessed dagger, asking if he wanted release.

The young death mage had, and he had *not*.

The Harrowed had received both.

A glimpse of the grey planes dispersed the memories of Brom's shed and the undercroft of Manalar. They didn't return, and Deshi straightened up, bouncing lighter on his feet.

The skin hunter was visibly unsettled by the Artist laughing, shifting their weight while standing on the balls of their feet. Muscles flexed, stark beneath leathery grey skin contorted with hooks and sutures.

"Mathias," they crooned. "The Elf is a magnificently splintered creature, shattered many times yet she keeps reforming with impressive tenacity. Something you have not yet done."

Distracted by the direct address, Mathias missed my discomfort in the Artist describing me so. While not untrue, how was it so obvious to them?

Or so admirable?

"The cracks are invisible to one with *your* mortality," they continued, "for you lack a proper vantage point despite your overlapping fascination with pain. It's not magic from which we sup but the purest will."

Deshi's killer knew better than to appeal to Jael or Mourn, both of whom stood between him and the vengeful spirit he'd created. Apparently, Mathias believed I was open to negotiation despite what I'd shown him.

"Look, Sirana," he began, extending a hand palm down as if he would keep a clinging mongrel from jumping on him. "You know what it's like backed into a corner by power-drunk mages thinking they're in charge of everyone. The more desperate they get, the nastier their methods, and both of us have had to get downright dirty to stay alive. I would have been *long* gone and out of your hair if not for Brom and his daughter. The last thing I wanted was to get in your way, but I didn't have a choice."

"A *choice*?" Deshi echoed, loaded with rage and incredulity.

Mathias projected louder to drown that out. "You wouldn't have come here, either, Red Sister, but others forced your hand, didn't they? You couldn't let go of that cursed dagger, couldn't drop it somewhere. Better to keep it close, know where it is than let it wander off from sight, right? Same thing with enemies." He shrugged with a sanguine smile. "And sometimes ... the pressure gets to you and you need to let it out. You *know* all about that, Red Sister."

~*I know, yes.*~ I glanced at Mourn with his ethereal wings, and at Jael, her eyes brighter and as alive as I'd ever seen them. ~*But I strayed from that path, I think.*~

"Ha!" Mathias barked with derision.

Yet, as I watched Mourn and Jael guard Deshi, the threats of the Temple dungeon and the Bishop's quarters, of every cranny of the Deepearth faded away. Replacing them were scenes of a diverse city by a grand lake, offering music, performers, and astonishing food amid greater cooperation than I'd ever known. The colors grew in vivid intensity as Deshi teared up seeing Yong-wen. Mourn smiled.

"You forgot the people shitting in the alleys," Mathias said, "the starving and beaten kids, the lives and livelihoods bought and sold for coins."

Jael shrugged, gazing curiously at the view new to her. "Have that back home. Not forgotten."

"Pretend all you want," the skin hunter sneered. "I saw the *real* you in that shed. In what you did to Brom. It'll surface when the pressure grows enough." Eyes flicked to Deshi. "Just wait."

The Artist tsked, the veil of tiny hooks and chains chiming as they shook their head. "Oh, Mathias. *That* is your excuse? You've learned enough to become a prodigy of torment, but you keep it in a cell whose lock you must pick yourself?"

"Hey, fuck you, whatever you are," the skin hunter snarled, finally addressing the Chenkyte, who offered a beleaguered sigh.

"Hiding in plain sight," they said, "is a useful, rudimentary skill when starting out. Eventually, one loses that cloak and cannot get it back."

"I said nail it, lunatic. I'm not talking to you."

Amber eyes gleamed. "You should be, Mathias. I am the only one here who would see you ascend by virtue of these chains of your own creation. The rest would see you cease to exist *because* of them."

"An intriguing offer," said a familiar voice which brought Mourn's white spines standing on end. "One I did not anticipate."

My eyes locked onto the black throne, the only feature which hadn't faded with the rest. The demon in crystal was still missing; someone else sat there now.

Lord Indrath. Poised as regal as if the throne belonged to him.

"*Shit*," Jael cursed.

"Ah." The Chenkyte turned and straightened. "The Herald mentioned an Infernal sniffing about my prize. Is that you?"

The Ice Lord waved his hand with nonchalance. "We do not have long to sort this out, traveler."

My heart pulsed with a panic overtaking my irritation seeing him again so soon.

What did he mean? What did his presence suggest about the red rune dagger at my belt in the waking world?

"Then make your offer, devil," the Artist said, "and I shall make mine."

"What *offer*?" the skin hunter demanded, looking between them with mounting horror.

Behind him, ghostly flames started licking Deshi's arms, accelerating the transformation from flesh to light. The disembodied threat came from all around.

"*He doesn't deserve one.*"

Mourn released the Harrowed either by choice or by necessity and before the glow enfolded him. Jael leaped out of Deshi's way and in front of me as Mathias spun around, his face paling, eyes going round.

"No — !"

The revenant cut through him like a battleaxe, air sheering in half as Deshi emerged out the other side. The strike filled our headspace with the power of violent, clapping wings, my mind buffering what it could to maintain the connection. Thoughts gathered cautiously only after Mathias had fallen to his knees, clutching his gut.

A wound.

Unlike with Amelda, I could see the gash Deshi had made in the skin hunter's soul. Vis and Vitas sagged like frayed silk along the edges and the potent, star-like center did not so much bleed as ... lose its light. Tiny motes drifted out, sparkling like sand floating on Sunlight before they faded. As if dying.

No, worse.

Unraveling, ceasing to exist in the recognizable, interwoven pattern that was *him*.

"Stop," Mathias whispered, eyes unfocused and filled with terror. "Stop ... no ... *no* ..."

Indrath stood up out of his throne, staring intently as Deshi turned around. The Harrowed's eyeless skull hid his intent if he meant to swipe again.

"Wait," the Artist breathed, their admiration clear as they opened a palm toward the Harrowed. "Grey Lady's savant, wait a moment. Let me witness this. We may reach an accord, you and I."

Deshi's form sparked and flared, a haunted echo asking, *"Why would I want that?"*

"Because in your ignorance," said the Ice Lord coldly, "and desire for *simple* retaliation, you may open a wound in your world that you do not know how to close." Indrath waited until he had our attention before adding, "Much like the Deathless. Would you make another of his kind, another world-eater from his long-time informant?"

World-eater.

Deshi spared a glance for the Infernal to acknowledge him but looked to me and Mourn, waiting for one of us to speak.

"Wen-yung?" he asked. *"Janshi?"*

"Gav ..." I cleared my throat. "The Deathwalker was warned about world-eaters by his Lady. He acknowledged their danger to me after a trance about Brom."

The Harrowed's flame dampened somewhat, and the Dragonchild spoke next.

"Your Lady has made you a legend, Deshi. You can torment whole cities for as long as you feed your anger, the same as I once did, but is that why you returned?"

The Guildsman hesitated. *"I just want Mathias."*

"That's not what you promised Nyx," I said.

A pause in which Deshi reconsidered. Indrath smiled at me while the Artist observed Mathias pulling himself together, pulling his wound closed with his bare hands. His expression conveyed nothing short of silent agony.

The Chenkyte shuddered with delight, joining him by tightening their blue-grey skin along a stitch line, tugging hard enough to pop a few before extending a grotesque hand touched with blood.

"Mathias. Come with me."

The man threw his body backward in full panic.

The Artist pursued. "I will teach you as my acolyte. I can *show* you what comes next."

Mathias scrambled on hands and heels toward the Lord on the throne, tossing a plea over his shoulder. "You said you could get me out!"

"I could," Indrath agreed, solid red wings lifting with curiosity.

"What would it take?"

"A contract, nothing more."

The skin hunter snarled, eyes snapping between the Harrowed and the Artist. "Could it include dismembering Amelda for dragging me into this?"

"Perhaps."

"What about Sirana?"

"I'm afraid not."

"Fuck me, Lord, come on."

"Not that, either. My other servants might. No children, though."

"Is *that* what you want?" the Artist laughed as Mathias grimaced. "After you've wriggled and writhed in trickery and bargains not yours, you'd make it insolvable! To serve *here*, restricted to the same dot of space alongside your undoing, instead of slipping away like a fish into the great ocean?"

A trapped and coveted man spun around, his face dotted with cold sweat. The vertical gash in his gut continued to close. "Th-that's not … ?"

The Chenkyte swayed closer, standing above him as if to present their crotch for admiration. "Your only way out *then,* my intended, is to be traded as a coin in the Hells for favors. I hope you enjoy the view from inside a war chest. You'd be seeing it *a lot.*"

"That is one way to describe it," Indrath said, lifting one shoulder in a blasé shrug. "Have no fear, Mathias. You'd stay under my protection."

"And meet the Harrowed later for a bored Lord's amusement," the Artist added with macabre cheer and a wave of their hand. "The Grey Lady's new creation is not leaving *this* world any time soon."

Mathias shook his head, staring up at the two debating his fate. "H-how do you know?"

"Ohh, he's … *hmm*, how would *you* put it, Dragonchild?"

"New guardian," Mourn stated.

"Insightful," said the Infernal by way of agreement.

"Guardian?" Deshi repeated.

The Dragonchild bowed his head formally to the Harrowed, whose cautious surprise came through despite the nightmarish visage. Cold flames calmed as his focus finally lifted off the man who'd killed him.

"The Elves are empowered to grant such boons," Indrath said proudly. "When events align."

Deshi turned to me, ghostly head tilting in a transparent suggestion of awe and wonder. It made me want to look away.

I didn't.

~*The pool,*~ I said. ~*The Hellhounds. Gavin and Isboern wait for us.*~

Abruptly, the Harrowed's fires went out, and a young man stood in simple clothing, choosing to bow to his chosen spirits.

"Take him," Deshi said, his nose wrinkling in disgust. "but should we cross paths, I promise nothing."

A wail circled the throne room, chasing the Chenkyte's eager giggle.

"Oh, fuck you all!" Mathias bellowed, clambering off the stairs leading to the throne, the soul gash barely visible. "I'm not a coin to toss around! I didn't pull this dung pile into your laps!"

Mourn drew closer behind me while Jael slid between the skin hunter and me, but Mathias stared past her with raw loathing. "And you, you fickle bitch, I tried to warn you away, didn't I?"

~*Let him,*~ I whispered as my Sister puffed up with insult.

"Well, you deserve what you get. Sarilis and Brom were working together before you ever showed up at the tower, and surprise! I'm sure they *both* know your Lord, here. Talking boons, are we? I bet that the old man is *daring* Gavin to come back."

Indrath sat down, placing his chin in his palm. He looked bored, and I couldn't tell if the accusation was true or not but wouldn't discount it.

"Amelda was stupid, as all cunts are," the man raged, "thinking they can lead any dick around, and so *stupid* to try to pin mine! Made fuck-damned sure *nothing* came easy for that noble bitch, and if you're wondering how she's claiming the Ascended would be at her beck and call if she expires too soon, look to your gorgeous Infernal dogging your every step!"

The Ice Lord smirked. Mourn lashed his tail.

"*He's* gonna slide that dagger in your kidney next," Mathias spat, winding up for his last purge. "And it's gonna be fucking soon or he wouldn't *be* here distracting you and wasting your time! You can't tell when to leave dangerous men alone! You walk into the den *every time* and have the gall to send them after me?! The only one smart enough to do as he pleases *despite* all you fuckers is fucking Divigna!"

The Chenkyte applauded with such enthusiasm their left wrist started bleeding. "Hurrah! Spit that spite and cleanse your palate, acolyte!"

Mathias rounded on them, fist ready to strike. *"Don't call me that!"*

They cackled with a disturbing obsession that stilled his arm. "But you know this is the only way out, Mathias. You *know*. Or you wouldn't have *snapped* all those petty silence spells just now."

The skin hunter panted, shaking with exertion, glancing at the Ice Lord, at me, at Deshi. He said nothing as the tall Artist closed the distance,

521

setting one semi-clawed foot between his boots, looming above him.

"Explore the shadow realm with me," they whispered, veil jingling a soft, alluring song. "I will get you out of this place."

Another glance around. None of us would issue a challenge to hold him. Not even Deshi.

Mathias ground his teeth, his jaw flexing. "Fine."

The Artist tilted their bald head. "What?"

"Get. Me. *Out*," he said, biting out each word.

Amid sudden mad and gleeful laughter, Mourn touched my shoulder.

"Wake up," he whispered.

Yes.

Before either Mathias or Deshi could change his mind.

CHAPTER 38

SUMMER IN PAXIA RETURNED IN THE FULL HEAT OF THE AFTERNOON WITHOUT cloud cover. I couldn't see in the brightness at first but grappled for my belt, confirming Soul Drinker sat in its sheath.

Yes. The coldest thing on my belt, its unnatural chill seeped through leather gloves.

The clopping of hooves, the shuffle and struggle of heavy bodies amid incomprehensibly loud shouting surrounded me as my nose confirmed who was with me.

Mourn, Jael, Mathias, even Deshi and the Chenkyte — everyone but Indrath — amid the sweat, dust, and blood.

~Isboern!~ I called. *~We're back!~*

~Gavin!~ he said with pure urgency. *~They've got Gavin!~*

~Again?!~

~The trade, remember! The other Hounds snared him as soon as we had Mathias. It happened fast, I couldn't shield both.~

Shit.

~Where are you?! I can't see yet!~

~On top of the wall. I can see you. Tami's growing a vine ladder for the others to climb while the Templari try to break the gate.~

~Alright, where in Hells is Divigna?~

I sensed the Godblood's amusement at the oath. ~*He's withdrawn closer to the Temple. The Hounds are dragging Gavin with them.*~

~*Still?*~

~*You weren't long in the trance, and they didn't allow him to volunteer. They just got him over the wall. If you're ready, I can shift my shield into their path and stop them.*~

Do it, Mourn cut in. *I have this. We'll be right there.*

~*Done. Meet you soon.*~

Pearls are open, Krithannia said as communication flowed, the noise by the wall intensifying on both sides.

Peeking from beneath my hood, I made out Jael gripping Deshi's jaw and force-feeding him some of her breath while he trembled. Mourn gripped one slider, his arm outstretched as his eyes swept the street. A man bound near my feet screamed in agony as someone dragged him clear of the Dragonchild's reach.

The Artist lifted Mathias by the Hellhounds' too-familiar weapon, the skin hunter writhing like a giant fish drawn out of a lake. The veiled tormentor crooned with delight, spoke something in the Dead tongue which I couldn't grasp without Gavin nearby. Nonetheless, they displayed all the motions of one finishing up a hunt.

~*Wait!*~ I said, reaching out through my pearl, my earlobe throbbing and bleeding from where they'd torn it. ~*You missed some chains, Artist. They've got the Herald.*~

Amber eyes narrowed, glowing sinisterly. I watched them consider calling the deal done with payment received.

You can't leave the Arena yet, traveler! Mourn snarled, the blade song slowing. *You may as well complete your bargain with the Herald and keep the Grey Lady amenable toward you on Miurag.*

The Chenkyte sighed behind their veil, bracing to lift Mathias and throw him over one shoulder. The skin hunter had injured something in his fall for certain, a shoulder or a joint.

Very well, they answered. *Show me.*

I spotted Tamuril crouching by the wall to my left, not far below Is-boern atop it. The Godblood had been watching over her and us while the

Druid built her net of clinging vines rooted in between the cobblestones. The Captain focused on Ma'ab protests beyond our sight.

~*This way,*~ I said, leading us to Tami's ladder with Jael dragging Deshi and Mourn guarding our rear. The blonde Naulor jumped with a shriek as the Chenkyte slipped in front of me first to grip the sturdy plants with one blue-grey hand.

"Sorry, sorry," I said, shifting into her view and waving my hand to draw her attention. "We need to use this. Thank you."

Tamuril made immediate room, managing a nod to me as the Artist passed by her, hauling a constantly groaning Mathias with disconcerting ease. I followed them up and over, Jael and Deshi staying close behind me.

"Where is Amelda?" Mourn asked the Druid as he reached the ladder last.

"With Krithannia and the Templars."

I wondered why he asked Tamuril instead of Krithannia herself through the pearls but then remembered Divigna could hear everything through them. Meanwhile, the Manalari were working to break down the gate, wearing too much heavy armor to slip over the wall like us. When my boots touched the courtyard, I found someone else was missing.

Vesram.

The Sathoet had likely followed Gavin and his captors, but we had no way to communicate with him or spot him if he didn't want to be seen.

Meanwhile, Indrath was around here somewhere watching us.

Goddess, don't let the ceiling fall in on this.

~*Hurry,*~ Isboern said openly, repositioning his relic as if to mirror his psionic shield. ~*They're trying to go below ground. I've slowed them but can't see the opening to block it.*~

"I'll get them," Deshi said, his form wavering once his bare feet touched the stone.

The Chenkyte spoke to him; it sounded like a protest or a command. The Harrowed understood although the rest of us didn't. At least Deshi didn't look insulted as he shifted his focus and his form, launching forward.

What did you say? Mourn asked, tail lashing. He couldn't hide his concern but chose to guard me and Jael rather than run after Deshi. Meanwhile, Jael drew both her borrowed swords, covering my other flank.

Mathias's new mastress hummed, lifting a free hand to summon three chains out of the nearest shadows. Loops of metal links wrapped the Artist's prize into a gouging, protective cocoon, the layers so thick an errant arrow was unlikely to breach it. The Chenkyte next stashed the skin hunter in the branches of the nearest tree where Mathias had a decent view to watch the performance in the courtyard. I was certain this was deliberate.

I said, the Artist answered Mourn at last, *that a 'guardian' should accept his role and find someone to guard. The Ma'ab hounds and their chains are mine.*

They stalked forward, one polydactyl hand held up with fingers curled, arm pointed downslope rather than ahead. Their presence withdrew from the pearls, vivid eyes intent on where the Harrowed had made an abrupt distraction of himself with this last Hellhound pack.

Deshi swiped at and bounced around Ma'ab who were well informed to keep out of his reach. This time the Harrowed showed restraint, his focus on forcing them to drop the chains wrapped around Gavin, who lay on the ground at the end of a long trail of black blood. If I didn't know my Deathwalker so well, I might have thought he'd dropped unconscious from the blood loss and vicious mishandling.

Instead, I was certain he was in a trance.

~What's his aura like?~ I asked, nudging Mourn without specifics.

The Dragonchild glanced that way but stayed alert, the hum of his blade dampening the sense of threat around us.

Active, he said by way of understatement. *He's not down.*

So I thought.

To our right, the Templars cast a collective spell which ruptured their own Temple's gate, pressing it inward and cracking the lock. Unfortunately, the Hellhounds had set either thunderstones or something worse at the base, which were set off by the mage force.

Light and sound enveloped our allies, sharp pieces of rock and metal darting past in my periphery, some deflected by Mourn's magic. I covered my ears and closed my eyes too late, deafened and blinded as urgency filled the courtyard and Mourn's alarm filled the pearls.

Krithannia!

I ... I can't ... !

Normally calm yet commanding, her voice seemed far away and distracted. The pearls' connections seemed tenuous, calls of concern from Wolf and his Hands distorted or dropping before a complete thought bridged the gap.

Is she ... ?

Where are ... ?

Watch out! The streets ... !

What in the fuck is hap — ??

"Shuiblith chikohk!" the Dragonblood snarled, aching to be in two places at once.

Before we could think of splitting up, however, a ball of chains holding ten screaming men rushed past the staggered Templars and through the open gate, spattering them with dust and blood. Taut lines of torture pointed toward the Artist, dragging the heavy Ma'ab as if hauled by a team of unseen battle horses.

The Hellhounds surrounding Gavin paused, their attention pinned to what was barreling down on them. They broke formation, scattering in a retreat attempt as the Artist's hoarse, maniacal laugh echoed off the Temple spires.

The Harrowed's flames vanished in a vapor, and Deshi used two Human hands to seize the tarnished chains, pulling the unresponsive Deathwalker behind a raised plant bed for cover.

~The Guild Hands have Krithannia,~ Isboern reported to me, running along the top of the wall with impressive agility for an armored warrior with shield. ~They have vials. I will aid them and my men.~

Mourn heard this through me, squeezing my shoulder as he tried to avoid using his pearls. *Confirmed. We will find Divigna.*

And Vesram, I hoped.

~Be careful,~ the Godblood said. ~Wait for us if you must. We will join *you soon as possible.~*

The blond man descended to the far side of the wall without using the shield's light-jumping ability, floating out of sight by the strength of his will. Abruptly, I understood how he'd kept his balance moving so quickly a moment ago.

I wanted to learn to do that.

"Behind me," Mourn said in Davrin, calling his second slider into his other hand, brandishing both. *"All senses open."*

"Check," Jael said, covering our rear with myself in the middle as the Dragonblood led the way.

We crossed the open courtyard, weaving through trees as the Artist used the open space to ensnare their final catches and bring them together with the others. A total of fourteen Hellhounds, five of which must have been captured from before I'd known where they were.

The Ma'ab bled from numerous wounds but were recognizable, all visibly exhausted and in pain, yet their bodies not as torn up as I expected from being dragged through the city streets wrapped in their own spiked chains. Their elite mage tattoos made that much of a difference, but at least none seemed ready to explode.

The Chenkyte took their time, anchoring a few chains to a broken window high above us. I recognized the spot where the Archbishop had pushed the Inquisitor out the window, and where I'd finally found Jael, alive but comatose after what the death mage had done to her aura.

Using a second anchor point, the shadow traveler applied leverage I couldn't see to hoist and secure the massive heft of many large men into a macabre design which struck me both as insects writhing in a spider's web and constellations in the night sky.

The disquieting chorus of distress grew louder as finer manipulation of the chains either positioned limbs at angles they were not intended to go, or the barbs dug deeper with gradual constriction to puncture tough skin at irregular intervals.

The Artist turned toward us as we got closer. *Well? How is this?*

We hadn't stopped searching for the leader of these men, but Divigna was nowhere to be seen.

You sense no other chains, Mourn said, a statement rather than a question.

I own all upon this mount but one, they answered, motioning toward Deshi working to disentangle Gavin. *The new guardian is in the way, but not for long.*

~Divigna doesn't have a chain?~ I asked, to which the Artist shrugged.

Apparently not, Mourn rumbled.

~And he left the rest to suffer and be defeated.~

A nod. *He's the only Ma'ab free on the mount.*

As the Herald is not present to answer my question, the Chenkyte interrupted, *why don't you tell me, Dragonchild? What is required for me and my acolyte to leave this Arena?*

The half-blood's tail stiffened, curving back and forth low to the ground. *You won't stay?*

Scar-laced arms folded over a grafted chest, pressing a line of deep sutures. *Why?*

Golden eyes narrowed. *What was it the Herald asked of you? Precisely.*

Another smile behind that veil. *To assist in disarming Ma'ab enemies of their chains and other weapons in a homebound conflict. Have I not done this?* After a pause filled with the collective groaning of captured Ma'ab above our heads, the Chenkyte added, *The tattoos which protect their skin and grant impressive endurance are not weapons.*

Agreed, Mourn granted.

And if your last Ma'ab was clever enough to drop his chain in my presence and not pick up another, and he is the one who's been … oh, how to say it? Tampered with by one of the Ascended, then I can only point out the deal never specified I must defeat every Hellhound. I am to begin teaching rather than fighting.

The half-blood's tail thumped. *Hm. So be it.*

Behind us, the able-bodied Templari and Guildsmen finally entered the courtyard, reluctant to approach the macabre display of bleeding men. Several Manalari murmured prayers and warding signs.

"*Profanota!*" Sir Erik bellowed with deep dismay as his Captain and Tamuril came to the front of the fighters, supporting a limping Krithannia.

Isboern bowed his head to acknowledge his lieutenant and approached us ahead of the Naulor, closing the distance with purpose clear upon his face.

"You must take those men down," he said to Mourn and the Chenkyte, blue eyes and chin up. "This desecrates our Temple, and we will not stand to let it linger."

Although Gavin's ally didn't understand the language, they chuckled and hummed me a thought. *No appreciation of the Art? A surprisingly common contradiction among war-makers.*

It is the location, Mourn said placidly. *Their place of worship.*

Is it? Worshipping whom?

Brother Sun. Of Miurag. Once the Grey Maiden, and perhaps her return.

Oo. Interesting.

~Will you please take the Ma'ab down?~ I asked, aware of the unrest spreading among the Manalari.

I will. The Chenkyte's eyes flickered slyly. *The moment Mathias and I are allowed to leave the Arena.*

I shared this with Isboern in a brief meeting of eyes, and the Godblood turned to Mourn. ~I don't understand. What arena? The mountain? The battleground?~

The Dragonblood sought out Deshi's progress, who was on the cusp of freeing Gavin. Only a few moments had passed.

"What's taking so long?" Jael whispered in Davrin, not part of the mind links and watching for trouble.

"Negotiations," I murmured.

"Again? Why?"

"The body-weaver wants to leave."

"So let them! When are we going after Divigna?"

A good question.

"Once he comes after us," I murmured, hearing her grumble as Mourn answered Isboern's question in full.

The Arena, he said, *is a magical barrier created by the Red Dragon of Manalar. He summoned it the moment you and the Ma'ab clashed at the wall. It does not prevent the comings and goings of all who live in this world but obstructs those from other realms, especially those aligned with the Eternal War. The Arena has been in place ever since our war started, Captain. It comes down upon a decisive victory, no matter who triumphs.*

Isboern's pulse beat in his throat. ~But ... we've seen no red brother of yours, legend.~

This does not matter. He sees us. Mourn raised a blade to indicate the death mages. *Only Outsiders invited by a native can enter. They likewise cannot or sometimes will not leave without involvement of either that native or the Dragon himself.*

I thought so, the Artist said with a sigh. *A good thing the Herald comes to his senses. Your 'Red Brother' does not seem talkative.*

The To'vah does not talk because he Sleeps. Golden eyes glinted as Mourn kept a wary watch. *Much better for us if he does not Wake in the middle of this fight.*

If you say, Dragonchild. No doubt it would be exciting.

Mourn chuffed as Deshi tossed the chain aside, his hands smeared with glossy, black blood. Gavin rolled over, bracing to push himself up.

I frowned at my unbidden thought. ~Who invited the Ice Lord?~

Mourn's tail flicked in annoyance, but he answered. *My guess is the Deathless. I witnessed the Infernal negotiating with the Grey Guardians once we sent him back to the Desert. I wager that's why he has enjoyed free movement in Manalar through this.*

The Grey Guardians. Gavin's mother, Ada. The Deathwalker warrior, Houda. The bulky and mysterious Oskar, and the little wasp girl. Why would they negotiate with an Infernal? Or, like me, did they not have much choice when push came to shove?

The Artist left without another thought, strutting toward Gavin with an arm outstretched and a snap of their fingers. Disconcertingly, I recognized Mathias's scream as he became unhooked from the tree in which he'd been stashed to be dragged along the ground much like the Hellhounds strung up like glistening red fish in a net.

That *could* have held my attention, but Gavin regained his feet with Deshi hovering to catch him as if he might faint. With his hood down, the Deathwalker's skin wavered perpetually between light grey and charcoal as the Sunlight and shade shifted together toward midday. Simultaneously, the hardened, black growths I'd noted at the redoubt — on his spine and ribs beneath his robe — had spread to visible areas. Sharp growths of pneuma flint created a jagged outline along his jaw, shoulders, and arms, his fingernails growing longer and pointed.

The Chenkyte bowed, presenting the crimson bundle containing the skin hunter and unwrapped it with a jangling flourish, leaving the raked, shocked man barely standing, his arms bound to his torso with Ma'ab rope. Deshi sneered.

Gavin's mercenary motioned outward, speaking the Dead tongue as they likely repeated the request to clear their deal. My Deathwalker listened, said nothing at first. He raised his chin and craned his neck, settling ice-blue eyes on the Artist's gruesome display above his head. I couldn't tell what he thought about it, but Isboern had lost patience, especially in front of his men.

The Captain left Krithannia standing next to Tamuril and Mourn, signaling his men to stay on guard as he strode alone toward the meeting of the tortured.

Krithannia poked my arm, whispering urgently. "Translate for him. Please. Don't let Willven force himself to read those thoughts."

Ah, shit.

I took off after him.

"*Hai!*" Jael called.

"*Come on!*" I retorted.

She ducked out after me, Mourn and Krithannia remaining in place.

"Wait!" I called. "*Willven!*"

He paused, just as he'd promised. Golden shield flashing, the God-blood turned to me, accepting a mindlink.

~Allow me?~ I asked, hesitant in the face of his determination. *~They can understand me. I will ask them to remove it.~*

~Please do.~ The Captain continued his approach. *~Tell them to take the Ma'ab down **now**. Before I do.~*

Gavin's piercing gaze focused on me, responding to my silent plea.

~Please, I must understand the Dead tongue!~

He opened to me.

"I have it, Herald!" the Chenkyte crowed in a strangely happy enlightenment. *"Yes, I believe I do. This bold young man coming to us must be Brother Sun's champion."*

"Correct," Gavin answered, clearly not a new idea to him.

"The Brother of Light. The Child of Dragons. The Sleeping God." They peered around. *"Are the Sisters' champions here? I haven't seen them."*

Sisters' champions?

The Herald hesitated. *"I don't believe so."*

I shook my mind free of distraction, projecting my thoughts through otherworldly vibrations. *~The Ma'ab must come off the Temple, or the Templars will do it themselves.~*

The Artist stiffened. *"Not wise to destroy a great work before its creator."*

~You have time to bring them down, but their patience thins quickly.~

"I do not fear them, child."

~But why resist and sour your exit? You've played, you have your acolyte. You've impressed me, but they don't appreciate your work, anyway.~

"Hmph." The Artist folded their arms. *"Vulgarians."*

"I release you," Gavin interjected, making eye contact with Isboern, *"Artist of the Exquisite Host. You have fulfilled my call and received payment in full. Are we agreed?"*

The Chenkyte admired Mathias as the man quivered with eyes on the ground, his face covered by brown, blood-stained hair. *"Oh, we are agreed!"*

"Then reclaim your chains," my Deathwalker said. *"Those are yours. Leave all the bodies but one, your new acolyte."*

"All? Do you need them?"

"I would study their hides."

"Excellent," they cooed. *"Dead or alive?"*

"Dead. They shall return to their masters soon enough."

"Done."

A few seconds had passed from Captain Isboern's arrival to the moment his Templars witnessed fourteen twisted Ma'ab brought down to the courtyard in a hammock of chains. The Hellhounds' weapons slithered about, looping around thick necks. Then, with a dramatic jerk of the Chenkyte's fist, one neck snapped. Many of us winced, realizing the gleeful rounds of execution would continue, one-by-one, as the Artist cackled.

Once the display was gone, the last of Divigna's men dead, and no additional blood had been spilled at the base of the Temple, I asked Willven awkwardly, ~*Um … better?*~

The Godblood's expression struck me with an emotion so deep as to be nameless. He whispered a private thought.

~*What can I say, Sirana? I long for this to be over.*~

~*One Ma'ab left, Captain. Just one more.*~

"*A pleasure as always, Herald of the Grey Maiden.*" The Artist took a bow which somehow included me and Mourn. "*You've all been intricately enjoyable hosts. Should you have need, recall the Artist of the Exquisite Host and invite us into this realm.*"

Gavin bowed in return, placing a flint-clawed hand on his chest. The thurible wobbled at his waist. "*I shall on behalf of my Lady.*"

"*Excellent. Come, 'Mathias.' We shall discover your new name after you've been spread on a proper rack as my new canvas.*"

The Artist dismissed the majority of their chains but used two to sever Divigna's ropes then wrap around the skin hunter's limbs, forcing him to walk, to follow after the Chenkyte.

"*N-no, no, wait,*" Mathias pleaded, speaking the language of the Nexus without realizing it. "*I … I've changed m-my mind! I want a different deal! Free me and we'll talk!*"

The Artist paused their progress, turning as the deepest shadows behind Gavin opened into a long corridor. They leaned closer to their prize.

"*Do you not understand?*" they said. "*You are free. You've slipped every restriction this world holds for you. I look forward to the expression of your soul when you see it.*"

"*I'm not g-going anywhere with a revolting bitch like you!*"

"*Very well, mortal. Let us start closer to where you are.*"

Another chain lashed out of the long corridor, snatching the leg of one of the Ma'ab bodies. The Chenkyte hauled the corpse closer, lifted it upright with boots scraping the ground, and spun to embrace it.

Stunned, we watched as the veil parted and wrapped around the Ma'ab's jaw, digging in and tightening until the two faces were brought together. With a sickening crack and several snaps, the lower jaw of the Hellhound's body came loose, disappearing behind the lines of slithering hooks like it had been eaten.

Once the Chenkyte lifted their bald head, however, the strong, masculine jaw poked out from the sides of their veil, and the larynx bulged in a noticeably thicker neck as they turned.

"Is this better, my acolyte?" they said with a voice so deep I barely recognized it.

Mathias stared in mute terror.

"Charming."

The Artist turned around, confidently leading them into the opening I wasn't certain was real at first. The depth extended farther than Mount Sonai itself, the darkness greater than anything I'd experienced in the Deepearth. Once Mathias and the Artist had gone deep enough, the Human's moans echoing in the eerie distance, a stray gleam from the Godblood's shield wove across the shadowy door, appearing to mend it.

A blink.

Before us stood nothing but the blank, unmarred stonewall of the Temple, its courtyard sprinkled with Hellhound bodies. Long moments passed before anyone spoke; in the silence, someone vomited. Mourn, Krithannia, and Tamuril drew closer.

~*The Arena is still up?*~ Isboern asked, his jaw set.

Yes, Mourn said. **But the Red allowed them to pass through. The Artist is gone from this battlefield.**

With a nod, the Captain made sure his men were alright and standing alert, passing a psionic order telling the Templari to spread out and secure the Temple entrances.

"We must find Divigna," he said aloud.

"And Vesram," I added.

Gavin frowned, a shard of pneuma flint pulling farther through parched skin. "Where is Amelda? The Sathoet had her last. Did he take her with him?"

Krithannia grimaced. "No ... He threw her at us as he scaled the wall after you. We lost sight of him and hadn't the time to secure her before the explosion. She pulled free and escaped amidst the disruption. Many of us were hurt, and I couldn't stop her."

"I missed that," Isboern admitted. "I didn't realize it until I'd helped to mend the worst of the wounds."

"I am certain she ran downhill toward the Guildsmen," Tamuril said nervously. "They will recapture her."

"We will see," Mourn grumbled. "Do not underestimate her desire to see us all harmed."

And claw back Soul Drinker.

"Vesram wasn't visible when Deshi ran to help Gavin," I said.

"Went after Divigna," Jael countered with confidence.

Most of us agreed, but no one suggested what the Sathoet intended to do should he catch up with the Eternal Hellhound.

"So," Isboern murmured, "now our opponent has neither of what he asked for? Not the Herald and his thurible, not Amelda, the Harrowed, and his blessed dagger."

Krithannia withdrew Deshi's weapon, offering it to him. "Here, just in case."

The Yungian accepted with both hands and a bow of his head, his face pale, tense, and unearthly as the blue in his irises glowed.

"Amelda seemed sure I shouldn't use Soul Drinker on Divigna," I said. "She claimed I could destroy both, and that it might ensnare me, too."

"I could see that," Gavin said, "but it doesn't explain Vesram's claim about needing the Black Heart to defeat him."

Mourn shook his head, showing a rare confusion. "Something doesn't align in this chain of thought. Not enough to risk either Sirana or another wielder of the relic to try."

"Agreed. We need to find Vesram."

I sensed a subtle, shared chagrin. Events had rolled in constantly to where none of us had remembered to ask him, and the former slave had a bad habit of disappearing on us.

Tamuril gasped, green eyes staring at nothing. "I see the lead Hellhound!"

"Where?" Isboern and Krithannia asked together, Mourn's tail conveying alarm as both Godblood and Dragonchild shifted to better shield us from ambush.

"O-or, *Pilla* sees him." Tami gazed at what little we could see beyond the spire-topped roof of the Temple. "He is on the path to the watchtower." She swallowed. "He carries Amelda on his back."

"Awake?" Mourn asked.

"Yes. She seems willing."

Fuck.

"Vesram?" Gavin asked.

The Druid shook her head. "Unseen."

The Captain exhaled. "Would you ... stay in the Temple?" He glanced at Krithannia as Tamuril's lips opened in protest. "And with Reprisal and *Hata Ri* while I take the Templari?"

The dark-haired Naulor narrowed storm-grey eyes in thought while her blonde sister waved a hand toward me, trying to articulate a reasonable argument.

"Sirana must follow commands whether we like it or not," Mourn interjected, saving me the throat-strangling attempt. "We will protect her. It will be easier if we know you are not also amid combat on the mountaintop."

"We have Pilla and the pearls," Krithannia granted, settling into reason as she stood with a reluctant Tamuril. "We are not fighters. There are other tasks we can do to help than hover near the danger, including watching for any doubling back."

"But ... Willven," Tamuril began.

The blue-eyed man smiled with a touch of shyness. "You've always kept watch on me from a distance. Keep watching for us, as no other in my life has."

Her cheeks bloomed pink, and all she could manage was a worried nod before offering me a hand-sized travel pouch and waterskin. "At least eat something?"

A good idea I accepted right away, for my stomach cramped at the mere mention.

"On the move," Mourn suggested.

"Sure." I poured nuts and dried fruit into the cup of my palm before tilting them into my mouth.

"Don't choke," Gavin said, peering at the top of the mount.

I smirked, finished chewing, and swallowed.

"I know which way he must have gone through the Temple," Isboern said.

"As do I," Mourn growled. "Let me check for thunderstones or other traps ahead of you."

A wince as he summoned the Templari. "Gladly."

"Wh-what will you do when you catch him?" Tami asked.

Many of us exchanged glances.

"We will do what he wants us to do," Gavin answered, his irises flickering in and out. "Put him down in a manner that doesn't betray his gods."

Captain Isboern led us through the Temple, circumventing the sanctum but climbing stairs in our path to reach the upper rear exits of the city. He and his men scanned the large, dirty boot prints over the fine rugs and flooring, their nerves on edge as damage to the architecture and adornments showed them how deeply the enemy had explored these halls.

Mourn, farther ahead and alone, cleared the way of threats. Draconic murmurings seeped through my pearl — a lighter tone, familiar but out of place for his seriousness of the last several days.

~Mourn?~

*I am well. Divigna did not have time to be elaborate on his surprises, and I *believe Vesram beat us to them.* ⋆

Key doorways had been set with eruptive thunderstones or spells throughout the wings of the building — those we must pass through regardless — but according to Mourn's nose, the Sathoet had either set them off or stolen them. I breathed deeply against a trembling belly, having to trust the Priestess's son would show himself when necessary.

The Sun was past its zenith, a warm wind rising as we left the Temple and made our way through the open gate in the highest wall. This led us to the rough path I couldn't call a road as it wouldn't support a horse-drawn cart, laid with an irregular stairway of broad stones wide enough to allow three men to climb together.

"Are we dead certain there are only two Ma'ab waiting up there?" Jael asked me.

A good question, one we relied on Tamuril's familiar to keep us informed should that assumption change.

"So far," I grunted, pulling a draw of water from my skin as I climbed another step.

The Templari armor made such noise, and the men worked harder to climb this final leg to the peak that I thought it a reasonable concern we'd be too tired to fight. Isboern tried to slow them down, but even his pace crept up its intensity as Tamuril confirmed time and again that Pilla had spotted none but Divigna and Amelda enter the watchtower.

⋆*And they haven't come out,*⋆ Krithannia said.

We were painfully aware the Hellhound could hear this, but he said nothing. If Mourn and Isboern thought this might cause him to grow overconfident to send hidden forces to meet us, we crossed the halfway point without any indication of barrier or resistance.

Mourn soon returned to ask the Godblood a verbal question. "Are there hidden passages or tunnels underneath that tower?"

"Some partial," Isboern panted. "Recent, unfinished. To get our watchers to different sides of the Mount unseen. But they don't reach the road. This is the only way up and down."

The half-blood grunted, eyeing our path skeptically when Pilla screeched from high up.

We see Amelda, said Krithannia, *and … I'm not sure if it's Vesram or Divigna.*

Must be Divigna, Mourn said, moving out in front. *I can sense my pearl ahead, about that close. I will clear the way for you to come behind me.*

We reached the three-quarters mark and the final bend below a higher outcropping of which we were wary. The Dragonchild passed under, saw the other side, and signaled the way with his sliders. Isboern and the Templari moved first, faster and spreading out while Gavin and Deshi stayed with Jael and me.

A boot scuffed the rock.

The only warning before something I could not see landed heavily next to me, crushing my chest in a two-armed bear hug.

"Alraid majua," the Ma'ab whispered, tattoos glowing green and blue as the muscled arms which held me appeared before my eyes.

A thunderous wave burst out in all directions upon the mount's trail, deafening me and shoving everyone away from Divigna with simultaneous force. My Sister shrieked, the Deathwalker and the Harrowed grunted, and all three started rolling down the laddered stone steps. Armored men toppled and knocked into each other, skidding off the beaten path and grasping for purchase. Mourn and Isboern had fallen off the bend; I couldn't see them. Were they alive?!

I could draw not one breath yet screamed in my mind.

~No!~

The Hound of the Physician seized me, lifted me off my feet, and sped into the brush away from the last road on Mount Sonai.

CHAPTER 39

WOODY BRUSH SPLINTERED FROM THE SPEED OF THE HELLHOUND'S PASSAGE, the sound strangely muffled. A broad, hard shoulder pressed uncomfortably into my swelling gut; I writhed to counter the jostling against my womb.

My spiders clung to me with every leg so as not to fall. They *wanted* to skitter away and bite him, but I forbade it. Their fangs wouldn't pierce his enchanted skin, and he might kill them.

I tried to breathe. *He* won't *kill me ...*

For better or worse, he wanted me alive.

No pressure points which had worked on Kurn worked on his sire. At least, not in the small pauses I had in between disorienting knocks to my head with the fat end of a stripped branch. His strokes were never hard enough for me to lose consciousness but readily disrupted attempts to send a message through my pearl.

Mourn. Isboern.

Jael.

Gavin and Deshi ...

They'd all been falling from the force of the thunderclap when I lost sight of them.

Let them be alright.

Mourn had sensed his pearl ahead of us at the watchtower, not right on top of us. Divigna might have given the token to Amelda as a decoy, an idea that flitted across my blurred thoughts with the hope that the Dragonblood could follow *my* pearl to wherever Divigna took me. The Hellhound must know he had little time unchallenged, so what would he do after taking this risk to abduct me from the others?

I waited until he found cover, entering one of those partial tunnels Isboern had mentioned. Intense heat and brightness broke, the relief undeniable. The Eternal Hellhound wanted me cognizant and less distracted for whatever would come next. As did I.

The urge to escape or fight with lethal intent had vanished by the time he set me down, my fear and anger quenched whether I thought it wise or not.

The Priestess …

The Valsharess had sent me to find her, and here she was.

"What is left of her," Mourn said.

Even Indrath had tempted the Davrin essence inside, offering a deal if Kreshel could obtain Soul Drinker from me. The Wargan had tried. I had not dared.

"What do you want this time?" I asked in Davrin.

A glimmer of recognition in those dark Northern eyes, but ultimately, he said, "Speak Trade."

I obliged him, unwilling to delay until we could be interrupted. "What do you want, Divigna?"

He tried to catch my gaze, but I kept drifting, tracing the innumerable black marks on his skin.

"To recover the soul blade and give you both to my gods," he said without emotion. "To let them choose what's best for our people."

A chilling but practical answer. I imagined the Prime Red Sister saying something like that, yet I didn't believe it was the only answer. Kreshel couldn't speak his true intentions any more than I could but he would accept the stated outcome.

I could not.

"How would trading for the Deathwalker and his thurible help with that?" I asked.

Divigna chased my eyes as I studied a dry shrub growing between two rocks at the tunnel exit. The stone seemed to weave in a mirage, and I blinked. Had I seen something, or wasn't it there?

The deep voice rumbled above me. "The heretic's knowledge is plenty. His unfettered existence an insult."

"You suggest a fettered existence would redress it?"

"It always does for our gods."

I inhaled through my nose, catching a whiff of someone familiar. Not Mourn, though. "And the revenant? His dagger drew your blood."

"The screamer is of great interest to the Physician."

I swallowed, glancing up. "Does she know that already?"

His mouth stretched into an uncanny smile, not a single crease or crinkle showing at the corners of his eyes. He would have answers to all my questions if I insisted on using *only* our tongues, but I could expect no surprises and gain only worries.

My heartbeat pulsed into my ears as Divigna craned his neck toward the exit.

"Vesram," he said. *"Anashi bik ral."*

The Sathoet hissed, his outline showing. "Ssspeak Trade."

Divigna paused, grasping as I did that the half-blood had been listening from the start. Whatever they said next, Vesram wanted me to understand.

"You will return with me," said the Hellhound with confidence. "We will bring her with us. We will confess everything."

I read the demonblood's expression; the temptation to accept *was* there. Vesram had spent more time with the Ma'ab than with his mother under the Valsharess. I'd seen nothing but forced loyalty when it came to the Davrin, against which this Sathoet had explicitly rebelled just hours ago.

The Sathoet might agree.

My chest tried to freeze, but I forced myself to speak. "You won't hold me long, Divigna. They will track you every step."

The Eternal Hellhound didn't argue; he didn't seem to care. Meanwhile, Vesram struggled to form his own words.

"Will … *not* go back with you," he said, a surprise and a relief to me, though my captor dismissed it out of hand.

"If I return," the Ma'ab rumbled, "so must you. As it has always been."

"Not thisss time."

Another pause.

"You will only make it worse, demon," said the Wargan. "Our gods can recover true your name from me." A fist tightened at his side. "They can *will* me to remember, and they will summon you."

Vesram's grey eyes held steady on us. "Not what Ada sssaid."

Divigna's lips tightened as if *that* was something worthy of his concern. "The heretic is not strong enough," he said slowly, as if the words needed an extra push. "Or he would have purged the silver and risen the Roh'ghast off the ground. He would not have needed the Chenkyte to defeat my Hounds."

"She never sssaid he would be alone." Bare and clawed feet shifted on grit as Vesram held his eyes on me longer. "*They* are strong enough."

Divigna glanced down, shaking his head to disagree. "Wishful visions. They are not enough to kill me."

"*Wargan!*"

I jumped and barely avoided blinding myself by looking at the exit.

"*Wargan, yujboni!*"

I knew that voice. *Amelda.*

Vesram's mane lifted along his spine as he snarled in annoyance. Divigna's dark Ma'ab eyes slid in her direction, out and up, then returned to me as I dared to look at his branded, hairless head.

"She may lead them here," I said.

"Or she may fall." The Hellhound shrugged with indifference. "None of you dare to kill her."

How I wished we did.

"Do you know what happens if we do?"

"I know what she said would happen," he replied.

Not the same thing, but worth noting. Vesram seemed interested, like even he didn't know.

"Tell me what she said."

"You cannot change it, Elf."

I shrugged. "I am duly helpless. Tell me anyway."

Divigna's mouth curled at one corner as Amelda called again. "She pledged to be a Ley beacon in her father's place, should the Deathless be defeated."

Beacon?

"What is a Ley beacon?"

"What it sounds like. A mage soul that helps our gods peer through the maelstrom of the Temple pool's disruption."

Twin pricks of excitement and dread touched my heart. Did he mean the Physician *didn't know* what had happened here?

Not yet.

Divigna had all but assured the Ascended would not claim Io'sulta unless they arrived to do it themselves. Surely, they would punish him for that should he return, yet he could not or would not choose Amelda's fate. At the wall of the Temple, Divigna had bartered with *us* to decide.

"By the will of my gods, or by my death. The one or the other ..."

Were the Ascended considered Outsiders to the Red Dragon? Had his Arena blocked the liches' direct interference thus far, or was that why none of them had joined the army on a critical conquest in the first place?

I wasn't certain. I knew so little about them, their motives, or their capabilities. I also knew nothing beyond what Mourn had said about Manalar's Sleeping Dragon. Not everything lined up in what had happened thus far, and I knew better than most how centuries-old sentients pushed events in ways which had no clear purpose in the present. Not until much later.

Even Divigna counted in that long game.

Regardless, Amelda *had* bartered with an Infernal following me, who was also involved with her father's creation. She would throw aside the veil in the event of her death, giving the Ascended a pathway in or at least a clear view of what had happened.

Whatever way the Red Dragon might see this, Amelda had granted an invitation to her gods.

"*Do not underestimate her desire to see us all harmed,*" *Mourn said.*

"*Wargan!*"

Three subtle draws of air filled the space after Amelda's call. No one answered, and Divigna gazed at me in that cave much as he had from across the stream as I'd been fleeing to the Dwarven Gate. He stared as he had atop the Lookout, asking for Soul Drinker, before Deshi had cut him.

The invitation remained, though I recoiled at what I might witness.

I don't want to do this.

But no one could translate his thoughts in my place, and the Valsharess demanded to know what happened.

Pebbles slid along the dirt outside, and I whimpered, barely audible. The Priestess and I were about to be interrupted.

Last chance.

"Alright." My stomach quaked as I stood up, our eyes locked. "Show me."

Divigna didn't approach but reached for me, grabbing my waist above my belt in two large hands. He lifted me off the ground.

"*Hai — !*" I squeaked, gripping his wrists, my fingers wrapped only halfway around. He pressed me to the scratched stone.

Vesram straightened with genuine interest as Divigna lifted his chin, his huge, patterned arms outstretched, and my gut squished in his hold. I braced my heels on his flanks rather than let them dangle, trying to form a mindlink, to dig past that stony gaze. The saphgar pendant warmed uncomfortably against my skin.

Despite mute permission, his mind resisted.

"Shielded," I muttered.

"Tattoos," the Sathoet growled, slipping closer, his mane puffed up, grey eyes wide and unblinking.

"Do you ... know which one?"

"*Let me see Mother,*" he bargained in Davrin.

"*What?*"

"*She is in there. Take me, too. I know which mark would block even mind-flayers.*"

Vesram stopped talking when Divigna's eyes shifted toward him in resentment. The Sathoet held his focus on me, easing my collection of his mental presence into an unfamiliar balance, as if we'd grasped hands and climbed onto the same small ledge knowing the Ma'ab's mind barriers would shove us off.

~*Which one? Show me!*~

Vesram guided our attention to an arched and dotted sigil over the Hellhound's right temple. Divigna's eye twitched as if we'd prodded it with a finger. A vulnerable pulse showed in his throat.

There.

As a silhouette slid into view at the cave's entrance, I drew the only weapon I had which would cut his skin for certain. Divigna's grip tightened as the red rune blade sliced a shallow wound from the front of his ear to his scalp. Blood poured down his jaw and neck, tiny crackles of blue and grey power tracing broken etchings in his flesh.

An unseen door burst open as if blown inward by an arctic wind. Links formed alarmingly strong as a terrifying depth *pulled* me to him like I'd been caught in his spiked chains. Struggle though I might, I could neither escape nor control the speed at which we descended.

The Physician's Hound dragged us down with him, falling freely into the darkness of an eternal and distant gaze.

THE STORIES WHISPERED ABOUT THE WARGAN WERE ALL TRUE, IF EMBELLISHED. The spread of overbearing cruelty justified the warnings told by generations of villagers, travelers, and city folk across the Far North, the Kurgan Steppes, and around the Great Lake.

Parallels to the shadowy tales of Morixxyleth were not lost on me, though I witnessed their reality from Kreshel's view. Mundanely horrifying in comparison to the mysteries of spirits and legends, their effects immediate and brutal.

Every Noiri, Kurgan, and Paxian woman made to spread legs for

Ma'ab men conceived when Divigna was nearby. His Elven essence, the inherent life magic bled through the branding of his body, his aura heightening the fertility of his men. He didn't *have to* plunge his own phallus into a captive, though he always did if she was mageborn.

The Physician had made certain he sensed mages like a stinging bee he couldn't ignore.

The *maknuut* Ada had discovered this one evening while the army was on campaign in the Kurgan Steppes. She drew Kreshel's life aura out from intense curiosity, a small, homely, mad woman too hungry for discovery to fear the danger.

Moments later, the Hellhound pressed her to the storage crate, his body forcing her legs open, muscled arms braced above the tiny death mage. His blunt cock threatened invasion of her dry cunt. He *would* impregnate her, as was his purpose.

Where life magic met death.

"*No!*" Ada cried.

He stopped.

For the first time in his existence, he ... *stopped*.

"Were you not commanding me, little sorceress?"

"No," she insisted, black eyes wild.

She was not.

"Leave me be, please," she whispered, gritting crooked teeth. "If you let me go, then my son will kill Vo'traj for us."

Kreshel stiffened his hips, pressed harder into a tense slit with his broad cock. She groaned as he forced her partway open and shook her head.

"Please!" she moaned.

It clearly hurt. The ugly *maknuut* did not welcome him in any respect. Why did he not take her anyway? He had hurt many women before; their pleas meant nothing.

What stopped him?

My son will kill Vo'traj ...

Spoken like the voice of an oracle about a son that did not exist. *Not yet.*

Dare he think it? Frighteningly, part of him *could*.

After decades, a quiet despair awoke within him. *She* believed that the *maknuut* witch saw some future truth. The Priestess accepted on his behalf.

Kreshel leaned over Ada, bringing his mouth close to hers.

"Kill her," he whispered, a glimmer of warmth breaking through the deep cold. "And kill me. Set me free."

"Y-yes," Ada agreed. "He will set you free. We swear it."

"You can't without confronting the Chirurgeon of Souls."

A delirious nod. "He will! We swear …"

The oracle's young voice quavered. She did not yet *see* this future, but her oath had been heard by *someone*.

The world may manifest it someday.

Kreshel withdrew without seeding Ada's womb, leaving it empty for another man. He turned a blind eye as she hid behind Vesram every day until she disappeared from camp.

My son will kill Vo'traj for us …

The Deathwalker of today had done much more than that, but it wasn't enough. The Hellhound *knew* it wasn't.

"My son will end this," said the oracle just days ago as she stood guard by the pool. Her voice did not quaver like before.

Vesram had heard it, too.

Not enough.

The mindlink shuddered. I lifted myself up from the male frustration so I could steady it.

Kreshel carried only a quarter of Mourn's years, but each contained a mountain's weight for how few days held joy in which to lighten them. I would not have recognized this prior to the Sisterhood, when I lived as a child at my Matron's House, my mind and tongue mage-locked much like the Ma'ab. Neither of us had expected levity within our longevity, so the weight had gone unnoticed, a necessary part of surviving for a century.

*But **was** it necessary?*

Kreshel sensed this. It was something *different* between us despite our similar age. He recoiled from it, not in fear but despair, gazing into this mirror before him. He and Vesram both ... so *envious* of the changes happening within me.

I met their potent stare swirling with emotions put forward through a cold wind of memory. I did not shrink but sat with them, having no answers. The pathway I'd walked lay invisible to them, indescribable even to myself. For them, this last century had formed a hard-beaten path, barren despite all the children born in Kreshel's wake, while I nurtured something unknown but lush.

Mother, Vesram thought, yearning to see her. *Pleassse ... *

I clung to my courage when it might have withered.

~Show me the beginning,~ I said as my presence shifted, moving up and out of the way to observe from somewhere small and defensible. ~Both of you.~

Memories formed from fragments, unveiling a tapestry so personal to my life yet one in which I'd been uninvolved. I hadn't been born when they first saw it.

The Ley Tower.

I recognized it from two perspectives at once. The first beheld a Priestess of Braqth fleeing toward it to escape capture from the Ma'ab chasing her and her Sathoet.

Vesram.

The second beheld the tower only after mother and child were surrounded and bound in chains.

THE DEMONBLOOD SON HAD GIVEN HER A CHANCE. HE HAD KILLED SEVERAL large pursuers to protect his mother, but then the small, pale females made their corpses stand up. He hadn't the endurance to confront them again, and he knew it.

Kreshel wasn't one of the walking dead. The young soldier ran on foot rather than horseback, bringing up the rear. He spotted the tower ruins while his brothers grappled with the strange, dark-skinned creatures.

The impulse to bring it to the attention of his sorceresses arose, to reveal the intended sanctuary of their captives, but their prizes swiftly proved dangerous and unpredictable.

"Don't stand there, Kreshel! Get them!"

For the safety of his mages and the goal of the expedition, he helped make sure the black witch and her demon couldn't escape.

The Blood Nobles Vo'jath and Vo'wry had been aching to turn back for weeks. Despite their promises and persuasions to either find a path to the far oceans or to discover something yet unseen, the women had complained on their expedition more than any. Kreshel and others were tired of hearing about it.

At last, the men could bring their women home without returning to their gods empty-handed.

Kreshel watched them together. The bestial creature whispered to her in ways suggesting comfort, not anger, and forewent several opportunities to cause chaos, either dying or escaping in the process. Controlling the delicate, knife-eared female was key to governing the demon.

An intuitive challenge for Kreshel and his elder Wargan, the pack brothers worked together day and night to make certain their clever and determined captives didn't gain an edge in a moment of unwariness. The men did not harm the black creature, nor did they share her pleasures amongst themselves, for such actions might work against them with the demon and served no purpose when they had their noble women to service.

Such violation might only anger their gods if accidental harm to this unique capture proved irreparable.

Such a long, long distance from those western mountains to the Far North. Their group was small enough to travel unnoticed yet often lacked the usual means to obtain supplies. If not for the Great Lake spanning half that distance and the less scrupulous boaters willing to carry them across for enough stolen objects of value, they would have been caught in a deadly winter in hostile lands.

Kreshel did not learn *her* name before they reached Ennikar, though this witch must have one. He learned Vesram's name and what he was from listening and observation.

The creature was not a demon summoned and bound to protect this mage, but a *son*. She was so small, and yet she was his mother who had given him birth.

Admiration.

Wherever these dark creatures had come from, they served a familiar power in a proper city. The Ascended and their Empire *must* find where this place existed.

Once the foreign mother and son were contained in the presence of their gods, the returned travelers were dismissed.

"We shall evaluate your gifts," crooned the Divine Artisan, waving impossibly long, white fingers toward the chamber doors. "You will be summoned if there is need."

Kreshel turned with the rest, careful to hide the confusion and disappointment the nobles dared to show.

"Wait. Him."

The Divine Physician ordered Kreshel to stay. She acknowledged him from the report as one most familiar with their behavior and tones of voice, learning bits of their language spoken and signed with their hands.

He did not speak but obeyed, standing closer to Vesram and his mother while avoiding eye contact as the rest of his group left. Not much later, he overheard his gods debating at the other end of the sanctum; they had no concern for his presence as long as he performed his function.

I will.

How could he not when so blessed and honored for his loyalty?

"This new sentient bears affinity to the magic of life from my studies," said the Divine Matron, her purple, fungal flesh intoning an exotic voice like no other. "She contains a potency unknown in our lands or among our people. The potential for this magic once fully understood —"

"Will take decades or more to become useful," the pale Physician interjected.

The gods stood before the Vermillion Lady on her throne with the Divine Warrior standing large and silent at her side.

"We have *centuries* to learn," the Matron rasped.

The Physician's sigil-marked head turned in a manner only possible without bones. "Does *she*? Or must she be made ... resilient first, so we may find the source?"

"Of all the possible realms from which to approach the problem," snarled the red-skinned Enslaver, the broad paws forming her feet taking a silent step closer, "you suggest soul-splicing yet again, Chirurgeon?"

"Skills mastered guarantee results, Hursesh, and the soul is the seat of memory. Can either you or the Matron promise *not* to waste this unique resource? To lose invaluable insights to raging insanity or invasive growths before we can find others for you to dabble around with?"

The pause seemed a hair's width too long for their crystalline Lady's patience, who tilted her head in the first acknowledgment of the exchange. The Matron and the Enslaver were unable to regain that edge, especially once the smooth tongue of the Artisan threw her noble sway behind the Physician.

"Our bloodlines grow stagnant," she said. "We would do well to enhance our newest births sooner rather than later."

The nape of Kreshel's neck itched. The last Ascended, the Divine Assassin, was nowhere to be seen but must be watching as the Vermillion Lady made her decision.

The young Ma'ab never heard her speak it.

"Give me forty days," said the Physician, a small, brilliant god forever followed by a gilded and bejeweled skeleton matching her stature. "I shall preserve them for eternity."

"Making life itself pointless," sniped the Matron, her bitterness apparent. "Destroying the cycle I must observe."

"Granting us the window to find the nest out of which they flew," the Third retorted.

"*Pfeh*! Much better to make her conceive!"

"Find me another and we will talk, Mother of Entrails. *My* way worked the first time. Why risk your *untested* theories before we have more than one prize on the table?"

Why, indeed?

The Physician claimed the inhuman captives from her sister gods, hiding them away in her study sanctum. She also claimed Kreshel and his pack brothers, detaching them from Vo'jath and Vo'wry for the first time in two years.

Over those forty days, Kreshel witnessed panic rising. The power of his gods was new to these creatures.

Wise though they may be in magic, they have never seen the like.

"A complex yet delicate pattern," murmured the Chirgurgeon of Souls in fascination. "Nothing like this can form in a Ma'ab's lifetime. Your souls are much older, yet the path to decay is obscured. We must not tear you ... until you prove you can mend yourself."

Her tone shifted toward delight.

"Then we shall tear. Gently at first. A little at a time."

In response to the bloodless wounds which made his mother cry, Vesram took escalating risks trying to free his mother. He attacked the Physician, trying to strangle her, but soon found she had no throat to throttle. She merely changed form, falling boneless, and engulfed his legs as her skin stretched like a sheep's bladder.

The demonblood paid for that one.

Yet still, he attacked the gilded skeleton next. Lacking weapons, he tried to shatter the joints with glowing fists. He could not, and the Physician's other half channeled a spell which drained him of strength until he could not stand off the ground.

Kreshel had not been commanded to defend his god from these captives, only stay and observe them. The Physician placed no blame upon him for these attacks; she wanted to see them, to study the pain in their souls.

Vesram would have died for his mother but the Physician would not allow this; nothing he could say or do was insulting enough to lose her focus. He became a nuisance, however, and with insights from the Enslaver, they learned how to control one with Abyssal blood.

Until even he knew he was a slave measures beyond what he believed before.

Perhaps Vesram suffered unnecessarily. Perhaps the demon son had accidentally provided a mage's insight to the Third Ascended as she persistently prodded the linked souls of the Davrin sorceress and her child.

"Forget, my bua," THE PRIESTESS WHISPERED TO VESRAM IN THEIR NATIVE tongue. *"These death mages must not learn of our home. This can't be what the queen saw for us."*

"Why protect them?" he asked, his growl nothing but pain and rage, his aura always inflamed. *"They culled usss. Rejected your magic … the queen sssent usss into exile."*

Her dismay offered him both dread and comfort. She recognized the truth. For that, she could be believed, unlike any other Priestess.

"The Priesthood rejected us, yes," she murmured. *"The Valsharess … I do not know. I asked her …"* She swallowed. *"But we have protected the Sisterhood, have we not? Jaunda and the others. Would you give them to this mad corpse?"*

He ducked his chin. *"No. Not give."*

"And that is all I say. Do not give it to them. I … I care for buas like you who do not deserve a fate worse than the place they were born."

Vesram embraced that old prick of jealousy for it reminded him of home. Nothing in his recollection held more authenticity than that. His mother *cared* for buas "like" him, but none would be so ugly. The motherless sons in the Sanctuary were all beautiful, as any with Elf-blood should be.

"Shyntre?" Vesram muttered.

The name of the infant his mother had nurtured before him.

Irrwaer swallowed but didn't lie to him. *"Him, yes. And the Consort healer, Sil. Many others with same choices you and I have right now."*

"Same how?" he snarled. This, he did not see.

She smiled, growing tired from always mending what the death mage tore asunder. *"We can learn about our captors. We might escape them. We will die eventually."*

Probably her before him.

The Sathoet shrugged, hiding his grief. *"I will not care for the sssuffering of buas far away if you are gone and I am alone. I might give her Sivaraus if it would save you.*"

Her shoulders drooped. She looked out through the iron bars of the Ma'ab cage. His mother said something other than what he'd expected.

"*I understand, Vesram. The choice is yours and always will be.*" She smiled, showing him the pride she had always held for him. "*Dead or alive, I cannot take it from you.*"

"WHILE HER DEMONBLOOD LIVES," THE PHYSICIAN SAID DURING A GOD-SHARE required by the Lady, "he enhances the Elf's magic."

"Not for long," the Enslaver chided, spying into every shaded nook of the lab while she could. "Her body is wasting. Even I can see their bond thins. You fail to maintain a simple vessel of flesh with your 'mastery,' Chirurgeon?"

"Hers is not so simple. I have learned much, but *she* learns as well."

"Oh?"

"She accelerates her own aura's decay, giving strands of strength to her child. I had not expected such an intriguing contest over a body only capable of healing. She pushes my hands!" The Physician chuckled, lifting an odd lump of black, faceted stone from the table with both pale palms. "But I shall win, nonetheless. See this?"

The Fourth god towered over the Third, closing her right, void-black eye to peer at the pneuma flint with her left of feline gold. "What is this?"

"I call it the Kor Nigram. Inspired by the Vermillion Lady which I have been working on." The Physician looked up, unintimidated by her warrior-like sister god. "I shall transfer the Elf's aura now, anchor it to one sigil at a time to this relic. When I am finished, her essence shall be complete but *not* whole, rewoven into a pattern that will fade no further no matter what she tries."

"Transfer?" the Enslaver sneered. "Where?"

The Third Ascended's flesh rippled to stare at Kreshel with moist, inky eyes, appraising his strength. She approached him, acknowledging his existence for the first time since he'd been stationed here.

"Kreshel Divigna," she said, her voice thrumming along his ears. "You have been watching from the beginning, You persist and bear witness to everything without flinching." She lifted the stone heart relic. "*You will bear this, today and forever forward.*"

Kreshel started to shake and did not understand why.

No ... !

He bowed, dropping to one knee before her, his fist closed on his chest, his birth heart beating in panicked terror.

"Thank you, my soul's mistress," he murmured.

When the Third sloughed around to check her work slab, the young man glanced at Vesram's black mother.

So sick and gaunt. Fasting toward death.

Her white hair had thinned, strands falling out to become lank without luster. Her scarlet eyes glimmered in delirium and a fever that would not break. Her heartbeat pulsed in her throat as if she understood neither of them would keep the dense muscles pumping blood through their veins, a birth rhythm deemed too weak and incompatible with their fate.

With our transition.

The maelstrom of emotion went unacknowledged, for it would change nothing for him. If his gods noticed the denial, they granted him grace in his weakness. Through his waning hours of mortality, Kreshel pushed himself beyond fear to elation, taking pride in being *chosen*.

Yes. I am chosen.

His soul would be empowered in ways he could not comprehend for a higher purpose, serving the Vermillion Lady under the expert hand of Her Physician.

So may it be.

Prior to his exaltation, Kreshel had earned a few mage's tattoos, as had most of his pack brothers. This imbued branding was a new process, their knowledge trickling down among the Bone Caste to soldiers who endured what was too painful yet for the Flesh Nobility Caste.

The Empire's Black Army tested these ways of enhancing strength and endurance among Ennikar's best hunters and protectors. The Enslaver herself would apply an abundance of fresh markings to Kreshel at the Physician's behest, preparing his body and soul for his humble ascension when they ripped out his heart.

The young man's howling echoed under stone as the Fourth scarred him with wicked edges of silver and hellfire steel. Her lips curled with amusement around her tusks.

"Baying like a true hellhound," she remarked.

Kreshel had no memory of what came next. Only the sound of cracking ribs and demonic fury would ever revisit him in the wells of his deepest rest.

The Divine Warrior met Kreshel Divigna for the first time when the young Ma'ab's sutures were fresh, and every point of skin blazed with entwined magic of life and death setting his tattoos into place. Kreshel trembled but stubbornly kept his feet after weeks on the slab.

"*Hellhounds,*" rumbled the god of war through a closed-face helm. "Our Lady has given me a task. I will see it come to pass."

"He belongs to me," the Physician hissed. "I am not finished."

"What do you need?"

"I need replacement bodies should the heart need a transplant."

"Then take the rest of his pack in payment for surrendering this weapon to the Bones. He is mine to train."

Kreshel quivered so slightly that none of the gods noticed. The Physician's work kept his torso closed as the Kor Nigram threatened to break it open again. The relic pulsed in his chest with something more than blood.

Much more.

Sometimes, his heart of pneuma flint threatened to dissolve his body. The "adjustments" from the Physician seemed never-ending, his suffering ever-present. When it did *not* end, it became a truth which a mortal man could only accept in madness, and a strange peace arrived when he unexpectedly learned her name.

Irrwaer.

Only then could Kreshel *feel* her son, could recognize the bua as the

Abyssal protector he had always been.

Why?

Because Irrwaer *was* Kreshel.

She is here, complete but not whole.

And, like him, never would be again.

"Let the demon help train our new Hellhounds," Kreshel suggested to the Divine Warrior, years after proving his mettle to his god. "I have witnessed his tricks. I have overcome them. We can use them to strengthen our tactics."

The Second Ascended considered his request, soon allowing Irrwaer's son to remain close to "her" whenever the Third did not interfere. The Hellhounds in turn grew strong and resilient to pain, their tattoos refined under Kreshel's example. The Eternal Hellhound led each generation; though his face would change into one of his brothers, he was still Kreshel, and he would never die.

In time, he forgot what he once looked like.

It does not matter.

Most of the continent quaked in fear when hearing of a new Ma'ab force coming to their valleys, their hollows, their farms, and their cities. Children swelled the wombs of the Bone and Flesh Castes as Divigna mastered his aura and those under his command. He need not fall between the legs of every woman at the center of their breeding packs to aid the Empire's fertility, but the nobles bragged about it when he did.

Yet, no matter how many Ma'ab offspring the Elf's magic quickened over the decades, Kreshel did not recognize these children. *She* felt nothing for the short-lived creatures, while Kreshel could not ignore his firstborn son as he could the others.

Vesram.

THE DEMONBLOOD WOULD NEVER LEAVE THE EMPIRE. VESRAM COULD NOT allow himself to die no matter the ill treatment. The Abyssal Elf sensed the Kor Nigram; he could always track it if he tried.

Vesram *loathed* that lump of stone. He wanted to cut the lich's prison from Kreshel's chest, to rip it out with his own hands and smash it upon the rocks. He had tried before but found only punishment. There never seemed a way …

Until recently.

My mind chilled with realization.

Kor Nigram.

In the Ma'ab tongue, it meant "Black Heart."

Gavin misunderstood.

Kreshel and Irrwaer shared a *heart*, a relic newly made. We didn't need the gatekeeper of the red rune blade to kill Kreshel, but the false organ beating in his chest.

A soul trap holding our Priestess captive for a century.

My guardian spiders strained to sound their alarm above the shrill, ear-stabbing shriek of a demon.

Yessss! Yeeeeesssss!

I snapped back inside my head, the impact of the waking world hitting hard enough to crack my skull. Divigna clutched my waist, pressed me to the cave wall as I braced myself. He stared with dark, vacant eyes.

Soul Drinker was halfway out of its sheath, opening a sliver of space as hollow and numb as if someone had severed my spine. Red runes blazed in the dim as a dread demon's cry grew louder. The handle, gripped by a familiar pair of small white hands, was framed by metal-blue sleeves and pale-yellow trim.

A hoarse, unrecognizable grunt escaped me. "Amelda, *don't!*"

My spiders had fled the safety of my nape, darting down my arms and along his like toward their prey. My aching eyes couldn't track them. I tried to kick her away. She was fixated on the blade when her body jerked, and I still missed.

"*Eeagh* — !" the noble cried, her boots scraping gravel as one hand slapped her embroidered collar.

I flinched, expecting my guardians' chime to fall silent. Instead, they sang louder as a blast of air erupted from the ground near my feet. The burst slammed Divigna from chest to knees, and he staggered, taking me with him. Soul Drinker left the security of my belt.

~*NO!*~

I lashed out, my boot connecting with Amelda's hand and sending the black blade spinning to the mouth of the unfinished tunnel. She clutched one hand with the other, staring with enough cognizance to confirm she wasn't in the gatekeeper's grip.

Suddenly, the noble widened her stance, weaving as if she were dizzy, then clawed her throat. Blood vessels showed in the whites of her widening eyes.

I had one antivenom left on my belt.

One left.

"Fuck, *fuck*, let me *go!*" I screeched. "She will die!"

The Eternal Hellhound had regained his footing and shifted his iron grip to my arms to hold me in place. The cut on his temple had scabbed up.

"Then it is decided," Kreshel rumbled, squeezing hard, digging his thumbs until searing pain wrapped around my arms like Tamuril's thorny vines.

My head pounded and light flashed behind my eyes. *"Arrrgh!"*

Amelda stumbled to her knees wheezing, pawing the ground, crawling closer to Soul Drinker. Kreshel dragged me by one arm, lunging to claim the dagger ahead of her.

Another large set of hands grasped my other arm.

"Got her," Vesram growled.

I didn't know who he was talking to until, behind me, a much smaller creature rattled on an inhale, his bright purple throat pouch inflating in my periphery.

Graul.

The shadow drake vibrated his own warning the moment before my spiders meant to return to me.

~*Hide!*~ I commanded. ~*Crevice on the wall! Now!*~

My babies fled, skittering toward the nearest cover when Graul's second blast hit the precise spot between Kreshel, Amelda, and the red rune blade. A cloud of dust and pebbles filled the tunnel, forcing the naked blade into sunlight where I lost sight of it. I choked on thick air, but Amelda was suffocating, thrashing in seizure as her throat swelled shut. The Sathoet and Hellhound pulled on my limbs, each attempting to jerk me out of the grip of the other. Neither succeeded, and it *hurt*.

"*Maekrix!*" Graul yowled in the dark, echoing.

Kreshel swept around, hurling a stone toward the voice. It smashed into a rock wall instead of an elderly, scaly body.

From another point in the dim: "*Maekrix!*"

And another: "*Maekrix!*"

With a quiet growl, the Hellhound stared at the Sathoet. "Let. *Go*. Before this does not matter anymore."

Vesram yielded to this vague threat, releasing me so Kreshel could loop one arm around my waist and pick me up like a small animal. The Ma'ab dipped and scooped up Amelda, too, before abandoning his hiding place.

The Sun blinded me, and Divigna kicked something metallic that tumbled down the mountainside. My spiders' chimes faded with distance. Relief and terror smashed together inside me. My guardians were *safe* against enemies too big for them, but I'd *lost* Soul Drinker and didn't know who would find it next!

Worse, I was too late to prevent Indrath's boon from happening for Cris's daughter. With Divigna on the move because Graul had found us, Amelda's decline hurled beyond the point where I had stopped Tamuril's.

~*Mourn!*~ I screamed. ~*She's dying! He's letting her!*~

He sounded startled. *What? Where is he going?*

The watchtower, Kreshel answered, his tone flat. *Have care not to strike your Elf to get at me. I can feel life in her belly.*

Divigna climbed fast, using no trail. Sheer power and momentum overcame the weight in his arms. I ceased struggling the moment my eyes saw past the glare and grasped how *far* we could fall.

Shit.

I didn't want to die.

Amelda's thrashing grew weaker, her gagging face dark red and blue around the lips. Bloodshot eyes stared, vacant. She'd stopped breathing, not quite dead but far too late for my antivenom. If Divigna might release her and we found some way to let Isboern take over, maybe his magic could save her?

"Then it is decided," he said.

I was fooling myself. Amelda would be dead before we reached the tower.

~*The Ascended … ?*~

By the will of my gods, Divigna agreed.

From the sound of it, even he didn't know what would happen next.

CHAPTER 40

GAVIN'S FEET LEFT THE GROUND FROM THE FORCE OF THE THUNDERCLAP, AND he tumbled with Deshi and Jael down the steep path. Up ahead, their brute fighters were all but shoved over the edge by Kreshel's spell.

The Hellhound stole Sirana in that helpless moment, his purpose unclear but not good for any Elf. Regardless, Gavin wagered her captor would not kill her unless by accident, should she act truly thoughtless and rash.

Unlikely ...

... what we have observed in her ...

... we have time ...

Long ago in the Nexus, Gavin had been solely responsible for preserving and strengthening his Vis without a body.

Meanwhile, fragments of pneuma flint had drifted on an unseen current, caught in a two-way vortex with his Vitas, tentatively linked to his homeworld from a ritual waiting to be completed. While they waited, his Lady had used this curiosity to set his body to rise and rebuild itself from his core outward, completing his transition once the silver dagger was removed.

His bones' density had increased three-fold since he had sat up in that shed at Troshin Bend, gaining a mass incongruent with his appearance.

Gavin possessed a weight akin to Mourn or Kreshel but without their bulk.

Lacking that muscle, the Herald should not have been able to stop his growing momentum quickly, if at all. Yet the obsidian bone spurs, thorns, and hardened plates had reemerged through his skin after his trance at the Temple. Hallowed whispers arose from the city's spirits, their strength coming to his aid.

With them, the Deathwalker clasped to the wild surges of magic flowing from the sacred pool. Like a many-limbed creature caught in rough seas, he brought his fall up short, grabbing Jael's belt with one hand while his other buried fingers into the parched, beaten path.

"Hurk!" she grunted at the sudden stop.

Deshi slowed himself another way, phasing from his solid state entirely as the Harrowed's black skull appeared, pale blue flames flaring up. He became light as the air he depended upon and settled gently on the narrow road as the shocking burst of sound faded.

The three of them were fine.

"Isboern?" Gavin called, peering where he'd last seen him.

Where is the mortal ... ?

... let it not be over ...

... not yet ...

The Deathwalker would be shocked if the Dragon's son had been killed in such a moment, but the Human psion could be vulnerable to a surprise fall. In such a case, Gavin must return to the Temple at once to touch *Pisc'sagrad* and see what could be salvaged. Sirana must take care of herself until the others reach her.

Regrettable ...

... but necessary ...

"Here!" the blond man called, grunting with effort as he climbed into view.

Yessss ...

... yesss, good ...

Mourn and Isboern had each used their talents and reflexes to catch themselves, but *all* the Templari found themselves in places their armor would not allow them to climb out. Their Captain and his legendary ally worked to retrieve each man and bring him to the high road, but some had fallen quite far and been injured in the process.

Concerning …

… will they slow us down … ?

"Please help us if you can!" said the Godblood.

"Coming!" Deshi answered, motioning sharply with his hand. "Come on!"

"But Sirana!" Jael began, holding her ears. "H-he … took her!"

He wants something …

… he will not kill her …

"An unavoidable delay," Gavin said aloud, waiting until the Red Sister focused on him with a snarl. "Isboern is the heart of this challenge, and Divigna is unlikely to harm your Sister. She is too valuable to the Ma'ab alive and pregnant."

Jael gritted and bared her teeth, an unstoppable growl pushing between them. Her body tensed up from the effort of withholding a punch at an unseen target.

The Herald understood her frustration. He would be heading neither to the Temple nor to help free his life flower.

Help the god warriors …

… it will shorten the delay …

Once, Gavin might have exhaled in audible annoyance. Today, he simply forgot to inflate his lungs to do so.

"Thank you for your aid," said the Captain, counting every Templar alive if not unhurt. "I cannot express my gratitude." He smiled. "You are stronger than you look."

Gavin grunted, standing with arms folded as Isboern set to praying to his Sun God so near the top of His holy mount. He focused on easing the last concussions and mending the bone fractures not attended to with what Guild potions they'd been able to salvage.

The Captain possessed many great gifts he had worked for years to develop and live in balance. A psionic mage possessed not only his life aura and mage aura, but a near-invisible crystalline power netted around and within both of them. The Herald recognized its presence from the void space entwined with familiar patterns, sharing a likeness to Sirana's unique essence, but with form and shape clearer now that Gavin knew what to look for.

But the Captain is not a healer-by-touch ...

... not as the Davrin know it ...

... not as the life flower has shown it ...

Both Sirana's child and the sire from her city possessed a healing talent beyond anything seen in Human mages, a potent form of life magic ever-present and striking in its adaptability to the world at large.

Deshi is proof ...

... the Harrowed is new ...

The Godblood held more in common with the Herald of Nyx. Gavin could manifest brief but potent enhancements through communion with his Lady. He had witnessed Willven Isboern do the same with Musanlo at the redoubt, observing this rare curiosity once again on this mountain. Soon, three critically injured Templari climbed to their feet.

To Gavin's left and farther up the steep path, Jael and Mourn argued in their native tongue, the hybrid's tail escaping his conscious control. Gavin could guess their point of contention.

Inaction ... tactics ...

... waiting ... always waiting ...

Sirana had released her bargain with her bodyguard, who had chosen to guard Isboern in this vulnerable moment for the greater among his goals. The younger Red Sister had no such restrictions and may run off on her own. The Dragonblood tried to convince her to stay for obvious reasons.

Strength and safety in numbers ...

Jael cared less than Gavin did where it pertained to her Sister.

Suddenly, a small, winged drake appeared out of Mourn's long shadow, and she yelped.

Sneaky ...

... how long has he been in the city ... ?

... saw him not ... never once ...

Graul the drake had been absent for the entire battle thus far but had managed to catch up with them. The hoarse, rattling squawks of the Deepearth creature joined the debate. Somehow, he extracted a reluctant accord from the young Elf. Jael stood vibrating but remained with the rest of the fighters.

Meanwhile, Graul slipped into the brush and disappeared.

Not waiting ...

... do we wait, or no ... ?

Gavin frowned and approached them. "What happens?"

"Sirana isn't answering through her pearl," Mourn said, his senses alert to their surroundings. "Though nothing changed in its magic. The pearl stolen by Divigna is moving. Graul volunteered to discover more."

"Are we going to the watchtower?"

"The Captain is. I think you and Deshi should as well." The Dragonblood motioned to his apprentice. "I would prefer Jael and I to keep watch unseen, until we know."

Bait for the Ma'ab ...

... purpose for the new guardian ...

Gavin sighed. "Very well."

The Templari were shaken but claimed an abundance of drive to follow their Captain to the peak of Mount Sonai. Whatever must be said occurred in swift silence, their group on the move without excess chatter or debate. If Isboern attempted to reach out to Sirana, he did not appear to find her. They could do naught but reach the summit.

The largest unknowns remained Vesram and Amelda.

We are in theirs and Kreshel's hands ...

Approaching the final bend, the Harrowed moved to the front of all, offering to take point. The Godblood accepted, their exchange made in crude hand gestures as the psion refrained from mindlinking any but the Templari at this moment. Mourn and Jael were nowhere to be seen.

Gavin couldn't know if any voice drifted through the pearls, be it from the Dragonchild, the Guild or their Mistress, or their missing Davrin.

Sirana ...

... she is a critical bridge in this quest ...

She had aided Isboern in leading that first battle to victory with her high view and clear voice.

She had healed and empowered a new servant of Nyx, assuring dominance over the Ma'ab camp and their rampart.

She had saved Vesram from the wrath of the Ice Lord, convincing the Sathoet to return with them to the Ley Tower.

She had communicated with the Chenkyte to a surprising level without much aid from the Deathwalker, blunting keen edges of mad joy in a way he could not.

Without Sirana, Gavin may not have come this far in his tasks of devotion. Losing her could be catastrophic to his Lady's vision to claim the Ley Tower from Sarilis.

We are not at that crossroads ...

... not yet ...

... bring the sacred pool to her ...

... let her return to Miurag ...

The Herald focused on the watchtower of Mount Sonai, his vision primed for any significant glimpse of life auras. Deshi had slipped inside the watchtower to clear it of danger.

"Empty," said Gavin, drawing Isboern's ear.

The psion sighed, his expression holding a strange focus. Gavin figured he listened for thoughts beyond theirs.

The bald mountain peak spanned wide enough for their force of twenty and then some, the clearing lined with pungent, waist-high shrubbery resistant to drought and intense sunlight. Not much cover beyond the circular two-story stand of stone. Aside from the main track leading to the Temple, vague pathways wandered away from the soldier's structure to steep slopes east and west while the side of the mount dropped in a sheer cliff of dark stone to the south.

The Harrowed poked his head out a first-floor window at their approach. "Amelda is not here."

"But she was," Isboern replied to which Deshi nodded.

... the pearl was moving ...

... Graul searches ...

"Our fastest trackers have left," Gavin said. "I imagine they are as likely to lift her trail as that of Sirana or Kreshel."

The Captain frowned. "We wait here for them?"

... in his hands ...

... the Physician's Hound ...

... she said you would end this ...

"We stand where the spliced soul invited us to meet him," said the Herald. "We should stay."

The Godblood chose eight Templari for their eyes and ranged talents, instructing them to secure the highest ground. The men knew what to do. This left Isboern with twelve subordinates surrounding him when a distant screech echoed in the valley to the east.

They spun around, swords and shields ready when the call sounded again.

"*Maekrix!*"

"Graul," Gavin said.

"Who?" Robi asked.

"The shadow drake. He found something and summons the Dragon-child."

Manalari exchanged glances, readying themselves for something to happen.

"Legend," Isboern said, extending his arm to stay unintended attacks when Mourn burst out of the brush carrying Jael.

"*He coming!*" the young Davrin blurted. "He has her! Both!"

"Both?" Isboern asked.

"Amelda dies from poison," the Dragonchild answered, coming out into the open "I will try to snare the Ma'ab sorceress from Divigna. If I succeed, Godblood, heal her if you can."

"Understood."

Isboern maintained his aplomb when others showed alarm.

They have every reason …
… Amelda's death …
… Indrath's deal …

"What happens if she dies?" Deshi asked him.

Gavin shrugged. "Nothing advantageous to us." He turned to Mourn. "Where is Vesram?"

"Unknown."

Heavy boots crushed woody limbs on their way to the crest. Gavin stepped toward it with Deshi slipping in front of him — annoying — and Mourn with Jael shifting to his flank. Kreshel's bald and branded head appeared moments later at a fast clip, hauling a female under each arm. Sirana's face reflected sheer terror as she clung to him. Her auras blazed with vibrant health and life.

"Sirana!" Jael shouted.

"She is well," Gavin said.

Amelda …

… not well … dying …

The swelling of her face and beneath her jaw left her unrecognizable. The Ma'ab noble hung limply, her fading aura confirming she barely lived but not much longer.

… venom …

… the Vitas burns its own anchors …

"The spiders," he murmured.

So this was what happened when they bit someone.

"Conf'ekess ve!"

Mourn's voice broke like thunder, tail lashing as he beckoned to the approaching trio. Sirana's thrashing allowed Amelda to slip free of Kreshel's grasp in an unwary instant, for the small Ma'ab woman glided toward them in a magical draw, landing on the barren ground between them.

At the same time, Isboern launched forward, his men spreading out.

Kreshel reversed his momentum once he lost the sorceress, slowing to a halt. He swung Sirana vertically before him, wrapping arms around her, holding her to his chest. A large hand seized her throat, restricting her breath to ensure cooperation.

"Stay back," he rumbled.

Sirana's sky blue eyes were wide but held no terror of imminent death.

"He won't kill her," Gavin said.

"Cuz we kill *him!*" Jael retorted.

The Hellhound paused, a corner of his mouth twitching as his dark eyes slid to Isboern praying over Amelda. "It's too late, Godblood."

Gavin glimpsed the thinning wisps of Amelda's Vitas slipping through the Captain's attempts to anchor them. Isboern knew his prayers weren't working. Even if Amelda's Vis clung on, her transition away from her body had progressed too far to overturn.

"No," Sirana wheezed.

Amelda's breath stopped, lips of darkest purple and blue, her flesh becoming that of a corpse. As the last vital essence passed from her, fleeing Gavin's gaze to rejoin the world, the Godblood ceased his prayers and returned to his feet. He was shaking, panting lightly, but unlikely to rail at the sky in denial.

"What happens next?" the Captain asked instead.

An instant apart, Gavin and Isboern met Sirana's eyes.

~Amelda bargained to become a Ley beacon for the Ascended.~

A thought conveyed with petrified confidence. Gavin could naught but believe her, and Isboern could not help but comprehend.

"Your rulers can see into the Arena," said the Godblood to the Hellhound.

"More," he said. "They can enter. If not now, then soon."

Isboern swallowed. "How soon?"

"I cannot see Ley Lines." The Hellhound tilted his head toward the Dragonblood. "Ask him."

Isboern's expression pleaded for something tangible from his legend.

"Between now and sunset," Mourn answered, tilting his chin toward the late afternoon sun. "I cannot guess better, I am sorry."

~Then you have time to get the Black Heart,~ Sirana thought.

Gavin frowned. *The Kor Nigram?*

~Yes!~

Isboern, Mourn, and Gavin glanced at the cursed dagger on her belt.

The sheath was empty, the blade was …

Gone …

… she does not have it …

What happened to Soul Drinker? Mourn asked, a valid concern as Sirana struggled for a full breath.

~*It fell to one side of the mountain.*~

What?

~*We'll get it later! Attack him!*~

~*Why?*~Isboern asked.

Sirana strained against the Ma'ab's hold. ~*The Physician's Hound has a false heart! She made it, and she'll want it back. She may come to retrieve it herself!*~

Comprehension broke like a wave at last.

Kor Nigram …

… not the gatekeeper …

… Vesram never meant the gatekeeper of the Elsewhere …

… he meant …

Kreshel's heart.

If not made of flesh and blood, it must be of pneuma flint. A natural soul trap from the Nexus like what laced his own bones. Had a mistress of death learned how to prevent an Elven soul's transition on Miurag? Was this how the Physician made him?

~*Seize it before his gods arrive!*~ Sirana commanded as if she weren't in the way. ~*You'll have a bargaining piece at least!*~

*But — *

Kreshel's left knee buckled. The Ma'ab emitted a grunt before his right one snapped forward. The large body stumbled, and another rushed him like a bull, at last becoming into sight.

Vesram.

Sirana, Kreshel, and the demonblood fell together to one side. The Hellhound snatched the Sathoet's mane with one fist, strangling Sirana with his other, his dead expression never shifting. Noise and voices exploded as Deshi shrieked forward to join the fight.

"Harrowed, wait!" Isboern called.

"Shield her from them, Captain!" Mourn barked, summoning his blades.

Deshi must have been linked to Isboern, or directly to Sirana, because the first punch he threw with his spectral fist landed square on Kreshel's sternum.

The Kor Nigram struck back.

An intense star of pale blue; an ethereal wail laden with pain.

"*Eeeeeaaaaa!*"

"*Watch out!!*" Jael screeched, leaping with impressive agility when the magical force knocked Deshi backward, sending him tumbling beneath her feet.

Oh, dear ...

Gavin watched the Harrowed come to rest, the Yungian's body condensing into deeply breathing flesh until he could gather his bearings.

... the last Ma'ab soul at Manalar ...

... locked in a fortress ...

Mourn and Jael sprang forward as Kreshel appeared stunned. He tried to roll over while Vesram scrambled blindly away. Sirana was clutching her face as pure force of will nudged her disoriented body farther from the fight.

Two Templari sprinted from the watchtower. Isboern's men did not hesitate, pulling the pregnant Davrin off the fighting grounds and granting her cover with them.

~We have her!~ Willven said. *~Sirana is safe!~*

Excellent ...

"Thank you!" Mourn growled, positioning himself to give Vesram a chance to escape as well.

... do it now ...

Gavin withdrew the thurible from his belt, gripped the iron wring in his left hand. Wisps of souls threaded in and out of the small holes like dancing fish. The voices of the dead within the relic, within his bones ...

All within him grew louder.

Even Amelda.

...find ...

... his ...

... weaknessss ...

Jael discovered that mage-heated blades would not cut Kreshel's skin. The Hound blocked her with his arms twice, nearly yanking the sword from her hand; only Mourn's skill stopped him.

The Hellhound then evoked another thunderclap which deafened and knocked down everyone outside the watchtower, including the Herald. Given his choice of targets, Kreshel charged the Dragonchild, justifiably the greatest threat yet not strategically vulnerable.

Kreshel must fight ...

... the Physician's Hound cannot yield ...

... will not surrender ...

Though the Wargan need not save the Ma'ab lieutenants from enough mistakes to wipe them all out.

~Gavin! Can you hear me?!~

The Deathwalker's lips pulled away from black teeth as he climbed to his feet, thurible secure in his grip. His ears overwhelmed with the rest, all sound muffled, yet another pathway had opened.

Crystalline clear, Sirana.

And I've shut down the pearls, Mourn said. **He can't hear us.**

And yet the voices of living allies passed through the Herald, flowing alongside those of the dead, never crossing, with him at the center.

Understood. We must find his weakness.

He doesn't have a tattoo in the same spot as the others, Mourn confirmed, demonstrably quicker of foot than the Hellhound as they danced around each other. **It's just not there.**

Would be stupid if he did, Jael snarled.

~He is shielded well from mental attacks,~ Isboern added.

~If you have a way to cut the skin,~ Sirana said, *~it's the dotted brand on his right temple that protects his mind.~*

No one questioned how she knew that.

Try a limb, Deshi, Jael said, **if you can't reach the heart.**

Yes, Janhuren.

Aware that Vesram was keeping an eye on him from the shrub line,

Gavin shifted his location on the mount at regular intervals, observing each offensive tactic taken.

The Harrowed avoided the same explosive knockback in his next attack, aqua-green flames flaring, spreading over tattoos before evaporating like a drake that had run out of breath. The former Guildsman somersaulted to one side undefended and struck while the Dragonchild held the bulk of the Hellhound's attention.

I can't tell if it hurts him, Deshi admitted.

You draw small amounts of Vitas from him, Gavin said. *It will add up, and meanwhile strengthen you.*

*Ah ... *

Keep hitting him — ! Mourn agreed, taking a hard fist to the gut to protect Jael.

Huaxia, Wen-yung!

The trio hemmed in their enemy, preventing Kreshel from withdrawing abruptly and charging into the Templari. The Hellhound made not one sound of frustration. He breathed, and he fought with his whole existence.

Meanwhile, the thurible had drawn Amelda's Vis to it — Gavin's one hope of obscuring the vision of the Ascended — but the Temple relic recognized nothing of either Kreshel or Deshi. All others were flush with untainted life, the blind spot in ancient death magic.

Gavin called forth Eynkis from his bones, but the young Ma'ab did not believe his High Wargan Divigna *could* be killed, much less recognize the tattoos created decades before he was born.

... you will be here forever ... until he wins ... or the Physician comes for him.

"Hm, let us try another way," he murmured.

~Let us have a shot, legend.~ Isboern sounded amused but keenly focused. ~My men and I are ready.~

On my mark, Captain. Try not to knock him off the mountain.

~Trust me.~

Then get ready.

The Godblood's golden shield flashed as it caught the sun. Sirana's recognition passed over Gavin's consciousness, laden with awe. ~Mit-

neh'thran.~

He blinked.

The relic had a name?

Mitneh'thran …

… Kor Nigram …

If only the thurible …

… might reveal its own name … ?

… to ussss … .

NOW! Mourn said, blades slowing their spin as he leaped back-ward.

Isboern vanished from view as his men whispered incantations. Deshi and Jael abandoned their offense at either side when the Godblood appeared behind Kreshel, opposite his men and facing them.

~Now.~

The warrior mages released their light spell full force as they had on the streets of Manalar, their Captain countering from the other side, his shield both enhancement and focus. Mirrored blasts caught the Eternal Hellhound between them, pure light enveloped him while a psionic shield deflected excess energies away from the watchtower and into the sky.

Mourn, Jael, and Deshi lay prone. Although Gavin refused to miss one tremor of this contest of auras, he took to one knee, crouching to make a smaller target while the Manalari held their spell long enough to char flesh upon bone. Some moments longer, and it might soften stone and glass.

Finally, within the intense globe of light, Kreshel began to roar. Gavin was uncertain if it was pain, at first, but then it swelled, and he recognized the sound.

Grief …

… for a life lost …

… too many lives …

~Do not waver!~ Isboern commanded when their enemy's lament swelled to a howl. ~*Templari! Take him down!*~

Sirana took a risk, quietly feeding memories she'd taken from Kreshel into the mindlink. They heard the same howl from elsewhere as the new immortal soldier lay upon the Physician's slab. They recognized flashes of decades around the Great Lake, recoiling at the sheer number of gutted and enslaved villages at which Divigna was present.

The Manalari received a voiceless confession in their hearts.

She said ... You will end this ...

~*Take him* down!~ Isboern repeated with a telltale trace of compassion when the scream grew louder.

Sirana's nudge paid off.

The sun warriors' light held steady, draining Kreshel of his strength, of all magic imbued to protect him. Flesh burned and cooked, water escaping as vapor where the Godblood's shield guided the power bleed-off. Finally, the heavy body collapsed, the howling stopped, its last echo fading in the valley below.

Their collective attack dispelled with a thought, a dozen gasping Templari collapsed to their knees, shaking with exhaustion. Isboern dropped to one knee, his shield braced upon the scorched earth as he stared at the massive Ma'ab body.

A large hand took hold of Gavin's shoulder.

"Get off!" He rounded on whomever had touched him.

Vesram tugged his arm next. "Come! His hearrrt! Need to reach the hearrrt!"

A moment's resistance — old habit — then Gavin allowed himself to be pulled toward the smoking corpse.

~*Gavin?!*~

Necessary Sirana.

How he wished he had his satchel and chirurgeon's kit, not to mention his grimoire. How would he do this? Ask the Sathoet to chew through the ribs while he dug with black, flinty fingernails? Ask the Dragonchild to donate a few fine blades?

Could the Deathwalker separate the Elven essence without removing the Kor Nigram? He doubted it. At least, not without tools on a bald mountain.

I need preparation ...

... somewhere safe and quiet ...

"*Is it over?*" a Templar asked his brother-in-arms. "*Have we won the pool?*"

"*The Dragon's Boundary remains in place,*" Mourn replied in their native tongue. "*The stewards of Pisc'sagrad are not decided.*"

Creeping dread slid up Gavin's spine.

Indeed ...

... How much time ...

... do we have ... ?

Kreshel's chest was still and oddly frigid to the touch despite extreme burns.

His life aura ...

So muted that Gavin might have missed it if pneuma flint weren't jutting through his skin. He could neither see nor hear the ghost which *should* be in transition this moment.

The hybrid soul within could not leave.

They are anchored.

The Deathwalker hadn't a thought on how to open the pathway for Kreshel to transition, despite his existential purpose insisting that it *must* be done,

The essence is cut off without a living body ...

... perfectly sealed away from the world ...

What if he simply *took* the Kor Nigram, as Vesram insisted? If he carried it with him until he had the Ley Tower in his possession and the time to commune — ?

Air tore atop that mountain.

~GAVIN!~

Lightning crackled, surrounding them, jolting him and the Sathoet and causing them to fall away from Kreshel's body.

"*Noooo ... !*" Vesram cried, the source of his terror unimaginable only until a dark passageway appeared before them.

An icy blast of Northern air hit them in the face. The dead within wailed, shrill and wary, except for one.

Eynkis howled in joy, rushing to the boundary of Gavin's bones, sensing the potent, familiar source of death magic. The Deathwalker struggled to hold on to him until he recalled his promise to the Hellhound we'd recovered from the Elsewhere.

Preparing for another fight, Gavin let Eynkis go.

The gods! the young soul cried. *The gods have come to take us all home!*

CHAPTER 41

~*What are we going to do?!*~

   First, no one panic.

   My fingers ached from how tightly I gripped the stone sill, my body swept twice over with fire and ice. Despite Mourn's calm, my heart thundered in my ears. ~*Easy to say.*~

   Isboern and his Templars regrouped around Mourn, Jael, and Deshi, desperation and fear trampling over their exhaustion from moments before. The Dragonblood extended his arm, pointing his flashing sword at Gavin and Vesram crouching in front of the gate.

   "*Conf'ekess vetra'!*"

   An invisible hand yanked our two allies backward and out of the pathway of whatever was coming through that portal. Isboern helped, moving the Deathwalker and Sathoet faster across the ground before erecting a psionic shield between them and the glimmering, oblong ring of power.

   I wished I could do the same from the watchtower. Instead, I hunkered down behind the stone and made sure the nearest doorway was open in case we needed to flee.

   Not that I knew where we'd run to.

   ~*If it comes to retreat,*~ Isboern answered with resolve, ~*we go to the*

Temple and the pool.~

Last resort. Best to face them here, Mourn said. *Maneuverability is as limited for them as it is for us, and their vulnerability is that portal.*

Agreed, we should not leave that gate open, Gavin said, on his feet with Vesram hiding behind him.

A gargantuan, masculine figure ducked his head and shoulders, leaving a sunless chamber to stand under the Southern sky. The body was so wide as to block the gate, his footsteps heavier than a team of oxen. His hairless head and trunk-sized arms displayed dark, embedded gems interconnected by blue iridescent pathways etched into his grey skin, leading to a red ruby in his forehead.

Wait …

Not skin.

~*Stone?*~ I asked.

That is a servant, Gavin said, *not an Ascended.*

He still moved away.

~*You are sure?*~ Jael asked, incredulous.

The Deathwalker turned one ear toward Vesram. *Toh-Rah Set. Hundreds or thousands of Ma'ab souls empowering a golem made of stone. A bodyguard for the gods.*

The work of the Physician? Mourn thought.

Perhaps. Perhaps not.

The giant had been sculpted, appearing to wear studded leather armor, including a pauldron on one shoulder with an odd, fanged skull staring out from underneath it. The massive hands clasped a thick metal sword and morbid black shield which were quite real, however, and too large for any of us to wield.

Somehow, the birthless creature possessed dark Ma'ab eyes, unfocused and staring past us. The mouth remained closed, a thin line carved into a solemn face. The golem craned his thick neck downward, focusing on Kreshel's corpse at his feet. He lifted his foot off the ground, slowly, and took a deliberate step over him. The crunch and grind of rock against rock lingered after the heavy thud.

The Toh-Rah Set stood between us and the *Kor Nigram*.

Between us and Irrwaer.

A wave of nausea broke over me, and I swallowed. *No.*

The Valsharess never said I had to recover the Priestess, only to listen for stories of what happened to her. I must only bring any half-bloods.

That was Her command ...

A pale form slinked around the shadowed space behind the golem, the motion foreign and unsettling. A quiet, throatless chuckle leaked through the ice-blue ring of power before a red-skinned warrior stepped into view, remarking on something I couldn't hear. Her bearing reminded me of Jaunda, and she was much taller than the free-flowing figure.

~The Fourth,~ I said, sensing the surprise that I recognized her on sight.

The Divine Enslaver, Gavin agreed.

Vesram quivered as the Ascended's powerful eyes turned toward us, one void-black and one cat's eye gold. Her lower tusks gleamed as she stepped through the portal, her leading foot a big cat's paw with red fur and ivory-white claws. She blinked, squinting in the Southern sunlight next to the Toh-Rah Set, touching the ground of Mount Sonai.

Fuck.

The Enslaver was as tall as Gavin, visibly muscled, her skin scarlet-red and marked with runes. Her head was half-shaven, the remaining dreads were snow white. Raw leather strapped down her scarred chest, and a primitive wrap decorated in bone and talon tied around her waist.

She gripped a coiled, black whip tipped with a pneuma flint blade and a few spikes, peering down at Divigna's body and then Amelda's. Towering over them, she scanned the rest of us, closing first one eye and then the other. I couldn't imagine how she might see us.

Snarling lowly at Gavin, her eyes narrowed in suspicion though seemed confused by Deshi. She might have lingered on him out of curiosity had she not paused on Jael, a new grin flooded her face with greed and glee. My Sister spat on the ground in response.

Sirana, stay hidden, Mourn said in earnest. *We may not get her to leave if she sees you. We may draw stronger forces here.*

I shrank down behind my wall.

We will guard her with our lives, dra'con, said the Templar to my left.

The agreement of the others passed through the mindlink, braced with Isboern's approval.

Thank you, but let me help you avoid testing that resolve. The Dragonchild crossed his blades, drawing the Enslaver's attention, scuffing his heel loudly and kicking gravel and dirt toward her. He growled in Ma'ab, enunciating every word. "*None of your army remains at Manalar, Enslaver. They are all dead, their Vis drifting toward Ennikar. Leave now with your failed Wargan. There is nothing left that is worth the cost.*"

"*No!*" Vesram protested.

Mourn's lips curled in annoyance as the Fourth glanced at the Sathoet, her golden cat's eye gleaming. Its black pupil shrank to a thin line as she considered Gavin's appearance.

"Hm," she grunted, unraveling her bladed whip to let it touch the ground. Her large paw scuffed some disdainful dirt back at Mourn. "*I will take the Wargan, the demon-Elf, and the young upstart. Then we will leave. Give me the dark Elf and the breathing corpse as well, and the Black Army will not leave the North for another century. I will see to it.*"

"*No deal,*" Captain Isboern said in her tongue, making certain the Sun's reflection on his shield annoyed the Enslaver enough to draw her focus. "*The war is over. We have won. Leave or be stranded here when I bring down your gateway.*"

The Enslaver appeared briefly surprised at a random Human's boldness but chuckled. "*I will flay your soul into shreds, little man. You and all your tender Paxians will cry for oblivion.*"

This wasn't going well. The Templari around Isboern had spent most of their strength and Vesram was terrified; he would not confront the Ascended. Deshi, Mourn, and Jael were ready to fight her alone but not unified if Jael should try, for she could be snared and thrown through the portal to Ennikar.

The Enslaver could see all of this. She waited, flicking her whip with a smirk, daring them to try.

Meanwhile, my Deathwalker stared at the portal. I could have sworn his obsidian growths had spread over most of his face and shoulders.

~Gavin? ... Gavin!~

*I hear them ... *

His multitude of voices seeped into the mindlink. Many of the Templari shuddered, looking over their shoulders as if expecting to be surrounded by ghosts.

Damn it. I couldn't let him fall into another trance.

~Can you use it against the stone golem?~ I asked, trying to ground him, ~Or the Fourth?~

My Deathwalker didn't answer but lifted the thurible toward either the Toh-Rah Set or ... the gate behind him?

The Herald stepped forward, and the Enslaver cracked her whip, the flint blade darting straight for him. The whip snapped upon Isboern's psionic shield. Her shoulders straighten, head cocking in surprise.

My eyebrows lifted. ~She couldn't sense it?~

Mourn replied, *No, but regardless, everyone stay out of her range.*

I hear them, the Deathwalker repeated.

Layers upon layers to his thought.

When Gavin might have taken another entranced step toward the portal, Isboern rushed to take his shoulder. He didn't react or try to shrug loose from the touch. I shuddered.

What do you mean, you hear who? demanded the Dragonchild, repositioning to catch the whip if the Ma'ab ruler attacked again.

The Deathwalker didn't answer as the Enslaver matched the next thunderous step of her golem, pausing at his flank to sniff the air, peering through each eye. She bared her teeth, thrusting forward her tusks. "What is this?"

"To'vah shield." Mourn smirked, his tail skimming Jael's leg in its lively lash. "You've entered the battlefield at a disadvantage."

"To'vah," she repeated with a sneer. "Quite troublesome, your kind, when you decide to show yourselves."

"You have your shields. We have ours. Test them, or don't. What will it be, Ascended?"

The Ma'ab ruler, unlike any other Ma'ab I could imagine, glanced back at the portal. She could have been listening to something — or someone — we couldn't hear.

~*Sirana!*~

I jolted in place. ~*Captain?*~

~*Stop protecting me from what you already know. Let me listen.*~

Was I? Against *him*?

From what?

The man exhaled, braced with his golden shield forward to defend Gavin's body. ~*I don't understand how you did it, but you've shielded the Herald from the rest of us. The voices of the dead from moments ago have slipped from the mindlink and so has he.*~

I tilted my ear. He was right, they were gone. ~*Shit.*~

~*You bore the madness of the Chenkyte for me. I understand why, but if the Grave Mother protects the pool and I am to revive it, I must understand the realm of her Herald.*~

Bold. Admirable.

But ...

~*Gavin hasn't ... agreed,*~ I thought, confused at the roil of tension within.

~*Then you must reach out to him, and you must lower your shields and not follow me. I need you to stay alert and keep everyone linked, even my Templari.*~

My fingers tightened upon the stone. ~*I can't.*~

~*You can. When I kneeled in the spring's waters after the rift opened, a wisp of death mixed with the brother of light, and all of Paxia lived less in fear. I know how necessary he is to see this change turn our way. Please. I must understand this, and you must take over the living bonds.*~

I swallowed, peeking over the windowsill.

Mourn's focus had locked on the Fourth in her distraction, his tail hovering above the ground, white spines lifting as an intangible tension rose. Jael seemed prepared to obstruct anything coming toward the exhausted Humans, while Deshi and Vesram whispered suspiciously to each other.

My Deathwalker's eyes had gone full black, and the pneuma flint had overtaken more of his parched skin for certain. Captain Isboern held his metal shield forward, holding tightly to Gavin's shoulder with his other hand. Bare fingers crossed several dark shards.

The Godblood had removed his glove.

~*Sirana. Please. We need to hear each other. The Sun Brother and the Grey Lady* must *talk*.~

The Enslaver turned her unsettling gaze from the portal to Manalar's defenders, her mouth set with frustration, one nostril curled in contempt. She lashed her whip upon the unseen shield again, smiling as it briefly shimmered, visibly thinning. The Ascended stepped behind the giant, dipping down to grip the Eternal Hellhound by one charred foot.

"*Tear it down,*" she said to the Toh-Rah Set in motion. "*Crush all but the dark female.*"

"*Whoa, hai!*" Deshi shouted as the golem charged forward, quicker than expected, with fist raised.

Everyone scattered. Jael backed away with the Templari, splitting from Mourn, who vanished into the Humans' collective shadow. Isboern dragged Gavin to one side as Deshi and Vesram sprinted around the other.

The mountain bore the full brunt of that first blow, sending tremors through the ground and a cloud of dirt into the air. With a hoarse laugh, the Enslaver dragged Divigna toward the gateway, and Ennikar.

"*Ssstop!*" Vesram cried.

~*Sirana!*~ Isboern called.

"Shhhhit!" I hissed, drawing a figurative breath.

Had to make it loud.

~*GAVIN!*~

His name pierced a veil, and the grey voices rose like a maelstrom.

There you are, the Herald said, mist and waving faces filling my head until I could see nothing of the battlefield.

~*The Brother's Champion wants to talk!*~ I said, desperate to see. ~*In private!*~

By all means. It's about time.

With the force and speed of a lightning strike, Willven and I changed places in the mists of Gavin's mind. As my conscious thoughts hurled into the daylight, I gathered up all willing threads of thoughts nearby.

Capitan!

Where are you?!

~Stall her!~ I cried, uncertain where that command came from but it felt right. ~Give your Captain every moment we can until they close the gate!~

Each Templari in and outside the watchtower came to attention as Mourn emerged in my periphery from the building's shadow. He sprinted to guard Gavin and Isboern to one side of the gate, the motion too fast to track until he attacked.

With a reach rivaling the Enslaver's, the Dragonchild became an obstacle between her and the two messengers, using his slider to sever Divigna's leg and leaving the Ascended holding a foot. She snarled and tossed the charred limb away.

The Harrowed in full flame screamed behind her, and she whirled partway, gauging the threat at her flanks. Meanwhile, Vesram darted in unseen, dragging Divigna's corpse toward Mourn faster than I'd thought he could.

"Inhelk rechana inhelk!" Jael barked then, releasing a spell through her humming blades which struck the golem in the chest, preventing another charge barely long enough for the split Templari to aim their own spells to avoid allies.

Two daylight blasts met on the golem's flank, tilting it off-balance. Sadly, it did not fall but recovered its footing during a spin meant to crush the Harrowed standing behind the Enslaver.

~Deshi, yield!~ I called.

The new guardian dropped back from the Fourth before he recognized the danger. Dust and splinters of rock exploded in his haunting face, then a second, slow swing passed right through him. The Harrowed wailed, clutching his head as the Toh-Rah Set straightened up, tilting backward, silently wavering above its scarlet mistress.

~You disrupted its flow of souls, Harrowed!~ I said. ~Strike the rock giant as many times as you can even if it doesn't react!~

Hai, Janshi! he acknowledged, gathering his mental shields against whatever he had seen or heard.

Suddenly, the Enslaver attacked with her whip, slicing Vesram across his maned back and forcing his visibility.

"Eeeeeeaaah!"

The Sathoet dropped the Hellhound's body, collapsing to his knees as the Fourth then summoned a cord made of red light. It formed a noose mid-air and snared Vesram around his neck. He dropped to his knees and did not — *could not* — struggle.

"Ours," she growled, drawing a muscled arm back, pulling it taut.

~*Mourn!*~

The Dragonchild barked a familiar command, lifting and tossing Divigna out of the Enslaver's reach, toward Jael and the Templari, before coming in with both sliders to sever the cord holding the demonblood. Vesram choked, scrambling up at once to vanish from view.

"You — !" The Fourth gnashed teeth, swiftly regaining her balance once the red cord dissolved. Her whip arm came to bear on the Dragon son alone as she pressed forward, three aggressive cracks forcing him to back up.

Mourn's ears twitched, his teeth bared and gritted as the snapping weapon tortured his ears and showered the hair with burning sparks. His blades turned the bite of the whip's blade several times but failed in their attempts to disarm her.

"Seize the Hellhound!" she commanded. *"Take him to the Physician!"*

The Toh-Rah Set withdrew from the Harrowed dancing around it, turning one long step toward Divigna's body.

"Shit!" Jael spun up her humming blade in one hand, extending her palm with the other, pantomiming the toss of a rock as she yelled. *"Thrae ternesj!"*

Draconic Words catapulted Kreshel's body. My Sister had aimed for the southern cliff — a good idea — but fell short. The giant golem kept moving, Deshi dogging him, cutting at his legs with ghostly hands as the massive arm reached out for the corpse containing the *Kor Nigram*.

~*Push the body off the ledge!*~ I ordered, hoping the Manalari had some way to do this and that Vesram wasn't in the way.

The Enslaver drew a rune midair, the air itself igniting into flame. Mourn's left slider vanished and a small shield appeared in his hand in response. The Ascended snarled a magical command, the burning flames darkening to black fire. She feinted as if to pitch the spell, pausing to draw his counter first.

He nearly fell for it as she changed her target.

~*No, protect Gavin!*~ I blurted.

Mourn snarled, speaking just in time to hurl his magic after hers. "*Cayosin'tiaf cayosin!*"

The two forces met in a crackling collision mere arms' lengths from the Deathwalker's spiny back. Only then did I notice my ally was …

Floating.

The fingers which held his thurible had become talons made of pneuma flint hooked securely around the iron handle. His shoulders bore a thorny mantle of black obsidian growths as other facets disrupted his jawline and the structure of his face. I barely recognized him. Isboern had a hold of one brittle arm, drawing the Herald closer to the gateway with Mitneh'thran pointed directly at it.

What are they doing?

"*Heave!*" three men called together.

The sound of a body tumbling. Silence followed in a freefall.

"Yes!" Jael hooted.

"Scatter!" Deshi wailed, harrying the golem to the edge of the mountain.

"*Fool, stop!!*" the Enslaver roared, this time hurling her black fire at the Dragon Son, one from each palm as the Toh-Rah Set ground to a halt at the cliff's edge.

Mourn dodged the first strike but not the second, black fire turning to gold and red as it spread over his arm and shoulder, swiftly engulfing him before my eyes.

~*No!*~

"*Navnikic di okraz, anyui!*"

The fire vanished as if snuffed by a waterfall, though no steam billowed into the air. Mourn did not appear harmed at all — not scorched or blistered, nothing he wore damaged in any way — but he was shaking, his Elven skin breaking into a cold sweat.

*Anyone else … and they'd be dead … * he thought.

I swallowed, my fingers aching from my grip upon the sill as a retaliatory storm of Words surged out of Mourn's throat on the rise to his feet. The spell smashed enough magical defense to knock the Fourth prone. She shouted in fury, leaping onto her feet without using her arms, cracking her whip in the wake of his retreat.

By then, everyone was out of range, including the Deathwalker and Godblood.

Suddenly, a short, bejeweled skeleton shining in gilded armor stepped through the portal, backed by the tallest Ma'ab male I'd ever seen. Red eyes glowed out the slit of a full-face helm, the massive body encased in exotic, magic-scripted armor formed from a blend of black metal and raw muscle.

The tiny skeleton joined us on Mount Sonai, casting a rope of blue light toward the cliff while the huge male stood in the doorway, sabaton boots braced wide on the stone floor in Ennikar.

The General ...

My body filled with ice as recognition surfaced. The General of the Undefeated Void. The Nexus warrior who once led forces in battle against a Greylord ... and won.

~The Second Ascended,~ I whispered in terror. ~If he steps through, we must retreat.~

Mourn glanced at the gate, shifting to place himself between the Enslaver and the Godblood. ~We've never seen this one outside Ennikar in my lifetime. If he comes leaves the capital, something beyond our ken has changed.~

~Are we wagering on him not coming through?~

Knowing the gamble, Mourn answered, ~Yes.~

~Splintered tits ... ~

Just when I believed we had sent Kreshel far from their reach, the skeleton pulled his corpse atop the mountain, dragging him across the ground like a huge fish wrapped in glowing blue netting. Power poured out from multi-colored gems embedded in the decorated servant, digging into Kreshel's torso to bind themselves to the false heart.

Mourn tried to sever the magic before the two met, but the spell-weave refused to break. *Shuiblith!*

"Vesram, get behind us!" Deshi called, having broken off from the immobile statue to guard Jael and the Templars.

The Sathoet hesitated one moment but ultimately gave ground, foregoing his heart's desire to keep his freedom.

Meanwhile, the Divine Warrior had settled his gaze on Isboern's golden shield, the only object between the two. The Godblood did nothing to acknowledge the threat, and I detected nothing of either's thoughts, not in word or motion as the warriors stood their ground.

A mystery how Willven *wasn't* soiling his armor, but the bigger question of his goal found our answer at last.

~*The gateway is shrinking!*~

What? Mourn looked.

The pathway must be powered by souls like the stone golem, for the Herald siphoned them off, wearing down the portal gradually. As he did so, the black flint on his body grew and grew, his feet repelled by the ground. No thoughts from either Gavin or Willven, but they must be linked with each other.

They weren't the only ones.

The Divine Warrior turned his helm to his right, a motion unnaturally smooth and quiet, acknowledging someone deeper in the shadow. Not the fluid lich, this time, for that one crouched behind his left leg, beckoning to the skeleton.

Something *must* be happening — or changing — elsewhere.

"Your Toh-Rah Set soon won't fit," Mourn snarled at the Enslaver. "Wait too long, and you remain here with us. What do you choose next, Divine Enslaver?"

Mismatched eyes narrowed into slits, her body language wary with the unsettling observance of the Second.

Once the gilded skeleton dragged Kreshel Divigna across the threshold — a concession we had to make unless we intended to invade Ennikar itself — the Second beckoned to his Fourth.

"*Hsreth sha!*" she jeered, cracking her whip in frustration.

The Divine Warrior said nothing, peered at Gavin and Isboern one more time …

And stepped back from the gateway.

I let out the breath I'd been holding. *~He's not coming through.~*

The Enslaver barked, *"Return to your goddess! Move quickly!"*

The Toh-Rah Set backed up, turning once the ground wasn't liable to crumble under his feet. The creature charged his own gate, and Mourn made room. Guarding Gavin and Isboern with sliders crossed, the Dragonchild murmured a shimmering spell onto their edges.

Once the golem got close, the Fourth grinned. *"Hit them!"*

The boulder-sized fist lifted up, feet thundering.

~Watch out!~

Mourn's eyes widened; all he could do was brace himself.

The bodyguard for the Northern gods smashed the magical shield, sending the Dragon son tumbling into his allies as both messengers called out in surprise. Whatever focus they'd held vanished.

The giant dropped to all fours to crawl through the collapsing gate, the Second moving far away to allow it. With a raucous laugh, the Fourth threw a crude gesture, cracking her whip with a flourish. On powerful paws, she sprang off of Mount Sonai.

Mourn covered Isboern with his body, as he had mine when the festering center of the warp rot had collapsed. An instant later, the gate closed in a sucking whorl, the air filled with the screams of an empire culminating into brilliant, silent light.

Our eyes saw nothing, but our ears heard everything as the last voice faded over the valley below.

So quiet.

Am I . . . ?

Alone in my head?

Wait.

I was. I released the breath I'd been holding.

They never saw me.

The Ascended had witnessed plenty; they knew how their invasion had begun and how it ended, but not everything in between. Enough distraction, enough warriors willing to fight, enough risks taken, other exposures chosen to cover up the hint of life magic such as Irrwaer had possessed atop this Mount.

They couldn't hear me.

Perhaps the liches of the Far North did not yet understand the mind mages on this world?

But maybe they'll talk to Kreshel.

My body started to shake. I fought it.

Don't.

I could not dismiss how I *had* escaped their notice just now. Not one ally had given me away when it most mattered.

No one!

My baby and I were safe.

And I still have a chance to be free of this geas.

I remained where I was when I started to cry, wet warmth draining down my cheeks. Lieutenant Robi had stayed with me while the others left to gather around their Captain.

"Are you hurt?" he asked, worried.

I shook my head. "Just ... frightened. The ghost of how it could have gone ... lingers."

"Ah. I ... the same."

He let the silence rest until, on the other side of the wall, Vesram began to keen.

"Lossst her," he moaned. "Lossst ... gone ... noooo ..."

"We ... tried, Vesram, I am sorry," Mourn murmured, exhausted enough that he did not stop Jael from leaving.

The keening continued, intermixed with growling which reminded me too much of the Sathoet's brothers contained in the twelfth floor of the Sanctuary. He was on the verge of powerful emotions which would not be held in check.

I didn't want to have to be the one responsible for controlling him, but Gavin was unconscious.

Please, quiet down …

He didn't.

"YOU!" he roared. *"You said he would **end** thisss!!"*

I jumped, spinning around to climb on my knees and look outside. *Who is he talking to?!*

A petite Ma'ab woman stood placidly among them wearing a black, hook-and-needle gown. She possessed a pneuma flint eye and enough hairless scalp to bear a few needles of silver. The Grey Guardian had appeared abruptly enough that several Templars were still backing away when I recognized her.

"He will end this," Ada replied, her pale hand stroking Vesram's mane, smoothing the puff hair down. "My son is not ready. I told you this. You chose not to listen, dear friend."

A low growl lingered, but the demonblood calmed himself before her, his grey eyes drifting to stare at the ground. "Kreshel sssaid he … wasss not enough … He watched. He knew."

"Kreshel always was practical. Like him, you shall have to wait. Though this is not done, *you* are free. As I promised."

Vesram quieted, if not comforted then at least dismissing the accusation that she'd misled him.

Meanwhile, Jael entered the tower with a sigh, Graul heavy in her arms. She came to sit with me so Robi could join his brothers-in-arms.

"*Hai,*" I whispered.

"*Mm,*" she grunted, settling down by the window out of the fading day.

Outside, the Templari, Deshi, and a bleary-eyed Isboern carried the comatose body of Ada's son closer to her in a hammock of cloaks.

"You are … away from the pool, guardian," the Captain said. "What does this mean?"

Ada's sharp, black teeth came on full display. "What do you think it means, Brother Warrior?"

Isboern swallowed. "Is it over?" He looked at Mourn. "Have we won *Pisc'sagrad* in the eyes of the legends?"

Mourn's tail swayed, a slow smile growing on his lips as he gazed at the sky. "The Red's Arena is gone. According to the pool's Guardian, Captain, you have."

"*Inomilu sancji*," he murmured, fist on his chest.

"*Inomilu sancji*," the Templari echoed together.

"You'll not want to wait long on the bonding ritual," Ada said, gazing at her unconscious son with obvious affection. "But you both have some time to rest."

"I understand, prophetess." The psion followed her gaze. "He ... showed me some sights. Patterns I'll not forget as long as I live."

Dark eyes glinted with joy. "Good."

"Are you leaving?" Vesram asked in dismay.

Ada slipped her hand into the Sathoet's palm, the delicate limb disappearing within gnarled, curled fingers. It surprised us all but especially him.

"Not yet," she said like a promise.

Jael sighed deeply, drawing my attention.

"Hm?" I asked.

She smirked as Graul churred, nestled on her lap. *"That was ... difficult."*

"Heh. Yeah, it was. But you did it. We both made it."

She shrugged. *"He did most of the fighting."*

Graul blew air through his nostrils, briefing rolling his eyes.

I chuckled. *"So? You stuck on him and me like a burr. I don't think you ever let down your guard. You cast real spells, and you didn't let your temper get in the way."* My smile faded. *"You ... stayed with me when I couldn't ... move. When I couldn't handle everything at once."*

My Sister frowned, lightly petting the shadow drake's wings for something to do with her hands. *"Mm-hm. Wasn't gonna leave you at your weakest. You didn't at mine. You could have. But ... we both rallied, I think."*

"We did. Thank you, Sister."

The smile returned easier than I expected, watching her lips through a brief pout thinking over the last fight.

"Kiss?" I asked.

Her head whipped to me. *"Huh?"*

I leaned in, eager to taste her lips. They were salty and touched with the grime of an all-day battle.

She inhaled with pleasure through her nose. *"Mm!"*

Graul squawked in alarm as her enthusiasm went straight up the tree, and she threw her arms around me. I gathered her closer, squeezing the drake between us to enjoy a long kiss.

"Hai!" he groused.

"Plenny ov shadow tah leave," I said through one corner of my mouth.

"Hmph!"

The drake stayed.

Soon enough, Mourn arrived as well, peering into the first floor of the watchtower which was empty but for us. *"Having fun?"*

"Bah!" Jael said, parting and thumping against the wall. *"Not yet! We still wear clothes!"*

"Indeed." His tail coiled with a hint of play. *"My regrets, but Soul Drinker lies at the bottom of a chasm."*

The image struck my chest like a club. *"Oh! You're right! And my spiders! They are still in the cave!"*

"Show me where. We must collect both without delay. The others are returning to the Temple."

"Even the Sathoet?"

"He prefers Ada's company."

"He better stay put," Jael grumbled, accepting Mourn's offer to take Graul for her so she could stand up.

I stretched after getting up, gathering thoughts while part of it all seemed like a dream. While events had been happening, I hadn't appraised all of the Dragonblood's wounds. Now I did.

Oof.

Cuts, burns, abrasions. A deeper slash wound, and several punctures from spike or arrow. None bled freely anymore, but some might with enough jostling.

Mourn paused in massaging Graul's shoulders when he noticed me staring. *"Ready?"*

"Are you well enough to go climbing down a whole mountain again?" I asked,

waving my hand from his shoulders to his feet.

"*I will be.*" He smiled. "*I want to show Jael a trick.*"

"*I thought you couldn't heal by Word.*"

"*True. But there is still aura shifting, and I expect to be carrying you most of the way down.*"

He meant we'd be clinging to him, Jael and I. Scenting him, feeling his warmth, his strength …

Listening to the hum of the mages' auras.

I exhaled, my earlier request for Jael echoing in my head. *Kiss … ?*

Damned web. That felt wrong with him.

"*Very well, then. I am ready.*" I swallowed. "*And thank you. For everything.*"

Golden eyes shone with warmth. "*Same, Sirana. For everything. I would not have seen the fall of the Bishops and won a rebirth for the pool without you. I know this.*"

My middle trembled with his words, a feeling I covered with both hands. I wanted to but had neither the angle nor the courage to kiss him then.

"*I obtained some food,*" he said, noting my hands on my stomach. "*You can eat while we climb.*"

Although retrieving my spiders and locating the naked rune blade took us until long after sunset, I appreciated the leisure for once in climbing around this mountain. Graul flitted from shadow to shadow while Mourn lifted me down by my waist, tucked me close to his front, or encouraged Jael to hold onto his back. Sometimes we'd switch places.

This was a lot of time to breathe his scent and enjoy his oddly warm, if dirty, blend of skin and scales. I enjoyed it while I could and knew Jael did, too, especially once Mourn demonstrated his "trick."

A careful, physical balance entwined with his breath which enhanced his endurance and hardened his scabs. The feeling reminded me of how he'd performed at the patriarch's house in Yong-wen, creating that song touching everybody there through motion and flow.

The "trick" was something Jael took to, which surprised me at first, but perhaps it shouldn't. My younger Sister responded well to physical lessons; I'd told Mourn that. He used it to find something that helped them both to recover a little faster.

"Can you sense it near, Sirana?"

"Unfortunately," I grumbled. *"That way."*

We discovered the cursed blade on an outcropping still some distance from the bottom, untouched by some other poor victim. The gatekeeper within wasn't free of the crystal, but sound was beginning to leak out.

★ *… hsssss … ..* ★

~*Disappointed?*~ I thought before shoving the point into the sheath. The blade fell silent, whole and reattached to my belt.

"Good," Mourn said, relieved. *"Good."*

"Good as can be," Jael said.

"Mhm." He craned his neck, searching the dark for the best pathway up. *"To the Temple? Join the others?"*

"Of course," Jael said, folding her arms. *"Where else do we go after a day like this?"*

"Need to get Krithannia and Tamuril caught up, too." I paused, adding, *"Are there baths?"*

The half-blood bobbed his chin. *"And beds if you like. Hearths for warm cooking or hot drinks, too."*

A grin stuck to my face before I knew it. If my former bodyguard meant to nudge us toward a few hard-earned spoils of war …

This is a good start.

Chapter 42

House of Matron Thalluen - Sivaraus

Jaunda approached Rohenvi's House from the main road, allowing herself to be seen with plenty of warning. The change from sneaking in would worry the Matron, as it probably should, but the Lead was relieved.

Penance is done. Get to stay home for a while.

No Red Sisters here to slap with until D'Shea called on her, but at least Shyntre was there to keep things interesting if she grew too bored. The bua tended to take on fights he couldn't win.

Auslan will be there, too. Hm.

The healer wasn't anywhere near the challenge the wizard could be once riled, and Jaunda wasn't in need of the Consort's magic for once. But there *was* that little comment D'Shea made while giving her orders …

"Watch everything, keep my buas safe, and I'll join you as soon as I can."

My buas. Jaunda shook her head. *What in the Drider piss is that … ?*

What had happened while the Lead had been prowling the Deepearth looking for the Black Dragon?

Suppose I'll find out soon enough.

The Matron didn't leave her walls to meet the Red Sister, but the House Guard were prepared with a standard greet and escort. One would never think anything was wrong with how cool they acted around her.

Was anything wrong? Why the vague sense it wouldn't be long before they saw trouble?

Jaunda huffed, smirking. *Because Shyntre's here.*

Any other bua that had raged through life the way he did would have been wrapped up and tossed into the Drider Pit decades ago. But the wizard was Phaelous's magic and D'Shea's willpower, raised in the Sanctuary with Priestesses, and never content from his first breath.

Shyntre had survived *a lot* of surly episodes, provoking, making demands, daring the Priestesses and even the Prime to do something about it. They'd retaliated every chance they could, had made his life miserable for sure, but they'd never seen him executed or assassinated.

Yet had the youth flaunted this in the elder females' faces, dancing behind the Valsharess's robes like a haughty brat?

No, not once.

Rather, he always seemed disappointed when they conceded. Those were the times he quieted down, like he was watching and waiting for the next time.

Definitely D'Shea's son.

Her fire in him was painfully obvious to the Sisters who knew about the Elder's stay in the Sanctuary. As the one who had escorted D'Shea in and out of the Sanctuary, Jaunda had always *liked* Shyntre in a bizarre way she couldn't explain.

So does Rausery.

That old feeling *almost* made sense after listening to the Headmaster speak with Elder D'Shea about the General's bloodline.

"Rausery and Jaunda?"

"The same influence. The Black Dragon. What Wilsira was trying to dig and exploit from commoners related to our General to create the Consorts."

The Conceiver had been after Dragon magic in addition to Abyssal for her Noble Davrin offspring. *Greedy cunt.*

"But," D'Shea said, *"you and Shyntre ... ?"*

"Not the Black. Another influence ... far older."

Phaelous meant a different Dragon. One from a time before the scrolls in his libraries, which *had* to be a long-fucking-time. Supposedly, the Ja'Prohn line had gold flecks in their red eyes because of this other Dragon.

How the piss did it happen? Jaunda could only presume she wasn't the first to fuck a To'vah and live. *Glad I insisted on not catching anything from Lethrix in our Bargain …*

"Lead Sister, welcome."

Focus. "Matron. Here on Sisterhood interests."

Rohenvi stepped gracefully down the steps of her mansion, wearing a simple garnet-red gown of good quality. Behind her, the cait Natia peeked out the door, standing by the leg of the governor holding the infant heir.

"Of course you are." Sirana's Mother bore a slight, tired smile before turning around to reclimb the stairs. "Follow me, if you please."

Jaunda breathed in deep the smell of other working Davrin, relishing it as she followed the Matron through familiar halls. Once out of sight of the rest of the House, she didn't keep Matron Thalluen sweating.

The Lead grinned as broad as she could. "Bluntly, nothing complicated, Matron. This is my stakeout. I'm supposed to guard Shyntre and Auslan for you until Elder D'Shea can join us."

Rohenvi blinked in surprise. "When will that be?"

"I don't know. She's juggling a lot at the moment."

"When *isn't* she?" The Matron exhaled softly. "You're not a subtle presence when kept in one place too long, Lead, and I imagine you're not as quiet when you aren't injured on a stealth mission."

Jaunda chuckled, shifting her weight to display her strength and health. "Yeah, you're right. The good news is you might as well let me and the wizard strut around your plantation. It's what the eyes that matter would expect to see and help warn others away."

"To what end?" Her face pinched. "I see no conclusion to this plot where I have any moves to make which matter. Me and mine are just a target for confrontation."

"Not my nuance, I'm afraid, but while I'm here, my skills are at your service."

Rohenvi paused with a slight softening of her tense mouth. "Shyntre said the same."

"Yeah?" Jaunda's grin widened. "If he said that, I'd believe him."

The Matron shook her head, rubbing her temples. "Wait. You … sound as though you respect him."

"As D'Shea's son, sure. As a bua who should have been dead ten times over before two hundred, even better. He'd make a good Red Sister if he'd been born a cait."

Sirana's Mother rubbed her mouth with a forefinger, looking thoughtful. "And Auslan? Is he still a secret?"

"Mmm, no." Jaunda shrugged. "Sorry. The Valsharess has Her eye on him as a battle healer."

Rohenvi's eyes widened. "B-battle? When?"

Oops.

"Uhhh, wait," Jaunda waved her hand, rubbing a temple. "You haven't had a healer born in your House recently, have you?"

"I have not."

"Touch healers always end up directly under the Queen. If She wants to retrain them, that's what She does. Just didn't have time for him after the Purge, and he wasn't safe with the Sisters or the Priestesses. There sure as fuck weren't many Noble Matrons we could trust with his health since he happened to be a Consort, too."

"Is that what happened?" Rohenvi wasn't pleased in the least but remained hungry for information. "So, with you and Shyntre here to guard him, the Consort could walk around and be seen?"

"If you decide to let him out, sure. I wouldn't let anything happen to them." Jaunda smirked. "Let the spies wag their tongues. The crumb trail eventually leads to the Queen, anyway."

Though not comforted by the revelations, the Matron squared her shoulders, smoothing the front of her gown with her hands. "I see. Well … Let me think about this. For now, I shall take you to them."

His BROTHER *had* BEEN RESTING, FINALLY, AFTER A LONG AND METICULOUS cleaning of the entire room which had exhausted them both but must have sensed them coming heartbeats before Shyntre did.

Auslan bolted upright, his throat closed as his hand grappled the empty air.

"Hey, I'm here." Shyntre rushed over, taking his flailing hand with a squeeze, pressing his shoulder with the other. "I'm here. What is it?"

The former Consort stared at the hidden door through which they received all their visitors. "D-Drake ... !"

"What?"

Matron Thalluen knocked in the soft code which identified herself, waiting a moment before she entered. Behind her was Jaunda, and ... no one else.

Rohenvi frowned. "Are you alright, Auslan?"

"Looks like he's seen a Drider," the Lead commented.

"A bad dream," Shyntre said when Auslan didn't — or couldn't — speak, glad they were both dressed. "You startled us."

Jaunda clearly didn't care, and the Matron didn't comment at first.

"Well," she began, "I've been informed that Elder D'Shea intends to visit us soon, but I don't know when or what to expect." Her head tilted toward the Red Sister. "Until then, she sent her Lead as your bodyguard."

Auslan blinked as if he comprehended that, and Shyntre couldn't hide his dismay. "You mean, her sitting in here with us?" He shook his head at Jaunda. "Lead, you'd hate it more than I would."

"Does it matter?" she replied. "Got my orders."

"Wait, clarify your thoughts, Shyntre?" Rohenvi asked in a tone which required a response.

Gladly.

The wizard met her eyes. "Matron, she'll make sport of us sooner or later in a locked room this small. It's what Red Sisters do, and this one isn't accustomed to long periods of stillness."

Jaunda made a face but didn't argue the point, merely looked at Matron Thalluen who didn't know how to hold her hands for a moment. Unusual. Shyntre wondered if they had had this exact conversation before stepping in here.

"I see." Rohenvi swallowed. "But didn't Auslan heal this same Red Sister thrice before?"

"She was injured," the wizard countered, "and you stayed present the entire time, did you not? You didn't trust her alone with him. What difference would it make if I'm here?"

The Matron breathed out through her nose, granting a nod. "And … if you were allowed to leave this room?"

Auslan shook his head in the negative, shrinking, his tongue mute.

"That would be better for the Red Sister," Shyntre admitted. "But it's been half a turn for Auslan in this room. Don't drag him out into the courtyard and expect him to make you look good, Matron."

"What," Jaunda remarked with a smirk, "would he faint?"

Shyntre pulled up straight. "Or fall into shock. Or panic at something unexpected." He looked between them, accusing. "Think about it! He was dragged out of his private quarters during the Purge, locked in a cell in the Cloister, tortured, then thrown sore and bleeding into this room! He hasn't left except to work for you until he fell ill. He might as well be coming out of the Queen's dungeon."

Rohenvi flinched. "I thought he was getting better under your care."

"His body is better, Matron," Shyntre said bitterly. "He's still having torture dreams. It's not your fault, but *please* don't coop us in here for cycles with the Lead. It won't help my efforts."

Sirana's Mother exhaled slowly, sorting through her worries and private concerns before speaking. "How about we begin by sharing a meal?"

The wizard grimaced. "In the dining hall?"

"No, in my private suites. With Natia, Vekika, and myself. They are spacious and safe. I have a chaise and comfortable places to sit if Auslan needs it, and room for Lead Jaunda to walk around if she likes." Rohenvi looked at Jaunda. "There is even a balcony."

The Lead shrugged. "As you like, Matron. Sounds good."

"Come with me, then." Rohenvi's eyes flickered to Auslan before meeting Shyntre's. "We will leave you alone to prepare and come get you when the space is ready. You have at least a mark."

Shyntre could do little but accept the proposal and wait for them to leave. Once their presence faded behind the wall, he sat down in front of his brother.

"Hey." He slid his palms in, cupping the healer's cheeks. "Look at me."

Auslan obeyed, but his eyes were moist. Shyntre didn't know where to start but decided not to go with the Sisterhood or the last time he'd been outside this room.

"You said 'drake' before you woke up. Do you remember why?"

A headshake. Shyntre took it as an answer at first, but then Auslan finally spoke.

"I was not asleep," he murmured. "I was awake when I said that."

The wizard bit his lip, passing over four useless thoughts before choosing his next. "Did you see one? Or sense it?"

"The Lead." Auslan's heart thudded in his chest; his face flushed. "She is ... different from when I last healed her."

Shyntre frowned. He hadn't noticed. *Yet.* "And you sensed it *before* she walked in the room?"

"I thought ... I thought something dangerous had arrived. I did not know what she was until I saw her."

"And what did you think had arrived?"

"Just ... a giant, dark drake. Gold eyes. Watching. Like in our dream."

" 'Our' dream?"

"Yes. The one with the runner who climbed out of the well and saved us from that unraveling spirit ..."

Shyntre didn't remember that.

"The drake took us across red sands to safer water," the healer continued, staring at the floor. "Where we met the red horse ... who carried us to the river. To Sirana."

The wizard swallowed, unnerved by how certain Auslan sounded about these dreams. He *did* remember that part with Sirana, at least. "Okay, um. So, it *wasn't* Jaunda that scared you so."

His brother shook his head. "Th-thank you for speaking on my behalf. I do not think the Lead Sister *harmless* but … no. Her aura scared me. Felt like a giant drake."

Shyntre bit his inner cheek, the words of the Valsharess leaking into his head. "*It is time for him to Awaken, We believe. He would not miss this. … Sirana ensnared his son and still carries yours …*"

Sons.

Why must *Her* darkest secrets always involve sons?

The wizard cleared his throat. "Maybe not a drake but … the Black Dragon?"

Auslan's eyes blinked several times, revelation breaking over his face. "Yes! That must be it! Did … did she meet the Dragon of the Deep somehow?"

"Maybe?"

Jaunda *had* been looking for something for quad-spans, ever since Rausery left with Sirana and the others for the Surface.

The wizard combed his fingers through his brother's hair, humming in thought. "I'll try to pay better attention at dinner."

None of the possibilities swirling in Shyntre's mind were *good,* but they explained the abrupt, changing circumstances.

We're coming out of hiding whether we like it or not.

ROHENVI HAD A TELLTALE WET SPOT ON THE FRONT OF HER DRESS FROM NURSING her heir, which suggested she had rushed getting things ready. Shyntre pretended he hadn't noticed as Auslan smiled, bowing to the Matron and Gaelan's daughter.

"Always a pleasure, Natia."

"Yeah! And food's ready!"

The child approached, taking firm hold of the healer's hand to lead him out of the room. Auslan exchanged some amusement with his brother as Shyntre motioned them forward.

"Go on. I'll be right behind you."

Matching pace with the Lead.

Not the worst way for the former Consort to finally leave his most recent prison. The House was largely awake, their small group observed by subtle eyes despite the relatively short walk through the halls. Most were presumed loyal to their House, curious but accepting of buas they knew were here, whether this was their first glance or not. The Davrin were nervous with the Red Sister present, a mood echoed in their Matron.

"Where is Vekika?" Auslan asked quietly.

"Already waiting," Natia answered brightly. "Maybe napping."

"Oh?"

Shyntre frowned. His first mental image of an infant heir alone in a basket waiting in empty suites *had* to be wrong.

Who else is in there?

He wouldn't find out until after they had sat down at Matron Rohenvi's six-seat long table in her meeting room. The resting and bathing quarters were closed off, and Vekika was too quiet to confirm if she lay within. Shyntre assumed she did.

"You appear calmer, Auslan," Rohenvi said as they took their places, Natia hopping into the seat nearest to her.

"Yes, Matron."

"Sit here, Auslan." Natia tapped the last chair on her side before pointing to another across from her and at Rohenvi's right. "Save that one for Vanry. He'll be here soon."

He? Shyntre's eyes narrowed as he took the only seat left. With the Matron and Lead at the short ends and the positions closest to the Matron claimed, he and Auslan sat across from each other but next to Jaunda.

"Who is Vanry, Matron?" the wizard asked, catching a whiff of warm food underneath the ornate metal covers. It made his mouth water.

"That's the governor I saw at the door, right?" Jaunda said. "The old male."

Old?

"And Natia's tutor for the next while, yes. A fortunate find and excellent help as I manage the grounds and my affairs."

High praise. Shyntre hadn't missed how the child's eyes lit up hearing this from her Matron. "So, he's not House Thalluen by birth?"

Rohenvi kept her eyes on the meal, moving her hands with practiced elegance to remove the covers of the shared dishes herself. "No, but he's well-vetted. Used to be a Deep trader but seeks something less dangerous."

She passed a purifying gem over the platters where they could see.

"I'll test first," Jaunda said, sounding hungrier than she might be concerned with poison as she helped herself.

The Matron allowed it, unhurried as she spooned portions of each dish for Natia, Auslan, and Shyntre while they kept their hands in their laps. Finally, she served herself, sniffing the plate with intent beyond relish.

"Deep trader," the wizard repeated, curiosity piqued. "Perhaps the source of your scribed book on the subject?"

"One of them," she replied, her smooth control of tone and expression suitable for Court, rousing suspicion. "I have many contacts of mutual benefit."

But few you'd leave alone in your bedroom with your heir …

No one else seemed to think this odd or care much if they did. Natia's smile was unguarded and genuine, innocent of whatever pasts lay outside her home. Auslan paid more attention to the cait's expressions and admired the platters despite being seasoned enough to note the Matron's behavior, wording, and omissions. Jaunda was stuffing her mouth with the appreciative grunts of someone who hadn't had hot and filling food in spans.

I guess I'll wait.

He filled his belly along with the others while he could, assuming this "old" Deep trader, Vanry, was listening to every word.

"Auslan," Rohenvi began.

He made sure to swallow his spoonful first. "Yes, Matron?"

"Do you feel well enough to leave your room?"

The healer took too long choosing his words.

"Yes or no, bua," Jaunda rumbled, one cheek full.

Shyntre frowned. "It's not that simple, Lead."

She smirked. "Fine. Is it 'yes, but' or 'no, but,' bua?"

"Yes, Matron," the Consort answered at once, "but …"

Jaunda snickered as Rohenvi leaned forward. "But?"

"I-I … would wish to cover my hair and continue wearing the clothes you've given me."

"The ones that hide your shape?" Jaunda clarified.

"Yes, Lead Sister. I … I was always …"

"Mostly naked," Shyntre grumbled, forcing himself to take another bite before he lost his appetite. "Wearing ornaments."

"Didn't like it, huh?"

"I did, once." He swallowed. "Not … anymore."

"That is fine, Auslan," Rohenvi cut in. "That is my wish, too. Secrecy isn't an option, but discretion always has its place."

He exhaled. "Thank you, Matron."

"What about Reverie?" Shyntre asked. "Could we lie down with the Red Sister guarding outside?"

"Reasonable," she replied, looking across the Jaunda to confirm.

"Bah," she muttered, scooping up a large bite of mashed root. "There are two exits out of that room. Can only watch both from inside."

"We could change rooms," the Matron offered. "Choose one with a single entrance. We can satisfy your requirements, Red Sister."

"Fine with me." Her teeth clattered as she bit down on the spoon, scraping it clean with the tight press of her lips. She paused to chew and swallow. "I have my orders, that's all, and I'm just glad to be home. If the food's always this good, I'll be fine until D'Shea gets here."

Shyntre's shoulders relaxed as he found it easy to take her words as presented. Jaunda had never been a good player of intrigue and kept secrets by keeping her mouth shut. But, since returning from her penance, her manner and body language were wide open, any hint of guile vanished.

Speaking of which …

Shyntre tried to see what had scared his brother so badly. Although she had a faint aura about her which implied she might have recently "merged" with a mage, nothing attracted his attention, even less to think the mage had been a Dragon.

Strange. I should be able to see something like that. Unless ... ?

Unless Auslan had experienced a vision despite his insistence that he'd been awake.

The wizard supposed he would have the time to prod her about it, but the fact that the Lead hadn't asked the Matron about providing available sex partners during her stay concerned him.

The table had fallen quiet for some time, Jaunda helping herself to seconds before a soft knock sounded at the far door; then it opened.

"Vanry!" Natia cried, spinning in her chair and flipping a morsel of her dinner onto the table drape without noticing. "Come sit with us!"

Auslan chuckled, cleaning it discreetly with his napkin as the older, commonblood male approached carrying Rohenvi's most precious possession.

"Apologies for the interruption, Matron," Vanry said. "Vekika is awake."

"I will take her," Rohenvi said, warmer than Shyntre expected. "Sit and eat while food remains."

"Indeed, I hope everyone has had their fill?"

Jaunda chuckled. "Better grab it while you can, bua. Leave it and I'll eat it."

'Bua' does not suit this one. But Shyntre didn't have another word to use as he stared at the new arrival.

The governor took the seat next to him, sitting at Rohenvi's right with a calmness only experience could offer, and reached to serve himself. Other than Headmaster Phaelous, Shyntre had never seen a mature Davrin male at Court or any of the Houses he'd visited. A first guess suggested Vanry was older than Jaunda for certain, maybe as old as D'Shea, and yet his bound hair was solid white without a strand of gold. This close, that detail didn't fit somehow.

The tutor *should* have some gold in his hair by now.

"How old are you, Vanry?" he asked.

"Shyntre," Rohenvi rebuked at once, an iron thread entering her voice. "My governor will keep his peace if he so wishes."

"Apologies, Matron," he muttered, one hand clenching, the other pushing food around with his spoon. "I ... never see elder males at Court."

She harrumphed, shifting her wide-eyed infant on her lap and taking a sip of taze. "There are more in the city than one might realize, though I am aware how quickly young buas disappear from public view once you can see their age."

Auslan lowered his head at that as if he'd shrink into his chair.

"I search for their true value only after that point," the Matron finished, lifting her chin as the Consort displayed obvious surprise. "In my centuries, I've grown impatient with thoughtless erections and vapid smiles."

Fine creases appeared in the other male's amusement. "And we are humbly grateful, Matron."

"Still pretty rare," Jaunda chimed in, sucking food off her thumb. "Think only Low Gate keeps the old males around to turn gold."

"I am from Low Gate," Vanry offered.

"Yeah?" Jaunda grinned. "Me, too."

"I can tell, Red Sister." He bowed his head with common politeness. "If I may be so bold, that is the quarter with the most caits making suitable recruits."

The Lead nodded, looking smug.

"Auslan has gold hair," Natia interjected with clear admiration, looking at Rohenvi. "Does that mean you see his true value, Matron?"

Rohenvi's face flushed hot as she tried not to show her real thoughts on that tender subject. Shyntre stopped tasting the food in his mouth as his brother's face cracked with pained horror. Jaunda shook her head and gulped water as Vanry kept his head down and ate a small first bite.

"What?" The cait peered around the table in confusion. "He's *valuable*. He's a healer! He saved Drani."

"Of course, Natia, yes," Rohenvi said, gathering her poise. "But he's also a challenge for any matron to care for." Her eyes flicked to him. "Too beautiful to go unnoticed wherever he stands, and the Nobles at Court do not like to be reminded of fading youth."

The cait deflated. "Is that why he's here? Because they pushed him out of Court and you accepted him?"

Gaelan's child was more optimistic than Shyntre would have guessed.

"Nah, it was the Purge," Jaunda said casually. "Time to overhaul the Priestess rank-and-file."

"Lead Sister, please," the Matron said, "that is beyond her understanding."

A shrug. "Not my fault. She'll need to learn some time."

Wide, garnet eyes swung around. "Learn what, Sister?"

"That your Matron resents the Court if you don't know the first thing about it."

"It's crumbling as it stands anyway," the elder male interjected, surprising Jaunda as much as Shyntre. "The Palace is in flux and we wait for the scrambling on the web to settle down. Why tell her of a pattern that is far and long irrelevant to a House servant."

The Lead twisted her mouth on a grunt. "Point." She looked at Shyntre, then Auslan, and finally Rohenvi, dissatisfied about something she saw in their expressions. "So ... a question, Matron."

Rohenvi had smoothed her face. "Yes, Lead?"

"Did you know this Consort saved your Third when she would have died?"

Dead silence, but for the mental groan in Shyntre's head. Auslan seemed petrified, hiding his hands in his lap rather than let any see they were shaking.

If D'Shea didn't see fit to tell Matron Thalluen that when she dropped Auslan here, then what in the Abyss does Jaunda think she's doing?!

Shyntre extended a hand, palm-down. "Okay, wait. We were both there, Lead. Some sensitive details on that mission the Elder hasn't approved for disclosure."

Rohenvi blinked. "You know what happened to her?"

Jaunda snorted, jerked her head toward the wizard. "Shyntre's the one that told us where shit had gone wrong, and told us where to find a healer, fast." She indicated Auslan. "This bua fucking did it but it cost him that gold streak and more."

Shyntre shifted in his chair, gripping the arms. "Lead, would you stop telling them everything?"

"I'm not telling them *anything*, mage. Maybe suggesting D'Shea made the wrong call, and the Matron who self-exiled from Court could appreciate a Consort crammed into her care for reasons past a favor to her long-dead Mother."

Rohenvi stiffened, glancing at Vanry in a moment of panic, who offered to take Vekika for her. The Matron accepted, freeing up her hands as Natia stared open-mouthed, fumbling to make sense of the adult talk. Auslan reached over to squeeze the child's hand, keeping his eyes fixed on the table, and Natia held on with both hands, grateful not to be forgotten. Shyntre heard several heartbeats overlapping around the table but wasn't sure whose they were.

Vanry spoke then. His voice was soft, soothing ears beyond the Fourth Daughter cradled in his arms. "Is this true? Did you heal the Matron's Third Daughter?"

Auslan blinked through his frozen panic. "S-Sirana?"

Vanry's brows lifted. He shared a glance with Rohenvi, who nodded to confirm. "Correct. Did you heal Sirana?"

Daunted by the effort to speak further, the Consort glanced at Shyntre, at Jaunda. The Lead waved her hand with nonchalance, and the wizard sighed.

"Answer the question," he said, giving up.

"Uh ... yes, I did," Auslan managed. "They ... brought her to me. I ... the healing was difficult. But she is cleansed and lives. I —"

"Cleansed?!" Rohenvi blurted. "Of what?"

Auslan flinched, falling silent. Shyntre leaned forward in his defense.

"A Sathoet got to her," he said, "tried to consume her in a ritual. He *failed*, and he's *dead*, Matron."

"We killed him for what he did to her," Jaunda said, pointing thumb at her chest with a wicked grin.

"Yes," Shyntre rushed ahead, "and I *promised* you that Auslan wasn't tainted. This is the proof! His magic purged the ritual magic so that her wounds would close properly."

"What?"

"None of my gems w-worked on her." he continued, cursing the abrupt tremor in his chest. "They weren't strong enough to overcome Abyssal magic. Few wizards can make them that way."

Rohenvi stared at the wizard, slowly clawing her way out of shock as she looked at Auslan. "So ... You *are* meant to become a battle healer?"

Dread in those gentle eyes. "A wh-what, Matron?"

"Aren't you to be trained away from only bed pleasures?"

"Uh ... I s-suppose but ... I never heard of b-battles."

Argh ... Shyntre rubbed his face as Jaunda chortled.

"By the way," the Lead drawled, "how *is* that training going, wizard? I was supposed to give you a reminder from your Mother."

"You were? Why?" He sounded irritable to his own ears. "You think this Priestess shit is something *I* can undo in a span?"

"Relax! The Elder doesn't expect a lot of progress yet. Just said to remind you that she hasn't forgotten."

"Argh!"

Vanry leaned in with caution. "I've been hearing things, Sister. At Low Gate."

Jaunda turned her ear to him. "Heard what, old bua?"

"That there could be concern for another outside attack. That the Ornilleth are riled up again. The Yutogul are acting oddly. Strange disappearances from established trade routes, some packing up and leaving."

"Heard all that, huh?" The Lead smiled less with joy and more baring of teeth. "Could be something to it. Can't hurt to keep an ear to the stone, right? What Low Gate does best."

Shyntre's stomach sank as the governor fell silent. Confirmation from a Red Sister, if he'd ever heard it. They both knew. Maddeningly, the Queen's ramblings spilled into his thoughts.

"You champion begins to learn herself, Mazdel. She will return in time. She cannot fail."

Return in time for what? The Ornilleth, whatever they would do after the mindflayer escaped the Priestesses? Had it returned to the nest, to its Elder Mind, riding the back of a Red Sister?

What one flayer knows, all *of them know.*

Now, something about Jaunda's long mission in the Deep had loosened her tongue to start talking to Sirana's Mother about her.

Why? The Sisterhood doesn't do that! It's always 'No demons but us!'

The only apparent benefit belonged to Auslan when Sirana's Mother seemed to reappraise him as he held Natia's hand.

"I seem to owe you a debt I did not realize," she said.

"No, no, Matron," he said, finally letting the cait go to lift bare hands. "You do not owe me."

A strong gaze traced the gold shock at his temple, recognizing it for what it was. "Well. You are free to walk around as you please with your guardians. Can I trust you to inform me of any concerns?"

"Yes! You can, Matron."

"And you'll not cause trouble in my House with intention?"

"Of ... of course not, Matron Thalluen."

She shared a tiny smile with Natia. "Very well. Have you any questions for me?"

The healer swallowed, gathering courage to ask something which surprised Shyntre. "Who *was* your Mother, that you'd take me in as a favor to her?"

Rohenvi's mouth firmed up to the point Shyntre doubted she would answer. The Matron pinned eyes on the Lead Sister across the table, who grinned.

"I *could* tell him," she said, somehow both an offer and a taunt.

Sirana's Mother relented with a sigh. "My Mother was Matron Siranet Thalluen. I named my Third Daughter for her. The old Matron and her Head Guard worked closely with Elder D'Shea for many turns when *she* was a Lead. I was quite young."

"Yeah, worked 'closely,'" Jaunda echoed with a lewd hand motion.

Shyntre caught Rohenvi begin a crude gesture of her own but refrain. Instead, she motioned his way. "You told me her son could have been a Red Sister if he'd not been born bua?"

"Uh-huh, did."

Shyntre rolled his eyes. How often had he been taunted for *that*?

"Well," Rohenvi continued, "had Siranet *not* been born a First Daughter with no path but to become Matron, she *would* be ranked above you right now, Lead."

Jaunda beamed outright. "Really! Ha! Bulging thought."

Meanwhile, Auslan blinked with eyes as wide as Natia's. "I … Is House Thalluen loyal to the Elder Sorceress?"

"Or the other way around," the Matron countered, lips easing into a proud smile. "After all, Varessa has no House anymore, and she named her son after one of us."

Shyntre jerked hard in his seat. "W-what?"

"Siranet's Head Guard. The third in their companionship."

His jaw sagged. "Third?"

"Varessa, Siranet, and Fyntre of House Thalluen." Rohenvi lifted her chin, proud of the Davrin bearing this name. "She was *my* Head Guard for my first decades as a Matron, before her passing." She waved a hand before rubbing her forehead. "This was all before the creation of the Consorts when everything changed."

"Yet now the Consorts are gone, my Matron," Vanry reminded gently. "And all changes. As it does."

She sighed. "Yes. As it does."

Meanwhile, Shyntre could not help but wonder. What might it have been like if, instead of imprisonment in the Sanctuary, his Mother had been allowed to place him in the House of her choice? The way it used to be for the Sisterhood.

D'Shea might have chosen to put me in House Thalluen.

He might have grown up here.

And the Valsharess might not have found me.

A flash of memory struck him from the first dream after Sirana had left. A young sorceress, breaking into a foreign hovel of pale stone he'd never seen before, *killing* his sire in front of him, brutal and merciless, before cornering him.

"Mazdel. It is you."

"I-I don't know who you are …" he whispered, *pleading.*

"I-I need to …" Shyntre paused, letting a shiver pass as everyone stared. "I need to go outside. For a walk, or something."

Rohenvi recognized that she had landed as heavy a load on his head as he had on hers in this conversation. She bowed her chin with grace.

"You are free to go anywhere you wish on my property," she said, including Auslan and Jaunda in her words. "Have care for yourselves and keep me informed for anything unusual you may detect."

"We will."

"Agreed," Jaunda confirmed.

Matron Thalluen smiled. "A new room will be ready by your return."

CHAPTER 43

THE CLOISTER - SIVARAUS

THE PRIME'S UPDATES FROM THE QUEEN LACKED ALL NUANCE, AS USUAL. Although essentially what Phaelous had conveyed, she integrated numerous and unnecessary snide remarks about Jaunda's actions to complete her penance.

"What is it with magic pricks making our best lose their minds?" the Eldest grumbled, eyeing the Sorceress pointedly. "I'll chain the Lead up myself if she caught from a fuckin' *lizard*."

"Jaunda isn't pregnant, Prime," Rausery stated.

"But goddess-damned Thena was! And her unit was *useless* for a span afterward!"

D'Shea blinked despite her best effort. "*Was* pregnant?"

The Prime's expression turned bitter and ugly as she focused on the Elder mage. "Don't know how it happened. For sure an accident. Good news is Thena *won't* be taken out of the fight for Sivaraus. She bled some but will be on her feet soon, and Qivni will put her through her paces."

D'Shea kept her mouth closed, her expression like stone as the Prime swaggered in getting herself something to drink. *'Accident,' indeed.*

What had she expected when once the next Red Sisters caught and Wilsira wasn't there to back them into a corner? The Conceiver hadn't left them a beneficial course of action in centuries. Sirana hadn't been able to escape the Queen's notice any better than D'Shea could in her time, but no one had known about Thena except those in the Cloister.

It's not the first time, even under my watch.

D'Shea had endured the rest of their meeting while Rausery kept the Eldest on track, finishing up with tangible goals moving forward.

Quite an achievement.

"I'll run the rounds this time," the Prime said. "Make sure the Queen's Army and Low Gate are up to where they should be in training and supplies. Rausery, get an updated headcount of the House Guards and fighting age Davrin at as many Houses will let you see for yourself. Tell me which ones don't."

The General dipped her chin. "On it, Prime."

"And you, Sorceress." Hard, red eyes slid to D'Shea. "About that healer Consort."

Here we go.

"Yes, Prime?"

"Heard there was a Noble in the dungeon with her belly stuffed by him."

"Curgia Itlaunaduv," D'Shea supplied. "The Second Daughter. Matron Itlaun obtained him at the last worship ball."

The Prime sucked on her teeth at the mention of an event she always avoided. "Want you to check on her."

"Why? Lelinahdara is handling the prisoners of the Purge."

"*That's* why. If the Queen insists you two play games with Wilsira's legacy — enough for you to be crawling around the old Consorts' dormitory — then at least see if that Noble has a clean bug ready to drop. The healer might be able to fake his taint, but the unborn can't, and *you* of all mages should be able to see that."

It's never that easy.

But it had also been a while since she'd heard anything of the commoner Bathila imprisoned in Wilsira's Forming Pit. Same concern there: how was the pregnancy advancing and what was Tarra learning about them?

I swore I would never go there.

And yet …

D'Shea chose not to persuade her superior in another direction. This time. "I will find out what the current circumstances are, Prime. Is there anything afterward I should investigate pertaining to our city defenses?"

"The Wizard's Tower, of course," said the Prime smugly. "And, if you dare, prod around for Auranka near the Pit. See how many Driders she has right now."

D'Shea frowned. "The Queen would know that better, and already. Seems a risk not worth taking."

The Eldest shrugged, pricking her with suspicion. "If you say so. The Mistress won't kill you, I know that much, and mage's eyes always see what the Abyss might be hiding from us. Maybe even from the Queen."

Bold claim.

But at least the old Davrin remained aware that demons were not to be trusted.

Rausery waited patiently, gauging her peer's response, probably planning her own route in her head.

"I will see what I can do before my next report," said the Elder Sorceress. "The Palace dungeon first, then the Wizard's Tower. Perhaps the Pit."

"Go at it, then. Three cycles max. Our Majesty says time's running short."

GUARDSVRIN DELGA OPENED THE FIRST GATE TO THE PALACE DUNGEON.

Welcome, Elder Sorceress, she signed, bowing with eyes down.

D'Shea tapped her boot twice, prompting her to look up. *Anyone new brought in since the Purge?*

No, Elder. Just three taken out. Deceased.

Names?

Delga gave them, and D'Shea frowned.

One of your own guard? she signed.

The Guardsvrin had as much talent for controlling emotion as she did name and face recognition. *The Confessor Lelinahdara must have been displeased with her during her last visit.*

Oh? How did she die?

The Priestess … fed her to her Sacred Son. He went feral on her. We found her later, after smelling blood.

Tarra's Sathoet? She let him out?

And the Priestess chose *not* to bring the guard to the infirmary but let her die in place. *Why?*

How long ago was this? And do you know her purpose?

About two spans ago. I do not know what she sought during that visit.

Has she visited since?

No, Elder. A tiny hint of relief escaped the Guardsvrin's tone.

D'Shea nodded. *That will be all, Delga. I will see myself down.*

The dungeon had gemstones embedded in the wall which informed the Guardsvrin of movement around the prison and sounded either minor or major alarms when certain doors were opened. High-ranking mages like D'Shea and Lelinahdara carried their own counterspell gem which allowed a blind spot in such magic, muting the pulses and colors which would follow anyone lower and mundane. D'Shea had expected that Delga would not know who Tarra had visited recently, but the fact that she had brought her Sathoet with her offered the Sorceress a hint.

Wager the same prisoner I am here to see.

Curgia could confirm if she was of sound mind.

"Itlaunaduv," she said after stepping inside the cell, fixing the door open but casting a silence spell.

Curgia peered up warily, lacking terror despite the circumstances under which she'd been arrested. The Noble's belly bulged through her white shift; her face and breasts confirmed she had been eating enough.

"Red Sister," she acknowledged, unable to discern D'Shea's rank and not recognizing her face.

Very good.

"I am here to follow up on the Priestess's visit from several spans ago."

"Of … of course. I am listening, Sister."

Any Noble playing games at Court would resist such an obviously vague lead, but this one had nothing to gain where she was, and her instincts seemed to have dulled in isolation. Rather, Curgia seemed hungry for interaction.

"Did you meet her Sacred Son?"

There was terror.

"Oh, please, don't let her set him on me again," Curgia murmured, covering her belly protectively with her hands. "I t-told the Conceiver what I knew."

D'Shea's spine prickled. *The Conceiver? She's dead …*

Killed by her enchanted spiders.

So is Kerse.

But might Tarra have played on those well-founded fears in this abused Noble? Taunting her with a younger Sathoet after forcible impregnation by the eldest.

Why? What did she want to know?

"You may carry a healer, Curgia, like your chosen sire," D'Shea spoke with confidence. "Queen's law is clear. You are safe to give birth and under Her protection afterward."

The Noble winced. "The Conceiver said that was undecided. She may simply take my baby and send me home."

"We'll see about that. Share with me what you told her. I know about her misuse of her Sacred Son with you. Perhaps I can block her intentions."

Curgia appeared hopeful. "Yes … the Sisterhood was there that eve … you would know …" After a silent moment, she continued. "She asked if I'd seen my Daughter's face. I have. She is as beautiful as her sire …"

A cait. The Sorceress felt oddly pleased. This may offer leverage.

"Whom she wouldn't believe is alive."

A chill swept through. *Uh-oh.*

Curgia smiled, her eyes filled with the bright mist of Reverie. "I wonder where he is. If he's escaped the eyes of the Conceiver such that she was surprised … Did you save him from the Purge? The Sisterhood?"

A clever question for a not-particularly-clever cait.

D'Shea smiled coolly. "Keep further your council on Enoquis, Noble. Loose lips cause tremors in the web you may wish to keep still."

Curgia's eyes widened; she nodded in earnest, taking the confirmation and advice at once.

"Though, do tell me what the Conceiver compelled you to share. Again, I can counter."

The young Davrin had no reason to doubt. "Oh … I … the eve I … miscarried the demon's child …"

"You remember this?"

"I'd put it out of my mind, but *she* reminded me. I only remember pain and void, something piercing me and draining my will to live, stealing something … important …" Curgia wrapped herself around her distended abdomen for comfort. "Enoquis gave it back, after the Sisterhood brought me to him." She looked up, eyes pleading. "Don't let him die, Red Sister. He is … so important to keeping the dark at bay, from it drowning us."

D'Shea frowned. "Do you … dream of him?"

"I see nothing. I only feel, believe. I *know*." Curgia's eyes took on the fervid heat of a zealot. "He is … *greater* than the Priestesses. They merely pretend, compared to him. He could heal the Queen Herself!"

"Does the Queen *need* healing?" the Sorceress asked blithely, tamping down contempt for the overblown faith.

Curgia sat on her cot, trembling.

"Maybe," she whispered, eyes turning vacant.

Bold.

Awareness returned. She licked dry lips. "Protect him, Red Sister, no matter what. I … I regret that I hurt him. I could have … c-could have k-killed …" She shuddered. "I will give up my Daughter how you see fit if you will keep her out of the Sanctuary and allow me to see them both again."

D'Shea face became a mask. "Are you renouncing the Daughters of Braqth, Itlaunaduv?"

Inexorable fear swept over Curgia's body, making it quake, yet she did not deny it by so much as a shake of her head. She wept loudly. "I-I have experienced two sires, their magic passing through my unborns … Enoquis draws his magic, gives *life* from another place, not the Abyss! He is nothing like the Sathoet! If Braqth's Daughters would claim his creation, I *know* th-they are false. The Priestesses are parasites, nothing more!"

We're in agreement there.

The Sorceress suppressed a smirk. If Curgia regretted her blurt in any way, expecting to hear a pronouncement of trial or execution for what she'd said after her birthing, she did not appear ready to recant it.

"I wish to tell him I am sorry," she muttered, wrapped in a ball around her baby. "That is all."

D'Shea blinked. "You … what?"

"He stopped my life from flowing out after Kerse's spawn. He *cleansed* me of that poison and gave me *her* …" Dark hands clutching her gut. "For no cost. No exchange. He asked *nothing*." The Noble's face twisted with bitter shame. "And I beat him for it … I had my *hands* around his *throat* … because he could not give me *more*. He would not stay with me for always … For me, he felt only fear, and I made it so. That … *that* is what the Abyss has made of me …"

The Elder stood in silence to listen to this unexpected confession.

Curgia blinked to clear her eyes as the sobbing paused, her cheeks soaked and nose running snot. She looked up at D'Shea. "Place my Daughter away from the Priestesses and let me see him to tell him this. I will accept any task, any charge or fate which comes after. Please, Red Sister."

D'Shea frowned at the unwelcome tremor in her chest; she breathed in, aware of the close scents of sweat and bad dreams.

All too familiar.

"I will see what I can do," she answered, "and consider your offer for the Sisterhood. You must tell no one about this, however. Do not speak of Enoquis to a Priestess as if he is alive. You have already made that mistake. If the rest of what you have said falls into her hands, I can do little about your fate. She will claim your Daughter, give you to the Drider Mistress, and go to find where your healer is hiding."

"No!" Curgia cried.

"Then be *quiet*. Be *still*. From now forward, do you understand? Do not reveal your true thoughts until *long* after the birth."

The Noble closed her mouth. With head bowed and eyes down, she did not move.

That will have to do.

Tarra would be annoyed ... if she bothered to come. Pitiable Bathila, held catatonic in Wilsira's Forming Pit, should be the Confessor's priority regardless. The dungeon Guardsvrin took turns feeding the pregnant Nobles all they needed to eat for healthy births. This one commoner — distantly related to General Rausery — had exactly four Davrin who knew about her.

Tarra, Phaelous, the Queen, and myself.

All too easy for them to forget about her in the twining plots and swirling conspiracies of the city.

But I have remembered. I shall check on her.

Despite telling herself she'd never go there again.

WARNING SPELLS DOTTED THE ENTIRE SANCTUARY AND WERE CHANGED ON A regular basis. Impossible to pass unnoticed even for the Elder Sorceress, but her explicit permission granted to visit Wilsira's otherwise forbidden quarters at least put speed on her side.

If I move quickly and directly, it may be enough time before Tarra follows me.

It depended on chance and where the Confessor was, what she was doing. If she happened to be in the ritual chamber, so be it. Having spoken with Delga and Curgia, D'Shea wielded a few verbal spars should they be required to talk.

The Sorceress secured the suite doors behind her and confirmed everything of import had been moved to the Wizard Tower once Phaelous had broken the cypher.

He would have told the Valsharess by now.

Tarra would have to leave the Sanctuary to double-check records whose secrets were removed from the plucking fingers of the other Priestesses.

Good.

D'Shea stood in the jump circle, heart pounding in her ears. Over two centuries ago, the pregnant Lead Red Sister had been stolen from the infirmary on the fifth floor, had been taken down here, as Sirana had been.

What had happened with Shyntre still in her womb? Why then, not earlier or after the birth? How might that Abyssal magic have affected her and her son? She'd not dared to give such times further light in her present mind before listening to Curgia in her cell, speaking of Auslan.

" ... *that is what the Abyss has made of me ...* "

Frightening to look at, especially so close.

But necessary if I shall recognize the spiders waiting to spring from their place on the web.

D'Shea exhaled and commanded the circle to move her down.

Into the pit where something had *happened*.

Something worse than a greedy Conceiver forcing herself between a Mother and her son.

SHE HATED THE SMELL. SOUR, HUMID, WARM ENOUGH TO LIE NAKED WITHOUT shivering.

When she stepped out of the ring, runes carved into all surfaces of the closed space reacted to her presence. They gleamed red in sequence, leading to the stained altar. D'Shea recoiled, eyes tracing the "safe" path toward the cage holding Bathila.

The door was open, a second body inside tending to her by the soft yellow light of a glowstone.

"Phaelous?" she said, annoyed at once.

The old Davrin stood up with care, tossing a soiled robe into a large bucket. He smiled. "A pleasure, Elder."

"What are you doing here?"

"Keeping our Queen's command. Tarra tends to get distracted from her patients but can't foist this one off on her acolytes. So, I come here once each cycle whether she cares to know or not." He paused. "I had not expected you to come here of your own volition."

The Sorceress clenched her fist, tempted to tell him some end-game reason in her competition with the Confessor. He would accept without question.

But he knows the truth. He just spoke it.

"I came to check on the surrogate," she admitted, "for the same reason."

Phaelous's eyes crinkled. "You are busier than Tarra, and you made time for Bathila?"

"No. Not for *her*."

Not exactly.

"Ah." Familiar, gold flecks in his eyes turned his gaze warmer as his guard slipped. "For yourself?"

Her jaw hardened. "For my son."

Her body flushed to know how she'd said it, all accusation and rejection. She tried to ignore the spark of pain the Headmaster did not bother to hide. It didn't work.

Ignoring him never worked.

"How do you mean to help him from here?" Phaelous asked, as if merely curious, kneeling to dampen a clean cloth in a fresh bucket he must have carried down himself.

D'Shea watched him continue the prisoner's bath. A fresh robe and large bowl of mash waited on a stool outside the cage. Witnessing the poor, witless wretch, her belly full to bursting, the Elder's throat ached suddenly. Her eyes itched enough to rub them.

"Varessa?"

She blinked him into clearer view, swallowing before she spoke. "It's the Dragon influence you uncovered. Isn't it?"

A few red runes vibrated as the Headmaster frowned. "I am sorry, Elder, but what is?"

"Wilsira used Rausery's bloodline to carry the Priestess Consort-Sons because ... ?"

D'Shea paused, willing Phaelous to fill the silence.

He will if he can.

"Because they were resistant to Abyssal influence," he answered, cradling Bathila's cheek with the damp cloth and studying her face. "This allowed the Conceiver more control over the results of her tailored births than she could by her magic alone."

His confirmation, and that tender touch for a naked Davrin oblivious to his presence, struck like a hot rock in her middle.

"But none of these common caits were mageborn," D'Shea said, crossing her arms. "Wilsira abducted me from the infirmary when I was about to give birth. She used *me* to fortify these runes, and I did from raw power and will to survive, but ..." She suppressed the urge to vomit. "The one Wilsira truly *needed* at that time, to keep the Void leashed, was Shyntre. Not because he was mine, but because he was *yours*."

Phaelous exhaled slowly, finishing the wipe-down and standing to get the fresh robe. "I do not know how the Conceiver made the connection. I did not grasp this counterpart of our mage heritage until I deciphered her notes, though I believe I witnessed signs for centuries."

"The Queen ... must know. The Dragon influence is why She has *always* protected you, and Shyntre, no matter what happened." D'Shea cursed the tremble in her voice. "This *must* be why She granted the Conceiver so much power over *all* of us. Wilsira discovered how to ... I ..." The Elder threw her eyes around the ritual chamber, around the runes forming yet another private prison in Sivaraus. "How to purify Abyssal magic, for lack of a better term."

"That works well enough, yes. And yes, Her Majesty knows of the Dragon magic among us. Moreso, I am certain she knows these two Dragons by name."

D'Shea locked eyes with him. "And once we report on these findings, as She has bid us? If Her Majesty keeps this secret and we tell Her what we've found?"

Phaelous hesitated, maintaining eye contact, letting her look at the metallic sheen much like her son's. "I ... I do not know what Her response will be to our discovery, Varessa. I am as worried as you."

He stopped. His lips suggested he might have said something.

If it weren't forbidden.

"Help me dress Bathila," he murmured instead. "If you would."

D'Shea acquiesced, aiding him to wrangle the warm, dead weight into a dry covering. She helped keep the surrogate's head up as the Headmaster spoon-fed her from the bowl of mash. At least the instinct to swallow the food remained.

"So you remember being held here," said the Headmaster, voice hushed.

"In fragments," she answered. "Mostly during Reverie ever since Wilsira died. I have only part of the answer I wanted most."

"What is the question?"

"*Why.*" She gritted her teeth in a snarl. "Why me, when I was most vulnerable? When it should have been forbidden to threaten a new baby ready to be born, why was it allowed? Why was I silenced and kept apart from my son?"

The Sorceress peered around the sequestered space, hugging herself. "If the Valsharess and Conceiver both knew what the gold in your eyes meant about your magic, then Her Majesty must have approved it all. She was planning to take him from me, anyway."

Phaelous swallowed, torn in what he both wanted to say and had the ability to speak. He focused on feeding Bathila with all the patience of the finest silk weaver.

"I am ... *not* certain the Queen approved Wilsira's action in advance," he said with care. "It may ... have been forgiven after the fact."

D'Shea sneered. "Does that matter? The end was the same."

He did not respond, and after a brief silence, she asked, tone mournful, "Did you ever see him as an infant? I ... never did."

Her chosen sire let out a breath. "Yes. I checked on him for you, for us both. Shyntre had an excellent caretaker his first decade."

"Oh?" D'Shea frowned, trying to recall anything from those early reports. "Just an acolyte, wasn't it?"

Phaelous smiled, eyes turning warmer. "A healer acolyte. Quite rare."

"A touch healer? Like Auslan?"

"Indeed. The assistant to his Mother, Priestess Juliran, who ran the fifth floor."

"Assistant?" D'Shea's face tightened as she allowed a few painful images from her Reverie further light in her thoughts.

A young cait, stern, and rarely smiling. An unusually hard worker, pragmatic and difficult to distract.

"Irrwaer?" D'Shea asked.

Phaelous's face brightened. "You remember. Yes. A true healer at heart, and not unlike Lead Qivni in some of her experiences and mindset growing up in the Sanctuary."

I remember her.

Irrwaer had visited regularly, taking seriously her duties in caring for D'Shea and Shyntre during the last turn of her pregnancy. Sometimes, the Sorceress had talked to her, taking her measure with the usual suspicions for anyone working for the Sanctuary. The acolyte kept her thoughts to herself, proved resistant to persuasion or manipulation, even when Priestesses like Tarra visited.

The healer seemed to have no agenda of her own to turn around and use, and yet sometimes she brought Jaunda to make contact in secret.

A deal the two of them had made.

D'Shea remembered the blood on the acolyte's hands during the birth. She heard screaming. Her own. Priestess Juliran and this acolyte, Irrwaer … the two females had had a pretty bua-child with them that eve when Shyntre was born. One who laid his hands on her belly when the pain had been greatest.

Was that … ?

Auslan. It must have been.

The Consort before he became one.

631

"I always saw Irrwaer carrying our son with her as she worked," Phaelous said.

The Sorceress narrowed her eyes, lips pressed with envy. "Why? And why always keep a baby so close?"

"I never found the opportunity to ask her. Perhaps she enjoyed it."

"And ... *this* is how Shyntre and Auslan met." D'Shea made a face. "I am displeased for having forgotten."

The Headmaster's smile grew. "You had reason for letting some things fade, Varessa. Extraordinary to me was that they reconnected later, after separation by expected events."

"Expected events."

"Of course. The acolyte became a Priestess, conceiving and birthing her Sathoet, then entering intense training. I understand the Consort is older by half a century, so he would have been coming of age for the worship ball around the same time. Juliran refused to care for him, so Shyntre was given into my care for a time."

D'Shea's jaw tightened as old rage flared up, threatening nausea as she imagined her bua thrown from one pair of reluctant arms to another. "I remember. I had ... wanted Irrwaer as our liaison between the Sanctuary and the Sisterhood. I even approved of Jaunda working with her Sathoet once or twice. *Ugh!*" She threw up her hands. "Instead, we got Tarra, and all that work spanning decades was undone."

The Headmaster arranged long, fiber-filled sacks to best support a pregnant Davrin's body and made sure the robe covered most of her. His experience leaked in from the past whether he wished it or not.

"Indeed," he said. "Irrwaer and her Sathoet vanished before Juliran could pass on the infirmary to her. I do not know what happened, but Lelinahdara was there to step in. I assume some plot of hers succeeded, and Irrwaer didn't have the defense she needed to counter it. Not long after, Wilsira's plot against Juliran also succeeded, and with realized healers gone, the Sanctuary fell farther under her control."

D'Shea ground her teeth. How different her web might appear had one acolyte-turned-Priestess lived and held her place.

As it always seems.

How often had D'Shea imagined a present where Matron Siranet had not died before her First Daughter was three decades into her second century?

Like shoving Gaelan or Sirana into prominent leadership roles before they built much of a web of their own.

Rohenvi did surprisingly well given the challenge, but the young Matron had ultimately been lured in by the Priestesses, entranced by their promises of 'revived' mageborns in every House. Of which she'd had precious few.

How dearly that gamble cost Siranet's once-strong House.

Before Jilrina and Kaltra were born by those Consorts, House Thalluen had seemed resistant to the Sanctuary's influence. A clear heart and simple desires had been part of what had made Sirana's Grand-Matron so attractive to the last survivor of House D'Shea.

I still miss her.

Not until Varessa had seen a potential ally in the Headmaster of the Wizard's Tower — seventy turns later — had she considered another close bond.

To speak of gambles costing us everything …

"Phaelous."

"Yes, Elder?"

The Sorceress rose to her feet first, staring at the Headmaster while he straightened up. "Who told Her Majesty first that I carried?" She suppressed the sudden urge to push him over. "*Was* it you, as I've always suspected? You *had* to tell Her, yes? Is that what you would say to me now?"

The wizard didn't answer, but regret sagged at the corners of his mouth.

She huffed. "You know what I find odd? I didn't even *hunt* buas until you. For centuries, I selected cait partners, *much* preferred to buas and who held not such undue risk to me."

His smile hinted at a hesitant return. "I remember. Matron Thalluen complimented you quite well at Court, Varessa. The two of you were a joy to observe from afar."

She flushed, taken aback by his simple and open expression. He wasn't jealous or resentful. Did she believe him?

"*Tch!* Siranet wasn't the Matron yet, fool."

"Mm-hm." He shrugged. "I could not help but discover, after House D'Shea disappeared from Court and you survived the trials of the Sisterhood, that you reconnected with Siranet despite the obstacles. Much as Shyntre has with his valued healer." His smile remained. "I have admired you for all your life, Elder Sorceress, and I am grateful our son takes after you in all the courageous ways you haven't been allowed to see."

D'Shea swallowed, forcing a breath past a tangle of emotion balled up in her chest. "Wh-why did you ... signal to me? The way you did."

He tilted his blond head. "Perhaps because you had finally noticed me? I was useful to you, and happy to be so."

No. No ... I saw more than a useful, golden pet ...

But had that been real or had something tricked her eyes? An illusion? Incense or a spell?

Had he betrayed me from the start?

The Sorceress bit her lip, displeased by the unruly sensations seeking the weak spot to break open her chest.

"A-Are we finished here?" she asked.

Phaelous hid split-instant dismay in a careful look around the walls. "Bathila will be alright for another cycle." He opened his arm in a guiding invitation to the jump circle. "I will see myself to the Tower. Do attend to your affairs, Elder Sorceress."

He gives up so easily. D'Shea refrained from wrinkling her nose. "I was supposed to visit you there next to discuss the Ornilleth defenses."

"Say that you have, and I will corroborate, if necessary," he suggested. "I have nothing new at this time, Elder, and will not unless someone visits the Fringe to learn about the Tragar weapons laced with saphgar."

Rausery could do that.

But she would be gone visiting Noble Houses in the wrong direction for three cycles.

Damn it. D'Shea sighed. This left her with all that time to fill, for she would not go report to the Prime alone. *Not this soon.*

Should she visit Shyntre and Auslan under Rohenvi's care? What did she have to tell Jaunda this soon after her return? After that final, unsettling report to the Valsharess?

The Headmaster asked gently, "What is on your mind, Varessa?"

"I am to …" She swallowed. "I am to visit Auranka at the Drider Pit next."

Phaelous showed his alarm in his eyes. "Why?"

"The Prime bid me." D'Shea shrugged, pretending calm she did not feel. "I said I would do it if I had time."

"To discover what, exactly?"

"How many Driders may be available to fight."

The Headmaster started to scowl. "The Valsharess already knows. Would the Prime have you struck down right before the Elder Mind attacks?"

The Sorceress felt the urge to smirk. "She claims to 'know' the Mistress will not kill me."

He scoffed. "Because Auranka can do much worse than killing, you *know* that. The Prime makes a grave and foolish mistake giving you that order."

D'Shea blinked at his tone. *Well, well. The old scholar's temper can be riled.* "Auranka can't touch *you*, though. The Queen Herself sent you and Shyntre to gather her milk. I accompanied you out of stubbornness, not because you *needed* me."

Phaelous's mouth twisted as though he wished to smile. Not their worst recent memory. "Indeed. Although, best not assume that protection will always be there."

"I never have. Have you any reason to think it has ended?"

"I do not." He watched her with long-familiar admiration. "Are you suggesting I come with you?"

The Elder shrugged. "My superior never said I need go alone. We count a few Driders. Jump back to the Tower and do some proper planning over hot taze before I surprise her by walking casually into the Cloister."

Yellowed eyebrows lifted with surprise, his expression at once pleased and cautious. "You still have questions for me."

"And you still have answers, I have the time. Why not seize it?"

Tempted, then reluctant, the Headmaster exhaled, his eyes drifting to the altar. "Please do not take the Drider Mistress lightly, Varessa. If we go to her domain this soon after the first, and not by the Queen's order ..."

D'Shea waited.

"She will take it as permission to press our vulnerabilities further," he finished. "It is both play and a meal to her. If it hurts you, it feeds her."

How true.

"Meaning we may not be in the mood for taze at once," she finished with a smug look, taking in every tick and nuance of his face. "You certainly know much about her moods."

His mouth twisted. A memory flickered behind those eyes that could not slip free.

"Perchance, sire of my son, does *she* know rumors or secrets that you do not wish *me* to know?"

"More than I could count," he answered at once. "But all secrets come to light in time. I may claim no choice for some of them, but ..." He looked down. "For all of them, I chose to wait."

"To wait? For what, old scholar?"

If he says, 'For you,' I will shove him.

"To know better."

D'Shea stood baffled by his response but intent on hiding it.

The Headmaster bowed to her, his body formal but his voice somewhat frightened. "I will accompany you to the Drider Pit. Whatever we find there, mata of my son, I will stay by you and see you out of her web."

CHAPTER 44

HIGHWALL, SIVARAUS – THE GREAT CAVERN

Here we are again.

Shyntre had been with them the last time she and Phaelous had stepped outside the city's boundary and into the deep darkness of this tunnel. Her bua had been silent and surly but listening to every word spoken between his parents.

I should have spoken to him instead of letting his sire irritate me and take all my focus.

Mostly, D'Shea had wanted to tell the Headmaster where he stood once she *could* say it to his face. She wanted to leave no doubt she hadn't forgotten his abandonment of her when she needed him most.

"Do be careful, Varesssa. Ja'Prohn tends to fail mustering the will to meet your passion the moment you turn your back."

The Drider Mistress had taunted her as if plucking the pain point from her mind like a festering berry. Phaelous had tried to warn her walking in.

If it hurts you, it feeds her.

The Sorceress did not want to think about afterward, when Auranka had flaunted feeding on Shyntre's dreams because no sacrifices were to be made until after the flayer threat was dealt with.

When I came to the Valsharess and saw him at Her feet, my bua looked so …

So much like Curgia in the dungeon, but far less fed and even more afraid.

He had bruises around his neck.

Tears of gratitude pricked D'Shea's eyes that she'd gotten her bua out of there and tucked him somewhere pleasant for the time being.

Is the Drider Mistress still feeding on his dreams?

She was likely to find out.

You will stay by me? the Elder signed. *No matter what she says.*

I will, the Headmaster answered, not the slightest tremor in his hand. *I shall be there this time, Varessa, even if you loathe me and want to strike me dead.*

D'Shea frowned. He had never expressed thoughts such as these before, but he truly believed she could want that. Maybe he believed he deserved it.

Another warning about everything he could not say.

They exited that first tunnel, walking along a cliffside path, one side descending to a holloway pocked with strands and web traps that only a fool would walk. Up ahead, the glistening web meant to contain the children of the Drider Mistress had been moved to the sharp crevice where that low path ended, leading to the Pit itself. The sticky strands glowed a subtle yellow and purple in the dark.

Cannot count the Driders if we do not get past that, the Elder signed.

Fire will dissolve it well enough, Phaelous answered, *but do not get close and hold your breath. She will be alerted to our presence, of course.*

D'Shea paused on the trail, her wizard stopping beside her. *Any way to ease through it without destroying it?*

The Headmaster slipped a hand into his robe, touching something he'd packed on their way out. *Yes, but she would know and after enough time, we'd be lacking the counterspell if she sprays her webbing.*

In which case, they could be caught in fresh spider's strands *and* blocked by the web, unable to run the way they came.

Did you also bring the purple elixir? she asked.

I did. It is not my first choice to give it to her.

What does it do?

He swallowed, his hand twitching. Of course, he could not say.

D'Shea changed the subject to another concern. *Burning the web gate could let the Driders out into the city.*

A nod. *Which will bring us at once to the attention of our Queen, who can usurp control from Auranka. Her Majesty may well ask what the Prime was thinking to send you here.* Phaelous paused. *I wager the Drider Mistress does not want that. She would rather deal with us herself. To do this, she must keep her children in check.*

Interesting wager.

D'Shea accepted the Headmaster's counsel and his faith in the Valsharess. *Fire it is.*

They wrapped layers of cloth over their nose and mouth before climbing down into the holloway, standing at the precise distance to the web D'Shea's spell could reach.

Hold your breath as we run in, the Headmaster signed, reminding her. *Close your eyes, or you may get dizzy or see things which may not be there in the flesh.*

Check.

The Sorceress cast without delay. She destroyed Auranka's gate with little effort or fanfare, the obstacle not designed to resist destruction but to extract a high cost in doing so.

Crackling lights and motes escaped the incinerated strands, coalescing into purple vapor. D'Shea seized the wizard's hand and squeezed her eyes shut, pitching forward.

Running blind through the crevice and into the Pit, haunting cries and shrieks enveloped them. The rock ceiling seemed to fall up and away, exposing them, nothing but empty space overhead, then on all sides. Her hand tightened on his as the passage tortured her ears and sense of balance, her other senses muted until she could hold her air no longer.

Phaelous jerked them to a halt, pulling her close, and pressed his masked mouth against hers.

"Breathe with me," he murmured.

Inhale.

She could smell him.

"We will ground each other, my Elder."

Another breath. The Sorceress clung to his shoulders, pressing closer to the only familiar thing in a terrible place.

"Do not look yet …"

His warning came in time. She kept her eyes closed from sheer will-power as the deceptively light touch of giant arachnid feet closed the distance around them. Her body flushed with sweat and fear.

"Gold …"

"Drink?"

"Nnno …"

"Hsss …"

"Day male … ?"

"Perhaps …"

They giggled.

D'Shea shuddered. *These aren't Davrin.*

She breathed with him, eyes closed. She *must* trust him in the Drider Pit. *No choice.*

"Varesssssa? Can it be? Welllcome!"

Eager heartbeats filled her ears as Auranka's laugh oozed down the walls ahead of her many legs

Phaelous lifted his mouth. "Open your eyes. Count them quickly."

D'Shea obeyed, stealing her will as she looked for the bloated, warped creatures who had left the Pit, forming a semicircle around them upon the upper ledge.

So many eyes, all tarnished yellow and rotting red, multiples crawling up elongated brows. White hair had fallen out in clumps, stubborn thatches clinging to the knobby skull, but all sported long ears arching backward. She focused on the pairs of ears and avoided the eyes, her count sweeping smoothly.

Thirty-eight.

And may the Prime choke on a Dragon's cock.

"Varesssssa …"

The Drider Mistress stepped delicately off her wall, chortling wetly as she joined her children on the ledge. Bare, swollen breasts swung low, nipples dripping yellowed milk as her spider-Davrin body angled to block an escape through the crevice.

Phaelous held her loosely as they stood their ground, keeping her within his aura as he strengthened it, pushing outward. D'Shea saw clearly how this kept the Driders back, hungry but wary.

"Enjoying the touch of a Ja'Prohnn?" Auranka cooed. "Forgiven him, have you?" The grinning, surreal face twitched. "You shouldn't. You have *no idea* what he has done."

The words spilled into her ears, growing claws which snagged at the barrier muting her doubt.

"Shall I tell you, D'Shauranti?"

The Driders closed in with their Mother.

"Will he *finally* allow you a Daughter?"

The snags turned into rips. Tearing.

"Wh-what?"

"Or will he interfere once more?"

"Run," the Headmaster whispered. "This will only get worse."

The Headmaster stepped backward, attempting to draw the Sorceress with him. She resisted.

He stayed.

"What did you say?" D'Shea snarled at the creature.

"Varessa, *don't*," Phaelous pleaded.

"Answer me!"

A mock pout of sympathy. "Aww. You don't *remember?*" Auranka's fanged face blazed with delighted madness as her children milled about her. "Do you think the Treasure Son you try so hard to know was the *first* to suckle at your womb, Queen's surrrogate?"

A secret inside the Sorceress's head swelled near to bursting. Crippling agony stole her breath, her strength as her legs faltered. Phaelous tightened his arms around her, bracing to hold her up.

A ... another?

Another geas. An older one.

Not Wilsira's.

I ... wasn't supposed to hear this.

By decree of the Valsharess.

D'Shea's body quaked, swiftly punishing her for scratching at the buried sore. For breaking its surface and spattering her memories with a sticky, horrible filth before filling her with a void.

She *had* been pregnant before. Phaelous had agreed to help her hide it.

Had she given birth?

No ... She had lost the baby.

A cait.

Not him, was it?

Oh, Goddess!

Impossible.

No, please! I will die!

Auranka cackled.

"Sh-Shyntre ..." she wept. What would become of her son?

"I will *not* leave you, Varessa. We will see our son soon."

"Hahaha! Always a coward, Ja'Prohn. Ssstanding there like your grandsires, holding the sorceresses helplesss as we have our way with them. Feeding again and *again* ... !" The Drider Mistress loomed. "Lay her down, Phaelousss. Go if you will not watch. She is oursss."

The Headmaster's hand reached into his robe, withdrawing a vial flashing purple and gold. "You want this, do you not, Auranka?"

A sharp gasp.

"Give me that!!"

The huge body struck a mage's barrier as D'Shea's Dark Sight unraveled into true blackness. She clung to the wizard with fading strength.

"I think not," he said with grave disapproval. "You disobeyed your Queen, and I now know what this is."

"Fool! It will turn your gutsss to rot!"

He snapped wax cap off the small bottle.

"Do *not* — !"

Phaelous quaffed the elixir himself. Screeches arose all around them as her once-close companion dragged her blind, weakening body away from them. The passageway tightened down around them as the darkness spilled inside her like a waterfall.

She lost all sense of touch, her strength spent as she collapsed into the torrent.

Help ... !

    I am here, Varessa.

Help me, Phaelous! I don't want to die!

    Then you shall not, beloved.

Her only hint of direction appeared as a golden thread, darting through an inky sea, thickening to a rope.

She reached for it.

Touched it.

Warmth.

An infrangible essence snared hers, halting her fall.

Stopping the hemorrhage.

    I have you. Come back to me.

A rhythm arose, rolling through the golden rope.

    Come home, beloved. Take what you need to lift yourself out. I am here.

A dependable constant she had not noticed until he was nearly out of reach.

    I am here, Varessa. I am here.

She grasped his shoulders, fingers digging in to warm, embroidered silk covering flesh. Lips sought his neck to taste the salt, painting her mouth with sweat as she drew in an intimate scent soured by the threat at their backs.

"Come," he gasped, staying his exhaustion to try to bring her to her feet. "We must reach the jump circle."

D'Shea shook too much yet to hold her balance without him, but the ugly wound from the geas was numb. She could think. She could function. Enough to try to climb out of the holloway.

"Phaelous!!"

Her ears prickled. A Davrin's voice? A real Davrin?

"Phaelous, please, where am I?!"

Weeping in terror. Such terror.

"Don't look," he whispered, pulling her arm when she would have peered over her shoulder. "Eyes up."

Bare feet scrambling over stone below them.

"Phaelous," D'Shea whispered.

"Keep climbing, Varessa."

Her boots dragged heavily along the stone, pins and needles spreading along the soles of her feet as she found one hold after another.

Finally, they reached the cliff's path. Phaelous had gathered a second wind from somewhere and pulled D'Shea's arm over his shoulder, holding her waist as he hurried toward the tight tunnel ahead.

"Wait!"

The Elder picked up her pace, trying to match his long stride.

"By Goddess, *wait!*" The pleading Davrin reached the path. "Take me with you! Don't leave me here! Take me to the Sanctuary!"

"She's catching up," D'Shea gasped.

With a sigh of defeat, Phaelous slowed before they entered the tunnel, turning around and placing himself between D'Shea and the approaching Dark Elf.

"Stop," he commanded, lifting his hand in a way only a mage could threaten. "Not another step."

She obeyed, blinking in baffled innocence. "Phaelous?"

D'Shea could not see beyond the appearance. The strange Davrin stood nude and dirty, as if she had been wandering in the wilderness for cycles. Her face ...

Like Auranka ... if she weren't a Drider.

Her hands covered her belly. "Phaelous? What happened to my

Daughter? Did she live?"

His heart pounded near her ear, his protective aura winding up to a notable hum. Only then did D'Shea notice the stretch marks and sagging skin on the Davrin's abdomen along with other fresh signs suggesting she had given birth only marks ago.

When the Headmaster did not speak, Auranka's face twisted with hatred. "*Answer me*, you conniving breeder! Where is our Daughter? Where is Wilsira?!"

D'Shea flinched like she had been struck, and Phaelous finally spoke, his voice cold.

"She died, Priestess. I am sorry."

The mata stood with mouth agape, shaking her head in denial. "No … No, she was vibrant in my belly. Strong and healthy! Someone must have *stolen* her. You see more than you tell, Consort, so where … *is* she?!"

"The Queen placed her for you, Priestess," he said, stepping into the archway of the tunnel. "Let her go."

"Let her *go?*" Auranka's face wavered, bending in extremes between sorrow, rage, and joy. She jerked her chin at D'Shea, creeping forward on bare, abraded feet. "You mean let *her* go, don't you? Replaced me so soon, did you, you little slut? Or have you been plotting with her in the shadows then smiling by candlelight in my bedchamber?"

Phaelous pushed D'Shea backward, a naked pain the Sorceress had never witnessed before on his face. Priestess Auranka drank it in, laughing, hunchbacked, fingers splayed like she intended to pounce on them. A dark liquid leaked from between her thighs as she limped toward them.

"Go ahead, bua," she taunted. "Turn your back on me as you have so many of us. See if you can run far enough to leave us all behind."

The elder wizard pressed them through the tunnel toward the jump circle. He did not turn around. Auranka's eyes glowed like molten topaz as she entered after them, glittering in twos and fours and eights. She shrieked, in agony and delight, filling the tunnel with piercing pain before her voice oozed along the walls.

"Nothing to say?" the Drider Mistress said in the shadows. "None was your fault? You did as you were commanded? You had *no choice* as a lowly male, to quicken wombs or wilt them ... or was it you feared the punishment of rebellion? Compelled to pain unto death?"

"All of that," the Headmaster said. "But not anymore."

"*Haha!* A worm's shield! I've heard it before!" Her fangs dripped, the venom sizzling on her breasts, causing her lips to curl in bliss. "To speak of disssobeying your Queen, Ja'Prohn, she'll not be pleased the surrogate has ssslipped her leash before obtaining your replacement. Perhaps she will take my council at last, that the Treasure Son *must* also be the Headmaster."

Phaelous clenched his jaw. "No."

Eight eyes blinked in mock surprise. "*No?* Do you think we do not know where he is? That we cannot smell that conflagration wherever he goes?" Auranka grinned, her shadow transforming behind her. "Do you think you will have a body with which to ssstop us?!"

"*Look out!*" D'Shea cried, diving for his pocket.

The Davrin vanished, and the massive spider attacked, filling the tunnel. Hooked feet snatched their clothing, held fast as fangs sprang into view above the Headmaster's head, abdomen arched at gut level, spinnerets seeping white, sticky threads.

"*Luthrenka'sha–A–augh!!*"

Phaelous managed to release his spell, singeing the bristling arachnid with an intense blast of heat which blinded neither of them. His full-throated cry, however, preceded the stumble by an instant. D'Shea withdrew the vial as he fell, keeping her own feet as she released its sparse contents over them both. A faint glimmer of magic surrounded them, and when the webbing sprayed over them, stretched by the thoughtless motion of a spider's legs, it would neither wrap around them nor stick to itself.

"*Phaelous!!*" Auranka shrieked, furious as the weight of her web slipped off them, slopping onto the stone.

"*Back,* putrid slit!" D'Shea roared, throwing every mote of anger and fear behind a gout of fire erupting from her palms.

"*Reeeeeeeeee — !*"

The Mistress scrambled away, climbing up the stone cliff as soon as the tunnel opened up, out of range for another hit. A demonic wail vibrated the walls, threatening to freeze them in place.

"The jump circle!" D'Shea pulled Phaelous's arm across her shoulders. "Now!"

"Y-yes," he gasped, his legs failing the first two steps as he turned. "You have to ... d-do it ..."

"Are you hit?!"

"B-bitten," he gasped.

Her wizard struggled for enough air after that horrid word, his skin clammy to her touch. She smelled rank blood beneath her nose, saw his shoulder swelling from two deep puncture wounds the size of daggers.

No.

"I'll get us there," she said, hauling him as fast as her fear-born strength would let her. "I will. Stay with me."

I'm here.

THE ELDER RED SISTER THANKED EVERY CYCLE SHE HAD MADE THE EFFORT TO enter Phaelous's private quarters unseen. She could barely think as panic threatened to crash into her body and render it useless, but she responded without conscious thought to the urgency.

Three jump circles later, D'Shea dropped her Headmaster onto his bed and stripped him to better see the injury. He couldn't communicate by then; she needed to use a smooth hose to let him breathe past the swelling in his throat. His hands clutched the blankets and he only focused on taking in air.

She had to do everything else.

"Antivenom," she murmured, rushing to his workbench. "Neutralize it ... make it water ..."

She had done this recently for Sirana, and the Headmaster always had components well-stocked. She had to do it from memory, though, and ... and would this work?

It's not just any spider bite!

D'Shea squashed the doubt, creating her potion in her best time and swiftly preparing her glass needle vial for injection. When she returned to the bed, needle in hand, D'Shea stared at his eyes, fixed wide open and unblinking.

Could it be?

I know him. I am not mistaken.

The metallic fleck had expanded, molten gold swallowing the red in his eyes. His body burned and sweated but the rot on his shoulder had not spread as much as it might have.

He counters the Abyss …

And D'Shea would do all she could to help him.

Phaelous had fallen unconscious as soon as Varessa had dared to remove the tube from his throat. Thankfully, he continued breathing on his own. She spent marks dressing his shoulder and dabbing his mouth with a moist cloth, easing as much moisture into him as he would take.

More than once, she thought of leaving him for House Thalluen, to retrieve Auslan so he might help accelerate the cleansing.

Though … I am not certain it wouldn't harm him further.

Or if Shyntre might be furious enough to draw the wrong attention, risking everyone in Rohenvi's House.

Might Auranka have gone after him at once?

The thought clutched her entire body in the worst cold.

Jaunda. Jaunda is there.

Touched by the Black Dragon.

Arytiss.

The Elder wasted not a moment longer. Her Lead wouldn't be able to reply at this distance, but D'Shea had the means from here to send her a message.

*My Lead. If you see the sign of Driders at House Thalluen, get my buas out. If Auranka is not present, bring them to the Wizard's Tower. If she is, do anything

necessary to inform Her Majesty. ∗

The spell worked, she knew, but only silence followed.

The Elder Sorceress checked the Headmaster's vitals for the twelfth time. *I can't leave him.*

Not even to report to the Queen.

Not yet.

And if that demon in the pit ran to the Palace to spew her lies to the Valsharess first, she would deal with it then. Once, D'Shea might have been scared and furious beyond measure to be caught in this web.

As long-ago memories drifted within reach, she cradled them in her mind. Without the whips and chains of multiple compulsions, the Elder Sorceress breathed deeper.

She wasn't afraid.

Not anymore.

When her Headmaster opened his eyes, his body was too weak to sit up. The gold flecks remained, having reverted to normal.

"Varessa," he rasped, his throat raw but his air passage clear.

"I am here. Please, drink."

Phaelous did not question what might be in it; he let her tilt his head up so she could hold the infusion of cold taze to his mouth. He swallowed gratefully.

"It should soothe the aches and the worst of your thirst."

"Thank you."

His eyes fluttered, his focus drifting as he took in their surroundings. She thought he might be on the edge of sleep, and that might be better for his recovery, but …

I have been sitting alone in my mind for quite some time.

"May I ask a question?"

He reined in his wandering eye, bringing his focus around to her with a turn of his head. "Of course. Any … or all that you wish."

Her lower lip trembled to imagine he might mean it. "Is … was Wilsira your Daughter?"

One corner of his mouth tried but failed to turn upward. "Yes. She was … given to House Tachna as an infant. I had no voice in her upbringing."

"Did she *know* you were her sire?"

"I do not … believe so." His brows drew down in concentration. "Perhaps she suspected … much later."

D'Shea twisted fingertips around her knuckles to massage them. "Hm. And … Who was Auranka?"

"Her Mother," he breathed. "A Priestess, before she underwent the ritual to become the Drider Mistress. What we call 'Auranka' is *not* the Priestess I knew. The … creature in the Pit merely enjoys reminding me."

She licked her lips. "Did you … admire her? The Priestess."

As you did me.

Her golden-blond wizard considered the question somberly. "I did. In her way."

D'Shea filled her chest, releasing her breath slowly. She didn't feel jealousy, not exactly. Just a distinctly uncomfortable comparison. "Are all the caits you've admired been targets for the Valsharess?"

He smiled tiredly. "Everyone is a target in Sivaraus, eventually."

True.

"And … the purple elixir. Why does the Mistress want it? What does it do?"

The Sorceress watched for any signs of pain or resistance to answer. The Headmaster only sighed as if to relax.

"I think …" he answered, a soft laugh slipping out, "it is a Dragon's favorite fermented flower."

D'Shea could not follow him. "Why do you think that?"

Phaelous's eyes began to wander. "The Great Cavern … used to be his. Some of the things which grow here are unique."

"And why would the Drider Mistress covet it as she seems to?"

He hummed, bowing his chin. "The potency of her Mother's milk relies on it. She can't feed on dreams or transform her children with as great a reward if she goes too long without it. She hasn't learned how to prepare it in all this time, for whatever reason. The Queen uses this as a form of control."

"What? What effect will that have on *you?*"

"It's Dragon magic, Varessa." Phaelous looked up at the ceiling, a glimmer of gold caught by candlelight. "It probably saved my life when she bit me."

D'Shea sat quietly for a time, turning over how much Phaelous had been able to say.

"Your geas," she murmured. "Is it ... gone?"

Shyntre's sire smiled with the warmth of a hearth warming stew.

"Auranka is right, you know," he murmured. "The Valsharess will not be pleased to discover we've both slipped our leashes. But, on the other hand, nothing we do or say from now on will be because She chose it for us."

He is right.

A terrifying thought.

Phaelous turned his head to meet her gaze. "Everything will be our fault and our joy, my Sorceress, so I will speak while I can." He breathed deep. "I love you more than I have loved any born in eleven centuries. I will not lie to you nor will I betray you ever again."

The sacred pool of Manalar awaits her rebirth. The victors stand hopeful but wary, long-held views of their world torn asunder in the violence of war.

I am here, residing in the Temple of the Sun, as part of the winning faction. Me and my allies bear an intractable responsibility for what happens next. Our choices will influence the continent for centuries, guiding generations not yet born.

Peace eludes us in the wake of battle, and the danger will not pass until we discover — and accept — who we really are.

Coming next: *Rising Guardians*: Sister Seekers Book 11!

Thank you for reading about Sirana and the Davrin Elves of the deep! Please support the author and help readers to find the dark fantasy they'll love by leaving a review for Sister Seekers on Goodreads, Bookbub, or your favorite retail site!

If you haven't read *Sons to Keep: A Sister Seekers Prequel* yet, now is the time! Get a Free Copy signing up at Etaski.com!

Coming Soon! *Tales of Miurag: Death*

Have you picked up the Tales of Miurag anthologies: The Desert and The Deepearth? Read about secrets lost in the ancient Queens of V'Gedra, and the entanglements of Valsharess and the Black Dragon.

I also have fantasy maps, timelines, and a glossary! Read extra tidbits about the characters and places in the story.

Visit Etaski's series lore at World Anvil!

Sister Seekers is an adult epic fantasy with an ever-broadening scope. Found family is a core theme throughout. Perfect for fans of entwined plots, challenging themes, immersive worldbuilding, and elements of erotic horror. Sexuality and inner conflict play into character growth with nuance, intrigue, action, and magic.

Follow Etaski and Subscribe to her newsletter at her website.

ACKNOWLEDGMENTS

My humble and grateful thanks to my friends supporting me up with all the virtual hugs I needed while I worked through a challenging year.

Eris Adderly, Axelotl, Dark Pulse, NecrosisBob, Pastor of Muppets, RainbowNight, Tone, and Vox Verina.

Much love and gratitude, today and tomorrow, with my Hubs.

Special appreciation for Doc Kangey, the anchoring presence working behind the scenes. Check out our hard work and lore yet to come at Etaski.com & Miurag.Etaski.com

THANK YOU, my Top Patrons who support all my efforts to see extra stories written to flesh the world out further!

Korfitz, Chris R., NotSoWeird, Pastor of Muppets, SirCumference, Axelotl, Jesse C., Leonard, Does, John K., Julie S., Paul B., Carla H., Briana R., Josanna, Ryan D., RainbowNight, Lesley PLAY, Kalculys-zero, Zenor , Kelly D., Raymond T., Zeroharas, Johnathon Matlock, Melwinne, Bradley L., Roy Meyer, Brian P., Tessa, and TheQuietOne.

ABOUT THE AUTHOR

Etaski has entertained herself with fantasy stories since the first day she sat on a school bus looking out the window. When hand-written letters were disappearing, she scribbled no less than five pages to be worth the postage. Her early stories were written by hand, and she had a writer's callus and three embarrassing novels before graduating high school.

She studied science, archaeology, history, and theater. Frank discussions of sexuality or death were rare growing up, so she wrote fantasies, theories, and observations within stories for deeper contemplation or just to be entertained.

History speaks little on sexuality, yet biology demonstrates how it sways basic choices. Drama reveals our strongest bonds but may fade to black at its most intimate. In the *Sister Seekers*, the sex and the story are inseparable, and their discoveries will change the journey of Miurag without cutting away.

Etaski's Website: etaski.com
Etaski's Book Page: etaski.com/sister-seekers
Etaski's Series Lore: miurag.etaski.com
Etaski on Patreon: www.patreon.com/etaski
Etaski on GoodReads: www.goodreads.com/etaski
Etaski on BookBub: www.bookbub.com/authors/a-s-etaski
Etaski on Facebook: www.facebook.com/asetaski
Etaski on Mastodon: mastodon.online/@etaski

www.ingramcontent.com/pod-product-compliance
Lightning Source LLC
Chambersburg PA
CBHW030919020726

47498CB00001B/34